ACKNOWLED

As always, my gratitude goes first and foren he privilege of subcreating, which I believe to be a spiritual exer ...agination. Next, I am grateful to my parents, Bruce Robert and Barbara Jean Balestri, for raising me in the faith of our fathers and inspiring me to pursue my historical and literary quests since childhood. I fondly remember my father taking me up to the Palisade Bluffs in Fort Lee, New Jersey, where Washington and Cornwallis waged their war of wills across the mile-wide Hudson River overlooking Manhattan. Such excursions planted within me the early seeds of fascination with the period.

My sincere thanks goes out to my beta readers, editors, proofreaders, historical fact-checkers, and encouragers from both sides of the Atlantic, especially Leah Fisher, Sean Earner, Christian Owen, Adeel Ahmed, Dominic Verdon, Greg Gorman, George Bray, Martina Jurickova, Lyle Dunne, Ashley Dewell, Franklin Valkenburg, Rob Jones, Michael Sweeney, Wesley Hutchins, Peter Webster, Steve Roque, Gabriel Connor Salter, Nathan Stone, Phillip Cambell, Eric K. Barnes, Christen Blair Horne, Hilde Van der Merwe, Veronica Lynn, Ted Lamb, Harry Cartmill, Tom Atwood, Michael C. Fraser, and David Maxwell. Ian Inkster, Alistair McConnachie, Duncan McIntyre, Jonathan Platt, Ian Smart, John Lindsay, Graeme Restorick, Guy Jackson, and Jonathan Moore also stimulated my creativity and increased my affection for the Mother Country which they call home.

I am grateful for various historical fiction and nonfiction authors and living history reenactors I've befriended over the course of the writing process, including Curt Radabaugh, Iain Cameron, Hannah Honneger, Joan M. Hotchstetler, Lynne Tagawa, Joanna Bogle, Stephanie Mann, Stephen Brumwell, Robert Lacey, Andrew O'Shaunessy, Nicholas O'Shaunessy, Marianne Gilchrist, Mary Beth Bailey, S.W. O'Connell, Lars Hedbor, Libby Carty McNamee, Marylu Tyndall, TJ London, Laura Feagan Frantz, Salina Baker, and Samantha Wilcoxson. In addition, I would like to thank my librarian and historian friends who have offered invaluable research assistance, including Kat Clements, Lisa Pickett, Steve McHenrick, Keith Greenawalt, Richard W. Hoover, Carol McNeill, Jim Swan, Ann Watters, Les Soper, Sheila Pitcairn, Deborah Gage. Special thanks also to my talented cover designer, Maria Teresa Carzon, for capturing the key elements of the story so beautifully in the visual layout.

I also want to extend my gratitude and prayers to the souls of the historical figures whose letters, memoirs, speeches, poetry and other literary endeavors I have quoted and adapted at length for this trilogy, including General John Burgoyne, General Thomas Gage, General Simon Fraser, General James Wolfe, Major John Pitcairn, Major John Acland, General Hugh Percy, General John Churchill, Baroness Frederika von Riedesel, Sergeant Roger Lamb, Sergeant James Thompson, and last but not least, His Majesty King George III. Without them posthumously on board, this novel would be a most sorry scrap of scribblings. They may not have chosen an adamant Papist to tell their tale, much less a 4'10" female one, shouting at herself in the mirror while striking military poses, generating dialogue in a variety of hit-or-miss British accents. But that's what destiny dictated. Where I have erred in my depictions of them, I hope they know that, to paraphrase George Washington, I have done so with my head, not with my heart.

This trilogy is dedicated to Catholic recusants across the British Isles and Empire who remained true to their faith across centuries of persecution and marginalization, as well as to British and American Loyalist participants in the American Revolutionary War who faithfully served their King and Country. To paraphrase Samuel Johnson's famous tribute to Flora MacDonald, if courage and fidelity be virtues, then the subjects of this saga should be remembered with honor.

AUTHOR'S NOTE

This story has been a long time coming. It first began to take shape when I was twelve and found myself simultaneously reading *The Autobiography of a Hunted Priest* by Father John Gerard, SJ, and *An Original and Authentic Journal of Occurrences during the Late American War* by Sergeant Roger Lamb. The 16th-century English priest who suffered torture and imprisonment for his Catholic Faith inspired me in one way; the 18th-century Anglo-Irish soldier who suffered privations and imprisonment for his King and Country inspired me in another.

Their stories of survival against the odds spoke to me down through the centuries and made me feel as if I had come to know both men intimately. Their hopes and fears bled through the pages, and their personalities burned brightly from the hearth of history. My youthful high spirits and intense emotions assured that their stories would overlap in my imagination to create a singular spiritual vision, dealing with the dichotomy of what it might mean to be, in the words of St. Thomas More, the King's good servant but God's first.

Other important influences on this story include the play/film *A Man for All Seasons* Thomas More's martyrdom; the film *The Miracle* about a Spanish novice who flees her convent to pursue a British officer during the Napoleonic Wars; the book and multiple screen versions of Leo Tolstoy's *War & Peace;* and three other memoirs, *The Life and Letters of James Wolfe, A Bard of Wolfe's Army* by Sgt. James Thompson, and *Baroness Von Riedesel and the American Revolution*. All of them deal with the high drama of warfare that brings about personal evolution.

In terms of my chosen focus and setting for this narrative, I have always found the British and Loyalist experience of the American Revolution particularly compelling because of my lifelong love of Britain and her multi-layered heritage. When I was in my tweens and early teens, before my family owned a computer or printer, I would save my pennies to pay for print-outs about historical figures at my local library systems. Most of these characters were "redcoats", British soldiers from the Age of Horse and Musket, clad in tell-tale scarlet tunics. I would compile whole folders of these biographies, then file them into volumes, and read through them regularly for story ideas I planned to someday spin. I would become invested in the ups and downs of each character's journey, and see them as not solely a part of Britain's legacy, but of America's as well, for there was a time when we were all one people, and perhaps on a level deeper than any of us are willing to admit, still are. On both sides of the sea, we remain the children of Lady Britannia.

The cultural roots of America, based in the thirteen original colonies, are an out-growth of Albion in the New World. This fundamental fact put the historical framework into perspective for me, especially as a native of Maryland, the only colony settled by English Catholics. The more I researched the Revolutionary Era, the more the division of the Anglosphere and cessation of America's ties to kingship seemed tinged by tragedy and drenched in kindred blood, a reality rarely addressed with the solemnity it deserves. Brother slew brother, but unlike in the case of the American Civil War, in which the Union won, we are taught to downplay this aspect when it comes to the American Revolution because separatists triumphed and the split is celebrated.

I, for one, could never help but grieve for the lost dual identity of British Americans, once proudly held and defended by so many before and during the war, and came fairly early to consider myself as a latter-day Loyalist at heart. I am an American, by birth and upbringing, shaped by my native land in countless ways, and yet I have always felt a spiritual tie to the kings and queens of Britain far more than any president because it appeals to a transcendent authority, an incarnational sacredness, and a historical continuity that stretches back beyond the year 1776 or '83. I do celebrate the 4th of July, but not so much in support for the Declaration of Independence as out of a general appreciation of America and all the good she has to offer.

Beyond this background, the reason I wanted to write a story focusing on the British experience of the Revolution was due to the very fact that they lost. In the great turning point of the war, the Saratoga Campaign, I cannot help but see a classical tragedy of fallen knights and broken tables, in which all the best and worst aspects of the British character were on full display. This apocalypse, brought on by pride and passion, is pregnant with the potential to explore correlating topics and profound truths that were important to me as a Catholic author. If the revolution resulted in a political schism, it reflected to some extent an earlier religious schism, when England severed herself from the See of Rome. The arguments made for both forms of separation could eerily parallel each other, and in some ways, they feel like a mirror being held up to one another other. I imagine Catholics inhabiting the British Empire at the time would have seen the pattern and reacted to it in different ways. This story explores one such possible reaction.

In some aspects, it is a retelling of the life of the famous Jesuit martyr St. Edmund Campion, put forward from the 16th to the 18th century, switching out a priest for a layman, and altering his career trajectory from that of a scholar to that of a soldier. As such, the premise is both quite original and quite familiar. St. Arsenios of Paros said, "The Church in the British Isles will only begin to grow when she begins again to venerate her own saints." This story pays homage to the tradition of hagiography, for the saint is the only true revolutionary in the world. Christ was creating the universe while dying on the Cross, and the martyr recapitulates all things in Christ through the witness of blood.

In other parts of this story, I strove to go back even farther than Campion's Elizabethan influence, touching upon the earliest consciousness of English identity and mythic history that permeates my Robin Hood series, *The Telling of the Beads*. I wanted Britannia to feel both thoroughly real and also more than real, with poetry infused into the mundane, for without a soul, the land is nothing. And if Britannia is nothing, America is nothing either. This is something sadly lacking in most fiction dealing with the American Revolution, which reduces the Mother Country to a cartoonish landscape generated by revolutionary propaganda as opposed to our very womb, where we gained our first understanding of liberty.

When it comes to the process of writing characters, I believe that every person is "an allegory," as J.R.R. Tolkien once said, "each embodying in a particular tale and clothed in the garments of time and place, universal truth and everlasting life." We can never completely de-mythologize history any more than we can fully de-spiritualize mankind, though our increasingly secular civilization may work its woe. I take this principle equally seriously when writing stories set during the Early Modern Period as I do with stories set during the Middle Ages. It is fundamental to us to believe that our stories are worth telling, for all their bitter glory, and I believe that each passing generation is simply another of a Mystery Play, unfolding the secrets of salvation in manifold ways.

Sr. Albert Marie Surmaski wrote, "No one lives a purely natural life with no invitation to the supernatural. Where there is someone trying to do that, there is a saying no to God, a closing of one's eyes to that further horizon. So any purely 'this-worldly' good is a partial, disordered sort of goodness that is particularly prone to snap in moments when our finitude and death come before our eyes." Perhaps the key to a truly Christian story, one that leaves a lasting impact upon an audience, is that it confronts that snapping straight on, with compassion for all of us easily deluded mortals who stumble into a dark wood and require the intervention of grace, often through suffering, to save us from ourselves and our distractions.

This, boiled down to creedal basics, is the power of Christ's dying and rising, which shall never be emptied. This is the foundational concept behind our trilogy and all those who pass by within it: Each man and woman finds themselves fighting the long defeat, living as crucibles of a fallen world, and to greater or lesser extents, being drawn into the drama of the Cross. When all earthly goods are despoiled, and death itself beckons the soul, they must confront the Absolute, the Hound of Heaven from whom they can no longer escape, for He draws all men to Himself from Golgotha.

Regarding my approach to historical fiction, I believe that respect for history should be paramount and that artistic license should build upon what we know as opposed to deconstructing it. We should always keep in mind our responsibility to past generations and avoid slander for the sake of sensationalism. I have a deep distaste for pointless shock factor, and I do my best to approach even the most intense subjects in as tasteful and empathetic a manner as possible while retaining the raw emotional impact that enables character development and thematic exploration. In terms of age appropriateness, the intended readership is mid-teens and up, though I suggest that sensitive readers who are disturbed by the darker elements of religious persecution and global conflict during the Long 18th Century proceed with caution.

For those like myself who believe in the workings of Providence and the everlasting nature of the soul, I will close this note with an old Celtic prayer for the departed:

"May God bless all the company of souls here. May God and Mary bless you. You too were here as we are now, and we hope to join you soon. May we all be adorned in the bright King of Heaven."

~ Avellina Balestri, July 2, 2024

Chapter 1: THE RECUSANTS

Edmund Southworth, born in the Year of Grace, 1756, had been named after two martyrs. The first was a pious king slain in ancient times, pierced by Viking arrows until he looked like a hedgehog, the psalms of royal David and the name of Christ Jesus flowing from his lips along with the blood. The second, called "Campion the Champion," was a Jesuit priest, butchered under Queen Elizabeth I, his bowels torn out while a prayer for her was still fresh upon his tongue. It was said that, before embracing his call as a missionary, he had received a vision from the Blessed Virgin Mary, who placed a lily between his outstretched hands, a prize of purity for any soul destined to pay the ultimate price in imitation of their Savior.

Both martyrs were Englishmen, born and bred. Edmund was proud of that, proud of his name, proud of his hills and moors, proud of his streams and sky. He was a Lancashire lad, attuned to the shire's ageless song from birth. He was in the land, and the land was in him. He was loyal to his country as well as his locality, a northerner down to his very bones. And he was a Catholic, as his forebears had been for as long as memory could be kindled, before King Henry VIII had declared himself head of the Church in England and severed his realm from the See of Rome. The Southworths were a noble family of recusants, set apart by their continued refusal to attend the Church of the State no matter how many fines they were forced to pay. Their dilapidated ancestral home stood as a testament to that sacrifice, stripped of its grandeur, full of cobwebs and phantoms alike.

The family was nearly as old as Mother England herself, yet also exiles within her very womb. Edmund spent many hours of his childhood curled up in yet another womb, the priest hole that had been built in their manor by Nicholas Owen, the master carpenter later tortured to death for his labors. The boy felt secure inside that sacred cell as he prayed upon his rosary beads in hushed tones, pretending that he was being hunted by the priest-catchers like his second saintly patron. But then, inevitably, he would imagine being pulled from his hiding place, condemned by a court, swung from a scaffold, and slit open before a crowd, bearing witness to the faith of his fathers till his final breath left his body. It was romantic, even as it was horrific.

Edmund could count a number of relatives among the slain, including John Southworth of Samlesbury Hall, known as the Parish Priest of Westminster. In London, during a plague epidemic, he had gained universal respect for tending to the sick and dying of every background and persuasion, administering the sacraments to suffering Catholics and raising money to aid all victims and their families. He was arrested multiple times but due to his popularity he was expelled from the country instead of executed. But he returned to his native land to continue his ministry, until at last, he was apprehended for a final time and accepted death rather than deny his priesthood.

"I was brought up in the truly ancient Roman Catholic apostolic religion, which taught me that the sum of the only true Christian profession is to die," Father Southworth said to the crowd gathered around the scaffold. "This lesson I have heretofore in my lifetime desired to learn; this lesson I come here to put to practice by dying, being taught it by our Blessed Savior, both by precept and example. To follow His holy doctrine, and imitate His holy death, I willingly suffer at present; this gallows I look on as His cross, which I gladly take to follow my dear Savior."

The agonies and ecstasies of such martyrdoms were never far from young Edmund's mind. Less than a hundred years had passed since the last Catholic priests were executed for treason, sometimes along with those who dared to harbor them. That was not very long ago for their blessed isle, as timeless as the ocean that surrounded her. And the few Catholics who still refused to conform to the Anglican settlement continued to be viewed with suspicion. Who could say that they were not spies for the Pope in Rome or the kings of France and Spain? Who could say their treason did not extend beyond concealing priests disguised as huntsmen or merchants to a violent overthrow of the government and the persecution of Protestants? Who could say if Papists truly bled British when cut?

As Edmund grew up, he could not help but grimace when he heard such talk.

His family…traitors?

Maybe so, if one counted cramped old priest holes against them. Maybe so, some decades before, when the Jacobites had fought to regain the triple crowns for the Catholic Stuarts, long since banished from their realms and replaced by Protestant claimants. Two or three of Edmund's cousins had donned the white cockade, symbolic of that ill-starred house, and battled on behalf of the dethroned royals alongside both Catholics and Protestant volunteers who chose to champion the Stuarts for their own reasons. Religion and politics, loyalty and self-interest, forced recruitment and hard cold coin all played a role in the movement. But that crusade was over and done with now, locked in the great treasure chest of lost causes and buried in the sands of time.

Their last chance of victory had been in 1745, when Bonnie Prince Charlie had raised his standard in the Highlands of Scotland, seven years before Edmund was born. Spurred on by the prince's vow to protect the Gaelic-speaking clans from outside interference, many men there had pledged their lives to him, and many ladies their hearts. They marched south, routed the government troops at Prestonpans, and captured Edinburgh, where the prince was feted in the shadow of Edinburgh Castle, still defiantly held by government defenders. Then Charles, bursting with self-confidence, had decided it was time to move south again, this time into England, where he hoped to recruit more support from the northern counties. Some men had materialized, though not in the numbers he had anticipated. Still, his spirits remained high as they marched into the English Midlands.

But it was all for naught. This rising, like the previous ones, was doomed to be a flash in the pan, with the Jacobite army marching only as far south as Derby before the Prince's council insisted upon retreating north again, back to the border, and thence to Scotland. Little did they know that, even as they turned back, the Hanoverian government in London was preparing to evacuate. The Young Pretender, as he was branded by his enemies, lost Edinburgh and was forced into the Highlands once more. The final battle unfolded at Culloden, where his supporters were beaten into submission, and the grass ran red with their gore. Elsewhere across the Isles, including in Lancashire, bodies hung from trees like rotting fruit. Scattered and slaughtered, they would never rise again until Judgment Day, though their legend lived in the very air, like sea-salt swirling upon the wind, while their bones moldered in common graves under the ground. As far as Edmund was concerned, despite the painful past, it was still good ground, *his* ground.

By now, most Catholics in Britain and Ireland had given up on any hopes of restoring the House of Stuart and bringing back the Jacobite courts from across the water. Recusants were just as likely to toast and sing "God save Great George, Our King" as their Anglican neighbors, and perhaps did so even more loudly to affirm their loyalty to the reigning House of Hanover beyond suspicion. Besides, as far as Edmund was concerned, German Geordie, the second of that name, was at least partly deserving of the victory over Bonnie Prince Charlie. The man had proven himself to be no coward, particularly by his willingness to put his own royal body on the line fighting the French at Dettingen. That, Edmund decided, made him a worthy Englishman at heart, even if his continental accent had been strong enough to cut with a knife.

Edmund always found tales of battlefield glory irresistible. To the consternation of his devout mother Perpetua and sister Teresa, he venerated war heroes almost as much as the saints in his boyhood days. His enthusiasm reached its peak when listening to stories about the conquest of Quebec, which the young British general, James Wolfe, had achieved against all odds upon the Plains of Abraham in 1759. Edmund would reenact the battle with his Protestant playmates, and they would pin scraps of scarlet cloth onto their shirts to appear like proper soldiers of the King. Then they would take turns impersonating the intrepid general, drawing up his men in a thin red line and ordering them forward in a triumphant charge. Whoever was playing Brave Wolfe would clutch his chest and reel around, and the other boys would kneel beside him reverentially. He would ask them how the battle fared, and they would reply that the French had been routed and the city was their own. The conqueror would smile and assure them that he died contented. Then their little game would resume from the beginning, with a new Wolfe ready for action. When Edmund would be selected, he treated it with the gravity of a Passion Play, and the other boys joked that Papists were incorrigibly morbid.

But the sketches and engravings had done the work of sanctification already, depicting Wolfe's body pouring out precious blood, outstretched and uplifted by his aides like the pierced Christ in his grieving mother's arms. Perhaps it was blasphemy, but Edmund was thrilled by the way heaven and earth reflected one another. He had always been struck by visceral images that insisted suffering must be redemptive, and could not help but call to mind one of the first verses of Scripture he had been taught: "O all ye that pass by the way, attend, and see if there be any sorrow like unto my sorrow."

This was the fate of Catholic England, his mother had told him mournfully, shaking her head and wringing her hands. Nothing was left to them but sorrow and shame in the land once called Mary's Dowry when Christendom enjoyed her golden age, before being torn asunder by factions. Edmund thought it was all strangely fitting, since the Lady was closest to the Lord in sorrow and in shame. That being said, he was not quite so pessimistic about his prospects in the outside world. Their Protestant neighbors were mostly decent folk who minded their own affairs, and though the local boys made fun of him from time to time, they included Edmund in their fun and games. He played with them so much his mother worried they would endanger his soul.

"Rotten apples spoil the good ones, and such is the consequence of keeping bad company," Perpetua would lecture her son. "Those boys you are always out roughhousing with, chant vile nursery rhymes against the Holy Mass and burn effigies of the Holy Father! They are little better than imps from the pits!"

Edmund had a feeling Anglican mothers lectured their sons in a similar fashion about playing with Papists. More than a few times, he and his playmates had repeated harsh sayings from their elders, and it led to blows. Such incidents became more frequent around the Fifth of November, when the failed Gunpowder Plot of Guy Fawkes and his fellow Catholic conspirators was commemorated with parades and bonfires. In 1605, chafing under oppression, the plotters had intended to blow up King James I and parliament in order to install a government favorable to Catholics. All they had succeeded in doing through their desperate scheme was to unleash a worse wave of persecution upon English Catholics, the vast majority of whom had nothing to do with the plot, but paid the price for it all the same. The long shadow of the debacle continued to cast itself over Edmund's youth.

But after the black eyes and bloody noses had been given and received, Edmund and his playmates tended to forget all about it and go back to their usual sport. Childhood was merciful that way. And the truth of the matter was that, whatever differences existed between them, their daily lives were similar enough, with private lessons in the morning and cheese pie for lunch and prayers before bed. All of them came from respectable families who could take pride in raising their children to be God-fearing, upright citizens, despite their boyish mischief. The lads seemed intuitively to understand how truly alike they were better than their frequently fretting mothers.

Then when Edmund was nine, one of their number unexpectedly succumbed after being soaked to the skin in a downpour. Edmund was devastated. He had always known William did not have the strongest constitution, having observed his sneezing fits when they wrestled in fallen leaves. But he never expected his friend's lungs to fail him so suddenly. Edmund blamed himself for being among the boys who insisted on staying outside even after the rain, initially no more than a drizzle, came down harder. He was sure it would pass over quickly so they could finish their game, and it had, as was typical of English rain. But not fast enough to spare William.

When Edmund's mother overheard his prayers for his playmate's soul, she told him it was improper and in vain. William had been a heretic, no matter how much Edmund had enjoyed trading marbles for tin soldiers with him, or how many lunches they had swapped under their favorite oak tree, or how many times they play-acted the Battle of the Plains of Abraham together. There was no salvation outside the Church.

"But he took communion," Edmund insisted. "Jack told me so. His father was called over from the vicarage, and he gave him the bread and the wine, even though he was too young, because…he was going to die…"

"False communion!" Perpetua blurted. "You know that, Edmund. It was not the Body and Blood of Christ. Why do you think we pay the taxes to avoid being forced to receive it? It would be scandalous for us to receive it as if it were truly the sacrament. No, we prefer to risk our freedom to hear the Holy Mass and receive the Holy Eucharist. I should not have to explain this to you, but that vicar's wicked boy has clouded your mind. He and his ilk will lead you into indifference, or worse, perdition."

And some of Edmund's innocence died along with William. He didn't understand anything anymore. No, he especially didn't understand God. What had his friend done to deserve death, much less damnation? What, burn a puppet of the pope for Bonfire Night in November? He had been a good enough boy the rest of the year, with kind brown eyes Edmund would never forget. He had eaten his vegetables with his lunch instead of throwing them in the bushes like some of the other boys did. He had prettier handwriting than most of them because he practiced more diligently to make his parents proud. He spent weeks caring for a bird with a broken wing one spring and wouldn't let any of his companions pluck its feathers for good luck. Surely all that had to count for something in the end. Surely God wouldn't just throw him away like spinach that left a bad taste on the tongue.

"It would be a wonderful thing to fly," William had mused, feeding the bird some seed from his palm. "No wonder she's so sad, stuck on the ground like this. At least I can make sure she has nice things to eat and no one pesters her until she's well."

There was something else Jack had said about William's death, through awkward sniffling, determined not to cry, something that Edmund dared not tell his mother lest she take it as a perverse triumph. After receiving communion, William had vomited up the bread and wine all over the sheets in his agony. Then he had called for his mother, and she tried desperately to calm her child as he burned with fever, but he kept having seizures of choking and spitting up, over and again, until his heart gave out. She would not let go of her little boy's body for hours, and the vicar had to be the one to gently pull her away. And Edmund found that he resented his mother, knowing that if he told her, she might have suggested it was a punishment from God.

Edmund's sister Teresa, however, was far more soft-hearted, kissing her little brother on the forehead and letting him cry on her shoulder. Six years his senior, she often acted like a second mother to him, one whose spontaneous warmth was contrasted with the dutiful aloofness of his first. Tessie was plain-faced, much like Perpetua, with messy brunette curls and slightly crossed eyes, but he was ready and willing to punch any of the boys who dared to say she would end up as an old maid. Any man would be a fool for not wanting his darling sister.

To make him feel even a little bit better about William, she agreed to pray the rosary with Edmund in the priest hole. That way they could offer whatever intentions they wanted without anyone else hearing.

"We can pray for anything imaginable in a priest hole, dear Ned," she informed him, using his family pet name in a whisper, as if it were a great secret just between the two of them. "It was blessed by the presence of the martyrs, so God will listen especially well to whatever intention we make while inside. Heaven can be brought down to earth in that tiny space, in like manner to how Christ is brought to us in a tiny Host. It is between us and Him, and no one outside will be the wiser for it. No, not even Mother."

Pray for Babylon, the Scriptures commanded. And so, the siblings petitioned Heaven on behalf of a heretic. For young Ned and his Protestant friends alike, ideas of eternal bliss were limited to lazy summer afternoons free from mathematics lessons and extra helpings of ginger cakes after supper. Their understanding of Hell, meanwhile, was shaped by the gold and purple flames licking logs through long winter nights. In any case, Edmund thought, in the world to come, surely no one would die from a cold. After his friend's passing, he became increasingly sensitive to death, and the fact one could not simply have another go at living afterwards, like in their games of Wolfe at Quebec. No, his friend would never get up again; neither would the real Wolfe, not until heaven really did come down and swell the earth like wind filling a ship's sails. Maybe that wind was what every mortal breathlessly awaited, something that would enable them to fly, as William had fondly imagined when tending to his bird. And when such thoughts struck him, Edmund rather wished he could become a priest, and bring God and Man together through the gifts of bread and wine and water and oil, grace building upon and transfiguring nature.

But he wanted to be a military officer too, desperately so. It was said that, before the schism, the majority of his male relatives had either been priests or soldiers, so it was simply a part of his lineage, some inherited determination to commingle spiritual and temporal realities. He dreamed of being clad in a blood-red tunic with glistening buttons, like his boyhood heroes, winning renown for king and country. He wanted to gain the respect of the men he would lead and be a father to them, as Wolfe had been. He wanted to die contented, having led a life of valor and victory. Perhaps, in this way, he might be a living sacrament, a little image of Christ, wounded in his resurrection. But he was a Catholic, and according to the law, a British officer he could not be. Perhaps, like oil and water, the two desires were destined never to mix.

His father, the elderly Francis Southworth, told him that the last time their family had served a crowned king was during the long and bitter civil war when Cavaliers and Roundheads contended for the supremacy of the king or the parliament. Their family had supported King Charles I against Oliver Cromwell, for Charles was a high church Anglican, fond of smells and bells, and tended to sympathize, at least up to a point, with the plight of Papists. He had a Catholic wife, Queen Henrietta Maria, who Puritans such as Cromwell decried as a French harlot for using her influence to lure her husband towards Rome. The colony of Maryland in the Americas, founded by the Catholic Lord Baltimore, had been named in her honor, which in turn honored her patroness, the Blessed Virgin Mary. Some of Edmund's relatives had migrated there over a century before, having been assured that it would be a haven in which to practice their faith. The promised sanctuary had not lasted. The Protestant colonists cast the Catholic colonists down and imprisoned their priests. Meanwhile, Catholics in the mother country suffered under the rigorous reforms of Cromwell, determined to make England a city on a hill by stripping away all popery. King Charles himself lost his head, arms stretched out cruciform, the ominous word "Remember" upon his lips. Yet despite historical currents running against the Southworth family, they refused to consider themselves on the wrong side of it.

"We Catholics had the last laugh, for we saved King Charles' heir," Francis recounted, taking a deep draught from his long Irish pipe. "We hid the prince in the hollow of an oak tree, and thus he remained protected from the Puritans in the same manner that Saint Simon Stock received his visions of Our Lady. That's the reason we celebrate Oak Apple Day every year, for without the risks we took back then, we would not have a king today! And without our kings, why, Christmas would still be outlawed! By the faith of my body, Ned! Any man who fancies his wassail should thank us, but it seems to slip their minds, the bloody ingrates!"

Edmund loved his father dearly, for all his eccentricities. It was said he had been a fetching man in his youth, resembling his son with eyes that were as gray as the sky before a summer storm, and hair like amber grain, ripe for the scythe at harvest. But he was worn now, like his wardrobe, which had changed little in style since the Jacobites were last on the march. They were not in a position to hire tailors, and Ned's own clothes were woefully behind the times, often hand-me-downs from his father. Francis had an old-fashioned sense of ethics to match his attire. He was rather famous in the county for lending, or outright giving away, more than he could afford to whoever asked, Catholic or Protestant.

"Courtesy, my boy," he told his son. "That's how they'll remember you're a noble, no matter what they think of the faith we keep. Bend over backwards, if you must, but never let yourself be outdone when it comes to a generous nature, a fair mind, and good manners. Remember these three things, dear Ned, for no one can take them away from you. Leave the rest to God."

His father would then tell the story of James Radcliffe, Lord Derwentwater, that pious nobleman in the bloom of youth who took part in the Jacobite rising of 1715. Hailing from Northumberland, he was beloved by friend and foe, turning away no man who came seeking succor at his ancestral hall, no matter their station or their creed. He lived and died a good Catholic, and few could bring themselves to fault him for it because he spent his days in deeds of kindness, giving bread to thousands. During the rebellion, he had led by example, stripping to the waist and digging trenches with the common soldiers. It always plunged a knife of sorrow into Ned's heart to hear how, upon the rebellion's failure, foreshadowed by Derwentwater's nosebleeds and the loss of his golden ring, he was denied clemency from King George I, though many pleaded on his behalf, including his disconsolate wife, mother of their two small children.

The young lord was offered his life only if he would retract his oath of loyalty to the House of Stuart and abandon his Catholic faith. He refused to do either of those things, though he did declare his willingness to swear an oath not to bear arms against the Hanoverian government again. His offer was rejected out of hand, and his execution date set. Spending his final days in prayer and fasting, Derwentwater took heart by reflecting on the Passion of Christ. Still, the young lord struggled through his own Gethsemane. He was so distressed the night before his impending beheading that several sympathetic Hanoverians, both wardens and visitors, seeing that he was trembling within his cell, chose to keep him company till morning. His fears notwithstanding, he met his end courageously, refusing a cup of wine to dull the pain, forgiving those who slew him with all his heart, and begging God to forgive him for his youthful sins.

With a small crucifix worn upon his breast, he told the axman to allow him to say "Sweet Jesus" three times, then to strike. And so it was done, his severed head held aloft, the blood gushing onto the platform. The folk in the north said the sky turned strange colors on the night following his death, which were dubbed "Derwentwater's Lights", for surely they marked the path his soul had taken to reach his reward.

Although she too revered the memory of Lord Derwentwater, Perpetua thought her husband Francis was overly concerned about what people thought of them. Instead of trying to win over Protestants through what she considered to be feigned courtesies, she preferred a mutual settlement between Catholics and heretics based on honest enmity. After all, she remarked, all the generosity in the world had not saved Derwentwater from the ax. She did not like the fact that Ned was naturally inclined towards his father's point of view, and worried that his efforts to please Protestants would lead him down the slippery slope to apostasy. Inevitably, he would long to possess the liberties that the Anglican ascendency took for granted, and she feared his noble blood would cause him to crave such privileges with increasing intensity over time.

She was not all wrong. As the boy grew to be a young man, he realized with renewed awareness how limited his future was bound to be as a Catholic. Most of his Protestant friends were off attending prestigious English universities and choosing respectable careers for themselves as lawyers or politicians or clerics or military officers. They were being introduced into gentlemen's clubs and taking the grand tour of Europe. But Edmund was shut out from these pursuits, either because of legal or financial restrictions, and so drifted further from his old circle of playmates. He could not even go fencing, hunting, or racing with them, for all but a few Catholics in the country were prevented from owning swords, guns, or horses. Nevertheless, he still found himself dreaming of being a soldier, in a scarlet tunic with brass buttons.

One activity he could indulge in was taking long walks through the surrounding countryside, often accompanied by his black-and-white sheepdog, Kip. Ned's ancestors had once owned a sizable flock of sheep, and Kip was a descendant of a long line of their sheepdogs. But the family had been forced to sell nearly all the sheep since Elizabeth's reign, as well as most of the grazing land. Only two small adjacent fields remained, used for all four remaining sheep to graze. Kip, at least, had a place to chase them around in circles and feel proud of himself. Perhaps he too was rather like a noble fallen on hard times, looking for excuses to still hold his head high.

On his walks, Edmund enjoyed chatting with the local farmers who worked their plots of land either as owners or tenants. Though the majority were Protestant, some were Catholic. Most came to view him kindly, for he talked to them plainly and without airs. He would discuss the weather and agriculture with the men, but the women would ask him to recite something pretty for them, and he did, for he loved old scraps of poetry from their medieval and Anglo-Saxon past. When he was not outdoors, he spent hours in his father's study, poring over such preserved works and committing much of the contents to memory. He grieved over so much literature having been destroyed when the abbeys were despoiled under Henry VIII, but he was determined to keep any more from being lost. Sometimes he would even tell stories of the ancient English saints to the farm children, Catholic and Protestant alike, while they took respites from their daily chores, and he was always gratified to see the look of wonder in their eyes as he spoke.

But beyond passing pleasantries, Edmund took his father's instruction seriously, and always asked how each family was faring and if there was anything he could do to help them through rough patches. The men were often too proud to reveal their troubles, but the women could be persuaded to tell, often tearfully, and Ned would find some way or other to ease the hardship without it seeming too much like charity to their husbands. He was good at getting away with it, for there was no trace of condescension in his bearing, and he could devise excuses that seemed believable. Like his father before him, they came to love him for his efforts on their behalf.

For all the limitations imposed upon him, Edmund tried to be satisfied with his lot in life, and remained deeply committed to his religion. He was pleased to be able to do some little good in his corner of the world and sew together the past and present of England through his refusal to recant. He was grateful that his family had at least managed to keep their house, for it offered the Catholics in the vicinity somewhere to gather whenever a traveling priest came to say mass. He could look forward to marrying some young lady of good character from another recusant family, as his mother heartily wished, and raise a brood of Catholic children with her to carry on the legacy. Yes, he could train himself to be content with the simple life of a modest country gentleman, and keep the faith, always keep the faith.

Or at least that's what he kept telling himself, determined to silence the voice inside him that kept screaming for more.

Chapter 2: GENTLEMAN JOHNNY

The year 1774, when Francis Southworth succumbed to apoplexy, was a bitter one for Edmund. Not only would the old man's kindly countenance be greatly missed by his family and the wider community, but it soon came to light that their finances were in a worse state than they had realized. "Pay me back when you can" had always been the elder Southworth's refrain to both Catholic and Protestant beneficiaries of his bounty, even though he had no easy way of replenishing his family's stores. As his wife often remarked in a scolding tone, he was no businessman. But the locals had adored him for his benevolence. This had been part of the reason that the local authorities continued permitting his family to retain their manor, even though on the books, their "foreign" faith should have prevented them from owning or inheriting property. Such allowances to ancient houses were not altogether uncommon, especially in Lancashire, where the Catholic population was at its highest.

But now that Francis Southworth was in the grave and the extent of his debts had come to light, a large part of the family identity, history, and heritage seemed doomed to be lost along with their ancestral home. This calamity had been a long time coming. From the time of King Henry's split with Rome, the family had lost their holdings a little at a time with each passing generation that kept the faith. First some of their fields were confiscated, then some of their flocks, then the horses, and then all manner of weaponry, even the decorative swords upon the wall from the age of chivalry. Then more of the fields and flocks were taken away. Now it seemed the sad saga of dispossession had finally reached its zenith.

In the aftermath of his father's passing, Edmund found his one escape from such dreary inevitabilities to be his long country walks along with faithful Kip, whose greatest happiness was barking at red squirrels in trees and flocks of sheep on neighboring estates. Ned could not bear to hear his sister weeping under their father's portrait, nor watch his mother staring blankly at the wall hour after hour, nor could he bring himself to tell the servants who remained that they soon might be out of work. He tried to be practical, contemplating how to make sure the servants could find other employment if the Southworths lost the manor. He thought about finding a cottage to rent for his family and seeking out a position as a clerk to keep them fed. Perhaps he could also make good on some of his family's old attempts at investments outside the country, though there were little enough funds remaining from which he might draw.

The harder Edmund tried to think of viable solutions, the more helpless and worthless he felt. He was the man of the house now. He should have been in a position to secure his family's needs, like other young gentlemen of his age and station. But they were Protestant, and he was Catholic, and the Law ensured that so many doors which had been opened to them would be closed to him. He could only pray that some secret passageway would be made known to him.

As Edmund walked home along the high road, he heard a carriage coming towards him at a faster pace than wisdom would have dictated. He was quick to get himself and Kip off the road, but not fast enough to avoid mud from the recent rainfall being splattered in his face and on his clothes. Then the carriage stopped short, and a handsome middle-aged gentleman in a plumed hat leaned out the window. Kip shook the mud from his coat and started barking at the stranger, while Edmund did his best to shush him.

"I say, lad," the man called from the coach, "do you know the way to the Southworth manor?"

Edmund thought he must be a buyer from the township of Preston, coming out to have a look at the place. "Just over the next hill, you should follow the road turning right," he instructed, pointing in that direction. "I am heading that way myself."

"Oh, are you in service to that household?" the man asked.

"In a way, yes," Edmund replied with a slight smile, trying to scrub the mud from his face with his sleeve. "I am the late owner's son."

The carriage door opened abruptly, and the gentleman stepped out into the road, using his ornate gold-tipped cane to test for puddles. "Ned? Little Ned Southworth? Last time I saw you, you were hardly taller than my riding boot!"

Ned's eyes widened as he beheld the man's brilliant scarlet tunic with glistening buttons, partially shrouded in a crimson velvet cloak. "General Burgoyne?"

Everyone in Lancashire gossiped about the misadventures of Gentleman Johnny Burgoyne, that dashing man-about-town with a record in the military, a seat in parliament, and a passion for the theater. He had been embroiled in any number of scandals, and his election had been so contentious, rioters took to the streets of Preston. But setting aside such scrapes, Burgoyne had won the respect of the nation for leading his beloved regiment of horse to victory on the continent, from France to Portugal. He also proved to be an outspoken force to be reckoned in political forums, standing out during the inquest of Robert Clive and the East India Company as one of their most savage critics. He had a gift for persuading people of his opinions and excelled at talking his way into and out of things. Women were said to find his charms irresistible, and even most men found his affability hard to rebuff. Though he had tended to brag about himself to an almost nauseating extent, none could deny that he was the life of every party, raising many a toast with the sparkling glass in his hand and a sparkle of fun in his eyes.

"Bless my soul, you do remember me!" Burgoyne said with satisfaction, walking over briskly and pulling Edmund into a quick embrace which the young man awkwardly reciprocated.

"Of course I do," Edmund assured. "You made quite an impression upon me as a child. I still recall the first time I saw you. Father and I were out walking across the moors when we heard the noises of the hunt. They grew closer and closer until you and your companions came into view. You were so poised upon your horse, so utterly at one with the chase. When you saw us, you reined in your horse and bowed low in the saddle, like a true Cavalier."

"Ah, there's nothing quite like the blasting of horns and the thundering of the hooves to thrill the blood of an old cavalryman like me, familiar with many-a-charge after Frenchmen and foxes alike," Burgoyne said.

"Believe me, it thrilled Father's blood too. He pined over not being able to partake. That's why it cut him to the quick when one of your companions made a snide remark about him being on foot whilst you all were riding."

"Incorrigible rudeness, that," Burgoyne sighed.

"You rebuked the man and said he should have his mouth washed out before he dared to call himself a gentleman again. He accused you of being a friend to Papists. You said, 'And what if I am? 'Tis none of your affair!' Then your companions departed without you. Falling out of the hunt, you dismounted and tarried and talked with us for a good quarter of an hour. Even at my age, I knew you were doing Father a kindness, restoring some small measure of dignity to him."

"And I believe I slipped you some licorice sweets," Burgoyne reminisced.

"Indeed," Ned confirmed with a smile. "You gave me a taste for it."

"Splendid!" Burgoyne exclaimed. "I always take pride in introducing my friends to new experiences they might not otherwise have had!" He tilted his head. "Tell me, how old are you now, lad?"

"Eighteen, sir."

"Eighteen…good age. So much ahead of you." Burgoyne stepped back and studied Ned, his eyes taking him in from head to foot. "Things haven't been easy for the family these days, have they? Oh, don't blush, it's just that you look like you've stepped out of the 40's! You haven't been hiding the Young Pretender in a priest hole all these years, have you?"

"No, sir, better than that," Edmund replied, tongue in cheek. "We're still hosting His Majesty King Charles the Second in one of our oak trees."

Burgoyne laughed. "You recusants are a strange breed, but I admire your pluck. Nevertheless, I feel compelled to notify you that time has in fact moved forward, and our illustrious King is no longer George the Second, but his grandson, the third of that name."

"So I have heard, sir," Edmund confirmed.

Burgoyne pulled out a fancy lace handkerchief and finished wiping the mud off Ned's face. "There, I've made you respectable again! But that shan't last long in this weather. Go on, get in the coach before this blasted drizzle makes drowned rats out of the both of us! My poor hat is already in sorry shape!"

Ned chuckled, seeing the way his plume was indeed drooping in the renewed rainfall. "Umm…do you mind…the dog?" He gestured to Kip, who was sniffing at Burgoyne suspiciously. "If it's not convenient, I would be just as content to walk…"

"Nonsense," Burgoyne said, as Kip shook his wet coat yet again. "We'll fit him in."

Ned smiled gratefully and climbed into the coach.

They whiled away the ride with small talk, as Kip, seemingly won over by Burgoyne's renowned charm, snuggled next to him on the seat and let him scratch behind his ears. Then the general went on to tell Ned how his late father had lent him a substantial sum of money after a series of unfortunate events befell him.

"I was in a wretched state, you understand," he lamented dramatically. "There was that misunderstanding during the election—I give a few speeches, buy a few drinks, and suddenly a mob has formed, God save us! Before I know what's what, I find myself hauled off to court for the debacle and berated for borrowing a regimental drummer to announce me at rallies and wearing pistols for my own protection at the polls. Then there was that prodigal son who turned out to be a sore loser and accused me of getting him drunk to cheat him at cards—I would have challenged the villain upon his honor had he stayed to face the consequences, so help me. And then there were a few racing horses not worth the bet…and at the time, I was in the midst of organizing a benefit for the care of military families, which was ruined by some prudes who failed to appreciate the entertainment. It had to do with mermaids, you see…a nautical theme! The production was forced to close early, and I had to make it up to the girls with lots of presents, and that just pushed me further into the pit of destitution! I ended up having to ask for a few of the more expensive ones back to use as collateral…a diamond necklace, in particular…you know how it is. That young lady was most cross indeed! So you see how scant my prospects were when I came to see your father about a loan. My supporters had all but abandoned me, and my opponents were baying for my blood. At the very least, I knew conscientious Papists such as yourselves had no stake in voting for or against me in the election, so it was worth asking. And he obliged me, dear man, though for the life of me I don't know where he got the money…"

"He sold a book," Edmund stated.

Burgoyne tilted his head. "A book, you say?"

"Yes, a very old book, saved from destruction when the monasteries were being ransacked under King Henry. It was an illuminated manuscript, and the cover was embossed with gold. I remember Father taking me on his lap when I was a tiny child and showing me the illustrations. I would name all the different colors, and he would tell me that I was very clever. It looked like a rainbow had been splattered all over the pages, the brilliant sort that sometimes comes out after it's been raining for days and then the sun finally breaks through. I would tell Father as much, and he would run my hand over the cover and trace my finger along the Cross in the center. That, he said, was the sign of the true Son."

Burgoyne bit his lip. "Your father thought very highly of such mementos."

"He did," Edmund agreed. "It was sacred to him."

"But he sold it," the general noted, mystified.

"Friendship was sacred to him as well," Edmund said. "He would never turn away from that."

"How did your mother feel about the sale?" Burgoyne queried.

"She didn't like it much," Ned admitted.

"I hardly blame her." Burgoyne was quiet for a while, then said softly, "Were you there when he passed, lad?"

Edmund nodded. "I…I was holding his hand."

He did not, of course, say that a priest had managed to slip into the house to give Francis Southworth the Last Rites of Mother Church. He did not speak about how he had kissed the old man's forehead, still shiny with holy chrism, and swore by the oil now moist upon his lips that he, too, would keep the faith of their fathers, true and unbroken, unto death.

Burgoyne roused Edmund from his melancholic memories by reaching over and laying his hand on the boy's arm, where the black mourning band was still tied. "I know, my boy. You miss him very much."

The genuine warmth in his voice and eyes touched Ned. He swallowed the lump in his throat and nodded.

"An old-fashioned sort, your father was," Burgoyne reflected, "like a knight from days of yore, who had grown infirm in the body, but still possessed all the faculties of the mind and powers of the soul. Best of all, he was a man of culture, like myself! Wouldn't you know it, I met him at the opening night of *Henry V* in Preston. Not the grandest production, particularly for those of us accustomed to London, but I was out to support it nonetheless. Your father was there too. You see, he shared my view of Shakespeare. The Bard of Avon, we agreed, shall yet be remembered as the greatest of our English playwrights, for he knew how to burrow through the many layers of man's nature, in comedy and tragedy alike. Anyway, when the play we attended had concluded, your father said aloud, not caring a fig for what anyone within earshot thought, 'Tan my hide, but this Henry was one of us, with a true love of Mother Church, and would surely have been a recusant in later days! Hear you all, they called him the mirror of Christian kings, and he had his soldiers sing *Non Nobis* and *Te Deum* when the field was won!'"

Burgoyne laughed, and Ned joined him shyly. Then the boy mumbled, "He wasn't wrong on that account."

"No, I suppose he wasn't," Burgoyne admitted. "Your father was the descendant of a knight who fought at Agincourt, was he not?"

"Yes," said Edmund. "Though we have many ancestors who fought in many battles."

"Ah, good soldier's blood!" Burgoyne exclaimed, and Kip barked as if to agree with him. "You should by all rights be in the service!"

Ned squinted. "By all rights, general?"

Burgoyne shrugged. "Well...if not for your religious scruples."

"I see."

"As I said, your father's pluck was priceless, and so we made fast friends, despite his attachment to the old faith. Perhaps he and I made up a pair of rogue knights, each upsetting the apple cart in our own way. If he had known how to ingratiate himself with courtly types, I imagine he could have used his good nature to exert considerable influence in areas of public life not prohibited to him. There are recusant families who have managed to do so, not least the Duke of Norfolk. The trick is to learn how to play well with a bad hand. Take it from an old gamester like me."

"My father was never adept at game-playing," Ned stated, "and most certainly not for the purpose of winning friends in high places."

"I know," Burgoyne sighed. "He was too true by nature, in what he stood for and against, to court anyone's favor. He was also too generous to the undeserving, but I cannot seem to fault

"Then learn to trust us more," Ned responded, taking her hand. "We treasure the pearl of great price, and have no intention of bartering it away for lesser goods. However, that does not mean all lesser goods must be abandoned, including courtesy."

Perpetua pulled her hand away. "You are tempted by Burgoyne's army stories. Admit it."

"I enjoy his company, madam, and am not ashamed to say it. He possesses a lively spirit and winning manners. But more importantly, he has a good heart."

"He's taken the Test Act, like every other officer of this king must do!" Perpetua reminded him. "It is weighed down with vows contrary to our faith, not least of all the injunction to apprehend priests, so they might be banished from this realm or cast into a dungeon for the rest of their days!"

"He will not happen upon any here, even if he came over unexpectedly," Ned assured. "Priests arrive in disguise, after all, and if they happen to be in the midst of performing their office when a guest comes to the door, well…we do not have priest holes for nothing. But in truth, I do not believe the general to be nearly so eager about priest-catching as you think. Such oaths amongst officers are merely a formality…"

"In the end, he will still abide by that formality to uphold his law and save his skin!" Perpetua predicted. "Mark my words, he will abide by it!"

Not long after this conversation, General Burgoyne took it upon himself to send several gardeners over to the Southworth estate. Undaunted by the brooding of territorial Tobias, and eager to keep Burgoyne as an employer, the gardeners successfully hacked their way through the burgeoning jungle outside, and in around a week's time, the general appearance of the yards had improved considerably. On the heels of this triumph, Burgoyne sent over a couple of servants to expand the Southworth household staff. Perpetua was adamantly against taking them on, since they were Protestants, and she feared they might report any number of legal infringements the family regularly committed. But Ned found it impossible to politely refuse them, so he did his best to learn more about them so they might be smoothly integrated into the household.

One of them was a sonorous voiced, middle-aged man named Hubert, who Burgoyne had selected as a manservant for Edmund. But the lack of staff over the years had caused Ned to become quite accustomed to taking care of himself, including tidying his own room and pressing his own clothes. Hubert became increasingly put out by this show of self-sufficiency from his new master, seeming to take it as a personal mark against his own services. Fortunately, it came to light that Hubert had formerly worked as a stagehand for a London theater which Burgoyne had frequented before it closed down. He had also been a part time actor, though his only speaking parts involved conveying messages or giving directions to main characters. To keep Hubert's morale up, Edmund promptly capitalized on his backstage talents by putting him to work as a handy-man around the manor. He seemed to be in his element reciting excerpts from *Hamlet* while hammering nails into boards.

"To be or not to be: that is the question," Hubert would dramatically query, "whether 'tis nobler in the mind to suffer the slings and arrows of outrageous fortune, or to take up arms against a sea of troubles, and by opposing end them…"

Perpetua had been known to reference that very speech in memory of their Jacobite cousins who had sacrificed everything trying to restore a royal house devoted to the See of Rome. She said that Shakespeare himself may have been a secret Catholic, not without sympathy for those struggling under Queen Elizabeth's persecution, even though she was his literary patroness. He may even have been privy to some conspiracies to dethrone her in favor of the Catholic claimant, Mary, Queen of Scots. Ned was not sure if that was true or not, but his mother's romanticism towards such drastic measures did not sit well with him. Schemes of that sort had never ended their troubles, but only increased them.

In addition to Hubert, the other newcomer in the household was a fourteen-year-old maidservant named Fanny. Her mother had been a small-time actress at the same theater Harry used to call home, and it was rumored Burgoyne had engaged in an amorous interlude with said actress backstage area after her performance of a sultry dance. Burgoyne took it upon himself to employ young Fanny following her mother's death, given the broad possibility that the girl might be of his flesh and blood. Ned observed that she had a very active imagination, talking to herself and twirling around in front of anything reflective, but she was a sturdy little thing and did her work well. While running a few errands into the village, Fanny befriended Jamie, a local stable hand who became a frequent visitor at the Southworth's servant quarters. Unfortunately, in addition to providing her with company, he also provided her with broadsheets full of stories of Papist assassins. Even though she couldn't read, the lurid illustrations were enough for her to get jumpy on the job.

Perpetua did nothing to ease Fanny's nerves, dead-eyeing the girl disapproving when they were in the same room. Soon, she was once again complaining about the situation to her son.

"Why did Burgoyne burden us with his disreputable theater acquaintances, one of whom is likely his ill-begotten offspring?"

"I believe it had something to do with charity," Edmund remarked evenly, as he scanned a newspaper article about more unrest in the American colonies following the closing of Boston Harbor. "I know you have become rather hostile to the world, Mother, but *caritas* remains chief among the virtues. Perhaps we could afford to extend a bit of it ourselves, even to those who may be, as you so delicately put it, ill-begotten."

"Do you not realize the risk we are taking?" Perpetua challenged. "That sort will do anything for a few extra coins, whether by means of betrayal or theft!"

"And what, thus far, has been stolen?" Ned asked.

"Agnes says she caught the little hussy stealing a lump of sugar from the bowl and stuffing it into her mouth before serving tea!" Perpetua declared.

Ned chuckled. "One day, a lump of sugar, the next day, who knows? The crown jewels of England, perhaps?"

Perpetua gave her son the same hard stare she had been giving Fanny. "The simple fact is that I don't trust Protestants under my roof. Even your father, as kindly as he was towards them, would never hire them for fear of their filing reports against us. Besides, it is our duty to provide employment for our poor fellow Catholics in this household. If there is any work to be done, they should be the ones doing it."

"These people were sent to us by our benefactor," Ned stated quietly. "We cannot simply dismiss them without good reason."

"I'll give you two," Perpetua shot back. "Firstly, how shall we ever be able to have mass said here again without monumental risk?"

"When the time comes for a mass to be said, we will give our Protestant servants the day off. I'm sure they won't complain."

"So very sure of everything, aren't you?" Perpetua snapped.

"No, I simply believe that…"

"Secondly, isn't your mother's discomfort reason enough for you to send these heretics away?" Perpetua demanded. "Or do Burgoyne's feelings matter to you so much more?"

"Madam," Edmund addressed her respectfully, "if I send Hubert and Fanny away merely for being Protestants, I would not be doing unto others that which I would have done unto me."

"You are a most imprudent master of this house," she ground out. "You say I raised you well. Yet this is not what I raised you to be!"

Edmund set his newspaper down on the table. "I would rather be imprudent than unjust."

A month later, Burgoyne surprised Edmund by inviting him to be his traveling companion down to London. At first Ned was hesitant, and the general accurately suspected it was in part out of deference to Perpetua's wishes.

"There now, your mother can't hide you behind her skirts forever," Burgoyne insisted.

"Respecting one's parents is all well and good, but you're of age, lad, and the master of an estate! You must learn to stand on your own two feet and take your place in the wider world!"

"There's more to it than that," Ned replied.

"Is there?" Burgoyne pressed. "Don't tell me you're afraid of me!"

"No, it's just…you've already done so much for us, and I fear I'd be rather a bore to you," Ned confessed. "I have…simple tastes, compared to yours. You'd start to hate having me around after a day or so, and it would become incredibly awkward…"

"You and your sister have too low of an opinion of yourselves," Burgoyne sighed. "You've been on your knees for too long, beseeching heaven for humility. Depart your sanctuary, young man, and test your mettle."

"Mettle?" Ned chortled. "I'm afraid I'm an incurable country mouse."

"Don't be coy," Burgoyne lectured him. "I can see in your eyes that you do not desire a wholly passive life. No, you crave a bit of action, for you are the descendant of knights, who held aloft their banners with grace and might of chivalry. And here I am, a fellow descendant of such knights, offering it to you! Won't you reach out and take it?"

Ned glanced down shyly. "I'd like to continue keeping you company, very much."

"Because you know that I know something of the world, dear," Burgoyne decided confidently.

"Because you have shown us kindness," Ned countered softly. "I want us to be friends. I mean…not just to repay a debt, or redeem my family name, but between you and me, for its own sake." He turned his eyes back up again. "You were right. I miss my father."

Burgoyne's eyes gleamed with pity, and he put a hand on Ned's shoulder. "A poor substitute for that saintly gentleman, I know. But I think we might have a bit of fun, all the same. What say you?" He extended his other hand for the boy to shake.

Edmund smiled, then after a moment's hesitation, he grasped Burgoyne's hand.

Chapter 3: A TRUE ENGLISHMAN

Journeying by coach from Preston to London, General Burgoyne decided that he and Edmund should make a detour into Oxfordshire. Using his connections, he obtained access to Blenheim Palace for the two of them. Impeccably dressed as always, this time in civilian garb with an elegant cravat and ruffled sleeves, Burgoyne was in his element amidst the almost dizzying array of baroque artistry. Edmund, feeling rather dapper himself in one of his new suits of clothing, could not help but smile over his friend's characteristic enthusiasm while they were touring the palace.

At last, they reached the set of famous tapestries depicting John Churchill, the Duke of Marlborough, triumphant at the Battle of Blenheim in 1704, at the height of the War of Spanish Succession. He seemed like a figure out of myth, at the center of his greatest victory against the Sun King, Louis XIV of France. Adorned in his flowing wig and claret coat, he sat astride his white stallion like Saint George about to slay a dragon. His loyal officers stood around him, seemingly in awe of their nearness to his greatness.

"Now that is a true Englishman," Burgoyne declared, pointing at one of the tapestries. "He knew how to choose the ground for his campaigns with the eye of an artist, dropping his lace handkerchief to indicate the spot before each battle, then seeking the handkerchief out and plucking it up again when he had chased the enemy from the field." He pointed to another tapestry. "There, you see, he is about to scribble upon a drum's head to inform Queen Anne and his wife, Lady Sarah, of the day's good tidings. A great man, he was, protector of our liberty and laws, whose memory shall live on while the British name and language endure, as it says on the column of victory outside…" He turned to his young companion and asked slyly, "Still bitter about the Glorious Revolution, Ned?"

Edmund shrugged. The momentous year of 1688 seemed long ago now, though also not so long ago, not for England, ever laboring under the weight of her past. King James, the second surviving son of King Charles I, had been the last Catholic to reign over the three kingdoms of England, Scotland, and Ireland. James had already suffered for his own conversion to the faith in various ways, including having his children taken away from him to be raised by Protestants and being dismissed from his beloved Royal Navy. Still, he proved instrumental in the deathbed conversion to Catholicism of his brother, King Charles II, and when he ascended to the throne himself, he used his power to push through laws which would grant religious toleration to dissenters from the established Church. This he intended to extend to both his fellow Catholics and most marginalized Protestant sects, except for the militant Scottish Covenanters whom he deemed to be enemies of his house and royal prerogative.

James believed, as the Jesuit martyr Edmund Campion had believed, that if only Catholics were offered freedom to debate, they would win their countryman back into the fold of the faith. To this end, he intended to assure Catholics would be allowed to return to the universities they had founded and serve in both the parliament and the military. Catholic priests and nuns would once again walk the English streets freely, clad in their religious garb, and the Catholic clergy and laypeople alike would be able to wear their rosaries and relics upon their person without fear. Gradually, the Protestant populace would grow accustomed to these sights and their attitudes would change. But James found his goals frustrated by opposition parliamentarians, prelates of the established Church, and the university dons, all threatened by this "encroachment" upon their supremacy. They cited the persecution of Huguenots under the Catholic king in France, and stirred up the people with dread of the burning times under Queen Mary I returning for heretics.

In response, James pushed forward his edicts more forcefully and put down subsequent rebellions more brutally. In his pursuit of tolerance, increasingly intolerant measures were enacted, and in the aftermath of the Protestant Duke of Monmouth's failed uprising, the Bloody Assizes under the ruthless Judge Jeffries were inflicted upon the offending west country, condemning all those suspected of treason to grisly fates. Monmouth himself was refused the clemency for which he pleaded, and was horrifically hacked to death by a clumsy axman. James, for all his good intentions, was not adept at the game he was playing.

The fiercely Protestant John Churchill, patronized by James from his youth, became increasingly disillusioned following Monmouth's downfall, even though Churchill himself had a hand in crushing the rising. At a crucial moment, he switched his allegiance from King James to his Protestant son-in-law William and daughter Mary, insisting that no man or king could be truly English and also be Catholic. James, afflicted by a terrible nosebleed, cast the royal seal into the River Thames, then fled the realm. William and Mary became joint monarchs, and the Bill of Rights established during their reign officially barred Catholics from ever sitting upon the throne again...as well as from bearing arms, or speaking in parliament, or holding a military commission. And they called this revolution…glorious.

But it had been a long time ago, everyone said…more than eighty years now. After William and Mary's reign, Mary's sister Anne had come to the throne, and after Anne's passing, the crown had been extended to her Protestant cousins from the House of Hanover. So many changes had been wrought in Britain under each successive monarch, cementing her place amongst the great powers of the world. Yet some things remained the same, and the long shadow of 1688 continued to fall over Edmund Southworth and all recusants like him.

Nevertheless, Ned responded to Burgoyne's remarks upon the subject tactfully. Gesturing up to Marlborough in the tapestry, he remarked, "Far be it from me not to appreciate the story of a French defeat, sir."

Burgoyne slapped him on the back. "Good lad! Your family was never shy about fighting the frogs, from Agincourt on!"

"No, indeed, sir."

"Besides, surely there are things to strike your fancy in Marlborough the man, regardless of his politics. Why, he was called the last cavalier! From the princes of Europe to the meanest born man upon the field, he was nothing if not courteous. Even to the enemy, he was marked out for his mercy."

"All to his credit," Ned conceded.

"He was quite the man for communion too," Burgoyne remarked. "I mean, the sacrament of the Lord's supper…well, you know what I mean! He took a high view of it…well, not high by your standards, certainly, but high, I mean, in that it was important to him to receive it…"

"A reasonable conclusion for all Christians to draw," Ned replied.

Burgoyne looked back up at the embroidered figure and smiled wistfully. "All that glory, and they say he just wanted to get back home. He yearned to walk in the garden with his lady and see his children grow up beneath the fruit trees…"

"Wouldn't any man exchange battle honors to be with their loved ones?" Ned queried.

Burgoyne chuckled awkwardly, even anxiously. "Yes, but…well, his wife reveled in all this, as any woman would do." He gestured around. "Her husband's renown reflected through her, like the sun through a prism, and she could bask in his glory, radiating all the colors of his triumphs."

"Yet surely she desired his presence above all," Ned said.

"You might be right," Burgoyne conceded. "The Duchess of Marlborough was an exceedingly ambitious woman, but my own experience with army wives indicates that…" His voice drifted off, and a look of guilt crossed his face. Then his features brightened again, and he nudged Ned in the side teasingly. "They do say Marlborough knew how to pleasure his lady, even with his boots still on! Now there's a gentleman to live up to, what?"

Ned giggled bashfully at Burgoyne's ribald sense of humor. "I hope I shall be invited to the tapestry unveiling when one is stitched together for you. After all, sir, your reputation proves that Marlborough was not, in fact, the last cavalier."

"Ah, yes, up with King Charles and down with Cromwell, lest all the theaters end up closed and I find myself clapped in irons," Burgoyne chortled. "But in all seriousness, such a commemoration as you predict might come sooner than later, especially if the colonials keep acting like whining infants, tossing their baubles out of the cradle. Then we'll have no choice but to play the part of a stern parent and pacify them."

"You really think the tax protests in America will lead to violence?" Ned queried with concern. "I know there's been the odd clash between mobs and soldiery for years now, including that awful shooting in Boston, but…"

"The Bostonians themselves were responsible for that unfortunate incident, provoking the soldiery to the breaking point with taunts and projectiles," Burgoyne reminded him. "It was nothing short of a mob in the end. Captain Preston did his best to restore order, but it was too late. In the confusion, one of the soldiers fell on the ice, and shots were fired."

"But I read that the soldiers were acquitted of murder by a colonial court, with only a couple found guilty of manslaughter," Ned recalled. "They were even defended by a colonial, Mister John Adams."

"The same Mister Adams who has joined his cousin Samuel in increasingly radical activities since that time," Burgoyne stated.

"That being as it may, surely his willingness to defend the King's troops provides some hope for a peaceful resolution to the wider troubles," Ned offered hopefully. "At the very least, we've not had a repetition of that ugly event."

"What was their little tea party last December if not ugly?" Burgoyne queried. "Wanton destruction of three full shiploads of tea, dumped into Boston Harbor because these incendiaries could not bring themselves to pay a three penny tax to offset costs from the last war, fought in their defense. The vandals caused such a panic, the Bank of England was forced to close its doors, and some men lost."

"Yes, I know," Ned said. "A gentleman farmer in our vicinity invested heavily in the East India Company, and his profits were to come from that tea. Father had to get up from his sick bed and talk the poor man out of taking a leap from his roof when the bad news broke."

"Did he also lend this unfortunate neighbor money he really couldn't afford to part with?" Burgoyne guessed.

Ned nodded. "Mother wasn't pleased with his decision, but…well, she rarely is. I was, though."

Burgoyne sighed. "He was too pure for this world. But no such generosity would have proved necessary had the colonists done their duty and reached into their purses. But instead, they resorted to mindless destruction. Now they complain about the closing of their port and make trouble for the King's troops stationed there. If they want their trade to resume and the soldiers to leave, they should simply pay for the ruined tea and expunge the radicals amongst them."

"Perhaps that may yet happen," Ned said, "or perhaps a royal delegation might be convened to get to the root of the unrest and find a solution palatable to all. Surely some settlement can be reached…"

"The King's government should never fall into the habit of settling with mobs, especially when it comes to the supremacy of parliament," Burgoyne reiterated. "If we spare the rod, we spoil the children. My experience makes me as qualified as the next man to put them over my knee and teach them to respect their venerable mother, Lady Britannia, and esteemed father, Georgius Rex."

"And you think such a spanking will inspire tapestries?" Ned asked dubiously.

"Oh, many disciplinary actions have gained the accolades of a grateful nation, Ned," Burgoyne assured. "I grieve the loss of British blood, even the diluted sort pumping through colonial veins. But if they mean to make a fight of it, I'm afraid we'll have to bloody their noses to put the fear of God and the King into them."

Ned bit his lip. "I pray they will not fight."

"Yes, well, never you fret, either way. There's always a silver lining to every storm cloud, my boy. If you can't see it, then be it."

"How, sir?"

"By becoming what you are meant to be from birth," Burgoyne answered. "I, amongst other things, was meant to be a soldier. God could not have made it clearer to me, and I've tried to make good use of the talents allotted me lest I disgrace the One that made me. Of course, I've always taken inspiration from the great figures of our past, so perhaps they made me too." He glanced up once again at the tapestry. "*Historia est vitae magistra.* Do you know what that means, Ned?"

"History is life's teacher," Edmund translated.

"Good, good," Burgoyne praised him. "You seem to have received classical education!"

Ned shrugged. "Something like that, sir."

After departing from Blenheim, the two travelers continued on the long coach ride south. Burgoyne continued to pepper his speech with Latin maxims, as if it were some sort of inside joke only his young Catholic companion would understand. The quotes were usually from Roman soldiers and sages, since stoicism was all the rage in officer circles and had caused the tongue of the ancient Church to come back in vogue, though not for the purpose of religious devotion. Burgoyne himself could hardly be called stoic in terms of foregoing pleasures of the flesh, but his reputation for fearlessness under fire certainly fitted the tradition. There were moments, sometimes even a split second, when Ned would look into Burgoyne's lustrous eyes and see his soul, burning for something beyond luxury, and he knew with perfect clarity why men followed him into battle willingly.

When Burgoyne and Edmund finally arrived in London, they booked a room for themselves in an opulent hotel which the general said that he frequented. Both the exterior and interior of the building were elegant, but Ned felt a creeping sense of unease about the establishment, complete with its sprawling gambling tables and gaudily clad female attendants. They were given a warm welcome by the matron, her powdered breasts puffed up at the bodice like two nestling doves and her tall powdered wig adorned with iridescent feathers and glistening gems.

"Our Johnny, returned to his home away from home," she twitted in an aristocratic Irish accent, extending a hand to Burgoyne. "What kept you away from the roost so long, you old gamecock? The hens have missed you!"

"Ah, I thought I was more closely modeled after Reynard the Fox when it came to this charming henhouse," Burgoyne said with a wink.

"Aye, a true-born lady-killer," she clucked.

"Indeed," he confirmed, kissing her fingers, "but I'm afraid as a man of state, business must come before pleasure, my dear Georgiana."

"Since when?" she challenged, and they both laughed.

"You're right," Johnny conceded. "I have not chosen the better part! But here I am, a penitent at your door! Now won't you pardon my grievous fault, or must I sprinkle ashes on my forehead before you'll grant me absolution?"

"Ha-ha. Perish the thought of you repenting of anything. But if you must be put through a cleansing ritual…" She took the glistening glass slipper that had been sitting on the bar, then poured bubbling champagne into it before extending it to him. "Purge yourself with this libation to the gods! Down the hatch, in one gulp!"

He bowed low from the waist, gallantly accepting the challenge. Then he took the slipper and drank down the champagne. He smirked upon finishing, and pretended as if he were going to hurl the slipper into the nearby hearth.

"No, you don't, Johnny!" she cried, snatching the slipper away from him. "That's my lucky piece, you know!"

"I thought I had the only lucky piece you needed, pet," Burgoyne laughed.

She rolled her eyes. "Why not let the lady decide? For that matter, why not give us businesswomen the vote?"

"Are you sure you want it?" he asked. "Politics is a nasty business. Good intentions count for nothing, and everyone hates you no matter what stand you take!"

"Dearie, being the proprietress of this establishment has taught me everything I need to know about being unable to please everyone, work my woe," she declared. "I still come out on top most times, as you well know."

"Alright, you've convinced me," Burgoyne decided. "I shall strike a blow to liberate the female population of the realm from the shackles put upon them by my ungrateful sex, if ever the vote should arise."

"You'd better. You know I'd find out if you betrayed us."

He put a hand over his heart. "'Pon my honor, madam! Now, will you be so kind as to direct my young traveling companion and myself to our room? This is his first time in the capital, if you can believe it, so I have quite a few plans for him!"

"Oh, I can well imagine." Her eyes twinkled as she gave Ned a friendly glance, and he awkwardly bowed to her, causing her to giggle. "My, my, as much a gentleman as his mentor!" She turned and slipped two keys into Burgoyne's hand. "The first is for your room," she said, "and the second for a massage. We have so very much to catch up about."

With that, she winked and sauntered off.

"She's the bastard daughter of a lord in Tipperary who managed to triumph over her natural birth with her natural endowments," Burgoyne informed Ned. "An endlessly intriguing woman, possessing brains and bosoms both…" He must have observed Ned's uneasiness. "Listen, my boy, you don't have to do anything you don't want to do here. But the run of the house is yours, my treat."

Ned stared at him for a long moment, then mumbled, "Thank you, sir."

"Of course," Burgoyne replied. "You are my guest."

"Then you wouldn't think your guest was appallingly rude if he chose to retire early?" Edmund asked.

"Oh…why, no…of course not," Burgoyne stammered. "No rush or anything."

Later that night, when Burgoyne returned to their room after an evening spent downstairs reveling, he came upon his young charge sitting on the side of his bed, reading from a Latin prayer book.

"Dear Ned, whatever do you think you're doing?" Burgoyne chided him, taking the little book from his hands. "You know it's not lawful for you to have this, whether it's been printed in this country or smuggled in from the continent. When in Lancashire, you might be able to get away with possessing such contraband, but here in London, people are less likely to turn a blind eye."

"Those are my daily devotions," Ned explained. "I didn't want to lose my place. Besides, I thought you liked Latin."

"Not at risk to my reputation." Burgoyne sighed, shaking his head. "Why can't you make your devotions like a good Englishman?"

Edmund winced. "Are you so sure I was not?"

"Don't be coy…"

"Is it not a fact, sir, that countless Englishmen of blameless reputation, down through the annals of our race, prayed in just such a fashion?"

"It is irrelevant here and now," Burgoyne insisted. "Hell's teeth, please don't tell me you brought any of those bloody beads to pray upon too! I know you've got all manner of superstitious odds and ends stuffed into dusty cupboards back home, but I had hoped they would remain there, safe from the light of sun and moon!"

Edmund swallowed back his frustration. "And what if the book were printed in English instead of Latin?" he pressed. "Would that be more acceptable to the powers that be?"

"No, worse," Burgoyne replied. "Then the intention would be not only to appeal to those already Papist, but to spread Romish influence among Protestant Englishmen."

Ned sighed, but said nothing.

"Now, then, I'm not going to ask you where you obtained this particular book, even though as an officer of the King, I probably should. But you must get rid of it, for both our sakes. We'll be lucky if some serving wench looking for a few easy coins hasn't caught sight of this and made a report to the nearest constable."

Ned's eyes widened. "What would happen to you?"

"I'd have to pay your fine and twist a few arms to get you released without further interrogation or sleepless nights spent on a cell floor, that's what would happen," Burgoyne sighed. "You're just lucky we've become so damn enlightened, or you might be at risk of getting your ears lopped off! But notwithstanding the reduction of the sentence, you wouldn't want me in a pickle for aiding and abetting your infractions, now would you?"

"Of course not."

"Right then."

Before Edmund could respond or react in any way, Burgoyne threw the book into the hearth. Ned involuntarily gasped and stood up from the side of the bed.

"There now, it's not in pain," Burgoyne exhaled, "unlike quite a few heretics who met an untimely end, courtesy of your inquisitors. How many did Bloody Mary fry in this country, in retribution for her father Henry's split with Rome? Three hundred, was it, of both sexes?"

Ned bit his lip, finding nothing with which to respond.

Burgoyne looked momentarily guilty as the book caught fire like kindling and curled up in the hearth. "Ned, I'm sorry I had to do that. It's just...it's the law. I'll get you another prayer book, if you'd like, one that's in English, as you said."

"One that's Anglican, you mean?" Ned surmised.

"Do you think God cares so very much if you pray like an Anglican for a week? I'm sure there's plenty you could find in such a book that would be inoffensive to your tender conscience. We're not that different, you know."

"It seems we are to the law," Edmund replied, staring into the fire.

Burgoyne went over and laid a hand on the boy's shoulder. "You know...I used to be like you. Not in all ways, obviously, but...well, prayer is not unknown to me. I am a Christian, Ned. Just not a very disciplined one. I'm afraid God and I...we don't talk as much as we should these days. I think I bothered Him too much with certain things in the past, without putting in much effort to please Him, and He grew rather cross with me. But...I still speak to Him, when I can put myself in a sober enough head for it. And when the occasion arises for me to take communion, I try to keep my thoughts pure, try to worship Him with a clean heart. Hard to believe I can manage that, isn't it?"

"No," Edmund answered simply, looking him in the eyes.

Burgoyne lowered his own gaze uncomfortably. "Are you cross with me now too?"

"No," he repeated. "You didn't have to take a recusant traveling with you at all."

"I took a friend's son with me," Burgoyne clarified. "One whom I now count as a friend as well. Now let's say no more upon the subject."

The following afternoon, Burgoyne whisked Ned off to the gymnasium of a nearby gentlemen's club, which parliamentarians frequented for recreation. Several pairs of men were fencing on the other side of the room, some with considerable skill.

"Have you ever fenced, Ned?" Burgoyne queried.

"You know I'm not allowed," Ned answered sheepishly.

"I didn't ask what you were allowed to do," Burgoyne clarified. "I asked what you had done."

"I've practiced a little, with the vicar's son," Ned admitted.

"Ha! Always the vicar's son!" Burgoyne chortled. "Bless him, for I intend for you to be my sparring partner."

"But surely putting a sword in my hands is of greater illegality than letting me keep a prayer book in my luggage..."

"Fie, fie!" Burgoyne waved his hand dismissively. "I'm making amends for being law-abiding last night by living on the edge this morning! Indulge my mood swings, boy!"

"But I'm not even good at this," Ned admitted. "Jack and I didn't practice often."

"Then I will have to sharpen your skills," Burgoyne replied. "I've crossed swords with many a Papist Frenchman during my time across the channel, and they were each better off for having been bested by me!"

And so Ned reelected to Burgoyne's persuasion. With fencing swords in hand, the young recusant proved to be just as bad as he had warned, lacking finesse in movement and making wild swings and thrusts.

"Please keep in mind that the goal is not, in fact, to stick me like a pig," Burgoyne panted, pausing to wipe the sweat from his brow with his handkerchief. "I'm taking my life in my hands with you, it seems!"

"Sorry," Edmund mumbled, lowering his blade. "I forgot myself."

"I think you're just a bit too true in everything you do," Burgoyne decided.

"What do you mean, sir?"

"This is a game, Ned, like life itself. We try to get a bit of thrill out of it without hurting anyone unnecessarily. We play pretend."

"You mean like acting?" Ned surmised.

"Just so," Burgoyne concurred. "The world is our stage, and we must do our best to be memorable before the curtain closes. As the ancients said, *non omnis moriar*. We shall not wholly die, providing our memory lives. But that sort of impression requires a bit of make-believe. *En garde!*"

Once again, their blades met, and the sound of clashing metal was pleasing to Ned's ears, for it represented an equality between him and the general which he had not expected to experience. It was the sound not of discord, but of friendship.

When the lesson concluded, Burgoyne took Ned out to the lounge for a drink. He greeted some other club members there, and with a sweeping gesture towards his charge, announced, "Gentlemen, meet my charming friend from the countryside, Master Southworth!"

A man who had just exited the gymnasium, whose gaunt face and bloodshot eyes belied the fact that he did not seem much older than Ned, came up behind Burgoyne and blurted, "Southworth? That name is mostly held by Papists!"

"Is that a fact?" Burgoyne chirped. "Well, whatever his creed may be, I won't let him stick you, Lord Gordon, satisfying as it might be."

Gordon pointed angrily at Edmund. "You have no right bringing a deceitful recusant in here and putting a blade in his hand!"

Burgoyne stepped between Ned and Gordon, his walking cane extended outward. "I am not in the habit of allowing my traveling companions to be insulted."

"You risk much, Burgoyne…"

"Oh? Were you concerned over my welfare in the gymnasium?" the general inquired cheekily. "How sweet of you. Though such worries were quite unnecessary, given my penchant for survival against the odds…"

"That's not what I meant."

"Hmmm…" Burgoyne said nothing more, but casually took a stance that revealed the pistol peeking out from under his coat.

Ned felt his throat tighten. "Please, sirs…" He stepped forward, intent upon intervening before the situation escalated further. "There's no need for–"

Burgoyne held out his arm, preventing Ned from getting in the way. Then he stared Gordon down unflinchingly, seeming to dare him to make his challenge or back down.

Gordon ground his teeth together. "You may be born in London, but you show yourself to be too much a Lancastrian by nature, accustomed to living amidst the festering sores of popery that have been allowed to bubble unchecked in your county for far too long!"

"Mine is a Lancashire family by ancestry, it's true, quite Protestant since the time of King Hal," Burgoyne stated coolly. "Nevertheless, I like to think I live up to the customs of that region in terms of hospitality towards all, regardless of creed. Your lack in this area does not reflect well upon your own Scotch ancestry."

"I would much rather be inhospitable than perverse!" Gordon retorted. "You're more likely to defend Papists than support the rights of our Protestant brethren in America! You are naught but a false Whig in the Commons!"

Ned saw Burgoyne's cheeks flush, and for a moment, he thought the general might be the one to issue a challenge. The other gentlemen in the lounge appeared to fear the same, their faces blanching. But Burgoyne seemed to think better upon it and suppressed his wrath.

"I vote as I see fit, whenever I see fit, and resist becoming a slave to the party line," he responded icily. "If that is a crime for a free-born Briton, then I am guilty. As for your own judgments, I cannot help that you deem it more appropriate to coddle presumptuous nobodies in the colonial hinterland than to show respect to a fine young man from one of England's oldest families." He placed a hand on Edmund's shoulder in a gesture of solidarity.

"I would prefer to keep company with the lowest born settler in the crudest log cabin than to associate with even the highest born sycophant of Rome!" Gordon declared. "We provoked our American brethren by denying them representation in Parliament and giving the Papist French in Canada rights which in this country are owed to Protestants alone!"

"So you want to bend the rules to appease every American complaint, but subjugate the Canadians in the most merciless manner?" Burgoyne countered. "No. You would be lenient with those deserving of discipline and harsh with those worthy of concessions. That is not in accord with our middle way. The refusal to bend ensures breaking. Take care of yourself, lest you be the one who ends up broken."

"We'll see who ends up broken in the end," Gordon growled. "The good Protestants of this empire will not be mocked!"

"Have your people contact my people if you wish to carry out your threats. Otherwise, I shall ignore them entirely." Then he turned to Edmund. "Come along, Ned. It's high time we got some fresh air." And with that, Burgoyne took him by the arm and hurried him outside.

"Who is this Gordon person?" Ned asked.

"A navy man with noble bloodlines and a place in parliament," Burgoyne said. "Gripped by enthusiasm, I'm afraid. He wants to change the world, perhaps for the better, but is going about it half-cocked. His sailors love him for trying to do right by them and improve their living conditions. But he's made enemies among his superiors through his opinionated nature and is now quite angry with the world. God only knows what's to become of him."

Ned remained silent, feeling decidedly unnerved now, and rather wishing he could go home.

Burgoyne seemed to sense his mood and squeezed his hand. "Now don't let him get you down. He's not quite right in the head, and everyone knows it." The general leaned over and whispered in Ned's ear, "Of course, if one must be eccentric, one could at least learn from me and be pleasant about it." He playfully nudged Ned in the ribs. "But let's not let him ruin our day when there's touring to be done. You're safe and sound with me; no matter what you may be, or what may befall us, you can always count on that much."

Shortly thereafter, the general called a carriage to take them to Westminster. When they alighted, Burgoyne took Edmund on a proper city stroll. Accustomed to plenty of room on his country walks, Ned found the crowded streets rather discomforting. He was not nearly as adept at bobbing and weaving through a crowd as Gentleman Johnny, who seemed to take it all in his stride, measuring distances between persons with his walking cane and tipping his plumed hat to every blooming beauty that passed by. Once or twice, he did become a bit too enamored with the fairer sex, following this or that feminine specimen with his eyes, and Ned worried that his guide might end up flattened like a pancake on Shrove Tuesday should he accidentally stumble into the path of an oncoming carriage. Alternately, the general might find himself confronted by a jealous husband unamused by his ogling, resulting in a showdown right there in the street and leaving Ned to hike all the way back north.

Fortunately, both potential disasters failed to unfold, and when Burgoyne's focus returned from womanly charms, he took Ned to see the inside of the Houses of Parliament, where he proudly represented the fair township of Preston. Edmund grew slightly ill at ease in Westminster Hall, where Thomas More, Edmund Campion, Lord Derwentwater, and other doomed Catholics of renown had been put on trial for their lives. His dread only grew when Burgoyne insisted they head for the Tower of London and, true to form, he made a few ill-timed jokes by Traitor's Gate, where the heads of the martyrs had been placed. The fact that Burgoyne then felt the need to insist he was only joking just made it all much worse. Ghosts of the slain seemed to pervade the very air in such locations, and with memories of that deranged man Gordon still assaulting him, Edmund felt as if the past was invading the present.

Things only got worse when they reached Tyburn, the infamous place of execution for convicted criminals and Catholic priests. A hanging was underway as they approached, with a handful of gawkers gathered to watch the sport. Ned saw the victim briefly, a small body twitching in mid-air, before turning away in disgust and hurrying away.

"Sorry, Ned," Burgoyne apologized, coming up behind him. "I suppose my dark humor got the better of me, but I didn't realize there'd be a hanging going on. You don't seem the type to enjoy watching condemned wretches swing."

"Are you?" Ned queried, a little more sharply than he had intended.

"Not particularly," Burgoyne admitted. "But the lower classes have a vulgar sense of what passes for entertainment. It can have a base appeal, watching someone else die, simply because they are someone else. The punishment is being meted out to another, which means, for the moment, the observers are safe, whatever their own trespasses. The law has long made use of that primal reality. It is a time-honored morality play to keep the general populace on the straight and narrow path…"

"Like disemboweling Catholic priests to deter others from saying mass for the faithful?" Edmund blurted.

"Or burning outspoken Protestants at the stake to deter others from voicing their opposition to the Bishop of Rome," Burgoyne replied. "I could take you over to Smithfield where the fires were lit, if you want…" He paused and sighed. "I know, I know, my bringing that up again is petty. None of it was your fault. But you mustn't blame me either."

"I think Christians killing Christians is a loathsome thing, whatever form it takes," Ned murmured. "It makes me sick…"

"Well, that boy you just glimpsed was almost certainly not being hanged for religious beliefs," Burgoyne stated. "Most likely the crime was petty theft…"

"Isn't it easy enough for poverty to lead to theft?" Ned asked. "Even the brief glimpses I have seen of it since our arrival here prove that it is so much worse here than anything at home. The poorest tenant farmers have it better than this, and we have not even strayed into the slums."

"Be that as it may, we must maintain a degree of order for anything to function in society," Burgoyne stated. "I know I like to play fast and loose with the rules ever and anon, but–"

"But must order so often lead to death?" Ned challenged. "Even for children, like that, who have likely known nothing but the deprivation and filth of the streets?"

Burgoyne was quiet for a moment. "If I had my way, we would find more humane solutions to many of our problems. Then again, if I had my way, I would be able to get you settled in whatever career you fancied, your Romanism notwithstanding. But I'm afraid this is the world we live in, and I don't always have my way. Perhaps someday, we may find avenues of reform to pursue in these matters, such as those I have pursued in the army. But until that day comes, I think we should still strive to indulge in whatever beauty life has to offer, in spite of its cruelty. And…I consider fellowship to be amongst its foremost beauties, don't you?"

"Of course," Ned confirmed.

"Good lad. Now…would you fancy a trip to the Abbey?"

Edmund's mood brightened a bit. "The Church of Saint Peter, Prince of the Apostles?"

Burgoyne smirked. "Yes," he said, "the Abbey."

So off they went, with Edmund genuinely eager to steal away a few quiet moments to clear his head and pray. But once inside Westminster Abbey, he was struck by a sense of hollowness that haunted him. It was the seat of an ancient ache, generated by the schism, where the ages lay interred and new monuments had sprung up, little shrines of the state, saluting the rising empire that had disowned her eldest children.

But even as Burgoyne spoke of his intention to be buried there after his own star had risen over the nation, Ned took some small comfort in one fact: Edward the Confessor was still resting there, for he was not only a saint of England, but a king of England too, the last Saxon sovereign before the Norman Conquest, when the old order was swept away by a new one, though they all shared the same faith. Not so now.

"I shall leave you, for a few moments, to your pilgrimage," Burgoyne whispered, then turned to make his exit.

"General?" Ned called after him.

"Yes, my boy?"

"Do you consider *him* to be a true Englishman?" Edmund asked, gesturing towards the Confessor's tomb.

Burgoyne laughed. "I'll tell you a little something about me, dear," he confided. "My idol is Richard, *Cour de Lion*. When I lived for a spell in France, I devoured romances about him and translated some of them into English to sharpen my scholastic skills. I even visited the burial place of his fearless heart in Rouen Cathedral. He was a bit of a madcap, the way he rode between the lines of Crusaders and Saracens, daring death to find him. He even claimed to have seen Saint George in a vision, mounted upon a peerless white stallion, spurring the English troops on to victory! But I suppose he's my kind of madman. Not only did he get his blood up in battle, but also when composing songs and seducing women. He could not help but put passion into everything he touched, if you take my meaning!"

"Including his religion," Edmund murmured, "and repentance."

"Yes, I gather he was the most pious of the Plantagenets, even with burning loins and bloody sword," Burgoyne conceded. "Our knightly ancestors were probably out there following him on whatever adventures providence allowed him. And believe it or not, his medieval popery, as primitive as I consider it to be, has not proven unduly off-putting to me. No, no, I still consider him to have been as true an Englishman as they come…for a Frenchman, at any rate!"

After Burgoyne left, Edmund remained inside before the Confessor's tomb for far longer than a few moments, reciting from memory the Latin prayers consigned to the hearth. When he finally finished his devotions and went back outside, he found the sun was dipping in the sky, casting streaks of gold and scarlet across the edifice of the Abbey.

Ned felt something small bump into him and a little hand reach inside his coat. Ned turned and saw a smudge-faced street urchin, who bit and scratched as Ned struggled to pry the pocket watch out of his hand. It was old, and hardly worked anymore, but it was from his father, and he was determined not to lose it. At last, Ned managed to pin the boy down to the ground, pulling his arm tight behind his back.

"Let go of it," Ned ground out, twisting his arm tighter yet when the urchin refused to unclasp his fist. "Let go!"

At last the boy squeaked in pain and released the watch. Then he just curled up in a ball, clearly too terrified to move, making a low growling noise in his throat like a wounded wild dog. How old was he? Seven? Eight? Ned couldn't tell. But he had a very slight frame, rather like the other boy he had seen earlier that day, meeting his pitiful end for the amusement of spectators.

"My God, Ned, you're better at scrapping than I thought, even if the opponent happens to be half your size," Burgoyne remarked, appearing behind them. "You keep holding the little miscreant down, and I'll call a constable…"

"No," Edmund retorted.

"But he robbed you…"

"No," Ned repeated. "Please…"

He yanked the boy upright, rummaged inside his own coat, and placed something shiny in the miniature thief's hand. Then Ned released him. It took several moments for the trembling child to realize his own freedom before dashing off into the shadows.

"You gave him a coin," Burgoyne observed.

"He needs to eat," Ned said. "I could feel his bones."

"You're soft, Ned."

"Because I don't want a boy to be hanged or left to starve? Because I will not turn in another, when I wish to remain free?" Edmund held Burgoyne's gaze for a long time. "I'm a recusant. I can't help but think like that."

Burgoyne sighed, shaking his head. "I fear you are destined to be like your father, forever more generous to others than they deserve or that you can afford. And probably incurring your mother's displeasure."

"She can be the most generous woman alive, when the beneficiaries are Catholic," Ned said.

"Yet you are not nearly so particular," Burgoyne surmised.

"No."

"Because of your father?"

"Because of Our Savior, who said we should love our neighbors as ourselves, yes, even those who hate us," Edmund replied. "Because of the Confessor, who laid the foundations of this Abbey, and gave freely of his treasure to all his needy subjects. Because only an accident of birth stands between me and that boy."

"Because it is your nature, Ned," Burgoyne finished, fondness shimmering in his eyes. "You cannot easily dispense with its sweetness. And I believe your father is well pleased."

Chapter 4: A ROYAL MEETING

The rest of the week in London was eventful for Edmund, filled with routine touring around the city during the day, lounging around at various eateries during the evening, and attending playhouse and opera house performances late into the night. Burgoyne always knew how to wheedle half-priced tickets, or even complimentary seating, from his theater friends, and Ned almost enjoyed watching his friend watching the plays and operas more than the performances themselves. The general tended to fall into a rapture when he enjoyed a production, mesmerized by the sensory spectacle.

When he and Ned returned to their hotel room past midnight, Burgoyne would either disappear to indulge in the vices of the establishment or stay up in the room he shared with Ned and demonstrate his memory for details by discussing and critiquing every aspect of the play or opera they had seen that night, from casting to props to lighting, at length. Then he would dig deep into the stories, comparing and contrasting the plots, characters, and themes with his own playwriting endeavors. Even when exhausted almost to death, Ned found this side of the general to be impressive and endearing, and chatted with him for hours until the older man finally ran out of energy and fell asleep. And Ned would tuck him into bed. And then their adventures would begin again the next morning.

When the weekend arrived, Burgoyne whisked Edmund off to an elegant garden party, where the general mixed and mingled amiably with London's elite as they admired some of the earliest spring blooms to peek their heads out from the warming earth. Ned, for his part, stayed out of the way as much as possible, awkwardly hovering over a punch bowl in the corner. For all his blue blood, the young man felt more at home at a harvest dance with honest country folk than lavish galas with glittering assemblies.

As Ned started to fill another glass of punch for himself, there was a sudden fanfare of horns, and then the garden grew hushed.

Burgoyne made his way over to Ned and whispered in his ear, "It's the King. Stand up straight."

Ned dropped the ladle of punch with a splash and clank. "You...you didn't tell me that—"

"Didn't I? Oh well. Surprise!"

Edmund had the sudden desire to hide under the table until the royal visitation was over. This was partly because he realized there was punch staining his white ruffled shirt, making it look as if he had been stabbed in an ill-fated fencing lesson and that his blood ran an insipid pink shade. The other part was the simple knee-jerk reaction of any recusant. Catholics might well sing about "Great George, our King" to ease the trepidation of their Protestant neighbors and dispense with accusations of lingering Jacobitism, but few would be entirely comfortable with said king showing up in the flesh to scrutinize them. They were, after all, marked by their refusal to acknowledge him as supreme governor of the Church in England, and the measures they took to keep the ancient faith alive made them dangerously akin to outlaws.

But it was too late for Ned to take refuge beneath the table now, much too late…

In the course of all that worrying, the King had already made his grand entrance, cut a path through the garden party attendees, making small talk with each one of them as he went, and planted himself in front of Burgoyne and Edmund. Ned imitated the general's low bowing and kept his eyes down, becoming increasingly fixated upon his stained shirt. He felt sure his face was turning as pink as the punch.

He looked up slightly as the King and the general exchanged courtesies. Burgoyne, as usual, was gushing and grandstanding, but Ned was in no mindset to process his monologue, beyond something to do with His Majesty's inestimable virtues, and Burgoyne's inestimable talents, and the colonial troublemakers needing to be put in their place. He did happen to notice that the King's clothes were formal but not showy, the kind any dignified country gentlemen would wear, as opposed to Burgoyne's ostentatious fare. And on his jacket was pinned a very pretty button.

After that, Ned recalled the King asking him a direct question, which his panicked brain failed to properly process. He found himself replying, "Yes, sire," followed by "pretty button," and was absolutely horrified by his own voice sounding so childish. He felt Burgoyne nudge him in the ribs, adding to his mortification.

The King was looking at Edmund full in the face now, his large blue eyes slightly perplexed.

"Your button, sire… it's very fine, very fine indeed…"

"Indeed," concurred the King, in perfect monotone. "It pertains to our patronage of The Handel Society."

"Oh…wonderful, I mean…well done," Ned replied, desperately trying to find some conversational footing. "I-I have always admired him, s-s-sire."

Joy to the world! He was stuttering now. But this did not appear to faze the King, who merely smiled kindly, warming Edmund inside.

"As you may know, our grandfather was the first to stand for the Hallelujah at the performance of Handel's Messiah in London," the King remarked.

"Yes, sire," Ned acknowledged, "because he found the power of the piece to be so moving."

The King leaned forward slightly. "It was not without precedent for our grandfather to slip into slumber during performances, however moving they might be. When he found himself roused, momentary confusion, accompanied by eagerness to suitably respond to what could have been the royal anthem, might follow…"

"Ahhh."

"We are not, of course, saying that is how it happened," the King stated tactfully.

"No, sire."

"Either way, we honor the tradition the late king set by standing whenever the Hallelujah is performed, and we are wide awake each time."

"Me too," Ned blurted. "I mean…I stand, and we all stand, because Your Majesty stands, and I think it's fitting that we should do so, for the King of Kings."

"We believe that was Handel's intention," the King said. "He said that he had seen the face of God, and so he made us see it too."

"And so we do," Ned concurred.

The King's expression grew wistful. "I recall meeting that great composer after a performance when we were still a young prince under ten years. He seemed flattered by our enthusiasm for his work and said, 'While that boy lives, my music will never want a protector.' We have not forgotten that moment, thirty years on, nor shall we whilst God preserve us. We have purchased his harpsichord. We play it, even."

"That's wonderful, sire," Ned responded cheerfully, genuinely pleased to hear the instrument was still in use.

"We hope the original owner does not mind too terribly, wherever he is. His genius was matched by a temper. Nearly ran a man through for touching the instrument."

"If there's anyone he wouldn't mind playing upon it, surely it would be Your Majesty," Ned insisted.. "You...you wear his button, after all…"

The King chuckled. "Do you play anything, hmm?"

"My sister does, though I am no good. I do drop everything and listen, though, whenever music of quality is being played. It's like…like a prayer, like everything we could feel…joy and sorrow and glory, and the brevity of here, and the eternity of there…" He caught himself rambling, and thought of some way to finish. "As you said, sire, it's as if God gives us a glimpse of His face, and we are left to marvel."

"Yes," the King said softly. "Marvel. That is the gift Handel gave us." He turned to Burgoyne, who appeared to have gone into a blank stare, finding himself no longer at the center of attention. "This young man…he's not the same as the one who was with you the last time, is he?"

"No, Your Majesty," Burgoyne answered, relocating himself. "I'm afraid not. He's not nearly as accustomed to garden parties, though he is fresh from the farm…"

"Afraid?" The King's eyes glimmered quizzically. "No need, sir, no need. We like things fresh from the farm."

Ned chuckled. "That…that makes sense, Your Majesty. After all…your name, it means…"

"Farmer," the King finished. "A tiller of soil, a tender of vines…"

"And what is England if not a farm with soil to be tilled and vines to tend?" Ned asked. "She needs a farmer to see to her needs, and nothing else will do. That's why our patron saint shares the same name, because the blood of the martyrs is the seed of the faith. Thus he served his Master as a soldier and a farmer, both. And he proved the guardian of kings in time of travail."

"And what does it signify to you that Handel shared the same Christian name as us?"

"That he sowed songs, Your Majesty," Ned answered, beaming. "One of the finest crops."

The King snort-laughed, then grew serious. "Heed our advice, young man. Do not abandon your own plot of land for the allure of the court. A simple, honest life spent close to the earth keeps a man's face bronzed and his eyes bright. Besides, the Creator deigns to reveal Himself to us through the book of creation, second only to sacred scripture, if we are but willing to look upon it with an inquiring mind and open heart."

"Agreed, sire," Ned replied with a smile. "I often feel God's presence most keenly when nature surrounds me, especially walking the hills of home."

"Good. This tour of the city seems not to have ruined you yet, though it might be wise not to risk too many more, what?"

"Indeed, sire," Ned chuckled. "I shall abide by your counsel and remain true to my roots."

"We are pleased," said the King. Then he unexpectedly took off his button, and extended it to Ned. "Become a member of the Society."

Ned blinked. "Are you quite sure you want me to take that, sire? It's a very fine button…"

"We have a box," the King replied simply.

"Oh…well...in that case…" Edmund reached out and accepted the button from the royal hand. "I am much obliged, Your Majesty."

The King gestured at the punch stain on Ned's shirt. "If you affix it *there*, it might cover *that*."

Ned felt his face burning as he did as he was instructed.

The King nodded in satisfaction. "We wish you success in your military career and continued good health wherever duty takes you."

"Umm…th-thank you, Your Maj–"

"Oh, he's not a recruit, sire," Burgoyne chortled, laying a hand on Ned's shoulder. "Faith, he cannot be, I fear! He is a Papist! Lancashire recusant family. Fine father. Lent me some coin when I was hard-pressed with the ponies and the ladies! Passed on, poor soul, and here is his lad, under my wing!" He pulled Ned a little close to him, and Ned tried hard not to appear unduly embarrassed, no matter how he felt inside. "We're two peas in a pod, he and I!"

The King glared at Burgoyne as if the man was touched in the head, then glanced over to Ned as if to determine whether or not the boy was being held hostage by a madman and required a royal rescue. At last, he turned back to Burgoyne.

"When next you see Lady Charlotte, pray tell your wife that the King, along with his Queen who shares a name with her, extend their fondest felicitations and pray for her good health."

Edmund blushed, recalling suddenly that Gentleman Johnny was a married man, and Burgoyne himself bore a chastened expression as he promised to relay the gracious royal greeting back home, whenever he got back home.

Then the King turned to Ned once more. "A recusant, are you?"

"Yes, Your Majesty," Edmund confirmed, butterflies in his stomach.

"Have you made any renovations to your house of late?"

"No, sire," Ned answered cautiously, guessing the query might well refer to priest holes and secret chapels. "Our space is sufficient."

"We see." The King squinted dubiously. "It is good to take care in such matters. Too many alterations risk unsettling the foundation, after all."

"We are very keen to keep our foundation solid, sire."

"And in terms of your daily bread," the King continued, "what is your source of sustenance up there, hmm?"

Edmund found himself saying, perhaps unwisely, "Very little to speak of, Your Majesty, save for the sacrifice of Christ."

Any recusant would have known the double meaning, would have known that he meant the sacrifice of the Holy Mass which they risked so much to attend.

But the King seemed unaware of it, or at least he chose to act as if he were. In fact, he seemed to approve of Ned's answer, and interpreting it in a manner applicable to all Christians, he replied, "That too is my dependency."

And in that moment, as the King departed from them, Edmund Southworth saw George the Third not only as his sovereign, but as a sinner, like himself, saved by grace. In that, at least, there was no separation between them.

As the King and his entourage left the party, the band struck up the chorus of "Rule, Britannia." Edmund glanced over at Burgoyne, and remarked cheekily, "From the masque of Alfred, called the Great, Father of the English Navy and Subduer of the Danes…a Catholic!"

The general chortled. "Like father, like son!"

Ned tilted his head. "So…who is the other young man you brought before His Majesty?"

Burgoyne smirked. "Jealous, Ned?"

"N-no, only…curious…"

"Oh, I'm teasing," Burgoyne assured. "He was just, well, one of my freshly plucked recruits, eager to go from boyhood to manhood, if you know what I mean."

Ned shrugged. "Perhaps I have different ideas about the meaning of manhood."

"Oh, most likely," Burgoyne conceded. "But you're…old for your age, somehow."

"Am I?"

"Yes…and young for it. I don't know. You're a conundrum, Ned." Burgoyne shook his head. "But at any rate, I…knew this lad's mother, so I promised her that I'd give him a helping hand upon his entry into the service."

"I understand," Ned said quietly.

"I'm not sure that you do," Burgoyne retorted. "He was not…what you have become to me, Ned. He didn't keep pace with my late night tangents nor tuck me in when I fell asleep."

"How did you know about the last part?"

"Oh, I'm a light sleeper, dear. Comes from bedding down on the open field during campaign season." He touched the boy's arm. "You're a good lad, Ned…"

He happened to glance past his young friend, towards the open house adjacent to the garden, where a portly officer was standing. Burgoyne proceeded to pull Edmund in that direction, then called over to the officer, "General Gage, sir! I've someone here for you to meet!"

Gage raised an eyebrow, casting a cynical shadow over his otherwise mild features.

"This is Edmund Southworth, my traveling companion. Ned, meet General Thomas Gage of His Majesty's Army. Dear Tom, I just had to introduce you both, given you come from the same sort of family, albeit yours is from the south and his is from the north like mine. I wouldn't be the least bit surprised if you turned out to be distant, or not-so-distant, cousins!"

"Not in the least," Gage responded dryly, scanning the boy with a suspicious eye.

Edmund bowed slightly. "Your family's history is still honored in our house, sir."

"But not our present inclinations, I take it?" Gage surmised.

Edmund remained silent. What was he to say? The Gage family had been one of the most faithful Catholic families in all of England until the general's father and his father's cousin relented and took the Test Act. In the process, they had betrayed all the recusants from Gloucestershire to Sussex who had depended on them for sustenance.

"Tom and I have known each other since we were twelve," Burgoyne interjected to break up the tension. "Old school chums, you might say!"

"You might," Gage admitted. "But while I busied myself with study, you snuck outside to bet on frog races and kiss that little golden-haired moppet who used to climb up a tree on the border of the school grounds."

"I learned how to climb just for her," Burgoyne laughed.

"You were never deterred from your antics, no matter how many switchings you received," Gage recalled.

"Ah, well, some things never change," Burgoyne conceded, "including my love for the theater! As I recall, when I was thirteen or fourteen, I even tried to get you involved in one of my amateur theatrical productions, but you wouldn't bite!"

"You wanted me to dress up as a donkey," Gage reminded him.

"But it was for *A Midsummer Night's Dream*, you see…"

Gage looked over at Ned, and stated in a comically deliberate fashion, "He wanted me to dress up as a donkey."

Ned couldn't help but grin.

"Oh, pish!" Burgoyne exclaimed. "Let bygones be bygones and all that sort of thing!"

"I'm working on it, despite my better judgment…"

"Good for you! Anyway, I'm off to make the ladies happy!" Burgoyne gestured to the voluptuous Duchess of Devonshire who was beckoning him from within the house, surrounded by her equally eye-catching friends. And in a twinkling, he was gone.

Edmund and Gage continued to size up each other on the threshold for several moments. At last, Gage motioned for Edmund to follow him inside.

When they found a quiet corner, Gage mumbled, "No doubt you've been told that my illustrious relations joined the Church of England for petty reasons, such as to prevent their prized horses from being confiscated by the government."

"Something to that effect," Ned admitted.

"Your convictions being what they are, I imagine you must do a lot of walking, whilst your fellows ride," Gage surmised. "It must bruise your family pride considerably. "

"I am pleased to report that my pride is intact, sir," Edmund said. "I do not resent keeping my feet upon English soil."

"Well, at any rate, the horses were a mere pretext in the case of my father and cousin. My family, like yours, wasted too much time supporting losing causes, from Bloody Mary to

Beheaded Charles. It took its toll. At the end of the day, my parents simply wished their children to have a future suitable to their breeding and free from foreign entanglements."

Ned restrained himself from remarking upon the dissolute reputation Gage's parents had earned. His father gambled away most of the family's newly acquired gains, and his mother's compulsively cheating on her husband gave rise to the saying, "when Lady Gage grows chaste." Burgoyne's mother had been similarly compromised as a gorgeous socialite at the center of endless gossip. Some even suggested that the general was not a true Burgoyne but the product of one of her affairs. Perpetua Southworth would occasionally remind her son of this. But it mattered not to Ned either way. A friend was a friend to him, regardless of origin. As for General Gage, regardless of his parents' indiscretions, he had long established himself as a faithful family man who, even in his youth, had avoided the vices of excessive drink, addictive gambling, and loose women. It earned him the nickname "Honest Tom" by those who liked him and "Timid Tommy" by those who did not. Ned, being who he was, could not help but like what he heard about the man. And as for his parents, rumors in recusant circles held that they had secretly reverted back to the old faith before their deaths, and Ned had no interest in judging their souls.

"It is for each man to choose his own form of entanglement in the end," Edmund replied to Gage briskly.

"A choice which may be wisely or foolishly made," Gage retorted.

"I agree," Ned concurred. "But then…you made no choice, did you?"

"I had the blessing of being raised Anglican, if that's what you're asking. Do you despise me for that?"

"I find it harder to despise a man for being loyal to his inheritance than a man who disposes of it, especially at cost to others."

"You mean the Papist peasants who could not afford to pay their fines without my father's support," Gage surmised. "I say it was better for them in the long run. It freed them from your unfortunate romanticism for a world that never really existed."

"Catholic England, you mean?" Edmund clarified. "But sir, I know she is real, for I have loved her like a mother, from the day of my birth…indeed, even from the day of *her* birth…"

"Birth from the womb of Rome, hmm?"

"Baptized by the waters that ran through Roman hands, yes. Augustine is the one who made angels out of Angles."

"You should not be so enamored by the Romish clerics of today as if they were all little Augustines," Gage counseled. "I have found from experience that those black-clad vultures are corrupt to the core with temporal ambitions."

"Even the ones who once huddled in priest holes your family has now plugged up?" Ned dared to counter.

Gage's eyes narrowed. "I meant the priests in Canada, where the Church of Rome has been given sanctuary for the sake of keeping the peace. I dealt with the French monsignors for years as governor of Montreal and saw how they manipulated the gullible denizens to maintain their princely lifestyles."

Edmund smiled slightly. "Then we must thank God for the blessing of residing in a realm where the clergy of the established church have so thoroughly transcended the distractions of the world, the flesh, and the devil."

Gage glared at him for several moments. Then the corner of his mouth twitched. "Shall we drink to that? It appears that you spilled your last glass."

Ned sighed, gazing down at his shirt. "His Majesty the King seemed to think that the button he gifted me would hide the stain."

"Our gracious sovereign appears to have one noteworthy flaw: near-sightedness." Gage went over to the refreshment table and filled a glass with Madeira, and extended it to the young man. "Go on, lad. Even I can see you're too sober for this party."

Ned accepted the glass as the general filled up one for himself. Then they clinked the glasses together and drank.

"So have you ever been to America, boy?" Gage inquired after the toast.

"No, sir."

"Good. Don't go."

"Do you believe there will be a rebellion in the colonies?"

"We would hope our cousins across the water would not be so foolish as to reap their own ruin. But the colonies are rife with hotheads and bullies from one end to the other, accustomed to an excess of self-governance which has turned into democratic despotism. I have lived among their kind for far too long, to the point of feeling like a stranger in the land of my birth. I could never be truly one of them...even if I sometimes wonder what I'm to do with myself away from them..." He smiled almost sadly. "They gave me the keys to New York, you know, after my tenure as their governor. A token of esteem. I'm afraid they possess other keys that keep me imprisoned too, the knaves."

"You love them," Ned blurted.

"I do not," Gage retorted.

"I think you do," Ned insisted.

Gage shook his head. "If so, love is one of the closest sentiments to hate ever to reside in the breast of man."

"What is your favorite thing about America?" Ned inquired.

Gage snorted. "My wife."

Ned smiled broadly. "I've heard you both are inseparable."

"Ten children later, I suppose it's hard not to be," Gage chortled.

"You met her during the last war, didn't you?

"Yes, a couple of years after that unfortunate run-in with the French and Indians under Braddock. Horrible time of it, that was. Such an effusion of British blood I hope never to see again. But I try to prioritize the better memories, the ones about winter and Christmas and Margaret in her fur-trimmed hoods and mittens while I was stationed at her home in New Jersey..." He smiled in spite of himself. "She's my rare bird, my rare American bird, untamed even sitting pretty in a gilded cage..." Gage's eyes grew hazy, partly no doubt from the Madeira, partly from something deeper. "Love, mistress is of many minds, yet few know whom they serve; they reckon least how little Love their service doth deserve…"

Edmund felt his heart swell. "That's from Robert Southwell, Jesuit and martyr."

"My cousin, you know, even if he did get himself strung up and disemboweled for nothing." Gage gave Edmund a hard look. "If you want to have a future, boy, don't resist the establishment. Make the move from death to life while you're still young."

Edmund was silent for a moment, then recited from Southwell. "My conscience is my crown, contented thoughts my rest; my heart is happy in itself; my bliss is in my breast."

"Is it, though?" Gage asked. "I think not, just by looking at you. For all your rehearsed answers, you will not die contented if you let history pass you by."

Edmund winced. "It is God alone who fixes our fates and makes use of our works."

"You mean like the works of Richard Challoner, the false bishop born in my family's manor house?" Gage pressed. "For years upon years, he has carried out all manner of illegality, teaching and preaching and publishing Papist propaganda, but continues to get away with it, this way and that. It seems the vagaries of fate alone have preserved him. You wouldn't happen to know where he lays his head now, would you?"

Edmund remained silent, deliberately maintaining a stony expression.

Gage laughed shortly. "No wonder you are a favorite of Gentleman Johnny. You have a good face for the card table."

"As you know, sir, recusants must be trained from the cradle."

"Oh, yes, they are old men even during their infancy."

"And that which is ancient, we keep new."

Gage exhaled. "I almost wish I could admire your obstinacy."

"We both have it in our blood, General," Ned reminded him.

"Well, I may need every drop of that whenever I'm sent back to the colonies to set straight these rabble-rousers."

"I will pray for you," Ned assured.

"Will you really?"

"I do not tell people I will pray for them and then not do it."

"Well, that's a good trait, I suppose," Gage said. "Do you pray for Burgoyne?"

"Daily."

"Good. He needs it." Gage rolled his eyes, and Ned laughed. "I may not spout theology, but I have some small reputation for being…straight-laced. I keep the law, a regular pew, and my breeches fastened around women who happen not to be my wife…"

"Thank God, General, that you are not like those other men," Ned replied, tongue-in-cheek. "There, but for his grace…"

Gage snorted. "Perhaps God's mercy shall extend beyond that blessing, and the troubles in America will blow over before our favorite patron of thespians finds himself honor-bound to join me in Boston…"

"Troubles?" came a gruff Scottish burr from behind them. "Send me to America, and by the faith of my body, these damned rebel bastards will disperse before I can get my sword out of the scabbard!"

Edmund turned to see a middle-aged man with wide brown eyes and a self-confident half-grin, dressed in an officer's uniform with an anchor decorating his moon-shaped gorget.

"Ah, Major Pitcairn, allow me to introduce you to General Burgoyne's traveling companion, who happens to probably be a distant relation of mine," Gage said, gesturing to Ned. "Mister Edmund Southworth, this is Major John Pitcairn of His Majesty's Marines."

Pitcairn shook Ned's hand so vigorously that Ned felt the need to check afterwards to make sure it was still attached to his wrist. "Come to join the service, lad?"

Ned cast a quick glance over his shoulder to see if Gage was likely to give away his recusancy. But the general kept his face suitably unexpressive. They were cousins indeed.

"I…have thought upon it, sir," Ned answered.

"There's a time for thinking and a time for action," Pitcairn declared. "When I was younger than you, I was out about my duty, and all the better for it. The only real downside was the government's unfortunate habit of disbanding the Marines, only to reassemble them, every other week. They seem to think we're good for nothing but slicing off pirate's heads and mopping the floor with Jacobite gore!"

"I think I might pay to see you personally confront pirates," Gage declared. "Or one of those dreadful reptilian monsters lurking in Scottish lakes, for that matter…"

"What, pay *me*?" Pitcairn checked. "I just want to make sure the compensation is flowing in the right direction…"

Gage barely managed to suppress a laugh. "You may have to check with the admiralty about such matters…"

"Ohhhh don't you get me started on that bloody ungrateful lot…"

"Now, now, my dear Major," Gage chided him. "You know how quick they can be to interpret everything as mutinous. But you've survived worse at Louisbourg, alongside Brave Wolfe."

"Yes, bottling up the frogs in their own damn pond, while they were shooting poisoned bullets at us, the Gallic curs!" Pitcairn snorted. "But we taught them a thing or two not to be forgotten, if they lived to remember, that is. Men of vision should have realized then and there the necessity of maintaining the Marines at all times. Someday we'll be called royal, as God is my witness, and a man of my age and experience will be able to hold his head high as a general, as would be the case if I settled for an army commission. Mark my words, we will be made a standing force, ever on call to forward the national interest with fire and sword…."

"Even if you remain the harshest critic of your own recruits," Gage chuckled.

"It's true that the damn animals passed onto me are never the easiest to train, but they always to me in the end, one way or t'other, and when we're finally put into action, we'll make any bloody revolutionary who dares to rear his ugly head submit to us." He jutted out his chin.

"What if the next batch of recruits are short of stature like the last batch?" Gage inquired. "I know you were rather perturbed over the prospect."

Pitcairn groaned. "I admit to having been hurt and mortified by their appearance. It can be a nightmare trying to clothe them in a manner not resembling clowns. If I have to blast out one more bloody Frenchman's brains for daring to call us *petits grenadiers*, God spare me…" He paused his lament and stretched out his hand as if to measure Ned. "You, lad, you're not too terribly short. Forsake the army, if they're the ones after you, and cast your lot in with us."

"I…umm…" Ned stammered.

"This young man and I were just having a religious conversation," Gage remarked, as he poured Pitcairn a brandy. "So tell me, Major, as the son of the esteemed Reverend David Pitcairn, do you consider yourself a Presbyterian or an Anglican? Your father may have been a Presbyterian moderator, yet you've taken the Test Act affirming the King as governor of the Church of England and have a history of attending services of both persuasions. Indeed, on multiple occasions, we've witnessed each other receive the Sacrament of the Lord's Supper under the auspices of the Church of England, yet when you are across the border in your native land, I hear that you still receive communion under the auspices of the Church of Scotland."

"I'm a damned Protestant," Pitcairn grunted, then raised his glass in a short salute. "If the King is the governor of the Church in England as well as a member of the Kirk in Scotland, according to the national settlement, my stance should be enough for any good Briton. Though I must say your King Henry was a damn greedy fellow…"

"No comment," Gage sighed, and Ned couldn't help but smirk.

"A bit of a loon too. Went through, what, six or seven wives? That's a man just looking for trouble, if you ask me. One is quite enough…"

"You just nurse a grudge against King Henry because your relation Andrew Pitcairn and seven of his sons were slain at the Battle of Flodden," Gage declared. "You blame us Englishmen for hammering the Scots again…"

"Perhaps I do," Pitcairn admitted. "Family loyalty is precious to me. But there are other points of contention as well."

"Such as?"

"The stuff that makes a real reformer," the major replied. "Our man, John Knox, unlike King Henry, did not enrich himself by way of religious upheaval. He said, 'None have I corrupted, none have I defrauded; merchandise have I not made.' And he had no headless wives to haunt him either!"

"Well, no, but perhaps a monstrous regiment of women, and royal ones at that…"

"It was Mary Stuart that got under his skin," Pitcairn specified. "She was Romish, through and through, and probably blew up one husband to move on to another…"

"But Knox even angered Queen Elizabeth in the south, a Protestant sovereign who might have been a source of succor for him, saying female rulers should be cast down," Gage said.

"He didn't mince words, I'll give you that," Pitcairn conceded. "But then again…"

"Neither do you."

"Neither do I," the major admitted. "That being said, Knox departed this veil of tears with his grieving wife by his bedside, reading Scripture to him as a good helpmate should. Also, like my father, I have managed to endure married life without any lethal explosions cutting short the experience. On top of that, my father was in the service of Good Queen Anne, so clearly, all's well that ends well with the women."

"So you people somehow charmed Queen Anne into forgetting your founder's sentiments?"

"Oh, we can be the most charming folk alive when we want to be. Comes with being among the elect, you know!"

Edmund could see how much Pitcairn was enjoying himself, and found his daring sense of humor to be infectious. Ned giggled, and Pitcairn flashed a glance at him, resting his hand on his hip. "Who knows? We might even bother to pull the less fortunate folk of this island on board the ark on the day of the deluge, if you treat us right!"

"Well, if anyone could redeem us, your father was surely the man," Gage said. "He will always be remembered not only for his piety but also for his gallantry as a chaplain in the Cameronian regiment."

"Aye, alongside Marlborough on the continent," Pitcairn confirmed. "He saw action at Blenheim."

Gage turned to Ned. "The Cameronians are the inheritors of the Covenanters, you know. Altogether brazen folks, who refused to accept anything deemed too Papist from King Charles before the Civil War. When he tried to force them to accept his high liturgical tastes in the name of the Church of England, they signed their names to a covenant in Greyfriars Kirkyard…"

"And signed Bibles in blood," Pitcairn finished, pouring some wine into his brandy.

"Good God, do the Cameronians still expect that sort of thing when it comes to the Bibles they give each new recruit?" Gage queried.

"Not expected," Pitcairn said, stirring his brand and wine with his finger. "But not unexpected either."

"Intense, that," Gage chuckled.

"Nothing else will do for us, I'm afraid," Pitcairn replied. "My father said it was our purpose to stand along the pathways of this world, crying, 'Stay, passenger, read what we have written with our right hand!'"

"Your names," Ned murmured. "That is what is written there, in your blood…"

Pitcairn smiled approvingly and nodded. "It's just like in the Book of Life, on the Last Day. My father taught me that the devil is kept at bay by the man who puts the flow of his life upon the Word of God. That is the covenant, pure and simple, between God and man, sealed in blood. God's blood. Our blood. That is everything in the end, aye, our last word upon any subject."

Like a sacrament, Ned thought, though he dared not say it. *An outward and visible sign of an inward and invisible grace.*

"Once hunted by kings, then put into the service of kings," Gage observed. "Quite an accomplishment for your people, Pitcairn."

"Aye, when the rights of the Kirk were restored under William and Mary, we responded with the fiercest loyalty to the crown, and have done so ever since," Pitcairn said. "But my father had greater hurdles to overcome than any past lack of royal patronage."

"In what way?" Edmund asked.

Gage shot Ned a look as if cautioning him not to press the subject, but it was too late.

"He nearly killed himself trying to get our bloody roof fixed, because the damn committee in Dysart were too filthy cheap to cover the cost of either repairs or extensions for the manse next to Saint Serf's church," Pitcairn declared. "It was nigh uninhabitable, vermin-riddled, drafty, and leaking all over the damn place when it rained! I remember listening to mice gallivanting about all night and then having to ring out my soggy clothes in the morning! God's bones! Five children and a maid in one room, that was how I grew up! No wonder I turned out like this! Pirates, Jacobites, and Frogs are nothing after being stuffed into a hole like bloody rabbits, and I was the youngest of the litter…"

"Oh…dear…" Ned managed awkwardly.

"Had to be christened the day I was born, and you know why?" Pitcairn pressed.

"Your father was a minister who could take care of the matter himself, and this auspicious birth occurred next door to the church to which he was assigned?" Gage offered.

"Besides that, though," Pitcairn huffed. "It was December, along the Firth of Forth, in that miserable, medieval hovel! They thought I might not last the night!"

"Having experienced the chill of Scotland even in the spring, I sympathize with your plight coming into the world in an even more inhospitable northern season," Gage commiserated.

"Indeed. The only thing that stood between me and an infant's casket was…"

"Was being who you are," Gage finished.

"Aye, was being who I am," Pitcairn confirmed. "Perhaps it prepared me for my calling. A soldier must scorn the effects of heat or cold when going about his duty, and I was already trained to do just that from my infancy. What doesn't kill you makes you strong and all that."

"The reaper does seem rather intimidated by you," Gage teased.

"Well, the reaper should have done us all a favor and paid a visit to the church committee," Pitcairn decided. "No matter how cramped the manse was, my father always had to leave a room open for any guest who might stop by, because he was just the generous sort. Same with tea, you know. He wouldn't keep more than a pound in the house without handing it out in charity to parishioners down on their luck, saying the house could not bear the excess."

"Oh, well, he couldn't have foreseen that a handful of Bostonian maniacs would cause a shortage," Gage said. "Otherwise, he could have set up a nice little side business…"

"Should have too, but you know, he was a good man, God love him, for he loved God well. The damn committee may have given him hell, but surely he's in heaven now, and I've made sure he'll be remembered with all due reverence here on earth. His children will forever cherish him, even if he had too many of us to remain fully sane…"

"Then you had ten," Gage remarked. "I am still trying to figure out how you managed it, being away from hearth and home so often."

"I have an internal clock that sends me back to the nest for mating season," Pitcairn declared, tapping his temple. "But your Lady Margaret has proven to be just as fertile as my dear Betty. And here you are today, with ten of your own. We play, we pay."

"You're right," Gage conceded. "Someone should shoot us. I suppose I've just grown accustomed to bringing her along with me wherever I go. Then…things happen."

"Is she still upset about the prospect of your youngest behind when you go back to Boston?" Pitcairn asked sympathetically.

"Yes," Gage admitted, "but it can't be helped. The baby is frail. A sea voyage might…" The general shook his head. "He is safer here."

Pitcairn nodded. "You know, Betty and I are not unfamiliar with such things. Been through it ourselves, twice, and hope to God not to go through it again. I think…you are right to take precautions."

"Most of the children are coming with us, so Margaret should not pine too greatly," Gage insisted. "They consider it to be going home. The bulk of them were born in the New World, after all."

"They're bound to be little trouble-makers then," Pitcairn twitted.

"Oh, they are, I assure you. In fact, they may need an exorcism to cast out some of that Yankee unruliness! Speaking of which…Pitcairn, you really must tell Youth Southworth here the story of Saint Serf and the devil. He's just the sort to appreciate such a pious yarn."

"I would, yes," Ned confirmed.

"Well, legend has it that the holy hermit came to Dysart, on the steps of the salt sea, and vowed to be the salt of the earth," Pitcairn began. "His intention was to commune with God and be the true salt of the earth. But Satan got wind of his presence and showed up in person to disrupt Serf's devotions. Of course Serf would have none of it, so he wrestled the devil inside the cave that had served as his cell. He won, too. Then he went on to save Princess Theneva whose cousin had brought her full with child against her will. Her father had set her adrift in a boat out of shame, but a school of fish guided her to shore where Serf took her in and raised her child. The boy was Saint Mungo, the patron of Glasgow. But Serf remained the patron of Dysart, and for centuries, the townsmen thought praying to him would ward off English pirate raids." Pitcairn squinted at Gage.

"I'm not apologizing," Gage declared. "Your people did the same to us."

"Well, we held our own in terms of defense as well as offense. The church still has a fine tower as a vantage point, with very neat slits for the arrows. You're welcome to take a tour if you care to come back up our way again." He made a gesture as if holding a crossbow.

"It's not one of my personal aspirations," Gage said.

"Not even as a pilgrim, General? I thought your family used to like that sort of thing," Pitcairn joked. "All sorts of folk used to come out on pilgrimage back in the day. They would leave seashells in the walls of the church, paying tribute to some Papist statue or other, long gone, though the niche is still there, alongside a carving of lilies."

Ned swallowed hard. "The niche…it must have been for…"

"The Lady," Gage mumbled.

"Aye, most likely. But as I said, the building is properly reformed now. Most of the Romish bits and pieces were pulled down long before my time." He smirked. "When we were children, my siblings and I used to throw stones at one of the broken ornaments left over on the arch outside. It was great fun."

Gage clicked his tongue. "Little vandals!"

"Little Covenanters!" Pitcairn laughed. "We used to muck about in the caves where Saint Serf was supposed to have dwelt. They were used for a wine cellar by then. We would pretend the bottles held the devil's blood, and make up rhymes, and swish it around while chanting them to ward off any lingering demons. Now I suppose I'll have to content myself with stirring damn Yankee blood instead. The seditious kind, you understand. I have no quarrel with loyal sorts nor those in the households of fellow kingsmen!"

"Well, you are rather too colorful in your language to be a saint, even if you would happily wrestle Satan himself, so perhaps your decision to focus on subduing earthly rebels is for the best," Gage remarked.

Pitcairn made a half-grin. "God's blood, General, but this is any old damn Thursday! I don't swear like this on the sabbath!"

"No, no, you don't," Gage admitted. "How, pray tell, do you manage it?"

"It's a damn skill," Pitcairn beamed. "I have impeccable self-control!"

"For one day a week only?"

"Yes, well, it's the Lord's Day," Pitcairn replied, with a sincerity that Ned found endearing. "Besides, I'm not fool enough to present myself at the Lord's Table to receive the Lord's Supper with a dirty mouth. My father would roll over in his grave. So I go on a fast from language from the time the sun rises till it sets."

"And you never forget yourself?"

"My son makes that impossible. You see, if I swear before darkness falls on Sunday evening, I lose money to him. But I never lose. So he has to pay me instead."

"A man of pure principle," Gage chuckled. "Just not enough to win Colonel Gardiner's approval, I'm afraid."

Pitcairn nearly spit out a mouthful of brandy. "God's wounds!"

"There you go again," Gage sighed. "He'd have you standing on pointed logs for that!"

"Well, back then, my tongue was even saltier!" Pitcairn laughed. "I went straight from the manse into the Marines, and my mouth went straight from fair to foul! I just made the mistake of showing off my newfound skill around the wrong man! Ate me alive, he did!"

"Was this the same Colonel Gardiner who distinguished himself during the last Jacobite rebellion?" Ned queried.

"Aye, that he was, a fellow Lowland Scot," Pitcairn confirmed. "He served as Sir John Cope's second-in-command when the damn Highland rebels took Edinburgh for the Young Pretender. Didn't think much of Cope's handling of the situation, but was resolved to fight or die for the security of his country."

"Cope, to my understanding, was a cautious but conscientious man who felt that he lacked support as a commander in Scotland because he was an Englishman," Gage stated. "He had a particularly unsatisfactory experience with two Edinburgh volunteers he sent out as scouts, only for them to stop off at a tavern mid-mission for a meal of oysters and sherry. They proceeded to drink themselves into a state of unwarranted euphoria and get themselves captured by a young attorney's clerk with Jacobite sympathies."

"To be fair, they were hardly older than the clerk themselves, recruited directly out of the university to deal with the crisis," Pitcairn recalled. "But I agree they deserved to be boxed about the ears. And Gardiner would have been the first man to do it. He was made of steel as surely as his sword and faced down the Highland Charge at Prestonpans without flinching. Even when Cope himself had fled the field, Gardiner stayed and rallied the survivors. The rebels took him down, but not before he received five bloody wounds in his body, the last one by a Lochaber ax! Still lived for many hours afterwards! Now that's a damn proper way for a soldier to go…"

"No need to emulate it too closely," Gage cautioned.

"Of course not! We should strive to do one better in the wound count!"

Gage rolled his eyes again. "Lest we falsely believe he had a death wish, it should be noted that Gardiner had complained about his horse being skittish before the battle. One cannot help but wonder whether his refusal to retreat was completely his own idea…"

"Seven hells! There's no way that Gardiner would have willingly gone off with Cope to bring news of their own defeat," Pitcairn countered. "He stayed because it suited his ferocity. Like my father, he took part in Marlborough's campaigns. We Scots and Englishmen were just upon the brink of union by way of parliament. But I say that our unity was forged first and foremost amongst soldiers, bleeding common blood. And Gardiner bled. Got shot in the mouth at Ramillies and was nearly bludgeoned to death by some scavenger knave. But a nun from a nearby convent intervened and nursed him back to health. He was only fifteen at the time, and to her credit, she treated him with maternal tenderness. She even tried to make a Papist out of him, but he had enough sense to refuse, though at the time, he hardly thought of God in any respect."

"Until his vision," Gage remarked, somewhat sarcastically.

"I spent little enough time with Gardiner, and I know some men called him mad," Pitcairn said. "But my father knew him better and believed God had touched his lips with hot coals, granting him the gift of holy violence to pursue the goal of lasting glory. That's enough for me."

"And his burnt lips also caused him to see things?" Gage surmised.

"There has been precedent," Pitcairn reminded him.

"What sorts of things did he see?" Ned asked, increasingly intrigued.

"Well, by the time the vision came to him, Gardiner was all grown up and leading a dissolute life," Pitcairn related. "One night, as he waited in his chamber to rendezvous with a married woman, he started to flip through a book from his pious mother to pass the time. *The Christian Soldier* by the Puritan divine Thomas Watson, I believe it was. As he read, he saw a strange light fall upon the open page. He turned his head, thinking the candle upon the table had flared, but then saw another thing." Pitcairn held out his hand, as if to indicate a mystery in their midst. "Yes, he claimed that he saw nothing less than Christ upon the cross, stretched out in His suffering, and he heard a voice, or what he thought was a voice, demanding, 'O sinner, did I suffer all this for thee, and are these the returns?' After that night, Gardiner abandoned his former way of life. He became devout, so much so, his friends questioned if a fall from his horse some time before had left him addled in the head."

"Plausible," Gage said.

"But not probable," Pitcairn retorted. "Not to my mind. From the night of his visitation to the day of his death, he kept up the practice of praying and reading scripture in the wee hours of the morning, even during campaigns. And his fury over swearing…well, if one had seen God, it's damn hard to lay the blame on him for that, even one such as myself. What he saw changed him, aye, in truth. And the manner in which the man fought testifies to something beyond himself. It's as Thomas Watson said, 'A Christian fights the Lord's battles; he is Christ's ensign-bearer. Now, what though he endures hard fate, and the bullets fly about? He fights for a crown!'"

"I have no desire to profane the sacred, believe me, but it seems strange in these latter days for God to simply show Himself in all His glory to one sinner, yet not others," Gage remarked.

Pitcairn shrugged. "The Lord knows what He is about."

"Yes, but I mean, you and I, we're church-going men, and we've not seen anything like that. Or have you?"

"Hell, no," Pitcairn chortled.

"There, that's my point. It smacks of enthusiasm on Gardiner's part, flights of fancy…"

"But He knows what He is about," Pitcairn repeated, pointing upward. "If it were good for such a man as you, or even such a man as me, to see God before Judgment Day, well, we would. And if not, we won't, and we'll wait. It's as simple as that."

"Is it?"

"I think so," Pitcairn said. "But whether you believe in Gardiner's vision or not, none could fault the man's guts nor his integrity. It's what made his friendships last, even with those who thought him daft. Aye, the man even gained favor with the royal family. It made his cruel fate all the harder for so many to bear, especially how his servant found him, nearly stripped naked by those Highland barbarians, and crumpled in agony under a thorn tree."

"Still alive, with five wounds?" Ned gasped.

Pitcairn nodded. "He was carted off to a nearby church manse where he was nursed by two young Jacobite ladies until he succumbed. His own home, a stone's throw away, had also been converted into a hospital. Bloody tragic, those times, with him leaving behind a wife and five children. You know, he settled down right well with her after his past dalliances. They suffered through smallpox killing a number of their brood. Broke something inside him, I think. The illness, mixed with the grief, certainly broke his health. But his heart never lost its courage. His faith would not yield even when his breath did. When my father heard of his fall, he quoted Knox, 'Live in Christ, die in Christ, and the flesh need not fear death.' That's the measure of a man, he said, that the spirit conquers flesh."

"You don't measure too badly yourself," Gage said, with a slight smile.

Pitcairn smiled in return and made a roof shape with his hands. "Above the door of the manse where I was born, an inscription reads, 'My hope is in the Lord.' And so, for all my bloody sins, I am sworn to praise the Lord of Hosts who made souls like me to fill the ranks of fighting men, on land and sea."

Pitcairn glanced across the room to where Burgoyne stood, leaning against a column, chatting it up with a young lady friend of the Duchess of Devonshire who looked positively enraptured with her wide doe eyes.

"Hell's teeth, if that isn't Gentleman Johnny, trying to get at it again. He's giving that lass no space to breathe."

"That noxious perfume he's wearing is likely compromising her judgment," Gage remarked. "She has only just made her coming out, you know, so this sort of experience is new to her."

"Now, then, she can't be much older than my youngest daughter Janet," Pitcairn said in distaste. "Soon he'll sweet-talk his way into slipping his hand down her bodice, or worse, her hand down his breeches!"

"That has been known to happen," Gage sighed.

"This will never do. She bloody well needs rescuing." With that, Pitcairn was off.

Gage gave Edmund a bemused look. "Every young lady should have a belligerent Scottish marine on hand, stuffed to the gills with paternal instinct, to save her from the wolves. He's quite a decent sort, once you get used to him."

"He seems like it," Ned concurred.

"He's akin to heavily salted oatmeal. Once you get used to the flavor, it's actually hearty fare, and even good for you. Just make sure to have plenty of water on hand to wash it down."

"Just not saltwater," Ned laughed.

"Well, no," Gage agreed. "Though that's probably the kind his people would try to sell us if we ever found ourselves in his neck of the woods. His own tongue certainly seems to have been dipped in it, in more ways than one. As you may have noticed, his accent can at times compromise his diction."

"I have not had any great difficulty understanding him thus far," Ned replied.

"Yes, well, you're not terribly far from the Scotch border, so perhaps you have an edge on us southerners. But then again, you've never heard him when he's truly animated."

"He seemed more than a bit animated to me…"

"Trust me, it can always get worse. At that point, his years stationed in England, which have moderated his burr somewhat, melt away like snow in the sun."

"Thank you for the warning."

"You should, you should thank me," Gage said, wagging a finger. "I'll even throw in a bit of advice for good measure. If you can't understand what he's saying, you have two options. The first is to ask him to repeat himself, which I would not recommend. It will only cause him to grow more animated. The second is to do what I do, which is to hang on every fifth word and pretend."

"Quite a precise method."

"Well, I've been at it for a while," Gage chuckled.

They overheard Pitcairn talking loudly from across the room, asking the girl where her mother was as Burgoyne attempted to circumvent the situation by inviting the pretty young thing out for a stroll in the garden.

"So, would you like to lay a little bet on who will win out?" Gage asked.

"In a duel?" Ned inquired cheekily.

"They really do wave their respective pistols around too much when their blood starts to boil," Gage exhaled. "But I am convinced they will remain mindful of their professional reputations…"

"You are?"

"No."

"Oh…"

"And…Pitcairn's won."

"I think he's proven his point about the marines being indispensable," Ned remarked, observing Burgoyne throwing up his hands in despair as Pitcairn escorted the young lady back to her mother across the room.

"I am under the impression that even our dear Burgoyne understands why the Romans needed to build Hadrian's Wall and does not wish to contradict their wisdom," Gage said. "Pitcairn and his fellow North Britons only appear to have two moods: a friendly sort of angry, and…angry, pure and simple. The latter tends to shorten lifespans."

Chapter 5: SPEAK DAGGERS

Burgoyne made his way over to Gage and Ned, grumbling under his breath about Pitcairn sabotaging his attempted conquest. "That man takes the air right out of the room…"

"You do get rather free with your hands when you're on your third or fourth drink," Gage noted, pouring himself another glass of Madeira.

"Does it take me that long?" Burgoyne chortled.

Ned gave him a disapproving look.

"Come now, boy! The lass was enjoying it! She was blushing like a rose!"

"Possibly due to that fragrance you're wearing, causing the air to thin to a dangerous extent," Gage clucked. He turned to Ned. "You see, I just become wittier on my third or fourth…otherwise, I remain the picture of stuffy sobriety…"

"But Tom, you've lived through some of the most exhilarating events in our generation," Burgoyne insisted. "Your initiation was the scattering of the Highland clans under the Young Pretender at Culloden…"

"You mean the slaughter of them," Gage replied bleakly. "Yes, I was there. A bitter necessity, and nothing entertaining about it. Believe me…"

"Then you fought beside General Braddock at Monongahela, only to find yourself in the assault upon Ticonderoga, before which the long-to-be-lamented Lord Howe was slain! You may be quiet about it, but your early life was anything but!"

"It's true," Ned concurred. "You must have many tales worth telling…"

"Spouting old war stories is simply not my style," Gage replied. "I am a manual man, and do my job by the book without excessive flourish. I can even make charging into wooden spikes and occasionally getting a French bullet lodged in my flesh sound dull. Perhaps because at the end of the day, it is…a bitter kind of dullness that I would prefer to forget." He cast a glance towards Ned. "One thing I'm afraid will not leave me is the memory of digging a bullet out of my leg while being taunted by the Cross."

"What do you mean, sir?" Ned asked.

"That cunning fox, the Marquis de Montcalm, took his victory on behalf of France as a gift from heaven," Gage explained. "So he erected a great cross to loom over our British dead, composed a few lines of Latin verse, and proclaimed God to be on their side. I suppose he thought we lost because we were heretics, and our dead were rotting in hell, with Lord George Augustus Howe foremost among them. All our men admired him, and not just because of his family name. He would have gone far, for he was feared and loved by every soldier who served under him, regular and provincial. Got me interested in raising light infantry through his own exertion. His youngest brother, poor Billy, almost starved himself over his loss. But then, well…" He drank some more wine. "The tables turned rather dramatically on the marquis, wouldn't you say? Apparently, with an upstart named Wolfe to howl at their heels, heretics can climb like goats, right up to the Plains of Abraham. God will just have to be on Montcalm's side in the crater where the nuns buried him. When I was governor, I got the impression that the man had become some sort of saint to the superstitious inhabitants of Montreal, no matter how many poisoned bullets his soldiers fired or how many captives and scalps his savages took."

Ned winced, trying to navigate his own mixed emotions. "Surely God is on the side of any soul that seeks salvation, nor the Cross is emptied of its power."

Gage shrugged. "I am no theologian. I just know I don't like to be mocked by the symbol of my own faith, not by French Papists or Scotch Jacobites. The latter set their crosses aflame to rally the clans against us…"

"I thought Scots were supposed to enjoy some mischief with the ladies," Burgoyne lamented, drifting back to his personal woes. "That's why they wear kilts, you know…easy to pull up and…"

"We are not like *those* Scots, with their primitive tongue and indecent attire," Pitcairn declared, coming back over to them. "Lowlanders and Highlanders are thoroughly different breeds. The Gaels in the mountains are rebels and rustlers, the lot of them. We, on the other hand, are a civilized people, perfectly content with good business practice and breeches. Even our Lowland bagpipes are more refined than theirs, outlawed for playing their bloody Jacobite tunes…"

"But there are Scots who straddle regions," Gage reminded him. "I was well-acquainted with Sir Peter Halkett and his two fine sons during the last war. Killed under Braddock, he was, and one of his sons beside him, trying to pull his father to safety when the fatal bullet struck him. Halkett was a Lowlander and a staunch Hanoverian, raised not far from your doorstep, Pitcairn. But he had interests in the Highlands, and when his surviving son found his bones, entwined with the bones of his slain son, the lad saw fit to bury them in Highland plaid. The Gaels respected Halkett, for he would not break an oath, not even one given to a Jacobite. After his capture during the '45, he refused to violate the terms of his parole by raising his hand against them again…"

"I rather think the Highlanders have their virtues as well as their vices, as Halkett understood," Burgoyne chimed in. "And the martial airs of their bagpipes are being redeemed, slowly but surely, within the service of the Hanoverian line and our glorious constitution."

"You're only saying that on behalf of your friends from those devilish clans," Pitcairn scoffed, "and because of that pretty post you gained at Fort William in the far north."

"If they are my friends, it is because they earned that friendship on the basis of my respect for their manly qualities, second to none in the world," Burgoyne declared.

"We might also spare a thought for those Highlanders who remained in the service of King George throughout the rebellion and another thought for those lowlanders who gave into the enthusiasm of the moment and tossed in their caps for Bonnie Prince Charlie," Gage said.

"You have cousins of that ilk, do you not, Major?" Burgoyne jabbed.

Pitcairn rolled his eyes. "Don't we all, if not by name, then by blood?"

Burgoyne, Gage, and Edmund gave one another an almost accidental guilty glance.

"Well, tan our hides," Burgoyne exhaled. "Even His Majesty has a smattering of Jacobite cousins, what?"

Gage groaned, and Ned cringed. Pitcairn laughed.

"I will do my best to forget that joke," Gage exhaled, "or that anyone laughed at it."

Burgoyne raised his hands in mock surrender. "I respect that!"

Pitcairn just shrugged, unrepentantly, and gulped down another brandy. "Well, my mother, God bless her, was the descendant of Bruce and Edward both, so I know something about royal relatives at each other's throats."

"The union in a life contained," Burgoyne summed him up.

"Yes, God help us all, driving each other mad as countrymen," Pitcairn snorted. "But folk along the borders still have rivalries…take that Northumberland man over there…" The Scotsman pointed at another officer, chatting to a lady at a table not far away, then shouted, "My good Percy!"

The officer turned around, his youthful face distinct with aquiline features. One hand was resting on his hip brazenly, and one foot up on a chair, showing off his knee-high riding boots and tight-fitting breeches, no doubt for the admiring lady's benefit. He continued nibbling nonchalantly at the chicken leg in his hand, one eyebrow raised as if to question why he had been interrupted.

"Are you eager to draw rebel blood with your ancestral sword?" Pitcairn inquired.

"In the colonies?" Percy surmised, tossing away the chicken bone. "Not especially. They are, after all, the sons of Englishmen, regardless of their location in the empire, and it is natural they should prove spirited when they perceive their rights to be threatened."

"What do they believe they are being threatened with, hmm?" Gage queried.

"Being treated as a conquered race instead of as our brethren," Percy responded. "Regardless of the distance between us, they believe that they carry England within themselves. As Earl Chatham similarly expressed, we are the most unfit people to do unto our children what we would not like done to ourselves."

"I'm sorry, but what rights do they feel are being robbed from them?" Gage queried. "The right not to be taxed for a war that we fought based upon their right to demand defense from the crown? Our victories against the French were for their benefit."

"For all our benefit, it must be said," Percy clarified. "But that is not the crux of the issue. As you well know, sir, the colonial land-owners believe it is their prerogative to have a say in the passing of taxes upon them. They appeal to the spirit of the Magna Carta and say they simply wish to be treated as equal British subjects, no matter on which side of the ocean they reside."

"It is a reaction based upon the excessive free rein we've allowed them in most matters," Gage sighed. "The Americans obtain many benefits from their position under the protection of both the crown and the parliament, including various opportunities which even here in the mother country are not as easily to be had. But as with everything in life, where there are gains, there are also losses. Constitutionally, the colonies are subordinate to the Mother Country. At no time has parliament reneged upon its right to tax our own colonies without going through the complicated muddle of their assemblies."

"Disunified their assemblies may be, but the Americans view them as their primary means to make their voice heard, since they have no seats in Parliament," Percy insisted. "Some amongst them have argued that their colonial charters were formed separately from our parliament, and therefore should be under the direct guardianship of the King, whose duty it is to secure their rights as much as ours, though distinct from each other."

"His Majesty, in accordance with the Bill of Rights, strives to fulfill his duties as a constitutional monarch, which is integrally connected with upholding the supremacy of Parliament," Burgoyne countered. "All other bodies of governance across the empire must be subject to it. Otherwise the civil wars and revolutions we endured down through the decades have no lasting resolution. We would be once more faced with the possibility of royal absolutism, or alternately theocratic fanaticism, both of which were curbed by our current settlement."

"The colonials view the disbanding of their assemblies that protest the government's acts as akin to the dissolution of Parliament under the Stuart kings," Percy said. "That, in large part, was what plunged these isles into generations of strife, with brother smiting brother. When we have refused time and again to consider further developments to our constitution, I fear we neglect this sorrowful history at our own peril."

"Firstly, we may be ancient, but our constitutional settlement, as it currently stands, is yet new, and thus in need of tender care," Gage replied. "Secondly, equity is not the same as equality. Each man should receive his due according to the law, but there is a rude rabble who would dissolve all distinctions for the ideal of democracy, even though it will never be realized. Such notions have always been manipulated and turned against the very people they claim to empower."

"Really, Percy, I cannot think of any self-respecting country that would give their colonies what our colonists are demanding," Burgoyne replied. "It is simply impractical from a managerial standpoint. Now, of course, we all want what's best for our subjects across the water…"

"Fellow subjects of the King, you mean," Percy corrected him.

"You know what I mean," Burgoyne dismissed. "We're each bound to them by blood or business or both, and none would deny they are the progeny of our national loins, but it's a radical proposal they are making! And I say this as a Whig, like you!"

"Well, Percy, we'll be on hand to swoop in and rescue whenever your Yankee friends decide to drown you in a bucket of strawberry leaf liberty tea," Pitcairn said.

"That's actually rather good, by the way," Gage remarked randomly. "I know they've used it to boycott real tea, but Margaret has a fancy for it, so…"

"Please do not misunderstand me, Major Pitcairn," Percy answered sternly. "My first and last devotion is to my king and country. I may dissent in my political views as part of the loyal opposition and lament that we have been brought to this point due to our refusal to compromise. But as a soldier of His Majesty, despite my regrets, I'll beat the Americans bloody if they carry out their threats to take up arms against the crown. Indeed, the destructive manner of their protests has appalled me of late, and if we establish further military presence, I say we should take a strong hand to quell such disturbances before they develop into something more deadly for everyone involved…"

"Och, no need to mount a defense," Pitcairn dismissed kindly. "We're soldiers under the same banner in the end, whoever the foe may be. And even if there are other quarrels you would prefer to have picked, at least it will get you out of the country for a bit. You've a fine service record, but these days, you seem to mainly be engaged in mortal combat with your wife…"

"Pitcairn…" Gage cautioned.

Ned just grimaced. As a northerner, it was impossible for him not to be aware of the tempestuous marriage between Hugh Percy, heir to the dukedom of Northumberland, and his Scottish wife Lady Anne Crichton-Stuart, the daughter of the King's former tutor and prime minister, Lord Bute. To press him upon the issue, even in jest, was to risk simmering his hot mix of Percy and Seymour blood.

Percy squinted at Pitcairn, then smirked sardonically. "This much I will say, sir: My people will fight the Scots, whatever brand they come in."

Pitcairn roared with laughter. "Will you indeed?"

"It's in our nature," Percy declared. "I'm afraid that both your people and mine took an ungenerous attitude towards hunting excursions traversing their respective sides of the border during medieval times."

"Ah, yes, the Chevy Chase," Pitcairn recalled. "Going to sing the ballad for us, or does it bring back unpleasant family memories?"

The young lady who had been chatting with Percy earlier clapped her hands together. "Oh, do sing for us, Earl Percy!" she coaxed him, batting her eyelashes.

Percy, obviously flattered by his female companion, bowed low in assent. Then he stood up on the chair, and to Pitcairn's bemusement, declared, "No well-fought battle is an embarrassment to an Englishman, even if it ends in defeat. Besides, the challenging Scotsman in this case was a deadman, even before he won his victory!"

"That's not a bad way to go in my book," Pitcairn chortled. "On with the song then!"

Percy bowed again before finally starting to sing. His voice was not bad, but neither was it the best. Nevertheless, it carried a certain ruggedness that brought Percy's own rugged swath of the country to life through this tumultuous tale of the warring Border Reivers.

"It fell about the Lammastide
When moor-men win their hay
The doughty Douglas bound him to ride
Into England, to drive a prey.

Douglas marched on down to Newcastle
'Whose house is this so fine?'
It's up spoke proud Lord Percy

'I tell you this castle is mine!'

'If you're the lord of this fine castle
Well it pleases me
For, ere I crossed the Border fells
The one of us shall die.'

'Oh, I will come,' proud Percy said
'I swear by our Lady.'
Then there I'll wait,' says Douglas
'My troth I plight to thee.'

'But I have dreamed a dreadful dream
Beyond the Isle of Skye
I saw a dead man win a fight
And I think that man was I.'

'Oh bury me by the bracken bush
'Neath the briar tree
Oh hide me by the bracken bush
That my merry men might not see.'

The moon was clear, the day drew near
The spears in flinders flew
Many's the bold Englishman
Ere day these Scotsmen slew.

This deed was done at the Otterburn
At the break of day
The buried Douglas by the bracken bush
And led Percy a captive away."

As Percy sang, Gage took Ned by the arm and escorted him out of earshot of the others.

"He's a proud young peacock, that one, with a fierce temper and a hankering after pleasure houses," Gage remarked. "But when you get on his good side, he's an impeccably mannered fellow and immensely generous with his wealth. His family's tenants and his enlisted men adore him. He meets regularly with his farmers and abhors flogging his soldiers."

"That's decent of him," Ned said.

"He takes after his mother that way. She loves gaudy attire and mummer performances, but she's made herself a favorite of the poor by speaking plain and to the point. She's so vulgar in her comportment, she passes on gossip from her coachman at seasonal galas and shakes hands with her cobbler for making her shoes."

"Well, on Judgment Day, I'm sure that cobbler's sweat on her ladyship's hands will be the millstone around her neck."

"Take care your sarcasm does not brand you a radical," Gage cautioned.

"Radical? Heavens no, sir." Ned tapped his chest. "This is not the metal of which revolutions are forged. I am a simple country gentleman who finds the greatest happiness telling stories to farm children as they work or play in the dirt."

"Stories of what?" Gage inquired.

"The saints of these blessed Isles."

"But what if they are Protestant children?"

"It is their heritage too."

Gage squinted. "You have more revolutionary inclinations than you care to admit. That sort of thing could tumble you into legal trouble…"

"Yes, it could, but hasn't yet."

"Yet?" Gage's eyes danced a little, dangerously.

"Yet," Edmund confirmed.

He glanced back over at Hugh Percy on the chair, singing of how his medieval ancestor had sworn oaths upon the Blessed Virgin, even though his branch of the family had joined the Anglican ascendency.

"I know, I know," Gage sighed. "As a Papist and a northerner, you remember the Percy Family for one thing especially…"

"Five, actually," Edmund retorted, holding out his hand to show all five fingers.

Gage shook his head in exasperation. "The Pilgrimage of Grace, with its banner of the five wounds, brought naught but death and destruction to this land. Sir Thomas Percy was a fool to lead it, and he paid the ultimate price for it."

"The northern lords desired nothing more than that King Henry should dismiss his errant ministers and restore to them their inheritance," Ned replied.

"The inheritance of the fat abbots, you mean," Gage scoffed.

"Their faith," Ned countered. "That was the inheritance. Death and destruction fell upon those caught with the banner because of their king's own bad faith."

"Take care when ascribing bad faith to royals," Gage cautioned.

"Major Pitcairn called him greedy."

"Well, I never told you to follow his example on everything…"

"Touching upon royals, Margaret Pole had ancient Plantagenet blood, yet she was martyred in her old age for possession of that banner," Ned recalled. "They chased her around the block and hacked her to death because she refused to lay her head down, which she believed would have been that same as a confession of treason."

"There was legitimate fear of foreign interference from Papist powers," Gage said. "Look at the Spanish with their Armada in 1588…"

Edmund raised a finger. "And the Dutch, with their armada, in 1688!" Gage gave him an annoyed look, and Ned added softly, "Men will do what they feel is right when they fear their people's ruin, whatever their religious persuasion."

"And what do you feel has been right in our own century?" Gage queried. "Would you have supported the Stuarts in the '45 Rebellion?"

"No, sir," Ned replied.

"How about the '15 Rebellion?"

Ned blinked. "Possibly."

"And what about when James was cast out by William? Would you have defended your reigning king?"

"The likelihood is significant, sir," he admitted, "though I don't suppose you would oppose me carrying that principle into the present and defending our reigning king now."

"Even though he is Anglican?"

Edmund glanced down at his Handel badge. "He is our king. *My* king."

"And once you give your allegiance to a king, Catholic or Protestant, you can't take it back?"

"Not under anything but the most drastic of circumstances, sir."

"Such as?"

"I don't know. But the slaughter of the innocents under King Herod might serve as a reasonable example. That having been said, one of my patron saints demonstrated a peculiar devotion to the queen who had him executed, praying for her before his end…"

"If he cared so much for her, the Jesuit Campion should have stayed in Europe where he couldn't cause her trouble," Gage replied.

"He cared for England," Ned stated. "He was willing to give his life to do her good."

"He did neither himself nor his queen nor his country any good. It was a futile endeavor."

"I think not," Ned countered.

"Of course. Recusants thrive on futility."

"Surely the hopes held by all Christians must seem like futility to the world. We cannot count the five wounds as being meritorious otherwise. Even a heart-wound could not prevent Our Lord from rising from the dead."

"Yes, but when shall there be a resurrection for recusants?"

Ned smiled. "God knows."

Percy's song finally came to a conclusion, and he bowed low as his audience offered him a round of applause.

"Noble descent, constancy, virtue, and valor in arms," Pitcairn complimented Percy, quoting praises offered to his house in ancient days. "You see? I am not one to withhold goodwill from the worthy vanquished!"

The Northumbrian beamed. "I am a Percy, in life and death."

Gage and Ned both looked at each other, realizing Percy had just quoted his doomed relation, the second Thomas Percy, who had been sentenced to death, just like his father, for taking part in a plot to install Mary, Queen of Scots, on the English throne. Thomas had been offered the chance to save his life by revoking his Catholicism, and he had replied with those exact words, demonstrating that his faith and family name were inextricably intertwined. But now it seemed the meaning had been all but forgotten by the present generation of his house.

"So are you two finished arguing about how much fire, or lack thereof, you hope to call down upon the colonials?" Gage inquired.

"If the transgressors are to be saved, I still believe it will be through fire." An eerie light came to Pitcairn's eyes. "It is cleansing when it brings the King's justice. Such was necessary when dealing with the Jacobites in Scotland, and it may be necessary again with the agitators in America. Every end is a beginning. From out of the ashes come new worlds, just as we must each return to ashes before we can rise again. Salt sowed upon the earth not only destroys but saves, so Scripture says."

"And you are ready and willing to spread around that flavor, in accordance with your upbringing?" Gage surmised.

"Aye," Pitcairn replied. "It's part of my calling."

"Well, as royal governor, it is my intent to act solely as the law informs me," Gage stated. "I shall not answer excess with excess and drag us closer to the precipice of civil war. We must not give the radicals any additional ammunition to unload on us. His Majesty agrees with me."

"You share his temperament, Tom," Burgoyne remarked. "Slow to anger."

"The King has shown great courtesy towards me in the course of my appointments."

"His friendship is a prize you have merited for your fidelity in matters great and small," Burgoyne complimented him. "Though patience on the part of honest men can easily be taken advantage of by unscrupulous knaves."

"Perhaps a bit of excess to begin with might prevent escalation in the long run," Pitcairn interjected. "I have such contempt for these villains who dare to challenge the King's peace, so hard-won by our forebears, that, if I had my way, I would march my men into the rebellious countryside and do as I pleased. One swift campaign, a smart action, and burning two or three towns would most likely set everything to rights. Nothing else, I am afraid, will ever convince these foolish, bad people that Britain is in earnest."

"You may be right, but humanity bids us to hold out hope it will not come to that," Burgoyne said. "We may have cause to speak daggers, but use none."

"Whatever happens, they've brought it upon themselves, just like the followers of the Young Pretender brought it upon themselves," Pitcairn said. "I am not ashamed of what we did, what we had to do, or what may come now…" He winced, then said in a softer tone, "Poor deluded people. God open their eyes."

Gage gazed at him sadly. "May your prayer be answered before it is too late."

"I believe it's too late already, and violence will bear us away." Pitcairn shook his head. "It's a judgment upon us, like hot coals touching our lips, glowing with the same fire that would not consume the Burning Bush."

"Yet God spoke from the Bush," Ned said.

"Yes, a holy, dreadful thing, which brings both peace and pain," Pitcairn responded. "My father understood that dichotomy, for he was raised on tales of the Killing Times under the Stuart kings. Bloody Clavers and his Highland brigands butchered us in droves to break our spirits. But we would not be broken, for we knew God chastises those He loves. Whatever agony comes may yet be our amnesty."

"Bonnie Dundee, as the Jacobites called Clavers, was punished himself, with a coat button drilled into his breast by the ball that struck him at Killiecrankie," said Burgoyne.

"Good God, man, do you think we cared about his damn looks?" Pitcairn huffed. "He was only as fair as the devil to us. You know, the Papists may have burnt a fair few of us, but it was Episcopal types like him who drowned us, even poor wee lasses like Margaret Wilson in Wigtown. They left her tied to a stake when the tide rolled in, then when she'd been submerged, they pulled her up by the hair and demanded she swear to the king's headship of the Kirk. She said, 'I will not, I am one of Christ's children, let me go.' So they did. It bothered me as a child when I heard about the wretched business at my father's knee. It only bothers me more now, having four daughters."

Ned found that the story bothered him too. This Presbyterian girl had perished for refusing to take the same oath which so many Catholics had been martyred for refusing to take. They may have had different reasons for their refusal, but the outcome was the same, as was their courage.

"Well, the Stuarts are no more," Gage stated. "Your father was able to proclaim 'Crown and Covenant' amongst his fellow Cameronians without contradiction."

"Just remember to be grateful we've come over to your side," Pitcairn said, wagging his finger, "and always be considerate of our tender consciences going forward!"

"In these isles, we have learned that compromise is our mainstay," Gage said. "It's how we avoided being trapped in the cycle of never-ending religious wars. It's give and take with everything here."

"Well," Pitcairn mused, putting his fist under his chin, "not…everything. If we compromised on all things, we would lose ourselves, and be abandoned by God, and then forgotten by the world. We must be willing to go all the way in essential matters. Besides, it is my family's way to burn brightly to the bitter end and make our enemies hide their faces from us. *Plena refulget*. That is our motto."

"Bright enough to endure the wet blanket that is Colonel Smith?" Burgoyne clucked.

Pitcairn groaned. "That man could suffuse any flame by boring it to death!"

"That's rather uncharitable," Gage said. "Francis Smith has dedicated his life to the service."

"It's true, though," Percy tossed in. "He's a fair enough career man, but his only hobbies seem to be taking long naps and collecting decoy ducks."

"Not even shooting at the blasted things!" Pitcairn exclaimed. "Just collecting them for show!"

"You worry me, Pitcairn," Gage said. "I get the terrible feeling you plan to launch a raid and blast his ducks off the shelf with your pistols."

Pitcairn raised an eyebrow. "I assure you, General, if such a thing were to occur, no one would know who fired the shots. The mystery would permeate military gossip for generations."

"Now, then, gentlemen," Gage sighed. "Being even-keeled is not a crime…"

"Though possibly the unforgivable sin," Burgoyne whispered in Pitcairn's ear, causing the major to laugh.

"You're not helping, Burgoyne," Gage said.

Burgoyne was undeterred. "I remember when Smith came back from a holiday in the Netherlands. I rather hoped he would bring back some tales of *amour romantique* amongst the ladies of Amsterdam…"

Gage groaned.

"…but no, he just trapped me in the corner of a gentleman's club, talking about flood prevention methods, for two hours…"

"Yes, he did that to me too!" Pitcairn recalled. "And then said I was 'a bit frazzled' by the end of it. Who the hell wouldn't be? Next he was going to describe the lifespan of a bloody tulip…"

"He also inferred my sense of humor was rude," Burgoyne sniffed. "I am many things, gentlemen, including risqué, but not rude."

"He never appreciates any of my jokes either," Pitcairn sympathized.

"Perhaps because they tend to be at his expense," Gage observed.

Pitcairn grinned. "Och, that's the fun of it!"

"Let's just hope he's not a man to hold a grudge."

"Ha! I'm immune from such fears!" Pitcairn boasted. "My Betty can hold quite a grudge, when she's of a mind. She still stews over our first fight."

"What was it about?" Burgoyne asked.

"Why the hell would I remember that?" Pitcairn retorted. "It's been some thirty years!"

"Probably about money," Gage decided.

"And what caused the first fights you gentlemen had with your wives?" Pitcairn challenged.

Burgoyne pondered for a moment, then admitted, "Money."

"The weather," Gage said.

"What? Why the weather?" Burgoyne queried.

"Because Margaret wanted to go for a sleigh ride."

"I'm not following this fight," Burgoyne said. "You didn't want her to go?"

"No, she wanted me to go with her. But, you know, it was freezing. Why have a blazing hearth indoors if you're not going to sit by it?"

"Ah, but snow!" Burgoyne exclaimed, ecstatically. "There's romance in it! Besides, the cold air can be invigorating for a man's lungs and, dare I say, his other parts too!"

"Unless you live along the Firth of Forth," Pitcairn said, treading old ground. "I nearly perished in the cradle…"

"But I thought you periodically went back up there to generate more offspring when your wife was staying with family during your absences," Burgoyne recalled.

"Yes, but…well, actually…you're right. I forgot about that part of my life for a second…I suppose I had simply gone too long without…"

"See? Cold can be refreshing for–"

"Can we possibly stop?" Gage sighed.

"…for having North American babies, like yours, sir!" Burgoyne waved his hand nonchalantly. "So much warmth can be kindled when a gentleman defers to his lady's wishes whenever possible! We may be men in authority, but our women still want their will!"

"You'll be pleased to know I yielded to Margaret's wish to go sleigh riding several days later," Gage admitted. "I am the sort who must have a wife who talks to me, or I grow sick of myself. That's even worse than catching cold."

"And as a result of this noble sacrifice, your newfound tolerance for lower temperatures equipped you for your rise to fame, settling the great shoveling feud of Montreal!" Burgoyne proclaimed.

Gage rolled his eyes. "All I did was force the thick-headed Gallic denizens to shovel out their own spaces and refrain from pulling carriages into their neighbors' spaces."

"And prevented them from bashing each other's heads in with said shovels," Burgoyne finished.

"There was that, yes. I don't have a problem with dead Frenchmen per se, but really, it was becoming an epidemic. Couldn't even get out of the office to watch a play without tripping over a shovel-clutching carcass in the snow…"

"You just reminded me what our first fight was about," Pitcairn recalled.

"Victims of shovel-related violence?" Burgoyne queried.

"No, not that! It was about going out to see a play…"

"Too expensive?" Gage guessed.

"No, no," Pitcairn grumbled. "I mean, yes, but that wasn't the crux of the quarrel. There she was, forcing me to go all the way out to an Edinburgh theater to watch the latest romantic comedy. I got about half way through the bloody farce and felt as if I was being smothered in feather pillows. I had to make a hasty retreat to a nearby tavern to erase all memory of my life for the past hour."

Burgoyne made a little squeak of dismay.

"Don't worry," Gage comforted him. "It couldn't have been any of your productions…"

"But still!" Burgoyne grieved. "The arts!"

"Damned philistine I be," Pitcairn agreed, not seeming too disappointed in himself. "In fairness, my marriage was somewhat more pragmatic than both of yours. Betty was a Dalrymple, you know, a kinswoman of my father's old superior, the Earl of Stair who served as an aide to Marlborough, distinguished himself at Ramillies, and built roads in Scotland with General Wade. It was a suitable arrangement that joined our families, but perhaps it left me unfamiliar with the finer points of wooing."

"Just because I married a colonial, it's not as if I did something truly madcap like elope!" Gage cast Burgoyne a knowing glance.

There was a glimmer in Burgoyne's eyes. "Ah, but my dear General, there are joys in madness the sane shall never know."

Pitcairn smiled mischievously. "Fortunately, I was wed to a woman who proved to be as frank as I am. We've come to understand each other very well."

"Except on the issue of plays," Burgoyne noted.

"Yes, well, as you pointed out, we have had other pastimes to share," Pitcairn chortled. He turned back to Percy, chatting with the ladies again, and shouted over to him, "And what was your first fight with your wife about, Earl Percy?"

Everyone cringed.

Percy stared at him for a long moment, then flatly answered, "Homicide."

"Right, then we'll leave that lie," Burgoyne chirped, and urged his companions to step a ways back and form a gossiping huddle, which proceeded to murmur about when, where, and upon whom said homicide was most likely to be committed. Burgoyne had decided it would make an intriguing play.

Ned, having listened quietly to the ongoing banter, noticed that the alcohol was clearly starting to have an effect upon everyone's intellects, and the conversation began to plummet into further silliness.

"I rather wish there was an artist on hand to commemorate our meeting with a sketch so it could be turned into a painting!" Burgoyne said. "We're a delightfully dynamic lot!"

"I, for one, would never turn down an opportunity to be immortalized on canvas," Pitcairn declared, puffing out his chest. "My mother said I cut a fine figure…"

"Your mother?" Burgoyne repeated.

"She was the one with the royal blood, bless her, and mighty proud to have passed on pleasing Hamilton features to her children."

"Well, Major, perhaps in America, your features will find their way into a propaganda engraving," Gage predicted. "Just prepare yourself to fill the role of villain."

"I'd not scorn it," he chuckled. "The bastards need a good villain to sort out their own brand of villainy."

"I suppose we can all be villainous in our own way if need be!" Burgoyne decided. "I'm the one with style!"

"And I'm the one who will be blamed for everything by default, whether I'm passive or aggressive," Gage sighed. "I'll stand in the center of the painting, to give it balance." He glanced over to Ned. "Will you stand with me, cousin?"

Ned laughed. "I should probably remove myself entirely."

"No, stay, we need young blood in this," Gage decided. "The rest of us are over fifty and probably having some sort of crisis…"

"But I'm too drab to be a villain."

"Look at who you're talking to!"

"Don't worry, Tom! I shan't forget you when I take over the world!" Burgoyne promised.

"Wait, what?"

"First the conquest of the West End, then the farthest horizon! We triumph through song!"

"Oh, right, this is about your musicals..."

"No, no, I'll take over the world with the Marines!" Pitcairn slurred, filling another glass of brandy for himself.

"Of course you will," Gage conceded. "You're amphibious and indestructible, like salamanders."

"Aye. We lose a tail, we grow it back. Woe to those who think they can disable us!"

Ned shook his head and threw up his hands. "The trouble for me, gentleman, is that I can't sing, and I'm not in uniform. So I might prove a hindrance rather than a help when it comes to your conquest..."

"I can remedy the latter, laddie," Pitcairn declared, tapping on his anchor-embossed gorget.

"Careful, Southworth," Gage warned. "The Major clearly has his heart set on adopting you, and you've not even heard half of what he's capable of when he gets around to drilling! Your virgin ears will bleed when he starts swearing you into shape!"

Pitcairn nodded and drank more brandy.

Just then, a young man, also in the uniform of the Marines, came up to the little group, bowed slightly to Gage and Burgoyne, then whispered something in Pitcairn's ear.

"My son tells me the hour is late and his mother intends for me to dine with the family," Pitcairn said, then made another half-grin. "He's the same one who buys me my Sunday drinks!" He gestured to Edmund. "William, this young friend of General Burgoyne may succumb to joining us bloody sea-soldiers, if I have anything to say about it. Say hello, William."

"Hello, Mister...?" William began, awkwardly.

"Southworth," Ned filled in, grateful that William's handshake was not quite as strong as his father's. "It's a pleasure."

"At least one of my children chose to follow my noble profession," Pitcairn said, slapping his son on the back. "My eldest boy David is learning medicine, like my brother William. I suppose I can forgive him for that choice. But God knows I shouldn't be on speaking terms with that black sheep, Thomas. Settled for an artillery post, he did!"

"Oh, Father," William sighed. "Grandfather was in the army, was he not?"

"Well, the Cameronians are a rare breed amongst army men..."

"You are rather making it sound like your prodigal son joined the ranks of the Ottoman sultan, or worse..." Gage glanced at Ned. "...the Pope's personal guard."

"Methinks Thomas fell under the influence of that hapless Cochrane fellow who married my daughter Kate," Pitcairn decided. "Another army man I have to deal with. From a fine family, but I swear, he's the sort who'll instigate a friendly fire incident or stick his head above a parapet during a barrage..."

"Charles is good to Kate, even if a bit, well, accident prone," William defended him.

"If I didn't think he was good to your sister, she would be a widow by now," Pitcairn snorted. "Let's just hope that what he lacks in brains he makes up for in manhood. After all, I'll be the grandfather of whatever he manages to produce, so I have a vested interest in him getting Kate sorted out sooner than later…"

"Father!"

"Come back to me when you've managed to do the same with whatever lass with a lump of land will have you for a husband," the major replied. "I'll rear whatever male infants you can make to be recruits from the cradle! And now that we've settled that, we really must away." He turned and bowed to his companions. "Sirs!"

"I'd be happy to walk you out, given I have pressing business to attend to with my young friend," Burgoyne said, gesturing to Ned. "I'm out to make a man of him!"

"At the hotel from hell?" Pitcairn surmised with distaste.

"What can I say?" Burgoyne shrugged. "I put down a pretty penny over there…"

"Just stay home with your wife, man," Pitcairn counseled. "Better for your body, your soul, and your purse!"

"He's right, you know," Gage remarked quietly, with just a tinge of contempt.

Burgoyne shrugged. "I'm afraid, unlike you two esteemed gentlemen, I have developed a taste for poison over the years, and when I deny myself my period dosage, I become a sorry specimen of a man."

"I don't believe that," Pitcairn stated, with a simple earnestness. "I hold to the damn opposite, in fact."

Burgoyne smirked grimly. "Just be grateful you didn't acquire the taste. Now, shall we depart in each other's company?"

"Very well," Pitcairn agreed. "I'll give you some recommendations for alternative accommodations on the way."

"How good of you," Burgoyne exhaled.

"Aye, it is. I know some of the most economical, but still reasonably clean…"

"So which one of us is going to call a carriage?" Burgoyne queried.

"Look, we can walk for a bit, like sensible people," Pitcairn snorted. "This damned city dabbles in rates of extortion…"

"But we came by carriage," Burgoyne argued.

"And I would have prevented you from doing so, had I been there. But better late than never. A brisk jaunt is good for your constitution! You learn that in the Marines!"

As Burgoyne and Pitcairn made their way to the door, Ned looked back over at Gage. The general smiled and remarked, "That little display of concern over our mutual friend's purse was proof Major Pitcairn is still more Presbyterian than Anglican, if ever there was any!"

Ned laughed, then muttered, "Thank you for not telling him that I'm…well…"

"I just didn't want him to light you on fire to avenge his ancestors," Gage replied. "He does rather like fire, you know, and can be a bit impulsive…"

"Is that a fact?" Ned queried teasingly.

"It's also a fact I don't much care for the smell of burnt flesh, so…"

Ned laughed again, nervously this time, wondering when Gage had last smelled it.

"Furthermore," Gage said softly, "I recognize that the colonial complaints we were debating must seem somewhat trifling compared to your own situation."

"Yes, rather," Ned admitted. As a Catholic recusant, even one whose ancestry stretched back to the very birth of England, tax upon tithe had been his family's lot, with no representation in parliament to be had. Furthermore, the very same Americans claiming victimhood now had been among the first to protest when Papists were allowed to hear mass unmolested in Quebec. Why should he be moved by their demand for greater liberties when they already possessed more than he did and would deny his fellow Catholics across the empire any relief?

"I…know how it was for my father, when he was a recusant," Gage said. "It's a bitter cup to drink for any man, especially one with a proud lineage."

"It is," Ned admitted. "But I do my best."

"Of course you do," Gage said, and there was a mix of sadness and even affection in his voice. Edmund found it impossible to carry a grudge against him.

"Thank you for talking with me," Ned mumbled. "It's made me come off as somewhat less of a fish out of water."

"If it makes you feel any better, London is an enigma to me too," Gage confessed. "Always has been. Strange place, even for work. Nothing manages to get done without a fuss. Either someone is running around trying to find me, or I'm running around trying to find them, and one or the other of us inevitably gets lost. It almost makes the Gordian Knot that is Boston seem comprehensible by comparison." The corner of his mouth twitched. "Almost."

Ned swallowed awkwardly. "I-I will pray for your child, the frail one. I know it must pain you to leave him behind as much as it pains your wife."

Gage appeared genuinely moved by this, and nodded. "Thank you." Then he smiled slightly. "Enjoy your walk."

Edmund chuckled, then jerked his hand up on instinct, unsure if initiating a handshake would be well-received or not. As a result of his indecision, he found himself waving oddly instead. Gage mimicked him.

As Ned hurried towards the door, he saw William Pitcairn had waited for him at the threshold.

"Fathers, am I right?" William teased, gesturing towards Pitcairn and Burgoyne who had strolled further down the garden path and were arguing over the merits of certain inns, with Pitcairn championing thrift and Burgoyne insisting upon comfort. "It is our filial responsibility to keep them safe, for they will utterly forget to look after themselves in the heat of things."

"Oh, I'm not the general's…I mean, he's not my…" Ned stammered.

"Are you sure?" William queried.

"Yes, quite sure. My father was friends with him, and he's repaying an old debt, that's all."

"But would you keep him safe?"

Ned paused for a moment, then found himself blurting out, "With my life."

"Then I repeat…fathers, am I right?"

Ned smiled and nodded.

"If you do join the Marines, though, my father shall be yours as well, and we will become brothers," William remarked. "He can be bloody strict, and you mustn't cross him, but he's also fair, and God knows, he does love us. And God knows, we love him too."

Ned turned his eyes down. "Whether or not I serve my country in the same manner as you, please know I would have considered it amongst the highest honors."

"I understand," William said. "Maybe Father doesn't always, but in his heart, he knows we each must follow our own path." He made a half-grin in good Pitcairn fashion. "Fortunately the old bulldog has at least one of his pups around to train, or he might have disowned the whole litter of us!"

Both young men laughed, then joined their "fathers" on their walk.

Chapter 6: DOWN AMONG THE DEADMEN

Major Pitcairn's walking route through London nearly caused everyone else's legs to give out, so Burgoyne finally took the initiative to flag down a carriage, promising to pay for all four of them. Pitcairn grumbled over the wasted coin, but ultimately relented and piled in with the others. After all, it would be unwise to miss supper with Betty, lest she start stewing. William and Ned chatted pleasantly for most of the walk, with William reminiscing about his childhood ever-on-the-move from Edinburgh to Cornwall to Kent, and Ned describing his stationary youth in the Lancashire countryside, with several noteworthy details left undisclosed. Finally in the carriage, the two of them gave each other knowing looks as the comedic drama unfolded between Pitcairn and Burgoyne. The two officers were rather too energetic to be contained in such a small space, as they veered between political agreement and disagreement, raising their voices and gesturing broadly.

Ned finally understood what Gage meant about Pitcairn being largely incomprehensible when truly animated, and he tested the method of hanging every fifth word out of the major's mouth and filling in the gaps himself. It was not uncommon to land on expletives. Burgoyne, meanwhile, made the mistake of asking Pitcairn to repeat himself, which only caused the old marine to become more animated and incomprehensible as his temper flared. William smirked at the scene, but would quickly wipe said smirk off his face whenever his father turned a sudden, sharp glance in his direction.

Then the conversation took other turns. Burgoyne began to describe a musical production he was working on, with the centerpiece being some sort of magic tree prop, and Pitcairn was reminded of a legend from his youth.

"The trees of Dysart are some of the oldest in Scotland," the major related. "The story goes they were planted by the three brothers Sinclair who founded the town. As the saplings were put into the ground, the Sinclairs pledged their undying loyalty to each other. But as fate would have it, they were later robbed in the woods, and falling upon each other in the darkness, they committed fratricide. Some say the trees they planted are cursed. I must say, walking past them as a child, I felt haunted."

"The inheritance of Cain and Abel," Burgoyne mused. "Brothers shedding each other's blood. The first civil war. We seem unable to escape its mark, even in the age of grace." He shifted in his seat. "Is it true what they say about Pontius Pilate having been born under a yew tree in Scotland?"

"I wouldn't know," Pitcairn replied, "but some claim his mother was a Caledonian tribeswoman who did favors for the Roman garrison stationed nearby. A scandalous conception, and a birth beneath the tree that stands for death."

"Yet out of death came life, through yet another tree."

"Yes, well, the holy book says where sin abounds, grace does even more, and so trust there will be a good ending to this age, blood-stained though it be," Pitcairn said. "My father loved to preach upon such things. It was the crux of everything he believed, that good can come out of evil, according to the Lord's will. It's the same with the trees of Dysart, in a way. Their curse became a blessing in disguise. I think that the people of the town made up for the debacle involving their founding brothers by showing greater loyalty to each other."

"You are nothing if not loyal to your roots, Major," Burgoyne agreed.

"Well, the town became quite prosperous under the shade of the very same trees. We're called the Little Holland, you know, because of how many Dutch merchants trade at the docks. Their language is spoken freely in the streets, in the taverns, everywhere. I can still manage fair enough with it myself. That sort of thing, among other traits, never left me, wherever I roamed."

"You miss it there, don't you?" Ned surmised. "I mean, you seem quite fond of it."

Pitcairn gazed out the window wistfully. "I'm fond of the sea, lad, and that can be found anywhere. It never stays in one place."

When the carriage reached the Pitcairns' temporary residence, William jotted down Edmund's address to send him whatever news might break in America, and Major Pitcairn once again accosted Ned with an aggressive handshake. Burgoyne received the same treatment, causing him to flex his fingers for a while afterwards to get the blood flowing again. Then, after a few final farewells, Burgoyne and Ned continued on to their hotel.

Once they arrived, Burgoyne decided to join in the nightly revelries of the establishment, and Ned, as usual, excused himself to retreat to their room. But Burgoyne prevailed upon him to at least sit in for a game or two at the card tables with him. Reluctantly, Ned agreed. Burgoyne was certainly in his element when gambling, his eyes glittering as he took steeper and steeper risks, seemingly lost to the thrill of it all. Edmund was less enamored by it all, but Gage had been right about one thing: the boy's upbringing made him rather good at keeping a straight face and his cards close to his chest. Burgoyne might say he was "too true" with a blade in his hand, but Gage read the subtleties of the young man's character better. Shared recusant heritage could not help but foster such understanding, even though they now found themselves on opposite sides of the religious divide.

I don't like what must be for me, Ned thought, gazing down at his poor hand of cards. *I don't enjoy deceiving my own countrymen, nor them fearing me. Perhaps Burgoyne and Gage are both right. I am too true for the games I keep playing. Yet play them I do, and play them I must, till my dying day. Or...*

With that thought, his concentration slipped, as surely did his expression, and he soon found himself being called out and losing the money he had managed to win. That effectively cured him of any attraction he might have found blooming in his heart for the precarious pastime. Burgoyne, meanwhile, uncorked another bottle of wine with his teeth and continued to play for very high stakes. Lady Luck seemed to be favoring him for the moment, as did two scantily-clad female employees of the house who slipped onto his lap. But Ned decided to sit on one of the vacant sofas behind the tables, just in case circumstances changed and his friend needed to be pulled away from his own ruin.

A drinking song started up among some of the other establishment denizens, and Gentleman Jonny joined in lustily.

*"Here's a health to the King and a lasting peace
To faction an end, to wealth increase.
Come, let us drink it while we have breath,
For there's no drinking after death.
And he that will this health deny,
Down among the dead men, down among the dead men,
Down, down, down, down;
Down among the dead men let him lie!*

*Let charming beauty's health go round,
With whom celestial joys are found.
And may confusion yet pursue,
That selfish woman-hating crew.
And he who'd woman's health deny,
Down among the dead men, down among the dead men,
Down, down, down, down;
Down among the dead men let him lie!*

*In smiling Bacchus' joys I'll roll,
Deny no pleasure to my soul.
Let Bacchus' health round briskly move,
For Bacchus is a friend to Love;
And they that would this health deny,
Down among the dead men, down among the dead men,
Down, down, down, down;
Down among the dead men let him lie!*

*May love and wine their rights maintain,
And their united pleasures reign.
While Bacchus' treasure crowns the board,
We'll sing the joy that both afford.
And they that won't with us comply,
Down among the dead men, down among the dead men,
Down, down, down, down;
Down among the dead men let them lie!"*

    Edmund couldn't help but think their moral and moderate king was unlikely to want to be associated with a place like this, even by way of praise. He certainly would not wish to be associated with a pagan deity of carnal delights, to whom the scantily-clad women were now comparing Burgoyne, since his surname, going back to the Norman Conquest, referred to Burgundy, the wine region of France. He seemed flattered.

"Not the sort to comply, my sweet?"

Ned turned to see their proprietress Georgiana elegantly lounging beside him on the sofa, like a pedigree cat, bred to please the wealthy. He found himself blushing and trying his best to rip his eyes away from her bosoms, powdered and pushed up as ever in her low-cut bodice.

"There now, dearie. I'm not so terrifying, am I?" she teased. "Johnny has told me all about you. Knowing him as long as I have, I'd say he was uncommonly fond of you, and wants nothing more than to see you relax and maybe even enjoy yourself a bit."

Ned glanced over his shoulder at the stairwell. "Lovely railing you have," he mumbled. "Whoever made it, it's…well-crafted…" He turned his eyes upward. "And the chandelier here, it really is…very nice…"

She raised an eyebrow. "And the carpeting?"

He turned his eyes down. "Yes, indeed, exquisite."

She laughed, a sound like tinkling silver bells, then opened a decorative fan to cool herself. The motion of the fan wafting the strong scent of her perfume towards Ned. No wonder she and Burgoyne got on. "Well, Mister Southworth, as you can see, I do have an eye for the finer things, which attracts customers with the same tendency, such as yourself."

He turned back to her, trying his best to focus on her eyes, a merry green. "It must have cost a pretty penny to put all this together."

"Indeed it did," she admitted. "My father, bless his wretched soul, did a bit of fundraising for me, as did the lascivious old man whose bed he plopped me into when I was a wee lass of thirteen. I had been educated for years to play the part with suitable charm as a cultured consort, not a mere street strumpet. Once the elderly fellow went down among the deadmen to keep his appointment with Lucifer, I ended up with a fair sum from his purse, as well as references. Soon I had more than a few paramours of rank, and I only continued to rise through my wits and willing manner." She winked.

Edmund found himself at a loss but stammered, "I-I am glad that you are…" He couldn't for the life of him manage to finish the thought, for he did not truly consider her to be doing well. "…that you are sitting with me." Was he though? Never mind. He continued, "It's kind of you to do so, since you are right, this situation is not to my comfort, and I thank you for…" Again, his voice faltered, before finally finishing with, "your company."

She gave him a rather pitying look. "There now, my dear. Johnny doesn't want you to feel uneasy. He knows you're the religious sort. But I can tell you appreciate beauty, even so."

"God is reflected in beauty," he said. "I am never far from Him when I praise that which is beautiful in this world."

"Even a railing in a house like this?" she chuckled.

"Yes, the color of the wood, and the skill that carved it," he replied.

"And the chandelier?" she continued in a teasing tone.

"Yes, the flame casting prisms through the crystals, and the crystals, falling like tears."

Something about the way he said that seemed to take her aback.

"And in people?"

"Yes," he said softly, meeting her gaze again, "in people most of all."

She hesitated for a moment, then resumed her previous gaiety, "And what sort of women do you find to be most beautiful?"

"Those who have merry eyes," he said, smiling at her.

She laughed again. "You are very different from Johnny, yet also much the same. I wouldn't be the least bit surprised if he were your—"

Suddenly, there was a commotion over at the tables. One of the gamblers had roughly seized the girl who had been dealing the cards by the arm.

Georgiana got to her feet and sashayed over. "Have a care, big man," she lilted, striking him in the side of the head with her fan. "No one handles my girls that way."

"This little wench of yours robbed me!" He shouted.

"You took the risks, and you'll pay the costs," Georgiana stated, pointing to the list of house rules hanging on the back wall. "I'll not coddle sore losers!"

"You're the whore behind this crooked house," the man growled, leering at Georgiana. "Give me back my money, you Papist mother of—"

"You had best watch your words, sir!" Burgoyne slurred, standing up from his own table. "Our gracious hostess may be many things, but the integrity of her tables I will defend with my blood, if needs be!"

"Besides, my name is Kelley, with an E!" Georgiana clarified, with a defiant toss of her curls. "That's Protestant Irish for you!"

A chorus of sporadic and rather drunken huzzahs went up from the house customers. Ned just sighed.

"My good fellow, it would be most advisable for you to remove yourself from this reputable establishment of your own accord, since your presence here has become about as welcome as a rat in a granary," Burgoyne said. "Otherwise…"

Before he could finish, the man had taken a flying punch at him, and several moments later, a brawl had broken out, with the other customers throwing punches at each other pell-mell.

Ned observed that the young girl who had been dealing out the cards was still seated behind the table, trembling with fright. Her eyes appeared like the petals of violets, and her cheeks were painted pink as rose blossoms. He wondered what color her real hair was underneath the powdered wig. And all at once, he felt deeply sorry for her.

He stood up, circumvented the drunken pile-on, and made his way to her side. Then he calmly took her by the hand and escorted her away from the insanity.

"Did that bully hurt you?" Ned queried, observing her bruised arm under the candlelight.

"Oh, it's nothing," she insisted, though it came out more like a whimper, and he handed her a handkerchief to dab her eyes. "You've got to get used to the odd incident."

"Do you?" Ned asked flatly.

She did not answer, but quickly composed herself and batted her eyelashes at him. "And what is my hero's name, hmm?"

Ned laughed awkwardly and shook his head. "Look, there are your heroes." He pointed to Burgoyne and a few of the others who were dragging the troublemaker, kicking and screaming, towards the door.

"But you do have a name," she said.

"Edmund," he introduced himself with a slight bow. "But you may call me Ned. And you are…?"

"Rebecca," she replied with a soft smile, accentuating her dimples. "But you may call me Becky." She glanced over at Georgiana, who seemed to be giving her signals of some sort with her eyebrows. "Shall we go upstairs, Ned?"

"Upstairs?" Ned repeated, trying to decide how to dissuade her without being rude.

"Yes, we can get to know each other better," she said. "And I'd be grateful to get away from all this for a spell. I feel a headache coming on…" She put a hand to her forehead dramatically. "You would be doing me quite the favor…"

Ned hesitated for a moment, then found himself relenting against his better judgment. Soon, she was briskly leading the way upstairs, teasing him for lagging behind when she was the one wearing skirts. Soon, they were in the hallway, standing in front of the door to his room. and she was batting her eyelashes some more and insisting he get out the key. He found himself reluctantly doing so, and soon she was sashaying about the room, chatting in a cheery fashion, and asking Ned to help her undo the back of her dress…

"Wait," he blurted.

She stared at him, tilting her head.

"Please understand…" His voice trailed off. "This is not something I wish to do."

She continued to gaze at him, seemingly mystified, then folded her arms over her chest. "Don't judge so fast, Ned. I may be small, but I know how to make a man happy, if he gives me half a chance."

"It's got nothing to do with your size…"

"What then?"

Ned sighed. "I'm sorry. I know I must seem rather silly to you, and possibly inconvenient. But it's just something I can't do with you, and…go on like it didn't matter…"

"What do you mean by matter?" she asked.

"I can't give of myself or take from you unless it means something, something lasting. I can't pretend it's just a late night game, like dice or cards, to be forgotten about in the morning. I can't gamble myself away, and tell a lie with my body. Do you understand?"

"No," she said. "What lie?"

"That we're bound to each other. That we've sworn oaths to each other and to none other."

She giggled. "You're a true romantic!"

"I suppose so."

She sat down on the side of the bed. "General Burgoyne thinks you're just not used to having fun. Brought up too strict or what not. Mistress Georgiana thinks so too…"

Ned chuckled. "I'm sure they do."

"Maybe I could get you accustomed to new things." She gestured to the other side of the bed.

"Get me accustomed to lying, you mean?"

"It's not lying," she insisted. "A girl in my line of work doesn't expect the sort of thing you're talking about…"

"But it is," he replied. "And you should."

"Then men lie to me all the time," she assured. "I'm used to it."

"You don't deserve that," Ned replied.

She was silent for a moment then burst out laughing. "Daddy should hear you say that! He lied to me like there was no tomorrow when I was little, promising me this, that, or the other thing. A right proper lord he was, with too many gambling debts to keep his word to a bastard daughter. Looking back, I don't mind. When he brought me here, he said I would be able to handle any man now, since I'd put up with him!"

Ned winced at how similar her story was to Georgiana's. "Becky…"

"No, no. He was right. This is home for me now. It's pretty, and clean, and Mistress Georgiana protects us from anyone who plays too rough. She knows what it's like to be one of us, so is sort of like our guardian angel. I wouldn't want to be anywhere else."

She beamed up at him, and Ned felt his heart sink, realizing she was sincere, and this was the best world she could envision herself inhabiting. He felt relieved to know that at least Burgoyne had gotten Fanny work as a house servant instead of selling to such an establishment where, no matter how elegant the facade, the trade remained rotten, for it trafficked in human beings.

"Want to play cards with me here for a while?" Ned suggested. "You're right; it's been pandemonium down there…"

"We're only allowed to use the cards at the tables," she replied. "House rule."

"Oh. Well, what about mind games?"

"Hmmm?"

"I mean, you seem like a clever girl for it," Ned flattered her. "Like Mistress Georgiana, I imagine you were educated enough to fit into all this…refinement."

"Now don't be mocking me," she lectured him.

"My apologies," he sighed. "But my mockery was not for you, it was for this place. You're too good for it."

"That's silly," she chided him.

"Alright, humor me then. Isn't the customer always right?"

She laughed into her hands now. "Alright. Tell me about your mind games."

He gestured to the nearby table, then pulled out a chair for her. "You try to guess what I'm thinking by asking me a set number of questions. We go back and forth however many times we decide upon, and whoever guesses correctly the most times wins."

Her eyes widened greedily as she sat down. "How much are we playing for?"

"The general said he would treat me to whatever I wanted to do in the house. So…you set the price, and we'll charge it to him."

"Haha!" She clapped her hands at that prospect. Ned bowed, then sat in the chair across from her. Then she hurriedly discarded her wig, revealing mousy brown hair underneath. "Not my finest feature," she admitted, taking out the pins holding it up, "but I can think better with it free-flowing, if you don't mind."

"Not a bit," Ned assured.

"Splendid." She brushed her fingers through her hair and shook her head vigorously. "There, now. Let the games begin! Which of us should start thinking of something?"

"Ladies first," Ned insisted.

"Alright." She closed her eyes tight. "I've got something. Ask me a question."

"Is what you're thinking of animate or inanimate?"

She leaned forward with a mischievous glimmer in her eyes, put a hand to the side of her mouth, and whispered, as if it were a great secret, "It's an activity."

Ned squinted at her. "Let's stick something animate or inanimate."

Becky pouted.

~

The next morning, Ned found that he had fallen asleep in his chair and Becky was also snoozing, using the table for a pillow. He sighed, still half asleep himself, reached for the pillow behind him on the chair, and gingerly pried up her head to slip it underneath. He accidentally pulled her hair in the process, rousing her.

"Ouch," she yelped, shaking her head.

"Sorry," he mumbled.

She yawned and stretched, her eyes hazy from slumber. Then they brightened, and she declared triumphantly, "Sheep!"

He raised his hands up, conceding her correct answer to the final round of their game.

"I would have guessed that earlier, but you said they eat carrots!"

"They do, though," he insisted. "My sister and I have even fed them carrot cake."

She laughed. "That's marvelous! I never would have imagined it!"

"That's because you're a city girl. It stunts your perspective…ouch!"

She promptly struck him with the pillow.

Just then, Ned heard someone clearing his throat at the threshold of the room.

There stood a rather disheveled and sleep-deprived Burgoyne, hat in his hands. "Well, Ned, how does it feel to have manned up a bit?" He tossed his hat onto his bed dramatically.

Before Ned could formulate an answer, Becky scribbled an addendum on the parchment spread out on the table, then handed it to Burgoyne. "My fee for the night's work."

The general's eyes widened. "What the hell did you do to him?" Then he turned to Ned. "Or what did you do to her? One or both of you terrify me."

"Think what you like," she said, fixing her wig back on her head. "Those are my earnings, fair and square!"

"I realize this was the first time for him and everything, but you didn't have to give him a complete tutorial for future reference!"

"I'll have you know, General darling, I won that tidy sum with my mind!"

Burgoyne blinked. "And some, I'm sure..."

"No, she's right," Ned confirmed. "She's quite good at the game."

"Well, yes, she's a professional..."

"Left me out on a limb more than once."

"What? I don't understand...that makes her poor at the game, not good at it..."

Becky started cackling, and Burgoyne stared blankly at her for a few seconds.

"Was he not being euphemistic?" the general queried.

"He couldn't guess what I was thinking, General, for all his questions! That was the game!"

The reality of the situation seemed to dawn on him. "Sink me, Ned! You're such a unicorn!"

"Now, don't be mean to him," Becky chided. "There's got to be some unicorns in the world! Remember, as the Bard said: 'Thus be it ever: To thine own self be true.'"

"But does he have to be true to himself at my expense? Couldn't he just have read his prayer book or something?"

"You burned it," Ned reminded him.

"Oh, right. Well, interior contemplation or whatever you call it?"

"I couldn't just tell her to leave without a penny more to her name," Ned protested. "It would have been rude."

"Well, I am sorry to disappoint you both, but I have been monetarily depleted at the tables. Maybe the bloody things are rigged, after all...you tell me..." Burgoyne shrugged.

Becky stood up and waved the paper under Burgoyne's nose. "That right there is a gentleman's agreement! It was made on your behalf! Now will you uphold your reputation in this house, or won't you?"

Burgoyne rolled his eyes. "Mind your manners, you mouthy little thing, and...be patient." He glanced out the door briefly. "I'll be back presently." Then he dashed down the hall.

Ned went over to the threshold and glanced down the corridor. "Is he going to abandon me here, do you think?"

"Probably not, given his hat is still here," she consoled him. "Besides, he rather likes to think of himself as a gentleman. Come to think of it, he sort of is, as they come. He's probably just gone in search of a loan..."

They both listened as the general argued with another one of the girls a few doors over. He seemed to want to borrow a present he had given her to use for collateral. She wasn't having it.

"Annabelle is one of the best dancers in the house," Becky said. "The general gave her a jeweled coronet for her birthday party a few months back. He said she was to wear it like a queen, even when no other adornment would be suitable for her!" Becky giggled. "She's ever so proud of it, in petticoats or out of them…zounds!"

There was a loud "crack" sound, and Burgoyne staggered back into the hallway. He returned to his room, nursing his cheek, and grunted, "Payment plan?"

Becky nodded. "Very well. Better put ice on that…"

"Can't afford it," he lamented.

"Oh, poor you," Becky sighed. "Let's see if I can't procure some from the kitchen."

"You're divine, Becky."

"Something like that." She turned back to Ned and pecked him on the cheek. Then she shook a finger at Burgoyne and repeated, "Don't be mean to him." With that, she was off.

"Peculiar little creature, but at least she's not violent," Burgoyne remarked, rubbing his face again. Then he turned back to Ned. "Alright, I surrender! Next time, we'll go to a boring little inn where you will be free from temptation, so long as you vow upon the ashes of your prayer book not to play mind games with the help."

Edmund laughed, then grew somber. "There will be a next time, sir?"

"Well, I find that I've grown accustomed to your sorry little country mouse face that could easily belong to a chaste knight in another age."

"Are you very disappointed I didn't...man up?" he asked meekly.

"No, not really," Burgoyne admitted. "But just because I can't make a sinner out of you, don't expect to make a saint out of me."

The corner of Edmund's mouth twitched. "God's will, General," he said. "God's will."

Just then, someone poked their head into the room. The face was familiar, and the rest of him was clad in nothing more than long underwear.

"Want a loan?" inquired Earl Percy. "I can make a loan."

Burgoyne beamed. "You, sir, are a godsend!"

Ned buried his face in his hands from embarrassment. At least it proved Gage's point about Percy being generous with his wealth.

Chapter 7: THE PLAY'S THE THING

After returning home to Lancashire, Edmund continued to see Burgoyne whenever he came north to tour his constituency and would regularly coax the general into taking long country walks with him and Kip. Burgoyne had developed a genuine affection for the sheep dog, who had in turn become quite accustomed to the scent of the general's perfume, associating it with his willingness to play fetch and feed Kip extra biscuits. But for all his kindness towards canines, Burgoyne would frequently cite the potential for soiling his fine boots on the dirt paths and try to get out of such excursions Ned, however, would insist, and his guest would reluctantly comply.

Once they embarked, Burgoyne would swiftly adapt to his surroundings and keep up as brisk a pace as he had in the city, brandishing his elegant walking cane and dramatically pointing to this or that natural feature along the way. He had to admit the fresh air was good for his thinking cap after being too long in stuffy quarters debating the fate of the troublesome colonies. Picking up from their time in London, he would pleasantly converse about his writing endeavors, asking the young man for input on story points he was weaving into wider plots to be performed on stage. Ned did his best to offer whatever constructive commentary came to mind and felt flattered to be consulted by Burgoyne, especially when the general referred to him as "a budding scholar" and praised his late father's literary knowledge.

Teresa looked forward to Burgoyne's visits as well, for he made her feel worthy of manly attention. He sometimes brought over sheet music intended to be performed in one of his theatrical productions written for balls and galas, and would insist upon Tessie lending her "enchantment" to the compositions by playing them on her harpsichord. Ned rarely saw his sister's face glow as much as when she was thus employed, and Burgoyne had a habit of presenting her with a bouquet of roses or some fancy trinket after each recital. The general appeared to enjoy giving these gifts as much as Tessie enjoyed receiving them.

Perpetua, however, stayed away from Burgoyne as much as possible when he came over the house, often locking herself in the hidden attic chapel for devotions, as if he were an evil spirit that needed to be warded off. She kept the Catholic servants on call to report to her about the goings-on downstairs, convinced that Burgoyne might try to deflower her daughter or launch an independent investigation of the estate for contraband, no matter how many times her son assured her that her fears were groundless. Burgoyne, for his part, seemed happy to ignore the discourtesy shown him by the mistress of the manor so long as her children continued to welcome him.

One day, during a long country walk, Ned brought Burgoyne out to a special grove of rowan trees he used to frequent as a boy. It was late summer, and the berries on the branches were as bright crimson as the general's cloak.

"My father used to take me here all the time," Ned said, unpacking the lunch he had brought along in his satchel. "He would tell me to look up at the berries and remember the blood of Christ and the martyrs."

"Always the martyrs, with your lot," Burgoyne chuckled.

"I was taught to live out my life, be it long or short, in remembrance of them," Edmund replied. "But Father would call to mind so many sacred things on his long walks. Every stream made him speak of the Baptism of Our Lord, when all the waters of the world were made rich with blessing. Every hill made him speak of the Transfiguration of Our Lord, when the prophets of God penetrated the veil and Doomsday was glimpsed. And every lamb he heard bleating in a meadow made him recite the *Agnus Dei* under his breath. Remember what His Majesty said about creation being like a second holy book? Well, that's what England was to Father, full of illuminations."

"Francis would have gotten along well with the King, I reckon," Burgoyne remarked.

"I think so too," Ned agreed.

"It's not unheard of for His Majesty to befriend Papists, as surely you surmised from his gentle treatment of you. He's even bent a few of his own rules for them, if he thinks they can be trusted. Once, he stopped over at the home of a recusant noble, and badly wanted to go hunting. Our king is a gentleman farmer and huntsman at heart, happiest when mending fences and chasing foxes. But he thought it would be terribly discourteous to leave his host behind. So he said, 'Can we put a gun in your hand for an hour or two and not end up with a bullet in our back and a cousin on our throne? What say you, man, what?' So upon offering his assurances, the host was whisked off on the hunt, and dare I say His Majesty knew from the beginning the man was no novice at it, legally or otherwise!"

Ned laughed at Burgoyne's imitation of the King's mannerisms. "You're really quite the actor, sir."

"Well, your father and I shared a dramatic flair, brought to bear in our own ways," Burgoyne recalled. "It's fully fitting that we met at a playhouse. The two of us always knew how to observe and to imitate, living many lives in the process. We could never help but see symbols in everything, meaning everywhere, and make the most of it. That's the essence of the arts. They are an appeal to beauty, sense, and truth. The stories we act out on stage must represent nature on some level, the sort that makes man what he is."

"What God puts in us," Ned mused.

"Exactly," Burgoyne concurred. "Telling stories, according to various mediums, is a means of praising the Creator. He is, after all, the Author of all."

Ned smiled wistfully, handing the older man some sliced ham on a piece of bread. "Sometimes, as a little boy, when I looked up at the berries here, I thought of scarlet tunics, and Wolfe bleeding upon the Plains of Abraham. I play-acted battle so often as a child, and wore any scraps of red cloth I could find to make a proper soldier of myself."

"Naturally," Burgoyne replied, nudging Ned with his elbow. "You love drama too, and don't deny it. By my soul, I really must get you to come down to one of my little romantic comedy performances. We throw the best midnight supper parties afterwards, since we don't know what to do with all the stamina we've built up for the stage!"

Edmund squinted. "Would I be scandalized?"

"Oh, come, boy, we theater folk don't solely languish in debauchery," Burgoyne insisted. "Sometimes we just spend hours around a harpsichord with cheese boards and wine glasses, trying to show off to one another how many numbers we have memorized! It's great fun! Besides, we're eccentrics, mayhap, but warm-hearted ones who can be positively devoted to each other during hard times. We won't let any of our own fall through the cracks, and have a soft spot for the plight of humanity. That's why we run so many benefits. We're a family of sorts, bound not by blood but by art. There's something wholesome in that, is there not?"

"Yes, there is," Ned admitted. "Perhaps I might accept one of your future invitations after all."

"That's the stuff," Burgoyne praised him. "Though, I must say, you do seem to gravitate more towards tragedies than comedies!"

Ned chuckled. "Keeping your company in any event would make me happy."

Burgoyne patted Ned on the arm. "Well, my dear, let me first tell you a little secret about comedies. They may seem like frivolous entertainment to dour Puritans in black apparel. But I say…yes, I swear, they are a reminder of the Last Judgment. You see, in comedies, everything comes right in the end. Love triumphs. Virtue is rewarded. And perhaps the errant may yet be reformed." He smiled as Kip began to wag his tail and make sad whimpers for scraps from the general's sandwich. "And every shameless beggar gets a bit of ham."

Ned sighed as Burgoyne fed Kip some meat. "He's taking advantage of your good nature, sir."

"I know," Burgoyne admitted. "But I can't resist those watery eyes looking up at me! They would make a marble melt!"

Ned shook his head, then relented and gave Kip some ham from his own sandwich too.

As they turned back along the path home, Ned caught sight of something that disturbed him. Across the meadow stood a local landlord with a riding crop in hand, brandishing it above a young girl about ten years of age, crouched on the ground. He was shouting and swearing at her to tell him where the hedge priest was hiding, and she was biting her lip, refusing to answer. Ned knew the girl. She was from one of the Catholic tenant families on the man's estate.

Ned saw the crop rise and fall on the girl's back and heard her start to whimper. Without a second thought, and ignoring the general's protest, he stormed towards the scene, his fists clenched.

"Stop it," Ned commanded, standing between the man and the girl.

"Not till she tells me where the damn Romish priest is off too!" the landlord declared. "I know there was one traipsing about on my land! I'm wise to your signs and signals, your pebbles placed in a circle and shirts hung on a bush!"

The man shoved Edmund in the shoulder, but could not move him.

"You'll not hit her again," Ned stated, refusing to budge.

"Back down, Southworth! You're as guilty as sin with the rest of them! I could have you hauled off to the magistrate along with your precious peasants!"

Ned turned to the shaken girl, tears glistening on her freckled cheeks, and ordered hoarsely, "Go home, Rosemary!"

She stumbled to her feet, ran a sleeve across her face, then turned and ran.

The landlord started to go after her, but again Ned blocked his way.

"You brazen Popish bastard," he spat, and struck Ned across the face with his crop.

Ned tensed, raising his fist slightly on impulse, then lowering it again.

"Ha! Go on! I dare you to strike a Protestant and get away with it! No, your only chance is to turn the other cheek!"

Again, he hit Ned with the crop, and Ned felt a trickle of warm blood run down his face.

Then something smashed into the landlord's side, knocking him off balance.

It was Burgoyne, gold-tipped cane in hand. Kip was at his side, growling and barking in defense of his master. With a single swift motion, the general yanked the riding crop away from the landlord and snapped it in two. Then he grabbed the man by the collar.

"You know," Burgoyne hissed, "I don't much like bullies…perhaps because it's simply another word for cowards."

"That one there is an avowed Papist, enabling Papistry to spread like cancer!" the man said, jabbing a finger at Ned.

"I only see one cancer here," Burgoyne ground out. "You struck my friend in the face, not once, but twice. Do you not think I'll break you for that?!"

There was something terrifying glimmering in Burgoyne's lustrous eyes, which Ned found to be wonderful at the same time.

The man winced. "I-I could have a lot of them arrested!"

"No, you couldn't," Burgoyne snapped, releasing his collar and wiping his hands along his cloak as if to cleanse them. "You have no proof, and their neighbors will not testify against them, not in this village, for they honor the memory of Francis Southworth. You know as much, hence the crop!"

"I…"

"You will get out of my sight this instant, lest I use all my clout to take you down!" Burgoyne shouted, so loudly and fully that it made Ned tremble. "Go!"

And so the man left, with Kip chasing a way after him across the field to make sure he kept going.

Burgoyne turned back to his friend. "Jesus, Ned," he murmured, and started to dab at the boy's face with his handkerchief.

"Sir, you mustn't profane Our Lord's name on my account," Ned lectured him gently.

"Oh, I'm sure Our Lord will forgive me. I'm in a state, Ned…in such a bloody state…" He shook his head and clicked his tongue. "You should have struck him back, be you Papist or no! I would have backed you up!"

"I used to scrap with Protestant boys as a child, but when I turned thirteen, Father said things had changed, and made me promise to restrain my temper, no matter how cruelly provoked,"

Ned explained. "I try to keep faith with his memory as much as the villagers who took his charity."

"Well, you should learn how to bob and weave, at least."

"I'm rather good at that when I want to be, believe it or not. But…" Edmund shrugged. "Better to let the man get the meanness out of his system on me than for him to beat a child."

"But it's not right, striking someone with noble blood like you," the general protested, "yes, even one in your current position. That vile man got his money from trading in tobacco and slaves. You, on the other hand, have inherited the memory of ancient honors…"

"Well, I don't suppose that makes the whip sting me any worse than it does a peasant or a slave," Ned replied.

"Now you sound like a Methodist, with their equalizing ways," Burgoyne sighed. "If you were not a Papist, I could imagine you attending their revivals."

"All have sinned and fallen short of God's glory, and thus we are equal in our dependence upon Him," Ned replied. "The King himself admits as much. It's not Methodist, but Christian. If the Methodists in particular are reminding us of it, more power to them."

"But Ned, returning to the point at hand, none of these Papist farm folk could relate to having a proud family name," Burgoyne countered. "I'm not advocating random brutality, especially against a mere slip of a girl like that, but they do not suffer the same indignity when being struck…"

"If I can hold my ground, even through indignity, then I win. Besides, my parents taught me that whatever remained of my inheritance should be used for the benefit of God's people."

Burgoyne titled his head. "*Noblesse oblige,* then?"

"If you like," Ned conceded.

"Yes, of course, I like," Burgoyne exhales. "It just angers me to see you mishandled."

Edmund smiled softly. "It seems you have a temper, sir."

"Yes, doesn't it?" Burgoyne's eyes sparkled. "Our blood is northern, Ned. It can run hot, if we let it. Came in use for me when fighting the Spanish dons…"

"But you try to keep it cool, most times," Ned observed.

"When it suits my purposes, yes. But good old-fashioned fury has its benefits as well."

"I doubt my own temper would be beneficial if I showed it," Ned said. "They would say I was the sort of Papist that had become dangerous."

"Well, then," said Burgoyne kindly, "I shall have to become enraged for both of us when the occasion calls for it. I can get away with it. Or at least I can try." He winked.

Ned chortled, then said sincerely, "Thank you for helping me."

"Tch, tch," the general clicked his tongue. "None of that." He continued to dab at the boy's face, and muttered, "You know, it twists me up inside, seeing you hurt." He tucked the handkerchief back into his coat and added, almost sadly, "Ned, you must never tell me certain things. I am a soldier and a statesman. I have taken oaths, time and again, that bind me."

"I'm aware, sir," Ned confirmed. "You are instructed by the Test Act to enforce the law against Popish priests and those who harbor them."

"I don't rush about, eager to implement it on that front, but still…" Burgoyne bit his lip. "You must keep me in the dark, that's all. I would hate myself if I ever had to hurt you. But I must have blinders kept on my eyes sometimes, or I would have no choice, before God or man, but to act as my duty dictates."

"I understand," Ned assured.

"Do you?" Burgoyne queried.

Ned hesitated, then replied, "Not about the law itself, but about you. I'll not let your integrity be compromised."

Nor any priest's safety, he thought, but kept it to himself.

"Setting oaths to the side," Burgoyne said, laying a hand on the boy's shoulder, "I think you'd make a fine soldier, Ned…not just as part of childhood play, but in truth. You've got the backbone for it. That's a part of your inheritance, from even farther back than the golden age of chivalry, which no one has managed to rob from you. Your eyes, your hair, your heart…you are a part of this land, Ned, and have been since it was first called England."

Edmund could not help but feel his heart swell to hear such praise, even as he knew a future for him in arms could not be.

Meanwhile, Kip had returned from the chase, running circles around his master until his energy was finally spent and he collapsed in a panting heap on the grass.

"Poor boy," Burgoyne sighed. "He's expended himself in your service."

"Something tells me he's also expended himself spooking other people's sheep," Ned observed, pointing to a handful of sheep in a neighboring field, milling around in a rather confused fashion.

"Well, everyone gets a bit distracted now and then," Burgoyne dismissed. "'Tis the thought that counts."

Ned exhaled and picked up Kip in his arms. "Alright, fine, I'll give you a ride, but only for a little while. All those extra biscuits and strips of ham have made you fat!"

Kip barked in a sort of agreement he may not have entirely intended as Ned and Burgoyne headed back to the Southworth manor.

The incident with the landlord ended up being a mere precursor of troubles to come. A month later, Teresa found herself apprehended by the authorities. She had been visiting several neighboring towns and villages on charitable errands. It was not uncommon for gentlewomen to engage in such missions of mercy if they had the heart for it, and Tessie certainly did. But this time she had been caught giving away more than food and clothing to those struggling with poverty. No, she had made a gift of something that branded her as a nonconformist of a troublesome disposition. She had given a sickly Protestant child a brown scapular, which had been given to her by a visiting priest newly arrived in England from Belgium.

Ned's first reaction upon learning of his sister's arrest was to send a message to General Burgoyne, begging for aid. Perpetua was against it, convinced that he would only make matters worse if he learned the reason behind her imprisonment. But Burgoyne's swift arrival eased a bit of Ned's anxiety. He knew in his heart Gentleman Johnny wouldn't abandon "a sweet young thing" like Tessie to her fate, and it became clear the general chose to chalk the scapular incident up to "womanly indiscretion and superstition," easily forgiven. So Burgoyne promptly volunteered his coach to take Ned to the town where Tessie was being detained.

When they reached the prison and were finally allowed inside, they found Tessie curled up in the corner of the women's cell, her face buried in her hands. Several of the other female prisoners were surrounding, some tearing at her clothes and hair as she pleaded with them to leave her alone. They just mocked her. Worse yet, beyond the bars in the adjacent cell, male prisoners were gawking at her, unused to seeing a high-born lady in their midst. Some started speaking filth, fantasizing what they would do to her if they could reach her. A couple even tried, sticking their lecherous hands through the bars, causing her to curl up further.

One woman prisoner sharing finally came to her defense. "Leave her be, ya bastards!" she berated her fellow inmates. "Poor thing's scared to death! What harm did she ever do to us, eh?"

"She's one of them Papists, ain't she?"

"Aye, she's some sort of Romish witch!"

"So?" the first woman snapped. "Gonna set ourselves up as judge and jury, eh? That's a laugh if ever there was one!"

The lecture appeared to do little good, with the other prisoners continuing their harassment.

Burgoyne's face was red as he demanded to be let in the cell. The gaoler jangled his keys and the door finally swung open.

"Teresa!" Burgoyne called her name in his booming theatrical tone.

She looked up, startled, and her eyes widened, seeing the general standing in front of her, resplendent as always in elegant attire, like a knight out of a storybook.

"Ohhhh…"

She struggled to stand up on wobbly legs then took several steps forward. A moment later she was in his arms, sobbing.

He held her protectively for a little while, casting a harsh glare upon the other prisoners. "If you dare accost this young lady again, I'll have your tongues and fingers!" he threatened. Then he turned his attention back to Tessie. "You can cry on my shoulder later, dear. But right now, our business is to fly!"

With that, he started to escort her out of the cell. She turned to the woman who had defended her and briefly grasped her hand. Then Burgoyne pulled Tessie out the door. Ned, overwhelmed with relief, immediately embraced her.

"Later," Burgoyne said again, urging them down the corridor.

"Not so fast, General!" the guard barked. "Return her to the cell immediately!"

"No," Burgoyne replied simply, continuing to direct his party towards the exit.

"Now, see here…"

Burgoyne turned and thrust out his cane, poking it into the guard's chest.

"Gaoler, would being struck by this indispensable fashion accessory upside the head make you more docile with your betters?" Burgoyne queried.

The guard gaped like a fish.

Burgoyne reached into his coat, produced a coin, and shoved it into the man's mouth. "There. A treat. Just bite down on that and let me hear nothing further from you."

Tessie, meanwhile, reached out and touched the guard's sleeve. "I forgive you," she rasped.

Burgoyne stared at her in shock for a moment, then pulled her along again.

When they finally made it outside, the constable was there, waiting for them.

"What do you think you're doing, Burgoyne?"

"Leaving, before I thrash you for tormenting a young lady of quality under my protection," Burgoyne stated, gesturing for his coachman to help Ned and Tessie into the carriage. "You should thank your lucky stars that I'm in a generous mood today. Now run along and shred all records of this debacle."

"She broke the law!"

"Yes, mistress of the underworld, this one," Burgoyne snorted, gesturing to Tessie as she huddled behind her brother in the carriage. "What did you expect for such an auspicious capture, eh? A ruddy knighthood?"

"I'll see you in court for this!"

"Please, do not insult my intelligence by trying to intimidate me with another lawsuit," Burgoyne said, rolling his eyes. "Been there, done that. Still going strong."

"You are forswearing your own oaths!"

"How dare you, sir!" Burgoyne bellowed, and the constable winced. "If you insist upon besmirching my honor, I will have no choice but to carry the matter to the field with sword or pistol, as is your preference! Unlike you, I do not make war upon women, but I have never been bested by a man!"

"Jack Brag," the constable hissed.

"If it's all just brag, you have nothing to fear," Burgoyne retorted, taking a step closer, so that their faces were nearly touching. "Try me, sir. I have no qualms about removing undesirables from polite society."

The constable glowered at him for several moments, swore under his breath, then turned and stormed off.

The general hopped into the carriage, leaned out the window, and shouted after him, "I thought so!"

Then he gave a signal, and the carriage sped off down the street.

"Well," Burgoyne sighed. "All in all, a good day." He glanced over to Tessie, who was holding her left wrist with her right hand. "What's wrong, dear?"

"Nothing, sir," she mumbled.

Ned felt his stomach flip and pulled up her sleeves. It was as he feared.

"What did they do to you Tessie?" he demanded, seeing the raw red rings and specks of blood circling her wrists.

"It doesn't matter now," she insisted. "The Lord was merciful to me."

Burgoyne's face blanched. "They put you in manacles?"

"For a little while," she said. "It was rather silly. I wasn't going to run anyway, and several pairs just kept falling off because my wrists are so small. The guard had to find smaller and smaller ones…"

"Was this during the interrogation?"

She hesitated, then nodded. "They wanted to know where I got what I gave." She turned to Ned. "They still don't know."

"Tessie, for God's sake, did they torture you in there?" Ned pressed, anger boiling his blood. "Did they hang you by the wrists? Did they hit you?"

Tessie folded her hands in her lap. "I was fortunate. Look at those prisoners with me, the poor souls. Skin and bones. I must make up some baskets when I get home."

Burgoyne and Ned met each other's gaze for a long moment in shared astonishment.

"Just don't pack any Papist trinkets in there, alright?" the general cautioned her.

Tessie didn't respond to that, but did move a little closer to Burgoyne, squeeze his hand, and lean her head against his shoulder.

Gentleman Johnny actually blushed.

Later that evening, Fanny confirmed that Teresa had bruises on her back, and Edmund felt overcome with wrath when he went to visit her chamber.

"They beat you, Tessie," Ned blurted, clenching his fists. "I should go back and give them the same treatment!"

"It wasn't really a proper beating," she insisted. "The reed was fairly thin. I prayed my rosary all the while, and it hardly hurt. They were just trying to scare me, I think…"

"No, they beat you!" Ned repeated, salt stinging his eyes.

"But Ned, dear Ned, whatever they did I take as a blessing," she replied, holding out her bandaged wrists. "I have offered so little on behalf of Mother Church. Let me at least offer this." Her own eyes sparkled. "The little boy who I gave the scapular to, the one laid up with a bad cough…he smiled when I told him the story of Our Lady of Mount Carmel, and Saint Simon in the oak tree, and the knights in the Holy Land. He smiled when I tucked the scapular under his pillow too. He's only five, and to him it was a treasure, whatever his parents thought of it. Oh, Ned. So many English children are growing up, not knowing their own heritage is filled with the presence of saints. So many of our people face sorrow and suffering without calling upon Our Lady to be their advocate. Yet this is still her dowry. That's why I don't repent what I did, not one bit, nor the penalty it incurred. I'm only sorry to have made General Burgoyne go out of his way…"

"Oh, I think he enjoyed playing the Lionheart with a damsel in distress," Ned assured. "Though I think you have a lion's heart yourself, sister. Would that I might measure up to the example to set!" He leaned forward and kissed her forehead, and she wrapped her arms around his waist.

When November rolled around, General Burgoyne invited Edmund back down to London for the opening night of his romantic comedy, *Maid of the Oaks*, at the prestigious Theatre Royal on Drury Lane. He even promised free tickets. Perpetua, of course, was opposed to this excursion, insisting that the more time he spent with Burgoyne in the hell-hole of London, the sooner he would be despoiled by the surrounding influences. But after all Burgoyne had done for the family, not least his rescue of Tessie, Ned had no intention of demonstrating ingratitude.

"I know how to keep my head above water, madam," Ned assured. "Besides, for all your distrust of the theater, General Burgoyne has been known to use the proceeds of his productions to help others less fortunate. His benefits for military families and infirm actors are famous…"

"And no doubt infirm harlots, too decrepit or pox-ridden to lure customers into their beds," she retorted coldly.

"So?" Ned challenged. "I do not hold it against a man from saving anyone from starving, harlots or otherwise. I will not scorn a man's generosity when we have so often been the recipients of it."

"Whatever he does is to make himself feel better about himself," she declared. "He is entirely consumed with his own gratification."

"Father said that the reason we feel good when doing good is because we are made in God's image," Ned responded. "I believe that."

"Your father was gullible," she scoffed. "And you are even more so!"

"So be it then," Ned declared, and exited the room to avoid further dispute upon the subject. He was determined to accept the invitation, regardless of his mother's complaints.

Upon arriving in London the night before the grand opening, and setting down his baggage in a room at a nearby inn, Ned made his way to the theater where the final dress rehearsal had just drawn to a close. The seating area was largely unoccupied, though he was surprised to see a gaudily-clad woman beckoning him over as soon as he approached. As he drew closer, he realized it was none other than Georgiana, her golden hair tucked up this time and buried beneath an opulent feathered hat. He was rather certain his mother would cook him for supper if she ever learned of this, but he went over to her anyway.

"So it appears Johnny worked his wiles on you too," she observed. "Oh, well, at least we have each other for consolation. I do not consider it too demeaning to suffer alongside a Papist for the duration."

"You don't much like the general's dramatic efforts?" Ned surmised.

"Oh, they're sweet little fairytales about mistaken identities and true love, following your heart and happy endings, blah, blah, blah," she chuckled, shaking her head, then mused softly, "Sometimes I even think he believes in them, in spite of himself. It's hopelessly endearing."

Ned felt sudden sympathy for her and the loneliness in her voice. "I'm so pleased you came," he said brightly. "As you say, we can keep each other company."

She beamed. "I shall be sure to nudge you throughout to make sure you laugh at the appropriate places."

"I've always felt we Papists had to cultivate a natural sense of humor in order to survive," he remarked.

"I wouldn't know, dearie," she replied. "Both my lines are Protestant Irish. Sailed over from England nearly two centuries ago. I'm high-on-the-hog Protestant through my Da, and down-in-the-gutter Protestant through my Mam, but Protestant, through and through, and no less Irish for it at this late date."

"Ah, but what's to be done about the rich and poor folk in your family tree who lived and loved before King Hal decided to switch out his women?" Ned quipped.

She snorted. "We forget about them, unless it's advantageous to remember them, like Johnny with his medieval ghosts, giving him a sense of purpose! Now, will you be so good as to escort this lady down to see our mutual gentleman friend?"

Ned bowed and proffered his arm.

They found Burgoyne backstage, sitting in a chair with his legs up on a crate that was dripping with brightly colored costumes. His feathered hat pulled down over his eyes, and his crimson velvet cloak draped over him like a blanket.

"Are you alive, Johnny?" Georgiana queried.

Burgoyne nudged his hat up. "Very much so, m'dear. God wouldn't be so cruel as to call me to account a mere handful of hours before my latest and greatest opening night!"

"How do you manage to survive, just cat-napping like that?" Georgiana asked. "I doubt you've been to bed in over a fortnight!"

"Are you inviting me into one?" he teased.

She smirked. "You'd probably nod off as soon as your head hit the pillow."

"I am a soldier, Georgiana," he reminded her, pulling aside his cloak and revealing wheels on either side of his chair. "We're used to napping with one eye open on the field, if need be, to skewer a few more dons if they set upon us. Surely, I could manage to rouse myself for more pleasant pursuits." He propelled himself forward with the wheels.

Georgiana squinted. "What is that contraption you're sitting on? Hypochondriacs going to take the waters in Bath use those in the infirmaries, don't they?"

"Now be so harsh on those of us who find the spas invigorating," he chided her, demonstrating how his chair could turn around in a circle. "As for my current throne, my old friend, the ever-controversial Doctor Franklin, suggested I needed one to maintain mobility during productions." He then started to demonstrate how far he could lean back in said chair.

"Did he also suggest a remedy when you end up falling out and breaking your crown?"

"Tut-tut, you worry too much, old girl," he scolded her, crossing his legs.

She narrowed her eyes. "You didn't need to say old…"

"I only meant it in the sense of fine wine…"

She made a grumbling noise.

Burgoyne finally noticed Ned, lingering in the shadows, and sprang up excitedly. "Bless my soul! You came, boy!"

"Your invitation was too warmly administered to decline," Ned said with a smile.

"Yes, but I heard your pope upped and died," Burgoyne said. "I felt sure your mother would force the household into some sort of a second Lent, and you'd burrow yourselves away from the world, eating only gruel and draping the mirrors in purple."

"The Holy Father passed away two months ago," Ned reminded him, then crossed himself and murmured, "*Requiescat in pace.*"

"Right, well, I don't know how you people handle such occasions," Burgoyne sighed, throwing up his hands. "I do hope you didn't don a hair shirt in mourning, though! Women don't like a fellow with rubbed-raw skin, and I'm still determined to get you manned up sooner than later…"

"Now, then, Johnny," Georgiana scolded him. "Push too hard, and you'll scare him off."

"Fine, the last thing I'll say on the subject is that I at least appreciate your lately lamented pontiff for having the wisdom to recognize our royal House of Hanover once the Jacobite Old Pretender bid adieu to the cruel world. Better late than never, what?"

"In my humble opinion, having done so, at least a reign ago, could have saved lives," Ned remarked.

"I thought you weren't allowed to question the pope," Burgoyne said.

"That is not true in every particular," Ned clarified. "There is a difference when it comes to the mode by which he exerts his authority in the Chair of Saint Peter…"

"At any rate, try *my* chair!" Burgoyne hopped up, and rolled it towards his guest.

Edmund couldn't help but grin. "Don't mind if I do."

"That's the spirit!"

Ned sat down, then wheeled himself forward a bit, before wheeling himself back. "I need one of these in the library"

"If the play is a smashing success, I'll rob a few coins from the charity proceeds and have one made for you to celebrate," Burgoyne decided. "Why let invalids alone enjoy the luxury?"

Ned chuckled. "Speaking of the play, how go the opening night preparations?"

"Swimmingly," Burgoyne proclaimed, "barring the odd incident, like a paper tree collapsing, and an overly energetic child from the chorus cracking his head on the birdbath."

Ned blinked. "What?"

"The little imp was running around like a maniac in stocking feet and slammed right into the thing!" Burgoyne declared. "Remind me how impossible it is to work with child actors next time! The male ones should really have been drowned in the Thames at birth…"

"Is the boy alright?" Ned queried.

"Yes, surely…quite…I think…we'll check on that…it's on my list of to do things…"

Ned and Georgiana both glared at him.

"Really, he seemed to have been adequately cared for the last time any of us saw him. One of the girls let him share her jar of sweets after she fell off the swing prop…"

"And how did that happen?" Georgiana asked, hands on hips.

"She took the foolish notion of actually swinging on it. You know, it just wasn't built for that sort of thing, but rather so the front row gentlemen could get a good look at the floral underwear…a work of embroidered art, you see…"

Ned rolled his eyes.

"And how is the second injured party faring?" Georgiana asked.

"Oh, well…I think they've gotten her properly buried by now…"

"What?!"

"…in ice to get that ankle swelling down," Burgoyne finished. "She has to dance around the magic tree during the druids and nymphs sequence! Perhaps this experience has taught her to lay off the sweets, as it no doubt contributed to the swing's untimely collapse…"

"You seem rather as if you've imbibed a healthy dose of sugar yourself," Georgiana observed.

"Chocolate, love," he specified, pulling a mug from out of the shadows. "I got it at that little Spanish around the corner, along with some pastries to dunk in it. Sorry I don't have any left, or I'd offer them to you…"

"I thought you had naught by animosity towards the Spaniels," Georgiana said.

"But m'dear, to the victor belongs the spoils! Besides, the establishments give discounts for theater folk, and there are none so meanly born with whom I would disdain to drink chocolate with for the cause of the higher arts!" He held his mug aloft dramatically.

Georgiana clapped at the monologue. "Well said! Now let me give you a massage. You clearly need to balance your humors."

At Georgiana's bidding, Ned hopped up from the chair and rolled it back over to Burgoyne, who plonked back down.

"Call this a courtesy," she said soothingly, starting to rub his shoulders, "for the complimentary tickets…"

"You know I adore your courtesies, *mon cheri*," Burgoyne cooed, taking her hand, sliding up her sleeve, and planting kisses from her palm to her elbow.

Ned thought it best to excuse himself before he became an unwilling witness to even more overt breaches of decorum.

The next evening, as the seats filled up with stylish theater-goers, Ned found Georgiana already guarding their seats. When she saw Ned, she beckoned him over and got him to assist her in setting up a parasol behind her own seat. While adjusting the parasol on a satisfactory angle, he noticed a picnic basket next to her chair. She smiled up at him, crossing one leg over the other.

"Johnny and I have a lovely professional relationship," she stated, "but no amount of fondness for him will convince me to starve myself through this extravaganza."

"I was under the impression that this theater only allowed purchases from particular vendors," Ned said.

"Ha! You think I'd let them charge me a pound of flesh? No thank you, young sir." She squinted at him. "Though I don't suppose you recusants can relate to committing any legal infractions, can you?"

Ned blinked. "Right, so…perhaps we could position the basket between us, and use your cloak to avoid exposure."

"Now you're thinking, dearie," she laughed. "Just for that, I'll not let you starve either. How does apple crisp sound to you?"

"Delicious," he admitted.

"Good. I brought along a surplus, as well as napkins too pretty to use."

"Perhaps we can decorate our little domain with them instead, so no one sits too near the basket," he suggested.

"Aww, you're adorable, Neddy!" she remarked. "I should sit you in my lap!"

"No, no, you really must make room for the edibles," he excused himself.

"But I could eat you up instead!" She winked.

Ned was saved from having to answer that by the musicians in the pit starting to play. The curtain opened, the audience applauded, and Gentleman Johnny appeared on stage to read the introduction and plead with the crowd to treat his play like a newborn infant, gently, instead of smothering it in the cradle.

Or drowning it in the Thames, Ned thought.

Then the production began in earnest. Two hours later, when the finale rolled around and the curtain closed upon the bowing performers, Ned felt rather as if he was being awakened from a strange dream, the kind he often had after consuming Agnes' questionable mushroom soup.

"You know, Johnny takes these things terribly to heart," Georgiana reminded Ned as she applauded along with the rest of the audience. "You must give him a stellar review, or he'll grow positively glum."

"I'm rather perplexed, in truth," Ned confessed, also applauding. "I mean, I grasped the gist of the plot…the wealthy man pretended his daughter was merely his ward so that the suitor would pursue her not for riches, but for love…"

"And the pure little country primrose is really the heiress to a great fortune. Virtue is rewarded, for shame!" Georgiana clicked her tongue.

"But what did all that have to do with…so many unrelated musical numbers…and dancing nymphs and magic trees…and a druid…?"

"It's a fantasy!" Georgiana reminded him. "Just praise the set pieces and the underwear!"

"Heavens, not the underwear," Ned sighed. "Besides, we couldn't even see it from here…"

"It may have been a perk for the front row gents only, but you can take a shot describing what was left to your imagination!"

Ned shook his head. "I'll stick with complimenting the magic tree."

Georgiana giggled gayly and punched him in the arm.

As it turned out, neither of them had more than two minutes to convey their compliments to the jubilant Gentleman Johnny before he was swept up into the aftermath festivities. Edmund ended up spending most of the lavish party escorting Georgiana around from gentleman to gentleman, feeling somewhat disconcerted by how many of them seemed well-acquainted with her. She could have abandoned him at any point to spend more time with the theater-going elite, but she kept Ned in tow and took him to a corner table to share a bottle of champagne. In her own way, she really was acting the part of a mother hen, and Ned thought it might be a good time to ask after Becky.

"She's getting on," Georgiana assured. "She's still in training, and has good and bad days, but she's getting on." She patted him on the arm. "I'll tell her that you fret over her. It'll bring a smile to her face."

"You know, I think I'm starting to fret about you too," he admitted.

She snorted. "I've gotten under your skin then! A good sign!"

As the night wore on, it was becoming evident Burgoyne was starting to descend from the heights of euphoria and needed a soft featherbed to crash onto before the immaculately polished floor became the alternative. The flowing punch bowl did not appear to be helping him maintain a steady stance.

"Someone needs to get him home to his wife," Georgiana told Ned, "and I'm afraid I'm not the girl for the job."

"Sensible," Ned agreed.

"Not that I'm her worst enemy," she insisted. "I've told him plenty of times that he should spend more time with her. She's ill, you know. The trouble is that Johnny has never been one to handle such things well." Her eyes softened. "They lost their only child to typhoid, you know."

"No, I didn't," Ned answered, a sinking feeling in his stomach.

"Little Charlotte, they called her, after his lady. He's never gotten over that. Losing the mother might…" Georgiana paused, then said, "She has his heart. He may have a poor way of showing it, but it's true nonetheless."

"Well, I suppose now is as good a time as any for me to meet her ladyship," Ned sighed, not at all sure if that was true. "I hope she doesn't take offense at his current condition…"

"Oh, darling, she's seen him far worse off than this! I'd like to think it brings out her maternal instinct towards him!"

"If you say so…"

"Just do us a favor and whisk him away from here before he makes one more speech insisting this play was for solely the good of mankind as opposed to replenishing his purse!"

"God help him balance those two goals," Ned mumbled, concerned about his extravagant friend's lifestyle choices.

"Go on, already! Fly away, country sparrow!" Georgiana coaxed him, then tapped her cheek with her finger. "Peck me goodnight."

He blushed, but relented, and kissed her.

"There now! I've made a man of you at last!" she laughed, and he tried not to roll his eyes.

Having bid a fond adieu to everyone's favorite hotel proprietress, Edmund set out to extricate the playwright from his party. It was not the easiest of tasks, but at last Burgoyne gave into his own exhaustion and intoxication, allowing himself to be pulled outside and pushed into a carriage headed for home.

Upon reaching Burgoyne's elegant townhouse, Ned worried Johnny would rouse the entire street as he began to sing lewd tavern songs quite loudly. He was relieved when a servant finally opened the door and helped to drag the general inside. Ned was additionally glad since it had turned bitterly cold, and Ned felt rather as if his nose was going to fall off as a final embarrassment.

Edmund caught sight of a woman coming down the stairs, fully dressed with her hair done up, as if it was the middle of the day instead of four in the morning. She appeared to be in her forties, with a comely face, a slender frame, and a firm step. Pausing midway down the stairs, she gestured for another manservant on the first floor to assist the general, which he did.

"Do set up a room for dear Ned here," Johnny slurred to the servants, patting Edmund on the back.

"There's no need, sir," Ned assured. "I have a room at the inn."

"Now don't be a pig-headed farm boy," he chortled. "We'll have your bags brought over. My home is your home for the week!"

Edmund gave the woman on the stairs an awkward glance, trying to gauge her feelings.

Her expression remained neutral as she nodded her head in assent. "As my husband wishes."

The servants escorted the general up to his room, which took the form of half tugging him, half carrying him. Then they took off his outer layer of clothes and tucked him in under the covers.

The woman sat down on the side of his bed. "John," she addressed him evenly. "This is Charlotte."

"Yes, I know, Charlotte," he mumbled, rather deliriously. "Hello, Charlotte."

"You remember me? Well, that's something," she exhaled, joining her hands in her lap. "Now, you must listen to me. You are extremely overtaxed and need to sleep."

"I don't feel like sleeping," he protested.

"Yes, I know you don't," she consoled, patting his leg. "But you have little choice, unless you want to get sick. Your bronchitis will start up again, and you'll have a cough for months. And besides that, your face will get all puffy. You hate looking at yourself in the mirror when that happens…"

"But I want to tell you about opening night," he insisted, sitting up a little. "I did it all mostly for the joy of telling you, Charlotte…"

"I'm sure you had enough attention from your many admirers to satisfy your needs in full," she replied.

"No, never in full," he countered, "unless I tell you everything, and I see you smile…"

"And so you shall," she assured, kissing his forehead. "Tomorrow."

"I love you, Charlotte," he murmured, falling asleep at last.

"You too, John," she said softly, very softly indeed.

Chapter 8: PHILOSOPHY WITH LOVE

When Ned awoke in the guestroom the next day, he found that it was nearly noon. One of the maids had already unpacked his bag and neatly laid out his clothes, for which he was grateful, given how much even his moderate intake of champagne hurt his head. He was then informed that the general and his wife were taking tea and scones downstairs, and he was welcome to join them if he wished.

Wondering whether it would be more impolite to show up late to their breakfast or not show up at all, he finally settled upon joining them. Entering the parlor, he saw General Burgoyne sitting very close to Lady Charlotte on the chaise. He had one arm snugly around her middle, and seemed to enjoy watching her daintily sip her tea. Then Ned overheard him starting to gossip about the tempestuous Percy couple.

"It's only a matter of time before one of them does in the other," Burgoyne insisted nonchalantly. "The real question is which one will get around to it first."

"And you are laying bets, dear?" Charlotte assumed.

"Well, no point in not making the drama pay," he replied. "And what about you, hmm? Which Percy do you think will be left standing when the smoke clears?"

"Don't put it past the ladies, husband," she said with a sly smile.

"Far be it from me, wife," he assured. "From my experience, your sex is altogether too temperamental to yield first."

"Perhaps we are grown temperamental from being tethered to our men," she countered, sipping more tea.

"You expect too much from us poor, miserable creatures, I'm afraid," he sighed. "Inevitable disappointment awaits."

"Yes, well…" She gave him a knowing look, then handed him her cup of tea. "You may be sure this one, at least, is not poisoned."

He grinned mischievously, then took a sip from it. "My lady is a vixen."

"And you are a fox. Always have been. Too cunning for your own good."

"Good enough to win you, though. You're the only prize that never loses its luster for this old hunter."

She blushed, her lips curved. This seemed to be a ritual between them, as old as their romance, which Ned was pleased to see still playing out.

Then Burgoyne caught sight of Edmund on the threshold.

"Oh, come in, Ned! Sit down, take some tea, eat a scone!"

"I…I didn't mean to intrude…" Ned stammered.

"Nonsense! You've not had breakfast. Sit!"

Gingerly, Ned did so in the chair across from them, and a servant was beckoned to fill up a plate and pour a cup for him.

"This is the young man I've told you about, Charlotte, the recusant I took to see the King! He spilt a ladle of punch all over himself, but still managed to gain the royal favor! Then Major Pitcairn tried to strong-arm him into joining the Marines!"

"It sounds as if my husband put you through a baptism of fire," she remarked, adding sugar to her tea and stirring it with a spoon.

"Yes, well, I suppose it prepared me for the world of the theater, madam," Ned chuckled.

"And you told me you loved it!" Burgoyne decided.

"The sets were superlative," Ned responded, following Georgiana's advice. "And I was quite pleased with the outcome for the heroine."

"I knew you would like her happy ending," Burgoyne declared. "She's to your taste."

"It is always heartening to hear of goodness rewarded with love, sir."

"And even more heartening, I should say, when love is blind, and smiles upon the unworthy," he mused, almost to himself. Then he abruptly changed the subject. "So what did you think of the guest room, eh? Comfortable enough for you?"

"Perfectly, thank you."

"You know, I spent some of my happiest hours while being put up in guest rooms." He leaned forward, a mischievous sparkle in his eye, and declared, "Courtesy of her brother's invitation, I shared an adjacent corridor with my lady when I stayed at their home as a young cavalry officer…"

Charlotte gave him a scolding look. "Now, stop it, John."

"Beg pardon, Lottie," he apologized, like a chastened little boy. "But, look!" He took her hand in his own and held it up, showing off her wedding ring, along with his own. "She made me an honest man! What other fair creature, amongst the whole of womankind, could manage such a feat but my lady?"

She rolled her eyes. "Not the easiest achievement, to be sure…"

"Well, all elopements have their little hitches, but still, we pulled it off, didn't we?"

Ned's eyes widened. "You eloped?"

Burgoyne nodded proudly. "I personally feel our wedding day was one of my greatest productions, planned down to the last detail…"

"We were almost caught two or three times before leaving the house because of the way you kept looking at me," she recalled. "It aroused suspicions…"

"And you were disappointed by the way I looked at you?"

The corner of her mouth twitched, even as she tried to look severe. "There's a time and a place, John…"

"Time and place hold no sway when you are with me, Lottie," he flirted.

"Well, you needn't have been quite so exuberant in your manner…"

"But 'tis my manner, dear!" he declared, thrusting up his hand demonstratively and splashing tea on Ned, who silently thanked God it had cooled somewhat in the cup.

"Jack," Charlotte lectured, "you're just as bad as the colonials when it comes to spilling beverages."

"Oh, that smarts, Charlotte…"

"Besides, you really mustn't gesticulate with the good china. Remember what happened the last time…"

"Ah, yes," Burgoyne said, gingerly setting the cup down, then as if speaking to it, intoning, "Alas, poor Yorick…"

Charlotte snorted, then handed Ned a napkin. "And this is what happens when you marry a theater man…"

"Never a dull moment!" Burgoyne proclaimed, kissing her hand. "Remember when we traveled the continent, and watched all the late night plays, then critiqued them mercilessly until morning?"

"Yes, and I dare say the endings we devised were vastly superior," she said. "But you were more likely to fawn over French literary flourish than I."

"Ever the Englishwoman, heart and soul," he chuckled. "I can't fault you for that, I suppose!"

"Of course not," she sighed. "I still followed you around the world, after all."

"You were the toast of Portugal," Burgoyne flattered her.

"I believe that was you, John," she replied. "Thus the king of that grateful nation bestowed upon you a precious diamond…"

"Only because I brought you around to dazzle him," Burgoyne insisted. "He knew he would have to give me some token to dazzle you with in turn!"

"It also had something to do with your cavalry checking the Spanish advance into his territory…"

"Invasions come and go," Burgoyne dismissed. "But your quality has not."

She blushed again. "Oh, John…"

"It was the same in France and Italy. All they wanted to see was my two jewels, you and the baby…" He stopped short, and she blinked. A moment of silence passed, then he took her hand once more. "We really must go traveling again when you're well, Lottie, like in the old days."

She gave him a blank look, that slowly changed to one of compassion. "Yes," she murmured, "we must."

And Ned knew in his heart, weighed down by sorrow, that it was never to be.

Over the course of his stay at their home, Edmund became keenly aware of the subtleties shared between the general and his lady. Sometimes they seemed estranged, not quite sure how to confide in each other beyond playful flirtation and shallow gossip. But then they shared the sweetest moments, like sunlight breaking through clouds, when a simple glance or passing touch seemed to speak for all that remained unspoken. Burgoyne seemed burdened by guilt that he tried to assuage with good cheer around her, and she seemed burdened with weariness that she tried to assuage with abiding fidelity to him. It was almost painful in its beauty. There was denial in the former, and exhaustion in the latter, and a bridge of love mixed with fear connecting them both across the chasm of their child's grave.

Burgoyne may have slept with many women for pleasure, but his eyes on his wife alone were so desperately sad, even when his voice was gay. And when the general was rambling to Ned about how the magnificence of his play's grand opening was just the beginning of the winter's run, or how the glory of British arms would intimidate the unruly colonists into towing the line come spring, she would just watch him, as if it was the first time, or maybe the last time, and she wished they could somehow start over again together. And Ned wished with all his heart they could do just that.

One afternoon midweek, Lady Charlotte invited Edmund to walk her around the garden, now grown barren beneath the late autumnal chill. Up until this point, Ned had spent most of his time out of the cold indoors, taking meals with the couple, playing board games with Burgoyne, and perusing the general's library which had graciously been opened to the young guest. Seeing just how much Burgoyne treasured books and manuscripts in English, French, and Latin made Francis Southworth's decision to save him from debt by selling a cherished book seem more justified.

Now outside with Lady Charlotte, Ned did his best to keep his teeth from chattering as she took the notion to test his ability in French. He was poor at it, which seemed to amuse her.

"I would think, being what you are, you would be more proficient in continental languages," she remarked.

Ned shook his head. "I'm afraid not, madam. I am more familiar with old Anglo-Saxon texts, written in what once was our own tongue, than with French ones."

"Surely you must have an affinity for Latin," she pressed.

"As your husband can confirm, it has its purposes," he said carefully.

"My John could charm the birds out of the trees in any language, if he set his mind to it," she chuckled. "Look him in the eyes for too long, and he'll have his way with you." Her expression grew suddenly more serious. "But still, he can be hurt."

"Naturally," Ned replied. "He is a man."

She gave him a long look. "I know my husband like I know myself, for better or for worse. He can be vain and impulsive and ambitious and generous and thoughtful and kind…" She winced. "And at times, altogether too trusting."

Ned wasn't entirely sure where the conversation was going, so he refrained from responding.

"I shall lay it on the line, Master Southworth," she stated flatly. "I do not trust you."

Ned felt his cheeks burning. "I am sorry that is the case, my lady."

"I have my reasons," she insisted. "I am not of Lancashire lineage, like my husband is. I am more likely to question the motives of Roman Catholics residing in this country…"

"Born in this country, madam," Ned dared to interject, "with lineage going back beyond memory…"

"It doesn't matter. The point I am making is that your kind has much to gain from notable Protestant connections, and it is inevitable you will manipulate them to secure your own ends. It is the difference between obscurity and prosperity for you. My time spent in the north has made me only more certain of the manner in which you and yours curry favor."

"My lady, your husband came back into our lives to repay a debt he owed my late father," Ned clarified.

"And from what I've heard, he has since repaid it many times over," she countered.

"Yes," Ned admitted, "in friendship. Has not General Burgoyne's own patrons aided him in similar fashion? Indeed, I was given to understand that you and the general have various Catholic associates who welcomed you into their homes and social circles on the continent."

"Some, yes, though I never trusted most of them, at least not fully," she said, with a wave of her hand. "Foreigners tend more towards immorality, and it influences the behavior of our English gentlemen."

Edmund had a bad feeling one of his eyebrows had shot up.

"Of course, some of them were decent enough, in their own way," she conceded. "But they were not trying to be two opposing things at the same time."

"Being English and Catholic, you mean?"

"Holding allegiances that put one at odds with their country."

Ned shook his head. "Or perhaps we are simply bound to the first England, before this second England ever came to be…"

"And here come the riddles you are trained to use, to deflect and defuse," she declared. "It is the usual way with recusants I have met in Preston. You wear masks to deceive us."

"Believe me, madam, we do not relish the necessity of wearing them," he replied, pain seeping through his voice.

"Well, I, at least, will wear none with you," she said, holding a finger up to him. "I tell you in all frankness: I won't let you hurt John, as has happened in the past with youths he's taken under his wing. It would only be worse this time. I can see he thinks the world of you. He believes you are something pure, something clean, a boy from the country who makes him feel innocent again. Do not climb the ladder with his help, and then…" She closed her eyes. "I know there are those who have benefitted from his patronage, yet still turn around and mock him behind his back. They join his detractors and call him naught but tinsel show. They claim he is a sail without a ballast, lost in his own flights of fancy. They do not know him, not really, nor have they tried to do so. If they did, they would honor his many services rendered to this nation under two consecutive sovereigns and praise the passion he brings to all his endeavors. But they cannot even manage to show personal gratitude. No, they only need him for what they can get out of him. Don't you see? I don't want it to happen to him again, I…" She wobbled a little on her feet. "I would rather be hurt a hundred times over than see him suffer."

Edmund felt his heart soften towards her, in spite of her prejudices against him. "My lady, I assure you–"

"Even if you are his natural son," she blurted, "that doesn't give you the right to use him."

"I am the son of Francis Southworth and no other," he shot back, a bit sharper than he intended. "The bond between your husband and myself is not one forged by blood."

"How can you be certain?" she queried, a certain strained resignation in her words. "In most cases, John remains uncertain."

"The simple fact, madam, is that my lady mother would rather die than bed a Protestant," he answered curtly, then thought better of it, and added, "She is a faithful woman, and was a faithful wife. Surely, as one who exhibits such virtues yourself, that is something you can appreciate."

She smirked. "Your recusant tongue is at work again, smoothing the rough places into plain. It is your training."

"Lady Charlotte, I swear, I–"

"I don't care what you may be, or not be, to him," she cut Ned off. "Just don't hurt him. That's all I want from you. Just don't..."

She wobbled again, worse than before, and placed one hand to her forehead and the other on her abdomen. Ned quickly braced her, putting his arm around her waist.

"I'm alright," she rasped.

"You're in pain," Ned countered.

He saw her bite her lip, confirming what he had said, even as she shook her head to deny it. She seemed ashamed to show any weakness in front of him.

"Please, take me back inside," she murmured at last.

As soon as Ned did so, she swooned on the chaise. When one of her maidservants managed to revive her with a cold cloth, another servant proposed calling for a physician. Lady Charlotte dismissed the notion as an overreaction.

But when Burgoyne learned what had happened, the blood drained from his face. Edmund watched from just outside the parlor as her husband rushed to her side.

"You should not have gone out," he said hoarsely, his hands bunched up in fists at his sides. "This weather does you no favors, you know that."

"I like to walk in the garden, even when there is nothing growing," she responded wistfully. "Except for the holly bush, of course...that is still green, and the red berries are blooming..."

"But, my God, you almost collapsed out there!" Burgoyne exhaled. "If Ned hadn't been there with you–"

"But he was, and now I'm sitting snugly with two blankets on my lap before the blazing hearth," she noted, gesturing to the fire. "You really do worry too much."

He sat down in the chair across from her. "You were always the one who used to worry over me." He gripped the arms of his seat tightly. "Shall I read to you, Charlotte? You used to like it when I did that. You said I had a natural voice for the stage, and that you enjoyed hearing me bellow commands on the parade ground. Yes, you flattered me, Charlotte..." He laughed shortly. "Your flattery was the only kind that ever really mattered to me."

"In truth?" she queried dubiously.

"In God's truth, so help me..." His voice took on emotion he had perhaps not intended, so he added cheerfully, "How shall I entertain my lady today? Say the word!"

"Will you read me...something in my hand bag?" She gestured to a calico pouch with a drawstring hanging up on the wall.

"Is it a shopping list?" he queried, standing up and retrieving the bag. "I remember in France, when the baby came along, and money ran low, you insisted that I go to the market instead of sending a servant so we could save some coin. You told me to be frugal...me, Charlotte! I don't know what you were thinking! Soon enough, you had hired help again, lest I should deplete our savings further. Thank the Lord your father allowed us prodigals to come home before we ruined ourselves beyond recall...but hey-ho, what's this?" He pulled out a piece of folded paper from the bag.

"Open it, and you'll find out for yourself," she coaxed him.

Burgoyne gingerly did so. He chuckled in an embarrassed fashion, shaking his head. "Is this one of my naughty verses?"

"No, one of your nice ones," she clarified.

"Even my naughty ones were nice, when you were the subject of them," he insisted. "I know, I know, I have a dirty mind, but in your case...it's just been my way of making up endearments for each and every part of you that I have loved."

She laughed softly. "Oh, how you used to make me blush!"

"And how it pleased me to see you blushing! Let's just say I was a good Christian boy who read too many of Solomon's songs and decided to pick up where that wise king left off!"

She shook her head. "Oh, John, if only you had written all of your naughty verses for me."

Burgoyne winced guiltily. "The naughtiest were all for you," he mumbled. "I swear it."

"Well, that one you're holding is fit for a Sunday social, as it turns out," she said, gesturing to the paper in his hands. "Will you read it to me anyway?"

"If it is your wish," he consented.

"It is my wish," she assured.

He sat next to her on the chaise this time, cleared his throat, and began to read in his best theatrical voice, "Such does my obstinate repine, and reason's voice reprove, still think him cold who would combine philosophy with love..." He paused, his eyes darting for a moment, then settling back on the paper. "Try then from yet a nobler source to draw thy wished relief; faith adds to reason double force, and mocks the assaults of grief..." His hand trembled slightly, and he muttered, "Fie, I'm getting old...may need spectacles soon. How would that be, eh? Your man past his prime? Handsome Jack with specs?" He laughed, and his hand shook more. Then he read on, in a much less performative voice, "By her, fair hope's enlivening ray, patience and peace are given. Attend her calls; resign, obey..." His voice cracked, and he again cleared his throat.

"And leave the rest to heaven," she quoted from memory.

He glanced over at her and swallowed hard. Then he continued, in a much weaker voice, bordering on a whisper, "The power that formed my Charlotte's heart, thus tender, thus sincere, shall bless each wish that love can start, or absence foster there. Safe in the shadow of the Power, I'll tread the hostile ground; and fiery deaths in tempest shower, and thousands fall around..." Again, he stopped, and this time remained frozen in time, staring at the paper, as if it were a death sentence.

"And when the happy hour shall come, oh, speedy may it be," she recited, reaching over and taking his hand, "that brings thy faithful soldier home, to love content and thee…"

He shut his eyes and let the paper fall to his lap, squeezing her hand. "Pure may our gratitude ascend to Him who guides our days. And whilst He gives with bounteous hand, accepts our bliss for praise." He swung her hand back and forth a little. "You really did like it, didn't you, Lottie? When I gave it to you, I mean, before riding off with my regiment. You kept it, all this time, and seem to have read it, more than once…"

"Yes," she said. "You knew I would."

"Yes, I knew…" He gazed at her longingly, and kissed her hand.

The last few days of Ned's visit saw Burgoyne being more attentive to his lady, even fawning over her, reminiscing about old times and trying, it seemed, to court her favor all over again. But business was beckoning him north to tour his constituency for the social season leading up to Christmas, and Ned could sense that the general was at war with himself, both wanting to stay and to go. Her eyes were pained when they lingered on him for more than a moment, but she also seemed resigned to the fact that there was nothing she could do to hold him back.

Charlotte treated Edmund courteously as he and her husband prepared to return to Lancashire in the same carriage. He knew she still harbored suspicions against him and his origins. But Ned was content to act as if their conversation in the garden had never taken place, and thanked her for being such a gracious host. She, in turn, offered him a smile which did not seem too terribly forced, enhancing her already comely features.

Burgoyne gave a gush of instructions to the servants regarding his lady's care. Then with an air of military decorum, he kissed his wife's hand, and started to leave the house. At the threshold, however, Burgoyne turned around and headed back into the sitting room where he had left Charlotte. Ned took a few steps in that direction himself, and spied him kissing her passionately. She appeared slightly flustered, half-pushing him away, half-allowing herself to be cradled by him.

"Jack!" she scolded him, but there was the faintest of smiles on her lips as she turned her head, playing at propriety.

Her husband was undeterred, taking her face gently in his hands and kissing her again, and again, and again. At last he let his hands fall to hers, clutching them momentarily. Then he turned and headed for the door.

On the ride out of London, Burgoyne fidgeted constantly in the coach, but remained silent, seemingly consumed by his own agitation. Edmund tried his best to pretend not to notice, no matter how uncomfortable it made him feel.

At last, Burgoyne blurted, "She's dying, Ned. Whatever shall I do?"

Edmund felt cut to the quick, completely at a loss for how to respond.

Burgoyne shifted slightly. "You know…I made love to her last night, like I used to…yes, we used to do it all the time, Ned…" He laughed shortly, awkwardly. "We were very…amorous. You know, once we did it three times in a night. God only knows how we managed to walk the next morning! It seems like yesterday, even though it was long ago, in the beginning…" A smile brightened his face, then it faded. "Not now, not now, she can't…it's a struggle for her to…and I don't want…" He bit his lip. "I can't stand it, knowing she's in pain. And she is, Ned. I know she is. I shared a bed with her nearly all week. She would wake up in the middle of the night…and asked me…to rub her back…" He exhaled shakily. "I'm sorry…I'm sorry I'm telling you all this. I'm in a poor way, Ned, so I hide away my feelings, even from most of my intimates…no one knows what it's like…in here…" He tapped his temple. "Perhaps only Shakespeare himself would have been able to plumb the depths of my condition! I go through so many hills and valleys, and struggle to find any even ground, any stable footing." He shook his head and repeated, "I'm sorry…"

"Do not apologize, sir," Edmund said gently. "You have been a friend to me, and I would be one to you, always."

"I-I'm not the kind of friend you would likely wish to have. I mean…I'm not very good, Ned….not very good to those I…love. I can be a faithless and fickle man…most of all to her, the faithfulest, tenderest, most amiable friend and companion a man was ever blessed with…" His eyes took on a strange shade. "The night when my child, our dear little Charlotte, was taken from this world, I was…I went to a brothel." He grimaced as the words left his mouth. "I thrive on distraction, you see. It's how I keep from falling into the chasm. It's a dark place, like a starless night, that has always threatened to swallow me whole, and I fear I would never be able to climb out again. That is why I know, with a dreadful certainty, that if I should hear my own dear Charlotte is gone…I will…do the same thing." He closed his eyes. "You must think me very wicked, Ned."

Edmund reached over and touched his hand. "I think you loved your child very dearly. And I think your wife alone has your heart."

"This is why…I had you come down," Burgoyne admitted. "It wasn't just…for the play."

Edmund nodded and squeezed his hand.

"Ned...don't ever tell anyone...about what I've said here…"

"You know I never would."

"Yes, of course...you're like one of your priests." He giggled, and poorly imitated the sign of the cross. "You must give me a heavy penance!" He took Ned's hand again. "Bad taste, I know…bad taste…forgive me, Ned…"

"It's alright," Edmund replied. "We're friends."

"Yes…friends. You…you're a fine young friend, Ned. Very fine…"

Halfway through the journey north, they spent the night at an inn where Burgoyne drank too much downstairs. His spirits buoyed by the alcohol, he laughed and joked freely, even flirting with the serving wench, getting her to sit on his knee while he slipped his hand, and a coin, down her bodice. By the time he went up to their room, a headache set in, his mood sank, and Ned had to help him get ready for bed. The general apologized several times for putting a damper on things, but Ned said he should think nothing of it. In the morning, the young man made sure to order extra coffee for his friend before the two of them set off north again.

When they finally arrived in Edmund's village that evening, he decided to give Burgoyne a little tour to take the general's mind off his troubles. Even though there were only two proper streets, Ned nearly got lost by departing from said streets, as almost all locals did, and trying to cut through some bordering woods, which may have resulted in him and the general stumbling around for hours until coming out on the other side, en route to the neighboring village. Fortunately, Ned managed to regain his bearings, escape the woods, loop around the church on the outskirts of his own village, and bring them both safely to The Cross Keys Inn. It was an old establishment from before the break with Rome, named after the papal seal. But times had changed. The family who had originally owned it were caught harboring priests during Elizabeth's reign. They were imprisoned and dispossessed, while their business was handed over to a Protestant cousin's family. The new custodians, however, didn't bother changing the inn's name.

Since it was Friday, Ned ordered battered fish and butter pie for himself and his guest. When Ned crossed himself quickly before eating, Burgoyne teasingly asked if he was putting all the food on the table under a Romish spell. Mister Vernon, the innkeeper, overheard the inquiry and assured his well-dressed customer that Ned wasn't planning anything diabolical. He was an old friend of the Southworths, despite his business success deriving from the past misfortune of Catholics, and insisted that they were "altogether decent, for Popish folk."

"For any folk, methinks, innkeeper," Burgoyne replied in a tone of sincerity, and Edmund felt warmed by it. "Now if we are to dine like Papists, I expect some mulled wine!"

"And fruitcake with crumbly cheese," Edmund added, beaming.

"Aye, with Christmastide just around the bend, we might as well get in the mood," Burgoyne agreed. "The hearty north is still in my blood and palette, no matter the charms of Londontown!"

Edmund knew Burgoyne often said such things for the sake of boosting popularity in his constituency, but he also seemed to be in earnest. Yes, whatever else divided them, they were both northern lads at heart.

When they had finished their meal and stepped outside, night had fallen and the torches were lit. They had just reached Burgoyne's carriage down the street, where the driver was already waiting for his employer, when two snowballs struck the general. He turned abruptly to see a handful of boys running away.

"Uncouth little ragamuffins," Burgoyne snorted as Ned, suppressing a chuckle, helped him brush the snow off his cloak. "Have their mothers not taught them to respect their betters?"

"I assure you, sir, it was meant for me," Edmund insisted. "You are simply the unhappy victim of friendly fire."

The boys could be heard chanting some rude verses about the hedge priests and Romish masses as they turned the corner and disappeared.

"Oh, hell's teeth," Burgoyne sighed. "That's not right…not right at all. You're still of noble lineage. It's a disgusting display…"

"It's what they've been taught," Ned remarked. "Hard to blame them for repeating what they hear bandied about by their elders. Besides, they're harmless for the most part. Just boyish mischief."

Burgoyne tilted his head. "Don't you ever tire of this sort of thing?"

Edmund shrugged. "Sometimes. But if that's the worst we get, I'm content with it. My grandfather was crippled by a Protestant mob in another county with fewer Catholics. We're left in peace here…well, at least for the most part."

"You deserve better than just that, Ned," Burgoyne countered. "You're a bright young man, and you…you're loyal. Yes, that's the truly fine thing about you. You're very loyal."

"And that, I suppose, is why I can put up with a few handfuls of snow tossed in my direction ever and anon," Edmund stated.

"I just…I could see your natural quality being put to many fine purposes, beyond this place." He gestured broadly. "Perhaps Lady Britannia needs a few more patriots such as yourself in her service."

"She has me already," Ned said softly.

"But not all the way," Burgoyne retorted. "I know, I know, you'll fight that, but…it's true. There will always be a division…this part of you for England, and this part of you for something outside of her, something at odds with her. You can talk all you like about days of yore, but we can't go back. There's so much to do and be, here and now…"

"Like being your friend," Ned said kindly. "I consider that a great blessing, which no handicap in my status has prevented."

Burgoyne exhaled. "Dear, dear boy, what am I to do with you? I don't want to be some sort of devil on your shoulder, as your mother surely thinks I am. It simply grieves me to see you…set aside."

Edmund glanced down at a nearby patch of snow. "It grieves me too, sometimes. But I do my best to endure it."

"It does you credit," Burgoyne admitted. "But if you ever should discover that God has made you for other purposes, then please…do not hesitate to seek my patronage. I will do all in my power to make sure that your talents are cultivated and your virtues rewarded."

Ned smiled. "Thank you. And I know you're not a devil."

Burgoyne laughed. "Well, maybe just a bit of one." He opened the coach door and picked up a parcel from among his luggage. "Here, a little something for Twelfth Night, if I don't see you before then."

Edmund blinked, taking the parcel from Burgoyne. "Thank you, sir."

"Go on. Open it early," Burgoyne coaxed. "I'm shameless about wanting to see people's reaction to my presents."

"Alright," Ned agreed, pulling open the wrapping. He saw in the torchlight that it was a beautifully embossed book of medieval romances featuring Richard the Lionheart.

"There, my idol and your co-religionist," Burgoyne said, tapping the cover. Oh, and I picked up something else too, for old times' sake…" He pulled a jar out of the coach. "I hope you still like licorice!"

"Oh, yes," Ned chuckled.

"So I did a good job?" Burgoyne asked eagerly, almost like a child trying to impress an adult. "I had to give it a good long think when it came to choosing gifts you might fancy…"

"I fancy them," Ned assured. "But you must know that, whatever you had given me, I would have treasured it."

Burgoyne beamed in satisfaction, and awkwardly asked, almost as a joke, "Want a hug then, Ned?"

Before Edmund could respond, Burgoyne was holding him very tightly, almost fiercely, causing both the jar and the book to fall to the ground. Ned heard the glass shatter upon impact. The general muttered apologies and started to pull away. But Ned would not allow it, sensing the intensity of his need, and squeezed him back for all he was worth. They lingered like that for a long time, till Edmund finally let the older man break free.

"Thankee," Burgoyne rasped.

Then they both knelt down in the street to retrieve the book, which had opened to an engraving of the crusading king, weeping over Jerusalem. They also scooped up the licorice, scattered in the snow that shimmered along with the broken glass beneath the torch's glow. Ned filled Burgoyne's pockets and his own with the sweets, insisting that sharing was part of the pleasure for him. Finally, after they had helped each other to their feet, and Ned had given him another quick hug, Burgoyne got into the coach and signaled the driver to head for his home in Preston.

Ned watched them go, a tear sparkling in his eye, and put a piece of licorice in his mouth, the flavor so full of memories.

Chapter 9: WAR'S ALARMS

For the first few months of 1775, hardly the only news Edmund received about goings on in America came from Lieutenant William Pitcairn, whose letters chronicled the tedium of hard marches, trouble with drunkards, bitter Bostonian weather, and exorbitant colonial tavern prices. He was, after all, his father's son. After commiserating with William's complaints, Ned had scribbled back to him about a robin that got trapped in their attic during the winter. Teresa decided to keep the poor little creature indoors till spring, feeding it candied nuts over Christmastide. Not long after she tearfully released it back into the wild, the robin nested in one of the trees behind the house, so Tessie could still hear its song from her window. There was a less pleasant bit of rural news Ned relayed as well, regarding a local farmer who had been savaged by one of his own dogs. The beast had to be taken out and shot in the yard the next day. It was a strange, sudden happening. The dog had always seemed so tame before. Some speculated the farmer had kept it too long upon a short rope. When it got loose, it went wild.

Ned would apologize for being so dull in his letters. William would assure that he had started it. And Ned would grin. And the back-and-forth would repeat.

In early May, Edmund Burgoyne stopped by the Southworth manor to announce that he had received royal orders to set sail for America, along with Generals Howe and Clinton, as the head of reinforcements.

"Has the situation gotten so out of hand that reinforcements are necessary?" Ned queried as they strolled in the yard.

"Nothing so dramatic," Burgoyne assured. "More or less a precaution. Still, my participation is a matter of duty. I can't just sit on my hands at home while some brazen fellows may take the notion to play turkey shoot with our lads across the water. The King commands, and I obey."

"What about Lady Charlotte?" Ned pressed. "How does she feel about this?"

A brief flicker of uncertainty came into Burgoyne's eyes, but he replied with forced cheerfulness, "She is a soldier's wife, as ever, and well-accustomed to me crisscrossing the globe on adventures."

"Surely she would rather you stayed by her side," Ned retorted. "I have heard that her condition has worsened."

"I assure you, young man, every possible attention is being paid to her health," Burgoyne said, somewhat curtly. "I would never leave her in any other way…"

"I don't doubt it," Ned replied. "But she loves you, and she'll pine for you."

Burgoyne's eyes glazed over. "It cannot be helped, lad."

"And what if a rebel decides to play turkey shoot with you?" Ned asked. "How do you think your lady will bear up?"

"With her piety," Burgoyne answered. "She is pure, unlike myself, and God listens to her. If I should be destroyed, her faith will sustain her, and the Almighty will bless her. If I lose her, on the other hand…" He shut his eyes. "I can't stay, Ned, for more than one reason. Please understand. I am useless to her here. I am too weak to watch her weaken. I must go somewhere that I can be strong. I must go where I can make her proud, even from afar."

Ned exhaled. "I have also heard rumors that your coinage has run low again."

"The story of my life," Burgoyne snickered. "But have no fear. I have written a letter to the King, to be opened in the case of my departure from this mortal realm. I have placed my dear Charlotte in his care. Our most gracious sovereign would never let her go without."

"But for the time being," Ned countered, "do you need anything? The Portuguese investments you helped us establish have been faring well."

"Ha! Want to put me in debt to your house once again, Young Southworth?"

"You know that you need only ask, and I would be pleased to give," Ned insisted. "That's how we treat our friends."

"Just like your father," Burgoyne chuckled.

Edmund glanced down at the grass. "You will write to me often, won't you? Because I'll worry myself sick if I don't know what's become of you out there."

Burgoyne smiled softly. "In truth?"

Ned nodded.

"Then I suppose I must write to you often," Burgoyne agreed. "Will you light your votive candles to the Virgin for my safe return, hmm? Familiarize her with my existence?"

"I assure you, she is already familiar with you," Ned replied, "and I add to that familiarity daily through my prayers."

Burgoyne sighed. "Incorrigible, you recusants!"

"Yes," Edmund agreed. "But there is a method to my madness. I believe that this land remains Our Lady's Dowry, in spite of ourselves, and that she remains the Star of the Sea, guiding mariners to port. Surely if anyone can bring you safely home from across the waves, she will."

And so, later that week, Burgoyne boarded his ship and embarked for the New World.

Then, in late May, before Burgoyne had even landed in Boston, news broke in England of a series of skirmishes that had taken place in the Massachusetts towns of Lexington and Concord on the 19th of April. Ned learned that General Gage, who had been doing all that was legally possible to keep the peace in Boston, had sent a body of troops to seize ammunition stores being amassed by insurrectionists outside the city. The mission, which hinged upon the element of surprise, was exposed by spies, and before long, riders from the so-called Sons of Liberty, a secret society of colonial radicals, had warned the countryside. Edmund's heart sank as he read how mutinous militiamen had lined up on the village green in Lexington and refused to disband when confronted by none other than the Marines' own fiery Major John Pitcairn, who shouted at them, "Disperse, ye rebels! Ye villains, disperse! Why don't you lay down your arms? Disperse, or you're all deadmen!"

Shots were exchanged, and militiamen killed. Later, there had been fighting on a bridge in Concord, and British soldiers were also slain. The route back to Boston devolved into chaos, with rebels shooting at the King's troops from behind every wall and tree. Several wounded soldiers, lying helpless on the road, even had their brains dashed out by farmers wielding axes. Poor, dull Colonel Smith, who had been in charge of the doomed expedition, was also wounded, and Major Pitcairn, animated as always, assumed command, only to be unhorsed while trying to rally the panicked soldiers. He had the misfortune to lose his prized pair of pistols tucked in the saddlebag when his wounded mount bolted towards the enemy. The only thing that had saved the King's troops from obliteration was dashing Hugh Percy, bringing up cannons to cover their retreat.

But that was not the end of the matter. Ned grimaced while reading about the brutal house-to-house fighting that had broken out on the long route back to Boston. Various Whigs in Britain, still sympathetic to colonial complaints, emphasized the atrocities that had unfolded, with civilians being harassed and sometimes murdered by roving bands of enraged soldiery who set their homes and barns ablaze. One particularly lurid tale told of how an old woman was bayoneted upon her own porch, and another told of a baby shot in the cradle for crying. The officers had tried to prevent such excesses, but order had disintegrated, and it was a miracle they managed to herd the bulk of their men back to Boston at all. Pitcairn, ever-dutiful, had been the last one to get in the boats crossing the Charles River to reach safety. Now the rebels had surrounded the city, with the soldiers of the crown trapped inside. And the number of insurrections ready and willing to bear arms had only swelled.

Some small part of Edmund still hoped and prayed war might be averted, even though the larger part of him knew such hopes would be in vain. Tessie did her best to comfort him, observing how deeply troubled he was over these developments. Perhaps everyone would take a step back from the brink, having been given a taste of blood. Perhaps Parliament would be persuaded to concede to at least a few colonial demands, and perhaps the colonials would come to regret having laid up stores to assault the King's troops. Perhaps they would all realize how sorry they were for what they had done, and repent what they were about to do.

But in his stomach, Edmund knew that the Mother Country and her colonies were set on the course for a terrible contest, in which countless families would be torn in twain. The outcome would surely be the ruination of America and the depletion of Britain. There would be blood, so much blood, running as deep as the ocean stretched between them, and his friend and patron, Gentleman Johnny, had cast himself into the midst of it, to sink or swim, to live or die. Just thinking about it made him feel sick.

Perpetua, meanwhile, felt that her son should put America out of his mind.

"This is not our war," she stated as she sat at her writing desk, making notes in a ledger. "The people involved on either side are not our responsibility, Edmund."

"Madam, how can you say that?" Ned exclaimed. "This is the first civil war between men of British blood in over thirty years!"

"Not upon this soil," she countered, "so we needn't fear it touching us."

"If it cannot be suppressed speedily, it will affect England, yes, every shire of her. Men from across the nation will be called upon to make war against their own cousins across the water…"

"Not Catholic men," she shot back.

He winced. "You would truly feel nothing for our neighbors?"

"I am not so easily swayed by sentiment as you or your father," she replied. "It will betray you as surely as the Protestants."

Ned felt a pain stab his heart. "You shed no tears, even when Father died. Tessie did. I did. But you only turned your face to the wall and fretted over the house."

She glared at him. "Tears do not restore what has been lost. All they do is distract one from what can be salvaged."

"I don't understand why you care so much about the house when you seem to care nothing for this country," Ned blurted.

"This house *is* our country, Edmund," she stated. "It offers sanctuary to our fellow recusants. That's why we stay here. That's why we hold on for as long as we can. We remain to serve God's persecuted people…"

"And to hell with everyone else, is that it?" Ned surmised. "Even a thought or prayer is more than they deserve from us, though we share the same plot of earth?"

"Yes," she shot back. "I do not consider them our neighbors, but rather our oppressors." She held up the list she was working on. "These are our neighbors, the Catholics in this vicinity who depend upon us to provide for their spiritual and temporal needs. That is where our focus must be fixed. The heretics can shift for themselves."

"Our Lord said we were to be like the Good Samaritan," Ned countered. "I cannot believe he intended for us to leave Protestants on the side of the road."

She exhaled and slammed the list down on the desk in frustration. "First, to our own. Rosemary needs a pair of spectacles. Her eyesight has grown more blurred, and she's struggling with her chores on the farm. Can you arrange it?"

Ned smiled slightly. "I can, and I will."

Even though Edmund did his best to assuage his mother's concerns by attending to the needs of local Catholics, as he always had, he kept as informed as he could about developments in the colonies, writing to Burgoyne regularly and fretting over his wellbeing. Burgoyne would reply when he could, making sweeping assurances they were merely dealing with a regional uprising of undisciplined provincials, armed with pitchforks and squirrel guns. Poor Granny Gage might be boxed in at the moment, but Burgoyne was confident that his reinforcements would be able to gain him some much-needed "elbow-room" sooner than later. He also promised to buy Tessie a new bonnet in Boston.

When July rolled around, shocking news reached England of a bloody battle that had raged outside Boston on the 17th of June. Ned devoured every printed account of the event he could lay his hands on. According to these reports, the rebels had started digging fortifications outside the city. The sounds of the shoveling had been reported to Colonel Smith around midnight, but true to his lethargic reputation, he dismissed the messenger and slipped back into slumber. By morning's light, the rebels had the high ground. Gage ordered a frontal assault to dislodge them. Some reports said the main attack was against Breed's Hill, and others said it was against neighboring Bunker Hill. Either way, it had been a bloodbath.

Three times, the King's troops tried to take the rebel works by storm. The rebels, meanwhile, played the tune "British Grenadiers" on the fife and drum, for it was second nature to them as Britons, even now, as the British Grenadiers advanced upon them. Twice, the assaults were repelled with heavy losses, including scores of officers. The rebels took deadly aim for them in particular, marking them out by their brilliant scarlet tunics compared to the brick-red uniforms of the rank and file. Israel Putnam, a hardened veteran from the previous war who was now fighting for the rebels, ordered his men, "Shoot for the red coats! Shoot for the reddest coats! Don't fire till you see the whites of their eyes!" Ironically, he was said to be armed with Pitcairn's captured pistols.

After the second charge, General William Howe was one of the only officers left unscathed. Before beginning their ascent, he had raised a glass of wine to his comrades and drank it down with a coolness of comportment that did him credit. Having thus fortified himself, he had promised his soldiers that they would be made to go no farther than he would go himself. But in the end, with his officers and men cut down like corn around him, he had to be escorted off the hill, shock having rooted him to the spot, his face stained with smoke and tears alike. Some speculated Howe had been deliberately spared, since his older brother, Lord George Augustus, had died in Putnam's arms during the last war. Whether or not this was true, it seemed that some part of Howe had died on the hill anyway, and it was unlikely he would ever be whole again.

At last, Major Pitcairn's Marines were called out from among the reserves to storm the rebel breastworks for a third time, their leader brandishing his sword and bellowing commands and encouragement to his men. "Now for the glory of the Marines!" he cried. "This day is ours!" Francis Rawdon, a young Irish lord of Protestant stock, had similarly distinguished himself, holding aloft the British colors while bullets whizzed about him and beckoning his men into the redoubt. The King's soldiers, inspired by their intrepid commanders and their own thirst for revenge, bayoneted and bludgeoned the enemy into submission or flight.

Dr. Joseph Warren, an infamous firebrand among the rebels, had met his fate in the final moments of the melee, refusing to surrender when Major John Small, advancing upon him with the King's troops, called his name. It was rumored they had once been friends, and Small desired to save the doctor's life. Warren simply offered him a parting smile. Then another soldier shot Warren through the head, while another prepared to bayonet him. Small, still hoping the doctor might be alive, knocked the bayonet away. But the reprieve was brief, and many British bayonets punctured Warren's body until he was all but unrecognizable. They then stripped him of his clothes and cast him into a ditch with other dead rebels.

But Major Pitcairn, too, though victorious, was among the dead.

At first, Ned felt as if his eyes must be deceiving him when he saw the name emblazoned on the list of slain officers. The hearty Scotsman was gone, like a flame snuffed out upon a wick, and the world was suddenly colder for his absence. He would never crack another colorful joke or make another half-grin or sit in another church pew and bite his tongue to keep from swearing on the Lord's Day. His wife would never more fret over her husband being late for supper with the family. His children would go without their father's gruff affection and protection. His marines would be without a leader, who fought so fiercely for them to be a standing force.

In that instant, Edmund felt as if the ground under his feet had swayed. It was a sudden shift, similar to the moment when he learned of his friend William's death as a child. Nothing seemed stable, and he found himself wondering what had become of his second friend named William, the son of the dead marine. He had received no letters from him since before news of Lexington and Concord. He was not listed among the slain, and yet Ned felt gripped with uncertainty as well as sorrow. If William lived, he was suffering. It seemed everyone was doomed to suffer now. Yes, it was as Pitcairn had said: Violence was bearing them all away.

They were indisputably at war now, and God alone knew how it would end.

Ned looked over the list again and again, desperately scanning for Burgoyne, and feeling faint with relief that his name was not to be found there. And yet his heart still ached for all those whose loved ones were not so fortunate.

Just then, Teresa came into the parlor and gasped, "Ned, what's happened? You look ill…"

Ned nodded, slumping down in a chair. "I am. I mean…there's been a battle outside Boston. Worse than the skirmishes this time. So many have been killed and wounded, both king's men and rebels, Tessie…and an officer I met in London, Major Pitcairn of the Marines, is dead…" He shook his head. "I knew the man for a few hours only, but I suppose I considered him a friend. I exchanged letters with his son, you know…"

"Oh, I'm so sorry, Ned," she said, taking her brother's hand. Then a look of concern crossed her face. "And…General Burgoyne? Dear God, not him…"

"Thank God, not him," Ned assured.

She crossed herself. "Surely he'll write to you as soon as he can."

"To both of us," Ned replied. "He never forgets you."

Tessie blushed. "I can never forget him either." She squeezed her brother's hand. "Shall we tell our beads now, for the quick and the dead who fought upon the hill?"

Ned smirked wryly. "Mother would be opposed if she knew of our intentions."

"Has that ever stopped us?" Tessie queried.

"No," Ned admitted.

He imagined that Pitcairn, true son of a Covenanter that he was, would not much care for their choice of devotions on his behalf. But he also hoped that beyond the veil, the Blessed Virgin would show herself a friend to any Christian soul.

And so Edmund and Teresa prayed the rosary inside their secret priest hole, forbidden beads slipping through their fingers, just like when they were children. The familiar Latin invocations eased Ned's heart, even as he felt a strange sort of guilt that he was safe at home while others had been sent forth to fight in the name of their king, and never returned.

Over a month later, Edmund received a message from Burgoyne's Preston home at the behest of Lady Charlotte, who was currently in residence there. It was an invitation to visit so they might discuss some matter of importance.

When Ned arrived, he immediately saw that the rumors were true and her condition had worsened significantly. She looked pale as a ghost, sitting stiffly on the chaise with a shawl draped around her shoulders despite the warm weather, and regarded him with a distant gaze.

"I wanted to ask you if you might have heard any news from my husband," she said in a reserved tone. "He's not on the casualty list, I know, but I haven't received any news from him."

Ned tilted his head, perplexed. "My lady, why would he write me before you?"

"Perhaps he's been wounded, and didn't want me to know," she offered, "or perhaps there are details he wished to share, man to man...you know the sort of thing..." She laughed weakly, then coughed. "It-it doesn't matter to me if he wrote to you about his...conquests," she insisted. "I just want...I want to know he's in good health, that's all."

"I have received no letter since before news of the battle arrived," Ned stated.

Charlotte folded her hands, pressing her fingers to her lips. "Oh...he might very well be injured, and not want either of us to know. He's done that sort of thing before."

"If so, it is because he cares too much for you to worry unnecessarily, especially now," Ned concluded.

"Because of my delicate constitution?" she sighed. "I followed him on campaign in Portugal, you know."

"Be that as it may..."

"I know, I know," she conceded dejectedly. "I'm not the woman I used to be. Not very much of one at all to him, I imagine."

He felt pity in his heart. "Don't say that, please. It hardly does justice to him or you."

She gave him a long look. "Then why has he not written?"

"My lady, you mustn't give into such thoughts. The mail is most likely just delayed by these dreadful circumstances, that's all."

She gazed at him for a moment, then smiled slightly. "Would you take tea with me?"

"With pleasure," Ned accepted.

The tea and scones with raspberry jam were mostly consumed in silence, until Lady Charlotte finally remarked, "I know you think me harsh."

"Not very, my lady," he assured.

"I want you to understand that my suspicion of you did not start as a response to your religious persuasion," she continued. "It was...well..."

"You love your husband," Ned finished, "and you've seen people use him. I understand."

"You bear an uncanny resemblance to another boy he brought around, you see," she said. "Tall, thin, light hair and eyes..."

"And he took advantage of his patron's generosity?" Ned surmised.

Charlotte nodded. "John took him everywhere, even to see the King. He wined and dined him and brought him home to me. And I knew right off what he was..."

"A charlatan?"

"John's bastard."

Ned stared at her for a long moment, not sure what to say.

"Oh, not that it's a provable thing," she said. "I asked John, and as usual, even he didn't know for certain. But he clearly thought it possible. So he felt…obligated. Besides, the boy flattered and fawned over John to his face, and my husband has always been susceptible to praise. But when John was not there…" She shook her head. "I heard him talking with his friends, partying in our house, at John's expense. I heard him mock the general as a simpleton and call me barren. And I hated him, with a new sort of hatred that surpassed my natural resentment of his origins."

"I understand," Ned assured her gently.

"That boy is in the army with John now, his protégé in the art of war." She gave Ned a long look. "But he loves you more."

Edmund felt his cheeks burning, and realized that, just a little bit, he had joined Charlotte in her jealousy over the existence of this other boy, this other son. "I love him too," he said simply.

She tilted her head. "You know…I think I'm starting to believe that. You may look like that other one, but…" She squinted. "Your eyes are not his eyes in any way but color. Yes…I didn't bother to notice that before. But…I do now."

When the time came for Edmund to leave, he felt comforted knowing they had gained a better understanding of each other. She even invited him to visit again soon, and he detected a melancholic loneliness gnawing at her soul. So he said that he would.

About a week later, a letter finally arrived from Burgoyne at the Southworth manor. It was only a few lines, but enough to ease the tension in Ned's chest. He decided he had best pay a visit to Lady Charlotte, so he took a carriage into Preston.

When he arrived at the Burgoyne residence, Ned knocked and rang the bell at the front door, but no one answered. Going around the back way, he noticed a rather unsightly nag tied up at a post. He also saw that the back door was slightly ajar, and some shards of broken glass lay on the path outside. As he drew closer, he heard a sound, like someone in pain, and pushed his way inside. There, he found a manservant, lying on the floor with a nasty gash on his head, blood dripping into his eyes. Ned crouched next to him and helped him sit up.

"What happened?" Ned demanded, using his handkerchief to soak up some of the blood. "Who did this?"

"It be the general's creditors, sir," the servant groaned. "They be looking for their pound of flesh, if you take my meaning. I tried to tell them off, but they weren't the sort to take no for an answer, as you can see…"

"Where are they now?" Ned demanded.

"Went to find the mistress, I reckon…"

Ned's heart pounded, and he stood up hurriedly.

"Careful, young man," the servant said. "They be a desperate lot…"

"I'm going to get them out of here," Ned declared. "Just staunch your bleeding with the handkerchief till I get back."

Ned rushed out of the servants' quarters and deeper into the house itself. He heard voices a way off and moved towards the parlor. Several maids, white with fright, were standing about in the hallway, listening to the goings on.

Turning the corner, Ned spied two bulky men, clad in dilapidated finery, planted in front of the chaise where Lady Charlotte sat, her hands twitching in her lap.

"I told you, gentlemen," she said hoarsely, the last word tinged with sarcasm, "you will have to wait to settle accounts until my husband returns from the service of the King."

"Well, m'lady, it seems your husband is all too often hiding behind royal robes or womanly skirts," one of the men snorted. "I hate to be indelicate, but he piled up debts at our establishment in more ways than one…"

"As I told you, the general pays his debts," she insisted. "He will do so, even when it comes to the likes of you."

"Is that a fact?" the other man snickered. "I'm afraid I'm not altogether convinced."

"Besides, m'lady, what if a Yankee bullet sends him to his judgment?" the first man inquired. "He'll charm his way into Lucifer's throne room, while we'll be rotting in the poor house. Does that sound fair?"

"We have a simple solution," the second man said. "Your ladyship was not unknown for cutting a fine figure in her day. Yes, dazzling, so gossip says, in every jewel her father and husband could lavish on her." He took a step forward. "Since m'lady no longer is able to mingle in society as she once did, it seems the reasonable thing to do would be to put such mementos towards maintaining the general's honor…such as it is…"

Lady Charlotte forced herself to stand. "How dare you! Villains! Knaves! Brothel bastards! How dare…" But she was so overwrought, she shuddered and slumped back onto the chaise.

"Methinks m'lady protesteth too much," the first man sneered. "And with such language!"

He took another step forward, menacingly. Suddenly, one of the maidservants, possessed of a courage beyond her slight frame, rushed in and put herself between them.

"Stop, you bullies!" she cried. "My mistress is ill, can't you see that? Leave her be!"

The second man seized her roughly by the arm, twisted it until she squeaked, then shoved her to the side.

"Susan," Lady Charlotte intoned. "Do not interfere." She stared at the men defiantly. "If you harm anyone employed here, or disgrace me in the least respect, John will take it upon himself to kill you."

They both chortled.

"If you do not think he will," she said, "then you do not know him."

"We could never disgrace you, m'lady! That's your husband's affair." Again, they took a step closer to the chaise.

She shut her eyes and clutched her belly. "Go, before it is too late," she commanded weakly.

"And who's to compel us, m'lady, in a house full of too many maidservants and not enough manservants?"

"How about a friend?" Edmund declared.

The men jerked at the voice from behind them, snatching a glance over their shoulders.

"Don't try to turn around!" Ned shouted, his right hand buried under the fold of his coat. "Not unless one of you wants to be bleeding from the back!"

They remained frozen for several moments, seemingly shocked by this sudden change of fortunes. And Charlotte's eyes were sparkling.

"Now," Ned stated, "you will apologize to the lady."

They hesitated, then mumbled some feeble words.

"And to her maid," Ned added.

"Just a minute…"

"Now!"

Again, they reluctantly obeyed.

"Good," Edmund said, taking several steps backward into the hall. "Get out."

When the unsavory visitors had been duly escorted out the door, and Ned made sure they left on the back of their ill-fed nag, he went back inside where the injured manservant was sitting on a barrel, still dabbing his head with the handkerchief.

"Feeling dizzy?" Ned asked.

"Rather, sir," he admitted. "But bless me! It did me mighty good to watch you show those bloody rascals a thing or two…"

"I'll send a physician in from town as soon as I leave," Ned promised. "Just stay seated and don't jostle yourself."

With that, Edmund headed towards the parlor. Susan, the maid, was standing in the hallway, like some sort of sentry.

"Sir, begging your pardon, but I don't believe her ladyship wishes to be seen by anyone at the moment," she said. "She's in such a state…"

But Edmund was undeterred and called down the hallway, "My lady, I have a letter from your husband! He's alive and well!"

Several seconds passed before Lady Charlotte called back, "Show it to me!"

Ned entered the parlor, and saw that Lady Charlotte's eyes were red. He pulled out the letter from his coat and extended it to her.

"I told you he was alright," he said softly. "He's just occupied with the aftermath of the battle and this ongoing siege. He promises to write to you in full as soon as he is able. It's only a few lines, as you can see…"

She scanned the letter up and down and let out a shuddering sigh. "Dear God, he'll be the death of me yet…"

"My lady, he didn't mean to…"

"He should know by now he can tell me everything, and I'll forgive him," she rasped. "But I must know everything, so I can prepare myself, so I can bear up with it. Instead, he tries to cover it up when he's gotten himself in trouble, and it gets worse for the covering of it. He should just tell me in the beginning. He should…" Her voice cracked, and she sobbed into her hands.

Ned felt sick, seeing such a proud lady reduced to tears in front of him. He sat beside her on the chaise, then pulled out the extra handkerchief Burgoyne told him to always carry in case of gentlemanly emergencies.

"I'm sorry," she whispered, accepting the handkerchief and wiping her eyes.

"Don't be," Ned said. "I'll tell the constable what happened. He'll make sure those ruffians don't dare come back."

"No, you mustn't tell the constable," she countered. "I don't want Jack to ever find out about this. Besides, you....you're not supposed to have a gun. You might get in trouble. I don't want that."

Ned smiled slightly, opening his coat to reveal that he was in fact unarmed.

"It was all a bluff then," she exhaled, shaking her head. "You're as much of a theater man as my husband!"

"Recusant masks and all that, my lady," Ned twitted. "But you can't blame me too much for wearing one on this occasion."

She chuckled softly. "No, Master Southworth, I don't suppose I can."

Chapter 10: MANY WATERS

After being rescued by Ned, Lady Charlotte once again invited him to visit her more often, which he did. Soon, he was doing so nearly every week, to his mother's predictable disapproval. But he had long ago become adept at ignoring her protestations. Over time, he noticed a pattern: the more Charlotte warmed to him during his visits, the more Perpetua seemed to sense that Ned was enjoying her company and grew even cooler towards him. It only made Edmund visit Burgoyne's Preston home more often. Little did she know that Ned was secretly settling a number of the debts owed by the Burgoyne household, carrying on the transactions through the servants so that the lady of the house would not find out. He felt it was the least he could do, given her husband's generosity towards his family, but he knew that his mother would disagree.

Lady Charlotte could be quite a pleasant companion when she put her guard down. She could be a wonderfully witty woman, full of opinions, observations, and the latest gossip she collected from various sources in London. Ned could easily understand why Burgoyne had found a soulmate in her, and could imagine the two of them spending many happy hours in each other's company, traipsing about Europe and settling into the comforts of home. Yes, he could imagine they would have made good parents too. And the thought made him sad.

When the mail would finally trickle in, Charlotte and Ned would discuss Burgoyne's latest misadventures in a city under siege. The general had grown bored and decided to interview many of the rebel prisoners. He came to the conclusion that most of these Puritan farmers and artisans were "men of good understanding, but of much prejudice and still more credulity." He was even in favor of pardoning the politically misled peasants unconditionally so that they could return to harvest their crops and maintain their shops. He hoped that such a show of royal clemency might set more colonials back upon the straight and narrow than would be the case if they were allowed to rot in prisons. He suggested dismissing them with the words, "You have been deluded; return to your homes in peace; it is your duty to God and your country to undeceive your neighbors." General Gage did not approve the naive plan. But Ned found Gentleman Johnny's humanitarian scheme endearing nonetheless.

Time wore on, Burgoyne grew bored yet again, and soon he was throwing his energy into launching a theater company in Boston, the first of its kind. The Puritan prudes, he complained, had left him no groundwork, and it was up to him, and him alone, to bring some artistic appreciation to the dour denizens of New England. Unfortunately, by his own admission, his efforts ended in a fiasco when it came to public relations with the Bostonians, who did not take kindly to his attempts to lure their comely daughters onto the stage, even if said daughters had been more than willing to go, due to his candied tongue. Burgoyne promptly turned his charms upon the beardless boys among the officer corps, who were eager to please him, even if it meant being trussed up in petticoats and tossed out on stage to balance out the cast. Charlotte rolled her eyes at this part of the letter, and muttered, "birds out of the trees," causing Ned to chuckle.

The farce the general had cooked up made a laughingstock not only of the Puritans, who Burgoyne would never forgive for shutting down play houses and gambling dens under

Cromwell, but also of the insurgents entrapping the King's troops in the city. He took particular aim at one George Washington, the newly appointed rebel leader who had once gained fame as an aide to General Edward Braddock during the massacre at Monongahela. He was the only mounted officer on the British side to escape unscathed that day, and distinguished himself by courageously riding back and forth to rally the scattered survivors and form a somewhat orderly retreat. It was said that he had hoped for a regular army commission, instead of a merely colonial one. It had not come to be. Now, apparently, he was out seeking revenge.

In addition to scraps of news from the colonies, Ned and Charlotte pored over news from London as well, most importantly a speech King George had made before Parliament, which had subsequently been printed for the general public. Ned picked up a copy himself and brought it over when he visited Lady Charlotte.

"'Lords and Gentlemen,'" he read aloud to her, "'those who have long too successfully labored to inflame our people in America by gross misrepresentations, and to infuse into their minds a system of opinions repugnant to the true constitution of the colonies, and to their subordinate relation to Great Britain, now openly avow their revolt, hostility, and rebellion. They have raised troops, and are collecting a naval force; they have seized the public revenue, and assumed to themselves legislative, executive, and judicial powers, which they already exercise in the most arbitrary manner over the persons and properties of their fellow subjects. And although many of these unhappy people may still retain their loyalty, and may be too wise not to see the fatal consequence of this usurpation, and wish to resist it, yet the torrent of violence has been strong enough to compel their acquiescence till a sufficient force shall appear to support them.'"

Charlotte leaned up. "Sufficient force? So…more regiments are to be sent?"

"I imagine so, my lady," Ned concluded. "But not only British. It is said that His Majesty has used his German connections to procure foreign aid."

"Either way, more bloodshed will follow," she murmured. "And…John is there."

Ned was not sure what to say in response. So he simply cleared his throat and continued reading. "'The authors and promoters of this desperate conspiracy have, in the conduct of it, derived great advantage from the difference of our intentions and theirs. We have been anxious to prevent, if it had been possible, the effusion of the blood of our subjects and the calamities which are inseparable from a state of war, still hoping that our people in America would have discerned the traitorous views of their leaders, and have been convinced, that to be a subject of Great Britain, with all its consequences, is to be the freest member of any civil society in the known world. Yet the rebellious war now levied is manifestly carried on for the purpose of establishing an independent empire. We dare not dwell upon the fatal effects of the success of such a plan. The object is too important, the spirit of the British nation too high, the resources with which God hath blessed her too numerous, to give up so many colonies which she has planted with great industry, nursed with great tenderness, encouraged with many commercial advantages, and protected and defended at much expense of blood and treasure.'"

"An independent empire," Charlotte mused. "Yet we are only beginning to consolidate our own. A rival come forth from our own loins, like Arthur and Mordred, destined to battle for dominion at Camlann."

Ned smiled. "The general married a woman after his own heart and taste."

"He would never settle for less," she chuckled. Then she grew serious. "I wonder if he will be a knight at our Camlann."

Again, Ned did not know what he should say, and simply read on. "'When the unhappy and deluded multitude shall become sensible of their error, we shall be ready to receive the misled with tenderness and mercy, and in order to prevent the inconveniencies which may arise from the great distance of their situation, and to remove as soon as possible the calamities which they suffer, we shall give authority to certain persons upon the spot to grant general or particular pardons and indemnities, in such manner, and to such persons as they shall think fit, and to receive the submission of any province or colony which shall be disposed to return to its allegiance. It may be also proper to authorize the persons so commissioned to restore such a province or colony, so returning to its allegiance, to the free exercise of its trade and commerce, and to the same protection and security as if such province or colony had never revolted.'" Ned looked up at Charlotte. "Well, that's at least hopeful, isn't it? The King wishes to bring a humane conclusion to this business as much as the rest of us. I expected nothing less from him."

"His Majesty sounds like my husband, who would release prisoners from their bands with a slap on the wrist," she said. "The assumption is that the Americans would appreciate such magnanimity and accept anything less than they have set their minds to achieving. There is no reasoning with the self-righteous. King Charles took a similar line with his rebels in his day, and they cut off his head, poor martyred soul, and his cavaliers were cut down around him in their fine, blood-stained clothes." She raised an eyebrow. "You are not as naive as you pretend to be."

Ned gave Charlotte a long look. "My lady, it is not for me to predict, only to pray."

"So you never form firm opinions, except in matters of faith?"

"And in matters of hope, and in matters of love," Ned replied. "As such, I hope for peace, out of love for my countrymen, on either side of the sea."

"So do you believe the colonials have a point then?" she queried. "Do you think, as so many Whigs think, that we are failing to treat them as our equal brethren by denying them parliamentary representatives?"

"I am in no position…"

"You have a mind. You have thoughts. You have drawn some conclusions."

"And you would have me trust you with them?"

"Yes, I suppose I would."

Ned smiled slightly. "I swear, madam, I have not attached myself to any opinion on the subject of colonial governance. Perhaps I will, someday, when my own people are emancipated."

Her eyes widened. "Catholic Emancipation is a bold notion, far bolder than colonial representation."

"Dangerous, some might say," Ned added. "But it exists in Quebec. And I would have it spread across the empire, to every colony and dominion, and upon this very soil."

"Even though Protestants are not shown nearly so much consideration in many Catholic countries, even those who are native born?" Charlotte queried. "I know. I've visited such places."

"Well, madam, I am afraid I am unable to impact the laws of France towards granting a greater liberty of conscience, for I am not French," he said. "As it happens, I am English, so it seems natural my commentary must start with England. Now, shall I finish reading, my lady?"

"Go on," she allowed, grudging admiration in her eyes.

And he continued to read the King's speech.

"'Among the many unavoidable ill consequences of this rebellion, none affects us more sensibly than the extraordinary burden which it must create to our faithful subjects. The constant employment of our thoughts, and the most earnest wishes of our heart, tend wholly to the safety and happiness of all my people, and to the re-establishment of order and tranquility through dominions, in a close connection and constitutional dependence. In light of the assurances we have received, and from the general appearance of affairs in Europe, we see no probability that the measures which you may adopt will be interrupted by disputes with any foreign power.'"

"He means the French," Charlotte said, "and the Spanish. Ever dangerous."

"And the Portuguese?"

"No," she snorted. "They wouldn't dare, not after all John did for them!"

Ned chuckled at the way she saw her husband as single-handedly saving nations. "He would surely show back up on their Mediterranean doorstep, pistols loaded, if they proved ungrateful."

"And probably catch the eyes of a few black-eyed beauties while he was at it," she sighed.

"But always come back to you," Ned said softly.

Charlotte nodded. "But always come back to me."

It was not the last time the unique dynamics of John and Charlotte Burgoyne's marriage would come up in conversation. One topic that had brought it to the forefront again was Thomas and Margaret Gage's marriage. With Boston still under siege, General Gage had been recalled to England to "deliberate over strategy" with His Majesty. The truth was that the poor man's career was all but over, no matter how hard the King tried to spare his feelings. General Howe, still recovering from his experience on Bunker Hill, was appointed to replace him in command of the royal troops in the city. Burgoyne, meanwhile, was free with his critique of Gage in letters home, saying he was not imaginative or proactive enough for the post. He also gossiped to Charlotte that Lady Margaret Gage may have been her husband's undoing. Hugh Percy had remarked to Gage his surprise that the inhabitants of the countryside had already been alerted to their plans when they set out for Concord, and Gage cried out in response, a strange sound from a usually restrained man. He then said someone very close to him had betrayed his confidence, for he had only told Percy and one other soul of the mission's intent in time for news of it to be divulged to the insurgents. He was convinced by Percy's own actions of his innocence in the matter, and settled upon that other singular soul as the guilty party.

No, there was no proof it was Margaret, and it was possible that Percy was exaggerating the story and extrapolating conclusions. Rumors told of his increasing dissatisfaction with Gage's cautious methods in Boston, which he may have blamed on the general's American wife. Alternately, Percy could simply have been bitter over his own failing marriage, and likely to see all wives as the root of every evil. Nevertheless, Gage had since sent Margaret back to England, and gossip could not help but circulate in many a social circle.

"I can't understand it," Charlotte sighed, shaking her head. "American or not, I cannot understand a woman who would willfully betray her husband, if she has in fact done so. Honest Tom was always good to her. A shy man, but a devoted one. He never looked at another woman. She was his whole world, whether or not he told her so in words."

"Perhaps her heart was broken by the prospect of her husband and her countrymen going to arms against each other," Ned offered. "People do strange things when their hearts are broken, even break the hearts of others."

"So what you are saying is that she is duplicitous, not whole in allegiance," Charlotte decided.

"No one wishes to be torn in two," Ned replied. "But it happens all the time."

She tilted her head. "You know that for a fact?"

"Yes." Ned folded the letter he had been reading to her and laid it on the table between them. "That is why I appreciate those who can be loyal even when that to which they give their loyalty fails them, time and again."

Charlotte glanced downward. "We've…shared a life together. Yes, we've brought forth life together. She's had ten children by her husband. I had one by mine. And yet…" She paused, then slowly rose to her feet. "Would you mind if I showed you something?"

"Not at all," Ned replied, standing up as well.

He followed her up the stairs and down the corridor until they reached a particular room–her daughter's room. Ned felt a lump in his throat as she opened the door and he saw how little seemed to have changed from the time when the child was alive, with clothing still laid out and dolls still sitting by the window sill. On the dresser there was a miniature of the little girl with her halo of golden hair.

"My husband will not enter this room," Charlotte said softly, picking up the miniature. "He hardly even speaks of her anymore. When I am gone, he will no doubt treat me in the same manner. It's rather terrifying, in its own way." She fumbled in the dresser drawer where letters and folded scraps of parchment were saved. "This room holds many different memories for me. Yes, I'm a silly, sentimental woman. But he could be quite sweet with his words. Well, still can be, but…you should have heard him in the beginning…" She glanced at one of the scraps of paper and smiled. "He could be pious and naughty all at once. He…he really seemed to believe God intended for us to be happy together…" She laughed lightly, painfully, then put down the paper and closed the drawer. "It was all rather romantic. Not just our elopement, but afterwards, flitting about the continent. We went everywhere, did everything together, and could stay up half the night gossiping and not grow tired of it. I thought I was the luckiest girl in the world…for the man who I had gotten for a husband was now becoming my friend."

"You fit each other, hand and glove," Ned remarked.

Charlotte chortled. "A scandalous analogy, that, especially when discussing John!"

Ned blushed. "I didn't mean to be…"

"Of course you didn't," she laughed. "But I suppose it might be taken as a compliment, either way!" She soon grew quiet, thoughtful. "He is very…carnal. It's part of his nature. As such, he has as hard a time controlling his urges, just like a child with a jar of sweets. He doesn't mean any harm, he just…forgets himself when seeking his own satisfaction. I used to be able to please him, to keep up with his passions. But then…" She bit her lip. "I have not been much of a woman to him of late, only a sickly burden he is bound to by oath. I told him as much, last time we were together. I told him I was sorry that I made such a poor comparison to his other women. But John looked miserable as I spoke, and took my face in his hands, and said, 'Incomparable, Charlotte. You are incomparable to me.' And I felt his hands shaking." There was a clicking sound in her throat. "Afterwards, he made sure to be especially gallant towards me, with silly romantic gestures. I like to think they are from the heart, no matter how theatrical. I like to think he is still in love with our lives, and so am I."

"You know that he is," Ned said. "I certainly do."

She closed her eyes and murmured, "It's like the Scriptures say: 'Many waters cannot quench love, nor can the rivers drown it.' Surely it is true, even now, with an ocean between us." She turned again to Edmund. "For all his faults, he is warm, Ned. You know as much. I do not think I would have done well with a cold husband. And he can be wonderfully tender sometimes, like when I was having the baby. It was almost comical how much he fussed over me. And he was so happy when the baby was born. I thought he might be disappointed it wasn't a boy, but he said a daughter was exactly what he had hoped for, so he could name her after me…" She winced, glancing over at the dolls still sitting on the windowsill in her child's room. "I…wanted so much to give him a son, or even more daughters. He was a good father, when he stayed at home. But…we lost the one, and there was no more…" She briefly placed a hand over her abdomen. "I…I don't think John knew what to do, losing little Charlotte. It was a hard thing for him to be deprived of his fatherhood."

"And you, of your motherhood," Ned added sympathetically.

"Yes, but…he is weaker than I am. Can you believe it? A strapping soldier and a delicate creature like me, and I am the stronger of the two!" She shook her head. "You know, the very closest I got to falling out of love with him was when he…he just stared at little Charlotte while she lay on her deathbed. She called out to him, and he just kept staring at her, as if he didn't even know her, as if she wasn't even real, and all the blood drained from his face, as if he had become a phantom. I screamed at him, and then…he went away. And she died while he was away. And I thought I had lost not only a daughter, but a husband too, for I felt sure I hated him. Then he came back the next morning, alcohol on his breath and his shirt buttoned all wrong, and he…" Her voice wobbled. "He-he was shaking so very badly, and asking me if I thought…she had died hating him. Then he asked…he pleaded with me to go to bed with him, so he wouldn't be alone. And…I did…for she was laid out in the hall, and he couldn't bring himself to look. I-I had her put in the dress that I ordered to be tailored for her tenth birthday, when I took her to her first opera…it was supposed to be the first of many operas, her coming out into society and…no, no, he could not look at her like that…" She swallowed back a sob. "It's not that he lacks affection…rather, he feels too much of it. And it wounds him, and it overwhelms him, and he runs away. But when he comes back…I can never let him suffer alone. I always try to ease it."

Ned felt lost for words at such intimate revelations from her. Then he asked haltingly, "Does he…does he hope to see her again, in heaven?"

"When I was young, and we were lost to each other so utterly, I asked if he believed in the immortality of the soul, for I could not bear to think of our love ever ending," she reflected softly. "He insisted to me that if reason and religion had not told him so, he would still believe in our ceaselessness, for love resides within lovers in being, and this love was stronger than death."

"Scripture is like poetry to him," Ned remarked. "It speaks for what he feels when other words fail him."

She swallowed hard. "Some time after our daughter died, I asked if he had changed his mind about the immortality of the soul…and he said…if he did not think, did not hope, that she was a little angel now, he would…" She inhaled shakily. "He wouldn't go on. I never saw him like that before, no, nor since. It frightened me. And I told him he must go on, he must, or I would die…" She wrung her hands together. "You see, Ned…it's still true. I would die upon his dying. But I do not wish it to be the other way around when time runs out for me…"

"My lady, please don't talk like that," Ned rasped.

"I am not about to delude myself, even if John tries to do so, for my sake as well as his," she replied. "Indeed, I tend to be more realistic than he is about many things. I know he will never be as famous as he wants to be, never reach that greatness he dreams about, as a playwright or as a general, no…nor indeed is he the best of husbands. But he will always be incomparable to me."

"That makes you the best thing that could have happened to him, and he knows it," Ned assured her.

She smiled again. "Here I am, taking you to this room where I don't take anyone. And here you are, comforting me, when you might be…his, by another woman."

"My lady–"

"I know, I know, you'll deny it yet again. But it doesn't matter now." She gave him a knowing look. "You are closer to him than you think. That's why he savors your company. He's bound to you, whether or not you are of his flesh. And I have given him no sons." Her eyes grew glassy. "I suppose I took you up here because I hoped that…if I could pretend, even for a little now, that you were ours…mine…" She touched his arm. "Perhaps I can make peace with what cannot be."

Edmund felt a lump rise in his throat, and then gingerly placed his hand over hers. "I'm here, my lady," he murmured, "for as long as I might be of some small comfort."

Sadly, the passage of time took its toll upon Lady Charlotte's health. One day, when Ned came to visit, he was informed by the maidservant Susan that her ladyship was too weak to rise from bed, but that he might sit at her bedside to keep her company. When he went upstairs, he saw a basket containing a purring mother cat and her five kittens, contentedly nursing at her side.

"It's Susan's cat," Charlotte explained. "She thought it might cheer me up to watch the kittens for a while."

"Has it?" Ned inquired, noting the look of melancholy in her eyes.

Charlotte gazed at the basket and smiled a little. "The mother cat fulfills her obligations, and so is in turn fulfilled. She knows what those obligations are by instinct, and has no cause to question them. She is to be envied."

"But human beings are more complex creatures," Ned reminded her. "We must glorify God, even through our questioning."

"You always have an answer," she chuckled. Then she gestured to the book shelf. "Would you mind reading to me? I fear I am rather weak for conversation today."

"Of course, my lady," Ned replied. "What is your pleasure for me to read to you?"

She raised an eyebrow. "Is it a sin according to Romish law to read the devotional writings of Anglican divines?"

"To my mother, yes," Ned admitted.

"And to your priests?" she pressed.

"Some would counsel against it, for fear that the reader might be misled by error or cause scandal to their fellows. Others are more open-minded on the subject. But either way, my father was a well-read man, and acquainted himself with many of your authors. He said that Christ could draw out wisdom from whomever he wished. I agree with him. If a man so fears reading the beliefs of others, he must have weak beliefs himself. Besides, I imagine, much of what they have to say is not at odds with my own faith. It matters not to me who penned a thing, so long as it is true."

So Ned read to her from her devotional books to help soothe her anxieties, and it became a common occurrence for her to request it during his visits. She said his voice was suited to such material. He was pleased to hear it.

When Edmund would return home from such visits, his mother would always interrogate him. He would answer her inquiries evasively, unwilling to volunteer any more information than necessary to mollify her. But she would not be mollified, insisting Charlotte was a bad influence on Ned. She proceeded to make a number of crude insinuations about John and Charlotte before their marriage and the reasons behind their elopement. From her perspective, Charlotte was an ungodly woman, tarnished by a conniving wastrel who had slipped his hand up her skirts with the full intent of eventually slipping it into her father's purse. After all, Charlotte's family was significantly more prestigious than his own, and he had used his marital connections to their full advantage when it came to his military and parliamentary careers.

Ned found the spreading of such gossip extremely distasteful, whether or not some parts were true. Lady Charlotte was a dying woman, who had been extraordinarily faithful to the sole love of her life, even when he broke her heart time and again. And Gentleman Johnny, whatever his faults, had utterly lost his heart to her, no matter how often he succumbed to distraction.

This tension between mother and son increased when the maidservant Fanny was caught rummaging around one of the manor's storage rooms which she and the other Protestant staff had been forbidden to enter. She screamed loudly enough to wake the dead when stumbling upon a skull, and Perpetua, storming down the hall, had smacked her good and hard across the face. Fanny responded with a panicked flood of words, assuring that if they did anything untoward with her, Jamie from the stable would come with his apprentice gang to her rescue from the Papists. This only earned her another smack from Perpetua, hard enough to knock her down.

"What's all this?" Ned demanded, entering the room himself.

"This is the thanks we get, taking in Burgoyne's bastard by a cheap theater hussy," Perpetua hissed, pointing at Fanny, who was nursing her flushed face. "He only foisted the consequences of his sin upon us because he assumed our house had no dignity left!"

Fanny suddenly broke down in tears, burying her face in her hands.

"Madam, don't," Ned said softly. "Whatever the girl's done, she doesn't deserve that."

"And why not?" Perpetua challenged. "That's what she is."

"What she is...is a child of God," Ned replied firmly. "No less than you or I."

Fanny suddenly stopped crying and stared at him for a long moment.

Perpetua shook her head. "What are you going to do about her then? She's a wicked little thing, a danger to this house..."

"Please go downstairs, Madam," he said calmly. "I am the master of this house, and I will assure its protection."

Reluctantly, Perpetua obeyed.

When he was alone with her, Ned folded his arm behind his back, and gave Fanny his sternest stare. "Was it Jamie who put you up to this intrusion?"

"He...he said Papists kept bones," she blurted.

"Whether we do or not is none of your affair, Fanny," he stated firmly. "You have specific tasks to accomplish in this home, and burrowing for bones in forbidden rooms is not among them. Indeed, it's a betrayal of our trust and a mark upon your reputation."

She swallowed hard, glancing at the cushion lying on the floor. "You gonna smother me? And stuff me in a crate?"

"I think not."

She gestured at the skull sitting on one of the crates with her chin. "Did *he* get smothered?"

"No. As should be fairly obvious, he was beheaded. And not by us."

Her eyes widened. "What did he do to lose his head?"

"It's not so much what he did as what he was," Ned said, "a priest. As for what he did, well, he offered mass, heard confessions, and cared for plague victims. And nearly a century and a half ago, the King's officials cut him open and decorated the city with his entrails as a warning to those of us who kept to the old faith. And as you can see, they deprived him of his head."

She grimaced. "Why…would you keep it?"

"Because the body is the Temple of the Holy Spirit," Ned replied, "and thus the remains of the saints are blessed."

"Is that why you burned heretics? So there'd be nothing left of the bodies?"

Ned sighed. "That was part of the reason it was done, yes."

"You gonna burn me?"

"No, Fanny. We probably couldn't fit you in the oven if we tried, with all those scraps you've been eating on the side. And let's not even start on the disappearing sugar cubes."

She made a guilty pouting expression.

"But there's a more important reason," Ned continued.

"What's that?" she asked.

"When that priest was having his heart cut out, with blood coming from his nose and mouth, he asked only forgiveness for himself, and for those who were killing him," Edmund stated. "Yes, he even prayed for the King."

She gave him a long look. "I don't think I'd have done that."

"But you see, Fanny, that is why his bones are blessed to us, yes, even more than because he died for his priesthood," Ned stated, "for had he died with hatred in his heart, his sacrifice would have been for naught." He gave her a long look. "Surely, then, we can forgive you. Besides, General Burgoyne is my friend, and he cares about your welfare."

Fanny blinked. "He-he does?"

"Yes. He told me he wanted you well taken care of, that your mother was special to him, and her death was a loss to him."

"She was gone quite fast after the fever put her to bed," Fanny mumbled. "After that, I didn't know where I was to go. I asked the manager if he'd like me to go out on stage and strip off some layers, on account that used to make mama coin, thrown right up to her, but he said my knees knocked together and my chest was like a pancake, so they'd not spend anything to see me like that. Turns out mama had some sort of an understanding with General Burgoyne, so he was sent to fetch me."

"She was wise to choose him for the task," Ned responded. "He has a good memory when affection is involved."

"Of course, that doesn't prove much about me," she insisted. "He may have just liked her shows. Besides, everybody at the theater had a soft spot for him on account of him always doing us favors, whenever he came into some money. You know, one year on Twelfth Night, when I was quite small, he won a bag of gold at the tables, and spent it on presents for the theater folk, because he's a proper theater man himself, you know. Mama got fancy silk stockings, and I got a doll…the nicest one I ever had."

"When the general decides to be generous, only the best will do," Ned remarked. "I know. I am a fellow beneficiary."

Fanny blinked away tears. "Do you think…the general is our da?"

Ned sighed. "Not mine, to be sure. Or at least…not by blood. In your case…I don't think he knows, Fanny. I don't think any of us will ever know. But…he clearly wanted the best for you, regardless. And…I don't think he wanted you stripping on stage for coin, even if the manager would have you. That's why he placed you with us. And, so long as you promise not to disobey us like this again, I intend to do right by his trust."

She nodded, then sniffled, and he extended a handkerchief to her.

"I don't believe you're a wicked girl, Fanny," he said softly. "And I don't consider your being in the house an indignity. And…although we are not siblings by blood, I believe God is our truest Father, and so we are all brothers and sisters in Him."

She stared at the handkerchief for a moment before taking it. "Thankee, Master Ned," she squeaked.

"You're welcome, Fanny," he returned. "Now go back down to the kitchen and help Agnes fix supper."

After she had curtsied and scurried out of the room, Ned went downstairs to face his mother.

"So? Are you going to send her away?" Perpetua demanded.

"It would only make things worse," Ned responded. "I've spoken to her, and I believe she is best kept nearer to us than farther away. If we turned her out, she'd be sure to make a fuss over the skull. I don't believe she will now."

His mother laughed bitterly. "It's because she has Burgoyne's blood. That's why you're keeping her on, because you feel beholden to him. Because he and his fine lady have seduced you with false friendship and worldly privileges. Yes, you feel so beholden to them, you would betray your own house!"

"That is uncalled for, madam!" Ned shot back. "I am no traitor to my kin or my faith simply because I will not hate all Protestants on your behalf!" He turned abruptly to go back upstairs.

"Ned…listen to me, please…"

Edmund turned back around in surprise, for it was the first time she had ever called him by his nickname.

She gripped the banister. "I…don't want you to be hurt like I was hurt. They won't protect you, not when the end comes. My mother thought she had Protestant friends. I did too, when I was a child. But when my father was beaten within an inch of his life, none of them helped us. They accused him of praying for the success of Catholic nations on the continent, and he was imprisoned and our home taken away. They even declared our family name null and void, just as they threatened to do to your father's name when they raided this house during your childhood. But there was worse to come, much worse…" Her voice broke, and for perhaps the first time ever, Ned thought she might cry.

"Tell me, Mother."

Perpetua clenched her fist. "We were taken away, myself, my brother and sister, and placed in the magistrate's house. He intended to reform us, to make good little Protestants out of us. But we resisted. I was the oldest, and kept the other two firm in the faith. The magistrate made it clear that until we obliged him, we were to be treated like servants, in a manner disgraceful to our rank. Still, we did not break, sleeping in the servants' quarters, fed on bread and water, switched whenever we were caught saying our 'Aves.' In the end, the magistrate came to the conclusion it would be best…to separate us." Her voice cracked.

Ned winced. "They sent them away?"

"Dominic and Teresa were assigned to other Protestant homes in different parts of the country. I knew they'd not be able to keep the faith without me, and even without each other. They were only seven and five years old, while I was ten. I had received the Eucharist; they had not. They locked me in the closet when they took them away, and I beat my hands bloody against the door. When they finally let me out, I told them that if I hadn't thought it a sin, I should have stabbed my siblings to the heart before letting them be reared by heretics. And…they beat me again."

Ned shivered. "Did you ever try to find them later on?"

"No," she replied. "I have no desire to find out what they became, nor what new names they were given. It would…break my heart." She pressed a hand to her forehead wearily, and leaned over the hearth. "The magistrate changed his tactics with me, trying to catch flies with honey instead of vinegar. He tried to…be a father to me. He tried to make me one of his children. I would have none of it. The magistrate's wife feared I would be a bad influence on her brood. Still, she did as her husband wished, and tried to mother me. Once, she came into the room they kept me in, sat down on the bed next to me, and started to comb my hair. She had no right to do that. She was not my mother. I screamed that very thing as I threw the brush at her. Only my mother had the right…" Her voice faded momentarily.

"When they tried to make me read from their heretical devotions, I cast the book in the hearth, and the beatings started again. When they took me to their heretical services on Sundays, I would shout at the minister and refuse to go up for communion, and more beatings followed. I relied on my faith alone to endure it. I hardly slept, on my knees, for as long as I could bear it every night, when I was less likely to be seen. Then one night, I woke from a dream about my parents, and decided to escape out the windows. But I fell and broke my ribs instead. The magistrate came in to see me after the physician put me in a brace. He looked at me with pity now…and that is what I hated him for the most, pitying me, of prouder lineage and nobler name than he was. And yet…I took advantage of it, and I begged him to send me back to my parents. He finally relented, saying that I was invincibly ignorant, and there was no point in torturing me any further like an animal in a cage."

"So you went home again?" Ned surmised hopefully.

"Home?" she repeated. "There was no home. I found my parents renting a tiny cottage, my father crippled for life and my mother sunken into despair for the loss of her youngest children. She barely remembered my name. Whatever I was before, I was never the same again. So you see, Edmund…I have no reason to be swayed by Protestant niceties. I have no reason to forget that they destroyed my family and perhaps my very soul."

Ned felt sick to his stomach and took a step closer to her. "Mother, I know now that you suffered a white martyrdom, in more ways than one," he said softly, extending his arms as if to embrace her, but she retracted from him. He winced, then added with emotion clogging his throat, "But even suffering for the faith will fail us in the end if we do not love our neighbor, Catholic and Protestant alike. I just told Fanny as much, regarding the martyrs…"

"There is nothing alike about them," Perpetua hissed. "Your equating them makes me lose all faith in you!"

Ned felt his cheeks flush. "Madam…why must you keep pushing me away?"

"You are the one pulling away, Edmund!" she declared. "You are the one tempted to conform! I see it in your eyes!"

"You see nothing of the kind!"

"I am your mother! I brought you into this world! I see you better than you can see yourself! I see everything that you will not admit to yourself!"

"Yet you are not God!" he blurted, turning on his heel and storming up the stairs before she could see and belittle his tears.

~

In November, General Burgoyne at last returned to England, escaping the sage still bottling up the rest of the army to confer with ministers of state. Charlotte set off to join him in London. Ned thought about going down himself, but Perpetua's moods had become so unstable since she divulged her harrowing past that he thought it best to wait for Burgoyne to come north to Lancashire. Charlotte agreed that his decision was prudent. But the year '75 turned to '76, and though Ned continued to receive letters from both the general and his lady, they did not return north. Ned reasoned Burgoyne needed to stay close to the movers and shakers of Parliament to make his ideas for coming campaigns heard. As for Charlotte, he had a feeling travel had grown more difficult for her since she left.

Meanwhile, more news appeared in the papers chronicling how the American revolutionaries made a daring play to capture Quebec. The assault had ended in disaster for the attackers, who were driven back by the British defenders under Sir Guy Carleton into the merciless embrace of the whipping winter snows, but the mere fact that the rebels had attempted such a conquest was startling. Worse yet, the rebels managed to maintain a blockade on the city. Ned was beginning to think that Burgoyne had been right about this uprising needing to be crushed swiftly for imperial survival. Indeed, one of the general's letters from London reiterated his sentiments. He was clearly concerned by the desperate state of things in Canada, and spoke broadly about how he would go about relieving Quebec.

But Ned could not believe he intended to return so soon, not with Lady Charlotte in such fragile health. Naturally, he would do everything in his power to stay for her. Burgoyne insisted that he should not fret so, for Charlotte was resigned to his soldierly duty wherever it might take him. Ned was worried by this seeming lack of awareness on Burgoyne's part regarding his wife's needs. He only wanted what was best for them both, and found himself increasingly missing their presence in his life as his mother continued to take every opportunity to question his fidelity to both his faith and his family. Burgoyne invited him down to stay in his London residence again, saying that Charlotte had taken quite a shine to him and was always cheered by his company. But Ned had a bad feeling his mother might do something drastic if he dared.

Then the day came when a messenger arrived at the Southworth manor, informing Ned that Lady Charlotte was failing fast. She had requested his presence in London, and this time, he did not hesitate to go south. Even Perpetua seemed to know she could not stand in the way.

When Edmund arrived at his destination, the house already seemed to be in mourning.

"She's taken a bad turn," Susan the maid sniffled, dabbing at her eyes with her apron. "The doctor came first, and bled her. Then the vicar was here. Had her take communion and all."

"Is General Burgoyne with her?" Edmund asked.

"The general left for Canada last month," the maid informed him.

Ned felt a knife in his heart. No wonder he had heard nothing from Burgoyne for such a long spell. Gentleman Johnny knew all too well that the young man would have given him a proper piece of his mind. His lady did not deserve to be abandoned in her hour of need, not for all the wars in the world.

Edmund was ushered into Charlotte's room, and felt his heart sink at the sight of her condition. She was ghostly white, except for the bruises under her eyes, and her hair, which she usually had the maid brush out even in illness, was splayed out against the pillow in a tangle. There was a blood-stained bandage on her right arm where the doctor had lanced her.

"Oh, my lady," Edmund murmured, sitting down in the chair by the bedside.

She opened her eyes, with some effort, and her pale lips twitched. "I hope I am not…too awful a sight…"

"You could never be so," he assured.

"Charming, like someone else I know," she remarked with a slight smile. "I'm afraid he went away, Ned."

Edmund swallowed hard. "I'm so sorry…"

"No, no, pity," she said. "I'm a soldier's wife."

"You're a man's wife," he blurted, "and that man should be here with you!"

She smiled gently. "Now, then…don't upset yourself. Here, I'll tell you a funny story." She leaned up on her pillow a bit. "According to letters from some of his comrades, Johnny's little production in Boston, mocking their religious forebears and rebel heroes, went on without him. Per his request, the play was open to the public at large, as opposed to restricted to the King's soldiers. My husband was determined to teach them how to laugh at themselves, come hell or high water. As fate would have it, that scoundrel Washington used the opportunity to launch a raid. Indeed, a messenger had to rush into the playhouse in mid-performance to announce the emergency, which the audience assumed was part of the satire. By the time they scrambled out of the building to meet the rebels, Washington's raiders were already on their way out with commandeered supplies. Ohhhh my dear, dear John…" She chuckled, then coughed.

Ned instinctively took her hand.

She squeezed it. "You know, I told him that you have been faithful in visiting me while he was away. He said you are the representative he would have chosen himself, and that I should call you if I ever…felt alone."

"I wish there was no need for any representative at all," Ned said, trying to hide his frustration with her absent spouse.

"Yes, well…I suppose I suspected for a long while I might go out of the world without…" She coughed again. "Without…husband…or child…perhaps for my sins, though God is merciful…"

Her words broke Ned's heart still further, and he kissed her hand. "I am here, my lady."

"Yes…you are a mercy to me." Her eyes glimmered as she gazed upon him. "It would have been a lovely thing…to give him a son like you. But…so long as he has you to look after him…I think I am content…"

"He always will, as long as I live, my lady," Ned assured. "I swear it to you."

She gazed softly at him. "A little piece of him…that's all I want now, for he will not return in time. I suppose I hoped against hope, but…now you will have to be that little piece to me."

Ned tried to respond but the words caught in his throat.

"You must remind him, sometimes, that he is a Christian," she insisted. "He must not despair over me…or himself…"

"I promise to remind him, and be your representative to him, just as I am his to you," Ned vowed.

She looked contemplative, then quoted from the old poem her husband penned for her years before, "Safe in the shadow of the Power, I'll tread the hostile ground; and fiery deaths in tempest shower, and thousands fall around…" She clutched her blanket. "Oh, if I could have one favor to bestow beyond this veil, it would be upon him! If love truly is stronger than death, it shall continue to shield him, wherever he goes!"

"I believe such things are possible, for God glories in sharing His grace," Ned replied.

She looked up at him with gratitude. "Tell your mother…I am obliged to her for lending her son to me for a little while," she said. "Tell her she raised you well…and always try to do right by her…"

"I will, my lady," he rasped, and his eyes began to burn.

She swallowed with difficulty. "May I…have some water?" She gestured to the end table, where a pitcher and a glass sat next to each other. "I…I'm afraid you must hold it for me…or I would spill it…"

"Of course," Ned assured, filling the glass with water, and helping her sit up to drink. She took a few sips, then leaned back against the pillow, seemingly taxed even from that small exertion.

"Dying…is a hard thing, Ned," she remarked weakly. "We must learn…to be like little children again. Perhaps that is the only way we might be fit for Heaven…like little Charlotte was fit for it…I-I so wanted her to outlive me, so John could see me in her, after I was gone. He would look at her, and remember…everything…but…" Her breathing fluttered. "When I took the sacrament earlier, I prayed…that God would not hide her from me any longer…that I could be a mother again…so that when John joins us, someday, we'll be a family again…" She gave Ned another tender look. "My dear, you're crying…"

Ned tasted salt tears on his trembling lower lip as he nodded.

She reached up and touched his face. "Oh, Ned…I see no mask at all now…"

Edmund sniffled, taking her hand again.

"I see why he loves you," she said. "You, too, are warm, like he is…" She smiled, again, faintly. "Read to me, won't you? Read to me about what is to come…"

And so he took one of her devotionals off the shelf entitled *Holy Dying* by Jeremy Taylor and opened it to the place where the ribbon lay.

"He hath taken away the unhappiness of sickness, and the sting of death, and the dishonors of the grave, of dissolution and weakness, of decay and change, and hath turned them into acts of favor, into instances of comfort, into opportunities of virtue. Christ hath now knit them into rosaries and coronets, he hath put them into promises and rewards, he hath made them part of the portion of his elect: they are instruments, and earnests, and securities, and passages to the greatest perfection of human nature, and the divine promises: so that it is possible for us now to be reconciled to sickness."

He flipped forward to yet another section:

"Let the sick man so order his affairs that he have but very little conversation with the world, but attend to religion, and antedate his conversation in heaven, always having intercourse with God, and still conversing with the holy Jesus, kissing his wounds, admiring his goodness, begging his mercy, feeding on him with faith, and drinking his blood: to which purpose it were very fit that the narrative of the passion of Christ be read or discoursed to him at length, or in brief according to the style of the four Gospels."

Then he did that very thing, reading the Passion narratives from John, hoping the length of it might lull her to sleep. It did so, and after John saw the blood and water flowing down as a mercy to the world, Edmund arose from his chair, leaned forward, and kissed her forehead. When he left the house, he knew in his soul he would never again see her on his side of eternity. And his heart bled for her husband, who had forfeited his last chance to say goodbye.

A couple days later, the messenger arrived once again at the Southworth manor to inform Edmund that Charlotte had died in the early hours of the morning. He also brought with him several of her devotional books which she had willed to him to remember her by. When Perpetua caught a glimpse of them, she expressed her displeasure that heretical material should have been brought into their house and told Ned that if he had any fidelity left to his faith or family, he should get rid of them.

"Do you not remember how many of our martyrs, including your own namesake, Father Edmund Campion, refused to pray with or to be prayed for by Protestants, lest it cause scandal and suggest apostasy?" she demanded.

But Ned simply replied, "These are different times, ma'am. And I am my own man."

Then he went up to his room and locked the door behind him with the books Charlotte had willed him cradled under his arm.

~

For months following Charlotte's death, Edmund felt no eagerness to keep up to date about news across the Atlantic. The fact that Burgoyne had left his wife on her deathbed still smarted, and Ned even hesitated responding to letters that came in from him, hardly mentioning his late wife except in the most passing manner, insisting upon his duty to the King taking precedence over every personal consideration. Ned was not deceived, though: Gentleman Johnny had fled from the shadow of death that had come to claim his wife, just as he had done when it came to claim his daughter. Ned worried that if he wrote back, his true feelings on the matter would come spilling out, creating a permanent rift between him and the general. Eventually, though, Ned found himself regaining his composure and continuing their correspondence. He could not help but fret over his friend, regardless of his failings, and thought it the best way to honor Lady Charlotte's memory and deal with his grief. He also took a renewed interest in the war.

Since the beginning of the year, so many things had transpired in North America. In early spring, General Howe's troops had finally abandoned Boston to the enemy, which many considered a slap in the face to all those who had perished upon Bunker Hill. Starting in June, Burgoyne and his reinforcements managed to break the blockade of Quebec, liberating British Canada and putting the rebels to flight. Then, in July, the self-proclaimed Continental Congress met in Philadelphia and drew up a declaration of independence, proclaiming their intent to dissolve the ties binding the colonies to Great Britain and absolving the inhabitants of allegiance to their sovereign. What made it all particularly distasteful to Edmund were snippets of the declaration which circulated slandering King George as royal brute and decrying him to the world as an unhinged tyrant. Subsequently, tearing down the King's statues, burning his likeness in effigy, defacing the royal coat-of-arms, and holding mock funerals for him while reciting Shakespeare's *Julius Caesar* proliferated across the colonies.

Ned had no time or patience for it. He had met King George in the flesh, and was convinced even by that single encounter that he was a good and God-fearing man. Besides, the King had given Ned a button from off his very clothes. Hence, if someone dared to regurgitate such treasonous drivel in Ned's face, he thought honor might compel him to illegally borrow a sword from someplace and take the blaggard to task. Ned guessed he would probably be skewered for his gallant effort, if his past fencing lessons were anything to go by, but at least he would die loyal. Otherwise, he would almost certainly face jail time as a Papist who had taken up arms, even if it was to defend the King's name. Ah, what a mad, mad world…

As summer turned to autumn, news reached England that General Howe and his brother Admiral Howe, at the head of an armada of ships, had sailed into New York City and wrested control of it from the rebels under Washington, putting him and his revolutionary army on the run. Loyal Americans now clustered in the city to be protected by the British military, since their property and even their lives were in danger of being forfeited elsewhere. Ned thought it utterly despicable that these so-called liberty-lovers were persecuting their fellow colonists for simply keeping good faith and refusing to betray their king. What crime did they commit by maintaining the allegiance of their forebears? Ned could not help but draw parallels to his own situation, and the pressure placed upon him in matters of religion.

Edmund could only guess at what might come next in the ever-intensifying series of events across the water. But Burgoyne's letters hinted that he had a plan in mind to cut short the duration of the conflict. What it entailed he did not say. Knowing Gentleman Johnny, Ned was sure it would be extravagant, daring, and perhaps just a bit mad.

Chapter 11: THE HIGHWAYMAN

Good Jesus, what shalt Thou do with my poor heart? Thou knowest I need nothing but to lose myself in Thine…

Edmund knelt in the attic chapel, hands clasped and eyes fixed upon the crucifix hanging on the wall, reflecting on this prayer from a Carthusian martyr. He had just received the Eucharist, and his heart was pounding in his chest as he considered the rarity of the opportunity. A priest had arrived three days before and taken refuge in their home, as was usual given their standing in the community. The word had gone out to the Catholic locals that a mass was to be said at the Southworth manor, with linen lying on the hedgerows and all other manner of signs and signals that had been used for centuries by the recusants. And so they had come.

As Ned prayed following the Eucharistic reception, kneeling beside his fellow Catholics, he felt the same thrill as when he first received the sacrament at the age of twelve, the same knowledge that it might result in his arrest, the same foreboding that he was branded by what he consumed. But it was worth it, in the end. And he felt a sudden intensity of union with the people who shared that room with him. There was no distinction between them there, whether they were noble or common, young or old, man or woman. All were equal in this secret supper and forbidden communion. The image of the Crucified One now imprinted upon his mind, heart, and soul, he closed his eyes and bowed his head.

Thee in me, and I in Thee, for time and in eternity, through Mary, Thy Mother, who gave Thee flesh upon which I feed…

This was his tethering to higher things, the melding of himself with the Savior in the most intimate way, through the incarnational mystery of the Body and the Blood. This is what the martyrs had sacrificed their own bodies and blood for, to bring the faithful to the foot of Calvary and join themselves to the Passion. It was also the connection between the present and the past, something which had been all but severed from the English people. Surely, they would never make sense of themselves until they once again partook in this divine feast of dying and rising.

Again, Edmund prayed.

When my last hour draws nigh, let me die for love of Thy love, as Thou wast graciously pleased to die for love of my love. Amen.

He then glanced over towards the window where a Catholic villager stood guard. It was young Rosemary's father, a plain-spoken farmer with a sharp eye. The attic was a good vantage point to see any horsemen who might be riding in their direction, though Ned remembered an instance from his childhood when they had been surprised by the back way. A report had reached the local constable that they were harboring a priest, and they had only just managed to shove him into a priest hole when they were raided. Poor panicking Tessie, only fifteen at the time, did her best to delay and distract the constable and his men, leading them to tear apart the wrong priest hole while the priest fled his hiding place and escaped the house through a secret passage in the cellar.

The constable seemed guilty over the whole affair, and awkwardly apologized to Francis Southworth for tearing through his home. Francis, undeterred, berated the constable for treating him like a common criminal.

"In what way have we given you offense or visited hardship upon your home?" he had challenged. "What have we done to be treated as petty thieves harboring stolen goods, or worse, traitors to our country, and the country of our fathers from before records were kept?"

"I had no choice," the constable stated. "We received information. I had to act upon it, as my duty dictates."

This part was the most terrifying: they had received information. Someone had reported them. The experience left a sense of dread in young Edmund, running over and again in his mind what could have happened to his family if the priest was found. Worse yet was the gnawing discomfort that they had been betrayed, more likely than not, by someone from within the tight-knit Catholic community. Why? For thirty pieces of silver? He could not imagine anyone he knew sinking so low. And most likely he would never know the guilty party, making him suspicious of everyone.

Now, a decade later, another priest had come to stay at the Southworth manor. He was a young and zealous man, fresh from schooling on the continent, with reddish-gold hair, bright blue eyes, and circular spectacles. His vestments were made from dress material Teresa had donated to the service of the Church. Almost all her best dresses had gone towards the adornment of priests and altars, while she kept only the plainest fare for herself. She would reverently stitch the patterns herself, and offer up every pin prick and drop of blood for the persecuted faithful. And now she looked on her brother with pride as the visiting priest clad in her vestments prepared to entrust Edmund with the highest of tasks: carrying the Eucharist upon his person to the imprisoned Catholics in York.

There was one Catholic prisoner in particular Ned had on his mind: Augustine Nevison, highwayman by trade. He was a strange man, clever and arrogant, bold and generous, vengeful and relentless. His father, a dirt-poor tenant farmer, had joined other northern English lads, mostly Catholic-bred, who chose to fight for Royal Charlie in '45. And alongside many of them, he was hanged. Augustine, only seven years of age, had watched his father choke to death, before being taken away from his weeping mother to be reared by Protestants, just like Perpetua Southworth. Despite his age, the memory of his loving parents and original faith never left him. Though he played at Protestantism for years, apprenticed to a hard-bitten stable master, he reverted to the old faith as soon as he was old enough to escape, on a horse he believed was owed to him for all the beatings both he and the animal received. He never lost his expert abilities in the saddle and could out-ride most folk in the county.

Alone in the world, he threw in his lot with criminals at a tender age, and though he became hardened to the lifestyle, the company did not suit him. He eventually abandoned them and made his own legend. The locals said that he returned to his native village to learn that his mother had died upon the open moor in the rain, driven to distraction by the loss of husband and son, hearth and home. She was buried where she fell, and a pitying villager had erected a crude headstone.

After paying his respects to her, Nevison had gone to visit the common grave where his father's bones lay moldering alongside those of his fellow rebels. He spent the night keeping vigil there, and at dawn he waylaid the judge who had condemned those Jacobite soldiers and ordered young Nevison taken away from his mother.

Pistols in hand, the outlaw bound the judge upon his own horse, then slipped a rope around his neck, with the other end tethered to a high tree limb. Nevison might have killed him then and there, and no one could have stopped him. Indeed, the judge reported that the highwayman had ridden away for a spell, intending to let nature take its course when the horse strayed to graze. But he had returned beforehand. According to Nevison's own colorful retelling, which made its way into a popular local ballad, the judge, in desperation, had begged and pleaded until he made an utter fool of himself. Then he threatened and cursed and wept. And the highwayman looked on, amused.

At last, Nevison had filled a cup with wine that had been stashed in his saddlebag and toasted King James and Prince Charles across the water. Then he drank a sip and poured the rest down the judge's throat till he choked and stained his clothes red. At last, Nevison unsheathed his sword and sliced through the rope binding the man to the tree, after which he cut off the judge's elegant beaded sleeves. The next time the highwayman was spotted, the wealthy Anglican victims who lost their purses described him wearing a pair of forbidden rosaries across his breast, including beads that matched those sleeves to a tee, offset by a simple wooden cross which folk said his father had given him before being marched up the gallows steps to swing for his rebellion. Meanwhile, the villager who had erected his mother's headstone found a pouch of gold sitting on his windowsill.

Nevison liked to spend most of his loot at taverns up in the hills or out in the moors, where he would invite the poor to sup with him at table. Some said such merriment helped him drown his sorrows. One thing was certain: It gained him useful allies. The rosary-touting outlaw was also famed for paying off the tithes of the pious recusants who refused to submit to the state Church. His main beneficiaries were his fellow Catholics, including Ned's own family when they were in a hard way. Farther north, near the Scottish border, he was known to extend similar courtesies to Protestant dissenters. He merrily dubbed them "a more honest sort of heretic", and was happy to help them avoid Anglican services.

Occasionally, he would even help the odd Anglican down on their luck, providing they had been more considerate towards Catholics than most. But it was a rarity. He had fostered a hatred for members of the Church of England from his youth and it showed no sign of abating. Presbyterians, Congregationalists, and even Baptists were, to him, "bloody fine opponents" whom he could not help but respect for their convictions. Quakers he called "dear silly lambs", and he would tangle with anyone taking advantage of their pacifism. Wesleyans, with their open-air revivals, he found amusing, eccentric, and indefatigable, much like he was; a colorful saving grace of the Anglican Communion.

But run-of-the-mill Anglicans of gentle breeding, who controlled the ascendency which ran nearly every establishment in the nation and filled their coffers at the expense of others, he despised with a passion. He reserved a special wrath for the dour-faced judges and starch-collared clerics, who he held particularly responsible for the persecution of his people. He robbed them blind whenever he could manage it, and sometimes, if he believed it was deserved, he beat them with a horsewhip or the flat of his sword. His raids were lightning fast, and he knew how to peddle in terror.

Once, Nevison assaulted a bailiff with a bullwhip in retaliation for beating a Catholic woman until she told him when a priest had last visited the estate. The information he extracted from her had resulted in the priest being seized and sentenced to a stinking prison cell for life. The bailiff's wife had thrown herself on top of her husband to prevent him from receiving further blows. She was probably the only one capable of saving his life, for Nevison would not strike a woman. He left, warning her to keep her husband closer to home or, next time, she wouldn't be able to recognize what was left of him.

Women seemed to hold a special place in his life. Perhaps it was because his career left him little time for softer things, and at heart he was still a motherless little boy. Perhaps it was because he venerated the Virgin Mary in the spirit of courtly love, and no one in Lancashire told their beads with more reverence. In his own eccentric way, he fashioned himself as a knight, defending his lady's dowry, and the illegal rosary beads he wore around his neck were his lady's favor. But he gained favor with earthly ladies too. He had a rugged appearance with hawkish features and wild copper hair down to his shoulders, contrasting with his fine velvet coat, doe-skin breeches, and knee-high riding boots. Women seemed to find his embodiment of contradictions appealing, and kept his secrets in their hearts and love-knots in their hair.

Although his female associates were plentiful, it was rumored one innkeeper's daughter came the closest to holding his heart in thrall. Bessie was brazen, buxom, and fifteen years his junior, the daughter of an Anglican father and a Catholic mother with a mind entirely her own. It was said she would ride out to her paramour with bread and wine for his hunger and thirst, disguised in an oversized coat with her long dark hair tied up under a tricorner hat. She would tryst with him in the moors, mists shrouding what passed between them, and then bring him back to the inn when no soldiers were about. He would gift her with trophies stolen from noblewomen and promise to take her with him someday to be the princess of his wild kingdom. When the night had given way to the day, gray light curling through the fog, he would vanish, leaving her watching from the inn door, cheeks rosy and eyes gleaming, a scarlet shawl draped over her white nightgown and her dark hair strung with a scarlet ribbon.

But Bessie was not Nevison's only protectress. Perpetua Southworth viewed him as nothing short of a hero, and regularly harbored him at the manor. She became a different person around him, almost approaching gaiety. Ned remembered being struck by her transformation as a child, and looked forward to Nevison's visits. He was always kind to Ned and Tessie, whom he treated like a beloved niece and nephew, showering them with attention and presents and regaling them by recounting his adventures. His visits became increasingly infrequent over the years, but Ned continued to remember him fondly as he grew up. Perpetua would stay up half the night conversing with him about the state of Catholics in the vicinity, and the two of them would hatch schemes to alleviate their suffering, through legal and illegal means. Francis Southworth tolerated Nevison's presence and accepted his monetary assistance out of obligation to the recusant locals who depended upon him, though he was far more skeptical of the outlaw's methods. He shook his head and predicted a violent end for him. Perhaps he was even a bit jealous, for his wife never smiled at him the way she smiled at that highwayman.

Amazingly, Nevison evaded capture far longer than most other outlaws of his class. This was partly because of the alliances he built up around him, and partly because of his keen sense of timing. He knew when to strike and when to recede into the mists. Not only would he hide in the hills, but he would also abandon England for Ireland, spending months living under aliases in Dublin or roaming the Wicklow Hills, occasionally holding up a gentleman traveler with a fat purse. He had a partner in crime on the Emerald Isle, a fellow Jacobite diehard named Cathal Boyle whose father had been slain in Scotland at Bonnie Prince Charlie's side. Boyle's grandfather had fought against William of Orange at the Boyne and later against Marlborough at Ramillies, fighting under a French flag.

Boyle's great hero was Count Redmond O'Hanlon, an outlawed Gaelic noble who gained both fame and infamy in the previous century for charging "the black rent" to the Protestants who had settled upon his confiscated ancestral lands in Ulster. It was in this way that he made good his own losses and kept his Catholic clansmen, who had been driven to the fern, fed. Though displaced, he held to the traditional code of conduct and courtesy cultivated by the Irish chiefs of old. The authorities in Dublin Castle put a price on his head, which increased along with exploits. He had a mixed relationship with Archbishop Oliver Plunkett, the Catholic primate of all Ireland, who had been opposed to his criminal activities and the collection of "the black rent", which he believed merely increased the animosity of Protestants and set a poor Christian example. Yet when the government offered O'Hanlon a full pardon in exchange for testifying against the archbishop, based on the trumped up charge of involvement in the Titus Oates plot, he flatly refused. He would betray no innocent man nor priest.

In the end, Plunkett was hanged, drawn, and quartered not for participation in any plot, but for spreading the faith of Rome. His prosecutor, the Earl of Essex, experienced a sudden change of heart, and pleaded for Plunkett's life before the King. But Charles the Second, son of a Catholic mother though he was, refused, saying that it was now politically impossible. Like Pontius Pilate, he said Plunkett's blood was upon Essex, who could have saved him earlier but would not, whereas the King now wished to save him, but could not. Essex was later implicated in a plot himself, and slit his own throat in prison. The outlaw O'Hanlon, meanwhile, was fatally shot by one of his own kinsmen who betrayed him while he slept.

But Boyle and Nevison, after years of companionship, trusted each other completely.

Papists both, the brazen brigands mocked the Anglican landlords who dominated Ireland as well as England and stole their good red wine. They guzzled some down in toasts to the King and Prince across the Water, and smuggled some to missionary priests at their "mass rocks" where the faithful would gather in secret, having alerted each other to the time and place with Gaelic riddles that Nevison, alone amongst Englishmen, had been taught by Boyle. Sometimes,

Nevison would supplement his income by joining ship crews for an odd trading venture or, indeed, smuggling operation. He had been over to France multiple times, as well as to the sugar islands and the Carolinas. But he always returned to his native Lancashire, risking life and limb to lighten the burdens of his people.

But for all of Nevison's precautions, his luck ran low in the late 50's. Seized and sentenced to hang in Lancaster, he was saved upon the gallows itself, so the ballads claimed, by the timely arrival of none other than General Wolfe, out recruiting manpower for his army, even amongst the condemned. Whether he had the noose already around his neck, or was simply plucked from a prison cell, Nevison did end up serving Wolfe as a keeper of horses and dogs. But he refused to don a scarlet tunic, for it would mean taking the Test Act. He might be a highwayman, but if push came to shove, he preferred death to dishonor.

"Why have you not gone abroad to fight for the French, then, if your heart belongs so ardently to the pope and the pretenders?" Wolfe had asked him.

"Because it has never been my way to shed an Englishman's life-blood, if it can be helped," Nevison had answered.

And Wolfe had respected that. So he let Nevison live. They struck up an agreement that the brigand would remain on the right side of the law and bring no disgrace to the regiment, and the general would protect him from his past misdeeds coming back to bite him. Ned agreed to abide by the arrangement for as long as Wolfe lived. By the time the general set sail to conquer Quebec, he and the highwayman had forged a unique bond.

"You'll die like a dirty dog someday, Nevison," Wolfe had predicted, "aye, dirtier than the dogs you keep."

"If so, General, bring red roses to my coffin, for Old Lancashire," Nevison had quipped.

And Wolfe, it was said, had laughed. But Ned was convinced he would have brought those roses had the one died before the other.

When news reached England of Wolfe's heroic fall upon the Plains of Abraham, plunging the nation in simultaneous rejoicing and mourning, Nevison considered himself free from his oath to the general, and returned to the King's highway, looping the mist-covered moors to ply his old trade. Although more cautious than he was before, he remained a living legend, appearing and disappearing like a phantom from a past age in his old-fashioned clothes, beloved and reviled in equal measure.

Edmund thought back to the last time he had crossed paths with Nevison a couple of months earlier. Heavy flooding had engulfed the vicinity, and he had headed out to the where the water had risen highest to see what could be done. Local farmers were putting their backs into shoring up a damaged dam with sandbags, and a number of prominent citizens, including the village vicar, Mister Randall, had turned out to oversee the situation. Sergeant Beeby, a domineering little man who liked to hear himself shout, was also at the scene. He had been called out from the nearest army garrison with a couple of soldiers to assist the locals with flood control. But his high-handed attitude did very little to calm the locals.

To Ned's dismay, the Protestant denizens seemed markedly unwilling to risk themselves on behalf of a Catholic farm boy who had been swept away by the flood. Only ten years of age, he had gone out to rescue a ewe, heavy with a lamb in her belly, fallen on her side and unable to get up when the waters rose. Both sheep and boy had been whisked away by the current, and now he could be seen at a distance, lying flat in the marshland on the other side of the coursing stream, presumed dead. Ned had begun stripping to the waist, determined to brave the flood himself if no one else volunteered to wade across.

"Don't be an idiot, young Southworth," the vicar scolded him. "You'd be taking your life in your hands, and to no good end. The boy is dead…"

"You don't know that," Ned blurted. "We'll never know unless someone is willing to take their own life in their hands. It might as well be me."

"Because he's Papist," the vicar surmised.

"Yes, if that's the reason none of the rest of you will lift a finger!"

Randall sighed. "It's not that way…"

"Yes, it is, you know it is, you're just not brave enough to admit it!" Ned gestured to the others on the bank. "I'm going in!"

The vicar sized his arm. "Listen, you," he huffed. "Whatever else I am to you, I am still your elder, and you will treat me with respect!"

There was a clicking sound from behind them, and Ned turned to see Augustine Nevison, with a pistol trailed on Sergeant Beeby. "Respect must be earned, preacher," he snickered.

The soldiers made a move for their guns.

"I wouldn't do that," Nevison said, pressing his pistol in Beeby's back. "Would you, Sergeant?"

Beeby swallowed hard. "You'll hang for this, Nevison!"

"Maybe so, sir, but don't you want to be around to watch?" Nevison queried sweetly. "If so, you might want to give your men the instruction to toss their firearms in the water. Now."

Grumbling, the Sergeant and his men did as they were told.

Gus knows his business alright, Ned thought. The outlaw proceeded to force Beeby to take up a collection from the prominent citizens standing on the bank. They cursed bitterly as they paid this variation of "the black rent", and grumbled even more as he ordered all of them but the vicar to roll up their sleeves and start helping with the sandbags. To his credit, he did not rob the farmers. Nor, indeed, did he rob Ned. And the panic over the faltering dam successfully distracted attention from the robbery, as water began pouring between the bags and Beeby's soldiers got involved with emergency measures.

"You should watch yourself, Nevison," Beeby growled. "It's wartime, and I represent the King's justice!"

"Ah, yes, England's war against her own children," Nevison remarked.

"Still a rebel in your black heart, Nevison?"

"An Englishman is never so true as when he dares to rebel," Nevison declared. "It's in our blood to take liberties. I am no lover of this establishment. So I say, let the Americans bloody your noses, though you think to bloody theirs! Let's see some Protestant on Protestant violence for the fun of it!"

"How dare you!" Sergeant Beeby squeaked whilst his own pockets were emptied out.

"Oh, shut your trap, Elmer," Mister Randall huffed. "He's doing it anyway."

"I have a record to maintain!"

"You and your intrepid underlings have done nothing of import to record, save marching about the countryside, stopping off at every alehouse along the route!"

"I must remind you, sir, that I am an officer and gentleman…"

"And I must remind you, sir, that I christened you!" the vicar huffed. "You had as loud a mouth then as you do now!"

"And I must remind you that I call the shots today," Nevison remarked, cocking his pistols. "In fact, you're both, shall we say, at mercy. But soldiers are safe enough with me, if they behave themselves. Clerics, on the other hand…" Nevison shoved Beeby down into the mud, and aimed his gun at Mister Randall instead. "I've decided to use you as my security till I'm safely on my way. I wouldn't advise any rash moves, or…"

"What? You're going to shoot me in cold blood?" the vicar blurted. "A man of the cloth? It won't go down well for you…"

"'Tain't my type of cloth," Nevison snorted. "To me, you're naught but an imposter and a church-napper, skimming the cream off the milk by tithing us Catholics into the poor house. Now move. We're going to take a nice little walk."

Mister Randall rolled his eyes, though he did start to walk along the bank, with Ned following after them to monitor the situation. "Say what you will about my office," the vicar challenged. "You're not going to shoot me, Nevison. Even you are not that much of a fool."

Nevison, still holding his pistol in one hand, unsheathed his rapier with the other. "Maybe not. Maybe I'll just…nick you a little."

A hiss of pain escaped the vicar as the tip of the blade made a small cut on his ear. "The devil take you!" he cursed, clamping a hand to the wound.

"It's not deep," Nevison assured, "not yet. But you know, it always bleeds a bit more when it's the ear. Maybe your kind needs to be reminded of blood. You've stained English ground with enough of it." He lifted the tip of his rapier to the vicar's collar, forcing him backward, with the flood behind him. The vicar slipped slightly in the mud and struggled to keep his balance lest he find himself pulled under by the rushing current.

Ned saw Mister Randall swallow hard as the blade cut a strip of the collar off, then hover dangerously close to his throat.

"Nevison…"

"Yes, Parson?" the highwayman replied, allowing the point to touch the vicar's throat, causing him to wince. When Randall stepped back, there was a crimson dot which dripped down his neck, leaving a stripe behind.

"There's…no reason for this…" Mister Randall rasped.

Nevison cut the other strip of the collar off. Then he lowered the sword, pointing it at the vicar's thigh. "You know what they say about celibate for the kingdom…some do so voluntarily, and some…are made so by others…"

"Be vulgar all you like," the vicar ground out. "You'll do no such thing."

Nevison laughed shortly. "Such faith…"

At this point, Ned felt the need to step in between them both.

"Enough, Gus," he pleaded. "You've drawn enough blood for one day." He cast a glance over his shoulder and saw the vicar dabbing a red-spotted handkerchief against his ear and then his neck. "Y'alright?"

"Never been better," he said sarcastically, stepping away from the water. "Why do you ask?"

Nevison sighed. "Methinks you're too lenient on this ilk, Master Ned. He'd have you as well as me strung up in a twinkling if he could manage it."

"Gus, please," Ned sighed. "For my father's sake…"

"Your father should have been more judicious about the company he kept," the vicar growled.

"Indeed, he should have been," Nevison declared, gesturing at the cleric. "Just be grateful the fine gentleman was forever doing his damnedest to be cordial to your family, regardless of your response. It protected them more than you knew."

"What do you mean?" Randall demanded.

"I've spied on your youngest girl many times, the little carrot-topped one who plays in breeches alone in the fields and woods behind the church," Nevison said.

The vicar looked suddenly faint. "Lizzie…has nothing to do with this…"

"Oh no?" Nevison raised an eyebrow. "Perhaps I might have wanted to teach you how it felt for a parent to have their child ripped away from them. It can make a mother or a father eat themselves alive with grief and guilt until there is nothing left to go on for."

"I'm not the one who took you from your mother!" Randall blurted.

"No, but you're the type to do it. Oh, you'd make some high-minded speech about it being best for the child, and for society, but if my mother's case had been brought before you, the result would have been the same, no?"

The vicar hesitated. "I…don't know."

"Yes, you do. You'd have put me in a Protestant house, to have my parents' faith beaten out of me, so you could rest secure at the top of the pile. You know I speak the truth."

Randall stared at him. "If that's what you believe…punish me. But not through my child. She never did you any wrong. She never…" He fought a twitch, a trembling lower lip, a loss of composure he seemed not to have expected.

Nevison smiled grimly. "I could have done anything to her, yes, anything at all, over a dozen times, and it would have been too late for you to do anything about it. But I never did. The elder Southworth would not have liked it, and he was a righteous man. Besides, I do not torment children, nor tear them from their mothers' arms, because I do not wish to be what you are. Think about that sometimes. Maybe feel some shame."

"On the subject of children," Ned sighed, pointing across the gushing stream, "there's a little boy that needs rescuing…a little Catholic boy, at that…"

"My God," Nevison blurted. "Why didn't you say so?"

"I was going to go in after him myself, but you interrupted," Ned sighed.

"Nothing doing," Nevison declared. "I'll go in."

"But…"

"I've had to dive out of a ship in the Irish Sea, lad. Water holds no terrors for me."

Soon, Nevison was fording the flood, swimming against the pressure of the current, with a rope he had brought along in his saddlebag tied around his waist, and the other end tied to his saddle. Ned held the reins of the horse, holding the animal in place as the rain started pelting the earth again. He heard some shrieking back at the make-shift dam, indicating some bags had come down, and the citizens and soldiers alike were scrambling to plug the gap once more. Ned prayed no one else would be washed away in the process.

At last, the highwayman managed to reach the limp form of the boy on the other side. Ned and Randall both watched as Nevison crouched down beside him, lifting the boy's head and placing a hand on his neck.

"It's futile," the vicar mumbled.

"We can't know that, not yet," Ned murmured.

After what seemed like a small eternity, Nevison slung the boy over his shoulder, and used the rope to pull his way back to the opposite bank. Though he struggled to maintain his footing despite the current, he finally made it across, crawling up the muddy slope on his hands and knees. Edmund rushed over and grasped his free arm to pull him to safety. The vicar, too, in spite of himself, went over and took the soaking bundle from him. Then Randall gasped, for the boy with the bloodied forehead stirred.

"The boy's not drowned! He was struck by debris, but his heart still beats!" Nevison panted, giving Randall an accusatory glare.

Randall bit his lip, his eyes were wide. He had been wrong.

"Restore the child to his mother, still a Catholic!" the outlaw instructed Edmund. "Give her my compliments, and God's!"

"I will, Gus," Ned assured.

"Good, good. Now, I am late for one appointment I wish to keep, and must away before I am forced to keep another I wish to avoid!" With that, he clambered up onto his horse's back, dug his heels into its flanks, and galloped off.

Nevison had indeed been late, Ned learned after the fact. He was supposed to meet with his Bessie. But King George's men got to her first. In the ensuing midnight melee, Bessie had been shot dead trying to warn him, and his waterlogged pistol had jammed as he tried to avenge her. He was then wounded twice and captured in the courtyard outside the inn. He had since been taken to York and was incarcerated in a prison there, awaiting trial. He was far too popular to pass sentence upon in Lancashire. Indeed, rumor had it they intended to move out of the north altogether and down to London. If he was to swing, it seemed likely it would be at Tyburn.

So Edmund resolved to visit Nevison in York before he could be taken south and bring him, and as many other Catholic prisoners as he could, the consolation of the sacrament.

But Perpetua's growing suspicion of her son since Lady Charlotte's death had not abated, and she made clear to the priest that she did not deem him worthy to be entrusted with the Eucharist.

"He harbors heretical books," she blurted. "He has been corrupted by the company he keeps. Do not entrust him with such a high responsibility!"

The priest glared at Ned gravely, "Do you realize the scandal implicit in the possession of such material? It is hard enough to keep the faithful among the common folk from falling away without landed recusant families showing sympathy for Protestant teachings."

"I was not aware that is what I was doing, Father," Ned responded in a low tone, wounded by his mother's accusations.

"Well, now you have been made aware," the priest stated. "We must not forget that for generations, the heretics have tried their best to trick pious Catholics into giving the appearance of apostasy. They have seized upon anything to that end, be it the reading of their books or the saying of their prayers or the sipping of meat broth on Friday. That is what they attempted to goad Lord Derwentwater to do during his last days in the Tower, for he was weakened from a terrible cough, but he would not break his fast nor speak with their minister, knowing as he did how it would be used to undermine the resolve of his fellow recusants. Besides, the content of heretical works makes them unworthy to own."

"But, Father," Ned replied, "firstly, I have not made it public knowledge that such books are in my possession. Secondly, these writings contain much that all Christians share…"

"They are like porridge mixed with poison," the priest countered. "Even a few drops mixed into the bowl can sicken or even kill a man."

Ned thought to argue that Francis Southworth had read Protestant books without qualms, and he was one of the most devout men of the last generation. Indeed, perhaps it was the strength of his faith that prevented him from being threatened by the others. But Ned could not bear to hear his beloved father scolded from beyond the grave by this missionary priest, too used to Europe to understand the divided loyalties Ned endured on a daily basis.

Thankfully, Tessie came to Ned's defense.

"My brother is as true in his faith as any Catholic in this shire, Father," she insisted. "The books were willed to him by a lady of good character, whom he kept company in her last days out of Christian charity…"

"Good character, indeed," Perpetua snorted.

Ned's face flushed red, but he said nothing.

"A general's wife," Tessie clarified. "Her husband was sent to America to deal with the unrest. He is…our friend."

"Beware such friends, dear daughter," the priest cautioned. "They can turn like a snake, based upon the wicked oaths they have taken."

"My thoughts exactly, Father," Perpetua chimed in.

"Without his friendship, we would not still have this house in which to shelter you," Ned rasped.

"And what do you think he will demand for recompense?" the priest queried. "There is always a price when you make a deal with…"

"The devil?" Ned blurted, then struggled to calm himself. "I assure you, Father, he has demanded no recompense beyond the bonds of affection that exist between us."

The priest squinted. "Make sure such affection does not obscure your vision, young man. Be vigilant against false loves. They can lead you into indiscretions, which you have already fallen into by keeping heretical literature."

Ned saw Perpetua had a look of triumph on her face, and he winced. No matter what anyone said, including this priest, he was determined to answer to his own conscience alone and keep Lady Charlotte's books. It would be disrespectful to her memory to do otherwise. Besides, the more his mother alienated him, the more he missed Charlotte. He would read her books whenever he felt himself assailed by grief, and through this act of remembrance, the maternal warmth she had shown him in her last days comforted him, as if her spirit visited him from beyond the veil.

"We pray for the general's salvation daily, in gratitude for the kindnesses he has shown us," Tessie said. "Surely that is not false love." She took a step closer to Ned, and placed a hand on his arm. "I would stake my very soul upon my brother's trustworthiness. He is incapable of betraying us."

"No one is incapable," the priest said darkly, his youthful face marred suddenly by pain. "A dear companion of mine, from the same seminary, was betrayed by his own brother, a Protestant, for trying to bring the light of the true faith to him. The judge who sentenced him was a cousin, eager to disassociate with him. He was imprisoned in Norfolk, and after hardly a year, he perished from the treatment in that foul place. He was just five and twenty years of age, and had always been a strapping, jovial fellow. So you see…we cannot trust anyone."

"I grieve for your loss, Father," Tessie said sympathetically.

The priest reddened. "We must…expect these things in the land of our birth. That is why I must not tarry here another night, unless patrols are about on the roads, and lay in wait for me…" His voice drifted off, and his eyes darted nervously towards the window. "One of the farmers said…word was out that I was in the vicinity. Some of their Protestant neighbors just shrugged, but others…"

Edmund found himself pitying the priest, seemingly too young to be titled 'father', and clearly afraid of what would happen to him when his time ran out.

He turned to Ned. "Whatever your mother's misgivings may be, circumstances make you the best candidate to reach the prisoners in need of holy consolation, especially those incarcerated for debts incurred for refusing to attend heretical services. I am afraid it would be highly impractical for me to go under the present circumstances. Ordinarily, this brigand Nevison you have told me about should not be receiving the Eucharist until he confessed his crimes and received absolution. No matter how hard-pressed we may be, we must not reduce ourselves to breaking the commandments through banditry and other misdemeanors."

"But he has saved the lives of many priests," Perpetua reminded him. "And kept poor Catholics out of debtor's prison."

"And thus, madam, if he makes an Act of Contrition, and shows true repentance for his transgressions, I am willing that your son should place the host upon his tongue." The priest turned to Ned. "Will you instruct him accordingly, my son?"

"Yes, Father," Ned assured.

"Then kneel to receive a blessing."

The priest raised his hands over Ned as he knelt and bowed his head.

"May Saint Tarcisius, who gave his life in defense of the Holy Eucharist during the cruel persecution of the Early Church under the Romans, strengthen you. May his shielding of the Body of Christ with his own body, even unto death, inspire you to emulate him."

"Amen," Ned murmured and kissed the priest's ring.

After the prayer was finished and the sign of the cross received, Ned was entrusted with several hosts, to be broken into tiny pieces for the prisoners to receive. Tessie reverently stitched them inside his shirt, then kissed him on the cheek.

"Please, do be careful," she begged him.

"You know I will be," he assured.

Then he hurriedly packed and headed down to the village to catch the carriage for York.

Chapter 12: BLOOD MATTERS

When he finally arrived in York, Ned could not help but be struck with apprehension as he approached the foreboding gaol. If something went wrong, and the Eucharist were discovered upon his person, this might become his new place of residence. Dread further clutched him as the guards pushed him up against a wall, tore through his clothes, and emptied out his basket. Thankfully, the stitching on the inside of his coat held true. When they had finished roughing him up and searching him crudely, even sticking a hand down his breeches, they shoved him into the gaol to be taken to the dungeon. Once they arrived at Nevison's cell and unlocked the door, Ned was horrified by the sight of the poor prisoner, beaten bloody, hung up by his wrists in shackles. The reddish-brown encrusted bandaging around his middle and on his right arm made Ned grimace.

"What are you doing to him?" Ned demanded.

"Shut your gob, Papist," one of the guards spat, shoving Ned forward.

"I warn you, do not touch me again!" Edmund commanded sternly, turning to glare at the man. "My family name is a good one no matter how you choose to denigrate my person, and I expect my questions to be met with answers. Why are you torturing this man?"

"He won't tell where he dropped off the loot from his last few robberies," the jailer stated.

Ned swallowed hard. Nevison was protecting them, from the Southworths down to the lowliest tenant farmer in need of coin to pay the tithes and keep the faith.

"Take the man down!"

"Why should--"

"I command it! Take him down!"

He straightened his back, standing up to his full height, with an air of authority. It was his inheritance, after all.

Marvel of marvels, the jailer relented and the guards took Nevison down and dropped him unceremoniously upon a pile of straw in the corner. He groaned, shuddering.

"Leave me to him," Ned ground out.

He waited, stiff as a statue, for the men to leave, for the cell door to close and the key to turn. He wrinkled his nose at the stench of decay all around him and broke into a cold sweat.

Then when he was sure they were alone, he rushed over to Nevison and went down on his knees beside him.

"Master Ned," the highwayman murmured through chapped lips, trying to force himself to stop shivering. "I...I..."

"Don't talk," Ned instructed, touching his forehead. "You're burning up."

He pulled out a blanket from the basket and wrapped it around him. Then he spontaneously lay down on top of him.

"Lad, no...your station..."

"Hush," Ned chided him. "You need warmth."

He heard a click in Nevison's throat, and then the man wrapped an arm around his back and pulled him close.

"They kept me down here alone for so long, when they weren't questioning me, I thought…I thought I'd never see a friendly face again…I almost looked forward to the hanging, where I figured a friend or two might appear to send me off…"

"Now none of that," Ned insisted.

"I…just want to talk, my dear…just to talk…I have been so alone…and the fever tricks me over what is real and what is unreal…"

"I am real," Ned assured, "and we will talk." He happened to catch a glimpse of the man's twitching hand and saw several fingernails were missing. "Dear God," Ned breathed, taking his hand. "What else have they done to you?"

"Oh, you know…some beatings, some dunkings…a few plucked teeth…" He grinned ghoulishly, revealing the gaps. "Don't worry, though. They got nothing more from me. And they shan't either. If they keep on like this, I'll soon be sent to God, before the rope has even graced my neck." He regarded the boy softly. "I'd never betray your house, Master Ned. Calm your mother's fears."

Now Ned was shivering. He kissed the man's forehead. "She sends you her blessings. And broth. And bread. And me, her son."

"Aye, you best of all," Nevison lisped, and touched his face. "My favorite godson."

"You called yourself the godfather of all the little Catholic children."

"So I did," Nevison admitted, "but you…well, you're special. You have a noble name, first and last, and I always thought it suited you." He touched Ned's arm. "Your mother loves you more than she lets on. I know. I remember my mother's love. She was showier about it, but it's the same love. And…the same scars left inside them, from wars they could not win."

"I worry over how many more mothers this trouble in America may scar," Ned murmured. "The conflicts amongst ourselves seem unending…"

"Yes, we've had many civil wars in this country, and since America was discovered, spilling over across the sea," Nevison sighed. "Perhaps it is our punishment, and we must be man enough to take it. I don't know. But my folk always stood up for the Stuarts, even when they were heretics. I suppose we always had an inkling that they would come around in the end, what with the second King Charles converting on his deathbed and the second King James banished for his convictions. So we took up arms for the first Charles when he fought against Cromwell, and saw his standard bleed when he first planted it. That was a bad omen, and we knew it. But still we fought. It's the way of recusants." He squinted. "It must be hard for a young man like you, always to be on the losing side."

Ned flushed, then nodded.

"And yet we each have an inheritance to uphold in our own manner," Nevison said. "My parents named me after the saint who first set foot in Kent, bringing the holy faith to these shores, and converting the king. Strange how much things have changed…" He shook his head, and recited bitterly, "'It has been found by experience that it is inconsistent with the safety and welfare of this Protestant kingdom to be governed by a papist Prince.' So says the Bill of Rights…Bill of Wrongs, if you ask me."

"But we must try to find some good in this country, mustn't we?" Ned queried, almost more to himself than Nevison. "Surely…there is some good left…"

"We must steal it for ourselves, if we can," Nevison chuckled. "I know, I know, bad joke. I made it to General Wolfe once. His folk used to be Catholic, you know, at least up to his grandfather's time. They were an old Norman family, straddling England and Ireland. I said that if his people had bartered away their faith for commissions, I might just steal it back for them, though they didn't deserve it. He was wistful. He said he was content with his ancient stoics. I think he lied." His eyes grew sad. "Sometimes I think of his mother, the poor woman. First she lost her youngest son, then her husband, then her eldest son. She couldn't have been very different from my own mother, and I shall never forget her tears. All the glory in the world couldn't possibly replace them…"

He coughed hoarsely, struggling to continue through the congestion.

"I'll remember that damn man till the day I die…skinny as a pole, he was, and pale as death. Always coughing in his sleeve and grumbling about this, that, or the other thing…but guts, damn, the man had them by the cartload. I never even saw him in battle, but I could tell easy enough, for often enough it was a fight for him to get out of bed, and keep at his work from dawn till dusk, and rush about with more energy than it seemed his puny form could hold, but he always did. And he knew a good horse, and he knew a good dog, and he knew a good man to have at his side and in his king's service." He winced. "And I am haunted by the possibility I could have won him over with the right word. Instead, death won him over."

"But his death was for the nation," Ned remarked. "He was…a martyr, of a kind…"

"Your father was far more a martyr, far more a sacrifice for the nation, though he never shed his blood," Nevison replied. "A white martyr, aye, but he suffered for the faith in so many ways, every day of his long life. Less glamorous, perhaps, then a fairly quick finish on the battlefield or on the scaffold. But that perhaps makes it more noble." He gazed at Ned tenderly. "I don't think your dear mother fully realized how blessed she was with him, and how blessed she is to have a son who shares so much with him. She thought I was more heroic, somehow, but that's never been the case. Your father and I…well, we just went about things differently. But whatever he thought of me, I always deemed him and his blood to have supremacy over me. That's why…I am so very, very glad you came, as if he sent you, to make our peace."

Ned felt salt stinging his eyes and cleared his throat. "Gus, I…" He leaned down closer to his ear. "I brought the sacrament."

Nevison's eyes widened. "Oh."

"The priest told me that you must make an Act of Contrition for your crimes before I can allow you to receive."

"Which ones?" Nevison teased.

"The ones you feel sorry for, I suppose."

Nevison pondered that for a moment. "I'm sorry I nicked that country parson, fraud though he is. I'm sorry I caused him to fret over his silly girl child. You must know she was never in danger from me. I used to leave her little trinkets, you know. She never knew they were from me, of course. She thought the fae folk left them for her."

Ned smiled. "Sounds like Lizzie. She's got quite an imagination. And she'd have given you hell if you tried to kidnap her."

"Oh, I know," Nevison chuckled. "I've seen her running through unseen adversaries with sticks. If it wasn't my morals getting the better of me, it would be my good sense." He paused for several moments, the mirth leaving him. "You'll tell her father I am sorry, won't you?"

Ned nodded. "I'll tell him."

"I...tried to say I was sorry to Bess's father, when I was lying in my blood outside the inn, and she was lying in her blood outside the door. He just spat at me. I don't blame him. Still...you don't know what I'd have given...to save her. I-I couldn't even run anymore when I saw that she'd taken the shot for me. I tried to shoot back, only for her. When that failed, I quit. No, I didn't want to escape. I...I wanted to die with her..." His eyes glazed. "I should have married her, Ned."

Edmund squeezed his hand. "Come on. I'll make the Act with you."

And so they did, whispering the prayer together.

"Oh my God, I am heartily sorry for having offended Thee, and I detest all my sins because I dread the loss of heaven and the pains of hell, but most of all because they offend Thee, my God, who art all good and deserving of all my love. I firmly resolve by the help of Thy grace to confess my sins, to do penance, and to amend my life. Amen."

Afterwards, Ned reached inside his shirt. "*Corpus Christi*," he murmured as he placed bits of the broken host into his friend's mouth, and bits into his own. Then they both clasped each other's hands again, in a silent unified prayer, closed their eyes and bowed their heads. When Ned opened them again, there were tears running down Nevison's face.

"*Domine, non sum dignus*," the outlaw murmured.

"None of us are worthy," Ned replied. "Christ comes to heal us."

"But you have better blood," Nevison countered.

"Our Lord is interested in the redemption of souls far more than the quality of blood," Ned assured. "We may be justified, regardless of lineage. Now come, let me feed you."

"But you mustn't..."

"Aye, I must," Ned insisted, pulling out the thermos of broth and a loaf of bread. He leaned him up and helped him to drink some broth, then tore up the bread.

"But blood matters, Young Southworth," Nevison whispered, "because it's what sustains life. Even without the honors in the world, there is still honor in your blood. Even without wealth or position, you would know who you are, and so would I. It's the culmination of everything that's been given to a man, and everything he is. The lineage cannot be erased, not from you, nor from your lady mother, bless her. That's why a king might abdicate, but never cease to have king's blood. It's stronger than any water that flows between him and his kingdom. And it passes to his heirs just the same. That's why my father fought for the prince as he did, why he was willing to swing from the neck till dead as he did…"

"That need not happen again," Ned blurted. "Not to you. You never committed any real treason to the government now established. Just took a few rich men's coins, folk who could well afford it…"

"That makes it worse of a crime to the court, for I have robbed nobles, not peasants," he replied. "You see…the blood again…"

"Any man with true nobility would not count his blood as higher than another man's belly," Ned retorted.

"Well, you see…that's because you are of a rare type, Master Ned. You know what it is to live with little, yet hold your head high. I'd wager that's what the faith does to you, and holding to it when it seems naught but madness. But you know…ending my life like this wouldn't be half so bad, if it were for something better than what I'll be swinging for. I lived a reckless life, squandering as fast as pillage came to me."

"You helped people," Ned replied. "We all know you did."

"And helped myself, and used others to help me…like my poor Bessie…" He shook his head sorrowfully. "God knows my sins, my guilt. I may never have taken a life by my own hand, but blood was shed because of me. I die in disgrace, as a warning to the people not to follow after me. It is not a gallant death, not like the martyrs, red or white. They gave their blood for Christ's blood, the one thing strong enough to wash out sin's stains…that which you brought me now, in God's mercy. They gave witness to the world with their very selves, just as my father gave his breath up for a higher thing, a Catholic king, who would free us from our shackles. You don't know how much I admired him, even as a child, yes, even as I watched him choked to death…how much I envied him…"

"Listen to me," Ned exhaled. "I have met King George, and I am going to beseech him on your behalf. I will plead for a reduction of your sentence."

Nevison chortled again, then broke down in a cough. "And why would German Geordie bother saving my neck? Look at what happened to Lord Derwentwater under the first George, bless his soul, and my father under the second. No mercy from the likes of the usurpers, no, never…"

"His Majesty now reigning is not German," Ned insisted. "He is a true king to all Britons. He receives petitions from his subjects regularly. So I will petition him in kind."

"You haven't answered why he'd want to grant a brigand like me even one more day to live, Master Ned," Nevison reminded him.

"Because," Ned replied, "I will fall upon his mercy."

"You're sure he knows the meaning of that word, lad?"

"Yes," Ned replied. "He's a Christian."

"A Protestant, sworn to put us down for our Popery…"

"Still," Ned insisted, "a Christian."

Again, Nevison laughed, lifting his manacled hands. "So are my tender gaolers!"

"He believes in his duties, though," Ned insisted.

"This is his duty, the punishment of the wicked…"

"And the forgiveness of sinners who repent," Ned blurted.

"Now then, that's a priest's job," Nevison remarked. "And only Catholic kings remember that they, too, are priests of a sort, by way of their anointing…"

"The King believes he is God's representative on earth, by way of his headship of the Church in this realm," Ned stated.

"But we don't believe that…"

"But he does," Ned declared. "Don't you see? That's what matters. He believes it. I saw it in his eyes, somehow or other. I could swear to that. And so I believe he can be persuaded to stay his hand. You were only caught because you stopped to save a child's life."

"A Catholic child," Nevison reminded Ned, "who nearly all the Protestants in the village were willing to let the floods wash away rather than risk their own necks." He tilted his head. "Tell me, did the boy recover from his injury?"

Ned nodded. "Good as new. The vicar and I made sure a proper physician attended to him and covered the costs. Randall…well, he's not a bad sort, really. He can't quite help being what he is. It's his rearing. But he knows, too, that you saved a child, and it matters. I can't believe the King won't see it in a similar light…" Ned bit his lip. "I will…try for you, Gus. Yes, I will try, in every way I can think to try."

Nevison smiled sadly, his eyes glimmering. "Tell your mother…her son is very much like her. Tell her she need have no fear for the estate with you as the master. Your blood holds true."

Not long after, Ned bid farewell to his friend, wrapping him up in blankets and kissing him on the hot forehead. Then he asked the guards to allow him to visit the other Catholic prisoners, so that he could distribute food and blankets to them. He managed to smuggle tiny pieces of the hosts to them, which they all received with expressions of awe. Then he asked them each for information on what caused them to be incarcerated, and promised to use family funds to help them in whatever manner was possible.

After leaving the prison, Ned went to visit the Ouse Bridge. The Catholic heroine, Margaret Clitherow, called the Pearl of York, had been horrifically martyred in the toll booth there nearly two centuries before. The best of wives and mothers, her crime had been harboring priests and allowing clandestine masses to be said on her property. When she refused to plead innocent or guilty, to protect her children and servants from being interrogated, she was sentenced to "the strong and enduring pain" of being pressed to death under her own door with a spike at the base of her spine, despite the fact that her belly was full with child.

Though the weakness of her flesh troubled her at this news, her spirit rejoiced greatly. She dressed herself as a bride going to meet her heavenly groom, even as her earthly husband, a Protestant, wept until his nose bled. She met her fate on the 25th of March, the Feast of the Annunciation, when the Lord's Passion was likewise commemorated. As guards piled heavy stones on top of the door, slowly crushing her to death, her last words, like Lord Derwentwater, had been the name of Jesus. At last, her rib cage and spine were broken, and she breathed her last. After her life, and the life of her unborn child, had been so violently ended, her remains were secretly buried by the authorities, but was later discovered by friends, who took her withering right hand as a relic.

So striking was the tale of her martyrdom, a Catholic priest who had apostatized to the state Church turned again to the faith of his fathers and was incarcerated in Bridewell Prison. He would be rescued by another Margaret, named Ward, later called the Pearl of Tyburn, who smuggled a rope to him in a basket and arranged for his escape from the window into a waiting boat. After being captured and tortured, she boldly declared that she had never offended the queen, but if Elizabeth had the bowels of a woman, she no doubt would have done the same, had she known of the ill treatment the prisoner underwent.

As for going to their church, she had, for many years, been convinced that it was not lawful for her to do so, and that she found no reason now to change her mind. Therefore, she told her persecutors, they might proceed, if they pleased, to the execution of the sentence pronounced against her, for death in such a cause would be very welcome to her, and she was willing to lay down not one life only, but many, if she had them, rather than betray her conscience or act against her holy religion. Another laywoman, Anne Line, perished similarly for harboring priests, insisting that so far was she from repenting of aiding and abetting one priest, she wished she could have done the same for a thousand.

The courage of these women made Edmund think of the Blessed Virgin Mary, safeguarding her dowry through their stalwart femininity. As fraught as his relationship with his own mother had become, he respected her cultivation of that same spirit.

After his devotions had been completed, Edmund saw no harm in attending a Handel concert, using the King's society button for access. It was Eastertide, and *The Messiah* was being performed at a church in the city. He had heard parts of it performed before in Preston, as well as sections of Handel's various other religious and patriotic works. But the lack of funds meant that attending concerts was a rarity and usually involved poor seating arrangements. Besides, it was discouraged by his mother who deemed it a form of Anglican worship. This was the first time he had the opportunity of listening to *The Messiah* from start to finish in one sitting, and was finally afforded seating where he could feel properly immersed in the experience. He was immediately drawn into the drama of desire found in the Old Testament prophecies foretelling the refiner's fire that would come among men, leading into the advent of the Wonderful Counselor who would be despised and rejected, only to emerge triumphant as the King of Glory. And when he stood for the Hallelujah, his hand upon the button over his breast, he felt as if King George were present at the performance as well, at least through the gratitude in Ned's heart.

The soaring music and accompanying voices left him awash with pride that his civilization could produce such astonishing work. There was so much robust wonder in the strains of song sailing around him, that he wished with all his heart to be more fully a part of it, to give himself over to it. His mother might say such beauty was merely masking the dysfunction of society, and yet in the midst of it, Ned momentarily forgot he was yet an outsider looking in through the glass of exile. Then, passing by Ouse Bridge again on his way back to the inn, he was reminded of the chasm with such keenness, he was almost in despair.

The next morning, Edmund took a coach back to his village. After hours on the road, he got himself a pint at the Cross Keys Inn, then began the long walk to the manor, with his knapsack of overnight necessities slung over his shoulder. Along the way, he ran into some local farm children watching their landlord's sheep. Two girls, who he recognized as Rosemary and Annie, the first Catholic and the second Protestant, were sitting on conveniently placed rocks that formed a stone circle, carding wool and gossiping. Rosemary was brown-haired and bespeckled, while Annie was blonde and fair-faced. They had grown up together much like sisters, tending the same flock and braiding each other's hair, seemingly spared from the shadow of distrust that tainted so many other relationships between those on different sides of the religious divide.

But as Ned drew closer to them, he noticed that Patsy, Annie's little sister, was weeping over a soggy looking rag rabbit.

When the girls saw him, they waved at him.

"Morning, Master Ned," they said in accord.

"Morning, girls," he said in reply, then he gestured to the child sobbing over the water-logged toy. "Why is Patsy carrying on so?"

"Our brothers drowned her rabbit in the water trough," Annie said matter-of-factly.

"Oh…oh dear. That does sound mightily wrong-headed of them."

"Billy sort of started it," Rosemary said. "Peter just kept it going."

"What was it about?" Ned asked.

"Our father's going to war and theirs isn't," Annie explained succinctly. "So Billy called Peter a name."

"Several names, to be fair," Rosemary added.

"Then it came to blows," Annie said. "I don't know why they went after the rabbit at all. But they ended up throwing it at each other, and then in the trough."

"They ran off home with bloody noses a while ago," Rosemary recounted. "I imagine they'll get over themselves sooner or later."

Ned sighed. He might need to have a talk with Peter about hitting Protestants in the current climate. Yes, Ned himself often scrapped with his Protestant playmates at Peter's age too, but times were fast changing. There was a rebellion underway now, and Catholics were always under greater threat of persecution during such circumstances.

"So neither of you are involved in your brothers' fight?" Ned surmised.

Both girls shook their heads.

"You're not upset that Rosemary's father won't be going to war then, Annie?"

"Why should I be when I don't want my own father to go to war?" Annie queried.

"That's sensible, to be sure," Ned sighed. "Though I'm sure your father is just doing his duty as he sees it. You should be proud of him, Annie."

"The landlord said he'd cut down on our rent," she explained. "That's all well and good, of course, but shan't help Da one jot when it comes to rebels shooting from up in trees. I hear that's how they do it in America."

"Yes, and I've heard the woods are quite large there," Rosemary joined in. "One could easily get stuck in the middle of all that, with wagons and all. It would be a bad thing, to be sure."

"And there will be wolves and bears and lions and the like in America, I imagine, especially in the woods," Annie added. "And savages. They cut off people's hair, right down to the scalp, so I've heard."

"Well, maybe they won't have to go through the woods," Ned suggested, to pacify them.

He then turned to little Patsy, who was still lamenting over her rag rabbit, and knelt crouched down beside her. "Oh, Patsy, this will never do," he said kindly, patting her on the head. Then he picked up the rabbit and started puppeting it to convince her that it had not, in fact, drowned. This had the desired effect, and Patsy had soon forgotten her grief and seemed quite convinced a rag resurrection had taken place.

"Alright, now that we've sorted that, I'm off home," Ned informed the older girls. "Do give the boys a good scolding for me. Tell them I think it's a fool's errand for them to fight against each other, especially during war time. We are all on the same side, all for England, whether or not we carry a gun. And if they ever drown a rag rabbit again, they'll have to answer to me. Understand?"

Both girls nodded in unison, then waved again.

"Ta-ra, Master Ned," said Rosemary.

"You take care of yourself, hear?" Annie joined in.

"I'll do my best, dears," Ned chuckled.

Then he continued along the road back to the manor, rather wishing the whole world could come to have the wisdom of babes. Perhaps that would be the only way Catholics and Protestants would ever make peace.

Chapter 13: A CHANCE FOR GREATNESS

As Edmund walked back to the family manor, he was surprised to see a familiar coach driving down the road in the same direction. He stepped to the side as the coach came to a halt, and the passenger stuck his head out the window.

Ned felt his heart back in his throat. "General Burgoyne."

The general smiled, a melancholy in it that brought tears to the boy's eyes. "My dear Ned."

"It's been so long," Edmund choked, taking Burgoyne's hand through the window.

"Indeed," Burgoyne rasped, squeezing his hand. "Far too long, but you've changed little enough. God, I've missed you!"

"Well, you're back in Lancashire now, and in one piece, Lord be praised!" said Ned. "That's all that matters…"

"Not back for long, I'm afraid," Burgoyne clarified. "As I mentioned in passing by letter, I've devised a plan to be implemented in the colonies. It's been approved, Ned. That means it's my duty to execute it, for the good of King and Country."

Ned blinked. "You mean…you'll be sent to America yet again?"

"In command, this time," Burgoyne replied with satisfaction. "Climb on in and I'll explain. No dog with you today?"

"No," Ned responded. "I've just returned from York."

"Ye gods! You've been in more hostile territory than I've been! I swear, they've yet to forgive us for besting them during the War of the Roses!" He squinted. "Merciful heavens, did the Yorkists give you that bruised eye and swollen lip? I should skin them alive, the sore losers!"

"Indeed, sir, they did, and we should!" Ned chuckled, climbing into the carriage. "But you'll be happy to know I ducked a few more times this round!"

"Good lad!" Burgoyne ushered to take a seat beside him instead of across from him, and wrapped an arm around his back warmly, draping Ned in his scarlet coat in the process. Then the general said tremulously, "By my faith, boy! I've been in such a state this past year, but…seeing you again somehow makes everything seem less bleak..."

"I'm glad," Ned rasped, and felt Burgoyne give him a little squeeze. Then he swallowed hard. "I-I don't know how to tell you…how very sorry I am about…"

"Don't," Burgoyne blurted. "It…won't bring her back. I…I had to go, Ned. It was my duty, you know…please, please believe that of me, I…" His voice wobbled. "Let's talk about…the future. It lifts my mood." He forced a grin, then promptly pulled out a scroll and opened it across both their laps. It was a map of North America. "The plan is rather simple, really. The colonies must be split in half by taking control of the Hudson River. There will be a three-pronged attack, with all of us converging at Albany. I will be leading the main body of my prong, with General William Phillips in charge of my artillery, and General Simon Fraser in charge of my light infantry. I have a history with both men, on personal and professional levels, and I trust them with my life. More importantly, I trust them with the fate of our peerless empire." He ran his finger down the map. "With my British regulars bolstered by Hessian and Indian allies, as well as loyal American and Canadian volunteers, I will lead them all south from Montreal, while a second column of troops under General Barry St. Leger makes its way east down the Mohawk River valley as a diversion. We will be met in Albany by soldiers from General Howe's army who will come out from New York City. Cutting off New England from the other colonies will be like cutting off the head of a snake. The rebellion will find itself in its death throes."

"It appears it will be quite a lengthy trek on your part," Ned remarked, tracing the route of Burgoyne's finger along the map, "through a great deal of densely forested terrain…"

"*Terra incognita*," Burgoyne admitted with a shrug. "But that should not hamper our progress too terribly, so long as we have Loyalists and Natives on our side who are familiar with the region. After all, both are under threat by the rebels and seeking protection as subjects of His Majesty. My responsibility is to assure that they have it, come hell or high water."

"So a crusade?" Ned queried.

"Of a kind," Burgoyne agreed, beaming. "I suppose a little idealism couldn't hurt us! Besides, it gives me a chance to put all inspiration taken from the old romances to some good purpose beyond the theater. This is…a whole new sort of stage." He gestured to the map once more. "I've always liked a bloody good challenge!"

After disembarking at the Southworth estate, Burgoyne and Edmund began to leisurely walk the grounds together.

"Ah, Ned, I must admit it's a beautiful country out here," Burgoyne said. "I would love to take you hunting someday. You know, a bloody proper fox hunt."

"As you know, I lack the accouterments," Ned replied. "Horses, guns, and blades are no less forbidden to me than they were to my father."

"Well, every disease has a remedy," Burgoyne replied, then changed the subject before Ned could press him. "You know, General Gage had me take over his correspondence on staff, so there I was in Boston, writing a grand manifesto to offer the knaves amassing outside the city a final opportunity to hurl themselves upon the King's tender mercies or face his righteous wrath. Oh, and I set to work writing that traitor Washington after he wrote us a poisoned pen letter, accusing us of inhumanity! I think poor Tom worried he might finally lose his famous composure, having been on friendly terms with the villain during the last war. He was terribly strained by the whole business in Boston by the end of his tenure there. He was just too dedicated to moderation, and the job proved too much for him."

"I'm sure General Gage tried his best to do his duty as he saw it," Ned offered in his defense.

"Please don't misunderstand me, Ned," Burgoyne replied. "Tom has always had a character replete with virtue and with talents. Even from his youth, he was better than me in some ways. Cleaner living, and all that. I can easily believe you to be cousins on that account. But he is simply not suited to this particular set of circumstances. He is better adept at peace than war."

"Perhaps that is to his credit," Ned murmured. "I wish the whole world were better at peace than at war."

"Yet honor bids us battle, when there is no other way to hold our heads high," Burgoyne said. "That, I suppose, is why God made men like me. We must do our duty, like it or not." The corner of his mouth twitched tentatively. "When it came to responding to that dastardly Washington, though, I didn't mind doing the deed one jot. It was rather fun, in the midst of all the tedium!"

Ned could only imagine how overblown such missives must have been. And at this point, how obviously unsuccessful. "Well, at least you enjoyed yourself, sir," he sighed.

"Yes, indeed," Burgoyne agreed, then queried in a darkly humorous manner, "Shall I tell you the tale of how our dear Major Pitcairn started a war?"

Ned could not help but cringe, both due to his tone and choice of words. "So even you are calling it a war now?"

"Well…it shan't be a long one," Burgoyne insisted. "We'll see to that."

Ned squinted. "It seems as if every time I am assured that it won't be too terribly bloody in the colonies, the situation gets dramatically worse."

"You mustn't blame me, Ned," Burgoyne replied. "The infernal rebels are full of surprises. But logic dictates that all their pluck is for naught in the end. But anyway…back to Pitcairn…"

"Yes, let's get back to him," Ned sighed.

"He had a real struggle sorting out his marines at first," Burgoyne said. "After bloodying the noses of both the army and navy to land them when and where he wanted, he had to lock himself in the barracks with them for weeks to maintain discipline and keep them from trading their kit in for cheap Yankee rum. He even had to flog several of them, something he didn't much like doing. He might call them 'animals' sometimes, but he was too humane to approach harsher punishments eagerly. He finally managed to drill them into shape, marching them hither and yon across the countryside and training them on the Boston common. Believe it or not, the inhabitants of the city took that crusty old Scotsman to heart. If they wanted a straight answer, he would always give them one, like it or not, and they trusted him to mediate disputes between them and the soldiery. Ezra Stiles, one of the radical propagandists, even called him a good man in a bad cause."

Ned smiled. "Maybe he liked a man with a strong handshake."

Burgoyne laughed. "Well, Pitcairn had enough opportunities to try it out on locals! He was seen around often enough, in Old North Church with his sons and son-in-law on Sundays and in coffee houses and taverns the rest of the week. You can well guess in which locations he swore, and in which he chose to bite his tongue! He would hold salon, and invite the whole street to partake, be they Whig or Tory. He even kept company with that incendiary Paul Revere, since they went to the same lodge of the Masonic Order, and even let the rebel paint him when he was off-duty. Revere lived next door to the Shaw Family's house, where Pitcairn was quartered. They were radicals too, but the major again won them over. Apparently one of his aides, a young Lieutenant Wragg, insulted Shaw's eldest son, who in turn threw a glass of wine at the lieutenant! A duel was on the brink of breaking out, but Pitcairn swooped in and managed to defuse things with his wicked sense of humor. He was the one for the job, I suppose, being the father of many sons."

"So he quelled disputes," Ned said, "yet started a war?"

"Well, you see, Pitcairn was just dying to get out of Boston, after Gage put him in charge of sweeping committees and, believe it or not, fire brigades! That's why as soon as Pitcairn realized the mission to Concord was happening, he volunteered, even though his precious marines were to have no part in the proceedings! His personality went from that of a boxed up snapping turtle to a lark in the open air! The colonials began to suspect something was afoot from him alone, even without the informant sharing General Gage's intimacy. Colonel Smith even had an altercation with a negro serving wench who seemed to know the whole plan, causing him to run off like the devil himself were after him! Pitcairn could not stop teasing the poor man about it!"

"I'm sure the colonel appreciated that," Ned remarked dryly.

"Oh, he did, as only he could!" Burgoyne chortled. "Anyway, off Smith and Pitcairn went off together on their not-so-secret mission. Meanwhile, that rascal Revere and his confederates rode about, rousing the countryside. As you know, Pitcairn ran into a right troublesome bunch lined up on a certain village green, and told them in no uncertain terms to stand down. Then there was shooting…from them, from us, God only knows who started. Some said it was Pitcairn with his pistols, but I don't even think he was that mad! He claimed he did his utmost to pull his men back into line, and I'm sure he did, but he was not the easiest man to understand in the best of times, and his Scotch blood was up. Got his horse shot up, and his hand too. But he handled things perfectly calmly in Concord."

Ned squinted. "I find that…hard to believe."

"You're right, I lied," Burgoyne admitted. "He punched someone during the search for weaponry. But you know, it was a tavern keeper, and Pitcairn was hungry, so at least he made up for the man's bruised jaw by ordering breakfast from him."

"Ah."

"Yes, made quite a scene of the whole thing, stirring brandy with his bloodied finger to disinfect it, then drinking the stuff so as not to waste good money on it, and vowing to stir the Yankee blood like that by nightfall."

"That does sound like something he'd say, yes," Ned sighed.

"Then a young woman in the street slapped him as if he'd been fresh to her, and an old woman in one of the houses lectured him like a schoolboy. Colonel Smith made a point of reporting such delightful details! Then the burning of munitions caused the courthouse to catch fire, and Pitcairn got to engage in his favorite activity of forming a bucket line to put it out! This caused the rebels to assume the town was being burned, so they charged down to the bridge and…well, as I say, you've no doubt heard the rest."

"Aye," Ned concurred softly. "And then came…Bunker Hill."

"Breed's Hill," Burgoyne corrected. "I was there, watching. It was Breed's."

"Lieutenant William Pitcairn and I exchanged letters for a number of months," Ned said, "but I have not heard from him for months now. Was he on the hill with his father?"

"Well…we'll get to him," Burgoyne assured. "But first things first…"

"Breed's Hill?"

"It was indeed a dark day, victory or no," Burgoyne said, his voice growing more somber. "The toll upon our officers was dreadfully disproportionate to that of the ranks because the villains on the heights mercilessly targeted them to break the chain of command. A disgusting display, lacking all decency and decorum! Meanwhile, belligerents across the river in Charlestown opened fire on our soldiers, only to suffer for their brazenness. We shelled them from our ships, and all the buildings went up in flames." He shuddered a little. "Looking on from my vantage point, I could see Howe's corps ascending the hill in the face of entrenchments, and beyond that, the large and noble town was in one great blaze, fire licking up the steeple of the church, the highest point. The roar of cannon, mortars, and musketry filled the ear, and the storm of the redoubts filled the eye. It was beautiful, and terrible, and so utterly overwhelming to all the senses, like a work of art that moves me beyond myself when I am distraught to the point of going numb. It was great, it was high-spirited, and while the animated impression remains, I almost wish I could quit it, before I remember…worse things..." He swallowed hard. "Do you understand me, Ned?"

Edmund winced. "I-I'm trying to, sir."

"I watched friends fall, never to rise again, and thought I might vomit," Burgoyne murmured. "Yet…I didn't. Something happened to me, beyond sickness. It was…a rush. I felt caught up in the drama of it, as if I had been hurtled into history itself, powerful and merciless. So many possible futures flashed before me, and I felt a sudden unreasonable dread fill my mind, that perhaps a final loss to the British Empire in America would leap from these flames. But it mesmerized me too. And then, after the first two charges were repulsed…the third charge wended its way up the hill, with Pitcairn at their head…" He shuddered.

"I saw a deadman win a fight," Ned mumbled, recalling the ballad that Percy had sung at the party, "and I think that man was I…"

"Yes, his fate upon that hill worthy of a poem or a play or a painting at that," Burgoyne remarked, his voice strange, as if deliberately putting the subject at a distance. "Pitcairn made a grand show of it, shouting and swearing, insisting he should have been sent out first instead of last, threatening to bayonet anyone attached to the army who refused to break and let his marines through. He was wounded twice, blood dripping into the sunburned salt-grass, but refused to quit the field, and scolded anyone who complained of the blistering heat." Burgoyne winced. "He fell, then, riddled with four more rebel bullets. His poor son William caught him as he collapsed, after which he carried his father down to the boats in the river. The younger Pitcairn kissed the elder one, then returned to the fight, as his father surely wanted him to do, and was wounded himself. Back on the height, the young Lord Rawdon stamped his fame for life, holding high our colors and leading the soldiers forward to take the hill. It was a ruinous glory. Any more such victories we cannot easily afford to win."

Ned shivered. "So Major Pitcairn was still alive, even after six bullets?"

Burgoyne nodded. "For another few hours, at least, while he lay in a bed in Boston. General Gage had sent over a young Loyalist doctor, his personal physician, in hopes of saving Pitcairn. He was no older than the major's own son who is training to be a physician, and as was to be expected, Pitcairn gave him a piece of his mind about how things should be done. The waistcoat had adhered to his wounds by then, and though he relayed his thanks to the general for this courtesy towards him, he insisted he was bleeding internally and that the doctor should attend to others he might be able to save. The physician insisted he at least be allowed to look, but Pitcairn would not allow himself to be touched until he had set his affairs in order. It was no small miracle he stayed conscious for as long as he did, but that's the man for you, to the bitter end. At last, he permitted the physician to undress him. But he pulled off the waistcoat, and tore open the wounds. Pitcairn began to hemorrhage. There was blood everywhere, staining the bedding and his floorboards. Not long after, his suffering ended."

Ned remained silent for several moments, then crossed himself. "By the shedding of blood, may he be given amnesty," he prayed. Then he asked eagerly, "And his son William? Did he survive the battle?"

"After the hill was taken, we next saw him wandering through the streets of Boston, dazed out of his mind and bathed in blood," Burgoyne continued. "Some people took pity on him, asking how badly he was wounded. But he insisted that most of it was his father's blood. 'I have lost my father,' he said over and again, and there was nothing that could console him. But some other marines nearby lamented, 'Oh God, we have all lost a father.'" He shook his head. "Such a tribute was well-earned. He loved his Marines. One of his last acts upon this earth was to write a letter back to London seeking monetary aid for the worthy but unfortunate under his command. And so they all donned black armbands upon his passing, as if a family member had perished. General Gage grieved for him, and the King himself proclaimed him highly praiseworthy. His body lies, for now, at Old North Church."

Ned felt the collective grief in his own bosom, and asked, "Where is William now?"

"I'm afraid he succumbed to illness not long ago," Burgoyne reported flatly. "Disease is ravaging our troops in America even more than Yankee lead. Though one could say it is the rebels who are the cause of both, and who benefit from both. Of course, it's also rumored the Yankees used poison on their bullets, just as the French rascals did at Lake George and Louisbourg…saps a man's strength, makes him susceptible to many ills…"

Ned felt his stomach flip, and he bit down hard on his lip.

Burgoyne must have seen the reaction, for he touched the young man's arm and said in a soft voice, far less performative than before, "Don't hurt yourself, boy."

Ned fought back the tears bristling in his eyes as Burgoyne ran his hand up and down his arm soothingly.

"I know, you…feel things keenly. I know that. I just don't like to see you in pain. It can't bring anyone back." The general cleared his throat, almost guiltily, and said, "Perhaps it was a small mercy that the father died before the son. Whatever his foibles, no one who knew him could doubt that he was the best of husbands and fathers. We…all might have done well to emulate him in that. His family, along with the Marines, was his life. He had already lost two sons, one to a childhood illness, another to the cruel waves when his navy vessel went down. William was his favorite, his marine son. Watching that boy die might have broken even his strong spirit. He was more tender-hearted than you might imagine."

"I can imagine it," Ned rasped.

Burgoyne leaned forward, and again, a certain theatrical air entered his voice. "I pity Mrs. Pitcairn most…to lose both her husband and son, and not even have their bones for visitation. They did send back her man's uniform buttons back, along with one of the fatal bullets they managed to dig out of him before the end. Paltry consolation, if such it be. I can't imagine that being an easy thing to show the children. His two youngest are still at home, you know…Janet at fourteen years of age and Alexander at seven. Then, I hear, more tragedy befell the family, for the major's daughter Katherine, who had come full with child by her husband, received the news of her father and brother's deaths poorly and lost the pregnancy. It turned out to be twins…"

"Please, stop…" Ned ground out. He clenched his fist, and felt a sudden flush of both anger and grief. *Damn rebels*, he thought. *Damn them, damn them.* He tried, only with partial success, to suppress such unchristian thoughts. "My heart bleeds for them…yes, for all of them…"

"Your heart bleeds easily, and often," Burgoyne sighed, resting a hand on Edmund's shoulder. "But Ned, I swear to you, they will be avenged, and their deaths will not be in vain. We will crush this rebellion, once and for all, and they will rest in peace."

Ned felt a surge of enthusiasm which he quickly tempered. Then he turned to Burgoyne. "We?"

The general squeezed his shoulder. "Won't you join me, Ned?"

"In what way, sir?" Edmund inquired carefully.

"On my staff, at my side during the whole of the campaign. As a British officer. You'd make a very fine one, I'm sure of it."

"As a Catholic?" Edmund pressed.

Burgoyne shrugged. "As I said, such circumstances can always be remedied."

"How, pray tell?" Ned queried. "By stripping me of myself, or by making the army conform to justice?"

"Careful, Ned," the general warned quietly.

Edmund lowered his gaze. "I apologize for my frank manner."

Burgoyne smirked. "You're a northerner. It's in our blood." He placed a hand on Ned's shoulder. "Come now, boy, surely you haven't mistaken me for a bloody Puritan trying to persuade you to cancel your Christmas plans," he chuckled wryly. "I've too much fondness for the theater and other men's wives to fall in with that prudish lot!"

The joke fell very flat, and even Burgoyne seemed to know that, his face twisting into a grimace.

"So soon, sir?" Edmund said softly, glancing at the black band of mourning still tied around Burgoyne's arm, since it was not yet a year since his bereavement.

The general took his hand away and let his eyes wander aimlessly around the yard. Then he abruptly changed the subject.

"Oh…you put a bench here," he remarked, gaily.

"Yes," Ned said. "I like to sit here, and listen to the birds, and think."

"And tell your beads," Burgoyne snorted.

"Or count with pebbles, or on fingers, or simply…in our minds," Ned replied softly. "Resourcefulness is a virtue. Can't arrest a man for that."

"I wouldn't even if I could," Burgoyne assured. "Come, let's make use of the seat."

They did so, chuckling briefly over the difficulty they both had to fit on the bench.

"We manage, as always," Burgoyne teased. Then he sighed. "Your father was a good man. No one would deny that. He clung onto things that were passed down to him, and in a way, I respect it. But is it fair to expect you to cling to them at the expense of your future?"

"What if I believe in them?"

"Do you, Ned? Is it really more fitting for a foreign prince to lead the church in this land than for our own king to do so?"

Edmund lowered his eyes. "Our Savior came for all lands. He wants us to be one."

"Like our island is one with the continent?" Burgoyne scoffed.

"Surely the steward of Christ, if there is such a thing, should have sway over a strip of water," Edmund argued. "It was always so before…"

"And with that sway, foreign influence would be pressed upon us," Burgoyne countered. "Foreign superstition. We have a blessing being separated from all that. We can set our own course and allow reason to guide us. That is why, if you do not take this step, your allegiance will always be in question."

"I have no allegiance to any temporal powers but my own country, nor have I ever," Edmund protested, balling his fist.

"Then own your king as the church's head."

"It's an old demand, is it not?" Edmund replied tartly.

"My God, you'd think I was out to hang, draw, and quarter you!" Burgoyne chortled. "It's not the old days. We're living in another world, Ned…"

"Yet similar, in many ways."

Burgoyne sighed, then changed tactics. "You're right, don't listen to me. I'm no good example of Christian living."

"You're a good man though," Edmund said quickly. "You've helped us."

"Oh, well…" Burgoyne chuckled. "I'm afraid my occasional goodness is more or less…acting upon whims."

"Acting upon grace, you mean," Ned replied. "God gives us every good desire."

"A better man, though, is your king," Burgoyne replied. "His Majesty took his time with you because he saw himself in you."

Ned lifted an eyebrow. "How so?"

"The King was once a shy young prince who had to be trained to greet every person in a room, and strike up little conversations with each of them, to overcome his stammer," the general recalled. "His varied interests were mooring points for him in such encounters, such as the music of the masters, and having always been of a particularly pious nature, nothing could win his favor more rapidly than finding another so inclined." Burgoyne smiled. "It is more than evident to me that he wanted to set you at ease because you are the sort that sets him at ease."

"I am obliged to His Majesty's courtesy towards me," Edmund replied.

"Say what you like about past monarchs, but our king has earned his right as supreme governor of the church in his kingdom," Burgoyne stated. "His personal morality is beyond reproach, which is the cornerstone upon which his domestic bliss is built. That he has shown his admiration for Major Pitcairn is little wonder, since he, too, is the best of husbands and fathers. He has eyes for no other woman but his queen, and does not deem it beneath him to play on the floor with his children. Perhaps it is because of his piety, which cannot help but make him both dignified and humble. He fulfills his role as sovereign with utmost solemnity, yet in his private devotions, he considers his salvation a matter for fear and trembling. They say he has scratched out 'George, our gracious king' and scribbled over it 'George, a miserable sinner.' You know, at his coronation, he removed his crown when he received the Sacrament of the Lord's Supper? He said it was unseemly, given how his savior had worn a Crown of Thorns. Yes...truly I say this, he is a true defender of the faith."

"I have nothing but respect for his person, and reverence for his sovereignty," Edmund replied.

"Ah, recusant evasion again! Think you are under a gallows tree, Ned? Stop trying to be one of your bloody martyrs." He shook his head. "I...like you, Ned, very much, you know that. And it's not just because your father took pity on my monetary indiscretions."

"A few indiscretions add color to a man's life, I suppose," Ned absolved him.

"See? You understand me in spite of your mild manners and country innocence. Beneath your seeming softness, there's a sharp wit and a stubborn will."

"Yes. Stubborn." Edmund kicked a stone with his boot. "Comes from being a part of the same land for so long."

"Well, you're a Saxon, Ned, with an older name in this country than myself or Gage or so many others of Norman stock," Burgoyne reminded him. "I suppose it isn't surprising that you are terribly old for your age. And this land, or what's left of it...gifted due to service at Agincourt, isn't that right?"

"Crecy, under the Black Prince. Later, we were at Agincourt, where knights put clods of earth in their mouths as a testament to their yearning and mortality, since they could not each receive the Eucharist." He gazed off into the distance wistfully. "Oh, we were in many places, either as knights or as priests or both..."

"There's little point in trying to be a knight for a broken fellowship, Ned," Burgoyne said quietly. "There's little point in being buffeted and spat upon for glories long gone."

Edmund looked into his eyes intently. "*Sic transit gloria mundi.* We were Catholics then, with honors. We are Catholics now, without them. And still, in the old Saxon tongue, my Christian name means 'defender of wealth.' We know where our treasure lies. *Deo gratias.*"

"Meanwhile, my people gained their prestige through joining King Hal's sacking of the monasteries," Burgoyne chortled. "An odd couple we make!"

"We are what we are." Ned crossed himself yet again. "God keep us."

"But in truth, Ned, with or without King Henry, the abbeys were growing mightily unpopular," Burgoyne insisted. "The corruption of fat abbots earned the people's hostility."

"And Henry, eighth of that name, was a champion of the people against corruption?" Ned queried flatly.

"That's neither here nor there," Burgoyne dismissed. "New religious ideas were taking root on their own. We've always been an independent-minded people, averse to too much foreign influence. It was only a matter of time before–"

"Ideas come from the continent, you say," Edmund remarked. "Foreign ideas, you might even call them."

"Now, don't get smart with me, Ned," Burgoyne sighed. "You know what I mean."

Edmund smirked. "Sir, if our answer to institutional corruption is to level every existing institution, and prop up new ones to take their place, well, then we are guilty of throwing our lot in with radicals. We don't want that, do we?"

"Oh, what's the use?" Burgoyne huffed. "You're a mule, young Southworth."

"Thank you, sir."

Burgoyne chuckled then tilted his head. "You know, Ned, when I was traveling the continent, I often remarked upon the industry of Catholic officers, including those from Ireland who enlisted as mercenaries. I said, now isn't it a damn shame, not putting their talents to use in the service of our gracious king. And of course, it's not just a matter of the ruddy Irish…right here, in the north of England, there are plenty of stout hearts, held back from the service only by tender consciences." He shook his head. "If I was running the world, I'd open quite a few doors for your kind. Yes, I think I might give you most things, save the crown and a few other high posts that I don't want the pope's nose poking in, just in case he decides to start roasting us again. A matter of self defense, you understand."

"Everyone would very much like to keep themselves alive, yes," Ned exhaled. "Even us, if you can believe it."

"Oh, I do," Burgoyne chuckled. "And I tend to think, if I had unlimited power, I could turn my genius towards fixing everything, since I just want the best for everyone. Not to sound vain or anything."

Ned raised an eyebrow.

"But you know, the simple fact is, I have limits put upon me, so my genius must be funneled into salvaging our rogue colonies from the brink of ruin instead of solving our religious problems at home," he declared, with a broad gesture of his hand. "All this just to tell you, Ned…I would fix things in so many ways if I could."

Edmund smiled. "Thank you."

"But I can't, you see, and that means your life will be wasted, unless you come over to our way of thinking," Burgoyne blurted.

Edmund scuffed at a stone with his shoe. "I'm afraid I am rather independent-minded."

"Are you, though?" Burgoyne pressed. "Or is your thinking simply conformed to the dictates of Rome?"

"There are some things I hold to as a Catholic, and some things I hold to by virtue of my own self," Ned replied.

"What do you mean?" Burgoyne asked.

Ned exhaled. "When I was a child, a playmate of mine caught a cold and died. My mother made it clear she counted him to be a heretic, and that there was no salvation for heretics. Well, the truth is…" His voice wobbled a little. "I believe God is of a more merciful nature than my mother."

"And yet you maintain her obstinacy, which will bring you nothing but grief," Burgoyne stated.

"We have certain beliefs we hold in common," he said. "Yes, *I* have certain beliefs, by virtue of my faith, and yes, by virtue of my self. Shall I spell them out for you?"

"You're not supposed to, you know," Burgoyne shrugged.

"Yes, I know. My namesake Father Campion challenged the Queen's councilors to allow him to debate in public. 'Campion's Brag,' they called it. And they caught him. And they killed him." He gave Burgoyne a long look. "But you are my friend, and I would speak plainly with you. So I tell you, I believe that man has sinned, and God has condescended to our form to save us through His precious body and blood, and that He has sealed the New Covenant by giving us that same body and blood to be our sustenance at the holy mass, no less than when He offered Himself for us upon the rood. It is the same sacrifice, in time and in eternity. He enters into us, and we are transfigured into Him, yes, his true body and true blood abide with us, and it is no mere symbol."

Ned took a deep breath. He could not remember when he had dared so much in his life, but it felt good to let all the masks he had ever worn fall off. So he continued.

"I believe that God does not hoard his grace, but is blithe that we should beseech his Holy Mother and the saints of the Church to intercede for us before the heavenly throne. Their holiness dwells with us even among their bones, pillars of the temple where the Holy Ghost dwelt with such felicity, and I believe in praying for the souls gone before us, whose attachment to sin must be purged by refining fire. And in all this, I believe in the unity of the Church under the successor of the Prince of the Apostles, to whom Christ gave authority upon earth. It is the Church that safeguarded the faith of Christendom, and her freedom was safeguarded in this realm under the law. Now the law lies a-bleeding, and has done since the schism, when More the Chancellor and Fisher the bishop stood their ground and lost their heads. But bloodied or not, we are still here. I am a recusant; this family is recusant. If we betrayed the faith, we would lose ourselves…"

"Look, such hyperbole is wasted on me, I assure you," Burgoyne sighed. "I'm not about to turn Romish through such old-fashioned arguments. I'm thinking of what's best for England. And if you'll spare a thought touching the current times, plenty of recusants in the local vicinity have seen the sense in coming around to the way of things, even in recent years."

"The way of things?" Ned repeated incredulously.

"Yes, during my election, gentlemen recusants by the dozens made the choice to take the oaths according to established law and cast their ballots. Then they went about their merry way, to practice whatever faith best suited them behind closed doors. This is England, not Spain, my boy. We don't have that hot-blooded inquisition streak by nature. Bloody Mary was a departure, being half Spaniel herself. The majority of us don't commonly care to look into the windows of men's souls. We English approach life by the middle way…"

"And thus become a middling people," Edmund ground out, his face temples pulsing with real anger now.

"Take care, Ned," Burgoyne extended another warning. "England has gained her renown the world over as the Mother of Liberty. Remember, the Magna Carta…"

"As I pointed out a moment ago, I fear we long ago forfeited our claims to liberality when we shredded the Magna Carta and the coronation oath when it came to the liberties of the Church," Ned replied. "It was put to death when one King Henry murdered Becket at his altar in Canterbury, and when another King Henry scattered his bones and stole his ring. The saint said that if all the swords in England were pointed at his head, no threats could turn him…"

"Ned, you know it is unwise to call into question the nature of the coronation oath," Burgoyne reminded him gravely. "Many would interpret it as only a step away from questioning the legitimacy of the King. Remember…what became of your grandfather…"

Ned gave him a long look. "If parliament tells me the King is legitimate, then he is. But when parliament strays from temporal settlements into religious rulings, then, sir, I will resist and I will refuse. It hath not the competence…"

"But Ned, the King…"

"…is the king," Ned finished for him. "Unlike you, sir, I do not split hairs in terms of the continental connections, be it Hanover or Rome."

"Ned…"

"I happen to think more than half the men in this realm are better than the oaths they take, contradicting themselves in their very essence, no matter how many good intentions they exercise. And you, sir, are better than to tell me to take an oath contrary to my conscience, which you would never do under any other circumstance. Not even your enemies would accuse you of taking an oath flippantly, yet you seem to believe I am lesser than you in this regard, because I am Catholic. You encourage me to emulate those who swear to one thing publicly, yet do another thing privately. I, sir, have as much pride in the integrity of my name as you do!"

"I'm trying to save your name, Ned," Burgoyne sighed, "to make it great again."

"Do you know what my earliest memory is?" Edmund queried. It was when my father held me in front of the oldest door in the manor, where there was an old rusted knocker. He said, 'My boy, put your hands upon it. There, now, you've claimed sanctuary, for the blessing has never been taken from it, since the day our home was proclaimed a sanctuary by the king and the bishop, in accordance with the rites of Mother Church. Four hundred winters are no more than the time Adam was bound in a bond, and merely a twinkling to our Lord God. Two hundred winters is less than nothing.'" Edmund gazed at Burgoyne steadily. "Unlike Lord Percy, we Southworths still remember what it was that made our house great."

Burgoyne was quiet for a long while. Then he laid a hand on Edmund's shoulder. "Ned," he said softly, "I-I want you to come with me…rather badly…"

"You will have that young officer you have been mentoring with you," Ned mumbled, "the one you brought before the King and who stayed at your house. Lady Charlotte says he has been with you in Boston and in Canada…"

"Oh, don't be cruel, boy," Burgoyne exhaled.

"How is that cruel? I thought you'd be proud of him…"

"He…is not you," Burgoyne said simply. "Yes, he's brave and energetic and lusts after glory. He is popular amongst his peers, or at least, those he deems advantageous to befriend. But, you see…he lacks patience, I suppose. He wants everything now. He also lacks patience for others. He lacks…love for others, if they gain him nothing…"

Ned felt the impulse to tell the general what Charlotte had told him about how the young man had disrespected her. But in Burgoyne's fragile state of mind, Ned deemed it unwise.

"Ned," Burgoyne addressed him again, his eyes pleading, "will you not come with me for the sake of friendship?"

Ned winced. "I had hoped that, in friendship, you would never put me to such a test."

"Pity me when I speak from the heart, boy, for it's all I have left to work with," Burgoyne blurted, and his voice was strained. "You think I care to argue with you over theologies? I've never had the wits for it. But God, Ned, I fancy myself to have some warmth left in me for those I love. And when I'm in pain, damn me, I don't know what else to do but lay it on the line…" He blinked several times. "Ned, I-I would be obliged to you if you came with me."

Edmund locked eyes with him, feeling increasingly ill by the second. Finally, he whispered, "Please forgive me."

Burgoyne flushed red and turned away. At first, Ned feared he had pressed him to anger, but a few moments later Burgoyne chuckled. "Well, it was worth a shot, eh?"

Ned felt his heart sink as the general began to compulsively fuss over the wrinkles in his clothes, including the black band on his arm. Ned gingerly reached over and ran his hand along the band, smoothing it out, then looped his arm through Burgoyne's, keeping it that way for a long while as they sat together in silence.

Then Ned saw something white sticking out of Burgoyne's sleeve. He lifted the sleeve slightly, and realized it was the edge of a bandage.

Burgoyne pulled his arm free.

But Ned would not be put off, and laid a hand on his arm again. "You're hurt."

"I was at a party, with some very powerful punch," Burgoyne said dismissively. "Made a foolish decision to try to shave when I got back home. My hand slipped."

"Is that the truth?"

The general laughed. "As good as any."

"You don't remember."

He shrugged. "It's easier that way."

"Could it have been…?" Ned began, but he could not finish articulating his thought, that it might have been deliberate, to punish himself, or get back to her.

"I told you, I don't remember, so help me," Burgoyne chortled oddly. He stood up from the bench, and tried to smile. "Now, cheer up. Do I seem like the sort to do myself injury? No, to be sure, I'm far too fond of myself!" He bit his lip, and said more seriously, "I-I don't want to do that to myself, Ned."

And Edmund knew then that Burgoyne was scared.

"It's the house, isn't it?" Ned surmised.

Burgoyne stared for a few moments, then nodded. "I was doing fair enough in Canada and London, concealing my anxieties, but now…"

"Please come here whenever you like," Edmund said softly. "My house is yours."

Burgoyne smiled. "Are you inviting me to dinner, boy? I do hope so, because I'm positively famished."

Ned smiled, and stood to escort him towards the house. As they made their way there, Burgoyne began to make casual conversation, as if this were no different than every other visit.

"So what caused you to be out and about among those God-forsaken barbarians in York?" Burgoyne inquired.

"I went to visit a friend imprisoned there," Edmund said. "Augustine Nevison."

"Wait, the highwayman?" Burgoyne exclaimed.

Ned nodded. "Family connections go back a long time between us."

"Of course," Burgoyne sighed. "Recusant stock."

Ned bit his lip. "They weren't treating him well. It wounded me sorely to see him in such a state…and to think of what his end may be…"

"Well, he has led a roguish life, Ned," Burgoyne reminded him. "Hard to imagine it concluding in any other fashion."

"I know he's done his fair share of mischief, but he's good at heart," Ned insisted. "I don't believe he's robbed anybody he didn't think could afford it. Helped out more than a few folks down on their luck too."

"Oh, I know his ways," Burgoyne assured. "He robbed me some years back."

Ned forced himself not to roll his eyes. Nevison had an awful habit of digging his own grave. "I could imagine you two having some interesting banter," he remarked, trying to keep his voice cheerful.

"We did, I assure you," Burgoyne confirmed. "I alternated between quaint pleasantries and calling down the wrath of heaven upon him whilst he pilfered my purse. He clearly had no idea I was one step from the poor house at the time, due to a bad run at the races, and I didn't dare tell Charlotte what had happened."

"Oh dear," Ned exhaled.

"But he discovered my misfortune somehow, and I found more than had been stolen returned to me, along with an extremely poorly written note. The man doesn't know how to spell…"

"He doesn't," Ned confirmed.

"Said I should buy something for my wife, so I got her some new fur muffs for the winter. She always looked quite pretty in muffs. And I got Georgiana some rouge, the pretty penny kind from France. And I treated myself to a meal down at a gourmet Italian place that had just opened up. It had the best wine and veal parmesan…"

"Sir, could you find it in your heart to intervene for Nevison?" Ned blurted. "Amongst Anglicans, he considers you one of the good ones because of your courtesy towards us Catholics. Could not that courtesy extend to him?"

Burgoyne raised an eyebrow. "You want me to try and slip his neck out of the hangman's noose, after he's dedicated himself to a lifetime of crime, including humiliating the officials of both the Church and State?"

"If it can be managed, yes."

"It is the King's prerogative if mercy is to be shown, Ned," Burgoyne reminded him.

"I know," Ned replied, "and you are just the man to present a petition, being the one he has chosen to reclaim the colonies. Would you? For me?"

"I thought we weren't going to press each other on the basis of friendship," Burgoyne replied, a little tartly.

Ned laced his arm through the general's once more, and waited.

Burgoyne was quiet for a long while, then sighed. "Well," he said, "can't hurt my reputation to try and save a self-styled Robin Hood, I suppose."

"Besides, sir, he's a fellow Lancashire man!" Ned added. "Can't let those infernal Yorkists misuse one of our own, can we?"

"Wouldn't be fitting or proper," Burgoyne agreed. "We beat them in the dynastic wars because our rose was full-blooded, while theirs was sickly white. We both come from the loins of those who sent them running, and I have no doubt that we'll beat them again, here and now, in this little matter of our native highwayman."

Edmund beamed as they neared the greenhouse. "One more thing."

"Yes?" Burgoyne queried.

Ned ducked inside the building and emerged with a pot of flowers. "Rose Campion, for His Majesty, in return for his button." He placed the plant in the general's hands. "Do treat it well. I know the King loves green, growing things."

Burgoyne squinted at the flowers as Ned handed him the pot. "Did I ever mention that, unlike His Majesty, keeping houseplants alive is not among my vast array of talents? They seem to once look at me, even from across the room, and wilt."

"Surely your servants can manage to sustain it," Ned countered.

"They do try, but again, the plant gets one look at me and…" He snapped his fingers. "*Finito de musico.*"

"Just talk to the plant sometimes, and tell it that it must stay healthy, because it's going to belong to a king soon," Ned instructed.

"You put stock in talking to plants then?"

"Father did," Ned replied.

Burgoyne sighed. "So much like him, the dear old man." He smiled sadly. "I wish he could have lived to see how the two of us have gotten on."

Ned smiled in return. "Me too."

"Well, don't just stand there! Deposit this poor plant into my carriage so I don't have to carry it about! The less immediate interaction it has with me, the better!"

Ned did as he was told, entrusting it to the coachman who tucked it up nicely with a blanket in the back seat. "Fare-thee-well," Ned bid the flowers adieu.

When he returned, Burgoyne was checking his pocket watch. "I assume you had a nice long conversation with your blossoms on the best ways to survive me?"

"I merely bid them well, knowing they were going to a loving home."

Burgoyne rolled his eyes. "Well, if they are anything like you, fresh from surviving an excursion to York, they'll muddle through the time spent at my humble abode somehow!"

"I knew I would make it out of York alright," Ned said. "I prayed to King Henry VI of the Lancastrians, patron of arts and education, whose resting place saw many miracles…"

"Fie, Ned, you do love the losers, don't you?" Burgoyne chuckled.

"It does not matter if he lost his earthly goods, his kingdom, even his life during the civil wars, not in the long run," Ned insisted. "What matters is that he loved God and loved his neighbor."

"Yes, but he was a weak king," Burgoyne replied.

"But a strong Christian," Ned countered. "That, in the end, is what counts. He might have been canonized, if not for that other king, tarnishing his good name."

Burgoyne shook his head. "Here I am, trying to lure you with the rising of our esteemed empire, going from success to success, and here you are, on your knees in the shadows somewhere, beseeching a dethroned sovereign."

"I wish nothing but good upon our empire," Ned stated. "But look at the empire of Rome. It seemed as if it would last forever. Now its ruins are everywhere. We cannot know how long our own fortunes will last. The Church lives because of those who lost everything, like saintly King Henry, yet called for his psalter in hand and the Eucharist upon the tongue, and forgave his enemies, and bore his suffering with patience. These are the things that last, the things that make England eternal."

"He asked for his lap dog and his song bird too, if I recall," Burgoyne remarked, "and spoke to the guards like they were his brothers. Mad, they said, gone stark mad."

"They called him a madman when he said no Christian man should be hanged, drawn and quartered," Ned noted, "and again when he dressed simply and would not be disturbed in prayer. But I think the world was mad, and he was sane. Or whatever madness he had was a miracle, in and of itself."

"So you'd hurl yourself in front of your feeble-minded, holy king, and defend him to the last, in the midst of all his losses, and the sword pointed at his head?"

"Mmm-hmm," Edmund concurred. "I am a true Lancastrian, as are you."

Burgoyne laughed. "God knows, I do love you, Ned!" His voice sounded as if the laughter might suddenly switch over to tears, and he wobbled a bit in his stance..

Ned swallowed hard. "Likewise," he murmured, then took his arm, steadying him. Burgoyne was not at all well.

All the same, they continued walking, the general seemingly determined to rise above it all, and Edmund feeling the need to play along with him.

"So tell me, Ned, what did you see today when you went roving over hill and moor on the long road home?"

"Puddles," he replied. "It rained something terrible last night. Oh, and a raven feather. It was floating in the water, and glistening in the sun. The black looked almost blue."

"Good luck or bad luck?"

"I don't know," Ned admitted, "but it was a thing of beauty to me."

"Of course," Burgoyne sighed, "to you."

"I also met a few of the farm children from hereabouts. They were out tending their landlord's sheep. The girls, going on ten years, were carding wool and gossiping."

"A pastoral idyll," Burgoyne declared. "Did they pass on any good gossip to you?"

"Oh…they were talking about your campaign."

Burgoyne's eyes widened. "Fame has found me at last!"

"They are rather worried about forests that may have wolves, Indians, and rebels who know how to climb trees…"

The general snorted. "They say the funniest things at that age, you know. I think it's because they start imitating their mothers…wives and daughters always tend to fret so…" He paused briefly, and Ned saw a look come over his face as if he felt a sudden pain in his side.

"Are you alright?" Ned asked concernedly, as Burgoyne leaned his weight more heavily upon Ned's arm.

"Just a stitch," Burgoyne dismissed. "Silly me, forgot my walking cane…I hardly ever do that…" They were just coming up to the sheep pen, and the general pointed at it. "Oh, look," he remarked. "A baby sheep."

"A lamb," Ned chuckled.

"Yes, exactly what I said," Burgoyne insisted. "Who made that adorable knit jumper it's wearing?"

"Tessie," Ned replied. "It's been a cold spring."

"Of course, dear Tessie," Burgoyne chuckled. "She has a maternal heart." He elbowed Ned in the side. "You finally got a ram in among the ewes, I take it?"

Ned nodded. "One of our neighbors agreed that one of his rams and our ewes should breed for a price. We didn't have the money before the Portuguese investments. The lamb, in a way, is your doing."

"I must admit, sheep are dazzling to the eye after the rain has washed their wool white…" He broke off from his musing and teased, "Are you going to make me feed them?"

Ned's mouth twitched, and he promptly hopped the fence.

"How do you manage to do it that fast?" Burgoyne sighed.

"Training," Ned replied, getting out a bucket of oats from the barn. "Come on over."

"Don't you have a gate, like any civilized sort of establishment would?"

"I want to test your mettle."

"Still trying to inflict Romish torture on heretics, I see."

"Really now…you were never in union with the Church to start with, so it's a bit hard for you to claim the title of a proper heretic!"

"Regardless, I'm getting old!"

"I don't believe that. Neither do you."

Burgoyne groaned, then reluctantly climbed the fence.

"There, you see? Not quite so old." Ned shoved a bucket of oats at him, and stepped away.

"You realize I was joking about feeding them, don't you? Oh, hell's teeth…"

Before the situation could be contained, the general was mobbed by several very hungry sheep.

"Just be assertive, and they'll wait their turn," Ned assured. "They can sense when you're not being assertive enough…"

"My arm is about to snap," Burgoyne stated flatly, as two of the sheep stuck their heads in the bucket simultaneously, munching away for all they were worth.

"My arm never snapped," Ned replied with a shrug. "You'll make it, most likely."

"Most likely?! I'm about to be eaten again, and you're just standing there! Oh…baby sheep…"

Baby sheep had indeed finally fought his way to the front, but instead of going for the bucket, obtusely started to nibble on the bandage poking out from Burgoyne's sleeve. For a moment the general twitched, and Ned thought to go over to him, but he quickly recovered himself, and laughed awkwardly through his teeth.

He tapped the lamb on the nose as some form of a reprimand, and muttered, "Silly Billy…"

And Ned felt his heart bleed a little, even as he saw a bit of blood seeping through the white edge of Burgoyne's bandage.

Ned whistled, and Kip finally sprung into action, chasing the sheep away from the general. Then Ned went over to his guest and started to pull up his sleeve.

"Now don't do that," Burgoyne grumbled, pulling away.

"It needs fixing," Ned stated, "and I'm determined to fix it."

"It was scabbing over so nicely, until your monster sheep got a hold of me," Burgoyne lamented.

"Sorry," Ned exhaled, starting to unwrap the bandage. "I just thought feeding sheep might make you feel...better. It usually makes me feel that way..." He winced at the sight of the cut trickling blood. "Oh..."

"You don't have to show it to me," Burgoyne sighed. "My own blood makes me feel ill. Just wrap it up tight."

"Of course," Ned replied, winding the bandage.

"Ouch, not *that* tight," Burgoyne scolded him.

"Sorry," Ned repeated. "I'll be gentler..."

Burgoyne chuckled, then reached out and cupped Edmund's chin in his hand. "You can't help but be gentle. You're like one of your lambs, Ned, with a white fleece after the rain."

Edmund blushed, then brushed off the bits of wool and oats stuck to Burgoyne's cloak. "Well, now that the sheep have eaten, it's about time we did the same."

He spied old Tobias, once more dragging about his mulch bag, and beckoned for him to go into the house to alert the family that a guest was there. The servant gave Ned a strange look before hurrying off into the house, and Ned worried something wasn't right.

After stalling for as long as he could with more small talk involving his tour of York, Edmund finally escorted Burgoyne inside the house. Kip was stationed between them and the stairs, and to Ned's surprise, he immediately flattened his ears and growled.

"Down, boy, down," Edmund scolded.

"I stayed away too long," Burgoyne chuckled, sadness glimmering in his eyes.

Ned felt an increased uneasiness. Kip seemed determined to keep anyone from going upstairs. He only acted that way when...

Burgoyne clicked his tongue and reached his hand out slowly towards Kip. His scent seemed to finally register, and the dog stopped growling. He even let Burgoyne pet him. Nevertheless, he remained slightly crouched, remaining at his post between them and the stairs.

A few moments later, Teresa came down to greet them, her hair particularly messy. Ned noticed a hair pin still stuck in one of the curling strands...the kind she would wear to keep her lace chapel veil in place during holy mass. His heart sank.

"Teresa, dear girl!" Burgoyne exclaimed exuberantly, taking her hands in his.

She had a rather stunned look on her face as she curtsied to him. "Sir..."

Burgoyne tilted his head, and remarked, with some palpable hurt, "You don't seem very happy to see me, Tessie."

"Oh, yes, sir, I am, truly, it's just...I didn't expect..." She brushed a loose piece of hair out of her forehead. "I-I didn't expect to see you today..."

"Not a completely unpleasant surprise, I trust?" Burgoyne chuckled, then glanced around him, as if he thought there might be other eyes watching him.

"No, no, General...I'm so glad...so very glad you've safely returned to us. I prayed for you every night..."

"In a veil, my little nun?" Burgoyne chuckled, plucking the pin out of her hair.

She blushed. "Sometimes I cover my head to pray, yes. Do you disapprove?"

"With my fancy for headgear, I don't suppose I can condemn you," he remarked lightly. "I do recall my lady wife was made to wear a veil when touring Romish churches on the continent. Had to purchase her a whole case of pins to keep the thing in place. She didn't much like it, lest she be mistaken for a foreigner. But you're a good English lass as ever there was one, aren't you, Tessie?"

She swallowed. "I like to think so, sir."

"You're just like your brother. Sweetly evasive."

Ned met his sister's gaze briefly. Was the priest still there? Had a mass been going on? Were the congregants in the attic? Yes, her eyes told him. Yes.

"Still keeping up with your music, love?" Burgoyne queried.

"Yes, sir," Tessie squeaked. "It is of great solace to me…"

"Splendid," he said, proffered his arm. "Then you will play for me? I fought off hordes of dissatisfied colonials and braved the raging seas just to hear you perform!"

Reluctantly, she curtsied and took his arm. He led her into the parlor, and she nervously began to sort through sheet music spread out over the top of the harpsichord. She seemed to see something that startled her and accidentally dropped it. Before she could retrieve it, Burgoyne, ever gallant, did so for her. Then he stopped and stared.

Edmund saw that it was an engraving of the Madonna and Child, no doubt illegally printed with a Latin prayer on the back.

"It-it's based off of a painting from Italy," Tessie explained hurriedly.

"I know," Burgoyne murmured, his eyes misty, fixated upon the engraving.

Ned inhaled, fearing the general would interrogate her or turn the image over. But he remained silent, staring at the picture, and Tessie touched his arm.

"It…is of great solace to me, just like music…yes, I look at it, and my playing becomes a prayer…"

He just nodded, and kept staring.

She tugged on his sleeve a little. "I…I'm so very sorry about your wife…"

He did not turn to her, but he did respond by reaching over with one hand and patting hers. His eyes were still soaking in the image.

Suddenly, Perpetua came rushing into the room and snatched the engraving out of Burgoyne's hands. "How dare you!" she spat. "Have you not taken enough from us? Where on God's earth will you leave us alone?!"

"Madam, stop," Ned blurted, fearing that her panic might expose them to greater danger.

"He's poisoned you!" she screamed at Ned. "He poisons everything he touches! He will drown in his own sin, and take you down with him!"

"Madam, you don't know what you're saying," Ned panted. "Apologize to the general!"

"I will never repent of speaking the truth!" Perpetua declared. Then she turned on Burgoyne again, who was staring at her in shock. "You already failed as a husband and father! You have no right to corrupt my son!"

Edmund grimaced at her cutting words, and the general's face turned red with rage.

"Take care, Madam, if you wish to keep your name!" Burgoyne shouted, full-throated and terrifying. "Take great care, lest you make an enemy of me, and I pull your roof down over your head!"

Teresa turned white, sank into a nearby chair, then burst into tears.

Burgoyne stared at her for several moments, then the color drained from his face too. "Tessie…don't cry…" he rasped, taking a step towards her. "You know I would never…wish to hurt you…oh, please, dear girl, don't cry…"

The general's voice broke as he reached a hand towards Teresa to comfort her, and Ned felt his own heart breaking.

Burgoyne had barely touched her cheek when Perpetua thrust herself between them. "You'll not lay a hand on her! Take the house, if you want! Take this land, take our name, take my life, even take my son, if he's sold his soul to the devil! But you'll not take my daughter too! You'll not tarnish her with your touch!"

"Mother, stop, stop, please, stop!" Teresa wept.

Burgoyne bit his lip again, trembling with rage. Then he glanced over to Teresa, pity cutting through the fury in his eyes. At last, he turned and stormed out of the room, towards the door.

Ned just stood there in front of his sister and mother, stunned for several moments, before turning away as well and following after Burgoyne. He was already well ahead of Ned, and nearing his carriage by the time the younger man caught up. He gave a terse wave to his coachman, who had been watering the horses at a nearby trough, and the coachman prepared to hitch them up again.

"Sir, please…I beg you…" Ned panted.

"Damn it, Ned, leave me a while," the general snapped, in a manner unlike himself as he shut the carriage door, and Ned stepped back a few paces, not sure what to do or where to go, but the tears filled his eyes.

A few minutes later, Burgoyne called over, "Ned, come to me."

He did so, though was not successful in stopping his own tears.

"Oh, look," Burgoyne sighed. "I made you cry too. This just isn't my day, I'm afraid…"

Ned could not help but notice Burgoyne's eyes were red.

"Please, sir," he whispered. "Forgive me for what was said…"

"It was not from your mouth," he stated quietly.

"But it was under our roof," Ned insisted.

"Indeed," he sighed. "But for your sake, and your sister's sake, I will not hang your house out to dry, regardless of your mother's disposition towards me."

A tear slipped down Ned's face. "Will I ever see you again?"

Burgoyne opened the carriage door, extended the handkerchief already in his hand, and brushed the boy's cheek with it. "I thought you knew, after all this time, that my affection towards you cannot alter, least of all after your kindness to my lady."

"It was my own good pleasure to keep her company," Edmund assured.

Burgoyne smiled slightly, letting his gaze wander. "The engraving, Ned," he said quietly. "I wasn't about to report it…"

"I did not think you were going to," Edmund assured.

"You must understand, when I appeared taken aback, it was out of some sudden surge of iconoclasm," the general clarified. "I am not quite so zealous. No, as a matter of fact…long ago, in Italy, I acted on another one of my whims and purchased a painting with a very similar image…as Charlotte told you, I had a bad habit of bleeding out our money when it came to art that I fancied, but this time…I-I bought it as a present…I meant it for her, because she had given birth to little Charlotte not long before and…oh…I was happier than I ever had a right to be, and I suppose I thought there must be something absolutely divine in it…"

"Surely there is, in every new life," Edmund replied quietly.

Burgoyne's eyes glazed. "Oh, Ned, sometimes I have dreams, such dreams…little paintings of my life, so much like that painting of yours.…with her, always her, and the baby on her lap. She was so young, and just became a mother, and there was still a glow about her, and she wore her hair loose…" He gestured awkwardly, as if frustrated with himself for being assaulted by such memories. "And she had a rattle, for little Charlotte…I can still hear it. I don't know where it is now. But I hear it. The baby, though…she was always more interested in playing with her mother's hair…" There was a click in the back of his throat. "And then I wake up from such dreams, such memories…and I don't have the desire for anything in this life. No, even my carnal appetites run dry. It's terrifying."

Edmund felt his eyes tear up again. "I'm sorry…"

"Oh…don't be. I'm a writer, Ned. When it's as bad as it can get, I start to make up stories in my head, just threads sometimes that are not at all tied together. But you know something? That makes me want to get up, because I must live to know how all the threads can be tied together. I like to tell stories, and fancy the whole world to be one great story, and I need to stay in it to find out just how the plot will unfold. It is my little salvation. Do you understand, Ned?"

"Yes," Ned replied. "I too see stories everywhere."

"And so we are friends," Burgoyne declared, taking his hand. "My best young friend." He smiled oddly. "And I suppose if the stories stop coming, the long slumber of forgetfulness may prove welcome enough in the end." He winced. "I…went into the baby's room, when I was drunk the other night. That was my undoing…"

Ned winced. "Remember, sir, that you are a Christian."

He laughed, as if it were a joke he did not really find funny, but wanted to make the one telling it feel good. "Am I?"

"Yes," Edmund returned firmly.

Burgoyne sighed. "She…told you to tell me that, didn't she?"

"She said you needed reminding sometimes."

"Astute in her observations as always, bless her soul," he sighed. "Though I suppose the long sleep is a more pleasant alternative to where I might be heading."

"And do you believe she's gone to sleep forever?"

"No," he shot down. "No, no, she's an angel, in heaven, with the baby." He touched his chest. "That I would believe, if I lost every other shred of faith allotted me. I suppose I just hoped that, if God was very unhappy with me…He would let it all go dark, but painless…"

"The dread of facing God is surely less than the dread of not facing God," Ned murmured. "We may not see the face of God and live, but what is life without the hope of seeing Him? No, no, I cannot ever lose that hope, not for me or you!"

Burgoyne smiled. "So you will keep reminding me?"

"Always."

"Even when I don't want you to?"

"Especially then."

Burgoyne giggled and shook his head. "Charlotte trained you well." He glanced over at the potted campion flower in the coach, and held it up. "I'll see that His Majesty receives this when I return to London in a fortnight."

Ned swallowed the lump in his throat. "I knew you would, sir."

After Burgoyne's coach pulled away, Edmund returned to the house, a long subdued anger boiling in his blood. He found Perpetua, kneeling in prayer, with the engraving in her hands, murmuring Latin under her breath, ignoring him.

"Poorly done, Madam," he choked. "Very poorly done…"

She continued to act like he wasn't there.

"Look at me, Mother!"

"I am not in the habit of having my devotions interrupted by anyone, much less my prodigal child," she replied.

"I am no child, but the master of this house, and you will hear me out!" he cried, clenching his fists at his side.

She finally turned around, her eyes cutting him to the bone. "So you have thrown out the fourth commandment altogether under that man's tutelage?"

"He is in mourning, Mother," Ned ground out. "You pressed him to the brink, and nearly brought his wrath down upon us! Brought his wrath down upon…" His voice grew quieter, anxiety drumming in his chest, and at last he whispered, "Is-is the priest still here?"

Perpetua's face remained unreadable as she retorted, "It is none of your affair! You have chosen your general over this family!"

"Have you gone mad?" Ned blurted. "I have refused all offers made to me! If our safety was at such risk, and a priest's life in peril, how could you have been so senseless as to provoke the general as you did?"

"If a priest was in danger, you would be the one responsible for bringing that man into this house! As such, you will never know, one way or the other from me!"

Ned felt a deep hurt in his soul at her distrust of him. "There was no reason to lash out at him as you did," he rasped. "He was not about to betray us. He was…suffering. He's newly widowed, mother. Could you not see his pain?"

"Pain, you say?" she repeated incredulously. "Yes, perhaps the only thing he keeps on him in the brothel bed is the black arm band…"

"How can you be so cruel? You don't even know him!" Ned blurted in disgust. "You don't know what goes on inside his mind!"

"And you do?" she pressed.

"We have confided in one another, under the bond of friendship…"

"Don't delude yourself, son. He'd abandon you when the first ill-fated wind began to blow."

"What I fear most is what he might do to himself," Ned responded. "He may go back to his house, and hurt himself, and it will be our fault!"

"He won't do any such thing," she scoffed. "He wants to be a hero for his heretic king."

Ned's face flushed. "Our king too, Mother."

Perpetua raised an eyebrow. "Is he? From an illegitimate line?"

"That's treason," Ned blurted.

"Yes, because that man brought you out to kiss the Hanoverian hand in London, and now you are besotted with spectacle."

"No, because our king is a worthy gentleman, who has earned his crown beyond mere birth, but by virtue of his comportment," Edmund replied, "and because the Jacobite cause is dead. Do not revive it amongst us to our peril."

"Are you going to arrest me for it, to prove yourself a good Englishman to Burgoyne?" Perpetua challenged. "We may be in this world, but we are not of it."

"Your platitudes do not absolve you of your callousness," Ned replied, gesturing at the engraving. "I know him, I tell you. He wasn't going to report us. He saw the Madonna and Child and thought of his family, gone down to the grave. You cut him to pieces with your words…"

"His child was likely as illegitimate as he was, and as his king is," she shot back. "They say Burgoyne is a false lord, yes, that his father was no Burgoyne at all! I've no doubt of it! His mother had a reputation for being as whorish as his wife!"

"Madam, I will not stand for this…"

"You see? You can't bear to hear anything against that woman!" Perpetua declared. "She seduced you, in God's truth, for all her pious pretensions! That man has a mind only for blasphemy, comparing her to the Blessed Virgin, and their offspring to Christ, conceived in God knows what circumstances…"

"Enough!" Ned screamed, and a tear ran down his cheek.

"You cry over them, but not what your own mother has been through!" Perpetua rasped. "No, you never shed a tear over that!"

"You use the torments of your childhood to jostle yourself into God's throne and judge the world!" Ned said hotly. "You believe that you alone have merited God's favor, but think little enough upon His grace! You make a mockery of your own faith!"

"You are one to talk of such things," she whispered, and her eyes were glistening too. "You have betrayed the faith…" She swayed a little, steadying herself with a hand against the wall. "It's all my fault…I should never have let you play with those heretics as a child…I tried so very hard, and still they came, as they always come, and took you away from me…"

"Mother," Edmund addressed her softly, realizing all at once that she was nearly as sick as Burgoyne, and going over to support her.

But she pulled away from him and shrieked, "Get out! Get out of my house! You are a prodigal, and bring nothing but shame to it and to me! Now get out!" With that, she broke down sobbing, burying her face in her folded arms, pressed up against the wall.

Ned stood there, stunned for several moments. Then, not wishing to upset her further, he made his way to the door.

Chapter 14: NATURAL ATTACHMENT

By late afternoon, Edmund found himself back in the village, having nowhere better to go until his mother's mood improved. Sergeant Beeby was on the village green with a handful of his soldiers, standing on a crate and trying to coax locals to take the king's shilling and sign up for Burgoyne's March. He seemed to be having some success, as young men of all backgrounds lined up to go and fight the rebels. He felt a sudden burst of local pride, undercut by a mix of guilt and concern. What would be their fate? Could he live with himself if he did not share in it?

Then he saw Jamie, the fourteen-year-old stable hand whom Fanny was sweet on, lining up as well. No, no, Edmund thought. He was too young, surely. But there were so many youths going. No, even so, he was such a small thing, tough yet tiny. He couldn't go. Maybe in a couple of years from now, but not now. He found himself going over to the boy, who was about as hostile to Catholics as they came, who had pelted him with balls of slushy snow and mud for many winters, and tried to reason with him.

"Off to war, when you've not even filled out your uncle's shirt?" Ned queried, gesturing to his grubby hand-me-down clothes.

"I be old for my age in all the ways it counts," Jamie declared. "I can hold me a musket better than you can, that's a fact. I've practiced with Uncle Barney's old one. You can't touch such a thing, because that you're a Papist."

"Holding a musket is different from fighting hand to hand with a bayonet to save your life," Ned countered.

Jamie shrugged. "I'm not a scaredy cat. Besides, fighting Yankees sounds better than mucking out stables and cleaning up Uncle Barney's vomit when he's soused."

Ned changed tactics. "You know what most boys your age and size are set to doing in the army? That's right…fetching for officers and tending horses. And you know what the Yankees are busy doing? Shooting at the officers. And you know who they're just as likely to hit? You! None too glamorous, being shot in the back while polishing an officer's boots or slipping a feedbag on a baggage mare…"

Jamie opened his mouth, then closed it.

"Besides, how will the apprentice boys get on without you here? You are their head."

"Well…aye, their brain," Jamie decided, tapping his temple.

"Right, so…don't you have a duty to them? Their masters might not be as willing to let them go off as yours has been, and they'll be left here…brainless."

Jamie turned his eyes down and kicked at a pebble with his worn shoe.

Ned lay a hand on his shoulder. "You know, Fanny likes having you here."

"She'd like it better if I did something smashing," he mumbled.

"No, she likes you fine as you are," Ned insisted. "She wants you to be safe. At least give it a few years, boy…"

"Ease up, Southy," came a sardonic voice from behind them. We Protestants like to make up our own mind without Papal interference!"

Ned turned to see Jack Randall, the vicar's eldest son, standing behind them in his scarlet tunic and gilded gorget. He possessed devilish good looks, with mischief glittering in his dark eyes, and an arrogant grin on his face. His martial kit suited his figure to a tee. He had been a fixture in Ned's life for as far back as he could remember, for good and ill, and was possibly the last person in the world that he was in the mood to see.

"Not today, Jack," Ned exhaled.

"Oh, beg your pardon, noble gentleman," Jack mocked him, making a sloppy sign of the cross to add salt to the wounds. "I'll beat myself bloody for my insolence towards a knight of old!"

"Stop it, Jack."

"Oh, that's right…you have no taste for blood these days. That's why you want us all to emulate your sanctity and hide behind our mothers' skirts now that the guns have started cracking. See, it's a form of old Romish magic to keep yourself snug in bed for the duration, though you've not been able to lure a companion under the sheets with you to make the wait warmer…"

"You've a filthy mouth," Ned ground out, turning and walking away from him.

But Jack pursued him a ways down the street. "Or is it just that our King isn't to your taste, hmm? You'll only swear fealty to the bloody Bishop of Rome, and to hell with the rest of us heretics, if we die today or tomorrow…"

"Jack, enough!"

"Maybe I was too kind, thinking the sight of our blood might bother you. Maybe British blood slick on the grass of Boston's hills and roads does nothing to you, on account that it's foreign to your veins…"

This was the last straw.

Overcome with a blur of emotions, Ned whirled around and punched him. The force of the blow knocked him against a nearby gate, and he struggled momentarily to stay upright.

Jack touched his nose, saw the blood on his fingers, and snorted. "Well, you know how to draw it, I'll give you that…"

Ned felt suddenly ashamed. He had not only broken his promise to his father, but also attacked his countryman in a time of war.

But before he could properly respond or apologize, he felt his arms yanked behind his back, and realized he was surrounded by Beeby's soldiers.

"You struck a Protestant subject of His Majesty, and worse yet, one of his newly minted officers!" Beeby declared. "It'll go hard on you, Papist!"

A small crowd had gathered along the street to observe the ruckus, and villagers and soldiers alike started jeering at him.

Ned felt his palms grow clammy. His grandfather's fate at the hands of a mob of former friends haunted him. Worse yet, he might be hauled off before a court, and the punishment for his rash action would fall upon his family.

"Jack," Ned rasped, panic spreading through his chest. "Please, Jack…"

Jack rolled his eyes, but after a few moments, he instructed the soldiers, "Eh, now, lads, you can loosen your hold on him."

"Why should they, Lieutenant?" the sergeant demanded.

"This one here's just feeling his oats, Beeby," Jack said. "Couldn't hurt a fly."

"Flies notwithstanding, sir," Beeby huffed, "this is wartime, and you are an officer."

"We used to tangle all the time growing up," Jack explained. "Brazen little Papist, I know, but I indulged it, and gave as good as I got. He's just not used to seeing me in uniform yet, is all."

"And what will get him used to it, sir, but a firm hand?" Beeby demanded.

"Oh, I'm all for a firm hand…"

Jack turned and threw a punch, so hard that it caused Ned to fall backwards onto the cobblestones, to the laughter of the crowd and soldiers who had been apprehending him. He put his hands to his nose, and was relieved nothing seemed broken, though he felt warm liquid trickling down his upper lip.

"There," said Jack cheerfully. "Fair's fair."

"Alright, we'll have it your way, Lieutenant," the sergeant conceded grudgingly, then turned around and shouted at the pedestrians, "but this is the last disturbance on the streets I'll tolerate from any of you lot!"

When Beeby had finally sauntered off with his soldiers, and the crowd dispersed, Jack extended a hand to Ned. "Buy you a pint?"

Soon they were both in the Cross Keys Inn, promised pints in hand. Jack had also purchased them cherry cobbler and slabs of yellow cheese. He was already running up quite a bill with Mister Vernon, which would need to be paid up, somehow or other, before setting sail. But Jack, touting his uniform for all it was worth, managed to take advantage of the proprietor's patriotic feelings. Ned had a feeling Jack's vicar father would be the one left behind to settle his son's debt.

"Now, then, no hard feelings," coaxed Jack as he munched on the crumbly cheese. "I didn't mean you to take what was said to heart…"

"Jack, if a man imputed cowardice to your name on a public street, you'd likely challenge him to a duel," Ned stated, dabbing at his bloodied nose with a napkin.

Jack shrugged. "That's different."

"How so?"

"Well, you're…"

"I'm what?"

Jack sighed. "If you don't want folk making sport of you, the best thing for it would be to cut ties with your hedge priests and come in with us. We'll fight the King's enemies together, and no one will dare snigger at you, even me."

"You make it sound so easy," Ned ground out, taking another deep drink.

"You want to strike a blow for Old England, don't you?" Jack queried, and there was an earnestness in his voice now. "I remember, you always wanted to play General Wolfe during our games…"

"What do you want from me, Jack? You know I'm not allowed!"

"I want to know if you're on our side, that's all," Jack huffed. "I've grown up with you, played soldiers with you, yet I don't *know* you. Do you have any natural attachment at all towards us? Do you have any natural attachment to this land…our land?"

"My family is as old as yours," Ned shot back. "This is my home as much as yours!"

"Then why won't you fight for her? For us?"

"Your people won't let me!" Ned replied bitterly. "Not without…betraying myself…"

"We are yourself, not Rome!" Jack blurted, and pounded his fist on the table. Then his eyes softened. "We are yourself, Ned. This place and this people. This public house where we drink three too many…"

"Yes, you tend to lure me into such indiscretions, ever and anon, then make fun of me for not walking home straight and claim Catholics simply have a weakness for the stuff from attending secret masses where Italian wine flows," Ned sighed.

"And the Pennington Barn where we have the harvest dances…"

"You like to corner the market on all the female attendees, and then tell me I will be a male spinster because my clothes have been feasted upon by Jacobite moths…"

"And the cow field where we pummeled each other when we were small…"

"You started those fights nine out of ten times," Ned noted.

"And won as many," Jack beamed.

Ned rolled his eyes.

"Then there's the stream where we threw stones and sailed our toy boats…"

"Yes, you threw stones at my little paper ships and sank most of them, pretending they were the Spanish Armada, because, of course, that's what my ships would be…and when I protested, you pushed me in the water and laughed…"

"But I pulled you out again," Jack added.

"Yes, but I could have caught my death, soaking wet…"

"And we mustn't forget our favorite hill, where we still have climbing contests," Jack continued. "Oh, come on, we do have fun at that, don't we? I can show you a good time when I want. It's a gorgeous hill. I'd be happy to be buried on that hill someday."

Ned swallowed hard. "Jack…"

"But there you have it. All those things and more, Ned. They're…us. That's because we can't really own a place that hasn't owned us first. It calls, and we answer."

Ned smirked. "Damn poetical of you."

"You know me, Ned. I'm an earth-bound creature. I must be able to see something with my eyes, feel something with my hands. I'm not the most devout lad when it comes to things I cannot see, try as my old man might. I love him, but I'm afraid I only give him grief."

"Well, I notice you still bless your meat pies, at least," Ned observed.

"I grew up in a parsonage, don't you know?" Jack grumbled. "Everybody watching everything I do. And God…" He pointed upward. "Well, He…He is a spy for my father!"

Ned nearly spit out a mouthful of ale.

"But anyway," Jack continued, "I don't know much about the ins and outs of theologies, nor tax policies, for that matter. But I say, God save the King, head of church and state, and I'm game to bloody a few damn Yankee noses in his name."

Ned bit his lip. "What if everything I've ever been taught is true, and God doesn't like this arrangement between the church and state one bit? What if He doesn't want me to go?"

"If He didn't want you to go, He wouldn't have had you born in Lancashire! We're fighters!" Jack declared.

Edmund felt sick to his stomach. "Tell me, Jack…why should the King be head of the Church? No…I know you are not proficient in theologies…"

"Because he's our head, that's why," Jack stated. "A body can't have two heads. And like a body, everything's connected. It's like this for me…the King is England, and England is Lancashire, and Lancashire is the village, and the village is us. And I'd be damn proud to fight, or die, among us, and for the honor of the King, that reflects back on us." He reached over and touched Ned's arm. "I-I reckon I'd be damn proud to fight with you too, if you threw in your lot with us…"

Ned stared past Jack, making no response, his heart at war with itself.

"Alright, fine," Jack snorted. "Go off to kiss the bloody pope's ring and become a bloody Swiss guard, for all I care…"

"You know what a Swiss guard is?" Ned queried, genuinely surprised.

"Go off and become a Wild Goose in the gardens of Versailles!"

"They were Irish, and I don't think I have extravagant enough sensibilities for Versailles…"

"Go to Spain, grab a torch, and join the Inquisition!"

"Look, we've all had a history of getting a bit overly enthused about bonfires…"

"Or maybe you'd like to join this war on the side of the rebels, and demand your liberation with fire and sword…"

"Jack!"

Even Jack seemed to know what he said could be dangerous, and he quickly covered for himself. "Naw, the Yankees wouldn't take you, I'm afraid. They've got little enough time for your kind up in Canada. And you've got too much pride to throw in your lot with a pack of good-for-nothing colonials." Jacked beamed. "So go back to your mother, shut yourself up in a priest hole, and knit relics into stockings for some saint or other's festival day!"

The corner of Ned's mouth twitched. "Alright, this is getting silly…"

"Of course, it is," Jack conceded. "That was my third pint!"

Ned laughed in spite of himself, and Jack broke down and joined in.

The sound of "God Save the King" being played rather badly on a harpsichord in the corner of the tavern was soon joined by the voices of local recruits, all with tankards in their hands.

"Well," said Jack. "I'll be with them. Come join us, if you care to."

Jack got up from the table, and Edmund remained seated there, all alone.

The moments crawled by, and the voices raised in song continued through the verses of the royal anthem. Finally, Edmund drank down the last of his pint. Then he, too, left the table, and joined the others. As he sang softly, badly, as he always did, he felt Jack put his arm around him. He made bashful eye contact with some of the other recruits, most of whom he knew from his youth, and although a few muttered japes under their breath about him missing out on the fun to come across the water, they let him be a part of their little clique in the moment. It was, after all, their village, held in common, come what may.

After the royal anthem and several subsequent patriotic songs including "Rule, Britannia", "See How the Conquering Hero Comes", and "Britons, Strike Home" had concluded, Jack stood up on a bench, raised his mug of ale, and started to sing a rural ballad with mysterious imagery as old as the land itself…

"John Barleycorn was a hero bold,
As any in the land!
For ages good, his fame has stood,
And shall forever stand!
And when the reaping time comes 'round,
And John is stricken down,
He'll shed his blood for England's good,
For Englishmen's renown!

There were three men out of the west,
Their fortunes for to try,
And these three men made a solemn vow,
John Barleycorn must die.
They plowed, they sowed, they harrowed him in,
Put clods all over his head,
And these three men made a solemn vow,
John Barleycorn was dead.

They laid him there for a very long time
Till rain from the heavens did fall,
Then Barleycorn sprang up again,
Which quite amazed them all,
They let him lie till midsummer,
Till he grew both pale and wan,
Then little Sir John, he grew a long gray beard,
And so became a man.

They hired men with scythes so sharp,
To cut him off at the knee,
They rolled him and tied him about the waist,
And served him barbarously.
They hired men with sharp pitch folks,
And pierced him to the heart,
But the loader he served him much worse than that,
For he tied him to the cart.

They rolled him and wheeled him around the field,
Till they came unto a barn,
And then these men made a solemn vow over poor John Barleycorn.
They hired men with crabtree sticks to strip him skin from bone,
And the miller he served him much worse than that,
For he ground him between two stones.

They put him in a cistern deep,
And drowned him in water clear,
And then they brewed him worse than that,
They brewed him into the beer.
Put white wine in a bottle, boys,
And brandy in a can,
And Barleycorn in a brown bowl,
Will prove the better man!

Here's little Sir John in the nut brown bowl,
And the brandy in the glass,
And little Sir John in the nut brown bowl proves the strongest man at last!
For the huntsman he can't chase the fox,
Nor so loudly blow his horn,
And the tinker he can't mend his kettles or his pans,
Without a little bit of Barleycorn!

Aye, English cheer is English beer,
Our own John Barleycorn!"

Ned clapped along with the others as Jack gulped down his pint. No one could deny Jack had been blessed with a good singing voice, far better than Ned's poor efforts, and he managed to make the strange song of the English soil sink into Ned's soul. He remembered his father telling him about the lyrics as a child.

"You see, dear Ned," he remembered his father saying, "We were pagans once, and during the harvest, we slew our own fellow villagers as a sacrifice to the earth. Barleycorn, the plant, stands in the place of the people. But then Christ came to us, yes, our true sacrifice to yield a rich harvest, and so we put away such practices and turned to him for salvation."

"But soldiers sacrifice themselves for England, Papa," Little Ned murmured.

"Mayhap John Barleycorn is a soldier, like in the drawings of Bold General Wolfe."

"Aye, we might see Barleycorn as a soldier," Francis conceded. "But even more so, what does he remind you of?"

Little Ned bit his lip. "A martyr."

"And who did the martyrs, such as the two Edmunds and Lord Derwentwater, imitate?"

"Our Lord Jesus," Ned answered.

"There, you see?" said the elder Southworth. "Christ Jesus is our John Barleycorn, shedding his blood for the good of England and the whole wide world, for He will be all in all."

"So we eat His body," young Edmund added, "and drink His blood."

"Yes, yes, my lamb!" his father confirmed, a look of rapture in his eyes. "You understand the truth of it full well!"

Ned was brought out of his reflection about his childhood days by the booming sound of the innkeeper's voice.

"Have you local heroes sorted out who'll be paying for the rounds?" the innkeeper queried, arms folded over his rotund belly. "Or do you intend to charge His Majesty?"

"Oh, we know how to sort that out, innkeeper," Jack promised, mischievously. "But to manage it, we need our mugs filled up again!"

The innkeeper rolled his eyes. "Young Randall, will you never knock that chip off your shoulder?"

Jack grinned and pretended to flick something off his shoulder, causing his friends to burst out laughing. "No, no, afraid it won't be banished, innkeeper, work my woe!"

He jutted out his chin and extended his mug. Reluctantly, the innkeeper refilled it. The young officer then walked boldly between his chortling friends, one hand slipped inside his coat and other raising aloft his mug, then belted out the chorus of a drinking game.

"Here's good luck to the pint pot!
Good luck to the barley mow!
Jolly good luck to the pint pot!
Good luck to the barley mow!"

Ned knew the game well. After each chorus, the lads would cry, "Good luck!" and take a drink. Then they would try to sing through the various drinks available at the establishment, adding a new one each round, and singing faster each time. Eventually they would wish good luck to the proprietor, his family, and the company. In practice the game usually collapsed beforehand, since the drunken singers would stumble over the list of drinks, and whoever stumbled first would have to pay.

This time, about four singers stumbled at once, rendering the result void.

"Well, innkeeper, there's only one tried and true method to break the tie…"

"Bloody hell…"

"Fetch the ferrets!"

How this tradition began Ned had no idea, but lads testing their manly prowess by stuffing ferrets down their breeches was a time-honored one. So out came the ferrets from the back room, coddled by Angie, the innkeeper's buxom daughter.

"You be kind to my babies, now, officers," she warned them, scratching one of the ferrets under its chin. "Otherwise, I'll give them permission to bite your privates!"

As she sauntered past, one of the intoxicated recruits got a bit handsy.

"Ey, ey, ey, don't you go pawing me none, soldier," Angie scolded him, smoothing out her skirts. "I'm only here for my babies and to judge your handling of them!"

"Your charms are wasted upon ferrets," he slurred.

"Better than weasels," she replied, and the tavern was filled with laughter. "Now you go first, why don't you?"

So the handsy one went first, with a ferret stuffed down each leg of his breeches. He only managed to keep them there for half a minute before one dug its claws into his flesh and he let them up. Down the line of officers the ferrets went, with some managing to hold them down longer than others, but none making it past the two minute mark. At last it was Jack's turn. The ferrets proceeded to almost instantly squirm around in his breeches, clearly annoyed about being passed around so many times, and before even reaching the half minute mark, Jack squealed, clutching his groin, and let the ferrets slither out to freedom, to the laughter of the inn.

"Shall I have a go then, Angie?" Ned queried.

"You?" Jack queried tersely, nursing his injury and his pride.

"Aye," Ned responded. "Me."

"As you wish, Master Ned," Angie complied. "But in the mood these little fellas are in, it's going to hurt."

"I can live with that."

"One minute and a half," Angie proclaimed, glancing up from her father's pocket watch.

"I intend to hold out past two," Ned declared.

"What are you trying to prove, Southy?" Jack demanded.

"That recusants can hold ferrets down their breeches longer than their conforming peers, apparently," Ned grumbled, wincing at the pain as one of the ferrets bit him.

"Symbolic of general stubbornness that flies in the face of personal welfare or something?"

"Maybe."

"Strange hill to die on, must be said," Angie remarked.

"Well, too late to abandon it now," Ned sighed as the other ferret made a frustrated hissing noise and started trying to claw through the material.

At last the two minute mark passed and the ferrets were released into the arms of their doting mother, who pecked Edmund on the cheek and declared him the victor. Ned glanced around at the officers and bowed in a lordly fashion. To Jack's credit, he was the first one to start the round of applause, quite an improvement on his tendency to be a sore loser in his childhood that could still periodically manifest itself. But not today.

At last, once all the wounded veterans were bandaged up, it was universally decided that the expenses incurred should be put on the vicar's bill. Everyone seemed confident he would pay up once Jack left town, to keep up appearances for the family.

Soon, Ned found himself being convinced to abandon his plan to purchase a room in the inn, since it would cost an arm and a leg, and instead follow Jack home where, Jack assured, he would find him suitable quarters for half the price. Ned was suspicious. But Jack was determined. And soon they were en route to the church property.

Out back behind the vicarage which the family called home, Jack's foxhound Brutus barked at Ned menacingly, and Jack praised him for being such a good Papist hunter, kneeling down and scratching his neck and back. Brutus appeared absolutely elated with this acknowledgement, and jubilantly licked his face. Jack had raised him from a puppy and liked nothing better than to go out into the countryside hunting rabbits with him. He had named him after the leader of the twelve wandering Trojans who came to Albion in the ancient days when giants still roamed the land. Once Brutus conquered these mythical inhabitants, he renamed the island after himself, Britannia, and became her first king. Jack seemed quite convinced his beloved hound was capable of taking down a giant just as well as a rabbit.

Having made it past the guard dog in one piece, Ned was taken further out into a field where a broad oak tree stood. Nestled in its branches was a rather spacious treehouse.

"There," Jack said, gesturing triumphantly. "For a reasonable sum, this luxurious apartment could be yours for the night!"

"I…don't know about this, Jack…"

"Oh, it'll be fun!"

"You're just trying to get a hand in my purse, Jack…"

"Think of it as…getting closer to nature and nature's God…"

"Alright, you stole that from something your father said, probably."

"Probably," Jack conceded with a shrug.

Just then, Jack's sister popped out from inside the tree fort, clad in a loose shirt and breeches. Lizzie was a nine-year-old tomboy with carrot-red hair, and on fire with territorial instinct over her domain.

"Don't you dare let him come up here!" Lizzie snapped, shaking a finger at her brother as she stood on the wood platform above. "He'll blow it up for something!"

"Lizzie, you realize how hard it would be for me to get gunpowder barrels up that ladder all by myself, don't you?" Ned queried.

"You could send for help," she sniffed.

"I'm fairly certain that sort of thing would attract the attention of law enforcement," Ned argued. "Also, as far as I'm aware, Parliament isn't planning to convene up there, unless Jack has found a way to expand his rental scheme…"

Jack punched him in the shoulder to shut him up.

"Law enforcement is busy at the May Fair, arresting pick-pockets," he stated.

"I thought the fair was over and done by now," Ned sighed.

"Last day," Jack said. "Everything's drab and muddy, the Morris dancers have packed up their kit, and the maypole's been taken down, but the vendors are still trying to squeeze a few more coins out of it."

"And the ponies are still there," Lizzie added.

"Yes, little Lizzie loves her ponies," Jack said, as if talking to a baby, and Lizzie stuck out her tongue at him. "And she has her dollies hidden away up in her tree, even though she's far too grown up to play with dollies…"

"None of your business!" she retorted.

"Yes, let's get back to business," Jack decided. "Look, Liz, I'm willing to put in a good word with Father about getting a pony if you're willing to let a Papist in your tree house."

"But my mice are up here," she declared. "How can I trust him with them?"

"I'm confused," Ned admitted. "What are you so afraid I'd do to your mice?"

"Feed them to the owl that shows up around here every night, looking to turn my mice into supper, the villain!"

"Umm…why would I do that?"

"Because," she said, "you're a Papist."

"Alright, that doesn't make any sense…"

It doesn't have to," she declared, folding her arms. "My house, my rules."

"Er…I suppose…"

She turned to her brother. "Why not just capture a wild pony from the moors for me to tame? Unless you're afraid of being trampled or something."

"Like you, they bite," he retorted. "Besides, Father would just make me turn it loose again unless we get his approval."

Lizzie groaned. "You do all sorts of things Papa doesn't approve of, and get away with it too, just because you're a boy!"

"Then I'm the perfect one to get Da to come 'round on the question of ponies! So how about it? Shall we shake on it?"

Reluctantly, she climbed down from the tree, and did so, warning there would be hell to pay if the deal fell through.

And so Ned ended up in the treehouse, hoping that the following day, he would have formulated a better plan for his future. Yes, he could storm back home and demand entry as the master of the house. Yes, Tessie would surely let him in, and perhaps even Perpetua would begrudgingly relent. But he felt that his own temper had been flared too far to face his mother again, at least for a while. And he had so much to think over.

Halfway through the night, it began to rain torrentially. The roof of the tree house was leaking like mad, and the mice were squeaking in complaint. Ned couldn't manage to sleep a wink, shivering under his soaking blanket. At last, Jack made his appearance.

"Have Lizzie's mice drowned yet?" Jack called up, holding a coat up over his head to deflect some of the rain, even as the lantern he was holding sputtered and failed.

"They seem very alive," Ned replied through chattering teeth. "I may not be, however, if I continue to be exposed to such conditions!"

"Oh, stop being a baby," Jack retorted.

"I'd just as well have stayed warm and dry in the inn for a few extra pennies!"

"Alright, look, warmth I can't promise, but if you want to get dry, we'll get you dry. There should be just enough room in the wine cellar for you and the mice to bunk up comfortably together!"

"Huzzah!" Ned groaned.

"Just bring the mice down with you, alright? Otherwise, she'll be off to spill the beans to the old man!"

Having been soaked to the skin from the tree house adventure, Ned came down with a cold the following morning. Jack set up a makeshift cot and smuggled him some blankets, which he said were compliments of the house. Then, after feeding the mice, he let the secret house guest nibble on some surplus shavings of cheddar cheese.

"You're all heart, Jack," Ned sighed.

"I know." Jack sat down on the makeshift bed and tilted his head. Ned almost thought he saw concern in his eyes as he touched Ned's forehead. "Y'alright?"

"What the devil, Jack?" Ned chuckled, then coughed.

"I mean…I just…" He sucked in a breath. "Remember what happened to William?"

"Yes," Ned said quietly. "I remember."

Jack bit his lip. "I suppose I was the one who badgered him into staying out in the rain, wasn't I? Said he was a sissy if he left before we finished with the ball game. Said he was his mammy's darling." He shook his head. "I…uhh...I didn't know he'd get so sick."

"None of us did," Ned murmured. "If you recall, I wanted to stay outdoors too."

Jack nodded. Then after a few moments, he mumbled, "I…should have gone over with Da, when Willie was failing. Maybe…I could have given the little mite such a hard time, that he'd have fought harder to live, just to prove he was no weakling, and so spite me. Or if not that, I could've just…" He shrugged. "Stayed with him, y'know?"

Ned felt a fresh melancholy, realizing how much Jack still grieved their long-gone friend. Perhaps what they were both grieving more than anything was their lost innocence, no matter how many years had passed since William breathed his last.

"I'd give much to be able to go back and hold his hand," Ned rasped. Then he reached over and took Jack's hand instead.

Jack blushed. "Look…you're not *very* sick are you?"

"I'll be fine."

"You sure?"

Ned nodded. "If you stop pestering me, and let me sleep, that is. It's bad enough with the mice always trying to talk to me."

He gestured to them as they began to make squeaking noises from their abode.

"Look now, I'm an educated man, with educated conversation to offer, which your rodent roommates o'er yonder simply can't hope to match!"

Ned couldn't help but giggle.

~

Ned awoke the following morning to the sound of voices shouting over each other upstairs. He had a splitting headache and sincerely wished they would resolve whatever family debate they were having. Then the cellar door creaked open and someone marched down the stairs.

"Pony purchasing negotiations sort of broke down with Lizzie," Jack panted, pulling the blanket off Ned and forcing him to sit up.

Ned groaned. "She tattled?"

"She tattled," Jack confirmed. "You'd better run out the back way before the old man finds you…"

But it was too late. The door opened again, and more footfalls were heard on the stairs. Soon the vicar was standing over Ned, his bushy eyebrows knit together in displeasure, his arms folded over his chest.

"My excessively loquacious daughter, Elizabeth, told me there was a feverish Papist holed up in our cellar. Evidently, the report was accurate."

"Good morning to you too, sir," Edmund croaked, his voice sounding very much like a frog.

Mister Randall gestured broadly at Jack. "What, may I ask, did my opportunistic son charge you to take up a secret residence here?"

"Actually, he was charging me for residence in the tree house…but it poured like Noah's flood, and nearly drowned Lizzie's mice, so…"

"I made him a special offer, Da, on discount," Jack stated. "You know…you taught me ethics over economics…"

The vicar rolled his eyes and cast Jack a harsh glare. Ned, meanwhile, coughed. The vicar huffed and placed a hand on Ned's forehead. "Lord, she was right about the fever." He raised an eyebrow. "Why, pray tell, are you not in your own abode?"

"His witch of a mother tossed him out on his rear," Jack snorted, "or probably would have boiled him for supper…"

"Jack," Ned growled. "Don't…"

"Alright, alright…but she did!"

"Why?" the vicar asked Ned.

Edmund shrugged. "Family fight, that's all. I meant to stay at the inn for a spell, but I had little enough coin on me, and then Jack said…well…"

"Yes, I can imagine," the vicar sighed. "I do hope you didn't bring any suspicious barrels down here with you. Lizzie was concerned."

"She was more concerned about the tree house," Ned sighed.

"Well, yes, she would be," Mister Randall concurred, with a slight smile. "She's the queen of her castle." It was no secret the youngest was his favorite child, and he indulged her eccentricities, though still seemed to be holding out on buying her a pony. "Now returning to the issue at hand…" He pointed a finger at Ned.

"I'll go back over to the inn," Ned sighed, sitting up with some difficulty due to his sheer fatigue and started coughing again. "Maybe I can arrange to get a room and pay later…"

"Oh, enough pride," the vicar huffed. "I may not have wished you to be here, but I shan't turn you out in such a state either. You're too sick to stand, and it's still raining cats and dogs. My son brought you here, so I cannot in good conscience wash my hands of you. Come along, you'll catch your death down here. We have a guest room."

Ned was moved by the vicar's decency, and responded, in a bit of a shivered voice, "Thank you, sir. I'll try not to be a bother…"

"Well, you are, but it can't be helped," Mister Randall sighed. He turned to Jack. "Help your friend upstairs, bundle him under some blankets, then tell the cook to fix him some chicken broth and some cherry juice with honey. Also have her make him up a poultice for his chest with garden herbs and mustard. It might be a good idea to steam some and have him inhale the vapors with a towel over his head too. That's a nasty cough."

Ned, again, felt touched, so much so he felt tears coming to his eyes. It felt good to be cared about in a manner that his mother seemed to have forgotten how to show. "Th-thank you…"

Mister Randall shrugged. "No point in being a half-measure host." Then he turned and went back upstairs.

Chapter 15: THE VICAR'S HOUSE

For the next few days, Ned remained buried under four blankets in bed, safe from the rain pattering outside the window of the plain but cozy guest room. He had taken all the remedies prescribed by the vicar, and he was starting to feel like himself again. Jack visited him every few hours to show off different bits of military kit he'd gotten and brag about what a hard time he and his local intimates would give to the rebels. Of course, he'd also tease Ned mercilessly about being a slug-a-bed.

Finally, the rain let up and clouds yielded to sunshine, which brought a smile to Ned's face as he gazed out the window.

"Don't you love the English sun?" Jack remarked, the light flashing on the gilded gorget he had been showing Ned. "It takes forever to come out sometimes, but when it does, it's the purest light in the world, and the sky turns from gray to the bonniest, brightest blue."

Ned smiled, seeing the light on his sometimes-friend's face. "Poetical, yet again."

Jack snorted. "If a man can't say nice things about their homeland and pretty girls, they are bloody well lost."

Ned chuckled. "So England is like a pretty girl to you?"

"In spring, most of all," Jack decided. "There's nothing quite like England waking up from a long sleep, innocent, virginal, with flowers in her hair. Then in summer, she stands up tall, like a warrior queen, ruling the water with her scepter, and she is beautiful and terrible. And then when the cold months come on, and everything bleeds out color and turns white with frost, she's old, old as the hills, and wise."

Ned tilted his head. "Do you think…the colonists remember such things? Do you think they…think of England?"

Jack shrugged. "I dunno. I don't think they'd be wanting to fight the King if they did. He's England when he wears the crown. And the crown is like the stone circles out in the fields, because we don't know who made them, but England does. It's her secret. We love them because of that, and so we love the crown, and would fight and even die to uphold its honor and splendor…" He glanced down at the gorget, running his thumb over the G and the R. *Georgius Rex*. The King. Edmund had met him in person, but Jack never had. Yet the King was England to Jack, and he loved England enough to die for her. And Ned felt a twist of guilt in his gut.

In addition to Jack's visits, Lizzie would periodically run down the hall, burst into the room, hop onto the bed, and blurt out, "You dead yet?" Ned would reply flatly, "Yes," and she would giggle, and usually inaugurate a pillow fight. Her father scolded her for being so unladylike with their house guest, but Ned insisted that she was like a little sister to him and could not help but brighten his spirits. Jack, meanwhile, would warn Lizzie that spending time around Ned in his condition would make her break out in purple spots and make her tongue turn green.

Another visitor Ned received was Jack's mother. Mrs. Agatha Randall was a gentle soul, with frayed nerves, given to constant fretting over her children. She had almost died several years before of a terrible fever, and it was believed the near brush with death had unsettled her humors and imbalanced her mind. She had a tendency to come off as rather airy, sometimes going off into her own world in a sort of trance. This made the rest of her family, especially her husband, quite protective of her, concerned about exacerbating her condition. But Ned's mild-mannered nature, in contrast to her own son's personality, seemed to be good medicine for her. She would come to the guest room to arrange fresh garden flowers in a vase on the end table. Then she would sit down beside the bed, set about her needlework, and talk to him as if she had forgotten he was a "guest", and instead had mistaken him for one of her own brood. He appreciated this more than he could say.

Finally, he worked up enough strength to accept an invitation to come downstairs to the breakfast board and share a meal with the whole family. They were serving pancakes with butter, honey, and jam, with beer and milk to wash it down, though Ned received more cherry juice. From the looks Jack and Lizzie exchanged with each other as they sat down to table, Ned was concerned a food fight might be about to break out in the midst of the vicar's grace.

As soon as the breakfast blessing concluded, Mariah, the second child of the family, started talking incessantly about her wedding to be held later that year, binding her to a rather well-connected gentleman from Cumbria. The third child of the family, Tommy, at age fourteen, was rather plump and somber, most likely destined to follow his father into the Church. At the very least, he seemed studious about the whole thing, if a bit fixated upon ceremonial propriety. He was reading one of his father's books open on the table at the same time as he shoveled forkfuls of pancakes into his mouth.

"Should we use bone or cream for the napkins for the wedding, Mama?" Mariah asked, holding up two samples to her mother to observe.

"How about goose-turd green, Princess?" Jack snorted.

"Jack, really," Mrs. Randall scolded him softly, shaking her head. "You mustn't torment your sister so."

"He's hopeless, Mother!" Mariah lamented. "Why didn't you drown him at birth?"

"Now, then, Sis, don't hurt my feelings," Jack pretended to pout. "From my earliest years, I've always been a great comfort at these tragic family affairs. Remember Aunt Lydia's wedding? Her husband was even punier than yours…"

"Ashley is not puny!" she protested, obviously more than a bit smitten. "He's as fine a figure of a man as ever there was!"

"If you have a fondness for twigs in wigs," Jack decided with a shrug.

"You don't even have enough taste to don a wig and cover that scraggly black hair of yours!" his sister scoffed.

"Wigs itch," he decided. "But as I say, at least your fella's got more meat on his bones than Aunt Lydia's man. He looked positively tubercular, but given his fat purse, maybe that was part of the plan…"

"Jack, don't say such a thing about poor Uncle Mortimer," his mother lectured him.

"But Mama…"

"You kept playing snapdragon with the punch at the wedding feast," Mariah sniffed. "Lit it on fire and challenged the boys to pluck raisins out of it!"

"I was celebrating! It's not every day a spinster aunt gets married!"

"The holy estate of matrimony is not only limited to those in the bloom of youth nor the peak of comeliness," Tommy intoned, in his best imitation of their father in the pulpit. "Indeed, even those worn down by the years may derive practical benefits from it…"

"Preach, Lumpy," Jack needled his brother with his hated nickname.

"That'll be enough from you, Jack," the vicar scolded him, adjusting the gazette he was reading. "You can thank your brother for giving me one studious son at least." He clicked his tongue, tapping the paper with his finger. "The American situation behooves me. I felt certain it would have ebbed out apace by now. What in blazes is Howe doing over there, besides treating all and sundry to drinks on the house?"

"Now, Charles, dear, you mustn't strain yourself over the news," Mrs. Randall cautioned him, her eyes worried, as they often were.

"I try not to, Agatha, but after the many ups and downs of the last war, everyone expected at least a little peace and quiet," Mister Randall exhaled.

"Don't worry, Da," Jack said, drinking down some cherry juice, and spilling it on his white shirt, which his mother started to fret over. "We'll go over there and make the Yankees see who's in charge, one way or another."

"I simply hoped they would have come to their senses earlier than this," the vicar exhaled. "We all needed more time to repair and replenish from the last war." He swatted at a fly with his folded gazette, then gestured to Jack and Ned with it. "You boys don't remember it half so well, no matter how much you played soldiers in the yard, but it was a bitter ordeal, and not at all clear which side would come out on top. I remember first hearing about poor General Braddock's command, slaughtered by those savages in league with the French. Then there was the news of dear Lord George Augustus, the shining star of the army and pride of the Howe dynasty, cut down in his prime. Then we heard of poor Colonel Munro, surrendering Fort William Henry to the Marquis de Montcalm in hopes of saving the lives of his soldiers and their families, only for that supposedly noble Frenchman to lose control of his Indians. Men, women, and children were butchered outside the fort in droves! It was horrifying!"

The vicar shook his head, seemingly wearied even by the memories of such hard times.

"Then suddenly, to all our surprise, things took a turn in our favor, with that ailing Scotsman Forbes capturing Fort Duquesne and, seemingly from out of nowhere, that young hero Bold General Wolfe sallied forth and conquered Quebec! Few enough of us had heard his name before his exploits at Louisbourg, and some whose fathers were peers decried him as the son of a common soldier. Then suddenly he was hailed as the nation's savior, and just as suddenly, we learned he was dead! It was such strange and sorrowful news carried over to us, and not only the army but the whole nation reacted as a family would upon losing their father, their friend, and their whole dependence. Yes, our breadwinner had been entombed, and we were left hungry in more ways than one. I don't think there was a dry eye in the parish when I read the news at the head of the church and attached it to the board, with all those casualties." He swallowed hard. "After such a surprising catharsis, having been blessed by the Almighty with dominion, it seems a shock and a shame for the empire to now fall to fighting itself. We are still weary from what we've been through."

"I can't imagine the colonials are over the cost of the last war either," Ned mused. "They shared in all the joys and sorrows…

"Then they should have paid their taxes in a goodly order, like the rest of us, instead of daring to take up arms against their sovereign," Mister Randall huffed. "I have no sympathy for them. They are some of the freest colonials in the world, having grown too accustomed to abusing the privilege by demanding equality with the Mother Country. It throws off the balance of things. Hierarchies are simply a part of life, on earth as it is in heaven, and we'd best get used to that, regardless of our station, or else subsist off of perpetual discontent. None of our other colonies and dominions have parliamentary representation, nor are the colonies and dominions of rival powers even remotely afforded such extraordinary considerations."

"But some loyal Englishmen, even in parliament and in the military, believe we should be the ones to set a different tone for all the world to follow," Ned countered. "They view England not merely as a matter of place, but of blood, and that an ocean should not prevent equality amongst kindred nor the proliferation of English liberty beyond the current limitations. I heard Earl Percy discuss the matter when I was in London…"

"Percy will stick his sword into rebel throats, just the same," the vicar assured, nursing his beer. "Yes, some men didn't wish to go over at first, amongst them the Howe brothers, Richard in the navy and William in the army, because they had colonial attachments. When the eldest brother, George Augustus, was slain in America, the colony of Massachusetts loved his memory so well, they raised the funds to erect his monument in Westminster Abbey. Lord George loved them too, it was said. Caused a bit of a scandal with his lack of formality and love of the wilderness. The Americans impressed him with their rugged ways. Hard for his siblings to set aside such sentiments, I fear. It has made Billy Howe sluggish in pursuit of that scalawag Washington. He should have been in the Tower by now, but he's still at liberty, being chased about like Lord Cornwallis."

"Cornwallis was also reticent to pursue this unfortunate conflict, was he not?" Ned asked.

"He's an outspoken Whig, with a history of swooping in to defend the colonials every time they cried oppression," Randall admitted. "'They're our brethren,' he said. 'They deserve the rights of Englishmen,' he said. But in the end, neither he nor the Howes were willing to forfeit their reputations over the matter. They would go where the King ordered them and put down any violent disturbance of the peace that afflicted the empire. It's what any sensible or honorable man would do."

"But some have refused to go outright, isn't that true, sir?" Ned pressed.

"Yes, a fanatical minority, like George Gordon and Ralph Abercromby…"

"Or a conscientious one…"

"Then they have a poorly formed conscience, to set the mob above the throne," Mister Randall replied tartly. "At least one British marine, a captain who served with some distinction in the last war, resigned his commission rather than bear arms against the colonists. This stems from a misguided attachment to our deluded and disloyal brethren. I realize that these men, now in arms against His Majesty, were the captain's former comrades arrayed against the encroachments of France, but that is no excuse. His duty bid him to carry the King's justice across the water, as the marines did so admirably under the late Major Pitcairn. It seems only yesterday they were all wearing mourning bands for their slain chief. Yet despite this noble example set for him, the captain set his own personal sentiments before his sworn oaths to serve wherever he was sent, by land or by sea. Otherwise, he should never have joined the service to begin with."

Ned could well imagine how Pitcairn would have responded to the news that one of his marines had refused to serve. Even if he had learned of the debacle on the Sabbath, choice language would have been spouted. No, even the fear of having to pay William out of pocket for failing in his Sunday resolution would not have stopped him. The memory of the little game between father and son hurt.

"I suppose some men find themselves at odds with themselves," Edmund remarked, "torn in two, in fact…"

"Very few among humble men who labor with their hands in this country," Randall said. "The rebels in the colonies fail to understand how unpopular their antics are with most poor folk here, taxed half to death already to pay for the last war. They haven't got any representation to speak of, but they pay, or go to debtors' prison. They, more than anyone else, believe the Yankees should pay their fair share. By my faith, the colonials in general are taxed lighter than the rest of us here at home! But are they appreciative? No! Instead, colonial smugglers, such as that John Hancock fellow, make themselves filthy rich through ill-gotten gain then pretend to be martyrs and forswear their rightful allegiance when the law catches up with them. They are victims of their own self-interest, and nothing more." The vicar squinted at Ned. "Don't tell me you sympathize with these so-called revolutionaries, boy."

"No, sir," Edmund retorted, defensively. "But I try, if I can, to understand what makes other men tick. In this case, it is the loyal opposition I seek to understand, not the radicals in America who have drawn a river of British blood in their effort to topple the crown. No, sir. I have no part with them." He turned his gaze downward. "I met both Major Pitcairn and his son, Lieutenant Pitcairn. I have nothing but contempt for their killers."

"Then why not fight them?" Jack demanded, pointing at Ned in an accusatory manner with his fork. Then he turned to his father. "Da, tell him it's his duty as an Englishman, whether he's from a Papist house or not."

The vicar looked over at Ned, then said simply, "Each man must chart his own course. It is not for any other man to turn the wheel for him."

Ned felt grateful, in a way, for Mister Randall's choice of words, but they did not relieve the weight in his heart. Where *did* his duty lie? What did duty even mean in such a case as this, when his faith and country seemed perpetually at odds? He always thought he knew. His faith should always come first, the things of God before the things of the world. But he felt that certainly slipping more by the day. If he could not be faithful to the things around him, what he could see, hear, taste, and touch, how could he be expected to remain faithful to invisible realities?

"Well, I'm quite worn out with all this war talk," Mariah pouted. "And I still haven't gotten any meaningful opinions about these napkins…"

"Your beloved dandy won't be going anywhere near the rattling guns, never you fear," Jack huffed. "His little brother's being sent out to represent the family instead."

"As it should be!" she said. "He's the firstborn son, the heir to his house!"

"As am I," Jack stated, lifting his beer mug in a salute, "and I'm proud to serve beside first sons, second sons, third sons, so long as they'll stand and fight for the crown against all who would put a dent in it!"

The vicar smiled slightly at his son's enthusiasm. Mariah just rolled her eyes and asked to be excused, intent on going to ask some of her friends in the village about their color preference for the napkins. Bobby also excused himself, determined to study in a quieter atmosphere. Jack, meanwhile, had his own plans for the day.

"I gotta see the match!" he blurted. "It's today, you know! Between us and the village over! Gotta be there to make sure those dirty dogs don't play rough!"

Ned squinted. "And *you* don't play rough?"

"Well…"

"Before I'm letting you rush off to join those football delinquents, destroying the manners and morals of this country, you must drink your milk," his mother decided, filling him a glass. "Good for the bones, dear."

He grumbled, but started to drink.

"Also, I must insist you first visit Mrs. Simmons," the vicar instructed. "Make sure she's getting on alright and help her with anything that needs doing."

Jack nearly spit out his milk. "No, not that! Anything but that! Burn me! Boil me! Peel my face off with a red hot spatula!"

"Eww," Lizzie grimaced, crinkling her nose and pushing away her plate of pancakes.

"Jack, really, you're being absurd," the vicar huffed. "She's a war widow and, frankly, if I believed in saints beyond the earliest years of the church, I would count her amongst their number…"

"But she's got twenty cats prowling around the place!" Jack blurted.

"You need to dispel this irrational fear of felines, once and for all," the vicar stated. "Besides, she doesn't have twenty…more like seven…"

"But they're evil!" Jack protested.

"You do realize you have a problem, don't you?" Ned mumbled through a mouthful of pancakes.

"Jack, dear, do be a good boy and do as your father says," said Mrs. Randall airily.

"But Mother…"

"I refuse to believe that a handful of vibrating fur balls can have this unhealthy hold over you," his father groaned. "You are now an officer in His Majesty's service…"

"Yes, to deal with rebels, not cats!" Jack countered.

"What are you afraid they'll do to you?" Ned queried.

Jack shrugged. "It's just…the way they move or something."

"You go to hangings for fun, Jack."

"Look, Black Bill made a bloody good death of it, what can I say? Like Dick Turpin, he jumped off the ladder on his own and snapped his neck right off, not like his accomplice, who begged for his life with gutless whingeing and took a full quarter of an hour to die!" Jack declared, finishing off the last of his pancakes. "I only wish they'd slit them open in the end, like they did with that other fellow down south…had that one on display for two whole days, with folk lining up to get a look at his innards…"

"Jack," the vicar scolded him. "You know I was opposed to that…"

"I mean, they didn't start cutting till he was done in, though!" Jack clarified. "Besides, folk like Black Bill would have had it coming. He may have been like Turpin in boldness on the gibbet, but he seems to have followed in life too. Right nasty stuff, I hear."

"I am aware, son," the vicar sighed.

"They say he ravished some lass under a tree in Westmorland and then cut off her finger with her betrothed's ring on it," Jack recalled. "When her man found out, he rode out after Bill, but never came back. They found him moldering in the marsh some months later. You know what else? They say Bill and his accomplice broke in on an old spinster with a hooked nose living alone on her father's farm. They said she must be a witch and roasted her bare bottom on an open fire, swearing to cut off her nose unless she gave them the dowry she never used to fetch a husband!"

"Jack, for the love of heaven," his mother exhaled, scandalized.

For some bizarre reason, the imagery of the story made Lizzie giggle.

"That's bad luck, Liz!" Jack declared, shaking his finger. "You're gonna become a spinster now, with a burnt bum!"

"I'd have been a spinster that knew how to use a pistol, and shot Black Bill right between the eyes!" She made a motion with her hand as if pulling a trigger. She turned to her father. "And I'd have used the dowry to buy ponies."

"You'll do no such thing, Elizabeth!" her mother scolded her.

"But Mama…"

The vicar very nearly rolled his eyes, but avoided addressing his daughter's pony obsession verbally. Instead he turned back to his son. "Men of violence deserve to meet a violent end under the law. But this tendency towards the desecration of their bodies I find disconcerting. They were temples of the Holy Spirit, no matter how poorly used."

"That Papist animal Nevison deserves a good cutting after what he did to you," Jack growled, bunching his hands into fists. "Alive, too, if I had to say anything about it!"

"No, Jack," the vicar said softly, flushing a bit at the memory of his own humiliation. "He is still…made by God…"

"But he made you bleed, Da!" Jack blurted, then pointed at Ned. "If it wasn't for this one here, you might have been cut up something awful! Besides, even if he never scratched you, he made sport of you! He deserves to be punished…"

"He's about to be, Jack."

"Well, I hope it proves a slow end."

"I do not," his father countered. "I must not, lest I lose myself to my pride. It's a dangerous thing to do for a sinner. That's why, if Nevison broke with Rome and asked for the consolations of the English church, I would attend to him. That's why, even when they've choked the air out of him for his crimes, I…I don't want him cut."

Ned felt his estimation for the vicar rise.

"But the sciences, Da," Jack reminded him. "They say this sort of thing helps physicians sort out what's what inside us. Maybe even save lives."

"Science is well and good, but not when it trumps the spirit," Mister Randall replied. "Then it becomes the tool of atheism, wherein a man is reduced merely to his parts but not his higher calling from his Creator. Without that, mankind is without dignity."

"So you're opposed to all cutting?" Jack pressed.

"I am cautious of the manner in which it is pursued, that is all," the vicar replied. "Remember that farmer's wife who had a stillbirth on the other side of the village a few years back? She called me in to stop the landlord's son from taking the babe's remains away for some experiment to satisfy his curiosity. He said this was the thirteenth she had, five being born dead, so it didn't matter what he did with it. It would just rot in the ground with the others otherwise. He said she had no right to stand in the way of science." The vicar gave Jack a hard look, and Jack turned his eyes down awkwardly. "No right. That's what he said over a grieving mother, put to bed with a fever. If that's what science makes a man, it is a dirty business."

"I agree, sir," Ned said softly. "And I believe you did right."

The vicar gazed at him for a moment, with some surprise that he had interjected, then allowed him a slight smile.

Jack was quiet for a bit, seemingly brooding over something. Ned thought it might be the fact that he had nearly lost his mother to fever not long ago, and his father's story struck a nerve. But he soon perked up again and declared, "Aww, this one's just sensitive about the subject because of his priests we got a hold of, alive and wriggling!" He shoved Ned in the shoulder jestingly, and Ned cringed at the poor taste. Then Jack turned back to Lizzie. "I could have taken home a nice chunk of Jesuit intestines as a treat for your treehouse rats!"

"My treehouse mice!" she clarified, sticking out her tongue.

"Jack, Elizabeth, enough! You're upsetting your mother," the vicar reprimanded them both, laying a hand on his wife's arm "Must I raise my voice to be obeyed?"

Jack and Lizzie both hung their heads and mumbled, "No, sir."

The vicar cast a nervous glance at Ned. "He…didn't mean anything by…"

"I know," Ned exhaled, just grateful the squabbling siblings had finally been hushed.

"Returning to the original topic of your fear of felines…Jack, would you like me to accompany you to Mrs. Simmons so that I might protect your person from a fate worse than what scientific experimentation has to offer?"

"Oh, would you, dear?" Jack's mother chimed in. "Follow him over to his silly ball game as well. Make sure he doesn't get injured by or injure any of those ruffians on the field."

"Mother, he'll ruin the fun of it!"

"Jack." She squinted at her son.

And that was that.

As they made their way to the other side of the village, Jack continued to grumble about the possibility of running late at the game, and Ned continued to remind him of his duty to his parents.

"You're one to talk!" Jack whined. "You're the one who got thrown out of the house by your monster mama!"

"Jack…"

"All I'm saying is that you have no bloody right siding with mine!"

"Look, I can't help that she seems to like me," Ned exhaled.

"She's probably forgotten you're not one of the family. She…gets confused, since the fever…"

"All the more reason neither of us should upset her, or your father," Ned countered. "He looks rather strained to me."

Jack shrugged, and a look of guilt came to his face.

"What is it?" Ned queried. "Is something the matter at home?"

"No, nothing," Jack mumbled unconvincingly.

"Is it your mother? Is she really out of danger now, or is she still at risk?"

"She's fine," he mumbled. "She'll be fine."

Ned tilted his head. "Everything alright at the church?"

"Now enough with your Papist prying!"

"It's you, isn't it?" Ned surmised. "I can tell…you're in some sort of trouble…that's why you're rushing off to don the king's livery…"

"I'm doing it because I'm proud to do it, and that's something you can't seem to understand!" Jack declared, turning on him sharply. "As for anything else, keep your bloody nose out of my business!"

"Can I help, though?" Ned asked softly.

Jack groaned. "No, alright? What makes you think you could?"

"I-I don't know," Ned confessed. "But…we've known each other forever, and if I could help I would." They had just climbed up on a small bridge fording a bubbling stream that ran down the hill in a picturesque waterfall. He smiled a little. "You sank my paper boat not far from here. I really should never have forgiven you for that."

Jack laughed. "But you did?"

Ned leaned over and scraped up two pebbles embedded between the planks of the bridge. He handed one to Jack. "Test your throw?"

Jack smirked. "Test? This is a foregone conclusion!"

Of course, Jack was right. He always had beaten Ned at these sorts of things. But as they threw together, Ned was at least satisfied that his pebble plunked into the water a bit farther out than usual.

They continued on in a companionable sort of silence until finally coming within sight of the widow's cottage.

Ned's eyes widened at the sheer number of cats lounging around the yard and pathway. "Alright…you were right, Jack…there are more than seven…Jack?"

He turned over his shoulder, and saw Jack running in the opposite direction. Ned groaned, then turned back to the path to see that an assembly of cats had gathered, meowing at his feet. One of the smaller bundles of fluff, complete with claws, attached itself to his leg and started trying to climb up.

"Ouch," he muttered, gently prying the kitten off and setting it back on the ground. "Nice kitty…nice, scary kitties…"

They meowed in a rather terrifying unison as more cats joined the throng, and Ned began to wonder if he should run after Jack and take his chance with football delinquents after all.

Fortunately, the sound of a voice back at the house caused the cats to scramble back down the path, leaving Ned to nurse his kitten-punctured leg and torn breeches. Soon Mrs. Simmons emerged, feeling her way out the garden gate with her cane as her furry companions surrounded her. She really did need greater supervision, given her fading eyesight. A maid came in periodically to tidy up for her, but she mostly liked to keep to herself and her cats.

"Is that you, Mister Randall?" she queried, accustomed to the vicar's visits.

"No, ma'am," Ned answered. "It's Edmund Southworth. Mister Randall sent me over."

"Oh, he should not have bothered a young man like yourself with an old lady like me," she chuckled. "The young should enjoy youthful pursuits."

"The young, ma'am, should cherish every moment they have with their elders," Ned replied. "Besides…my father would wish me here as surely as the vicar."

Ned was soon whisked off to the parlor, where the portrait of the venerable lady's husband, the late Major Bartholomew Simmons, stared down at him disapprovingly. He had never been particularly enamored by Papists, though he had spent a reasonable amount of time with Francis Southworth, playing chess or darts down at The Cross Keys Inn. It was said he was almost pagan, obsessed as he was with his favorite Greek and Roman philosophers, but decidedly leaned Deist, treating divinity as a distant force. He attended church infrequently, to his wife's pious chagrin, and received communion even less so. But he still called himself an Anglican because he was patriotic, and liked to think of Britannia as Romana reborn to reorder the world.

Upon the onset of the last war with France, Simmons' behavior towards the elder Southworth took a turn for the worse. He became suspicious, almost paranoid, of everything Francis said or did, convinced it was a portent of Papist treachery. An army man since the tender age of fourteen, Simmons had a brutal streak when he believed himself or his country threatened. One day it all came to a head, and to Francis' shame, Simmons had him publicly searched, declaring loudly that this "Romish gentleman" was in league with France. It had been an awful scene, with Francis shoved up against a wall of the inn with a pistol pointed at his chest, his face flushing crimson as his former friend searched through his clothes in front of everyone, robbing him of dignity.

"Bart, please," Francis had begged. "Bart, please, I've done nothing of which I should be ashamed! Bart, you know me!"

But Simmons would not heed him.

The innkeeper, to his eternal credit, had finally come to Francis' defense, saying that too much drink had gone to Simmons' head and that he should leave the establishment before tormenting any of his other loyal customers. Perpetua once related that upon returning to the manor, Francis had been so distressed by the encounter that he locked himself in his study and sobbed for most of the night. Perpetua, meanwhile, predicted an ill fate for those who had humiliated her noble husband.

And so it came to pass. Simmons and his eldest son sailed off to participate in General Edward Braddock's campaign to wrest control of Fort Duquesne from the powers of France. The march ended in a massacre. It was said by a French prisoner that both father and son were wounded in the fray, Simmons having been shot down trying to reach his boy. The Indians got a hold of them, and made sport of them, scalping and mutilating the son in front of his helpless father before finally cutting the boy's neck.

By the time the French managed to reign in the excesses of their native allies, Simmons had been divested of all his arrogance and reduced to fits of weeping over the corpse of his son, kissing the place where his boy's handsome face used to be before it was all but torn off. Then he begged for the French to kill him where he lay, and when they hesitated, he picked up his own pistol, placed it to his temple, and pulled the trigger. It was not as swift a death as he could have wished for. The horror continued for a quarter of an hour with him writhing convulsively on the ground, clutching his head in agony, asking for the Frenchmen to clean the blood out of his eyes, and if it was night or day, and if he had overslept and missed his own wedding. And the blood kept gushing out of his nose till he was dead.

When news reached the Southworth estate, Perpetua declared it an act of God, seeming particularly taken by the man ending his own life, and Francis shouted at her to hold her tongue, appearing as if he might faint. He rarely shouted, and it shocked her. Then he went immediately to the widow and spent hours consoling her. Most of these details were deliberately concealed from Mrs. Simmons. As far as she was aware, her loved ones had simply died, quick and clean. But she was a broken woman, fretting desperately over her second son, who was still in the field.

Then came the Battle of Quebec, and yet more tragedy falling upon the house of Simmons. The youngest son was wounded upon the Plains of Abraham, but wrote home assuring that it was only a scratch. The truth was that he hesitated to have his leg amputated for so long, the limb became putrid, and he died a miserable, excruciating death in the Ursuline convent. He told one of his comrades he kept seeing lights, pretty lights of all different colors, sometimes in the midst of the pain, and it brought him peace. Folk around the village still spoke of him as a budding artist, loving nothing more than to go out into the moors and experiment with his paints and brushes. He died with his head in the lap of one of the nuns who had been nursing him, twitching convulsively, racked with fever and fear, confusing her with his mother, and she told him, "*Oui, oui, oui, je suis ta mère…*"

When his heart gave out and his eyes emptied, it was said the young nun panicked, suddenly gripped with fear that the poor boy had gone to hell for his heresy, and clutching his corpse, she wept and prayed that she might take his punishment instead. Perpetua had no such impulse, and though she did not speak when the news broke the second time, the expression on her face still horrified her husband as he rushed out again to see the widow, and then the vicar, with whom he hatched a scheme to secretly support her lest she lose her dignity. She had lost far too much already, they both agreed.

And Francis had prayed. Yes, even decades later, he could be caught mumbling, "Lord Jesus, I must speak to Thee of Bart…"

Now, years after Francis' passing, Edmund sat in the Simmons parlor with a tray of tea and crumpets in front of him as his hostess described how she made use of her monthly "allowance", which she fully believed came from some financial investment her husband had made down in London.

"Each of my dear children donate to the church on a given festival day of the liturgical calendar," she explained, gesturing to the purring cats that had blanketed Ned on the chaise as if he were part of the furniture. "One for Michaelmas, one for Christmas, one for Easter, one for Pentecost, and so forth through the year."

Ned could not help but smile at the woman's simple goodness after all she had suffered, and petted one of the fluffiest cats as it drank out of his teacup. He also felt an abiding guilt as she spoke movingly about duty.

"We all have duty, that's what my dear Major used to say. We must give whatever we have towards it, whether we have been given much or little."

By the time Ned bid a fond farewell to Mrs. Simmons' cat sanctuary and relocated runaway Jack, he appeared sorely in need of medical attention, with black eyes and a bloody nose. He was also walking in a manner that indicated he might have sustained a nasty blow beneath the belt.

"Your mother is going to have my head," Ned sighed, taking Jack's arm and putting it over his shoulder.

"Bloody cheaters, that's what they are," Jack grumbled.

On the way home, they ran into yet another sheep fallen on its side, full with lamb, a common enough sight along the slopes outside the village. Both Ned and Jack quickly set about helping her up. It was part of their upbringing, a sort of honor code of the countryside, knights assisting a lady in distress. Ned did his best to calm the ewe, anxiously panting as she stood again on wobbly legs.

"Easy does it, my girl," he said soothingly, rubbing her nose. "You'll be right as rain now."

"She's late in the season to bear such a load," Jack remarked, pulling briars out of her wool. A faraway look entered his eyes as he regarded her, the same Ned had seen earlier. "Isn't it a strange thing, how no matter how many things perish, there are always new things being born? It's like magic, of a kind, in trees, and in beasts, and in us. Father talks about how we're all fallen into sin, unlike the plants and the animals, but this much we can still do like the rest of creation, if we live long enough…make new life…" He slapped the ewe on the rump and she trotted off to find her flock. "You'll have to write to me, Southy, and tell me how all the lambs are faring…"

Ned found himself at a loss for words, so simply responded with a melancholic nod.

Continuing on their way home, they passed one of the old stone walls weaving through the pastures. Ned smiled and clambered up on top.

"Come on, Jack, walk along it with me," Ned coaxed.

"You've always loved that wall, haven't you?" Jack snorted as he climbed up as well.

"It was built by our ancestors, the Angles and Saxons," Ned stated, stretching out his arms to balance himself as he walked. Then he turned to Jack and began to recite a stanza of poetry in the old Saxon tongue, something his father had preserved in his library.

"What's that about?' Jack asked.

"Battles," Ned said. "Old ones."

Jack blinked. "Dammit, we might have fought shoulder to shoulder, back then."

"Aye," Ned said softly. "We might have indeed, Jack."

Just then, gray clouds dappled the blue sky, and cold droplets splashed Ned's face. But the sun was still peeping out defiantly, a pale ball of light hovering above the horizon of purple hills, determined to outlast the latest shower. Both Ned and Jack remained standing on the wall, foolishly perhaps, with the rain dripping down from the heavens and making the grass turn even deeper green. Their watch was rewarded by a curve of colors slicing through the sky, causing them to let out a spontaneous cheer, as if they were still little boys. Then they both made wishes, each one refusing to tell the other what they had wished for, lest it not come true. The rain finally stopped, and the sheep standing in the meadow shook themselves dry as Ned and Jack wended their way back to the vicarage.

When they arrived, Ned took Jack to the kitchen where they dried off their rain-soaked clothes by the stove and Ellie, the cook, tended to Jack's scrapes from the football match by smearing lard on them. Afterwards, they went outside and sat on the stoop, watching the sunset bathe the countryside vista with a golden glow. Ned always found the view behind the church one of the prettiest in the village, flowing out from Mrs. Randall's garden, weaving between the old lichen-covered headstones in the churchyard, and then cascading out into the wild. He could just make out the stream trickling in the distance, and the bridge where he and Jack threw pebbles. Yes, it was a good view. It was home. Surely, he had to believe, even in the new world, the colonists remained England-haunted.

As they sat there, watching the evening sky turn pink, Jack continued to nurse his black eye with a slab of cold beef, cut off from the meal being prepared for the family, and the two of them shared a pot of honey with a very sticky set of dipping sticks. The sweet substance had been obtained through the vicar's backyard beekeeping, a tidy little side-business to help with church repairs which was renowned to be the vicar's all-consuming passion. Some even said it was his true religion. Ned recalled Jack putting some in a jar as a child and releasing them in the church during one of the most fashionable weddings of the season. Jack got good and walloped for his trouble, but the image of the weak-kneed groom nearly fainting into his bride's arms and needing snuff to bring him around still inspired vicar's son to call the incident "bloody brilliant."

But now the vicar's son revealed recollections of a more somber nature.

"See, over there?" Jack said, pointing to a grave near the gate, aglow with orange rays. "Our Willie's getting to sleep in the sun. He always liked the sun, just not the rain…" He bit his lip, and Ned put an arm around his shoulder. Jack cleared his throat. "He would have loved to get a uniform, you know, and a sword all his own. He would have fretted over having to kill the rebel bastards, but I think he'd have been brave, push come to shove."

"I think so too," Ned said softly.

"We all played army so many damn times. Hard to believe it's real now."

"I know," Ned rasped.

Jack sucked in a breath. "I-I'll think of him when I'm there. I'll think of him, and…do it for him, you know? I'll make them all remember the Lancashire lads were there." He gave Ned a look. "I-I'll think of you too. I mean, it doesn't seem quite right without you there, somehow. So I'll have to just…make you be there through me."

A lump rose in Ned's throat. "Jack…"

"Oh, look, here comes old Harry!"

Henry Cartmill, a wiry forty-year-old groundskeeper who had served in North America during the last war, was busy trimming the hedges nearby, singing a jaunty old army song under breath.

"Come, each death-doing dog who dares venture his neck!
Come follow the hero that goes to Quebec!
Jump aboard of the transports, and loose every sail,
Pay your debts at the tavern by giving leg-bail!
And ye that love fighting shall soon have enough!
Oh, Wolfe commands us, boys; we shall give them hot stuff!

Up the river St. Lawrence, our troops shall advance,
To the Grenadier's March, we will teach them to dance.
Cape Breton, we've taken, and next we will try,
At their capitol, to give them, another black eye.
Vaudreuil, 'tis in vain, you pretend to look gruff,
Those are coming who know how to give you hot stuff!

With powder in his periwig, and snuff in his nose,

Monsieur will run down, our descent to oppose.
And the Indians will come, but our Light Infantry,
Will soon oblige them to take to a tree.
From such rascals as these, shall we fear a rebuff?
Advance, Grenadiers! And let fly your hot stuff!"

"Let's hear the verse about the French nuns, Harry!" Jack chortled, nudging Ned in the ribs. Ned rolled his eyes. He knew exactly the bawdy lines being referred to, in which the conquering soldiers informed the abbess of the Ursuline convent that her sisters were now their booty.

"Oof, I'd dare not go there," Henry countered. "Your father would say it ain't fitting to be repeated on church property. Besides, some folk say the author of the piece, Sergeant Ned Botwood, had hard luck over his jesting! God sent a musket ball to cleave his heart in two for his vile tongue, so the Frenchies were quick to claim!"

"Oh, we can't trust anything the Frenchies say!" Jack protested. "And as for Father, well...I'll be gone for a soldier any day now! I'm not a little boy who needs his ears to be covered around army talk anymore!"

"Ha! This new crop of recruits you're marching off with don't know nothing about real soldiering," Cartmill declared, continuing to trim the hedges. "I was mustered upon the Plains of Abraham, you know."

"Tell us about meeting General Wolfe again," Ned requested. He had heard the story from old Cartmill almost a hundred times since childhood, and could probably recite most of it from memory, but still never tired of it. "Tell us, what was the general like?"

"The general...well, he was a noble fellow, called the officer's friend and the soldier's father, for he was extremely tender to, and careful of them, to the very end," the groundskeeper said wistfully, setting aside his shears. "I was a sergeant back then, standing in the thin red line. I saw him pass me by in his scarlet cape and silver walking cane, calm as a man gone for a country walk. Then I felt my chest on fire. Shot through the lung, I was, and thrown onto the ground, spitting up blood, sure I was done in. I closed my eyes and thought never to open them again." He took a deep breath, showing off the whistling sound that remained from the wound. "All of a sudden, I sensed a presence, somebody hovering over me, kneeling down beside me. I opened my eyes, and there he was, Wolfe himself. I could hardly get a breath, but managed to spit out, 'Sir, I be drowning!' He lifted my head up and squeezed my hand, and I squeezed back, as tight as I could manage. He said, 'Look me in the eyes, brother soldier.' So I did–blue, like ice, they were, but also warm, like flames."

"Like an English sky," Ned murmured, "when the sun comes out."

Jack smiled at him for remembering his words, and Harry nodded.

"Even so, Master Ned. His hand was the same...cold to the touch, yet the touch warmed me, nevertheless. So help me, I'll never forget the way he looked at me, for he really did see me, you understand? He saw right through to me. Then he said that I was brave...and he ordered me to fight to breathe, fight to live. 'You have good years to come,' he told me, and promised there'd be a promotion for me afterwards. Aye, he even took the time to pass on the message to another officer, in case he should be slain in the fight. I thought, no, he will not die, no, he must not die…" He ran his sleeve across his eyes. "He said, 'Take heart, and remember me.' I didn't know what that last part meant. Everything was fading for me. Last thing I felt was him patting my hand, and then he was gone. When I next woke up, I was in a hospital tent, all bandaged up. They didn't know if I would live or not, but I knew that I would. He had given me a reason to. And then I heard…the battle was won, but he was gone, gone for good. He had died as he lived, with his face to the enemy. And every soldier that received the tidings was inconsolable, for we loved him beyond measure. And I cried myself to sleep."

Ned felt a lump in his throat at the end of the retelling. He felt, somehow, that he had met Wolfe himself, and shared in the loss.

Soon, Cartmill had abandoned the hedge work entirely, and was calmly puffing on his pipe, spinning more yarns about his glory days in Wolfe's army. Lizzie came out on the porch to listen, wide-eyed, and proceeded to lick the honey pot clean. The groundskeeper always had a soft spot for her, and soon, just for her, he had switched from telling stories about his own (no doubt exaggerated) past to retelling her favorite story of her namesake, Queen Elizabeth, making a grand speech to her troops at Tilbury, amassed to oppose the invasion of the Spanish Armada.

"'Let tyrants fear,' the noble princess said, riding among her soldiers," Cartmill recounted, taking another draught on his pipe. "'I have always behaved in such a manner that, under God, I have faith in the loyal hearts of my subjects as my safeguard. I have come here resolved, even in the heat of the battle, to live and die amongst you all. I would lay down my honor and my blood, even in the dust, for my God, my kingdom, and my people.' Then she said, 'I know I have the body but of a weak woman, but also the heart and stomach of a king, aye, and of a king of England too, and I have naught up foul scorn that Spain, or any prince of Europe, or even the bloody bishop of Rome should dare to invade the borders of my realm. If need be, I myself will take up arms, and be your general, judge, and rewarder of every one of your virtues in the field.'"

Lizzie clapped her hands together enthusiastically, then turned and punched Ned in the shoulder. "So much for your pope!"

Ned rolled his eyes. He thought to make a remark upon the fate of Mary, Queen of Scots, which helped set the Spanish invasion into motion, but swallowed it back. It might have seemed appallingly unpatriotic, even if the whole island was now united, by crown and parliament.

It was nightfall by then, with the stars appearing like holes poked through dark blue velvet. God was on the other side of the holes, Lizzie decided, which is why they were so bright. As if to confirm her musings, a swirl of colors, not unlike the earlier rainbow, wove its way between the patches of starlight. Bright blue and green streaks overlapped in the sky then faded into purple and burst into pink before disappearing in the expanse. What future did the lights foretell? Whose souls would pass through that shimmering velvet in the year ahead? Were those already slain in the war gazing down through the stars at the young man soon to follow them? And what of Lord Derwentwater? Was the martyr watching over Ned with shining eyes, anxious to see whether or not he would keep the faith?

After Ned, Jack, and Lizzie spent a while longer with Harry as he pointed out different constellations that had helped guide him and his comrades through hostile territory during his army days, Mrs. Cartmill came out of their cottage on the church grounds and very nearly dragged her husband inside by the ear, knowing full well his tendency to chatter. If he didn't have a human audience, she huffed, he would be sure to start talking to trees!

But all those stories of blood and glory had an unintended effect, because well past midnight, when everyone was snug in their beds, Ned was awakened by the sound of Lizzie, in the hallway, calling Jack's name and pounding on his door. She sounded rather like she was crying.

"Dammit, Lizzie, what's all the fuss?" Ned heard Jack grumbled, then asked concernedly, "Anything wrong with Mama?"

"Don't…don't go, Jack," she choked.

"What? Why?"

"I had a dream…you were all covered in blood. There was so much blood, Jack, I couldn't even see your face."

"Then how did you know it was me, hmm?"

"Because I'm your sister! I'd know it was you no matter what!" She pleaded in a softer voice, "You mustn't go, Jack…you just can't! I won't let you!"

"Oh, carrot…"

"Don't 'oh, carrot' me!" she squeaked. "It was real! It was so real!"

Ned peered out the door, and saw Jack kneeling down and Lizzie throwing her arms around her brother's neck and sobbed into his shoulder. "I…don't want you to die…oh, Jack, please…please don't go…you'll die!"

Jack, in response, squeezed her tight. "Love you too, carrot," he mumbled, ruffling her red hair. "Come on. Back to bed with you."

Ned slipped out the door and down the hall, and saw from the crack in the door of Lizzie's room the brother lulling his sister to sleep, still in his arms, as he sat in a rocking chair. Her arms were still around his neck and her head pillowed against his shoulder. He was telling her a story about witches and wild ponies on the moors. Glancing up, he saw Ned, and smiled slightly.

A quarter of an hour later, Jack came into Ned's room, set down a tray of milk, beer, and cold chicken on the end table, and fell backwards onto the bed next to Ned, hands folded behind his head, staring at the ceiling. "Damn my eyes, that was rough going."

"Is she alright now?" Ned queried.

"I got her to nod off," Jack said, reaching for a drumstick and starting to gnaw on it. "I was always good at that, even when she was a baby in a bassinet. She was always feisty."

"Like you."

"Aye, like me. Two of a kind in the family." Jack gestured to the tray. "Go on, Papist. Eat heartily for the gallows!" He laughed at his own dark jest, but Ned could tell it was his way of dealing with his own worries.

Ned lay a hand on Jack's shoulder, and Jack reddened. "Want to talk?"

"No, to sleep," he yawned, then added, "just…not by myself."

Ned nodded in understanding and tossed part of the blanket over his companion.

After lying together in silence for a bit, Jack murmured, "When I was little, I used to count the wood knots on the ceiling when I couldn't sleep. I thought it would bring me good luck and a long life. That's what the nursemaid told me." He paused. "I don't know if that sort of thing works when it comes to war."

Ned felt a lump form in his throat, then turned and spontaneously gave Jack a hug. He didn't fight it.

"Southy, if you were to have a baby, what would you want it to be? Boy or girl?"

"That's an odd question," Ned observed.

"Humor me."

"I think I would be just as happy either way."

Jack nodded, and said no more about babies. Then he mumbled, "If I don't come back, well…I'll let you keep most of my shirts."

Ned winced. "Don't say that, Jack."

"Why? Not my fault you're a Popish pauper and could use more shirts! You should be thanking me for putting myself in harm's way! A Yankee bullet could do wonders for your wardrobe and love life!"

"Damn you, shut up!" Ned buried his face into Jack's shoulder.

And they cuddled awkwardly. And they both fell asleep.

~

That Sunday, Edmund sat in the pew at the back of the church. He wasn't supposed to be there. It was a scandal for any recusant to be caught at a heretical service. But he felt a need to be there, somehow, to see if he might be able to find God there.

"God grant to the living, grace," prayed the vicar as the service concluded, "to the departed, rest; to the Church, the King, and the Empire, peace and concord; and to us and all his servants, life everlasting; in the name of the Father, and of the Son, and of the Holy Ghost, Amen."

"Amen," Ned said along with the congregation. Surely that was no great sin.

After the service had concluded and the parishioners filed out, Ned just sat there alone, trapped somewhere between thought and prayer. Since his childhood, he had been aware of how the medieval building had been altered by the fervent heretics of old, hammers in hand. The alcoves once dedicated to the saints, including the Blessed Virgin, had been emptied. There was still the remainder of several carvings not so easily detached from the walls, but the faces were defaced or the heads were cut off, a common occurrence in so many houses of worship throughout the land, great and small. Ned found it strange how they could be so impassioned to banish the holy ones of God from His sanctuary. Despite this, there was still a golden cross standing upon the altar.

"Oh, God," Ned murmured. "Tell me what to do…"

Just then, he sensed someone else in the church, and turned to see Mister Randall standing in the aisle, studying him. The vicar gave him a stern look, then instructed, "Move over."

Ned scooted further down in the pew, and the vicar sat next to him.

They remained in silence for several minutes. Then Randall whispered, "As you know, I am the youngest son of a noble family, much like yours. When I was fifteen, my father told me I should choose a career for myself. The military, the bar, or the church, he said, and told me to go be by myself for a while and sort it out. I went riding, and then it rained, so I stopped off here, and sat down, in this very pew. And I mulled it all over, and thought…all three options had something in common. If I were an officer, I would be giving and receiving orders. If I were a judge, I would be interpreting and implementing the law. And if I were a cleric, well…I supposed I would be charged with upholding the honor of God. That gave me a fright. But then I looked up at the gold cross on that altar, and I thought of…honey. Yes, there was a passage of scripture that stuck with me, about the law of God being as sweet as honey. My fascination with bees went all the way back, you see. And I thought perhaps preachers of the gospel are similar to them in the task God gives them. And I fancied God had given me that task too. So I chose the Church. Most of the time, I don't regret it."

Ned looked over at him, slightly perplexed. "Are you trying to tell me something, sir?"

The vicar sighed. "Don't be difficult, boy. I just…I suppose, for whatever reason, I don't want you to think I am thoroughly useless in my role. It's not because of my pride. I really don't care what your kind think of me. But I also do, because…" He gestured broadly. "I don't want to be the reason you reject the settlement to be…me. Does that make any sense?"

Ned nodded. "I…always sensed you were trying your best."

"For an imposter, you mean," Randall grumbled. "Well, maybe you and Nevison can afford to view my position that way, seduced by the romance of nonconformity. But I cannot. I have too much work to do running this parish and, sometimes, this village. It could drive me into Bedlam some days…" He winced. "I will admit, though…the outlaw was right about the boy in the flood. I had given him up for dead too easily. Perhaps I really was lacking in moral courage, the willingness to risk or command others to risk themselves on the behalf of a Papist peasant."

Ned was quiet for a moment, then confessed, "I saw Nevison in prison. He…said sorry, about his handling of you, I mean."

"Did he?"

"Yes, he…really wasn't going to hurt you any worse than he did. And what he said about Lizzie…well, he just wanted to scare you…"

"He succeeded."

"He shouldn't have done it. It wasn't Christian. He knows that now." Ned sighed. "Do you accept his apology?"

"I suppose I really must. It's part of my duty." He adjusted his posture. "I didn't tell Jack what Nevison said regarding Lizzie. If I did, he might have gone off on some foolish foray to take the bandit down. Or he might have unreasonably blamed you. I didn't want either of those things to happen. I believe in the rule of law. If a man is to suffer for his crimes, it must be through the proper channels. And I don't want others caught up in that, either you or Jack."

Ned swallowed hard. "I am trying to get a reduction of Nevison's sentence."

The vicar raised an eyebrow. "How?"

"By royal appeal, through General Burgoyne."

"Why would His Majesty be inclined to spare him, do you think?"

"I-I don't know," Ned admitted. "But I owe Nevison that much. I have always considered him a friend. Do you think very ill of me for that?"

Mister Randall looked down. "No."

"Thank you."

"It takes a certain bravery to own unsavory friends," the vicar conceded. "That's another reason why, well…whatever others may say…I don't think you're a coward. I knew your father for a long time, through many ups and downs, and cowardice was foreign to his countenance. I find it highly unlikely that his son would be any different. I've seen you going on foot for your whole life, while others rode, looking down on you, and often thought…that is brave, in a way, as well."

Ned sighed. "Well, it got me very good at clambering over walls and fences."

The vicar snorted. Then said quietly, "Has it ever occurred to you that this recusancy of yours is a wall you could climb over?"

"You should want me to stay Catholic," Ned replied. "You benefit from our tithing."

"Now, you know that's not fair," Randall exhaled. "Yes, I take a salary to feed my family, but I'm not simply pocketing it all. The tithes go towards running the parish."

"The parish you took from us," Ned clarified.

"You're never going to move on from that, are you?"

"Why should we?"

"Because the past is in the past."

"That's an easy thing for you to say."

"No, living in the present isn't easy at all," the vicar retorted. "It requires a willingness to see things as they are and work within the confines of them without indulging in flights of fancy about alternative histories. It means accepting what is and making the best of it, for the good of the nation."

"Submitting religion to politics, as a servant of the settlement," Ned shot back.

"Is it evil in your eyes to try and prevent more civil wars in this country, or to struggle to make a compromise stick, or to hold at bay atheistic notions coming over from the continent?" the vicar demanded. "Yes, I am a servant of the settlement, and have labored my whole life to continue implementing it, because it has brought peace to this land and given Englishman a manner in which to be Christian without being sucked under by the depredations of Europe."

"Peace for what price?" Ned queried.

"The price of trappings, for whatever they were worth," Randall replied. "At the core, we are still Catholic, in the truest sense, which is not dependent upon union with Rome. Perhaps it is not who heads the church which constitutes the Christian life, but rather simply living it. That is the universal struggle amongst all the faithful…to live it."

"Father lived it, as you know. You say you respected him, and yet you would have me break the vow I made to him on his deathbed…"

"Edmund," the vicar said softly, "no one can reasonably deny that your father was a good man. But I believe his attachments were unworthy of him because they proved contradictory in terms of allegiance. As such, your vow to him and your desire to be a patriot are at odds…"

"And what in my father's life, spent in philanthropy amongst his own people in his own country, could be called contradictory?" Ned snapped. "Tell me he was not a patriot!"

Randall was silent.

Ned exhaled, and remained quiet for several moments. "I remember the day the news broke about Quebec."

"Do you?" the vicar queried. "You were a tiny thing then."

"One of my earliest memories, I fancy. Our neighbor, Mister Harrison, came to the house weeping. His son had already been killed in the defense of Fort William Henry, and we thought at first he had lost the other one, like poor Mrs. Simmons."

"Poor man has had a train of bad luck from birth," Randall remarked. "His wife ran off with a charlatan, his son became the victim of a massacre, his monies were sunk in Boston harbor along with the shipments of tea. Always a bit emotional, wearing everything on the sleeve, and shedding copious tears. He was lucky to have your father as a friend to help him bear such misfortunes. I think he would have done away with himself otherwise."

"One of Father's last acts was to lend him money to tide him over from that madcap tea party," Ned sighed. "But I don't know…that day, so many years ago, when news of the battle came, made him seem almost transformed. Yes, he was weeping, but his eyes were shining like orbs when he announced a great victory had been won upon the Plains of Abraham. The strange name charmed my ears even then. Father asked anxiously if his son was alright, and he said that he had indeed survived, but he was weeping for all the youths who had not, aye, weeping for General Wolfe. He cried so bitterly then, Father embraced him, and Tessie, who was watching them along with me, started to cry too. Then I started to cry. What a strange moment that was, but mirrored up and down the country! We were all one then!"

"Indeed," the vicar croaked.

"Then you came riding up later in the day to tell us the same news."

"Part of my job, making sure everyone hereabouts was informed," he said.

"Your throat was hoarse, and cracked during certain words, like when you said Wolfe was dead. I remember that part the most. Then Father asked you in for a drink."

"It had been a long day of reading things aloud from the pulpit, and shouting things at people's windows," Randal recalled

"It looked as if you'd been crying."

"As I said, it had been a very long day."

"So you and father drank from the vintage wine he kept only for special occasions, and you toasted to the victory and to the fallen…"

"Yes," the vicar concurred, a hazy look in his eyes. "We toasted to England."

"I will never forget it, as long as I live," Ned vowed.

He recalled something else too, the way his mother had later lectured his father over partaking in such toasts, the way she said that at least the French were not heretics, and worthier of being mourned than the dead English general and his dead English soldiers, who were beyond any help or hope now. Outside the Church, she said, as ever she had said, there was no salvation. And Francis Southworth had admonished her, proudly proclaiming that his family had gained the land their house was built upon under Edward III, founder of the Order of the Garter, in exchange for their devoted services rendered to him against the foes in France. Besides, he said, no one could know with certainty, no, not the Holy Father himself, whether any particular soul was damned, including their English general and all his English dead.

Then Francis said that, if the reports were true, Wolfe had used with his dying breath to offer God praise for the victory, while the ground upon which he lay shook from the booming of the big guns. That, the Southworth patriarch insisted, was keeping faith with an older custom, one stretching back to Henry at Agincourt and far beyond, when Catholic Englishmen up and down the centuries, scrubbed from memory, sung the *Te Deum* and received white hosts upon trembling tongues. No matter if everyone else forgot, no matter if his own household lost hope, Francis vowed he would never forget England as she was seen from eternity, still the Lady's dowry, wealth worth defending.

"I remember you and Jack as mere infants, always pretending to be soldiers under Wolfe's command," the vicar remarked. "And when you were older, your voices cracking with young manhood, I caught you playing with swords."

"And scolded us for it," Ned recalled.

"Yes, of course I did, for it was not lawful for you," he sighed. "But it did prove your pluck. You were not as belligerent as Jack, but never shied away from him either."

"You say that you don't consider me a coward, and yet you would counsel me against sitting out this war," Ned surmised. "Isn't that right?"

"Britain must ask of herself the merit of her progeny," Randall said. "It is only through their willingness to serve her with an undivided heart and a strong arm that we shall remain united, strong, and free."

"You want me to go because Jack wants me to go," Ned said tersely.

"Yes," Randall blurted. "Jack wants you to go. As much as I did not approve of the two of you keeping such close company as children, I see now…" His voice trailed off. "He…relies on you. Perhaps you are, in some respects, more grown up than he is. And I worry for him. There. You've exposed a hidden motive. Are you proud of yourself?"

Ned felt himself burning up, but mumbled, "Jack can take care of himself."

"Yes, Jack can take care of himself," the vicar repeated in a tone of bitter sarcasm, turning to leave. He paused, seeming to think better of it, and turned back around. "I…know that you abstained from communion today, but…would you like me to bless you?"

Ned stared at him suspiciously.

"For God's sake, I'm not trying to entrap you, boy," Randall exhaled. "I do not have witnesses poised to spring upon you at an unsuspecting moment. I just…this is my job." He glanced at the floor for a long moment. "Whatever you think of my ordination, it cannot possibly be sinful for one baptized Christian to receive a blessing from another…"

"It might be, if it causes scandal," Ned replied.

"Boy, you came here of your own accord, to my house and to my parish! Am I really so scandalous to you that even my touch is a curse to you?"

Ned suddenly felt convicted. He could not hurt this man after he had been treated with kindness and hospitality. So he found himself awkwardly clambering out of the pew and kneeling down in the aisle to receive whatever blessing might be bestowed.

"Must you be so Papist in everything you do?" the vicar sighed.

"Afraid so," Ned mumbled.

Randall shook his head, exasperated, then placed his hand on Edmund's head.

"The Lord bless you and keep you; the Lord make His face to shine upon you, and be gracious to you; the Lord lift up His countenance upon you, and give you peace."

Ned felt a sudden swell of emotion overcome him, and a tear rolled down his cheek. He wished his father was still alive, wished it so very badly. But Francis was gone, and Mister Randall was in front of him, placing a firm but not unkind hand under his chin and wiping the tear away with his thumb. Then he traced the sign of the cross upon Ned's forehead.

About ten minutes after the vicar departed, Jack came into the church, carrying a pile of parcels in his arms.

"Fancy finding you in here, pondering like a good Protestant," Jack teased.

"This place used to be Catholic, you know," Ned noted.

"Maybe God doesn't want to be locked up in a church, whether it's Catholic or Protestant," Jack argued, sitting down in the pew next to Ned. "Maybe…He wants to be outside. Maybe…He wants to go where we're going…"

"Oh, Jack," Ned exhaled.

"Well, Jesus was outside almost all the time, except when he wasn't," Jack said.

Ned giggled. "Alright, what's in the boxes?"

"Things," Jack replied.

"Yes, I gathered that much…"

"For you, to keep for me, maybe for a few months, maybe for bloody ever."

Ned felt a sinking feeling in his chest. "Don't, Jack…"

"What? I worked hard on wrapping all this up for you! At least don't be an ingrate!"

"I'm not, I just…"

"I even gave you the shirts with ruffles for dances," Jack said. "I'm risking the girls losing their minds over you."

Ned rested his hand on a lumpy package. "This isn't a shirt."

"'Course not, egg-head!"

He squinted. "Why on earth would you give me your football? I don't even play."

"Because," Jack said, "most of the players are going off with me, so…well, it's safest in your keeping, I'd wager. Just don't kick it. You'll hurt your puny self."

Ned rolled his eyes. Then Jack shoved another package at him. It felt hard.

"A book, Jack? Really?"

"Not the village idiot you thought I was, huh?"

"Alright, I'm opening this now," Ned decided, tearing open the parcel, "or I'll be eaten up with curiosity…" He squinted at the title. "You read George Herbert, Jack?"

"I'm a parson's son," he replied with a shrug. "Besides, he said, 'For all may have, if they dare to try, a glorious life or grave.' Worth remembering, I think." He glanced down at the floor. "Also, 'old men go to death, but death comes for young men.'"

Ned felt a chill run through him and opened the book to distract himself from his friend's dismal musings. His eyes fell upon words that felt amazingly familiar to him.

Oh all ye who passe by, whose eyes and mind
To worldly things are sharp, but to me blind;
To me, who took eyes that I might you find:
Was ever grief like mine?

O all ye who passe by, behold and see;
Man stole the fruit, but I must climb the tree;
The tree of life to all, but only me:
Was ever grief like mine?

Such moving lines about the Passion of Christ, and from an Anglican. Edmund had never harbored the delusion that they lacked literary prowess, but somehow it struck him in a new way today, and he saw an opening in the high wall he had not allowed himself to imagine before.

Might not God be found here, now, in this place, with these people, as they are? Perhaps there are some hills I must climb, some sacrifices I must make, to follow Christ in a manner that will do greater good to my neighbors, which I dared not imagine before…

"Go on, take a look at this one too," Jack said, shoving another parcel at him.

Ned did as instructed, and was shocked to see a finely crafted figurine of a horse.

"But you idolize this, Jack…always have done."

"And you always wanted a horse," Jack mumbled. "A dream come true, hmm?" He offered a lop-sided grin. "If they bring my carcass back with ever so many holes in it, well, you can bury it with me, like the ancient kings…"

"Stop, Jack!" Ned blurted. "If you keep on like that, you'll make it happen!"

There was a misty look in Jack's eyes, a sadness that stabbed Ned to the heart

Yes, Jack can take care of himself.

The vicar's bitter words rang in Ned's mind. He shivered.

"If they don't bring me back, well, you can just keep it."

"I could never bring myself to look at the thing if you didn't come back," Ned rasped.

"Then give it to Willie," Jack blurted. "He always liked it too. You can prop it up on his grave for me, and tell him I thought about him when I fought…I thought about everything here when I fought…"

"Stop, Jack, please…"

Dear God, tell me what to do! I'm not brave enough to be a coward!

"I'd let you have Brutus too, but he might gobble up that sheep mutt of yours, and have you for dessert…" Jack laughed, but it came out forced. "Then again, maybe you can teach him to like the smell of Papists, if you spend enough time with him…or maybe just wear one of my shirts…you can assume my place as the village master of hounds…"

"Enough!" Ned shouted, his voice echoing through the church, his resolve crumbling away. "I'll go with you!"

Jack stared at him for a long moment. "No, you won't…"

"Yes, I will! I can't bear it otherwise, I can't…" Ned buried his face in his hands, praying God would somehow understand. "I'll go to your war with you."

I'm sorry, Father, he thought. *I'm so sorry.*

He heard Jack breathing in a funny way, then felt a hand on his back. When he looked up again, he saw Jack's dark eyes were shimmering more than usual.

"Our war," the vicar's son rasped.

~

The next morning, Ned's sister finally arrived at the vicarage, her brow wrinkled with worry.

"I am sorry I didn't come sooner," Teresa apologized. "I thought you might have needed time by yourself to think things through."

"I did, Tessie," he said softly.

She winced. "The vicar told me you intend to go south after General Burgoyne. He said…you see it as your duty."

"I do," Ned replied. "And I must."

"Ned, what you're toying with is nothing short of apostasy…"

"A crime which Mother condemns me of, innocent or guilty," Ned exhaled, "and one which I find increasingly less egregious compared to cowardice or treason. We're all in this war together, rise or fall. England is our mother, and her honor is in jeopardy. Jack has helped me see that."

"You mustn't take advice from Jack in such a grave matter as this," Teresa protested.

"Why not?"

"Because…he's Jack!" She glanced over her shoulder. "No offense, Jack."

Jack, who was behind them, munching on a sandwich made from the roast beef leftovers, just shrugged his shoulders. "You're still carrying a grudge because I wiped my nose on your dress when I was five."

"That was my good dress, Jack."

"I had a cold!"

"You were being deliberately naughty! You could have just asked for a handkerchief…"

"Not as fun."

"Jack, really…you've not improved one jot! Must you keep wolfing down your lunch at a moment like this?"

"Sorry, but I'm not about to starve on account of your familial dispute," he mumbled, taking another bite. "Need to build up my energy to slaughter some rebels…"

"You already have an excess of energy," she exhaled. "And why must you men try to solve everything with slaughter?"

"Because…" He pretended to think about it for a moment, then finished, "It's fun!"

She shook her head in despair and turned back to her brother. "Ned, you mustn't join him…"

"I have to do this, Tessie, for all of us, to redeem our reputation," Ned murmured. "I'm sorry, but I cannot hide from the world any longer, using the faith as some sort of shield to crouch behind while others do the fighting for our nation's good name."

"But you are named after the two Edmunds, king and priest!" Teresa protested. "Their consecration has been upon you from the day of your christening, when the treasure they died defending was entrusted to you! You cannot escape your patrons, nor scrub out the blood of the martyrs! If you don a scarlet coat at the price of your conscience, the color will only remind you of the wound in your own soul! If you sign away the faith of your fathers, all lesser goods will be forfeited too!"

Ned felt a sudden sickness overwhelm him. "I-I'm sorry, Tessie…I have a coach to catch…goodbye…" With that, he stormed outside, not even looking back when she called his name, one last time, her voice contorted with anguish.

Jack followed after him until he reached the garden gate. "Look…I know that was rough on you, and it's going to keep being rough on you, but…"

"Please, none of your philosophies right now, Jack," Ned blurted, wrapping his arms around him to stifle a chill.

"No philosophy," Jack assured. "I just wanted to say…I'm proud to know you, that's all."

Ned squinted, shocked his voice sounded sincere.

"What I mean is…you've chosen us, over everything else." Jack bit his lip. "It makes me feel…better about everything. Whatever's out there, we'll face it together. And Willie…well, I'm sure he's proud of you too, if he can see us. I feel sure he can, somehow. I'm sure he's cheering us on. And for that alone, I feel like…well, it's the right thing, what we're doing. And who knows? Maybe Tessie will get to understand that too, in time, once you've made a bloody hero of yourself."

Ned glanced down. "I doubt it."

Jack sighed, then leaned over and gave Ned a typically awkward hug.

"You're such an odd duck, Jack," Ned muttered, returning the embrace.

"Ha! You're one to talk." He leaned up and pinched Ned's cheek. "I might have to protect you from those lusty rebels with your pretty baby face! God only knows how desperate they get out in the wilderness!"

"Oh, hush," Ned groaned. "For a parson's son, you've got the naughtiest mind."

Jack laughed heartily. "No help for that, I'm afraid!" Then he grew suddenly pensive. "We…we'll make it through alright, together, hear? It's what I wished upon the rainbow."

Ned felt his throat constrict, sensing Jack was trying to convince himself of that more than anyone else.

"Of course, Jack, we'll be fine," Ned confirmed, touching his friend's arm. "It's what I wished for too."

Chapter 16: THE TEST ACT

When Edmund finally arrived back in London, he went in search of Burgoyne, only to learn that he was scheduled to make a speech in parliament that very day. Ned promptly joined the crowd making their way towards Westminster Hall to listen, and soon found himself sitting in the gallery, surrounded by men and women craning their necks and peering through opera glasses.

Ned spied Burgoyne below, resplendent as ever in his scarlet uniform and feathered hat, gesturing grandly with his decorative cane like an actor on stage, voice booming.

"While we remember that we are contending against brothers and fellow subjects, we must also remember that we are contending for the fate of the Empire," Burgoyne declared. "The colonists must be reminded of their allegiance to the mother country, lest anarchy triumph over law, and we become the laughing stock of all Europe! The rebels cannot hope to stand against an army such as the King has placed under me, and will melt like snow in the noonday sun as we advance!"

"The honorable member from Preston may pontificate to his fellow Whigs about our patriotic duty," another parliamentarian replied, "but in making his coming campaign sound like nothing more than a parade through Hyde Park on a summer's eve, he proves why he has gained the moniker Jack Brag!"

Some in the chamber laughed, and some booed. The gavel pounded three times and the Speaker of the House called for order.

"If I brag, it is based upon the quality of my countrymen, with hearts of oak," Burgoyne insisted. "Is there a man in England–I am sure there is not an officer or a soldier in the king's service–who does not think the Parliamentary rights of Great Britain a cause to fight, bleed, and die for?"

"Then you admit there will be blood," the parliamentarian pointed out. "How much, pray tell? A river's worth? An ocean's worth? Will it be like the deluge in the times of Noah?"

"I believe we should each be willing to put our blood at the disposal of the national interest," Burgoyne proclaimed, "but I am confident this campaign will be a swift and clean one, so long as we strike in concert from our respective positions, and drive the wedge home to split the colonies in two! *Carpe diem*, I say! *Carpe diem*!"

"I stand with General Burgoyne!" cried Major John Acland, a young member of parliament from the West Country, famous for his fiery speeches.

"Of course you do," the opposing Whig sighed. "Your biases against the Americans are well-known. Indeed, you have shown yourself so fiercely opposed to compromising with them in any respect, you have fallen into the habit of upsetting the equilibrium of this House, requiring the King himself to reprimand you!"

"I bear no undue ill-will against the Americans," Acland retorted. "I only burn with a righteous indignation at their affronts against the Crown, whose cause I know to be just! We must proceed against these so-called revolutionaries with resolution, and spare no cost in subduing them, if we wish to hold our heads high among the great powers!"

"It was my hope that England, the Mother of Liberty, who planted and nourished these colonies, would remain intertwined with their fate through ties of affection, not subjection," the Whig retorted. "It was my hope we might bind up the wounds opening ever wider between us and perhaps stop the bleeding…"

"That which is generosity and magnanimity after victory is timidity and foul disgrace before it!" Acland shot back. "We must make a stark choice, gentlemen: either we acquiesce to the independence of America, sacrificing the honor, security, and advantage of the British nation, or we enforce their submission to this country by vigorous measures! I must maintain that it would have been better for this country that America had never been known, than that a great consolidated American Empire should exist independent of Britain to rise up and displace her!"

"Or worse," Burgoyne added, "that our former colonies should be manipulated by our enemies, especially France, and used to bring about our downfall! This is a matter of self-preservation!"

"Self-preservation, you say?" the Whig queried. "And are you so bold in your plan to save us all that you would gamble with the flower of Britannia's ranking youth, educated to be the next generation of our leading citizens? You have summoned them to your side with promises of smooth sailing and a hero's return, even though their houses would be left to falter without heirs, and this nation without progeny, should tragedy unfold!"

"Yes, I am so bold, because my vision of the future is strong!" Burgoyne cried, his eyes gleaming in a strange sort of ecstasy. "We will overcome all adversity! So sure am I of the outcome, I will lay you a wager in gold, before all here assembled, that we will have this business settled, and I will have returned home in triumph, by Christmas day in the morning!" He pulled a coin from his pocket and held it up dramatically. "Be assured, I will put my money where my mouth is! My fortune, and very life, are at the service of my country! By the King's head upon this coin, I swear it!"

Again, there was a cacophony of noise in the chamber, cheering and booing and banging on the benches, before shouts from the Speaker and the pounding of his gavel finally restored order. Ned could not help but roll his eyes, given Burgoyne's history of gambling gone wrong. Also…the general did not have much of a fortune left to speak of anyway. That, of course, would not stop him from publicly speaking of it.

"I, too, will not hold back even a farthing," Acland declared. "I have already set about rousing my native west country to arms, putting my private fortune at the disposal of those answering the call. Personally, I shall be pleased to offer my sword to General Burgoyne, to serve in his glorious campaign to the best of my ability, should His Majesty give me leave!"

Burgoyne bowed gallantly in reply. "I could not ask for more spirited company!" He turned back to the opposing parliamentarian. "It is not seemly for Englishmen to shirk from a fight, nay, not since our warrior ancestors first set foot upon these shores!"

The parliamentarian raised an eyebrow. "Then surely our offspring, the Americans, are molded from a similar substance. They will ready themselves to meet you, and use the land itself against you." He shook his head. "Mark my words, General Burgoyne: when next you set foot upon English soil, I fear it shall not be at the head of victorious hosts, but as a prisoner on parole."

Burgoyne visibly flushed, and for once seemed at a loss for words. Then recovering himself, he bowed again, and said crisply, "Let history decide."

Later in the day, Ned tracked Burgoyne down to a large back room of a tavern where the general was involved with a number of other officers. A map of America was spread out on a table before them. When Burgoyne looked up from the map, he finally caught sight of Ned, standing on the threshold. His eyes widened momentarily, and Ned saw him mouthing some excuse or other to the other officers, assuring that he wouldn't tarry long. Then he strode over to where Ned stood and ushered him out into the hall.

"My God, Ned," Burgoyne exhaled. "Whatever are you doing here? Is something amiss? Do you need anything?"

Edmund swallowed the lump in his throat. "Sir, I…" He inhaled shakily. "I've come to join you, if you'll still have me."

Burgoyne just stared at him for a moment with an unreadable expression on his face. Then he pulled him into an embrace. "If I'll have you," he chuckled. "Silly goose!" He leaned the boy up again. "Just got off the road, didn't you?"

Ned nodded.

"Well, go ahead and order what you will for supper. Tell the proprietors you're my guest…nae, my recruit! Now tell me, where are your rooms?"

"The White Hart Inn," Ned stated, "just across the way."

"Excellent," Burgoyne replied. "I am rather in over my head with meetings for the next few days, but we can meet on Friday evening at the inn to discuss the paperwork."

Ned felt a thud in his chest at the reminder of what he would be asked to do, and Burgoyne placed a hand on his shoulder.

"Now, then, you mustn't worry about it," the general insisted. "It's mainly a formality. Think of the spirit of the thing as opposed to fixating on every letter. They just want to know you're a loyal Briton. And you are. I know that."

Ned nodded reluctantly. He wanted that to be proven, once and for all, more than anything else. He had to keep telling himself that, had to keep up his nerve.

"Good, good. Now I must scurry back…"

"One more thing, sir," Ned blurted, taking hold of Burgoyne's sleeve. "I must know…did you give His Majesty my plant?"

Burgoyne chuckled, and patted Ned's arm. "I did indeed, at my last royal audience. He knew exactly who you were when I mentioned you…the Papist farm boy with a good taste in music!"

"And did His Majesty like the plant?"

"His Majesty promptly set it beside the window where it was sure to get the sunlight it needed to thrive."

"And did you ask him…about my friend?"

"I said that I would, and I did," Burgoyne assured. "It comes down to this, Ned…if Nevison wishes to save his life, he can fall upon the King's mercy, which is bountiful indeed, and don the scarlet tunic in his service. I had a message sent, informing him of his options."

Ned reddened. "But…it would mean him taking the Test Act…"

"Yes, well, that comes with the kit," Burgoyne said with a shrug. "It is his only way of blotting out his crimes in the King's eyes."

"But sir, I know you may find it hard to believe about a highwayman, but he is a Catholic, and a devout one…"

"Then perhaps, Ned, it might be sensible for you to jot him a little message yourself. It might help him see the light."

Ned swallowed. "Would you…send the message on my behalf? Tell him that Edmund…wants him to live. Tell him that Edmund has gone for a soldier, and has come to believe God does not look with scorn upon it, if it is done in the best interest of the nation. Can you write that for me?"

"I can and I shall," Burgoyne assured. "Everything will be taken care of…I promise, Ned." He smiled sincerely. "Thank you for coming to me. You don't know what it means…" He cut himself off, squeezed Ned's shoulder, and said, "Until Friday, then!" Then he turned to return to the table.

The next evening came, and with it Burgoyne, swooping into the inn with a bundle of papers under his arm. But he didn't pull out the papers just yet. No, he insisted upon buying his young friend a drink. Not food this time, just a bottle of wine. Ned knew he should have suspected something from the start. Perhaps he did. But he allowed himself to be deceived, allowed the wine to flow, allowed his reality to become blurred.

The next thing Edmund remembered was sitting in his room, staring down at a very specific parchment, his watery eyes causing the words to swim in front of him like black eels. He was drunk, yes, the drunkest he had ever been in his life. Burgoyne mercifully had seen to that. But all the alcohol in the world could not completely blot out the pain of what he was about to do, nor could it scrub those terrible words out of his mind.

I, N, do utterly testify and declare in my conscience that the King's Highness is the only supreme governor of this realm, as well in all spiritual or ecclesiastical things or causes, as temporal, and that no foreign prince, person, prelate, state or potentate hath or ought to have any jurisdiction, power, superiority, pre-eminence or authority ecclesiastical or spiritual within this realm. So help me God, and by the contents of this Book.

Yes, those same words, proffered to the pious for generations, and refused by martyrs unto death. The denunciations and abjurations continued as the eels swam upstream, against the sacrifice of the mass, the doctrine of transubstantiation, and invocations to the saints, especially the Virgin Mary. Worse of all, perhaps, was the vow to report any Papist priest he might discover for punishment before lawful authorities.

"I can't," Ned rasped. "I can't…"

"Ned, you must," Burgoyne begged. "Your whole future is at stake!"

"Stop…it hurts…" He pressed both hands to his forehead.

"It won't hurt anymore once you've gotten it over and done with," Burgoyne insisted.

"But-but…I can't think…I can't…"

Edmund felt Burgoyne take his hand and clamp it on top of the Bible lying between them on the table. He felt the embossed cross burn his palm.

"I can't," he repeated, trying to pull his hand back. "I can't lie to God!"

"Listen to me, Ned," Burgoyne intoned, a thick desperation rising in his throat. "Do you want to go through your whole damn life branded as a coward at best or a traitor at worst? Do you want to abandon every manly obligation to your king and country and sever every tie of kinship with your fellows who are willing to seal their duty in blood? And all this for a pope who doesn't even know you exist?! Is that really what you want?!"

Ned leaned forward, burying his face in his crossed arms.

"No, look at me!" Burgoyne took him by the shoulders and forced him to sit up again. "This is your last chance! I can't help you after tonight!"

Edmund shut his eyes tight and felt the tears hot on his cheeks.

"Ned, please…I don't want to have to hurt you like this…but it's the only way…" Again, he took the boy's hand and placed it on the Bible. "God knows your heart, lad." He slipped the quill pen into his other hand. "Ned…trust me…it's for the best…" Then he started to guide it along in the signing.

Edmund heard the scratching sound of the pen against the parchment, and found himself resigning to its motion and his destiny.

And then it was done.

He was a true Englishman.

So they said.

But it was not over.

No.

Not yet.

He remembered, still in an alcoholic haze, being pushed into a carriage and driven to the outskirts of the city. The first clear image in his mind was sitting in a pew. The church was old. It had been Catholic once, surely. He tried to stand up, but a hand was on his shoulder, holding him down.

"Ned," Burgoyne said, putting a hand on the boy's shoulder. "You must take communion in front of a witness to make the papers legally binding. The Reverend Manderly and I will be your witnesses."

Ned touched his chest, where once he had carried the Eucharist, consecrated by a Catholic priest, the Body of Christ for the imprisoned to feed upon. Yes, he had carried it reverently over his heart, and now he felt his chest was aching for its presence once more. But instead, he was about to take Anglican communion, a sign of conformity to the Anglican Church.

"It's a counterfeit," Ned choked.

"A counterfeit of what, Ned? We simply reject the concept that communion of any kind is body and blood in substance. Whatever you were schooled to believe, great minds hold different views on what it might be. At worst, it will only be bread and wine to you, but still a sacred symbol of the Last Supper. At best, there is more at play, and Christ is present in the receiving of it." Burgoyne bit his lip. "I believe that last view, Ned. I only wish I was like you, pure of heart, and could receive without fear. It's a blessing, don't you see?"

Ned swallowed hard. "I-I cannot see…anything…"

"Look, I'll take communion with you, alright?" Burgoyne offered. "I haven't had the chance since coming home, and…Charlotte would want me to. Besides…fellowship and all that…"

"I probably shouldn't give the sacrament to either of you Saturday morning tipplers," said the vicar, who Ned only just realized was standing over them with his arms folded, his garb wrinkled, and his wig at a quizzical tilt. "But it's four in the morning, and the bed beckons me back."

"There's a good career cleric for you!" Burgoyne chirped. "Remember, I did obtain your ne'er-do-well brother a slot in the cavalry before he proved the ruination of your family name. I also put in a good word or two with Lord and Lady Fulbrook, your patrons…"

"You don't have to remind me," the vicar sighed. "I've struck more than a few deals with the devil to be a respected man of God. One hand washes the other with us. So far that has included baptizing bastard babes and now regularizing this wine-soaked Romanist…"

"He is my friend," Burgoyne retorted, suddenly defensive. "Now perform your office, Mister Manderly."

Again, Ned only remembered bits and pieces of what came next. He was down on his knees next to Burgoyne before the altar. He liked to think he had protested a few more times out loud, but perhaps the words were only in his mind, and the taste of wheat and wine upon his tongue. Anglican communion did not taste terribly different from Catholic communion. And yet his chest was not only aching now, but burning. What was he doing to himself?

Where is He? Where is my Lord? Where have they taken Him? For He is not here…

Ned heard the vicar mutter words and heard Burgoyne mutter a response, taking communion too, as he had promised. After a few minutes he took Ned's arm, and whispered, "Help an old soldier up, won't you? My knees are smarting!"

Ned did so, and the two of them hobbled to a pew at the back of the church and sat together. Burgoyne kept clinging to Ned's arm the whole time they remained there in silence, and Ned felt that he was trembling, and heard him murmuring the Lord's Prayer in a voice heavy with sorrow. Something about it made Ned's heart bleed.

Then at last Burgoyne rasped, "I-I used to receive…with her. Even when I felt unworthy. I thought God would be lenient on me, because she would loop her arm through mine, while we sat in the pew afterwards, and I felt forgiven…" He shifted in his seat. "You know…when I first knew her, in the flesh…I was unworthy. I felt like I was casting a lily into mud, for she was a good girl…a good Christian girl…and I was…" He shook his head. "She was trembling in my arms and didn't always know what to do that night. I wasn't used to that from most of the women I had lain with. But she was quite young…and a virgin. I didn't dare say anything naughty the whole time, lest I hurt her feelings. Later on, when we got to know each other better, we could be playful about it, and she laughed at my naughtiness, but not then. She didn't even seem to know there would be pain the first time. I felt guilty. She was so vulnerable to me, and I…I took what I wanted from her…"

He winced, and continued only with difficulty.

"I-I calmed her. I made her feel pleasure to distract her from the pain. I am good at that, you know…making women feel things. And it was easy to make her feel new things. Then in the morning, when I awoke…she was leaning up beside me, looking down at me, and the sun shining through the window was flowing through her hair. It was much lighter in color when she was younger, Ned…it looked like spun gold in the dawn, forming a halo. And her eyes were as clear as crystal, and she was telling me that she loved me, yes, me…that she was mine in body and soul, and she would die loving me…and that surely it was a holy thing, to feel so alive with love…surely the Lord, who Himself was love, would not scorn it, and we might take the sacrament together…" He shuddered. "Dear God, Ned, it broke my heart. I thought…if I destroy her, may I be stricken from the Book of Life!" He clenched his fists. "I-I tried to do right by her…I tried…for though she loved me with a greater love than I fear I am capable of, I think…I could still die for the love of her…but…" He squeezed Ned's arm. "Dear God, dear God," he prayed. "Do not hate me for receiving as I am…do not hate me for having loved her as I am…do not hate me for bringing the boy here, or at least, do not hate him, whatever his conscience tells him…for he is good, I swear it…"

Ned felt tears fill his eyes as he helped his friend to stand. "Come, General," he whispered. "We must rest now…rest in the mercy of God…for what we have done, and failed to do…"

~

When Ned woke up the next morning, he found Burgoyne had already gotten a lieutenant's uniform in Ned's size laid out for him, along with a long scarlet sash. There was also a gilded copper gorget, the last vestiges of medieval armor, embossed with royal coat-of-arms featuring the lion of England and the unicorn of Scotland. Above the two beasts were the letters "GR" for Georgius Rex, a sign of utmost fidelity to the sovereign.

The sovereign, yes…

Head of Church and State.

Ned had sworn to the titles, with his hand upon the Holy Book.

He remembered it with surprising clarity through the haze of his hangover.

And the memory caused him to shudder.

The general seemed genuinely excited for Ned to try his uniform on, which he did. It felt strange, like slipping into someone else's skin, but simultaneously and paradoxically like something he had done before, so often it did not feel new. Burgoyne, grinning, held up a hand mirror for the boy to admire himself, and Ned squinted when the glistening buttons reflected in the glass. Then he presented Ned with a surprise: a set of pistols, the first he had ever been allowed to own. He could not help but feel a lump in his throat as he held one of them in his right hand, testing the weight.

"You look so fine, Ned, so very fine," Burgoyne murmured, and Ned saw that he too was swallowing hard. "You have put away childish things and become a man. Your father would be proud."

Ned stared at him incredulously. "Would he, sir?"

"Well…he was, of course, an old-fashioned gentleman, about many things," Burgoyne admitted, gesturing broadly. "But…surely seeing you like this would make any father proud, and your father had enough knightly blood in him to be charmed by the look of a soldier's livery. Besides, if you were mine, I…I'd be so proud, I'd unman myself with tears…" He sniffled involuntarily. "Well, then…do you like them, Ned?" He gestured to the pistols. "I picked them up for you as soon as you told me you were with us. I could hardly wait to give them to you."

Ned smiled softly, and on a compassionate impulse, touched the older man's face. "I told you already. Anything from you, I would treasure."

Burgoyne cleared his throat. "Your new life will take a bit of getting used to, young man. You've led a fairly sheltered one thus far…"

"In some ways, and not in others," Ned replied.

"Yes, but, well…the point is you'll be subjected to vulgar language and coarse manners, and I don't think that's the usual on the farm. The army is full of hard-bitten men and their modes of being. Black humor and barbed tongues. And, often enough, blasphemy. Not that I encourage that sort of thing…I generally don't like hard swearing on staff, as I find it uncouth, but still…"

"I will do my best to adjust," Ned assured.

"Of course you will," Burgoyne agreed. He smiled again. "I have another little something for you. Now close your eyes and hold out your hands."

Ned did so, unable to keep himself from smiling at the way Burgoyne took such joy in giving presents. He felt something long and steely placed in his hands, and when he opened his eyes, he saw it was a sword, yes, his very own. Again, he winced, this time at the reflection of the candlelight in the steel, which caused the tears he had been holding back to finally swim in his eyes.

The following day, the general took Ned with him to the Sunday service at the same church. It was full of recruits, with fresh faces and scarlet tunics. Even though the gifts from his mentor had moved him, Ned had returned to feeling dead inside, sitting in the pew, listening to the vicar's monotonous voice wash over him, unable to comprehend the nature of the words nor their meaning. Neither Edmund nor Burgoyne received communion this time. Indeed, most of the recruits did not approach the altar either. Ned assumed they had already done so the previous week to validate their paperwork, and felt no pressing need to receive again.

But one young man, at the last moment, when the other parishioners who intended to receive had already done so, sprinted out of his pew, almost tripping over his own feet, and made his way up to the altar. He knelt down, his cupped hands extended, and after receiving, he remained kneeling there for a very long time. Only the sound of the vicar's voice saying the concluding prayer seemed to rouse him from his meditation. He then returned to his pew and sat down next to a woman who appeared to be in her late thirties. She gave him a warm smile.

After the service ended, the recruits were invited to breakfast in the vicarage. Edmund would have preferred to skip it, but Burgoyne was in his element, being idolized by the young recruits, and the general was soon sitting next to the vicar at the head of the table, bantering with the boys as Ned struggled to fit in, feeling utterly alien.

The recruits seemed quite cocksure, bragging of how they would scatter the rebels like frightened rabbits. The vicar's two teenage daughters, Phyllis and Cynthia, seemed thoroughly enamored by the local young men in uniform who were seeking their attention. The vicar's son Nathaniel, meanwhile, seemed to be in a less cheerful mood. He was the youngest, just twelve or thirteen by his looks, and he periodically asked in a sullen tone why he couldn't join the campaign, at least as a drummer. But each time the vicar simply intoned, "No", and the boy continued to mope and play with the scrambled eggs on his plate.

As the recruits continued to boast and the vicar's daughters continued to flirt with them, Ned found himself lost in the shuffle, unable to eat or converse, just playing with his food like Nathaniel until he haphazardly dropped the knife he was using to butter a muffin. He found that he was too embarrassed to go looking for it.

A few moments later, however, someone reached over and placed another butter knife alongside his plate. He turned to the young recruit sitting next to him, who he recognized as the one who had gone up for communion. There was a knowing smile on his face, similar to the smile of the woman who had been sitting next to him in the pew. He had auburn hair, warm brown eyes, and prominent front teeth.

He reached out a hand to Ned. "Lieutenant Paul Jennings, at your service," he introduced himself, and Ned noticed the boy had a lisp that made every *s* sound resemble *sth*. He found it somehow endearing.

"Oh…thank you, I mean…I…" Ned stammered, shaking his hand, and Paul chuckled a little. "Southworth, Edmund Southworth…a lieutenant too, as of yesterday…"

"Ah, splendid," Paul said. "We're all fresh off the presses here. I got my uniform only the day before that."

"It looks fine…very fine indeed," Ned said.

"No finer than yours," Paul returned brightly. "I admit to being nearly giddy with gladness. Mother said I could not join up until my sixteenth year. I'd have gone off to join my uncle in the service two years ago, for a nice early start, but she is the most stubborn woman alive. Well, anyway, my birthday was on Thursday, so off I go to finally make something of my small self."

"Oh…happy birthday…belatedly," Ned replied, and cringed at how awkward it came out. Paul just giggled.

"We must become fast friends, you and I," Paul decided. "Yes, the first to be made on our first tour of duty."

"Y-yes…I would like…"

Ned got distracted by the sound of the others arguing and wagering over how many Yankees they were going to shoot, and Paul patted his arm.

"Don't let them upset you. They get loud, but they mean well. Zeal for King and Country consumes them." Paul leaned over a little closer and whispered, "And zeal for the Manderly sisters, it seems! But I grew up with them, so I'm immune to their charms…or lack thereof…ouch…"

Ned smiled to see that the younger sister Cynthia had apparently overheard and flung a half-eaten muffin in his direction. Then she stuck out her tongue.

"I meant that you're like my sisters!" He tried to patch it up.

"I still haven't forgiven you for making a kite out of my petticoat!" she sniffed. "You stole it right off the clothesline!"

"Borrowed, not stole," Paul sighed, "but it's good to know your memory is as flawless as your hearing." He then retrieved the half-eaten muffin and started eating it himself. He turned his attention back to Ned. "So I heard General Burgoyne say you had been his traveling companion in London before."

"Yes," Ned affirmed. "Last spring. It was most generous of him."

"Wonderful. Where did he take you?"

"Oh, the usual places…the houses of parliament, the Tower, and Tyburn…" Ned paused, then added in a faraway voice, "There was a hanging going on."

"Uncle Martin took me to see a hanging there," Paul stated matter-of-factly. "It was a horse thief, around my age now, by the looks of him. He used to be an apprentice to a saddler. Then off he went with one of his master's mounts, saddled and bridled and all! I imagine he intended to escape the county and sell the horse at a market elsewhere. But he didn't get far enough fast enough."

Ned swallowed a mouthful of muffin with difficulty. "Did he die well?"

"Not particularly," Paul admitted. "He was crying when they put the rope around his neck. He shouldn't have done that. It didn't help his cause, just made people in the crowd throw handfuls of mud and rotten vegetables at him."

"I suppose sometimes…it just happens," Ned offered.

"No, any man worth his salt should be able to control it," Paul countered, reaching for a piece of toast. "That's what my uncle said. It's the measure of a man, especially at his end. We only have one death to die, after all. Some men have naturally weak characters though."

Ned shifted in his chair. "May I tell you something, even if it leaves you thinking of me as having weak character?"

"I highly doubt I will," Paul said kindly, eating a piece of his toast.

"I don't like hangings. They make me sick."

Paul smiled sympathetically, then leaned over to him. "Truth be told," he whispered, "I did not like it much myself. In fact, I felt unwell by the end of it. It dragged on for so long, they finally pulled down on his legs to break his neck. A mercy…but that sound!" He shuddered briefly. "All the same, I couldn't let on to my uncle. I'm just glad he didn't decide to take me over when they opened the dead man up and had him displayed like that for a day or so. His own family wouldn't have anything to do with the body, because he had shamed them so in life, and the officials said the decision was made to satisfy the curiosities of science. But umm…I doubt most of the people looking were quite so high-minded. Either way, I don't think I'd have handled the viewing well, and that would have embarrassed Uncle Martin, so altogether best avoided." His gaze flitted briefly to the other recruits, chatting it up at the table. "You won't tell on me, will you?"

Ned shook his head, relieved that he was not the only one with reservations about such lurid showings. Then he found himself asking, "If your servant stole something substantial from you, would you…?"

Paul looked at him quizzically. "My man would not do such a thing," he assured.

"Yes, but if he did…"

"But it's not in his nature," Paul insisted. "I know…Amesbury has been around for as long as I can remember…"

"But…"

"No," Paul blurted. "It's a nonsense question."

Ned felt rebuked. "I'm sorry."

Paul sighed and patted Ned's arm again. "Don't be. I'm the one who kept going on about hangings after you made a passing reference. I'm afraid I have a vivid memory and imagination, even by way of suggestion, and Amesbury, well, he's my…" He shook his head. "Never mind. We'll talk more about your journeys with the general. Is it true you met the King?"

Ned nodded. "I hadn't expected him to be at the party General Burgoyne took me to, but there he was, and before I knew it, I was talking to him, and he was talking to me."

"Ohhh, do tell me what about!" Paul pressed him eagerly.

"Music, mostly," Ned replied. "We have common tastes, it turns out."

"It's times like this I wish I kept up with my flute," Paul sighed. "Hurt my lip once, and then got lazy, and never returned to it."

"I don't play anything myself," Ned clarified. "I just like listening to recitals and the like, especially the works of Handel…"

"I like listening too, for a while, then I start fidgeting," Paul admitted. "I'm poor at sitting still for a long time. But you, lucky you, to have royal tastes!"

"Yes, I suppose," Ned chuckled. "His Majesty was kind enough to give me a button from the Handel Society."

"Oh!" cried Paul, clapping his hands together once. "He was carrying it on his person then?"

"Wearing it upon his breast, yes," Ned confirmed.

"Well, of all the truly splendid things," Paul remarked. "You must have made quite the impression."

Ned shrugged. "The King is generous." He paused, then mumbled, "I had General Burgoyne give him a potted plant from me in return. But I also…asked a royal favor."

"What favor?" Paul asked eagerly.

"I…would rather not say just yet," Ned answered. "You see, I don't know how it's going to turn out and…well, I'd just rather not say…"

"You're afraid you'll hex yourself," Paul chuckled. "No matter. I can wait to find out. From what you've told me, I believe this matter between yourself and His Majesty must have a happy conclusion."

"I hope so," Ned murmured, wishing he had the same confidence as this boy.

"I'm afraid I'm not as cultured as you are," Paul confessed. "Therefore, if I am ever to meet the King and gain royal favor, which I should like, I will first have to do something suitably heroic upon the field. It would make my uncle very proud too."

"I'm sure he's proud of you already, in your new uniform," Ned remarked softly, thinking back to the way Burgoyne had looked at him the day before when he first put on his red coat and held his pistols.

"Yes," Paul admitted. "Yes, he is. People say he's a harsh man, but they don't know him, not like I do. You see, I lost a father, and he has no sons. So we fill in where the other lacks. And making him proud is one of my highest hopes." He glanced over at the vicar, then whispered to Ned, "Perhaps he will spare a prayer, or at least a good thought, for me too, even if I was a bother to his daughters growing up!"

Manderly, meanwhile, seemed to be trying to steal some attention back from Burgoyne by reminding everyone that he, unlike the general, had actually been to America and could offer a realistic appraisal of the continental terrain and colonial temperament. His illustrious patron, Lord Fulbrook, had investments in the colonies, and Manderly had traveled with him to tutor his lordship's son and heir, ten-year-old Master Jeffrey. The vicar quite liked to brag about Fulbrook and his progeny, and just how much trust the nobleman placed in him as a teacher, and how much of a scholar Master Jeffrey was becoming under his care.

But the teenaged recruits at the breakfast table seemed far more enraptured by Burgoyne's romantic tales about fighting the dons in Portugal to pay Manderly's meanderings about America much heed, even though he was their host. Paul seemed to feel sorry for the vicar, and asked him a number of questions about American wildlife and savage tribes to make him feel important. Manderly happily indulged him, though Ned could not help but wonder how much the vicar had seen for himself, and how much was based on books he had read in his own home study.

Soon Manderly was distracted, fussing over a spoiled jar of strawberry preserves which the maid had failed to seal properly, and scolding her at length. Paul again intervened, insisting the butter was good enough for a spread, and giving the mortified girl a chance to escape. Then he managed to gently nudge the vicar into bragging about the new shelves that were installed for various jams from the pantry. Ned got the impression Manderly viewed himself as a connoisseur of canned goods, and Paul was a longtime expert at humoring his fruit based obsession.

After the breakfast had concluded, most of the youthful attendees congregated outside in the yard. Manderly grumbled about how they should not tread on the grass, but since everyone was already cavorting on the lawn, he moderated his rule to merely not trampling the garden, which Ned noticed was an odd blend of green cabbages and purple petunias. Paul just assured the vicar that he would protect the petunias with his life. Manderly actually cracked a smile, and said Paul's mother had raised him well. Paul assured he would relay the compliment to her.

Ned, meanwhile, trailed behind Burgoyne as he joined Manderly strolling down the garden path towards the gate.

"I do hope you know what you're doing, General," Mister Manderly remarked.

"Why shouldn't I?" Burgoyne queried. "I am a professional."

"Yes, I am aware. I also am aware that these are boys, silly, sheltered boys, the lot of them." The vicar gestured to their rough-housing antics on the lawn, with his daughters squealing and cheering them on. "Almost all between sixteen and nineteen…"

"Perfectly suitable ages to serve His Majesty and win honors for themselves, their community, and their country," Burgoyne assured. "Granted, it shall hardly be a proper war, such as when we've campaigned against the frogs or the dons, but even this small service quashing errant colonials will get them off to a good start…"

"I fear you underestimate the resolve of the Americans who have risen up against the government, just as your fellow Whigs in parliament have warned you against doing," Manderly said. "When I accompanied Lord Fulbrook to America, I got a sense of the inhabitants and their independent nature. They believe that they were being forced into this war by our refusal to heed their complaints, and now they maintain they are only fighting for their rights against unjust encroachment."

"I know all about their nonsense arguments," Burgoyne scoffed. "I do not believe they hold water. Parliament has never relinquished the right to tax the colonies. It is the same with nearly all the nations of Europe in colonial affairs."

"You don't seem to be taking my full meaning," Manderly countered. "Whatever you may think of their arguments, the colonists will see your march as a further encroachment upon them, a hostile invasion which will further inflame their passions already set alight by coffee house orators. Your plan to include savages in your ranks will further stoke a panic. Men who sat upon the sidelines will join the struggle to rid themselves of you and secure what they hold dear."

"On the other hand, there are many Loyalists who will flock to us as an army of liberation," Burgoyne countered. "And as for the savages, I intend to keep them on a tight leash. They will not molest any soul unless I tell them to do so. I will not have a hair harmed upon any man's head unless he gives us just cause by impeding our march."

"The rebels will fight just as hard as the savages the whole way," the vicar predicted. "Yes, perhaps even like demons. You have no way of knowing the number of Loyalists who will commit to helping you at their own peril. Furthermore, you will be struggling through vast stretches of poorly charted territory. I spent some small time north of the city of New York. The risk you are taking is colossal…"

"Some element of calculated risk is inherent to all military operations," Burgoyne replied.

"I must reiterate the question put to you in parliament: just how well have you calculated your chances against so many lives, General?" Manderly queried, gesturing again to the lawn.

"Sir, since I have not endeavored to instruct you on how to conduct yourself as a cleric, I advise you not to endeavor to instruct me on how to conduct myself as a soldier," Burgoyne replied tartly. "If you wished to have a say on military matters, you really should have gotten over your fear of blood and donned the scarlet tunic. Instead, you chose a quaint little vicarage and vegetable garden and a stable annuity in the bosom of the nation's church."

"I know you have little enough respect for me in the cloth," Manderly mumbled.

"Well, what do you expect? I made you what you are, as a friend to your family. You were not any more religious than the next man, but you said you thought it might suit your temperament, and that God would largely ignore you just as you largely ignored Him. Yes, you said you knew how to make yourself socially acceptable to superiors, on Earth as it is in Heaven. You would do anything to keep a tidy little shop here, no matter which kings might reign, like the legendary Vicar of Bray. It wouldn't surprise me in the least if you were a secret Deist."

Manderly winced. "I am not the exact same man you made."

"Aren't you?" Burgoyne queried. "Do we still not do each other's dirty work, ever and anon?"

"Losing a wife does something to a man, as surely you know," Manderly stated bitterly. "It makes him think…yes, even one like me." Manderly glanced over towards the young men again, then said solemnly, "I know for a fact how many fine families across this country are sending off their sons with you because you told them it was a good way to initiate them into the service with minimal risk. I know how many mothers in my parish will be left to mourn if anything goes amiss. Now all their fates are bound up with your ambitions, for good or ill…"

"You need not remind me of the preciousness of their lives," Burgoyne shot back. "I take my responsibility to them more seriously than you know. But I am a soldier, and to fulfill our duties, we must keep our eyes upon the prize, and not be held back by our private dreads, like old women fretting by the fire…"

"Forgive me for dreading the prospect of poor boys being forced to kill other poor boys, with the same blood running through their veins, in a war that should never have happened," the vicar ground out.

"Spoken like a true Whig!" Burgoyne snorted. "And how do you propose to quell the armed rabble? Through sweet talk? General Howe and his brother, the admiral, tried that in New York with Adams and Franklin. It went nowhere. Those obstinate rebels would not treat them unless their independence was recognized!"

"They would not treat because the Howes had no formal authority to negotiate any settlement that would be remotely satisfactory," Manderly countered. "All the Howes could offer was some sort of gentleman's agreement to suspend hostilities."

"And what settlement do you think would prove satisfactory?" Burgoyne pressed.

"Representation in parliament," the vicar replied. "It might not be too late to stop this fratricide…"

"If they had parliamentary representation, they'd be constantly out-voted, and they know it," Burgoyne argued. "The radicals simply used that as a disingenuous rallying cry to pursue other ends."

"Then surely some other system might be established that would prove satisfactory in terms of representing them," Manderly countered.

"If we falter on the point of parliamentary supremacy, the empire will be divided piecemeal into squabbling bodies politic," Burgoyne insisted.

"I have heard talk of all manner of things, including the creation of an imperial parliament in which all our dominions were proportionally represented. Even if such efforts involved trial and error, it would be worth it to maintain the empire and avoid a further bloodbath."

"Such foundering would do nothing but weaken us in the eyes of the world, eager to see us fail. If the British constitution is suspended, we are lost…"

"If it is indeed a constitutional crisis, then surely military action will not solve it," Manderly exhaled. "We are placing our troops in a terrible position…"

"Our troops will do their duty with alacrity," Burgoyne replied. "And as for the 'constitutional crisis', as you call it…if these colonial troublemakers truly wished to avert fratricide, they should have sat on their hands for a spell and obeyed the law until people of your persuasion came to power, then petition the hell out of you."

The vicar sighed. "I know many have been given to hyperbole, both when exaggerating parliamentary abuses and maligning the sovereign's character. Some among them, clearly, have behaved rashly, promoting senseless violence and stirring it up amongst their usually peaceful fellows. And of course others are simply using circumstances to get a leg up in the world…I know something about that. But dear God, still…"

"Still, you don't like blood," Burgoyne concluded.

"If that's a crime, then I am guilty," Manderly declared.

Burgoyne shook his head, then muttered, "Look, you know I'm sorry about your wife. She ran things very well here, and dare I say, she managed to make you happy. I never wished anything else upon you."

Manderly looked down. "I don't think I appreciated Catherine as much as I should have while she lived. I suppose I took her for granted, like the house and garden. Part of the upward climb, a marriage to make Lord and Lady Fulbrook happy. They wanted their chaplain to have a nice docile bride for the sake of respectability. And it was a respectable match. But…" His voice drifted. "I made a mistake. I became unduly attached to her. Not that I ever said it. But there you have it. And I find I do not do well alone…" He glanced at his son, moping on the porch steps over being too young to join the recruits. "Not as a father, certainly."

"Oh, the boy will get over it," Burgoyne assured. "There will be other wars."

A hazy look passed over Manderly's eyes, and he said sadly, "No doubt."

Just then, Edmund felt someone tap him on the shoulder.

"Are you quite tall, or am I just that small?"

Ned turned to see Paul standing next to him, measuring the distance between their heights with his hand. The boy was noticeably shorter when standing up than he had looked when sitting down. Major Pitcairn would most certainly not have sought to recruit him into the Marines. The very thought of the affable Scotsman, slain across the sea, made Ned feel melancholic.

"Well, I'm not tall enough to make a grenadier," Ned replied, "but I have bumped my head on a low doorway or two."

"Oh, good," Paul chuckled. "Makes me feel a bit more substantial! Mother used to measure my height by having Amesbury cut markings in a cherry tree that grows in the yard. But I seem to have stopped growing for years now. So I'm stuck with what little amount of me there is."

"It saves you headaches," Ned reminded him, and both laughed.

"My house is just down the opposite street," Paul said, pointing in the general direction. "Would you care to take tea with me?"

"Didn't we just have a late breakfast?" Ned chuckled.

"You hardly ate more than a bite," Paul observed. "You were too nervous. Too many strangers around. But I'm just me. You'd be hard-pressed to be really nervous around me."

"But didn't you eat breakfast at least?" Ned queried.

"I'm hardly the type to scorn sharing a second one," Paul chirped. "I've always had a healthy appetite. Besides, there's cake leftover from my birthday, and I can't eat it all by myself…or maybe I can, but I'd rather share it with you. It's more fun that way."

Ned smiled. "I'll ask the general if he wouldn't mind my tarrying."

"Of course he won't," Paul assured. "We're about to be brothers-in-arms, and must give each other a proper send-off!"

So Paul grabbed Ned's sleeve and dragged him over to the general.

"Ah, you two found each other!" Burgoyne said upon seeing Ned and Paul together. "I suppose it was meant to be."

Paul nodded. "Yes, he dropped his butter knife, so I've adopted him."

Burgoyne laughed, then turned to Ned. "When he was a lad of ten years, young Master Paul impressed me by quoting chunks of 'The Faerie Queene' when I was over the vicar's for supper!"

"My mother used to read it to me as a bedtime story when I was much younger than that," Paul explained. "I just sort of remembered it naturally after a while, for I always asked her to read over and again, I loved it so much"

"And in return for your recitation, I bought you a tin soldier to add to his regiments displayed on the shelves!" Burgoyne recalled.

Paul nodded. "My lucky piece."

"Do you still have Edmund Spenser's works up in your noggin by any chance, Lieutenant Jennings?"

Paul cleared his throat, then recited:

> *"A gentle knight was pricking on the plaine,*
> *Ycladd in mightie armes and silver shield,*
> *Wherein old dints of deepe wounds did remain,*
> *The cruel markes of many's a bloudy field;*
> *Yet armes till that time did he never wield:*
> *His angry steede did chide his foming bitt,*
> *As much disdayning to the curbe to yield:*
> *Full jolly knight he seemd, and faire did sitt,*
> *As one for knightly giants and fierce encounters fitt."*

Burgoyne clapped. "Bravo, boy! My faith in you was not misplaced! And now, look at you! A gentle knight in mighty arms, preparing to wield them for the good of the realm!"

Paul smiled broadly, revealing his overbite. "I hope for nothing more than that I shall bear and wield them with honor and do my family name proud. Then I know you will be proud of me too, which would make me very happy."

"I have every confidence it will be so," Burgoyne assured.

Paul turned to Ned. "May I borrow Lieutenant Southworth for an hour or so, General? He didn't eat properly at breakfast, you know, so I want to get some tea into him. What say you?"

"Very well," Burgoyne chuckled. "I'll be at the inn in the meantime."

"Thank you, sir," said Paul brightly, offering the general a salute then bounding off.

Burgoyne leaned over to Ned. "He's a precocious youngster," he whispered. "Loves his books and model soldiers. Can give a man a bit of headache when he gets to chattering, must be said! But I think you'll take him to heart. Very sweet-natured. A bit naive. Just needs a bit of grounding. Maybe you can help with that. Now run along. He'll certainly take your mind off…" Burgoyne's voice faded out.

Ned winced, but simply replied, "Thank you, sir," and turned to follow Paul, who was already partway down the street.

Chapter 17: TEA AND CAKE

After Ned had procured permission from Burgoyne, he followed Paul across the street to his house. They were met at the door by a maid with dark skin and a shapely form, waving her mop at them. "Not this way, Master Paul! You go 'round the back way with those boots!"

"But they're not dirty, Cassie," Paul insisted.

"No buts, Master Paul," she insisted, nudging him out with the mop. "This floor is clean enough to eat off of, and it's going to stay that way for at least a day, so help me."

Paul rolled his eyes. "Fine," he conceded, "but we'll be requiring tea and cake in the parlor."

"*That* I can do, Master Paul," she assured, pointing out the door again. "Around the other side!"

So Paul and Ned made their way around to the other side of the house.

"Cassie can be so domineering," Paul huffed. "You'd think she owned the place sometimes!"

"Is she…?" Ned started, then restrained himself.

"A slave?" Paul filled in. "We're not supposed to have them in England, you know."

"I know," Ned conceded. "But families with vested interests in the sugar islands often smuggle enslaved Negroes home with them."

"My mother abhors the trade," Paul replied. "Says it's corrosive to the soul. Uncle Martin fights with her all the time about it. You're right; he has investments in it. He's the one who bought Cassie for us when she was only nine. We were struggling with money matters at the time, and he thought she could give the housekeeper a hand. But mother was fit to be tied. She said she didn't want an African child brought to her from an auction like a Jersey cow. Uncle Martin said that if she refused, the girl would go back on the block, and then…she might have a worse fate. Mother relented, but handled the whole thing more like an indenture, only to last for seven years. She even taught Cassie reading and religion in the meantime. Then two years ago, when the time was up, Mother freed Cassie and gave her a choice to stay or go. Cassie chose to stay part of the household, and since then, she's been paid alongside the other servants. As I said…Mother doesn't take kindly to the business. My uncle says she's too soft-hearted, and that such commerce is necessary for the greatness of the nation. He lectures her for…being a bad influence on me…"

"And you? What are your thoughts?"

Paul shrugged as he opened the back door for the both. "Mother could never be a bad influence on anybody. But…I don't want to be called soft, I suppose, nor a detriment to the national interest. Besides, I stand to inherit certain holdings from my uncle. He is quite enthused by the prospect, and the last thing I was to do is disappoint him. All the same, I don't like…" He paused nervously. "I…don't discuss it. It's for the best, I think. We'll cross that bridge when we come to it."

When they had taken their seat in the parlor, beside a cheery fire crackling in the hearth to ward off the cool spring air, Cassie came in with tea and cake for them both. But while Paul delved into the cake eagerly, Ned still had trouble finding his appetite. He felt as if he had become more a ghost than a man, conscious yet disembodied, desiring no food but forgetfulness.

"Keep stirring your tea like that, and you might dissolve the spoon."

Ned was roused from his morose thoughts by his younger companion, who had a kindly smile on his face.

"I'm sorry," Ned apologized, setting the spoon aside. "I suppose I'm proving to be very poor company, aren't I?"

"No, you're just shy, like me," Paul decided. "Ask anyone who knows me. I'm either quiet as a mouse, or I start rambling and no one can shut me up. It's nerves, you know?"

"You don't seem nervous now," Ned observed.

"That's because you make good company." Paul patted him on the arm, and Ned felt genuinely comforted. At least he would not be completely without friends on earth, even if he may have forfeited heaven. He winced at the thought and decided to change the subject.

"Have you ever been outside England before?" Ned inquired.

"Yes, twice. I was with my uncle in Dublin for a couple of weeks when he was recruiting for his regiment there. And before that…" An uneasy look came to his face for a moment. "He took me to the West Indies when I was twelve. As I said, he has…business interests. It was a short trip, but it was…" He paused and shook his head. "Well, it was the farthest I've been from home. How about you?"

"I went along with my father on a business trip to Edinburgh when I was ten. We were putting some of our sheep up at auction there. Our finances have never been the best…"

"We've seen so very much of the world, haven't we?" Paul teased.

Ned chuckled. "You more than me. I fear I shall be sick at sea the first time out."

"Oh, I know I shall be from experience," Paul affirmed. "But you look rather heartier than me. Besides, they say the stomach adjusts after a number of voyages."

"Does it though?"

Paul shrugged. "That's what they say. If not, we will just have to get used to being sick sometimes. A soldier's life, and all that. Would you like some more cake?"

"Oh...yes, thank you. I-I suppose I'm getting my appetite back."

"Yes, I noticed," Paul said, handing him a plate. "You just got overwhelmed before. Too many recruits from a single place, trying to outdo each other by talking at once and showing off how much they know about America in one sitting. They would make anyone's head start to spin, bless them!"

"I'd never thought much about the Colonies before knowing General Burgoyne," Ned admitted. "We did have some cousins who sailed over to make their home there, but that was over a hundred years ago, and we've lost touch. I wonder if their descendants are in arms against us now…"

"Not necessarily," Paul countered. "From what I've heard, there are only a small portion of incurable traitors. They're just very loud, like some of our recruit friends, and have made themselves popular among the more gullible folk by talking about things they know little enough about. But I don't believe most of their followers are beyond recovery if their leaders are struck down. The rest of the Americans are loyal. Some are just too cowed by the rebels to show it. That's why we must go, to show that the king's troops will protect them and their property."

"Yes, I see the necessity of it," Ned agreed. "I just...I suppose I have wanted to be a soldier since I was a child, and yet now that I am fitted and kitted, I am still getting used to the idea of shedding blood, rebel or no. And in this case...it will be British blood flowing from their veins."

"I fear the guilty have brought punishment upon themselves by their own actions," Paul said. "We should not feel guilty for having to implement it." A reflective shade entered his eyes. "My mother and uncle don't often agree, but they both went down to see the soldiers who came off the ship, from the fight on the hill. Mother spoke with Lady Gage for a spell…hard to believe the rumors that she betrayed her own husband. If she did, the sights of those poor men on the ship must have been even more terrible for her, for she would partly be the cause. Mother kept going down to the makeshift hospital where lots of them were dropped off and proffered her services to tend them. They said she was a lady of a respectable family, and shouldn't expose herself to the filth of the men's bodies and the crudeness of their tongues. She would not be deterred. Mother is a very stubborn woman. And she said there were women and children in need of tending as well, some widows and orphans, or nearly so, since their menfolk were alive, but shot almost to pieces." Paul winced.

Ned smiled slightly, sadly. "My mother…she can be a stubborn woman, too, when it comes to helping those she feels bidden to help."

"That is a fine trait," Paul said. "Fine, indeed. They make us better people."

"Yes," Ned agreed, with ever-deepening melancholy.

"Like with Mother…soon, I went down there with her, to help, if I could. I was changed by it. What wretched sights and smells! And so very many leg amputations, it haunted my dreams. The rebels had aimed their cannons low, stuffed with rocks and nails when they ran short of ammunition. And the bullets that were left to them seemed to have been coated with some sort of poison, so I'm told. Caused all sorts of convulsions before men struck by them died. It's horrible to contemplate that our colonists would sink to such methods as were used by our mortal enemies in the last war. Have they forgotten that we are no foreign foe, but their own brothers and cousins, the servants of their own king? I know not how they justify themselves before God! Surely, they should not present themselves for the sacrament in such a tarnished state…" He shook his head. "I talked with quite a few of them, and listened to them, as best I was able. Mother says I am good at it. I don't know if that's true, but I do try."

"I agree with your mother," Ned said.

Paul shrugged. "They deserve to be heard. Some have said, such souls who form the rank and file are vagabonds, not gentlemen. Does it matter? I think not. They have shed their blood for this country, and my uncle says each and everyone, therefore, is his brother. He does everything in his power to help those left to suffer. Even Mother says that is the very best part of him, however else they disagree. Many of the soldiers are illiterate. They can't petition for themselves, nor write home. Quite a few of the men I met did not wish their families to see them in such a state, so I promised I would write whatever they wanted to send to send home. I hoped it would give them some small measure of peace. It made me glad God gave me the knowledge of reading and writing."

"It is a double blessing when it becomes not only a gift to one's self, but to others," Ned agreed.

Paul's eyes grew wistful. "There was one soldier in particular I shall always remember, a decent fellow by the name of Randon. I penned his last letter to his wife, for he was too weak to hold a pen, and even if he could, he said that he wasn't very good at that sort of thing. He had some schooling as a boy, on one of the estates where a teacher was provided for, but he didn't know how to write prettily. I promised I'd try to pretty up whatever he wished to tell her."

"What was the crux of it?" Ned asked.

"He had…been redeemed, it seemed to me," Paul explained. "In America, he had given himself over to the mystery by which men are saved, and he saw the necessity of a holiness of heart and life. He said…God had spoken peace unto his soul. Can you imagine what it must be like, to be so sure that God had spoken to you? He burned to tell the whole world of it, but he was dying, and could tell only me." Paul closed his eyes. "I thought it a dreadful responsibility. Perhaps I was even jealous. Dying would seem like a small enough thing if God had spoken to a man's soul, don't you think?"

"A small thing, or a greater thing than it seemed before," Edmund murmured.

"Yes…yes, I think you're right," Paul conceded. "It did seem a great thing to him. That's why he needed to pour himself out to those he loved best. He begged me to write to his wife that, if ever he was dear to her, she should give herself up to God and be found among those inquiring after salvation. He wished her to bring up their dear little ones in the fear of God, and told them never fix your heart upon the vain and unsubstantial things of the world, for heaven was the only thing that demanded our hearts. He pleaded with me to write to his children, though they had only an imperfect knowledge of their father, to meet him in the realms of bliss. He said the world was naught but sin and sorrow, but that the key to bliss was in our own breasts because God is the solace of a reasonable soul, and God is everywhere, and so we should all be happy. That's how any sort of love amongst us here below shall be consummated, refined, eternalized…" His voice faded out. "You know, it rather reminds me of another part of 'The Faerie Queene.' There he was, common rank and file, but I fancy he had the heart of a knight, and his faith was what sustained him through the shadow of death."

Paul took a deep breath, then recited:

"On his brest a bloudie Cross he bore,
The deare remembrance of his dying Lord,
For whose sweete sake that glorious badge he wore,
And dead as living ever him ador'd:
Upon his shield the like was also scor'd,
For sovereign hope, which in his helpe he had:

Right faithfull true he was in deede and word,
But of his cheere did seeme too solemne sad;
Yet nothing did he dread, but ever was ydrad."

"That's beautiful," Ned said.

"Isn't it?" Paul agreed. Then he grew wistful again. "You know, I think the man would have said much, much more to me, but his life ebbed out apace and his tongue ceased to perform its office. I sat by him the whole time and wouldn't leave him, poor man, though it had grown dark. I wouldn't leave until I could no longer hear his breathing. I hope to God I made his words pretty enough for him, though I don't think any alterations were truly necessary."

"I'm sure he was grateful," Ned assured.

Paul shook his head. "There was so little any of us could do for the sufferers. Some soldiers brought to that miserable hospital could not speak at all, but stared at the ceiling, stuck, I think, upon that hill. It must have been a truly awful spectacle, and they had no words, just no words…" Paul bit his lip. "So you see, we must…put an end to this thing, this wretched affair in America. We must not allow the suffering of our countrymen to be without merit. We must not let those who caused it get away with it. So you see…I am happy to go now."

Ned was quiet for a moment. "How much punishing do you think will need to be done?"

"Please God, order will be restored quickly," Paul replied. "I have every confidence it will be. Then surely the crown will offer mercy to the erring who show true repentance. As you say, whatever separations exist between us and them, we are of one blood, and it is good and true."

"Yes," Edmund said wistfully. "Good blood…" He cleared his throat. "You come from a military family then?"

"On my father's side, over a century of service, going back to the Royalists who fought for King Charles. At the beginning of this century, they served under the Duke of Marlborough. In fact, I have a story I must tell you." He leaned forward in his chair excitedly. "My great-grandfather was a sergeant at Ramillies. He saw Marlborough before the battle, and he and his fellows tossed up their hats for 'Corporal John', which they called him fondly, because the Duke's care and attention extended over all the ranks. He made a lasting impression on men of high and low degree with the irresistible charm of his manner, which was grave yet gentle, forgetful of his own deeds and attentive to the needs of others. His looks, his bearing, and his address were said to be just as conquering as his sword. And so they watched as the great man went down on his knees to receive communion from his chaplain. It was a sight to behold, for he always dressed impeccably, but…there he was, kneeling in the mud, not caring how his fine clothes were dirtied."

Ned thought back to the medieval custom observed by knights, placing a clod of earth in their mouths if they could not receive the Eucharist, Christ's flesh unto their flesh, and their flesh unto the earth…everything was connected, everything redeemed, even as it was bathed in blood. Did Marlborough, who proclaimed that it was impossible to be both English and Catholic, know of such things? Did he understand his own impulses when facing his possible end, knit into him from generations past? Would Ned ever be able to escape that forbidden longing himself?

"Then the Duke mounted up upon his horse, and dropped his handkerchief, as he tended to do before battles," Paul continued. "He was everywhere at once during the fighting, and got that same horse shot out from under him, and his aide was shot down as well. But the Duke just mounted up again, calm as the surface of a lake untouched by wind. After the battle was won, he called out to his soldiers, 'A coin for the man who fetches my handkerchief back!' Well, my ancestor was the one to fetch it. He won not only the coin, but the handkerchief too! It was terribly splattered and tattered, but I still have what's left of it in a box. My uncle gave it to me for my tenth birthday."

Ned smiled at Paul's enthusiasm. "No wonder you wanted to join up for the service so young. It's in your blood."

Paul nodded. "Every mother's son among us was either with the army or navy, so far be it from me to miss out. My father was navy, but my uncle made sure I went with the army. My dearest friend Michael has gone into the navy, though. He is serving under Admiral Lord Richard Howe in New York City. I felt utterly gutted when he left at age fourteen, and I had to wait to make use of myself for two whole years before Mother relented to my leaving. We still write to each other all the time, and he tells me how life is upon Black Dick's fleet. He says the admiral is a hard man to figure. His orders can be confusing and his temper can be ferocious. Yet most of the sailors adore him, for he keeps them well cared for, from his own stores and treasure, and calls them 'fellows.' He takes promising young midshipmen under his wing as well. Michael has benefitted from that. Why, at this rate, he'll be a captain sooner than later. I can sense it. We used to be inseparable growing up, and I always knew he had greatness about him. It's a hard life on the sea, but he comes from sea-faring blood. Now at least I shall have proper news to exchange with him, who knows? Maybe we'll meet in New York. It would make me so very happy." He paused for a moment, then remarked wistfully, "I do wish Mother could understand just how important it is for me to go. Otherwise, I'm not truly a man…"

"What about your mother's side of the family?" Ned queried. "Any military men from there?"

"A little but, on the other side of the civil war, serving under Thomas Fairfax and John Hampden and Oliver Cromwell. Aside from that, though, I'm afraid we're rather nobodies on that side. Clerkish sorts from Kent who kept the dullest sorts of records for magistrates and vicars. But you know something? My mother was born in Westerham, same as General Wolfe, whose father Edward served under Marlborough. And funnily enough, Marlborough's father was from a Royalist family, and his mother from a Roundhead one, just like mine! So you see, everything is interconnected and fitting, for if she had been born a man, surely she would have been a conqueror too! Instead, she was born a woman, and is curtailed to commanding me! Usually her instructions have something to do with divesting me of excess possessions. But I'm like a squirrel. I hoard things as if they were acorns in my hollow tree, and don't want to leave.

At the same time, though, I want to be a hero too and have great adventures far away from all my comforts. So you see, the two sides of me hopelessly quarrel with each other, and I want altogether too much from my silly life."

Ned snorted, starting to understand what Paul had meant by his tendency to chatter non-stop. This, and his appearance, could not help but make Ned think that the squirrel comparison was very apt. "I suppose I like to hoard books," Ned confessed.

"Oh, yes, I am obsessed with hoarding books too," he agreed. "But you know something? I consider it a sign of quality, for both of us!"

"Me too." Ned smiled. "So what are your favorite things to read about?"

"Oh, most anything," Paul replied, taking another piece of cake for himself. "Plants, animals, the ocean, the stars, tribal rituals in the far corners of the world…you name it, I'll read it. But best of all, I like to read about the history of our nation. I am quite fond of the reign of Queen Elizabeth, as you must have guessed from my quoting Spenser for General Burgoyne. It was the cusp of a new age, charting our own course. She said something I've thought about often as we prepare to do our country honor: 'My mortal foe can no ways wish me a greater harm than England's hate; neither should death be less welcome unto me than such a mishap betide me.'"

Ned glanced down at the floor. "Yes, I…well, I feel England is a lady. We must protect her honor…"

"Exactly! Just like all great Englishmen of the past did!" said Paul. "I would sometimes imagine, when growing up, that I was among those men, serving Eliza Gloriana, in all her splendor…Francis Drake, in the Golden Hind, and Lord Willoughby, on the fields of Flanders, but most of all, I think, Sir Philip Sidney."

"Why him the most?"

"Well, they all singed the king of Spain's beard, like our dear General Burgoyne. But Sidney, well…he was more than a soldier…"

"A warrior poet," Ned filled in.

"Yes, he understood the lofty principle that, in victory, a hero seeks the glory, not the prey," Paul said. "For him, it was a matter of becoming what one ought to be, so that all other goods might proceed from it. He said a brave captain is as a root, out of which, as branches, the courage of his soldiers doth spring. And it's not simply courage to engage in violence, but rather to choose that which is noble over that which is base. He said, 'With a sword thou mayest kill thy father, and with a sword thou mayest defend thy prince and country.' That's the heart of everything, isn't it? What we do with what we're given."

Ned nodded, but the quote haunted him in a manner he had expected. In taking up the sword for his prince's honor, had he not simultaneously slain his father's legacy?

"But Sidney was more still," Paul continued. "Not only did he fight to free the Protestant Dutch from a bloody inquisition, but in the end, when he lay dying of his wounds, he gave a cup of water away to another soldier who he insisted needed it more than himself. That, I think, shows the purity of his heart and cause."

Ned remembered hearing of how Sidney had met with Father Edmund Campion while they both were on the continent, and the two had discussed and debated theology. Campion had thought him to be a soul disposed to at least considering the faith, though Sidney may have been using Campion to gain information to relay to Queen Elizabeth. Either way, Sidney was known to be sincerely religious, composing poems with his sister based upon the psalms and seeking the prayers of all men of good conscience.

Was Edmund a man of good conscience anymore?

"A cup of cold water to the least of these," Ned murmured. "Yes, that is what it means to be Christian."

"Indeed. You understand my way of thinking!" Paul beamed. "So now that I've gone on about myself and my pastimes to an incorrigibly dull extent, tell me more about you. You must come from a very fine family. The general wouldn't be touting you all over the place otherwise, would he? You must come from one of those marvelously old lines from up north. I can tell, you still have an accent, though you're trying very hard not to have it."

Edmund blushed. "Some things die hard, I'm afraid."

"No, I like it," Paul replied. "You mustn't kill it altogether. Besides, it's very proper, the way you speak with it. That's another reason your family must be very fine. Have you many soldiers amongst you?"

"Not…recently," he replied. "But-but long ago…we were, yes, I mean we did…we were knights. At Crecy, and Agincourt, and other battles, we fought…we received lands. But that was…well. Ages ago, wasn't it? Worlds apart, then and now. These days, we're sort of…reduced in circumstances…quite a lot, really…" He bit his lip, once again sustaining a wave of guilt, wondering what his Catholic ancestors must think of him now, since none in their line had broken faith but him. "Now I'm the one rambling, aren't I?"

"There, now, it's still in your blood," Paul said. "I mean, being a knight. You don't need wealth for that, do you?" Again, he patted his arm. "You will make the finest sort of soldier. I know that. And who knows what opportunities might come of it? You have General Burgoyne's favor, and he's not one to forget friends. Victory will just make him more generous. Have faith. And until then…well, you do have people who think well of you as you are. I have known you all of a day, and I think well of you."

"Thank you," Ned said softly, and meant it.

Just then, they heard Paul's mother calling for the housekeeper to help her pack yet another knapsack. Paul sighed. "She's getting altogether too involved in this. Did your mother try to over pack you?"

"No," he replied quietly. "I'm afraid not."

Again, Paul seemed to detect his emotions. "She got angry with you before you left, didn't she?"

Edmund nodded.

"Well, mothers will do that. I swear, they'll worry themselves into an early grave, no matter how many assurances we give them."

Edmund swallowed hard. "I don't know if she will ever forgive me."

"Oh, of course she will," Paul insisted, pausing to finish the last of his tea. "They don't have it in them to hate us, not really. We were inside them once, after all. They can't easily forget it."

Edmund smiled a little at his choice of words. "I do hope that is true."

"Don't just hope," Paul countered. "Believe that it is. Besides, they may not say it to our faces, but I think we're making them just a little proud. And they'll have to be proud of us anyway in the end, restoring the colonies to their allegiance and upholding the king's honor."

Edmund rather wished that were the case, but his young friend had no idea the depth of the chasm that had been opened between mother and son when he put ink to paper on the Test Act. Besides, Paul seemed far too secure in the love his own mother had for him to imagine any other state of affairs.

Paul glanced over in the direction his mother had last been seen. "Best check up on her before she tries to pack a whole bed frame. Come on."

Edmund felt odd about being drawn into their family's private world, but reluctantly followed Paul down the hall. They came to a bedroom, which Ned assumed belonged to Paul's mother, and he lingered outside as Paul went in. He just glanced in from around the corner to see an elderly woman with silver hair and heart-shaped face, whom Ned assumed was the housekeeper, helping Paul's mother to pack various odds and ends, spread out across the bed.

"Mother, you really mustn't," Paul sighed. "I know I'm a bit of a collector here at home, but in the middle of a campaign, I'll survive just fine without all this…"

"Your general, it's been said, is packing more than half his house," his mother pointed out, finger upraised.

"And plenty of frilly things for his party women to boot, from what I hear," the older woman snorted.

"And champagne!" his mother added. "Enough crates of it to sink a frigate!"

"He's a general," Paul said with a shrug. "He can be extravagant without it being embarrassing."

"A few extra pairs of mittens shouldn't bring you too much shame," his mother huffed, rolling her eyes.

Paul squinted at the contents of the bag. "Are there…ten pairs in there?"

"Don't be silly," she replied.

"Alright, are there nine pairs in there?"

"Are you trying to win one of those count the sweets in the jar contests?"

"I was always quite good at those actually…"

"Yes, because…well, sugar," she decided. "You could never get enough of it. Still can't. The sugar bowl inside is empty from one round of tea and half the cake is gone…"

"Eight pairs, is that it?"

She made a slight groaning noise. "Seven. You're losing your touch, my clever boy."

"Mother, I don't need seven pairs of mittens on a campaign. We must learn to rough it a bit…"

"Mrs. Dilby and I knitted them, and you're going to take them," she declared, like a commanding officer giving an order. "You've got hands like ice, Paul!"

"I can't help that!"

"There, Master Paul," consoled the housekeeper, tying up the bag. "Cold hands, warm heart."

"They say General Wolfe had cold hands," Ned remarked. "Perhaps it is a conquering sign."

"Thank you?"

"But you can help it," his mother countered. "Wear mittens more often!"

"But they're cumbersome!"

"Oh, you're just not trying hard enough. I'm sure you'd get used to them…"

Paul sighed, then leaned over and kissed her on the cheek. "I'm in a losing battle…"

"You've already lost, dear."

"Oh, speaking of losing things," Paul started, "did you pack away my lucky soldier?"

"That's something you'll have to ask Cassie," his mother sighed. "She keeps up with your latest collections better than I."

"Fine, I'll take it up with her. Oh, and Mother, this is Ned…" He gestured out the door. "…a friend."

Ned smiled bashfully, and Paul's mother smiled knowingly in reply.

"My son has a habit of making fast friends…"

"A gift, Mother!" Paul corrected her, then bounded back out into the hallway.

His mother gave Ned a look, then said softly, "You're older. Take care of him."

He could have retorted that he was a staff officer, not attached to any fighting regiment, and would be unlikely to see much of Paul in America at all. But instead, he found himself saying, "I promise, Madam."

She seemed instantly relieved.

After he left the room, he found Paul kneeling down by several trunks piled at the end of the hallway, and rummaging through their contents.

Just then, Cassie turned the corner, and her eyes widened. "Whatever are you doing, Master Paul?"

"I'm looking for my lucky piece," he grumbled, pushing aside the first trunk and digging through the second one. "You buried it somewhere."

"Wait, please," she sighed, "let me have my moment…"

"Your moment?"

"Yes," she confirmed. "I take pride in bringing order out of chaos, including these trunks, which I put together for you with so much care…ahh…" She gave a little yelp as he tossed things haphazardly on the floor. "This isn't necessary! I can just tell you where to find everything, if you'll just be patient!"

"Alright, then, if you know everything there is to know about everything, where did you stuff my lucky piece?" he challenged. "I must have it in hand!"

"You have a million lucky pieces, Master Paul!" she retorted, resting her hands on her hips. "And a million unlucky ones! You really need to stop yourself from collecting so many things that just end up collecting dust or going missing. Your mother, she thinks you have a problem too!"

"It's a female conspiracy," he decided, rummaging to the bottom of the third trunk. "Ah, found it at last!" He produced a small tin soldier and held it aloft triumphantly. "Now I have a better chance of not being blown to bloody pieces!"

"Don't say that!" she snapped, perhaps a bit more forcefully than intended. "Yes, and no one would be able to find all the pieces. You'd keep things a mess to the end, Master Paul."

Paul chortled. "You'll miss me though?"

She rolled her eyes. "Seeing the house remain tidy day after day will bring grief to my soul."

"But you will," he pressed.

She sighed. "Maybe." Then she added softly, "I have taught myself how not to miss things, you see. It is easier that way."

A momentary look of guilt flickered in Paul's eyes. "And it's the same with people?"

"Especially so with people."

Paul seemed uncertain how to respond to that, so simply changed the subject. "Shall we introduce Ned to our bird, Cassie?"

"If you wish, Master Paul," she sighed, leading them both back towards the kitchen.

There, Cassie gestured rather proudly to a cage in the corner containing a mourning dove. It was preening its feathers, with one wing extended stiffly in a rather sorry fashion.

"How did its poor wing get ruined?" Ned inquired.

"Hannibal," Paul and Cassie said in accord.

"Who's Hannibal?" Ned queried.

"Oh, you'll have to meet him too," Paul said.

"Had to beat the beast off with a broom," Cassie stated matter-of-factly, opening the cage and slipping in some millet inside.

"To be completely fair to Hannibal, he must have seen us eating roast duck last Christmas, and thought it only right that he should partake in the feast on his own terms," Paul said.

"No excuses for that one," Cassie countered. "He's an imp, attacking doves because they remind him of the Holy Ghost."

"As you can tell, Cassie is very religious," Paul chuckled. "Though there's something of the heathen in her still, when it comes to seeing all sorts of portents in animal behavior."

She squinted. "And then you went and fed that beast part of the duck I cooked!"

"He was sulking on the window sill over his dinner being rescued away from him," Paul explained. "I had to do something to cheer him up…"

Cassie seemed not to be listening to his excuses anymore, stroking the back of the dove with her finger, making a cooing noise, to which the bird responded. Then she started to hum, an undeniably soothing sound.

"She's quite musical too," Paul bragged to Ned on her behalf. "She sings quite prettily in church, and makes up ditties at home, like one about the dove, and another about the tree in the yard, and all sorts of things. She's been at it ever since we were small. I think she has a natural rhythm. Maybe all Africans do…"

"Some do, and some don't, like your people," she sighed. "But this is my own gift."

"She still sings African language songs too sometimes, with sounds no one else can make," Paul added.

"Plenty of other people can make them," she sighed. "Just not you, Master Paul."

"Well, I did help teach you how to rhyme in English, to my credit, so you could make up new songs here," Paul noted proudly. "What are the words to what you were humming just now?"

"It's about a sinner on Judgement Day, trying to run away," she stated matter-of-factly. "He asks the sun, and the moon, and the stars to hide him, and the ocean to swallow him up. Then he asks all the animals to take him in."

"Of course, animals," Paul beamed. "Sometimes I wonder if you still secretly worship them."

"Not Hannibal," she snorted.

"Well, yes, definitely not Hannibal…"

"He's an evil spirit covered in fur."

"You believe everything has a spirit, good or evil. Even Mister Manderly couldn't lecture it out of you."

She shrugged. "Is it so very hard for you and yours to believe that the Lord would put a spirit in everything?"

"No, I suppose not. Though perhaps that's because you bewitched me into seeing it your way from my youth!" He slapped his knee. "So what happens to the sinner in the song, who keeps trying to run away?"

"The sea tells him no, for it's running dry, and the moon tells him no, for she's bleeding red, and the stars tell him no, for they're falling from the sky, and the sun tells him no, for he's burning out. And the animals, hoof and horn, feather and fin, have no time for him, for they know nothing of sin. The sinner has a choice to make: either he gets down on his knees and starts a-praying, so the light will hide him, or the Satan will come fetch him off, and hide him right well in the darkness." She started to hum the melody again, then softly sang the words, "Oh, sinner-man, where you gonna run to? Oh, sinner-man, where you gonna run to? Oh, sinner-man, where you gonna run to, all on that day?"

"And no matter where the sinner-man goes, the animals all go off to heaven, is that right?" Paul teased her.

She made a face. "Not Hannibal."

Paul laughed heartily. "Well, with your knack for this sort of thing, I'd wager that if I manage to die a heroic death, you'll be the one to make sure I'm immortalized in song…"

"Why must you keep saying such things?" she scolded him.

"Why not? I think it'd be fun to be the slain hero of a ballad! Uncle Martin would be right proud, if it got proper circulation…"

"Please…" she rasped, sounding genuinely pained now.

"Oh, don't take it so to heart, Cassie…"

"He has no right to take you away," she blurted.

Paul raised an eyebrow. "What?"

She winced. "Your uncle…he-he has no faith in higher things, so he must make you turn into him, in hopes that he will live on through you. He is not a godly man. If he were, he would not be taking advantage of your—"

"Cassie, you're out of line," Paul stated, suddenly stern. "It's not your place to speak ill of a captain in His Majesty's service, nor of my own choice to be commissioned, especially in front of another soldier who is my personal guest."

Ned felt himself growing red from referred embarrassment, having witnessed him pulling rank on her.

Cassie gazed at him for a few seconds, seemingly hurt, and even contemplating a retort, before glancing down at the floorboards deferentially. "I'm sorry, Master Paul. I forgot myself."

Paul, too, looked down at the floor awkwardly. "We…all do, sometimes, I suppose." He shrugged. "But Uncle Martin isn't godless. No one is, when all is said and done. He just…fears enthusiasm as a detriment to the nation. He is vigilant for her tranquility."

"Yes, Master Paul," she mumbled, scrubbing the countertop with a sponge. "Whatever you say."

Paul exhaled and shook his head, seemingly exasperated by her, but then appeared to think of something funny, and asked her, "Remember the prank we played on Uncle Martin when we were young? There were ceramic frogs in the teacups. No one could see them all filled up."

"Yes, I remember," Cassie admitted, a smile touching her lips. "You spent the whole of your allowance on them."

"I fear I was never very good at holding onto money, even then," Paul admitted. "Speaking of which…what shall I bring you back from America, Cassie? I plan on going to the shops in New York."

"More sponges?" she suggested dryly, holding her sponge aloft.

"I was thinking of earrings," he said. "You told me you wore them as a girl before you came here."

"Yes," she conceded wistfully. "Made from river pearls."

"Alright, pearl earrings it is, then, even if it costs me the whole of my wages. I've always thought I'd quite like to see you wearing a pair."

"Always?" she queried dubiously.

"Yes, since you first told me you'd worn them…"

"When you were eight?"

Paul nodded. "And you were ten. Is it difficult to believe? We were inseparable."

"That's mostly because I had to clean up after you," she declared.

Paul giggled. "Even before you spoke English, you were always trying to teach me how to put everything away in its proper place. I'm entirely sure it worked."

"It didn't," she sighed.

"But you used to tell me stories too, when I asked, and I wouldn't understand half of them, because you kept mixing up the languages, but I asked for more anyway." There was a soft light in his eyes as he continued. "I suppose I fancied you were once an African princess, draped in pearls, and couldn't get the image out of my head. It suited you, even when telling me stories with my head in your lap or when scrubbing the house with a sponge." He smiled fondly. "Do you remember how, sometimes, when we would play make-believe, I would have you sit on a chair with a lace-fringed cushion, and pretend you were Queen Elizabeth?"

"Yes, Master Paul," she said. "You were very silly."

"I would pretend to be Raleigh or Drake or Willoughby or Sidney, and swear fealty to you."

"As I said, very silly," she reiterated.

He was quiet for a moment, then began to recite in a soft tone.

"Upon a great adventure he was bond,
That greatest Gloriana to him gave,
That greatest Glorious Queene of Faerie lond,
To winnie him worship, and her grace to have,
Which of all earthly things he most did crave;
And ever as he rode, his hart did earne
To prove his puissance in battell brave
Upon his foe, and his new force to learn;
Upon his foe, a Dragon horrible and stearne."

Cassie raised an eyebrow. "Speaking of dragons…I believe you wanted to show off Hannibal to your guest, for reasons beyond my poor understanding," Cassie reminded him.

"Might as well," Paul exhaled.

So off the three of them headed towards Paul's room.

"Prepare to face horror, sirs," Cassie announced as she opened the door.

Ned immediately noticed the sheer amount of paraphernalia stuffed inside the room, including shelves full of books and tin soldiers, buckets brimming with an assortment of pebbles, bark, and sea shells, and walls plastered with maps of the world and engravings of heroic deaths. And in the midst of it all, there sat a cat, on the bed, looking very much like a giant gray dust bunny, with yellow eyes gleaming malevolently. It took one look at the humans entering its conquered domain, leapt off the bed, and started to hop towards them, hissing. Cassie let out some African exclamation, and she and Ned both retreated back into the hallway.

"That thing you've adopted, Master Paul, is a shadow demon," she declared. "You cannot convince me otherwise!"

"Hannibal, really," Paul lectured the cat, shaking a finger. "You must behave more gentlemanly, or I'll be forced to lock you up in the closet again without supper."

"He doesn't believe your threats!" Cassie exhaled. "You always end up feeding him anyway!"

"Yes, but he doesn't like the closet one jot," Paul reminded her. He went over and sat down on the bed. "Now, Hannibal, we need to deal with this in a civilized manner…"

Hannibal promptly leapt up on the bed, attacked Paul's coat, and just hung there by his fangs and claws, making growling noises.

"He's not really angry," Paul assured, scratching him behind his half-chewed-off ear. "He's just…unwinding."

"What does that even mean?" Cassie sighed, exasperated.

"He gets anxiety, you know. He's not used to having a family quite yet, but he's getting there." Paul worked out some of the tangles in the fur with his fingers. "He's much more docile than when he first came to us…"

"You mean, when he gave me this?" She extended her arm, revealing scratch scars.

"I said I was sorry about that," Paul exhaled. "But you know, you do come from a land with lions, so I figured you might have some experience…"

"We don't take the lions inside, Master Paul!" she huffed. "We also don't make a point of feeding them, if it can be avoided!"

"Yes, but…well, he was hurt," Paul insisted. "Those other cats in the alley scratched him up good. And he was too weak to go hunting. He would have starved for sure."

"And that would have been a great tragedy?" she queried resting her hands on her hips.

"For him, yes," Paul replied, tranquilizing the ferocious feline by rubbing the spot between his eyes until he was almost purring.

Her eyes softened a little. "Well, you can make a gentleman of him if anyone can, Master Paul. But without you here, I am not sure who will put the time into training him."

"Oh, you mustn't throw him out, Cassie," Paul replied, gesturing to Hannibal, still hanging from his coat, in a position of comfort. "He needs us."

"He knows where his bread is buttered, that's a fact," she sighed. "Since the day you coaxed him indoors, he's become a squatter on your bed."

"He's rather nice to have around on winter nights," Paul remarked, as the cat finally released his hold and hopped down onto the pillow. "All that matted fur is like an extra blanket." He pulled one of the regular blankets up over Hannibal, as if to give him a sense of additional security, and the miniature lion growl-purred some more.

She shook her head. "Look at how you spoil him!"

"Everyone should know someone cares for them, even if it takes until they're old to find out," Paul said. "I don't think it's likely to spoil very much. Only lack of feeling does that."

She turned her eyes down briefly, as if his words touched some nerve. Then said quietly, "Hurry back, then, while my patience for the abominable beast holds out."

Ned smirked, thinking of the reaction Jack would have to Hannibal if he were there. He'd probably have a fainting spell, and Lizzie would laugh him to shame.

"I like to think all my efforts to navigate the many moods of Mister Manderly prepared me to deal with our dear Hannibal," Paul stated.

Ned laughed. "You have quite a way with the vicar, I notice."

Paul shrugged. "It took some practice over the years, but I knew I should be prepared just in case he ever worked up the courage to make his play for Mother's hand."

Ned raised an eyebrow. "He's shown an interest?"

"Oh, for years now," Paul confirmed. "It's obvious to everyone but possibly himself."

"Too true," Cassie confirmed. "It's why he keeps inviting Mistress Mary to help him with anything and everything over at the church, and giving her that look, if you know what I mean."

"Well, what eligible man in his right mind wouldn't give Mother that look?" Paul queried. "She's radiant!"

"I don't think he's near good enough for her," Cassie decided.

"Well, no one is," Paul replied. "But he really should give Mother the chance to accept or decline a proper offer, you know. I think he's just afraid of the worst outcome, poor man. His hesitancy almost has me swung over to his side. I like underdogs. Besides, he is a good man, after a fashion. It's really up to Mother whether or not she thinks he could make her happy."

"And his daughters are already like your sisters," Ned observed.

"Oh yes, for ages."

"I think the elder one used to wish you would pay her a different sort of attention, Master Paul," Cassie chuckled, kneeling down to pick some cat hair off the rug. "Then she just gave up on you."

Ned gave her a brief, wistful look. "Oh, well…a man's entitled…to his own tastes in feminine beauty, I suppose."

The way he said it made her cast him a glance over her shoulder, and he gave her a rather bashful smile. Since she was African, Ned could not tell if she blushed or not, even as Paul got to his feet and lent her a hand up.

After bidding adieu to the shadow demon, Paul and Ned went back into the parlor.

"I am so thankful General Burgoyne brought you to church with him," Paul said. "I couldn't have spent the day in a more pleasant way. I think we shall be great friends, providing you don't mind too terribly my being thoroughly common, and you with knight's blood!"

Ned smiled. "You don't seem common to me."

Paul laughed, seeming to catch on to the double meaning quickly. "No, I suppose neither of us are. We're odd ducks, and so we're bound to understand each other." He beamed at Ned. "The general must think a lot of you, as I'm sure you know. The other young men he's toured about, he doesn't bring to church."

Ned winced a little bit unintentionally.

"He and my father…they were friends…yes…even with their differences accounted for, there remained respect and affection…"

"All true friendship is like that," Paul replied. "And now the general keeps faith with what he felt for your father by looking after your interests."

Edmund did not respond directly to Paul's comment about Burgoyne. Instead he said simply, "I miss my father, still…yes, almost as much as when he first left this world. I-I don't feel whole without him…" Even as he said this, some secret part of him felt relieved that the elder Southworth had not lived to see his son take the Test Act. It would surely have broken the old man's heart and spirit.

Paul touched Ned's arm sympathetically. "I can only imagine. You see, I was too young to remember when my father was lost at sea. He never even saw me, for I was born when he was away. I've never known what it's like to have a father, so I did not think much of it as a child, except that most other boys had fathers, and I had none. Maybe that's why Anthony and I became such good friends. He had no father to speak of either. But at least I had Uncle Martin. He has always tried his best to make up for the loss." He smiled a bit sadly. "I'd like to think that the poor dying soldier was right, and the dead can watch the living. That way, even though my father never saw me as an infant, he can see me now, in the King's livery, and be proud that he had a son. I-I intend to do everything that I think would have made him proud, at any rate."

"I'm sure you will," Ned said kindly. "Does your mother speak of your father much?"

"Maybe not much, but that's because…well, it was sudden, his death," Paul said. "They'd been married for such a short time when his ship and all hands were lost. I don't think she's ever quite gotten over it, or the thought of him drowning, alone. But she did tell me he knew I was coming. She said the day before he left, she let him know. She was going to wait, because it was early on, and she'd miscarried before me. But then she thought better of it, and told him, and they went to church and took communion together. I-I received that day too, you might say. And she said…he was very happy. And God knoweth how, after all the pain she suffered, I came into the world on her birthday. She said it was like a present to soothe her loss, and a sign we would be one, even more so than most mothers and sons. And it has always been so." He smiled again, trying to be cheerful. "I must say I feel rather good about myself now that I've communicated this morning."

"To validate your papers?" Ned remarked, incapable of disguising the tinge of disdain in his voice. Fortunately, Paul seemed not to notice.

"No, that was last week. This time…it was just for me." He tapped his chest. "I don't usually take the sacrament with such regularity. Mother says I overthink every Sunday. I probably do. But I consider how small a thing I am, and lose the courage to present myself for communion. Does that ever happen to you?"

Ned felt strangely moved. "It probably should," he rasped.

"Mother tells me it would do me well to receive the sacrament more often. She communicates at almost every service. And well she should. She's really quite divine." He smiled. "But you know, many parishioners do not present themselves nearly as regularly. For me, it would be a pleasure…but I am shy. Thank heavens for the Test Act, I suppose, for it's gotten me over my scruples, and I shall do my best to be more regular from now on."

"What do you feel like when you receive?" Ned queried.

"Oh, I…I feel like I've taken myself in my hands," Paul explained, joining his hands and extending them. "Then you give yourself away, and God makes up for the loss. So you see…if something were to happen to me in America, though I don't think it will…I want to go prepared. I want to be where God is present, and God to be where I am present…whatever happens. That's what receiving is for me, and I think it's why Marlborough went down on his knees in the mud to receive, when he thought he might die. He was…taking himself in his hands…" He chuckled awkwardly. "That was a clumsy way of putting it all, wasn't it?"

"No, it wasn't," Ned assured. Then he blurted, "What to your mind happens if, say, you were sick, and vomited it up, would it still count, do you think?"

Paul looked perplexed.

"I-I'm sorry it's just…I had a friend when I was a child…and you remind me almost too much of him…if he had lived longer. Yes, you even have his eyes…" Ned swallowed hard. He hadn't expected the emotions to be so raw after so many years.

Paul laid a hand on his arm. "If the bread makes God present to us, in some special way beyond our kenning, well, He cannot be thrown up," he said softly. "It's a thing of the heart, even more so than of the mouth. We live and die only in God. That's what Mother has always said."

Ned brushed a sleeve across his eyes. "My childhood friend…he-he took care of a bird, and had tin soldiers, just like you. We…traded for them with marbles sometimes…"

Paul pulled his tin soldier out of his coat and placed it in Ned's hand. "There. It's yours."

"But…this is your lucky piece…"

"Oh, pish! Like Cassie says, I've too many for her to keep track of," he insisted. "Besides, General Burgoyne gave it to me, and it's clear he favors you."

"But I've no marbles to trade for it!" Ned chuckled.

"You can repay with some grand gesture on the field of battle!" Paul teased. "Or maybe just reach for something too high for me on a shelf in a shop when we reach New York."

Ned bit his lip. Then on an impulse, he hugged the boy. And the boy hugged him back. It made Ned feel just a little less numb.

Just then, a skinny middle-aged man in a neat black outer coat and white waistcoat, with a wig perched atop his head, entered the room. There was a polished wooden case tucked under one arm and a package of groceries held in the other.

"Amesbury, at least!" Paul exclaimed. "I thought you'd fallen in the river!"

"Apologies, Master Paul," the man replied as he set down the groceries on an end table. "It was sheer madness getting in and out of the city today. But I'm pleased to report that your pistols were ready on time."

Paul excitedly took the case from the manservant and opened it up, revealing two monogrammed pistols.

"They're stunning," Paul said in awe. "It must have cost my uncle a fortune."

"I believe you're worth that and more to him, sir," the manservant replied.

"Well, then Amesbury," Paul said, a tinge of emotion in his voice, "you'll soon have the opportunity to see if I'm any good at using them." He gestured to Ned. "Oh, and Amesbury, say hello to our guest, Lieutenant Southworth. As you can see, he's going overseas, just like us."

Amesbury bowed promptly towards Edmund, and muttered, "Sir."

"You'll be going over with Lieutenant Jennings then?" Ned queried.

"'Twould be unseemly for Master Paul, or any young gentleman like him, to be without an attendant in that savage country, sir," Amesbury replied.

Paul gave a quick glance over to Ned, and seemed to immediately ascertain that Ned was not bringing a manservant with him. Ned had thought about sending for Harry from back home, for the sake of appearances, but some gut instinct prevented him. He didn't want to drag anyone else into the unknown with him. Besides, he was used to taking care of himself.

"Well, good help is hard to find, especially nowadays, as you always tell me, Amesbury," Paul insisted, seeming to think Ned's lack of an attendant had to do with financial troubles.

"Mmm-hmm…true it is, Master Paul," Amesbury agreed, setting down the packages and starting to judiciously organize them. "'Tis a generation full of slackers, I say."

"And you have put them to shame by always being very particular about your work," Paul praised him.

"Old bachelors are particular by nature, Master Paul," Amesbury chuckled. "We get set in our ways without a wife to nag us into compromise."

"Well, I have grown so accustomed to your particularities, I could not do without them." Paul turned back to Ned. "Before we had any other servants, Amesbury was here. I'm afraid I'd be rather helpless off the field without him! But I've been training him since I was three years old for such a time as this, with my tin soldiers!"

Amesbury smirked. "So you did, sir."

"I used to make him play army with me for an hour or more before bed," Paul chuckled. "It could be rather hard to get me down, couldn't it? Stubborn streak from Mother, I think…"

"You could be a tad rambunctious, Master Paul," Amesbury admitted. "I had to make up martial stories to pacify you."

"Yes, about all the little soldiers and their adventures." Paul smiled. "And now, at last, we'll be having some of our own now." He placed the open pistol case lovingly on a nearby shelf to admire the contents. "So, Amesbury, why was London sheer madness today, or at least more so than usual?"

"There was a hanging going down at Tyburn, and a mighty large crowd turned out to watch," Amesbury explained. "Lucky if I'm not black and blue from all the shoving."

"Oh dear," Paul sighed. "Do you know what poor devil was condemned for?"

"The fellow was a highwayman up north. Had to take him down here to avoid trouble from his friends. Made quite a scene at his sentencing a few days ago."

"What sort of scene?" Paul queried, eager for gossip.

"Well, it seems he stood to be pardoned if he took the King's shilling for service in the colonies, but he'd have none of it."

"That doesn't make sense," Paul remarked, shaking his head. "Surely a man would not prefer a certain death of dishonor upon the gallows to the possibility of an honorable death in battle."

"Ah, but he was a Papist, Master Paul," the manservant clarified.

Ned felt as if someone had punched him in the stomach.

"That explains it, I suppose," Paul exhaled. "They are treacherous by nature and choose evil over good. No point in trying to help them, since they will not be helped."

Ned snapped his gaze on him, feeling affronted to his very core by the young man he had just taken to heart, but simultaneously being wracked with guilt for his own actions over the course of the fortnight. He forced himself to suppress his own emotions, and asked Amesbury, "He's dead then?"

"Yes, sir. He thrashed about for a bit, but not as long as some. Less than ten minutes."

Ned could not help but twitch at the thought of it. "Did…did he say anything on the scaffold?"

"Only heard part of it from where I was standing," Amesbury said. "What I got from it was that he knew his own sins and had made his peace with the Maker, so nobody had power over him anymore, for only God could send him to heaven or hell. Then the general spoke to him…"

"The general?" Ned blurted.

"Aye, Burgoyne himself was there. He told the condemned man this was his last chance for clemency, or he would die in the manner of his rebel father. The brigand replied that he fully intended to die in the faith of his father. The general then said he shouldn't entertain romantic notions about being a martyr, for he was only paying for his crimes. The outlaw said he didn't deem himself worthy of that title, but that he had been branded guilty all his life on account of it, before he robbed as much as a ha'penny. The general lastly said that better men than the brigantine had signed the Act and taken the shilling. And the highwayman replied in a wobbling voice, 'Let them live with their conscience, as they may, and let me die with my conscience, as I will!' Then, to everyone's surprise, he kicked the crate out from under himself."

Paul gave a little gasp. Edmund was stone silent.

"I wonder how courage can be so misplaced," Paul murmured, "to embrace death out of devotion to a foreign power rather than to serve one's country. What makes them like this? Is it superstition alone?"

"Don't ask me, Master Paul," Amesbury said with a shrug as he unpacked the store items. "I don't keep company with their foul kind. But I'll give that Papist a nod for dying bloody well."

"But for nothing, or at least, nothing worthy," Paul countered. "What an utter waste of a man!"

Ned felt himself going numb all over again as Paul got up to scour through the package of groceries Amesbury had also brought home. "Oh, good, you got more for the bowl in the parlor," he chirped, holding up some sort of candy. "Ned, would you like a piece…?"

"I must go," Ned rasped, knowing all too well the rudeness of it. "I-I'm sorry, but I must…"

"Oh…" Paul blushed a little. "Of course. It has gotten rather late. I didn't mean to keep you if you needed to be somewhere else. I'll see you out…"

"There's no need…"

"But it's no trouble."

When they were outside, Paul touched Ned's arm.

"I'm sorry," the boy apologized. "I truly am. I know you said hangings upset you, and this man was from the north too. I should have stopped Amesbury from going on about it and not asked him questions." His face was a little bit sad, a little bit hurt, guessing at what he'd done wrong and trying to make it better. "We are still friends, aren't we?"

Ned gazed into those big brown eyes, innocent and oblivious of the turmoil in Ned's heart. "It's not your fault," Ned mumbled.

But some part of Ned felt that guilt did rest upon this boy, and every other privileged Anglican, dwelling in their comfortable little world of ascendancy and forcing him into a war against his own soul.

Those fierce sentiments passed away quickly, however. Something about Paul told Ned he was far too open for his own good, and his sweet nature, combined with his thoughtless naiveté, could easily be used to wound him.

"It's not your fault," he repeated again, this time more kindly. "You have been nothing but generous to me all day. Forgive my moods."

"But are we still friends?" Paul checked again, his voice tentatively hopeful.

"Of course," Ned assured.

"Then there's nothing to forgive," Paul assured. Then he handed him the candy he had kept clenched in his hand. "For the road," he said with his unfailingly warm smile.

~

That evening, Edmund stormed into the inn room he shared with Burgoyne and found the general in his waistcoat, poring over more maps he had spread out over the table, a half-emptied bottle of champagne standing nearby.

"Ned," Burgoyne gasped. "You startled me. It's late. Thought you'd up and deserted or something. What kept you out…?"

"Walking," Edmund replied tersely.

Burgoyne tilted his head. "Whatever is the matter, boy? You look as red as a beetroot…"

"You knew Nevison refused, didn't you?" Ned demanded. "Before you got me drunk?"

"Listen to me, Ned," Burgoyne insisted, folding up the map. "I tried to save him, believe me, I did. So did you. We both did our best. It was his own obstinacy that killed him."

"You didn't even let me know when the sentence would be carried out!" Ned protested. "I couldn't even be there for him in the end!"

"There's nothing more you could have done for him, I tell you," Burgoyne replied. "Why torture yourself?"

"Because I was his friend!" Tears burned Ned's eyes. "You didn't want me to know because you thought I would change my mind about signing the Act!"

Burgoyne exhaled, and came closer to him. "Ned, I swear to God, I tried to get him to come around, even upon the scaffold. I take no pleasure in a brave man meeting such a fate. Besides, I owed him a little something too, as you know. But at the end of the day, he was a criminal, with a lifetime of bad decisions behind him. You have a future which is a clean slate under the law…"

"One which you are dictating for me!" Ned shot back.

"That's not true…"

"You deceived me!"

Now Burgoyne turned red. "I never lied to you, boy. Keep a civil tongue in your head."

"You manipulated me," Ned grounded. "Indeed, you have proven to be a master at it!"

"I didn't clap you in irons and drag you down to London against your will," Burgoyne retorted, his temper flaring, "although I suppose I could have, if I'd thought to call the constable over to your house the last time I was there!"

Ned winced.

"You seem to have taken me for a fool, a harmless, brainless jester, only adept at prancing nimbly upon stage, as so many do," Burgoyne returned, his tone bitter. "Well, I'm not. Not only was there likely a priest in the house, but you probably had a bloody host in your bloody pocket and smuggled it into that bloody highwayman! Isn't that right?"

"I will not answer," Ned rasped.

"Tell me the truth, Lieutenant!" Burgoyne sneered. "There was a hedge priest in the house, wasn't there?"

"I told you, I will not answer…"

"Yes, you will!" Burgoyne spat, slamming the map down on the table. "That was part of the oath you took! I am your commanding officer now, and you will answer to me, not to Rome!"

"I will answer to God!" Ned cried, pain choking him. "May He have mercy on me!" The tears spilled over onto Ned's cheeks and he whispered, "Sir, you are right, I signed my name upon the parchment, yes, my name in my own hand, with my other hand upon the holy book. I will do my duty to you, as best I am able, even if our friendship should end tonight. I will do my duty to my king and my country, even if my family curses me till death. But I would rather be flogged and carted than to betray a lamb to the wolves, no matter what that parchment read!"

"You see the King's justices as wolves?" Burgoyne asked, his voice softening slightly.

"Make what you will of it," Ned retorted, trying not to sob. "I shall not talk."

Burgoyne gazed at him for a long while, his expression softening further. Then he brushed a tear off the boy's cheek. "You were right not to tell me. I…spoke in anger." He turned his gaze down guiltily. "I should have told you about Nevison, to let you say goodbye. I just worried you would…" He shrugged. "I never expected you to come south to find me. I suppose it seemed too good to be true, and I didn't want anything spoiling it. I…wanted you with me, so very much. Then there was Nevison…"

"You were there. Did he suffer?" Ned asked brokenly.

Burgoyne hesitated, then said, "A bit, yes, though not as badly as some." He gestured broadly. "I don't know how to lie to you, Ned. He was getting his throat crushed. Of course he suffered. It was…an awful thing to watch and listen to. I rather wished I could have given him a few breaths myself. But he went limp faster than others who thrash about for nearly a half hour. And I think…" He hesitated again. "He died for something he chose to die for, in a place he associated with the death of your martyrs. A foolish thing to cling to, and an ungodly place to do the dying, in my estimation, but I think it brought him some portion of peace."

"A peace that should be coveted," Ned murmured dejectedly. "Did he leave me any message?"

Burgoyne hesitated.

"Sir, if you have any affection for me left, please…"

"He said you should not have tried to sway him," Burgoyne stated. "He said that you knew better."

Ned swallowed hard. "Did he die hating me?"

"No, I'm sure he didn't," Burgoyne replied. "He said that he'd pray for you to return safely to your father's house, even from Purgatory, where they would no doubt put him to work mucking out stables and polishing coins he couldn't pocket." The general smiled a little. "He kept his wit intact, facing the end. That's a credit to him."

"Is he…still hanging there?" Ned asked.

"Yes, but…they'll take him down before first light, so another crowd won't have the chance to gather and gawk. I made sure of that."

"Then into a Potter's Field with him?"

Burgoyne looked down. "Someone had suggested…using his remains for scientific studies and public display…"

"No!" Ned yelped.

"I told them no already," Burgoyne assured. "As for a Potter's Field, unless someone were to suggest otherwise…"

"I suggest otherwise," Ned stated, struggling to keep his voice steady. "My mother would happily give his remains a place to rest beneath our land, even if she would scorn a similar placement of my own corpse."

"And you would approve of this for him?"

"With all my heart."

Burgoyne sighed. "It can be arranged. Mind you, though…well, they'll strip him when they take him down…part of the payment…you'll have to pay for…"

"I'll pay for anything necessary to preserve his modesty, if that's what you mean," Ned rasped, his eyes burning again.

"And I'll pay for the wagon," Burgoyne said softly.

"There's no need. I can afford…"

"You pay to clothe and shroud him, and I'll pay to transport him. Fair?"

Ned nodded wearily, then felt his knees buckling. "May I sit down, sir?"

"Of course, dear," Burgoyne answered, seeming to take note of the fact that Ned was now treating him as a commanding officer, and that alone. He was getting what he asked for, but it was obviously causing him pain, and causing Ned pain in turn.

Edmund sat down on the side of the bed and buried his face in his hands, trying to hide more tears. After a little while, he felt Burgoyne sit down next to him. Then after another little while, Ned felt the general loop his hand through his arm.

"Damn it, Ned," he murmured. "I've hurt you. And so I've hurt myself." There was a click in his throat. "I once told you that I wasn't the sort of friend you would want. It seems I was right. And yet…" He let out a shivering sigh. "Don't hate me, Ned. Or worse, don't…grow cold to me. I deserve it, for all sorts of things I've done and failed to do, but…I n-n-need you, Ned."

Edmund looked over and saw that Burgoyne was shivering, his eyes glassy.

"I'll get your tunic, sir," Ned said.

"Damn the tunic," he muttered. "You damn well know it's not going to help, not this."

Edmund gazed at him for a long moment, then said softly, "I hurt you, and it hurts me. Yes, it's the same for me, I'm afraid."

Again there was a click in Burgoyne's throat. Impulsively, yet also gingerly, he leaned over and embraced Ned.

And Ned embraced him in return, even as he recalled his mother's words about putting no faith in Anglicans like Burgoyne or Paul, and about the punishment awaiting apostate Catholics like himself, and he wondered just how much he had erred by not heeding them.

Chapter 18: FIRST STAFF

Edmund found the Atlantic crossing to be harrowing. He vomited over the side more times than he could count, and when storms tossed the ship to and fro, he threw up in a bowl beside his cot, clinging on for dear life lest he be flung against the wall. He was just grateful to finally set his feet on dry ground again after one and a half months, only to find that it seemed to slip out from under him. He found himself flat on his face, with other newly minted officers laughing at him until their cheeks were as red as a rose. Canada was sure to be a learning experience.

Life on the staff of General Burgoyne was slightly less exciting than he expected. While Burgoyne haggled with the Governor General of Quebec, Sir Guy Carleton, over campaign preparations, Ned's duties mostly consisted of running around to prepare for the parties Gentleman Johnny was so fond of hosting with his fellow military top brass and the upper-crust of Canadian society, both of the new British establishment and the old French vintage. Indeed, he loved showing off his proficiency in the language and culture of France, though truth be told, his French had much to be desired. His handsome features compensated with the ladies however, especially the voluptuous wife of one French Canadian volunteer officer with whom Burgoyne seemed particularly enamored. Rumor had it that he intended to take her with him as a "companion" on the campaign.

But one thing the long sea voyage and his time in Canada offered Edmund was the chance to get acquainted with some of the other staff officers who he now worked alongside on shore.

Lieutenant Jonathan Rawcliffe was, simply put, unremarkable, or at least he seemed that way at first. He was in his early thirties, and while he was not obtrusively fat, he was also not especially thin. He came off as soft-spoken and withdrawn when Edmund first met him. He had the appearance of a store clerk more than Edmund's vision of an army officer, complete with ink-stained fingers, a poorly powdered wig, and spectacles he was regularly cleaning and pushing up his nose. Edmund rather hoped he liked to read, but Jonathan said that he had few high literary tastes, just plodded through his job, keeping tallies on the general's luggage and counting up costs. Edmund steeled himself for the boredom that he would have to endure, even as he got the distinct impression the man viewed him as something of a noble spoiled brat, eating out of Burgoyne's hand. The fact that Ned had been raised Catholic no doubt contributed to the reception lacking in warmth.

But with time, Edmund came to see more beneath the surface. Jonathan could be funny in a dry, self-deprecating manner, and slowly seemed to warm to Edmund when it became clear the boy was not about to sit too high on his horse. Eventually Edmund learned little things about his comrade. His father had been a soldier, killed in the Seven Years War by a French musket ball, and his stepfather was a doctor, doing his best to break fevers and birth babies and train his stepson to be a competent assistant. Now, Jonathan had a wife usually called Elizabeth, or Betsy when her husband was affectionately annoyed, or Bitty when he was consumed with homesickness. They had two children, Emma and Jeffery, the girl sensible and the boy mischievous, and lived in a village near the New Forest where Jonathan had grown up shooting ducks and getting into trouble with gamekeepers. He did not seem at all remorseful. Indeed, in spite of his spectacles, Ned was startled by what a good shot he was with a hunting rifle, which he showed off practicing in a field just beyond the main encampment. Each of the bottles he had erected to test himself were shattered where they stood.

"Not bad for four eyes," Jonathan remarked, and Edmund laughed.

The clerk then proceeded to take it upon himself to teach Ned how to properly hold and shoot a pistol, a musket, and a rifle without allowing his "recusant inhibitions", as Jonathan delicately phrased it, to get in the way of his performance. It took him quite a while to get the hang of it, but he had a patient teacher and proved to be an attentive pupil. After weeks of daily lessons, Burgoyne had to admit that Ned surprised him by the naturalness with which he drew his pistol, as if he had never been forbidden to hold a gun. Ned winced at the memories of his past life, but thanked his commander all the same.

Jonathan's closest friend on the staff was Lieutenant Gavin Jones, a ruddy-faced Welshman who could be as prickly as a bramble bush. He was a native of Cardigan, and his father had been a part of the fishing industry from a young age, working first with his own hands on other men's boats, then eventually saving up enough to buy his own and eventually hire others. Jones would boast about his father's ability to make a new man of himself, and how he had bought a nice house in the nice part of town to rear his family. It was clear that Jones had inherited that spirit of industry, and was undeniably a hard worker. He was always swearing under his breath in the old language of his fathers, since Burgoyne disapproved of vulgarities spewed out around him in English. Conversely, he also liked to sing hymns, and would brag about his place in the male choir back home which leaned towards Wesleyan worship.

Apparently his father, having achieved middling worldly success, had gone through some sort of spiritual crisis which led him to attend a revival meeting featuring none other than John Wesley. The experience changed his life, and he ended donating generously to the so-called Methodists. He also sought to place his newfound brand of faith upon his children. No matter how cantankerous Gavin could be at times, that religious streak fostered by the preaching of Wesley was still evident. Indeed, this had the side-effect of making him far more vocal in his disapproval of Ned, not just for his pampered background, but also for his past papistry. But Jonathan usually managed to get him in a better mood and get him back to work if he became too fixated upon lampooning Ned. After all, Jonathan and Gavin were two peas in a pod, teasing each other relentlessly as part of their daily routine and taking pride in being two of the only sober ones on staff.

"We just enable the fancy pants and their excesses," Gavin would jest. "But apparently we're too dull to be brought in for a spot of fun."

"We would put them all to sleep faster than the wine," Jonathan decided. "We're too faithful as husbands. Kills the mood they're going for."

"Shall we start cheating then?" Jones suggested.

"Elizabeth may be tiny, but she can handle a pistol. So no."

"Jemima hates blood. She would probably have me drowned in a laundry bucket."

"See, this is the importance of weighing costs against benefits…"

"Are we cowed by them? Is this why we haven't become captains yet?"

"The way I see it, we're simply sensible men who appreciate the passion of our wives and have rubbed elbows with paltry few important men at garden parties. Best be satisfied as is for the time being."

The third officer Ned met on staff would come to be his routine nemesis. Lieutenant Eli Thompson had ice-blue eyes, a pock-marked face, and the twang of Ulster on his tongue. His Scots-Irish father, descendent of the Covenanters, had come from hearty farm folk in County Antrim while his English mother, he would proudly proclaim, hailed from Huntington, the birthplace of Oliver Cromwell. Her father had ancestors among the Roundheads who claimed the head of King Charles as well as colonists who set out to make themselves a city on a hill in the frigid wilderness of Massachusetts; her mother was a Huguenot lady whose family had fled persecution under the Catholic king of France and been given sanctuary in Protestant England.

Both his parents had died when he was still a child of the same contagion that scarred his cheeks, and he had been taken in by his grandfather who raised horses for the army in Carrickfergus. Whenever Eli mentioned the old man who had reared him, it was with deferential awe. He had taught the boy to pray and work in equal measure, to shoot and ride and read the Good Book. He had trained the boy to be frank and frugal and never falter in upholding Protestant liberty and laws. And it was through him that his grandson had learned to dread being murdered in his bed by the bloodthirsty Irish populace who clung to their Papist perfidy and spurned the covenant of the Lord.

With a burning passion that made Gavin's own sentiments seem tame, Eli abhorred the abominations of Roman doctrine, from the saints to the sacraments, and refused to believe that Edmund had truly abandoned his Popish errors. The fires of Smithfield which had fed upon the flesh of those condemned for heresy, kindled by the Catholic queen he knew as Bloody Mary, blazed on in him with a brilliance Ned doubted would ever be put out. For he, like Edmund, had grown up with his own stories of his own martyrs, burned at the stake or drowned in the bog, and he could quote much of Foxe's book by heart. His grandfather had read from that almost as often as from the Scriptures.

Eli had also been taught to revere William of Orange, the savior of Protestants, whose reign had enabled the signing of the Bill of Rights, preventing Papists from ever again sitting on the throne or gaining other powers through which they might betray the Isles to the Pope in Rome. They had been disarmed for the security of the realm, and Eli wished that Ned, too, had remained weaponless.

"I took the Test Act," Edmund would retort defensively when accused. "I received the Sacrament of the Lord's Supper. What more do I have to do to convince you I'm not a threat?"

"Aye, with your mouth you swore and received," Eli spat. "But not with your heart! Your eyes speak of your tongue's deception!"

Eli's irascible nature, punctuated by occasional loud outbursts, did not endear him to the majority of his comrades. The mostly irreligious soldiery tended to mock his fervor behind his back, especially after he would give those working under him impromptu sermons when they failed to live up to his work ethic or simply when the inspiration struck him. He would commonly use earthy analogies, such as salvation being akin to foaling, and the struggles of life being the blanket to wipe the blood away. Ned found himself rather struck by the simplicity of it which nevertheless rang true, even coming from an adversary, but even most of Eli's fellow practicing Protestants tended to treat him as a hard case of enthusiasm. They said it was likely that the fever had left him touched in the head, a fanatic at odds with mankind, who took solace for hours every night, standing head bowed, hands clasped, beseeching heaven in the silence of his heart. Another strange habit he had was to occasionally let out bursts of short laughter at the oddest times, as if something were striking him funny which no one else could see. Then he would seem to catch himself at it, especially if anyone was staring at him, and the scars on his cheeks would turn a bit redder than usual.

Yet even if he struggled to interact with people, he seemed to become a different man around animals. His eyes were warmer and his voice sweeter as he calmed horses and tended to their needs, just as he had done back in his grandfather's stable. It was undeniable that he had a natural way with them, and they quieted easily as he murmured to them in the Ulster Scots dialect he hardly ever used with people. His fondness for creatures went beyond horses. Once, he made quite a scene reprimanding a soldier for grabbing a stray tabby cat by the tail and throwing it out of a wagon.

"She's not a sack of rocks, but a living thing!" he snapped.

"But cats always land on their feet, sir," the soldier insisted.

"I'll land you on your feet, you dolt!" Eli threatened, and the soldier meekly apologized, promising to amend his ways.

Eli then went off to find the frightened feline, whom Ned was fairly certain he wouldn't be able to track, given how she had bounded off and likely climbed up a tree. But track the cat down he did, returning to the camp with her sitting snugly in his arms. She purred in pure contentment as he scratched behind her ears.

Ned also had the opportunity to finally encounter his "twin", the one who Lady Charlotte suspected might be Burgoyne's illegitimate son. His name was Lieutenant Isaac Caldwell, the son, so it was said, of an aristocratic but impoverished widow. Burgoyne had seen promise in him, so the story ran, and had taken him under his wing. He was, as Charlotte said, tall and fair, and even Ned was slightly startled when he first saw him, feeling momentarily as if he had caught a glimpse of himself in the mirror. Of course, upon closer inspection, their looks were not as similar as it initially seemed. But that fleeting confusion still haunted him, and he could tell it even momentarily disturbed Caldwell. But he quickly laughed it off, saying that Ned had the face of a country bumpkin.

Ned remained unnerved, even as his attempts at courtesy with Caldwell tended to be rebuffed with haughtiness. Perhaps it was because he saw something in Caldwell's eyes, a shadow, yes, the shadow side of his own self. He liked to brag about how he had seen combat in Canada the previous year, a brief skirmish, it was true, but action. The balls whizzed about ears, he claimed, and he had been commended for his courage. Even Jonathan had to admit Caldwell had shown fearlessness under fire, but that didn't make his humorless bragging any more bearable. At least Burgoyne added a certain theatrical flair to his own boasting that could prove charming. Caldwell could turn on the charm if he put his mind to it, making fast friends with various young officers from privileged backgrounds who liked nothing better than an evening spent with cards and liquor. But he was a climber, the worst kind, who would use all those he encountered merely as rungs on a ladder to step on, one after another. And to those he couldn't get anything from, he was arrogant and even cruel. He regularly made the clerks, such as Jonathan, his chosen target, inferring that they weren't real soldiers. Jonathan for one bore up with it patiently, refusing to show himself flustered.

One day, however, Ned was working with Jonathan filing boxes of the general's belongings when they heard what Jonathan described as "angry Ulster noises" outside. Heading in the direction of said noises, they soon discovered Eli tangling with Caldwell, who was cackling and dangling a locket from his hand. Inside of it was a miniature of Queen Mary II, the consort of King William of Orange, Protestant hero of their Glorious Revolution.

"Well, well, in spite of the craters on your face, you managed to find yourself a lady love!" Caldwell laughed, holding up the locket. "And a royal lady too!"

"Give it back!" Eli ground out, coming at him, only for Caldwell to poke him back with his sheathed sword. "It's not yours! It's a sin for you to steal from me!"

Caldwell only laughed harder. "Oh, for shame! I must make amends for my errant ways!" He mockingly blew kisses at the locket.

Eli grimaced. "She was one of our greatest Protestant queens, and a good God-fearing woman! How dare you disrespect her!"

Caldwell raised an eyebrow. "Hell's bowels, you really are jealous! But as it turns out, she's a bit too prudish for my tastes. So she's all yours to fantasize over, lying awake at night, seeking satisfaction…"

Eli charged into him, managing to land a flying punch on Caldwell's mouth, causing them both to yelp. Caldwell had a bloody lip, and Eli had bloodied knuckles.

"You pock-marked bastard!" Caldwell spat, then seized Eli by the collar and punched him multiple times.

"Enough," said Jonathan, pulling them apart and standing between them. He was rather stronger than he looked, when push came to shove, and suddenly was dominating the scene. Then he held out his hand towards Caldwell. "Methinks it's time you gave Lieutenant Thompson back his miniature."

"It's none of your affair, four eyes," Caldwell sneered. "You wouldn't appreciate a good joke if it walked up and bit you."

"I'm afraid I'd be obliged to bite back," Jonathan replied. "Now give it over."

"Why should I?"

"Because it belongs to him, and means something to him," Jonathan countered. "Just hand it to me…"

Caldwell jutted out his chin. "Who's going to make me?"

"Lieutenant, I'm just an honest Hampshire man," Jonathan said calmly but firmly. "I'm not canny enough to bother with who you think you are, or even who you think your father is. But this much I'm certain of: the general doesn't take any more kindly to bullies than I do. And your sort of bullying reminds me an awful lot of my five-year-old making off with his sister's doll. You know how I sorted that?" Jonathan took another closer to Caldwell, until their faces almost touched. "I put him over my knee and walloped him. Sometimes that's the only cure for it."

Caldwell snorted. "You'd have my fist in your face first."

"Ah, but Lieutenant," said Jonathan evenly, "it's not gentlemanly to strike a man with spectacles. And as you know, our general is quite the gentleman."

The two soldiers stared each other down, neither one backing up. Ned wondered if Caldwell might yank off Jonathan's spectacles to disorient him and then land a punch on him. But the truth was that Burgoyne valued Jonathan, and Caldwell knew he would not take well to the loyal clerk being physically assaulted, no matter what other infractions Burgoyne allowed Caldwell to get away with. So with a dismissive shrug, he yielded the locket to the clerk, and stormed off.

Jonathan turned and delivered the locket back to Eli, then took out a handkerchief and dabbed at the Ulster boy's bloody knuckles.

"Thank you," Eli mumbled. "He has, well, sharp teeth."

"Makes sense, in light of his tongue," Jonathan sighed. "But I think we held our own for this round."

Eli nodded, stuffing the locket in his inner coat pocket. "It…it was my mother's, you see…she kept it because, well…she admired the queen, our great Protestant queen…"

"I understand," Jonathan assured, now cleaning Eli's bloody nose.

"I-I suppose as a child, I almost thought they were one and the same. Even now, sometimes…" His voice drifted. "Do you think that's very odd?"

"To still love your mother and revere those whom she revered for their virtues? No," Jonathan answered, handing him the handkerchief. "Blow your nose, dear."

Eli did so with a goose-like honking noise.

"Feel better?" Jonathan asked.

Eli nodded again. "Thank you, again."

"No worries. And now that we've settled that," Jonathan exhaled, "I'm starving. Let's have breakfast."

Eli blinked. "You mean…you'd have it with me?"

"Of course. Come. I've just got another haul of croissants from the shops, as well as some fresh eggs to fry."

"I like eggs," Eli conceded awkwardly.

"It's settled then."

Over the course of the breakfast making, it became increasingly clear just how much Eli liked eggs and how very seriously he took frying them in a pan over the fire, which clearly left

Jonathan bemused. He became even more when he said quite randomly yet ceremonially, after cracking the last egg, "God save the King."

Jonathan gave him a puzzled look, then smirked, raised his flask of watered down beer, and returned, "Long to reign over us. And may his breakfast be as fit for royalty as this one is."

"So," Eli mumbled meekly, stuffing pieces of egg and croissant into his mouth at the same time, "are we sort of friends now?"

Jonathan smiled. "I don't see a reason why we shouldn't be."

Eli sat there for a spell, as if pondering the meaning of Jonathan's words deeply, then he let out one of his odd laughs.

From that day on, Eli was attached to Jonathan at the hip. He would just appear during lunch to eat with Jonathan, and became increasingly loquacious as time went by, offering his scattered commentary on all things under the sun. Jonathan did his best to be absorbent with his newfound accomplice, even when it proved draining. After all the hard work it took to bring the young man out of his taciturn shell, Ned wondered if Jonathan sometimes wished he might go back in again. But Jonathan seemed to intuitively sense how adrift Eli was since his grandfather's death, and remained ready to offer him a listening ear and helping hand.

On one memorable occasion, Eli managed to recruit Jonathan to help him care for an injured flying squirrel he found flapping about on the ground in pain from a torn fleshy wing. It was an odd task for Jonathan, whose huntsman's instincts would be likely to view the rodent as a potential stew. But his time as a physician's assistant pulled on his heartstrings, and he tempted fate by opening the crate Eli had trapped it in. The squirrel went just a bit ballistic, leaping up and swatting Jonathan in the face, leaving scratch marks on his cheek. Eli, in typical fashion, blamed Jonathan for scaring it and cuddled the creature into submission so the unenthusiastic medic could stitch up the wing with scarlet thread. It still couldn't manage to climb, much less fly, and didn't seem to want to, since Jonathan had taken to feeding it scraps. It turned out to be a she on closer inspection, so Eli christened her Jenny and let her adopt him as her godfather.

Then there was Freddie the messenger boy. He didn't like to be called that, of course, but young Frederick Kerr was universally patronized by those whom he served. He was all of twelve years, and easily distracted by everything, from strange insects to uniquely shaped rocks. This caused him more often than not to be late or get lost and get a sound switching from officers over him. He was also chastised for forgetting to polish the buttons on his uniform. How exactly he landed a job on Burgoyne's staff was a mystery, but these days he was mostly put to the generally harmless work of conveying Burgoyne's party invitations to and from wealthy French Canadians with whom the general sought to curry favor. Jonathan, however, found other ways of employing him on behalf of the rest of the staff by sending him off on scouting missions into the vicinity's bakeries to sort out sale days and pick up a regular supply of pastries for them to devour. Freddie inevitably would get delayed, and Jonathan was fairly certain by the smeared cream filling on the boy's face why, but decided to accept the bounty as it could be obtained.

At several of the parties General Burgoyne hosted, Edmund was instructed to check guests at the door while Jonathan and Gavin scurried around obtaining whatever the general wanted from his baggage cart or the shops in town. He would never forget the early and grand arrival of a stout and sturdily built Highland officer, whose broad chest and shoulders were bound by a plaid sash that stretched down to his knees as a kilt. A mere glance from this man made Ned feel in awe of him. The officer intoned in a thick Scottish burr, "Tell General Burgoyne that Fraser of Balnain has come out for him."

Edmund turned to do just that, but Burgoyne, who was not very far from the door, called over to Ned, "Tell the gentlemen to be more specific as to his identity. That clan breeds at an incalculable rate!"

Fraser's eyebrow rose up. "Tell the general…the Christian name is Simon."

Again, Edmund turned to relay the message, and again he was cut off by Burgoyne. "Come, now, that's no good! Never have there been so many Simons in one family tree since the time of the apostles!"

Fraser smirked, and pushed past a befuddled Ned. "Never have you been known to forget a face, John. Are you going to start now?"

The Highlander, his posture perfectly erect, bowed low at the waist, and Gentleman Johnny, also with impeccable posture, responded in kind. When they stood up to their full heights again, they were both beaming at each other.

"So then, will you pass the flaming cross in my name, as is the custom among your race when you turn out to do battle and swear fealty to your chosen master?" Burgoyne queried.

"Perhaps," Fraser replied, "if you remember me."

Burgoyne put a finger to his chin. "Ah, yes, I do seem to recall you now. You're the husband of that fine German lady, dear Margaretha. God knows what possessed her…"

"The best of wives indeed, and better than her poor husband deserves," Fraser admitted with a genuine smile, then added softly, and more solemnly, "not so very different from dear Lady Charlotte."

Burgoyne blinked, but did not respond.

Fraser tilted his head. "And how are you faring?"

"Not in Bedlam." He grinned oddly, and Fraser's own expression fell flat. "Oh, I'm joking. Can't you tell when I'm joking after more than eight years?" He slapped his friend on the back. "I'm keeping busy! That's the important thing. We'll both be very busy bees and give the cursed rebels a right proper sting like we did when they tried to press north. Now it's our turn to press south!"

"I'm convinced you left Canada last winter just to escape the cold," Fraser stated, wagging a finger.

"I'm not the one who occasionally appears without breeches," Burgoyne replied, gesturing to his kilt.

"You're the one who wanted a Highlander by your side when you drain the honey from the Yankee hive," Fraser replied. "I'm afraid you must take my poor self as you find me, or else beseech London to send you an Englishman or a Lowlander…"

"Your poor self," Burgoyne snorted. "Everyone in London sings your praises!"

"Everyone?" Fraser folded his arms.

"Everyone who matters," Burgoyne started with a shrug. "And you know for a fact I hold no one in greater esteem, and I have impeccable judgment in all things!"

Again, Fraser smirked. "Impeccable."

"Indubitably."

"Well, as long as you can whisk me away from the Pharaoh Carleton, I will be singing your praises in turn," Fraser declared. "That man is altogether impossible to serve with any enthusiasm!"

"He does rather have the personality of a snapping turtle," Burgoyne agreed.

"An authoritarian one too!"

"Yes, though not devoid of honor or humanity," Burgoyne offered in his defense. "After all, General Wolfe was friends with him, and he never offered friendship to a man devoid of virtues. Carleton may yet have more to offer our cause in this conflict…"

"To the colonials, aye, he's humane to a fault, turning loose prisoners and bundling them up for the journey home. But with us? No. And the colonials hardly appreciate his gestures of goodwill anyway."

"Well, Roman Catholics in this country seem to view him as their champion, at least, which helped keep them loyal during the invasion last year. Whatever he may think of them, being a Protestant Irishman, come hell or high water, he has upheld the Quebec Act."

"Good for him," Fraser snorted. "I'd still take you as my superior over him any day. You know how to give your people leeway."

"I'm flattered beyond words," Burgoyne beamed. "But who knows how long I'll be a superior to you, given how you're rising in the ranks!"

"John, they've only given me a temporary promotion, applicable solely in the American theater…"

"It won't stay that way, though!" Burgoyne assured. "The best things are yet to come!"

"Always brimming with confidence…"

"In you? Yes!" Burgoyne replied. "It's why I like you so much, Balnain. You've never learned to stay in your place."

Fraser smirked. "Nor have you."

"We shake things up. It's great fun."

"Rebels, in our own right."

"Yes, indeed. But if those in charge expect us to save the day, they really can't force us to toe the line."

"I don't think we ever learned how to manage the latter."

"That's because we've got skin in the game, and we're not afraid to play, behind closed doors, or with them swung wide open for the world to see. And it's their own game we're beating them at, Balnain."

"Our devilish ways have aggravated some people, to be sure," Fraser remarked with a smirk. "But they haven't managed to take us down yet."

"And we still have adventurous types willing to lay bets on us getting our names in all the papers!"

"For good or ill?"

"My dear Balnain, I don't believe in bad publicity!" Burgoyne declared. "Besides, I'm convinced the two of us combined can charm our way out of any fix!"

Fraser smirked. "And where does General Phillips fit into this?"

"Well, if our charm fails us, he can throw a wild punch and give us the chance to escape!"

Fraser laughed heartily. "Let's drink to that, shall we?"

"We shall!" Burgoyne poured him a glass of champagne. "Let us eat, drink, and be merry, for tomorrow…"

"Careful, Johnny," Fraser cautioned.

"We win," Burgoyne finished, clinking his glass against his friend's. "You mustn't fear to test the Almighty so much. We are wed to the army, so it is part of our natures by now!"

"Call me superstitious." He drank down the champagne. "Och, this is bloody weak stuff, John."

"You see, a bullet hasn't been made that can do you in," Burgoyne chortled.

"Oh?"

"Well, not outright at least. You'd flop around for an ungodly amount of time shouting curses at the sky…and probably at me. You remember I told you about another Scot, Major Pitcairn of the Marines."

"Ah, yes, a Lowlander," Fraser noted.

"But as tenacious as all your lot," Burgoyne insisted. "When he led the last charge up Breed's Hill, it took six bullets to take him down! What a painting it would make, or a scene in a play…"

"Good God, John," Fraser sighed, shaking his head.

"I can't help it! It's how I see the world! It's how I…make sense of it." Burgoyne glanced down to the floor momentarily.

Fraser did the same. "Is Pitcairn buried on this continent, or has he been taken home?"

"Still in Boston. Why do you ask?"

"I just…wondered." His eyes glazed. "So many of our own, sleeping here, on this far side of the water…"

"But not us," Burgoyne assured, his voice cheerful once more. "We'll live to be dirty old men and die in our beds, hopefully next to much younger women, with our names forever etched in the book of time by destiny's golden pen!"

Fraser paused for a moment, then lifted his glass again. "To growing old with Margaretha." With that, he drank down the last of the champagne.

"And now…your mail, sir," Burgoyne declared, picking up a bundle of letters lying on a nearby table.

"Ah, you remembered!" Fraser exclaimed, fingering the letters. "I rather you'd have given it to that addle-headed, cross-eyed boy to drop off, instead of him just sliding your invitation under the door…"

"Entrust your letters to Freddie?" Burgoyne clicked his tongue. "No, no. Our friendship means more to me than that. Besides, he's terrified of you."

"As he should be," Fraser snorted. "He's a Lowlander by the sound of him, and however hearty some of their folk may prove to be, mine can still eat them for breakfast."

Burgoyne rolled his eyes.

"Why in the name of all that's holy did you attach him to your staff to begin with?" Fraser queried. "He's not the most reliable messenger…"

"His father is a gentleman from Roxburghshire who I lost a small fortune to," Burgoyne confessed.

"Horses?"

"Roosters. I didn't much like all the blood, but I couldn't manage to tear myself away from the pot of gold, until of course, it tore itself away from me…"

"Damn, Johnny."

"Well, this Old Gamester knows how to make the most of things, even unfavorable ones. We'll make a man out of Freddie yet."

"We?" Fraser sighed. "How did I get mixed up in this?"

"I like to mix you up in my misadventures, Balnain!"

"So I've noticed…"

"At any rate," Burgoyne interrupted, "I told you I'd deliver your letters in person, and I have, just as I did when we were in Ireland. You were always getting too much mail, what with your twenty siblings and all…"

"As usual, you exaggerate, but as you know, my father was married twice. Lots of half-bloods out and about, having mostly had prestigious broods, but they're Frasers still, so I find it my duty to look out for them as best I am able."

"It's all about who you know in this business," Burgoyne said, nudging him with his elbow.

"My clan has little other option," Fraser admitted with a grim smirk. "But I'll be sure they make good use of their opportunity, or they'll be swimming back to shore without transport or recommendations from me."

"I have every confidence you'll make good soldiers and honest Britons of the lot of them," Burgoyne replied. "Even those few still fondly gaze across the water in search of princes and pretenders."

"And I have every confidence that my knowing your own honorable self will continue to fill my life with additional color," Fraser returned.

"And glory!" Burgoyne insisted, taking him by the arm and leading him into the dining room.

During the party that evening, Burgoyne, full of bubbling enthusiasm for the campaign to come, sat quite near to Fraser and nearly talked his ear off. Fraser seemed to be genuinely amused by his friend's exuberance, talking far less, but always making the remarks suitably clever to keep the game going. When pressed for his opinion about Burgoyne's grand scheme to split the colonies in two, however, Fraser first declined commentary, as he had accepted the job, and that alone should have been enough as a matter of duty and endorsement. But when pressed again by Burgoyne as they began to play cards, he conceded simply, "Yes, it will succeed, should the fates favor us, and the cards fall into place."

"The fates favor the King, God save him," declared Burgoyne, revealing his four kings.

Fraser snorted and passed on his hand. But Ned had seen over his shoulder it was aces. Highland superstition, perhaps. It would be unwise to defeat the omen of victory.

Chapter 19: PATHS OF GLORY

When the time came for Fraser to hold salon, he invited Burgoyne and various other officers to the house where he was quartered. Ned went along as part of Burgoyne's staff, and found himself struggling to carry over a crate of Burgoyne's champagne.

"Really, John," Fraser sighed when he saw it. "It's my party. I'm providing."

"I don't trust your Inverness stealth," Burgoyne stated. "You'll coerce me to drink that horrid concoction that makes any normal man feel they were about to spontaneously combust."

"Don't tell me you're striving for normality after all this time," Fraser quipped.

"I want to enjoy myself, not become bedridden," Burgoyne protested. "Besides, if that occurred, I'd be trapped here with you. We wouldn't want that would we?"

"Ach, you risk your good health in all sorts of enjoyment, General," Fraser scoffed. "Besides, perhaps you can guzzle down a crate of champagne, but I'll handle myself better with the same amount of stronger substances."

"Do you really want me to have to summon the chaplain for you when your insides are falling out?" Burgoyne queried. "I'm really not good at standing around for that sort of thing…"

"I don't let anyone call chaplains on my behalf," Fraser snorted. "That's a decision for me to make alone, and believe me, knowing the chaplain we've got, that won't be happening…"

"Simon, the Reverend Brudenell is a good man…yes, a very good man indeed!" Burgoyne insisted.

"I thought you tended to be cynical about Church of England clerics, given your history of making and breaking them," Fraser remarked. "This one seems common enough for the cloth, preaching the party line and little more."

"Not this one," Burgoyne replied. "He is sincere. I would stake my life on it."

"How do you know?"

"Because," said Burgoyne, "I know. Besides, he's our dear General Phillips' cousin, and I don't believe that bloodline churns out shirkers in their chosen careers."

"Perhaps he's just too dedicated for my tastes then," Fraser sighed. "You know as well as I do the way Brudenell can fixate upon the letter of the liturgy, if you take my meaning. Damn, you couldn't get that man to cut short a service if he were under a barrage! It borders on a hostage crisis for the congregation!"

"Then don't let your insides fall out," Burgoyne teased his friend, pointing to the bottle standing on the table.

"That, sir, is what makes my bowels so steely!" Fraser declared. "As I said, I'm happy to keep pace with your drinking, as you see fit to test me."

"Want to put your money where your mouth is, Balnain?" Burgoyne challenged.

"I'm not one to speak empty words," Fraser replied, reaching into a coat pocket and producing a coin. "And more where that came from!"

Burgoyne gasped dramatically. "My dear Fraser, surely your hand will fall off…"

"My Scottish sensibilities are more than assuaged by kenning full well who the winner will be," he insisted.

"If the fates permit," Burgoyne quoted him sarcastically. "It does my heart good to know you are more positive about this wager than our professional reputations."

"I'm more positive of this than that our mothers were…"

"Careful…"

"Women, that our mothers were women!"

And so the contest carried on through the long night, the alcohol flowing liberally and the generals imbibing it freely. General William Phillips of the Artillery joined them. A proud and choleric Welshman who served as Lieutenant Governor of Windsor Castle, he took every opportunity available to boast about his ancient warrior ancestry, and Fraser, who was his long-time friend from their time spent together warring on the continent, joked that a few more drinks would make Phillips claim to have the blood of Arthur in his veins. Sooner than later, the wine worked its magic, and Phillips launched into a recitation of his lineage.

"I come from a line of Welsh nobles, the eldest of the Britons, before Arthur's age, when the Romans ruled," he declared, knitting his heavy eyebrows together and jutting out his angular chin. "Their power lay in Dyfed when William called the Conqueror first set foot in Pevensey. Cadivor ap Collwyn, his son Bledri, and his grandson Rhys ap Collwyn all bound themselves unto him by the flow of their blood, and so it remained between his descendents and theirs. When the Lionheart called upon his lords from all regions of his realms to take up the Cross, Aaron ap Rhys donned the crusader's dress and set forth to reconquer Jerusalem. He stood, unyielding, at the Siege of Acre, and likewise at the Battle of Arsuf, and was praised for the greatness of his gallantry when holding his ground against Saladin of the Saracens. The Lionheart bestowed upon him the Order of Knighthood of the Sepulcher of Our Savior and crafted for him a coat-of-arms that bore the lion. Amongst his heirs was Thomas ap Philipps, who survived the War of the Roses to serve the first Tudor, who was the seventh Henry, and escorted his corpse to its resting place in the halls of kings. Under the eighth Henry, Thomas toppled the French at Tournai, and upon his knighthood, became Lord of Picton Castle and all the lands lying around it."

He turned suddenly to Edmund, who had been mesmerized by the poetry of his words, and Ned found himself now captured by the magnetism of his eyes.

"They call me proud in my bearing, boy, and fierce in my temperament. Of all men, do I not have a right to be?"

"Aye, sir," Ned answered breathlessly.

And Phillips' smile was so real and warm it cheered and charmed Ned's heart.

"Perhaps I shall include your ancestor who fought with the Lionheart in a play about the illustrious king," Burgoyne proclaimed.

"Another play, John?" Fraser sighed. "Please don't tell me it will be a musical. Although if it is, I suppose you could get Phillips here to assist with production…"

"I may have organized the artillery band, but I am no mummer!" Phillips protested.

"More's the pity," Burgoyne exhaled. "I could have cast you as Blondel the minstrel, who discovered where Richard was being held captive by playing a tune they had composed together under various fortress windows, awaiting the King's voice in song."

"The only tune that will please me now is the sort to make the Yankees do a jig," Philips replied. "It will be in rhythm to the rattle of my big guns."

"I'll drink to that," Fraser chuckled.

"How can it be otherwise?" Burgoyne queried. "The rebels don't have a prayer, given the opposition. Look at us: an Englishman, a Scotsman, and a Welshmen, representing the whole of the Isle, arrayed to uphold the right! When has there ever been a people such as us, ready to take on the world with zeal and bayonets only? Who can hope to stand against us and live? Albany shall be our Jerusalem! We shall have it, and nothing less!"

"Departing from the legacy of the Lionheart, then?" Fraser queried. "He made great boasts, but failed in his conquest…"

"We will realize his goals, and he will be proud of his children!" Burgoyne raised a toast. "That Lady Britannia, along with Cour de Leon, smiles upon us, their favored sons! Our names shall be in the flowing cups of posterity, freshly remembered by each passing generation, across our united empire!"

As they toasted with their sparkling glasses, the glow of the candles made the wine appear like liquid rubies, complimenting the officers' dazzling red tunics. The light flickering across their faces turned them into phantoms, trending the thin line between history and legend, and their lips were dyed crimson as they drank.

When they finished, General Phillips refilled his glass and turned to Major Acland, who had been sitting several chairs down from the others, having made good on his speech in Parliament by embarking upon Burgoyne's campaign. "For industry, we must particularly commend the rising of the English west country, which one of Welsh descent such as myself cannot help but appreciate, given its closeness of proximity to us! I say we toast the man in our midst responsible!"

"As you know, gentlemen, I hold nothing back, not my time nor my talents, not my monetary solvency nor marital bliss, " Acland bragged, clinking his glass of wine with Phillip's and then draining the contents, his face flushing as he grew more intoxicated.

"Indeed, you have even brought along your lady wife and loyal hound," Burgoyne remarked. "Surely there's a song in that somewhere!"

Fraser stared for a moment, then said, almost scoldingly, "I would not bring Margaretha."

Acland cast a sharp glance at Fraser. "It was Lady Harriet's desire to come. She said that she would brave any hardship to remain at my side. She knows I am no mere adventurer or place-hunter, but rather alight with sentiments of patriotism, which she shares."

"Does your dog share in it too?" Philips jabbed.

Acland made a crooked grin. "He's got a fine red coat, has he not? And he doesn't answer to the name of 'Rebel' either!"

The table erupted with laughter, given the fact that Philips had adopted the dog that once belonged to the rebel general, Richard Montgomery, slain while attempting to wrest control of Quebec from the British the previous year.

After the laughter died down, Fraser grew serious again. Then he lifted his glass in another toast. "To Lady Harriet, whose beauty is only matched by her fidelity."

"Hear, hear!" Acland cried. "And may I fill her with a strong boy child sometime between now and Christmas!"

Burgoyne and Philips chortled, but Fraser did not. He simply added, "May she be fruitful when all her needs may be met."

As midnight drew near, Fraser leaned over to Burgoyne and stated, "Two of my young lieutenants are keen on performing for the general and the other guests."

"Performing what, pray tell?" Burgoyne inquired dubiously.

"A sword dance. It infuses their blood with martial ardor."

"And strives after gracefulness, akin to the movements of the Highland stag, isn't that right?" Burgoyne responded.

Fraser nodded. "I compliment the general's memory."

"How could I forget, Balnain? The stag is one of your clan's signet animals."

"So it is."

"Clear of eye, swift of hoof, sharp of horn..."

"Nothing less will do."

Burgoyne glanced over at some of the other officers at the table, many of Lowland and English extraction, then back at this friend.

"So your lieutenants were the only ones who wanted to do this dance?" Burgoyne queried, tilting his head. "You didn't, by any chance…suggest it to them?"

"Don't you remember being young, John?" Fraser asked, evading the question. "They want to show off!"

"Or you do," Burgoyne replied, "because you can."

"Aye," Fraser conceded, with a sneaking smile. "Perhaps because I can. As you know, the military offers allowances for my people which they do not always have at home. Pipes, tartan, and swords upon the floor…why, it is almost as if Britain had accepted them in lands apart as symbols of herself."

"Just not universally welcome in Britain herself, especially when it comes to particular clans with rebellious histories," Burgoyne surmised. "That's the point you aim to make, isn't it?"

"Perhaps we should let old wars die the hard death they deserve," Fraser replied. "That's the point I've been aiming to make for much of my life. Now indulge me like I indulge you and your plays!"

"Alright, Alright, I'll protect you from the Edinburgh contingent," Burgoyne conceded. "Snobbish Scottish southerners are more likely to get their feathers ruffled than us Englishmen!"

Fraser sent a manservant outside, and a few minutes later, two young men in Highland dress appeared in front of the table, along with a piper who helped lay out two pairs of decorative broadswords on the floor.

Fraser leaned over to Burgoyne and muttered, "That bonny one on the right with the yellow hair bears the name of Stewart, Donald Stewart. Still blessed with the royal touch among ladies…and God only knows, perhaps also among men…"

Burgoyne elbowed him, and cast him a scolding look, causing Fraser to laugh.

"You'd best cheer on your own blood," Burgoyne chided him, "for I take the other to be your kinsman, young Alan."

"Indeed, another wild one from us, offspring of the half-siblings…I do my best for the lad, but…ah, they're starting…"

The two contestants took their positions and leapt from one to the other side of the crossed blades, going around the square formations, synchronized with each other. It was strangely mesmeric, striving to embody a blend of confidence and grace. Both dancers seemed to be handling it with utmost seriousness, like warriors of old, proving their prowess.

Fraser kept glancing over to Burgoyne to watch him watching the dance. There was a mischievous smirk on the Scotsman's face as he did so. Then he winced as Alan made a misstep and knocked one the swords out of place, swearing under his breath in unison with his nephew as the young man disqualified himself.

Young Stewart, however, continued his dance, closer and closer to the cross, and the piper's tune picked up its pace. The sound of his shoes clacking on the floor lent additional rhythm. At last, the skirl of the pipes ended without him having been disqualified.

Lieutenant Stewart, clearly pleased with himself, bowed low, and the attendants, some amused and others irked, were all obliged to clap once Burgoyne started them off.

"*Mealaibh ur naidheachd!*" Fraser congratulated the victor in Gaelic, clapping along with the rest. Then he stopped suddenly, a strange look coming to his eyes. "Donald," he called over, and the young man came over to him, smiling proudly. The general spoke some more words in Gaelic to him, and the young man touched his nose, which was bleeding. Fraser discreetly gave him a handkerchief, and put on a brave, congratulatory face as he shook the lad's hand for his success. But Burgoyne had sensed his friend's shift in mood.

"Enough with your superstitions," he sighed, tugging on his fellow general's sleeve in a scolding manner once the lieutenant had departed. "As you say, he's got the royal touch. Nothing can harm him. And as for your young kinsman, he suffers from no curse except clumsiness!"

"Entirely my half-brother's doing," Fraser snorted, then paused, staring momentarily into space, before returning to himself and drinking more whiskey from the jar.

As most of the party attendees departed for their own billet, Edmund remained with Burgoyne and Fraser, still at their little drinking game. He knew the alcohol was finally starting to take its toll when Burgoyne started teasing him about whether or not he wore anything underneath the kilt or if the rumors about uncouth Highlanders were all too true. Fraser quipped that if he was so dead set on finding out, then he would have to take a peek down there to find out. Burgoyne replied that he dared not take the risk, lest their eyes be perpetually scarred. Fraser said it was for the best, lest Burgoyne should start to fret over comparisons. Burgoyne then made a comment about the lengthy jeweled sword pin keeping the kilt modestly closed, and whether perhaps it was a form of "compensation". Before he could even finish the last word, however, the Highlander retorted "counterbalance."

When their banter finally ran its course, Fraser glanced over to Ned, who had started to gather together Burgoyne's things for whenever his superior decided to depart. "The general tells me your family was Papist," the Scotsman remarked.

Ned winced. "Yes, sir. But I…I've taken the Test Act, sir."

"Yes, obviously," Fraser chortled. "But there's no need to be shy about your origins. My clan has had our fair share of Papists. One who shared my name is surely on your mind…Simon Fraser, Lord Lovat. Last man to be beheaded in Britain."

"Don't scare him with the story of that old double-dealer, Balnain!" Burgoyne chuckled.

Fraser smirked. "But his last words, John! We must live by them in our own profession! *Dulce et decorum est pro patria mori…*" He glanced over to Ned. "Know what that means?"

"It is sweet and seemly to die for one's country," Edmund translated.

"Very good."

"Not so good for Lovat, though," Burgoyne snorted. "He died, alright, but not for any higher cause. He simply fell prey to his own mistakes."

"Well, we all have cause to bob and weave a bit in this world," said Fraser, "but might as well go out expressing higher sentiments, at least, even if we failed to embody them."

Indeed, Edmund knew about the infamous Lord Lovat, nicknamed "The Fox". Over the course of his career, he had switched back and forth between identifying as Protestant and Catholic, Hanoverian and Jacobite, too many times for his own longevity. It was said he exemplified a certain self-serving trait common to the Fraser clan. After all, the son of the Fox, also named Simon, had quickly recovered from his father's execution and accepted a commission to raise the Frasers on behalf of the Hanoverian government. Rumor had it that he had deliberately delayed arriving at Culloden and withheld reinforcements from Charles Edward Stuart to assure that his line would endure. Sure enough, he had since found favor with the ruling regime and been acknowledged as clan chief. Simon Fraser of Balnain, who sat studying Ned with a perceptive eye, was the chief's cousin, for good or ill.

"I suppose I should count myself lucky to still have a head, if little else," Fraser stated with a wry smirk. "Quite a few of us lost our lands when the last Stuart was sent back across the water. As a young man without a country, trying to make the best of my exile, I decided to sign up for the Dutch service, which I continued under for some eight years."

"But you returned to Britain as soon as the Highland regiments were raised, and have spent a good twenty years with us now," Burgoyne said, slapping the tabletop. "You've bloody well redeemed yourself!"

"And I was fighting the French the whole damned while, under Dutch or British flags," Fraser noted. "Up to my boots in their blood, most times…"

"And your own," Burgoyne noted. He turned to Ned and added, "This fool doesn't know the meaning of pain when wounded, and will stomp about refusing care long enough to test the patience of saints."

"I believe it is within a man to train himself to deal with pain," Fraser said. "The Stoics were wise in such matters." He turned back to Ned. "They taught that a man is what he disciplines himself to be. I believe that holds true no matter his starting point. Whether one is an emperor like Marcus Aurelius or a slave like Epictetus, an honorable life is possible."

Edmund cast his gaze down self-consciously. "Thank you, sir."

"By the way, I hear tell that you are a great admirer of General Wolfe, the hero of Quebec," Fraser remarked.

"Who is not, sir?" Edmund replied nervously. Even after his encounter with the king, he was still getting used to meeting important men and found himself often tongue-tied.

"It may be common knowledge I took part in that campaign myself," Fraser informed, "but you may not have heard I was in the boat with him that took him to the heights."

Edmund perked up. "I was unaware, sir."

"Then sit, and I shall tell you…"

"Not again," Burgoyne groaned.

"Ignore him," Fraser sighed, gesturing at his fellow general in annoyance. "I shall tell you how it was, since you are not so jaded…"

"Alright, I surrender then," Burgoyne grumbled, standing up and staggering over to the chaise on the other side of the room.

"What? Just like that?" Fraser twitted. "That's not sporting!"

"I have a headache," Burgoyne whined, collapsing on the chaise. "I'm indisposed."

"So you're just refusing to leave the house then?" Fraser rolled his eyes.

"Be good enough to have some coffee brought in for me in the morning…" Burgoyne mumbled, and put a pillow over his face as some sort of headache cure.

Fraser sighed and shook his head. "Where was I? Oh yes…" He turned to Ned. "It was quiet, that night, like death itself. Only muffled things could be heard…oars in the water, and words in poetry. I was near enough, though, I heard what General Wolfe was whispering as we got into the boat. He'd received a poem from his lady, one written by Thomas Gray."

"Elegy in a Country Churchyard," said Ned, then turned red as Fraser chortled.

"Ned is like me," Burgoyne mumbled from his couch. "A connoisseur of the arts! He'd not have stirred from his father's library…had it not been for my gentle persuasion."

"So what did you fancy reading most then, hmm?" Fraser queried.

"Very old things," Ned laughed softly.

"The classics of Greece and Rome?"

"No, the jottings of our ancestors and their meddlesome monks," Burgoyne joked.

Ned glanced down briefly. "The saints," he admitted softly. "Our saints."

"Ned has an old Saxon name, you know, not Norman names like ours!"

"Mixed breeds, I imagine, the three of us," Fraser said. "For me, Norman and Gael, for the two of you Norman and Saxon.

"I imagine that is right, sir," Ned replied.

"Ah, but the name," Burgoyne repeated, "that's held out for him. It characterizes his love of ancient things. Ye gods, he reads manuscripts in the old tongue."

"Can you speak it too?" Fraser queried.

"By way of some quotations I have committed to memory, sir," Ned replied.

"Show me."

Ned swallowed hard, then quoted, in Old English, Saint Caedmon's Hymn, then the beginning of the Dream of the Rood. He did not deem it necessary to translate.

Yet even without translation, Fraser seemed to sense the nature of the piece. He studied Edmund for a long moment then nodded. "Yes, you have pure eyes, as the general has remarked upon. Beware he doesn't corrupt you."

Burgoyne chuckled sleepily. "You North Britons...must truly be wizards...to read souls..."

"Yes, wizards," Fraser remarked dryly, taking another gulp from his glass. "The young men see visions and the old men dream dreams." He smiled over at Ned again. "But I'd wager you can quote Gray's poem back to me, can't you, lad?"

"Some parts, yes," he replied bashfully, and cleared his throat. "The boast of heraldry, the pomp of power, all that beauty, all that wealth e'er gave, awaits alike the inevitable hour: the paths of glory lead but to the grave."

"Well done," Fraser praised him. "That's the part Wolfe recited."

Ned nodded, knowing the story well. Then he added softly, "It's not my favorite part, though. That would be the ending."

"The ending?"

Ned nodded again, and recited quietly, "No longer seek his merits to disclose, or draw his frailties from their dread abode; there, they alike in trembling hope repose: the bosom of his Father and his God."

"Of course, you would gravitate to that part," Burgoyne chuckled. "That religious streak, still as strong as ever..."

"It makes sense of the rest of the poem," Ned stated, a melancholy creeping into his voice. "If all the beauty, wealth, and glory fail, then...we must all hope that..." He swallowed hard and shook his head. "My apologies for going on about it too long."

"Don't be," Fraser responded, his voice wistful. "You know, General Wolfe said to us, 'I would rather have written that poem than gain the victory tomorrow.' Of course he couldn't have meant it...or at least we must assume not, mustn't we?"

"I-I'm not sure," Ned said softly. "Perhaps the wound inflicted by the pen is more lasting than that of the sword, and perhaps it brings not only a hurt, but a cure."

"No wonder General Burgoyne is fond of you," Fraser remarked, and turned to Burgoyne on the couch. "Well, what do you think, John? Eh, John? Are you listening to me?"

Burgoyne groaned, roused from his stupor. "What do you want?"

"I'm asking you a question," he slurred, with finger pointed. "I'm asking you if you'd rather win this campaign, or write something…something that would make you immortal…"

"Both," Burgoyne replied. "That's the trouble with you, Balnain…you try to put limits on me while putting none on yourself…"

"I help keep you from getting hurt is what I do," he stated.

"Like you kept Wolfe from getting hurt by those French sentries when his boat passed the embankment?"

Fraser smirked. "So you do remember."

"You've told it often enough."

"Like you've told me often enough about how you heroically saved the virtue of that bevy of nuns in Portugal?"

Ned couldn't help but laugh briefly.

"Ah, he's filled your ears with it too, I see," Fraser exhaled. "But getting back to the boat, I never said it was I who befuddled the sentries. All I said was that a Fraser in the general's boat, with characteristic quick wits and fluency in the French language, managed to trick the sentries into thinking we were their own."

"And we all know how you love to show off your flair for linguistics," Burgoyne noted. "French, Dutch, German, and that rustic Highland tongue of yours…"

"Now, as you know, there were many Frasers in the king's livery, then as now, lacking not in education," Fraser reminded him.

"Yes, yes, and many Simons," Burgoyne sighed.

"Just so! But of course, Wolfe was taken to heart by our kind in a special way."

"In what way, sir?" Ned queried.

"We've always had an affinity for chiefs who lead by example and get his own hands dirty," Fraser stated. "Such a man was the young general. It was said, rightly, that he was the son of a soldier, and the parent of soldiers, an ornament to the army for his humility and humanity as much as for his zeal and courage. Whenever he came nigh our camp, every mothers' son amongst the Highlanders would turn out, prompt and eager to be of service to him, and we would say one to the other in the Gaelic tongue, 'Here comes the red-headed corporal,' for as surely you know, he would not cover his tawny hair with a wig, and he made a habit of taking walks clad in plain clothes. He would greet the men as 'brother soldiers,' ask after their health, and tell them to be of good cheer. And his azure eyes would shimmer, like light upon water."

Fraser laughed, seeming to find some memory amusing.

"There was one rogue, Duncan McPhee, who used to rustle cattle in Scotland and sell them in England. The only way to keep himself from being hanged was to join the army, but he proved his worth as a fighter, and Wolfe promoted him first as an orderly and later as a sergeant, never to be broke!" Fraser laughed. "So McPhee took it upon himself to act as Wolfe's bodyguard when the general went out walking. But since he only spoke Gaelic, he could not take orders without the assistance of his fellow sergeants! It was sheer mayhem, but no one could make him budge from the general, not even the general himself!"

Ned smiled briefly, then grew serious. "Tell me, sir, if you would, about the general's death."

Fraser's face grew grave, and his eyes glassy. "He was wounded in the wrist, and quickly wrapped it in his handkerchief. Then he received a shot in the belly, but struggled to hide it. Not long after, however, he received a shot full in the chest. He staggered, not wishing his soldiers to see him fall. The young volunteer who helped him off the field reported that the general smiled at the sight of his own blood. 'My dear, don't grieve for me,' he said, 'for I shall be happy in a few minutes. Take care of yourself, for I see you are wounded. But tell me, how goes the battle?' Then a few other officers came over and told him the French had given ground and our troops were in full pursuit of them, even to the very walls of the town. This seemed to strengthen him, for he raised himself up, smiled again, and said, 'God be praised! Now I die contented!' They say they slipped away without a groan, and the smile never left his face till he died…" Fraser's voice cracked on the last word, and he swallowed hard. "It still feels like yesterday, even after all these years. Time takes all, they say, but it will never dull the keenness of that day, in its joys or its sorrows…" He paused, then pulled something out of his pocket. "General Wolfe made presents to many young officers to remember him by. This was what he willed to me."

Edmund's eyes widened at the sight of the compass. "Oh…may I hold it, for a moment only?" he pleaded before he even knew what he was doing or how much like a little boy he sounded.

Fraser chuckled softly and handed it to him gingerly. "No dropping it now."

"Never, sir," Ned assured, running his fingers along the initials "J.W." cut into the back and feeling a lump form in his throat. He squinted, noticing an image underneath it, and smiled. "Is that…a wolf's head, sir?"

Fraser nodded, running his thumb over the image as well. "He was the leader of our pack, and led us in the hunt for red meat. Such a noble fellow, great and ever-memorable, ever to be lamented…" His voice faded as he took the compass back from Ned. "We found him to be so kind and attentive to our needs that we would have gone through fire and water to have served him. Poor General Wolfe…"

Silence settled over the room for a few moments. Fraser glanced over at Burgoyne, sleeping peacefully on the couch.

"Glory and the grave," Fraser murmured, "we chase the first, yet tumble into the second. And nothing in this world can save us."

Then the Scotsman stood up, walked over to the chaise where the seemingly unconscious Burgoyne was lying, and tossed a plaid blanket over him. A smile touched Fraser's his lips. "Sleep well, Sassenach."

"I heard that…"

"Wheesht! Sleep, why don't you?"

And Ned could not help but smile.

~

The time drew near for the great campaign to begin. Ned had watched from a distance for months as the rank and file were drilled relentlessly by their officers. Long marches into the countryside, bookended by musket and bayonet training, had comprised the soldiers' daily routines from dawn to dusk. Some were crack troops, but so many others were green. Now they were all about to be put to the test.

As Burgoyne and his generals prepared themselves for the final parade of their regiments, Fraser stood dressed now in the clothes of any other British general, scarlet coat and snow-white breeches, shedding any Highland distinction. The hilt of his ceremonial sword and the gorget around his neck sparkled in the sun. Burgoyne stood a little ways off, in his finest dress uniform complete with a feathered hat, conversing with General Phillips about the gun salute. Edmund found that the brightness of the day made their tunics even more brilliant, burning his eyes. He blinked, trying to keep them from tearing as he prepared to assist Burgoyne to mount his horse.

He heard a cawing sound and turned to see a raven sitting on a branch not far from where Fraser stood, spreading its wings as if preparing to launch into flight.

The Scotsman snapped his head up, a strange glint in his eyes, then in a single motion pulled out one of his pistols and squeezed the trigger.

Ned jumped a little at the suddenness of the shot.

The raven fell to the ground, its black feathers now bathed in red as well.

"My God, Balnain!" Burgoyne half-snorted, a look between shock and amusement in his eyes. "What treason did that poor carrion ever commit?"

"Unless the enemy has chosen to use such creatures for messengers, and only Fraser knows about it," Phillips threw in teasingly, "and he was trying to reform him by making him into a loyal bloody-back like us!"

Fraser just shook his head, and stated bleakly, "That was not the one."

Without any further explanation to either man, Fraser was helped onto his gray mount by his aides, and rode forward to inspect the troops under his command. Burgoyne and Philips likewise mounted and followed after him.

Reverend Brudenell was already on the field to consecrate the muskets and regimental colors as the fifes and drums of the military bands played lively martial airs. The sight of the regiments in their formations could not help but dazzle Ned's eyes and cause his heart to swell with pride at the flawless presentation of his country's fighting men. The sky was crystal clear without a cloud, bringing out the blue field of the Union flag, and the scarlet coats of the soldiers brought out the red cross emblazoned on the banners. And also, he felt some strange and sudden terror, as their weapons glistened under the sun and the chaplain, clad in raven black, stepped up onto the platform that had been erected for him to give his sermon.

"The Britons are a highly favored people from amongst all the nations of Europe," he intoned. "They have ever been renowned for their bravery, their courage, their magnanimity, and generosity; their ardent zeal for liberty and freedom, their eager thirst after military glory, and their constant success in the day of battle; their kings were heroes, their ministers were patriots, and their parliaments uninfluenced by anything but the interest and glory of the people whose law and liberties were committed to their charge. May the courage and intrepidity of these troops be a continual terror to the enemies of the King."

Ned caught sight of Fraser rolling his eyes at the wildly hyperbolic and blatantly inaccurate speech. The Scotsman turned to Burgoyne, sitting on his horse beside him, and mouthed the words that Ned surmised were "the same." Burgoyne just shook his head, with a small smile on his face, as if privy to something he kept close to his chest. Ned had to admit he agreed more with Fraser; this chaplain seemed little different than the run of the mill sort sent out to rouse patriotic fervor, with genuine religion only as a distant secondary concern.

"While inferior professions hold out sordid views as a spur to emulation, the object of the military is of the most sublime nature," the chaplain continued. "You are charged to perform gallant actions that shall gain the approbation of your sovereign and superior officers, the gratitude of your fellow subjects, and the admiration of posterity. Happy those who shall have arrived at this exalted summit! To gain it, the greatest men that ever existed did not think it too much to sacrifice interests, ease, and even life. Such lofty goals are not inaccessible to private soldiers, whether as a collective body, or as individuals any more than to officers. Who then does not feel the influence of that divine spark, which prompts us to rise above the common level? Who has not ambition to transmit his name with applause to posterity? Who does not wish and pant for the opportunity to signalize himself? The esteem and rewards of their country will not be wanting, and they will spend the decline of life in tranquility, ease and comfort, recollecting the memory of gallant actions with companions of former dangers."

Ned felt a sudden uncertainty rise in his breast, even as the vicar promised them a glorious return home and happy years of retirement. He did his best to suppress it, like a rock sunk down into the depths of water.

The chaplain gestured to the muskets that the men were holding. "The brave soldier should entertain the most ardent regard for their arms, and to wish that even in death they should not be separated. Thus it was a maxim with the Spartans, to return from battle with their arms, or laid out upon their shields. Epaminondas, one of the best generals of antiquity, being mortally wounded, was only anxious lest his arms should fall into the enemy's hands. The arms of the Roman soldiers weighed sixty pounds, and it was death to throw away any part of them."

Now the chaplain gestured dramatically to the regimental banners, fluttering in the morning breeze along with the sleeve of his black robe.

"But the colors are above all things the object of a soldier's particular regard, attention, and attachment. This was the case in warlike nations at all times. Romans worshiped and swore by them, and to lose them was to incur certain death. We have many instances in ancient history of commanders, in a doubtful engagement, throwing the colors among the troops of the enemy, knowing that the courage, ardor, and exertion of the soldiery would instantly redouble, beat the enemy, and retake them. Though we do not worship the colors as they did, yet the awful ceremony of this day proves that they remain the object of peculiar veneration. They hold forth to us the idea of the prince whose service we have undertaken, of our country's cause which we are never to forsake, and of our military honor which we are ever to preserve. The colors, in short, represent everything that is dear to the soldier. At the sight of them, all the powers of his soul are to rouse. They are a post to which he must repair through fire and sword, and which he must defend while life remains. To desert them is the blackest perjury and eternal infamy: to lose them by such an accident, even as one might otherwise judge unavoidable, is not to be excused, because to lose them, no matter how, is to lose everything; and when they are in danger, or lost, officers and soldiers have nothing for it but to recover them or die. Penetrated therefore with innate eagerness for glory, mindful of the fame of your ancestors, emulous of the luster of your countrymen, you are bound not only to transmit their honor and colors unsullied to posterity, but let every individual think himself entitled, nay bound, to aim at something that may deservedly shine in the page of history."

As the chaplain moved along the lines, reading prayers over the arms and colors, Ned, Jonathan, and Eli took their post by the general's baggage carts at the side of the parade grounds, observing the goings on from a distance

"That was an all-but-pagan speech," Eli mumbled.

"How so, Thompson?" Jonathan inquired, reaching out and brushing some of the wrinkles out of Eli's coat so he would not be censured. Eli was always one for cleanliness, but not necessarily tidiness, tending to focus more upon the neatness of the horses than himself.

"Did you not hear it yourself?" Eli queried. "Where was God in all of that?"

"I know the sermon was theatrical, but pagan still seems rather harsh," Jonathan countered. "I'm sure the chaplain meant well…"

"But I ask you, when did he press us to remember the Lord in preparation for the Judgment Day?" Eli demanded. "Where was the talk of our daily sins and mortal span? What of the second birth, the one water and the spirit and blood? What of the reprobate's punishment and the life eternal? Anything less than that is empty preaching, not fit to fill the hearts of men!"

"Well, the sermon was of a certain type, intended to encourage the men to behave righteously under arms and spurn any conduct which might sully the nation's honor," Jonathan replied.

"The nation's honor is already sullied if she has forgotten what gives her worth," Eli retorted. "We are called to continue the work of reform and make the name of Christ glorious throughout the world! It is not for any merit of our own that we are chosen to rise up as a city on a hill. It is only this: The Covenant, and that alone, given to a stiff-necked people. Either we keep to it, in blood, or the scepter passes away. If we will not be fire, we will be nothing!"

As Eli spoke, Ned could not help but think back upon Major Pitcairn, with his talk of blood and fire.

"I do not like it," Eli murmured. "Things are not as they should be. And our general taking another man's wife on the road with him…"

"I do not like it either, but there's little to be done about it," Jonathan sighed. "I think before we worry ourselves about the sins of the general, or of the nation, we should perhaps try to see the better parts of them, and the worst parts of ourselves. Then I'm sure we will find plenty that needs doing within our own reach. Besides, there are blessings we would be remiss not to count. We live in a country where the rights and liberties of Protestants are upheld. And whatever missteps the general makes, he treats us well, and the men love him for that. That is the better part of him, the gentlemanly part which feels the pains of others. Surely God smiles on the good to be found even in us, poor miserable sinners. Surely we can pray the good will win out."

"It cannot win out," Eli blurted, "not by our will, which is rotten to the core. No, we cannot win…unless God should deign to spare us."

"May God right our will," Jonathan replied softly, almost like a prayer.

Eli cast Ned a look of displeasure. "The general has also suffered us to have Papists amongst our ranks…"

Ned turned, trying to think of some retort, to deny the accusation, but he found the denial itself would cause him more pain, and it stuck in his throat.

"Oh, enough, Thompson," Jonathan chided him. "I won't let anyone bully you, but I won't let you bully him either. He made his mark and took communion. That should be good enough for all of us…"

"No," came a sarcastic voice behind them, and Ned saw it was Lieutenant Caldwell. "Only the judgment is good enough for us. Isn't that right, my scarred saint?"

Eli's face burned, and Caldwell extended a hand as if to mockingly pinch his cheek, but Jonathan pulled his hand away.

"None of that, now," he said, softly but firmly.

"Oh, so you're still playing his bodyguard?" Caldwell sneered.

"This is neither the time nor the place," Jonathan hissed. "The general is about to make a speech."

"Can't blame Caldwell," said another young lieutenant, who was frequently seen in Caldwell's company. "He's a bloody Puritan, he is. Surprised communion even slid down his dissenting throat…"

"True that, Jackson," Caldwell snorted. "Lucky he didn't choke on it."

"I believe the King is appointed by God to be the defender of the Protestant faith," Eli rasped. "That's what I thought upon when I took my oaths."

"Of course you did," Jonathan replied sympathetically, patting his arm. "We all did."

Then Jonathan walked a few paces back, leaned over to Lieutenant Jackson, seeming to believe him of a more reasonable nature than Caldwell, and whispered, "Lieutenant Thompson had the fever as a child. It left its marks on him. It's not his fault if he's a bit addled, don't you see? Have a care, and be kind, if you can manage it…"

Jackson made a snorting noise. "I didn't give him the fever, now did I? Just because he got the pox or whatever it was, doesn't mean I have to put up with his bloody rantings…"

"Have a care, Pip," Jonathan groaned in exasperation.

"And don't call me Pip! Only my mother and the general call me that…"

"Hush, now, Pip," Caldwell interrupted him. "Our illustrious commander-in-chief will expect us all to cheer on his speech as if it were something out of Shakespeare, or we might be sent to bed without supper…"

Ned cringed at the cynicism in his tone, reminding him once again of Lady Charlotte's impression of him.

Then Burgoyne rode out onto the field, resplendent in his finest dress uniform, and the soldiers roared like the ocean's roll, "Huzzah!"

"Soldiers of the King!" Burgoyne cried. "You have been sent to this far continent to represent the power, the justice, and when properly sought, the mercy of His Majesty. You should on all occasions show yourselves patient, obedient, disinterested, and generous in the discharge of your duties in His name. The cause of our country and the devotion to our sovereign spurs us on to restore the primacy of the Constitution. We also are come here to answer the melancholy appeal of the King's loyal American subjects who have suffered greatly under the completest system of tyranny that ever God in his displeasure suffered for a time to be exercised over a stubborn generation. The powers behind this present unnatural rebellion have assaulted the most peaceable denizens, without distinction of age or sex, for the sole crime, often for the sole suspicion, of having adhered in principle to the government under which they were born, and to which by every tie, divine and human, they owe allegiance. They have implemented arbitrary imprisonment, confiscation of property, and persecution unprecedented even in the Inquisition of the Romish Church!"

Edmund could not help but wince as he felt Eli's steely glare upon him. Burgoyne knew how to play to his audience, and such rhetorical stoking of Protestant fears could not help but make Ned's stomach flip. Whatever freakishly in-between thing he was now, he still worried over his family's welfare, even if he was as good as dead to them.

"These flagrant injustices are inflicted by assemblies and committees who dare profess themselves as friends of liberty," Burgoyne continued. "The profanation of religion is added to the prostitution of common reason, with men of the cloth leading their flocks down a path of destruction. The consciences of men are set at naught, and multitudes are compelled, not only to bear arms, but also to swear subjection to a usurpation they abhor. To these long-suffering souls, we come as the true liberators. But to those hardened enemies of Great Britain and America, whom I consider to be one and the same, we shall be messengers of wrath that will await them in the field and overtake them wherever they lurk. In consciousness of Christianity, my royal master's clemency, and the honor of soldiership, I am determined to strike where necessary, yet also anxious to spare where possible. But if these vile offenders refuse to repent of their treachery, and the frenzy of hostility should remain, I trust I shall stand acquitted in the eyes of God and Men in denouncing and executing the vengeance of the state against the willful outcasts! No stone of theirs will remain upon another, nor a head of wheat upon their stalks! With such a body of men as this, in full powers of health, discipline, and valor, animated by all these considerations, the long-awaited judgment cannot help but fall upon them in all its fury!"

Ned could not help shiver as a cheer rose up from the ranks and Burgoyne rose along the lines again, his feathered hat held high, and he heard Eli murmur strangely, "Judgment…he hath said it…oh…"

Fraser turned to the soldiers, hand upon sword hilt, and cried out one injunction only: "Ready yourselves, for fire and blood!"

Then he, too, rode along the lines, and troops let out another cheer.

But through the din, Ned heard Eli praying. "Judge Thou me," he rasped, "and make me Thine own prisoner!"

Again, Caldwell and Jackson berated him.

And Jonathan said, "The fever, I told you. Pity him…the fever…"

Chapter 20: ARK OF THE COVENANT

Not long before the army's departure, there was a Eucharistic procession through the streets of Montreal, attended by the French Catholic inhabitants, of high and low degree, reverently kneeling and crossing themselves as the great golden monstrance held aloft by the monsignor passed by. Ned noticed one man in particular dressed in fine attire, clearly a gentleman of some means, kneeling beside poor shoeless townspeople in the mud, a rosary with crystal beads and a jeweled cross slipping through his fingers as he led the people in prayer.

"*Ave Maria...*"

"*Sancta Maria...*"

"*Ave Maria...*"

"*Sancta Maria...*"

"*Ave Maria...*"

"*Sancta Maria...*"

Some of the British soldiers, out of boredom, turned out to watch as well. General Burgoyne had given them strict orders to comply with the Quebec Act and avoid interfering with the religious practice of the inhabitants. Much like the command not to bother local women, however, this did not stop them from snickering and making crude jokes amongst themselves as the procession made its way towards the church.

Others, though, were more contemplative about the proceedings. A young sergeant from Dublin, Roger Lamb, was a middle-class Anglo-Irishman serving in the Royal Welsh Fusiliers, and a proud Protestant to the core. Yet he seemed intrigued as opposed to scornful of the proceedings.

"They must see it as the Jews saw the Ark of the Covenant in the Old Testament," he mused, scribbling in the journal he took with him everywhere to record his observations abroad. "The presence of the Lord, as they perceive it, gives them pause."

"But Sergeant, sir, aren't these Frenchies toting around naught but a pack of superstitions we've done away with for good reason?" a Welsh soldier nearby queried.

Lamb shrugged. "I...don't know. Perhaps we of the reformed faith should consider the impact of such ceremonies upon man. We are sensual beings, after all."

Several Gaelic Irish soldiers among the ranks furtively crossed themselves, their faces suddenly aflame and their eyes moist with guilt. Surely they had been raised in the faith, but turned their back upon it to take the shilling. Ned nearly followed the same pattern, on instinct. He was horrified by the reflex, still so ingrained in him. Worse yet, he was spotted in the act.

"*Etes vous Catholique?*" an old Frenchwoman next to him asked, crossing herself with her rosary beads. "*Catholique Anglais?*" She sounded shocked, as if encountering a rare beast rumored only to exist in myth.

"*Non, madame,*" Edmund blurted. "*Non...*"

"Of course he's Papist," Lieutenant Caldwell said mockingly, coming up from behind him. "Once a Papist, always a Papist. The general should have thought twice before allowing you to infiltrate his staff."

"How dare you! I swore to the Act with my hand upon the book!" Ned blurted, failing to keep his voice from cracking with guilt. "I am a loyal Briton, and have torn asunder all other bonds to prove it!"

"It has yet to be proven, under fire, whether or not your blood runs British," Caldwell declared. "Perhaps your continental sympathies will make you weak-kneed before the revolutionaries. It's said the French put them up to this. Perhaps you're in league with them, along with these bead-rattlers here." He gestured to the crowd.

Ned wanted to strike him, or at least shove him, or maybe say something derogatory about his conception. But the procession had reached them now, and the monstrance was passing them by, and Edmund glanced up.

A white circle, surrounded by a halo of gold. White and gold, alike, were glistening in the sun, emerging after showers, warming the mud and scalding his eyes. Yes, he felt weak-kneed now, his heart pounding, his mouth watering. And he saw the crucifix held high, body bronze, wounds garnet.

Hoc est corpus meum.

Edmund covered his eyes with his hands, then turned and staggered off into the alley.

He leaned against the wall of one of the buildings, his chest heaving. He tried to dispel with the memories of secret masses in the attic, of the crucifix above the altar, and the host upon his tongue. He tried to forget the sound of Kip barking, ever vigilant, keeping strangers at bay, seemingly privy to mysteries beyond human ken. Yes, the dog was far better than he was…

Ned heard someone coming into the alley, and prepared to rush off again.

"Wait, young man, please. I wish to speak with you."

Edmund turned to see the gentleman he had observed kneeling in the mud, leading the rosary. His voice was calm and refined, as Ned expected it would be from his bearing, but his accent was a surprise.

"You're…English," Ned exhaled.

"'Tis true," he returned with a smile, "and as one Englishman to another, I tell you there is nothing to fear in what you just saw."

Ned winced. "I'm not afraid."

"Then why are you trembling?"

Edmund touched his chest, where once he hid the Eucharist, under his coat and over his heart, but said nothing.

"I've seen many Protestants react poorly to our Catholic ways, as if we were engaging in a pagan ritual," the man said. "But, son, we are not. Nor indeed is it as foreign to us as you must think, certainly not to our ancestors." He tilted his head. "Are you religious, lad?"

"I…used to be," he replied. "I…try to be."

"Yes, I thought so. Sadly, many religious folk react the strongest of all against us. But the love of Christ is what unites us. We Catholics just have certain beliefs about the manner in which Christ manifests Himself to us, Body and Blood, Soul and Divinity. Yes, we have certain beliefs about the manner in which salvation is extended to us in our daily lives, through common things transfigured. God is mindful of our senses, lad. We are fearfully and wonderfully made to see, hear, touch, smell, taste, and see. That's what the sacraments engage with, whilst imparting graces to us. Thus, he gives us the sacraments, uniting us ever more closely to the Cross…"

"Yes, I know," Ned cut him off. "I know…all of it. Dear God, you don't know how much…" He fought to stop shivering, but could not manage it, the sight of the monstrance burned into his soul.

"Oh, my poor boy," the gentleman murmured, a sudden realization dawning in his eyes. "You are one of us…"

"No, no, not anymore," Ned insisted. "Please, let me go…"

"No one is holding you, lad," he insisted, "except yourself…"

Ned grimaced, then ran away as if fiends of hell were chasing him.

An hour later, Edmund remained sitting alone on a crate, next to a pile of them that still needed packing and labeling for the road. His heart was so heavy with doubt, he feared his legs would give way if he tried to stand.

Then he jumped a little, feeling a hand on his shoulder.

It was Jonathan Rawcliffe.

"I saw you at the procession."

"Did you?" Ned mumbled dejectedly.

"I know it must be difficult for you going from one religious disposition to another. What you see around here in Canada is everything you've known and loved from childhood. So you mustn't rush yourself or your feelings. It's going to take time to adjust to your new life."

Ned swallowed hard. "Shall I ever be able to adjust to my family counting me as a deadman for what I've done?"

"We're your family now," Jonathan assured. "Even General Burgoyne thinks of us that way, all members of a family. And maybe I don't say it outright much, but I consider the three of you– Jones, and Thompson, and yourself–as family to me especially. We're a dull little quartet of sorts, more familiar with pen and parchment and horse tack than guns. So we must put up with and look out for each other, as families do."

"I don't think the others will ever see me as family," Ned replied. "I will always be a Papist spy to them."

"No, Ned," Jonathan assured. "You will prove them wrong, and show that you are as loyal a Briton as the rest of us. You have made the right decision coming into fellowship with us, and with time, they will fold you right in and take you to their hearts. I already have."

Ned looked up at Jonathan's kindly face, and felt a stabbing pain through his own heart. "You have?"

"Yes," he confirmed. "I didn't think I'd get on with you at first, given some of the general's past young friends…"

"You mean Lieutenant Caldwell?"

Jonathan raised a finger to his lips. "Careful…he'll likely be a captain in no time at all."

Ned smirked a little. "Poor us."

"Indeed. He'll never let us live it down. Though I suppose we mustn't judge him too harshly for his weaknesses. Something tells me it was a part of his upbringing. But…you are not him. And God knows I'm glad of it. You've got good manners with everyone, whether they are your superiors, equals, or inferiors. Moreover, you don't complain about tasks that lack glory, and make no fuss in getting them done. You show dedication, as if it was the most important work in the world to which you had been assigned. Lastly, you take insults on the chin, and control your anger. You have clearly learned not to fall into the traps set for you."

"It is part of being raised recusant," Ned murmured. "We cultivate simple virtues, and accept that we are rarely in a good position to strike back."

"I am a simple man, and appreciate simple virtues, including those of your upbringing," Jonathan stated. "Don't think the general lacks awareness in this either. He is shrewder than he lets on, and knows the stuff of which a good officer is made. He knows the stuff men follow. I would not at all be surprised if you went far. You have a future with us."

Edmund swallowed hard. He wanted to believe him so much it hurt. And yet…

"Was it the right decision, Jonathan?" he queried. "Taking the Test Act?"

"Of course it was," his friend assured.

"Tell me why," Ned pressed. "I need to be reminded."

"Because," Jonathan replied, "you are an Englishman, and I believe a true one. It makes as little sense for you to commit your spiritual allegiance to Rome as to St. Petersburg. No, it is a straightforward thing for me. Our own king makes a far more fitting governor of the Church in England than any foreign prince."

"But did not Rome foster us?" Ned rasped.

"Yes, in our infancy, when we were first brought into the fold of Christianity," Jonathan reasoned. "But now we have matured, and are capable of handling our own religious affairs. Besides, it is part of our national character to go down the middle in most things. We strive to take the best of that which is Catholic, and the best of that which is reformed. A happy medium, in which different persuasions are held together as true Englishmen."

"Perhaps you're right," Ned responded, then added softly, "Perhaps…"

Edmund had little time to ponder further on the question, though, for there was to be one final supper party at the home of one of Quebec's elite, and Burgoyne would want to come prepared with gifts from his store.

To Ned's shock, their host turned out to be the very same Catholic gentleman from the procession. It turned out he was a leading architect in Quebec who had assisted in building fortifications to defend the city against the rebel assault.

General Fraser stopped and stared when he first saw their host, and Howard responded in a similar manner, a flicker of fear crossing his eyes. They had a history; Ned could see that plainly enough. But it seemed not to have been all bad, for after the first awkward moments passed, Fraser stepped forward and, as if overcome by impulse, embraced him. Howard seemed stunned at first, but then returned the gesture with the same warmth.

"You two go back aways?" Burgoyne queried.

Fraser nodded. "Aye, aways." He offered no further explanation.

Though English himself, Howard's wife was a slightly plump Frenchwoman with a pleasant face. Looking close to forty now, her husband still paid her as much attention as if she were still a blushing young bride, and blush she did over his affections, in addition to the flattery in French contributed by General Burgoyne. Ned overheard several of the officers at the party whisper among each other that their host must have abandoned himself to the dictates of Rome just to appease her.

When the time for toasting came, the wine flowed freely in praise of King George, Queen Charlotte, the host, the host's wife, the host's children, almost every major officer present, their families, and also the dog begging for scraps under the table.

Then Fraser himself rose, holding aloft his glass, and intoned, "Lest we forget—Brave Wolfe!"

Howard swallowed a lump in his throat and raised his glass in accord. "Brave Wolfe!"

"Brave Wolfe!" the cry rang out around the table, punctuated by the clinking of glasses.

Then Fraser glanced over at their host's wife, who seemed to have become somewhat downcast. He filled his glass again and raised it once more. Then he said some words in French, in a far more proper accent than Burgoyne could manage, finishing with "Marquis de Montcalm, *adversair honorables!*"

She appeared very pleased with this, blushing more than ever, and Howard cast Fraser a grateful glance. Burgoyne, meanwhile, rolled his eyes, as if the Scotsman was the worst possible show-off. Fraser just beamed back at him.

After supper had concluded, Edmund watched as Fraser and Howard stood in the garden, golden-hued in the setting sun of late spring, chatting together like brothers.

"Well, Howard, you've done mighty well for yourself under the Quebec Act, it seems," Fraser said, gesturing to the house. "The blessings of the New World!"

"The blessings of God," Howard responded with a smile. "My dearest Rachelle is a queen among women, and she has blessed me with a posterity." He laid a hand on Fraser's arm. "Thank you, by the way, for making things easier on her during the toasting."

"It's a pleasure for me to do any favor for a fine woman like your wife, if I can," Fraser assured kindly.

"She lost a father and brother, both fighting under Montcalm, and the marquis himself was a guest at their home many times. She has fond memories of him as a good Christian gentleman very much in love with his wife and devoted to their children. He was always talking about going home to the family castle in the French countryside and enjoying some small measure of peace with his loved ones, though war was the bane of the Montcalms, all the way back to the Crusades. She saw him ride back to the city after the lost battle, and the women cried to see his wound, but he comforted them, saying, 'My friends, this is nothing.' Strange thing…she told me he had a black band on his arm for one of his daughters who passed, though he knew not which one, and it grieved him, for news came so slowly, and often contained more rumor than fact. As you recall, General Wolfe was wearing his own black band for his father just passed…" Howard bit his lip. "They were much alike, in pride and passion, cool heads and warm hearts…enemy brothers…"

"He was a much set upon man, the marquis," Fraser recalled. "A faithful son of France, betrayed by colonial officials claiming to serve his king, whose corruption was as rank as the sewers. They preferred that their enemy should take the city before Montcalm could report their misdeeds. He should probably have remained within the city, but sallied forth to meet Wolfe on a point of honor, and paid the ultimate price. I have long pitied his position."

"I don't think he was too much to be pitied," Howard remarked.

"He died a slow death in agony, aware of his defeat, unable to save his people from conquest, grieving for his family, who were left without a husband or a father," Fraser recounted. "Surely he was to be pitied, from one soldier to another!"

"Yes, but he said he was ready to put aside the things of the world, as we all must do in the end," Howard said. "He dictated his last messages to each member of his family, even the daughter he thought most likely to be dead, and sent his concession and compliments to Wolfe, asking him to care for the French wounded, though he was already dead. Then he called a priest and received holy viaticum and was buried in that crater carved out by one of our shells in the Ursuline convent. He didn't scorn such a fate, but embraced it. Perhaps, he won his own victory in the heart of defeat, dying as he did on the Feast of the Exaltation of the Holy Cross."

"I recall he raised a wooden cross at the foot of the breastwork on the Heights of Carillon," Fraser remarked, "and inscribed it with his own Latin poetry…"

"'*En signum! En victor! Deus hic, Deus Ipse, triumphat,*'" Howard recited. "Behold God's sign, for only He hath triumphed here."

"But God abandoned him in short order," Fraser blurted, "just as, at the time, He abandoned the lately lamented Lord Howe."

"Just as God abandons God upon the tree for our sake," Howard replied.

"So it is not capricious to you?"

"No," Howard replied. "We must be crucified, each in our own way. It is the only path to Heaven, when all tears will be wiped away. God uses even our own violent impulses against each other to redeem us. Montcalm understood that. It's why his lips never stopped moving in prayer, all night, until he was dead at dawn."

"And what of our general, hmm?" Fraser pressed. "Have your feelings altered for him?"

Howard cast a look at Fraser, as if wounded by the insinuation. "I can still feel his hand, cold to the touch, in life and in death…" His voice broke. "God, I miss him."

"I suppose we all do, in our own way," Fraser admitted. "He was the blacksmith, and history was the anvil. He left his brand upon friend and foe, never to be removed."

"And I suppose never to stop burning our flesh," Howard murmured. "He fairly won our hearts, then broke them."

"His destiny was to be the hero of our age," Fraser said. "The martyr, even. It is for us to bear the cost, each in our own way."

"I suppose if the nation did not have some cultus to cling to, some sacredness left unscripted, it would cease to exist," Howard admitted. "A land without a soul is a corpse."

"But you despair of Wolfe's soul more than that of Montcalm, your co-religionist?"

"I do not despair of any man, least of all those I love," he rasped, crossing himself. "The exaltation draws us all. May it be our final conqueror."

Fraser cleared his throat, then remarked with a forced cheerfulness, "Well, I'm glad you managed to conquer your own bit of war booty, at least. Your lady seems to have gone with you willingly enough!"

"Her widowed mother never approved of her marriage to me," Howard confessed. "Her sister, a nun in one of the nearby convents, has been more generous towards me, which has given Rachelle some resolution. But…they all suffered during our conquest. So many did."

"Aye," Fraser sighed. "You always had a heart for the settlers hereabouts."

"These people know what it is to endure defeat and still stay true to what they are," Howard stated. "They not only suffered expulsion from Acadia for their allegiances, spiritual and temporal, and the destruction of their fishing nets at Louisbourg, but also bore up under the shelling of Quebec and the scouring of the countryside by our men at arms. Afterwards, they saw the statues of saints being taken down and replaced by those of our military heroes, much like what happened in our own cathedrals back home."

"Montcalm and his contingent were willing to unleash the dogs of war upon British colonists just as readily," Fraser reminded him. "Look at what happened at Fort William Henry, as one example amongst many. The Indians went on a rampage, for all the promises made by the marquis. They terrorized the frontier."

"We could all afford to give repentance a try," Howard sighed. "And perhaps…learn from our mistakes…"

"You mean involving Indians?"

"I mean involving ourselves in wanton brutality, whether we are red or white."

Fraser circulated his shoulders. "Now then, you're a Papist, not a Quaker, and it's a brutal world. Little enough to be done about that most days. But look, at least the inhabitants of these parts have been granted the freedom to keep their faith. You enjoy the same here."

"Yes. The population appreciates the reasonable treatment they have received under British administrators, and most distrust the rebellious Americans who decried the Quebec Act. Old wounds are being forced to heal between us, at least somewhat. God only knows what will happen if France interferes on behalf of the southern revolt, though…" Howard raised an eyebrow. "And how are your wounds healing, Balnain?"

Fraser shrugged. "Soldiers must do their best to numb themselves to such things and do their duty as it appears to them."

A wistful look came to Howard's eyes. "I remember you, fresh from service in Europe, a pardon in your pocket to serve as an officer in the 78th Regiment."

"Fraser's Highlanders," Fraser recalled with a smirk. "Raised by the son of our beheaded chief. Yes, the fox kit knew how to survive."

"A clan trait?"

"Perhaps. Even the regiment seems to be canny about such things. The 78th may have been disbanded, but the 71st was reborn. Fraser's Highlanders march on. Switched their kilts out for trews, these days, but kept the pipes!" Fraser smiled fondly. "I miss being amongst my own kindred sometimes, you know."

"You have done them proud," Howard assured, "even as you have risen beyond them."

"It seems only yesterday I was told I could not command anyone but fellow highlanders. They said the unruly clans would only listen to men cut from the same cloth. That's why we were pardoned…to keep them in line, even as we were to be kept in line."

"Yet look at you now," Howard said. "You command men of every stripe and stand as an equal amongst peers with the likes of Burgoyne and Philips."

"They…helped me," Fraser explained. "But others have not been half so keen to see a man of my origin rise to where I am. They will take note of me from afar, judging my every move, to determine the result of the experiment…"

"And you will banish their doubts, as you always have."

Fraser smiled, then thanked him in Gaelic, "*Tapadh leat*."

"*Se do bheatha*," Howard replied, and Fraser laughed.

"God's blood, you remembered what we taught you!"

"A man should never neglect the language taught to him by his sworn brothers, nor the language taught to him by his wedded woman," Howard stated. "Hence, I set aside a space in my mind for both Erse and French."

"I imagine your lady found more pleasurable ways to school you in her tongue, though," Fraser quipped, and both men laughed.

"And what about you, my dear General?" Howard said, slapping his friend on the back. "Still a bachelor?"

Fraser snorted. "No. Beware the feeble sex, I tell my young aides! They are not to be resisted indefinitely, no matter how stalwart you think yourself to be!"

"And have you children to complete your good fortune?"

Fraser shook his head. "Not yet."

"I have six myself, the oldest two with families of their own now. I wish you could have met the youngsters, but Rachelle insisted they go to bed…"

"Tell me what they fancy, and I shall send them presents from New York," Fraser promised. "Yes, I'll purchase something for your Rachelle too, if it doesn't make you overly jealous."

Howard laughed and shook his head. "You'd make a good father. You should try for a family as soon as you're home again. Wolfe wanted children too, but then…" He swallowed hard. "I sometimes grieve that he never knew the comfort of a wife," Howard murmured. "He was softer than he sometimes acted, you know…he wanted children…a house, a garden…" His voice trailed off. "Damn, after all this time, we should be over it."

"But we aren't," Fraser mumbled.

"No…" Howard made a gesture towards his companion. "Do you still have what he gave you, Fraser?"

Fraser smirked and drew forth his compass from his coat. "And you, Howard? What have you got to show for yourself?"

Howard in turn reached inside his coat and pulled out a handkerchief, purple and white, which he reverently extended towards his friend.

Fraser looked at it for a long moment, his eyes shimmering, then he touched the edge of it. "We are like two little boys, aren't we? Showing each other our treasures…"

"He cared for you, no matter what he said about your people," Howard assured.

"And for you, no matter what he said about yours," Fraser replied. "Off duty, he let you call him 'Jemmy.' Now that's something indeed!"

Howard smiled. "We were young then, yes, young and guileless, and gave our love easily, like the gray-eyed boy with Burgoyne…and as I lost my innocence, I looked up to you for solace."

"Up to me?" Fraser scoffed. "A Jacobite mercenary fresh from the continent, the ink not yet dry upon my pardon?"

"Yes," Howard assures. "You were always kind to me and kept my secrets."

Fraser shrugged again. "One outsider can't afford to judge another."

"Will you do me a favor then?"

"Ask it."

"Look after that boy, who once was a recusant," Howard said. "Look after him as if he were part of your own family."

"But he's part of Johnny's family, not mine," Fraser countered.

"You think much of General Burgoyne," Howard observed. "More than simply as a commanding officer."

"Aye," Fraser agreed. "He has earned my affection as well as my esteem."

"Your affection is worth more than you know," Howard said quietly, "which is why I ask you to look after that boy, as if he was a part of your own clan."

"Good God, that's going a bit far, isn't it?" Fraser chuckled.

"He needs to be taken in by someone who knows what it is to be different," Howard insisted. "He needs a father, especially given what's to come. And perhaps…you cannot afford to wait for a son…"

"What do you mean by 'what's to come'?" Fraser queried.

"You may think the world of Burgoyne as a person, but not of his plan," Howard stated. "I can read it all over your face. It will be a bloody road to victory or defeat."

"I've never feared blood," Fraser stated resolutely.

"Either the shedding of it, or the bond it creates," Howard agreed. "That's why I ask you to treat the boy like kin, for my sake. I trust you to show him the same understanding that you showed me, and to keep whatever secrets he may hold close to his breast."

"You think he may return to his Romish ways, don't you?" Fraser surmised.

"I think he is suffering," Howard stated. "I think he will need you."

"Well, if such an occasion should arise, I'll do my best to be of service and knock some sense into his head so as not to throw away his military career over religious stipulations. But no one appreciated it when I gave such advice before, did they?"

Howard smirked. "They appreciated you, nevertheless." He gazed at him quizzically. "I remember how you crossed yourself, at the same time that I did, when we first saw the general's corpse. Will you never tell me the truth of your upbringing?"

"The truth is that my clan is mixed," Fraser stated. "Aye, that's the Gospel truth of it."

Howard nodded, accepting the answer. "Do take care of yourself, Simon."

"It's ever a Fraser's talent to take care of himself," the Scotsman chortled, then the men shared a second embrace.

"It's been so long," Howard murmured. "And now you are going into the fire again. I wish to God you were not, for seeing you again has burdened my heart."

"Well, you were always one for saying your prayers before bedtime," Fraser remarked. "I could probably use a mention."

Howard nodded. "I do that already. Always have done since we last parted."

Fraser smiled softly. "Do you…pray for the dead too?"

"What do you think?" Howard challenged. "My faith aside, I do not think God would be so cruel as to prevent us from speaking to him about those we have loved best and lost soonest."

Fraser nodded. "I…understand."

"Do you?"

"Aye, that much I do."

"Then you have made me a very happy man," Howard said. "It is so often a struggle to be understood, and your understanding gladdens my heart, even as you have burdened it. I'll have to content myself with both."

~

At last, on the 20th of June, 1777, Burgoyne's March began in earnest. Though, in fact, it started off with a fair amount of rowing, as the British flotilla moved from Cumberland Head out onto Lake Champlain. The morning was bright and clear, sun glistening upon the water and the uniforms, the gorgets of the officers and buttons of the men resplendent. Burgoyne was himself clad in his very finest military attire, for this would be his greatest performance, and he fully intended to make the most of being center stage. Edmund's heart swelled in his chest to be amongst them, listening to the martial airs played upon fifes and drums. Whatever misgivings he still harbored about the Test Act, at least he would be with his people, upholding the honor of king. He was a true son of England, just like his knightly ancestors, and whatever sacrifices had to be made, he would make his island proud and prove his courage. He placed a hand upon his gorget reverently, his fingers tracing the imprint of the noble lion and the pure unicorn, and vowed in his heart never to disgrace it.

The British were not alone, either. They had allies. Hessians from Germany with their long mustaches and pointed caps were there, singing deep-throated Lutheran hymns, as were native tribesmen, fierce in their colorful war paint and equally colorful beads, letting out periodic war-whoops. There were also American Loyalists, come out to assist in their own liberation from the revolutionary government, and more shockingly, Canadian volunteers and foresters, many of French Catholic extraction.

Ned was shocked to find that the French Canadians had been allowed to bring a priest along with them. Eli, of course, was livid.

"It's an abomination!" he declared. "How can we expect the Lord to bless us with victory if we tolerate these devil's disciples and persecutors of God's people? If our Israel is to remain true to the covenant, she must have naught to do with idol-worshippers!"

"Eli, we're in the midst of outright pagans," Jonathan reminded him, gesturing to a canoe of Iroquois. "Surely we can put up with a Papist minister in our company. They can't all be wicked men through and through, can they?"

"I'm not happy about the heathens being here either," Eli declared, "but it's the black-hearted clergy that stirred up the Gaels in Ireland and the Popish mobs in France to accost us. Our general is permitting this outrage because he has been seduced by that Papist adulteress who shares his tent!"

"It's out of respect for the Quebec Act," Jonathan insisted. "If these people wish to fight for the Crown against the rebels, I don't see why we should deny them the privilege…"

"Then why do we deny it to Papists in Britain and Ireland?" Eli demanded.

Jonathan shrugged. "It's just different."

"How?"

Jonathan cast an almost accidental glance in Ned's direction, who felt his heart sinking. "It just is, dear," he doubled down. "It would hardly be practical or humane to evict all French Catholics in Canada, as was done in Nova Scotia, so it is best to incorporate them wherever possible into His Majesty's service as loyal subjects."

"But not in England?" Edmund murmured.

"The Mother Country and her colonies may be united, but they are still distinct," Jonathan replied. "Everyone would be better off if they remembered that."

"And so…?"

"So England is Protestant," Jonathan countered, "and so she must remain."

"What is most important is that we secure for ourselves a godly nation, and rear for ourselves a godly people," Eli stated. "Otherwise, the name Protestant is empty. It must be about reformation, or it is worthless."

"That is fair, but we must be cautious not to veer to extremes," Jonathan replied. "There is no such thing as perfection in this world, so we do the best we can with what we have to work with that includes areas of compromise."

"Compromising with offenses against God?" Eli challenged. "I think not. The state of a nation, lost to its own sin, is like riding on a sinking ship, or being wed to a drunkard wife. Such, I fear, is a sign of the times, which we are called to purify, first in ourselves, and then in society."

"You sound Cromwellian now," Jonathan sighed.

"I intend to. He was right. Our work is to usher in the day of the Lord. Everything else served only as means to an end."

"Even the King?" Jonathan queried wryly.

"Aye, even the King, in as much as he is a man who must answer to God and be checked by the faithful. Samuel Rutherford wrote of such matters in *Lex Rex*."

"The rebels in these colonies have been known to make such arguments for conditional loyalty to the sovereign," Jonathan said.

"As is their right," Eli replied. "Whether they are right or wrong in this case is another matter."

"You might want to be careful who you share such sentiments with, Thompson," Jonathan cautioned. "You could be mistaken as a radical, or even supporting regicides…"

"Cromwell did not rush to kill Charles, but considered it a cruel necessity after that treacherous king betrayed the good of the nation by calling for foreign aid from Papist nations, under the influence of his Jezebel queen," Eli said. "Cromwell did not play the part of a madman. He merely proved that the King is not about the law of God nor of God's people."

"He became a military dictator, and conducted heinous massacres," Jonathan countered. "In Drogheda and Wexford, his soldiers slaughtered Irishmen and Englishmen alike…"

"He harmed no one who did not first refuse his terms, causing the towns to be taken by storm," Eli pushed back. "And as for the Gaels, well, they deserved it."

"Eli…"

"They did! They butchered us in the north! Cromwell avenged our blood, and drove them out to protect us! King Charles was the one who enabled their perfidy! Aye, he emboldened them through his own extravagance!"

"And yet you wear royalist livery now, though you would not have done so then," Jonathan surmised.

"Even Cromwell would have been largely satisfied with the settlement we now have," Eli said. "He was not opposed to all kings, just ones who forced Popish trappings upon the people yearning to be cleansed of such baubles. He even considered becoming king himself, though he realized he had the power without the title as lord protector and could better avoid accusations of avarice. He was not interested in pomp and splendor. He sold off the King's art at public auction and set his wife's cows to graze on royal hunting grounds."

"Art, ceremony, and liturgy have their place, though," Jonathan insisted. "Such things mark man's striving towards the divine, and humanity's achievements across the annals of history…"

"But does it glorify God in worship, or distract from him?" Eli demanded. "That is the question upon which all else rises or falls. The Scriptures warn us against making graven images, for we are a sinful people, susceptible to idolatry. We should not innovate when it comes to the straightforward modes of worship based in the Bible. God does not need gold and lace to be adored, but only a humble heart receptive to His Word."

"I believe one may have both a receptive heart and an eye for beauty," Jonathan replied. "It's not mutually exclusive, but a matter of rejoicing in the Lord through all the senses He gave us."

"I say we have a proclivity for corrupting what God has given us, all the way back to the garden," Eli countered, "If the defense for Romish frippery is merely a nod to human achievement, I say tear down every stitch and stone and pray in an empty chamber, or outside in the dirt. We are but miserable worms, and should come to God unburdened of our pretenses, so he may unburden us of our transgressions."

"I consider myself to be a moderate, in politics and religion, who can count relations on both sides of our civil war under Cromwell and the King," Jonathan stated. "I am not the sort in favor of lighting candles and burning incense, but I don't want the cross taken from the altar nor the stained-glass windows smashed. As for praying alone in a room, well, yes, one should do, but what of the Sacrament of the Lord's Supper?"

"There is a time and a place for it, in remembrance of the atonement, through which we have our salvation," Eli stated. "Yet it is not the bread and wine which contain power in and of themselves, but rather obedience to the Savior's command to present ourselves before His table with a penitent heart and a lively faith. It is in this way He deigns to confirm and seal us up in His promise of the life eternal."

"Surely, there is something more to the sacramental substances than that," Jonathan countered, "even if the exact nature of it remains a mystery to us. As Lancelot Andrews said, 'As to the real presence, we are agreed, but as to the mode, we define nothing rashly, nor anxiously investigate.'"

"John Knox himself conceded that the Lord's Supper was a mystery, but playing with such language overly much only obscures what should be plain for all good Protestants," Eli retorted. "If Christ is present to us while we reenact His last supper, it is through the keeping of His commandment, which knits together the Lord and the receivers and lifts us up into heavenly and invisible things. We must have enough zeal and commitment to rely upon scripture alone and do away with the embroidered doctrines of Rome."

"But there must be room for differing points of view on such subjects amongst reformed Christians," Jonathan insisted. "Even your own heritage has its contradictions, for Puritans and Presbyterians were sometimes friends, and often foes."

"Yes, it is true, mostly in terms of organization," Eli conceded. "But on the important points of doctrine, we were in agreement."

"Remember, the national settlement exists for a reason, to bridge these organizational gaps," Jonathan reminded him.

"I am not convinced that is a good enough defense of Elizabeth's settlement," Eli shot back. "I favor the course of her brother Edward, the Young Josiah, and her martyred cousin Jane. It is a pity they perished so young, for both understood the sword of spirit which is necessary for governance, and that is the primacy of the Holy Scriptures. I also favor William and Mary, who were shaped by a sturdier Calvinism."

"Especially Mary, it seems," Jonathan remarked, somewhat sympathetically, aware of Eli's attachment to her through his mother.

"She was a righteous queen and a woman of frequent prayer," Eli said. "She would spend hours on her knees in the chapel, and saw God's hand guiding all earthly affairs. Yes, she saw the Glorious Revolution as a gift from heaven, an opportunity to show the world what we could be as a reformed people. She believed in us as a city on a hill, a light to the nations. She wanted to convert the Papist Irish and the heathen Indians within her dominion through education. But she feared that all her great dreams of godliness reigning supreme in our isles would come to naught through our fickle natures. The covenant would be shattered through our sins."

"But again, we must accept that there will always be sinners amongst us until the end of the age," Jonathan reminded him. "I wish it were not so, but I must count myself as the primary offender, and thus pray God would continue to tolerate our stumbling and even our settlements, for the common good."

"You speak of allowing for disagreements amongst reformed Christians, but only to a point," Eli replied. "I don't believe the vestry taxes placed upon dissenters in England and Ireland are fit to be enforced upon fellow Protestants whose consciences keep them from the state church," Eli said. "Nor do I lack sympathy with the inhabitants of colonies that have similar laws, such as Virginia and the Carolinas."

"It's a matter of maintaining general uniformity," Jonathan argued.

"But conspicuously absent in Scotland," Eli observed, "because of the settlement."

"Well, yes, it's the way things worked out, because of specific considerations pertaining to the union…"

"And absent in diverse colonies, such as Pennsylvania and New York, and last but least, in Canada," Eli finished. "I say we suffer from a lack of imperial consistency."

"Empires must accept some diversity from one region to another if they intend to endure," Jonathan said. "Individual circumstances must be addressed. These American colonies each have a different founding story, and are composed of different sorts of people…"

"They seem to put aside their differences now," Eli remarked.

"Please don't tell me you sympathize with the source of this unity," Jonathan sighed.

"No," said Eli simply. "I do not believe our King has violated his oaths to the people of God. If I thought he had, I would never have submitted to the Test Act, though at first I was loath to take it."

"What persuaded you?" Jonathan asked.

"My grandfather said it was permissible, if my conscience would allow it, and I deemed governorship of the Church to mean the King's obligation to maintain Protestantism within his realms and secure the rights of his Protestant subjects."

"And that is why the priest coming along for this march bothers you so?"

"The Quebec Act as a whole bothers me so," Eli replied. "However, that is an exception to the King's fulfillment of his oaths. He has proven himself to be an earnest head of the faithful. The question of tax procedure pales in comparison to that. So I will fight, and die, if need be, to defend his prerogative, so long as he continues to promulgate the reformation of the Church."

"Are you two ever going to button it?" Gavin sighed, returning from carrying a message from the general about the immediate disembarkation of his wardrobe from the flotilla. "You've been talking about religion and politics since before I left."

"The lad has a good mind for debate," Jonathan said, gesturing to Eli, who blushed. "It's proven stimulating!"

Gavin just rolled his eyes.

"Well, why don't you bother weighing in, Jones?" Jonathan prodded him. "Share your Wesleyan wisdom!"

"I am not as proficient in such arguments," Gavin replied. "I view faith as a simpler thing."

"Do tell," Jonathan insisted.

"I have little to say, except…perhaps we have our priorities wrong."

"What do you mean?"

"I shall quote John Wesley upon the subject, since he has a purer turn of phrase than I," Gavin stated. "He said, 'Whosoever therefore thou art, who desirest to be forgiven and reconciled to the favor of God, do not say in thy heart: I must first do this; I must first conquer every sin; break off every evil word and work, and do all good to all men; or, I must first go to church, receive the Lord's Supper, hear more sermons, and say more prayers. Nay, but first believe! Believe in the Lord Jesus Christ, the Propitiation for thy sins. Let this good foundation first be laid, and then thou shalt do all things well.'" Gavin touched his chest. "Perhaps we spend too much time debating the particulars, when the necessary thing is within our reach, for me, for you…" He pointed to Jonathan. "And you…" He pointed to Eli. "Aye, and even you…" He pointed at last to Ned. "Perhaps, whether we are Protestant or Papist, we should become Christians first!"

Jonathan smiled. "I dare say we needed that sermon today."

Methodist intervention notwithstanding, Eli's paranoia of Papists under every rock only grew as the army's march south began in earnest. Perhaps it had something to do with the environment they had entered, densely forested with unpredictable terrain. The air was thick with the almost suffocating scent of living and dying foliage, and strange noises reverberating through the night made it difficult to sleep. The soldiers could not tell whether the sounds emanated from man or beast, and the mystery left them all the more unnerved. The painfully slow work of the foresters with their axes and sickles, blazing a trail forward for the train to follow, fighting for every inch of open ground, did little to relieve the gnawing claustrophobia that plagued the ranks.

To make matters worse, hordes of insects and reptiles were roused by the troops trudging through their domain, and soon found their way into the wagons and tents. General Burgoyne himself had an unexpected guest in his quarters in the form of a six-foot-long black rat snake. He nearly fainted dead away on his cot, while his mistress responded more proactively by screaming so loudly, the creature beat a hasty retreat, slithering back in the woods. General Burgoyne, meanwhile, had to be revived with smelling salts, a fact which neither General Fraser nor General Phillips would ever let him forget. They even questioned if the initial blood-curdling shriek came from the lady alone.

Whatever animosities had existed between men before the march only seemed to intensify due to the challenges of the natural environment. And so, multiple times in the following weeks, Eli filed reports on Ned, trying to get his pay docked and his arms confiscated as a "secret Papist" based on spurious evidence. Ned almost wished he was doing what Eli feared and covertly practicing his old devotions. But that would surely be duplicitous, after taking oaths to the contrary. It would be violating yet another covenant. No, he would just have to bear up under the scrutiny and force himself to adjust to being Anglican, just as Jonathan assured he would. Burgoyne, to his credit, just crumpled Eli's reports against Edmund into paper balls and used them to pelt Freddie the messenger boy with when he slacked in his daily duties.

"Never fear, dear Ned," Burgoyne consoled him. "My chivalrous cavalier blood will keep that incorrigible roundhead horse boy at bay!"

One thing had to be admitted, even by his worst detractors: Burgoyne proved to be an enlightened superior. As overbearing as he might be in some theatrical venues, he knew how to handle those under his military command with a light touch and a winning manner. He led by example and encouragement, never failing to give praise where it was merited, and treated his subordinates as thinking beings, not dumb brutes. He knew how to crack the odd joke and chat about home without losing his air of authority, and had a knack for making direct orders seem more like recommendations and requests. He learned about each member of his staff individually and proved himself to be a shrewd judge of character and talent, placing each man where he believed they could be of most use within his "family", then giving them the space to exercise their skills.

On every occasion, he showed himself to be the soldier's friend, demonstrating a genuine attentiveness to the welfare of those under his command, especially his aides, who received his particular protection and paternalism. This was exemplified by his remembering to bring along five extra pairs of spectacles, just in case Jonathan needed them, and his willingness to share the pastries that his faithful clerk foisted on him in a show of fellowship, even though they made the general "feel fat" and fret over the possibility of the ladies noticing. Jonathan insisted that having a few extra pounds had never prevented him from having fun with his Bitty, because she wasn't the superficial sort, and the general turned purple over the imagery that the awkward but endearing remark inevitably conjured up.

    Ned observed firsthand that Gentleman Johnny's humane leadership caused young officers to idolize him and the whole army to hold the warmest attachment to him. Whatever they all would have to face over the course of this harrowing wilderness campaign, and whatever shadows still haunted Edmund's soul, he was proud to serve under this man, with his wondrous mix of virtues and flaws, who he was bound to in friendship as well as duty.

Chapter 21: SAVAGE PEOPLES

Upon the onset of the campaign, General Burgoyne composed a proclamation to be spread across the countryside, for the purpose of encouraging the loyal and admonishing the rebellious. Ned was put to work taking dictation for him, and the language the general chose reminded him of the Old Testament, Richard the Lionheart, and William Shakespeare all rolled into one.

"I invite and exhort all persons, in all places where the progress of this army may point—and by the blessing of God I will extend it far—to maintain such a conduct as may justify me in protecting their lands, habitations, and families," one section read. "The intention of this address is to hold forth security and not depredation to the country. To those whose spirit and principle may induce them to partake in the glorious task of redeeming their countrymen from dungeons, and reestablishing the blessings of legal government, I offer encouragement and employment; and upon the first intelligence of their associations I will find means to assist their undertakings. The domestic, the industrious, the infirm, and even the timid inhabitants I am desirous to protect provided they remain quietly in their houses, that they do not suffer their cattle to be removed, nor their corn or forage to be secreted or destroyed, that they do not break up their bridges or roads; nor by any other acts directly or indirectly endeavor to obstruct the operations of the Kings troops, or supply or assist those of the enemy. I have dwelt upon this invitation, and wished for more persuasive terms to give it impression; and let not people be led to disregard it by considering their distance from the immediate situation of my camp. I have but to stretch out my arm to the Indian forces under my direction, and they amount to thousands."

Fraser snorted when he read through some sections, for the bombastic flourish and was laid on thick, "like too much jam upon not enough toast," the Scotsman decided, and worried the theatrical threats might push the inhabitants in the opposite direction, just as Burgoyne has managed to do with his offer of terms to the rebels besieging Boston. But Gentleman Johnny was both sincere in his extravagance and unwilling to edit it down any further before release.

"I've spent too much time on the point already, and wasted a sinful amount of parchment and ink on drafts," Burgoyne decided. "At the end of the day, an author must have confidence in his craft and quit the business altogether. Otherwise, he can end up editing away his own genius. And besides…I loathe editing."

"Some things commonly loathed are actually healthy," Fraser argued. "Like drinking milk, for example…"

"Please restrain that pesky maternal instinct of yours," Burgoyne sighed, "especially given the likelihood that you were raised on whisky from the cradle…"

"My point is…surely the most important thing is how this missive is likely to be received by the populace," Fraser argued. "I ask you, General: are you willing to carry out your threats, particularly pertaining to the Indians? Because if not, making them puts you at a disadvantage."

"While I am more than capable of inflicting punishment upon the erring, I do not intend to stain myself with crimes against humanity," Burgoyne stated. "I will keep the tribal components of this army from straying into barbarism."

"How?" Fraser queried. "They may be allies, for the present, but they remain highly unpredictable, as too many European commanders have discovered to their peril."

"Those other commanders lacked the necessary skills of persuasion," Burgoyne decided.

"It has little to do with persuasion," Fraser retorted. "You're letting a bear out of a cage. What makes you think you can control it afterwards?"

"Because," Burgoyne stated, "I can. The Indians are by nature simple-minded and impressionable. All they require is a benevolent but firm hand to maintain discipline."

Fraser tilted his head. "So…you'll be writing up a speech for them too?"

"Oh, already been working on it," Burgoyne stated. "But you needn't appear so apprehensive at the prospect."

"Just make sure you don't find yourself making a Shakespearean soliloquy to an unappreciated audience. Pearls to the swine and all that."

"I choose language not nearly based upon its meaning," Burgoyne replied, "but also how it sounds when read aloud. Shakespeare, I wager, might yet tickle heathen ears, though nary a word was comprehended. The Scriptures translated under King James might soften even a hardened heart by their aural quality. And so when you say I spread my jam thickly, I say there are reasons to leave it be. My business is communication, in contour and substance, combined to affect a greater persuasion." He raised an eyebrow. "You are not such a stranger to flourish yourself, Balnain. Perhaps of a different type, but it is in you and, dare I say, in your enjoyment of sword dancing!"

Fraser smirked. "I suppose we all like to get our point across."

"Indeed, we do," Burgoyne replied.

"Just remember that not every stage has the same audience," Fraser reminded him.

"Perhaps," Burgoyne conceded, "or perhaps all the world is a really single audience, some in the front row and some in the gallery, but all with eyes to see and ears to hear and mouths to cheer or boo. It is up to us now to infuse some virtue in them, as best we might."

The commander-in-chief had the opportunity to test his abilities during a ceremony in honor of the Indians who had sworn to serve the Crown. A translator among the Iroquois was on hand to render each section into the native tongue as the general progressed. True to form, Burgoyne's mode of address was unmistakably theatrical, and Ned found himself drawn into his leader's performance.

"The Great King, our common father and the patron of all who seek and deserve his protection, has considered with satisfaction the general conduct of the Indian tribes from the beginning of the troubles of America. Besides a few apostates, the collective voices and hands and hearts of the tribes over this vast continent are on the side of justice, of laws, and of the King. His clemency has been abused; the offers of his mercy have been despised; and his further patience would in his eyes withhold redress from the most grievous oppressions in the provinces that ever disgrace the history of mankind. It therefore remains for me, the general of one of His Majesty's armies, and his representative in this council, to galvanize you."

Ned watched as Burgoyne dramatically drew his sword from its sheath, laid the blade across his open palm, and extended it towards the Indians sitting cross-legged before him.

"Warriors, go forth in the might of your valor and your cause! Strike at the common enemies of Great Britain and America, disturbers of public order, commerce, peace and happiness! The chiefs of His Majesty's forces, and the princes amongst his allies, esteem you as brothers in this war. In glory and in friendship, we will endeavor reciprocally to give and to receive examples. We know how to value, and we will strive to imitate, your perseverance in enterprise, and your constancy to resist hunger, weariness and pain. Yet be aware it may also prove our task, from the dictates of our religion, the laws of our warfare, and the principles and interest of our policy, to regulate your passions when they overbear, to point out where it is nobler to spare than to revenge; to discriminate degrees of guilt; to suspend the up-lifted stroke; to chastise and not to destroy."

He sheathed his sword once again, the steel slipping into the leather with ease.

"This war to you, my friends, is new. Upon all former occasions in taking the field, you held yourselves authorized to destroy wherever you came, because everywhere you found an enemy. The case is now very different. The King has many faithful subjects dispersed throughout these provinces. Consequently, you have many brothers in these parts, who are persecuted or imprisoned wherever they are discovered or suspected, and as such are deserving of pity from every generous mind. Persuaded that your magnanimity of character, joined to your principles of affection for the King, will give me fuller control over your minds than the military rank with which I am invested, I enjoin your most serious attention to the rules which I hereby proclaim for your invariable observation during the campaign."

He placed his right hand over his heart, and raised his left, finger pointed to the heavens, as if preparing to transmit a divine oracle.

"I positively forbid bloodshed when you are not opposed in arms. Aged men, women, children and prisoners must be held sacred from the knife or hatchet, even in the time of actual conflict. You shall receive compensation for the prisoners you take, but you shall be called to account for scalps. In conformity and indulgence to your customs, which have affixed an idea of honor to such badges of victory, you shall be allowed to take the scalps of the dead when killed by your fire and in fair opposition but, on no account, or pretense, or subtlety, or prevarication, are they to be taken from the wounded, or even dying; and still less pardonable, if possible, will it be held, to kill men in that condition on purpose, and upon a supposition that this protection to the wounded would be thereby evaded."

Ned glanced over to where Fraser was standing, and saw a hazy look coming to the Highlander's eyes. Ned wondered if was thinking back to the suppression of the last Jacobite rising, when such humane codes of conduct had been cast aside by the government troops, bayonets dripping with blood. Would Gentleman Johnny have justified such slaughter? Ned hoped not.

"Base lurking assassins, incendiaries, ravagers and plunderers of the country, to whatever army they belong, shall be treated with less reserve," Burgoyne continued, "but the latitude must be given by order, and I must be the judge of the occasion. Should the enemy, on their part dare, to countenance acts of barbarity towards those who may fall into their hands, it may be yours also to retaliate. But till severity shall be thus compelled, bear immovable in your hearts this solid maxim: It cannot be too deeply impressed that the worthiness of your alliance and the sincerity of your zeal towards the King, your father and never-failing protector, will be examined and judged upon the test of your steady and uniform adherence to the orders and councils of those to whom His Majesty has entrusted the direction and the honor of arms."

When at last Burgoyne concluded his address, the Iroquois translator stood up alongside the elderly chiefs and sages. He appeared to be in his thirties with keen dark eyes and his hair shaved off except for a single strip. He wore a white fringed shirt of deerskin, an elaborately beaded wampum belt, a gold ring in his nose, and streaks of war paint along his cheeks. One of the old men began to speak in his native tongue, which the translator then rendered into English with a thick accent.

"I stand up in the name of all the Nations present to assure you that we have heard your words, and they will abide in us. We receive you because when you speak, we hear the voice of our great father beyond the great lake. It is for his honor that our hatchets have been sharpened, since he has promised to preserve us upon our land, though the Bostonians and the Virginians have sought to claim it for themselves. Our whole villages have come forth to fight in your company. The old and ill, our wives and infants, alone remain at home. With one voice, we agree to obey your commands upon the road, and pray that the Father of Days gives you many and success."

Burgoyne, his eyes shimmering with delight at his own perceived success, bowed low from the waist.

After the ceremony had concluded, the Iroquois translator came over to where Jonathan stood and mumbled, "Your chief of war…does he talk like that always?"

"When he makes speeches, he tends to," Jonathan sighed. "He spends much time reading the works of our great sages…"

"Shakespeare," the translator said. "That's the name of one often recited, yes?"

Jonathan nodded. "Indeed. The general is also a writer when he's back home, so seeks to imitate him."

"I think…they both use too many words to say what they mean," the translator chuckled. "I did not understand everything tonight."

"It's alright," said Jonathan kindly. "I dare say you are worlds better at handling our language than most of us are doing with yours. But if you'd like, I can try to help you make sense of the odd bits of the general's speech. I'm quite a plain-spoken soul by comparison."

The translator nodded. "That's why I came to you."

Jonathan snorted. "I have a frank face?"

"Yes."

"It's settled then." Jonathan extended his hand to the translator. "I am Lieutenant Jonathan Rawcliffe."

The translator hesitated, then took his arm in deference to the custom. "I am Red Elk. Or that is what white men at trading posts call me. We have our own names in our own tongue."

"Of course," Jonathan said. "Perhaps you can teach me to say them in time."

"Depends how long we share this road," Red Elk replied, an ominous note in his voice. "But if you wish, you are welcome to break bread with me by the fire tonight."

"I would be honored," Jonathan replied. "Might you be willing to have my colleague Lieutenant Southworth join us? He has known the general longer than I, and may have some insights regarding his manner of speech."

"If he does not eat too much," Red Elk snorted.

"I won't," Ned promised, causing both Jonathan and Red Elk to laugh.

At the campfire, the British soldiers were treated to a stew made of rabbit meat and squash. Ned joined Jonathan in doing his best to answer any questions the translator asked regarding the words Burgoyne had chosen and his intended meaning. Ned had a mind to counsel Burgoyne to resist his Shakespearian urges when addressing their native allies in the future, but he knew it would go in one ear and out the other. He found himself gaining an increased appreciation for Red Elk, who seemed eager to learn everything he could and offered his own thoughtful commentary on the elements of the speech they discussed.

"Your chief speaks like a holy man, but he sleeps with another man's squaw," Red Elk observed. "That is against your religion, no?"

"Yes," Ned admitted.

"Then tell me, if you can," Red Elk began, "how are my people to obey his word if he does not obey the word of his own god?"

Ned and Jonathan gave each other a look. Then Jonathan answered, "Our God came to redeem sinners. We are all at different points in that redemption." He cleared his throat. "I heard you speak of 'The Father of Days.' Is that…the name of God among your people?"

"Yes, we believe in the Great Spirit, who is greater than everyone and everything."

"So you do…pray?" Ned asked hesitantly.

"We speak to the Great Spirit by burning tobacco. The smoke carries our prayers to the lesser spirits of good who then carry them to the Source. We believe all things have a spirit, you know…the animals, the trees, the rocks, the water, the earth…us. We are part of everything, in its beauty and violence. We are all a part of the land."

Just then, a little girl around six years of age with hair and eyes like raven's wings came running over to the fire and climbed on top of Red Elk. He sighed in frustration and scolded her in his tongue. She seemed unaffected.

"My sister Tall Willow's daughter," he introduced her curtly. "She's nothing but trouble."

"Oh, I'm sure she's not that bad," Jonathan insisted brightly, "or at least no worse than my little Emma can be…"

"You'll find out soon enough…"

She scrambled down from her uncle marched resolutely towards Jonathan. Then she started talking rapidly at him in her native language.

Jonathan turned to Red Elk. "Are you going to translate?"

"No."

"Oh."

"I did my work for the day," he said, sopping up the last of the stew with cornbread and stuffing it into his mouth. "I can't understand her half the time anyway."

"Fair enough."

She said something in an emphatic tone now, pointing at Jonathan.

"She wants your extra eyes," Red Elk remarked.

"What?"

Without warning, she snatched Jonathan's spectacles off his face, and ran away laughing.

"I say…can you get those back for me?" Jonathan inquired of his host desperately. "I mean…she might break them…"

"Eh, she usually doesn't break what she steals," Red Elk said, not showing any signs of going after her.

"This happens often?"

"Why do you think we call her Little Crow?" Red Elk queried. "She loves shiny things and flies away with them."

Jonathan blinked, disoriented. "Does she ever fly back with them?"

Red Elk shrugged.

"I…need those to live."

Ned heard the little girl giggle as she hung upside down from a tree limb like a monkey, wearing the spectacles.

"Should I go try to…?" Ned started to suggest, concerned the child would fall and face-plant.

"No, we mustn't cause a diplomatic incident," Jonathan mumbled. "Maybe…I'll adapt to being blind as a bat…"

"General Burgoyne has brought along extra pairs for you, if worse comes to worse," Ned informed him.

"Oh, well, that's jolly good of him," Jonathan said, "though this particular pair has gotten to fit my face so well over the years. Takes time to break them in, you know…"

Fortunately, intervention came from another quarter. A tall woman with gold hoop earrings, long black braids, and a belly swollen with pregnancy came rushing over, shouting at the child in the tree. Little Crow reluctantly came down. The woman continued to lecture her as she draped a beaded shawl over the little girl's shoulders. Then she went over to Red Elk, and began to harangue him as well. He rolled his eyes, and they both fell into a lengthy argument.

Meanwhile, Little Crow came over to Jonathan and voluntarily surrendered the spectacles, sticking them back on his face herself.

"Thank you, Little Goblin," Jonathan sighed, adjusting the spectacles on his face.

The woman was marching away in a huff now, and Red Elk exhaled in exasperation. "Want to have that translated too?"

"Oh, I know a scolding when I see one," Jonathan chuckled. "I have sisters too."

"So do I," Ned chimed in.

"She thinks I am too lenient with the children," he sighed. "What does she want me to do? Chase them around in circles like a squaw?"

"And I'm guessing the children know that's how you feel, so favor your guardianship."

Red Elk shrugged. "They have no father. He was killed six months ago, by Bostonians. They think the last war gives them rights to our lands. Your chief across the water says he will uphold our claim, and so we fight for him."

"You are under his protection, just as we are," Edmund assures. "Our King is a father to all his subjects and will not go back upon his word nor your rights."

Red Elk glanced in the direction of the Iroquois camp followers. "After what befell her husband, my sister was unwilling to be parted from me. A dream came back to her many times that her husband wished her to be here. He is still going through the ordeals, you see."

"What do you mean?" Jonathan queried.

"Every spirit must go through ordeals for a year before it comes to rest in the Sky World," He explained. "That is why she is still in mourning for him. But at the end of the year, there will be a celebration for that spirit's arrival." He stirred the fire with a stick. "We do not take dreams lightly, especially when the dead appear in them. But your Holy Book speaks often of dreaming, does it not? I remember hearing a story about a man who dreamed of the stars bowing to him and famine stalking the land. He had a colorful coat…"

Jonathan nodded. "Joseph in the Old Testament."

"And Joseph in the New Testament followed after him in his dreaming," Ned added. "An angel told him of a wicked king sending soldiers to kill the Christ Child…"

"Did he have a colored coat too, if he fostered a god?"

"I-I don't know," Ned admitted, "but in heaven, he surely does, for he was a just man."

"Just men are hard to find, and treasures to be found," Red Elk remarked, then added, "so are good coats."

"Would you like one of our coats?" Jonathan asked. "As a token of our alliance?"

Just then, a youthful voice came from behind them. "We need no coats."

Ned squinted, and saw an Indian boy, around ten or eleven, with dark hair down to his shoulder and dark eyes glinting golden in the firelight, the flickering flames dancing across his bare bronzed chest.

"I will fight as I am, when it is time," the boy declared. "I will live, or die, for our people."

Ned was struck, all at once, that this boy was no different than he had been at his age, desiring to uphold the glory of his people.

"This is Running River," Red Elk introduced him, "my nephew. He will be a great warrior someday, if he learns patience. He does not know how to wait to shave his head for war."

"Few of us did at that age," Jonathan admitted. "You taught him our language, I assume?"

Red Elk nodded. "It is best for us to know what you're saying, whatever may come."

"That is fair," Jonathan replied. He looked over at the boy. "Even if you do not need a coat, the exchanging of gifts I believe is common to our peoples. Refusing them is generally taken poorly by either side. You should remember that if you expect to be wise enough to gain allies."

"No allies came when my father was killed," he said.

"But you have allies now…"

"And you will not bring him back to us."

"No," Jonathan admitted. "I'm afraid we cannot. But perhaps we might ensure that you are given a measure of justice in his honor."

Just then, Little Crow inaugurated a dance around the fire, seemingly to get attention back on her and her beaded shawl.

"She's just like her mother," Red Elk sighed. "Always showing off."

"Well, she's a girl," Jonathan said. "She deserves to show off." He leaned forward and addressed her, "That's a very pretty shawl, Little Crow."

Her uncle translated, and she smiled, revealing several missing baby teeth.

"The beads tell the story of the first days," Red Elk explained. "We do not write things down in the same way your people do, but we remember things all the same, and pass it down through speaking it."

"I would be interested in hearing your story about the beginning of things," Ned said, "if you wouldn't mind telling it in English instead of Iroquois."

Red Elk shrugged. "I will tell it in both tongues." He set down his empty bowl of stew and straightened his posture. Then he beckoned for his niece and nephew, and they sat down on either side of him. Her dark eyes were full of wonder, and his full of solemnity. And so Red Elk told the story, first in his own language, and Ned found that his vocal tones and hand gestures seemed to speak to him beyond the words. Then he repeated the tale, this time in English.

"In the Sky World, where there was no birth or death, a great tree planted by the Father of Days was the source of all life," Red Elk recounted, gesturing to the beaded tree design on the little girl's shawl. "But when the tree was uprooted, the Sky Woman fell through the hole left behind. She landed far below, in the great water, and might have drowned, but two swans heard her cries and helped her onto the back of a great turtle." Again, he pointed to the beaded swans and the turtle upon the cloak. "A muskrat dove under the water to put mud over the shell of the turtle, and from that mud, the earth took shape." He pointed to the beaded muskrat. "The Sky Woman was pregnant when she fell, and upon the turtle's shell, she brought forth two sons: one good and one evil. The good son made good things, but the evil son made evil things to thwart that which his brother made. The good twin challenged the bad twin to do battle with him." He pointed to the crossed axes on the shawl. "The good brother won, and his evil brother was banished to the underworld. He became the ruler of the land of the dead, but still strives to spread evil in the world. After the Sky Woman died, her good son planted a seed in her body that grew into the first corn to nourish the first people." He gestured to the last beaded design, which was a corn stalk, and Little Crow whirled around again to show off the whole shawl.

Ned could not help but think back to the days when he told ancient stories of the Anglo-Saxon saints to local farm children, just as their Anglo-Saxon ancestors had done around the open hearths of their villages, Catholics all. He missed those days.

Over the next few weeks, Jonathan and Red Elk formed a closer bond based on their mutual candidness and love for shooting. They would test their skills against each other at target practice and go hunting together for all manner of game, including bear, which Jonathan had long desired to track since setting foot on North American soil. The latter venture nearly ended in disaster when Jonathan's gun jammed and the creature turned to charge him. Fortunately, Red Elk was on hand to shoot instead. But things went from bad to worse when the wounded animal reared and charged the Iroquois, swiping angrily at his arm. Fortunately, Jonathan managed to get his rifle working again and shot the beast dead. Then he rushed over to staunch his ally's bleeding.

"You should ask permission from the spirit of the animal before killing it, Englishman," Red Elk lectured Jonathan as the redcoat applied a tourniquet to the Indian's arm. "You did not. That is why your gun failed you."

"So why did it start working again, pray tell?" Jonathan queried.

Red Elk smirked. "Because I asked for both of us."

"Fine," Jonathan sighed. "You can keep the bearskin, just so long as I keep the creature's teeth to send home to my son."

"Don't go giving him notions about settling here," Red Elk huffed. "There are enough of your kind milling about as it is."

"Oh, heavens, no," Jonathan chuckled. "I just want him to be able to tell his little school friends that his clerkish father is secretly brave."

Over time, the other Iroquois grew fascinated with Jonathan. This was in part because Red Elk had informed them that Jonathan's biological father was a warrior but his adopted father was a healer. The implied dual power of taking and restoring life was meaningful to them, and due to this, they allowed Jonathan to see certain dances and other rituals which no other whites were allowed to attend. Jonathan tended to find the displays deeply perplexing and rather discomforting, especially when it came to the manner in which they imitated animals to a startlingly accurate extent, in movement and calls. He would report such sentiments to his comrades succinctly with the phrase, "Right, that was odd."

Red Elk seemed amused by Jonathan's befuddlement over their customs, but Jonathan, for his part, got his Indian acquaintances to come over to the British camp to listen to Gavin's singing. The prickly Welshman was initially reluctant to perform for a lot of painted pagans, muttering something about throwing pearls to swine, but Jonathan reminded him that the original Britons were also painted pagans, and they shouldn't hold their noses too high in the air. And so, at least somewhat chastened, Gavin would belt out his rousing choir hymns. The Indians were impressed by his range, even if the meaning of the lyrics largely eluded them, and decided it was good medicine to drive evil spirits away. Indeed, they were quite fixated upon what might attract good and bad powers into their lives, and were not shy about pointing out their judgments.

"That dog is no good," Red Elk declared one day, pointing at General Phillips' canine companion chasing a squirrel. "I hear he already got his first master killed. The second will follow suit."

"Well, thank you for being so optimistic this morning," Jonathan chirped, drinking his morning coffee. "Really makes me want to embrace the day with verve."

"Why else are we here if not to point out warning signs for your train, since your people seem altogether blind to them?" Red Elk demanded, accepting the cup of coffee Jonathan offered him and taking a long sip from it.

"I mean…I thought you were here to translate…"

"I am not...how do you say it...a pony with only one trick…"

"Close enough," Jonathan sighed, "and point taken. I just feel like maybe you should give our resident doomsday dog a chance. He's quite friendly…"

"I do not need more…friendly friends who bring bad luck." The Iroquois pointed to his injured arm from the bear hunt fiasco.

"Awww. Must you make it so personal?"

"You should get rid yourselves of that black robe," Red Elk said. "He too is bad luck."

Jonathan squinted. "The French priest?"

Red Elk nodded. "We have put an end to his kind before and were better for it. One reason we get on better with you English is that you are not so eager to send your holy men to us, regardless of your commander's speeches. It upsets the spirits who guard our nation when foreign preachers are allowed to come to us. If your god is jealous, ours are too."

Jonathan winced, but said nothing. Over time, however, he expressed increasing distress to his comrades about the animosity the natives showed towards Christianity. He also seemed to be harboring some underlying guilt over the lack of missionary zeal on the part of his countrymen. For all his critique of enthusiasm, Ned sensed that Jonathan was rather more sympathetic to evangelism than he let on.

The French priest, for his part, had stayed mostly among his own people, saying masses for the Canadian volunteers on Sundays and hearing their confessions the rest of the week. However, a handful of Irish recruits, Edmund observed, got up enough courage to scurry over to him for spiritual succor late at night, kneeling in the damp moss and confessing their sins in Gaelic. There were quite a few soldiers from Ireland on Burgoyne's march, most of whom were Protestant, either Scotch-Irish like Eli Thompson or Anglo-Irish like Roger Lamb. Others were of Norman or Gaelic extraction, but who had changed their faith generations before, often intermarrying with British settlers and adopting their cultural norms.

Still, there were quite a few who had been recruited straight from the Irish peasant class, Catholic tenant farmers accustomed to grinding poverty and secret masses and the Erse tongue. They had been made promises of a better life if they took the King's shilling, a chance for adventure and self-respect. If their landlord was raising a regiment, their rent might be reduced and their families promised better fare than potatoes if they enlisted. So they paid the same price of conscience Ned had paid, and suffered the same regrets. Occasionally, those regrets gnawed away at them until they succumbed to a dreadful repentance and cast caution to the wind.

Oftentimes, their officers would turn a blind eye to such "lapses of judgment." But other times, they chose to make an example of "obdurate Papists" in their ranks. On the books, punishment might be docked pay; or it could be a flogging; or it could be arrest and dishonorable discharge. Ned shuddered to think what might become of those discharged. Would they be allowed to go free, or end up on prison hulks? It no doubt varied, depending on the national mood and the men in authority. Burgoyne made a point to be as lenient as he could in such cases. He took no pleasure in persecution. But he had taken the Test Act many times over, and was compelled to submit to the law on occasion and make an example of the offenders.

Ned had made no attempt to approach the priest himself. It was not in his nature to lead a double life. These Irishmen had sworn to one thing before witnesses, but continued to practice another in private. It seemed like some sort of adultery to Ned. No, whatever his misgivings, whatever his guilt, he intended to be true to his word and learn from Jonathan how to be a good Anglican. That being said, he would never report those mad Gaels who gambled everything to visit the priest. His fellow staff members, however, were not likely to be as understanding.

One evening, Ned overheard Jonathan berating one of the young Irish soldiers he had caught returning from the Canadians' camp. Ned spotted yet another Irish soldier, watching in the shadows. He knew this one in passing. He was older and smarter than the boy being scolded. He seemed to know how to get away with things. Rumor had it that he'd been to prison for petty theft. Might have been hanged, too, if the landlord's daughter hadn't intervened and convinced him to join her brother's regiment. The brother, now an officer on the march, was a rather plump, lethargic fellow, whose main hobby in life was collecting buttons in a tin. Rumor had it that he hated the army and only purchased a commission after his father threatened to disown him and throw his buttons in the local lake. But as harmless as he seemed, he had no problem with ordering the lash to be laid on heavy when it came to Popish regression. After all, it reflected badly upon his noble family name.

"You know you shouldn't have done it, boy," Jonathan scolded the young recruit, "not after you swore an oath to God to uphold the King's titles, spiritual and temporal. Don't tell me you want to get yourself flogged again? I know this wouldn't be your first time…"

"I don't be wanting…" The boy paused, struggling. "…be wanting to go…go to hell, sir. I don't…" He paused a second time. "I don't…have enough…English words…"

"For heaven's sake, I know heathen Indians who speak better English than your kind. But you have had far more opportunities than they have had to become civilized, to learn and adapt out of your former condition, if you did not despise us so. Is it just obstinacy on your part that keeps you tethered to old superstitions?"

The boy blinked. "I don't know what that means…obstinacy….or superstitions…"

Jonathan sighed. "You're even more difficult to handle or make sense of than your cousins in the Scottish Highlanders. Still, I…" He winced. "I don't take any pleasure in the thought of your being flogged again. You must just be healing up from your last punishment."

The boy swallowed hard, but repeated again, more intensely this time, "I don't…be wanting to go…to hell…" He buried his hand in his coat pocket.

"That's what Romish clerics want you to believe, so they can keep you under their thumb," Jonathan said. "You don't need what continentals have to give you. Whatever our differences, we are from sister islands, and have been joined at the hip since the Normans conquered both. More to the point, the water equally separates us from Europe. Surely it would be more sensible for us to be on the same side. What could these foreign priests possess that we do not already have?"

"God," the boy blurted, raising up his hands indicative of the host being raised. "They bring us…God."

Ned felt his heart catch in his throat, even as he saw Jonathan shake his head despairingly.

"What are you reaching for, boy?" Jonathan took a step closer to him and stretched his hand out. "Give it over. Now."

Ned couldn't make out exactly what it was being surrendered, but he could easily imagine.

"You really are close to the Indians with your talismans," Jonathan sighed.

"It's a cross," the boy said.

"It doesn't look like one I've ever seen." He squinted. "That's the whole problem. It's nigh impossible to distinguish Christian from pagan with so many of your habits."

"It's from *Muire na nGael*."

"Who?"

"*Muire na nGael*, sir. *Tá sí i measc na naomh ar neamh.*"

"What?"

The boy ceased trying to speak English at all, and blurted out an additional flood of words in Erse, clearly trying to offer some sort of explanation, although the language barrier was never more obvious.

"I don't…I really don't know what…any of this means…you really need to stop…" Jonathan stuffed the item in his own coat. "Now, look. I'll not bring up any of this, if you promise me something."

The boy blinked.

"I want to teach you more English. You shouldn't just go on like this as a soldier in the British army. All sorts of things can go awry, and it's just a bad look. Understand?"

The boy reluctantly nodded.

"Good. And stay away from that priest."

The boy did not nod then, but mumbled something, which Ned could not distinguish as being English or Gaelic, but offered a quick salute, seemingly to distract Jonathan from trying to interpret the meaning.

The following day, Jonathan declared his intention to have a long talk with the priest himself. He came upon the black robe collecting plant specimens in his satchel and taking down notes about the flora and fauna in his journal. It was the hobby that consumed most of his time when he wasn't going about his priestly functions. Born and raised in Montreal, he was unaccustomed to trekking through densely forested land, even more so than Jonathan, born at the borders of the New Forest. He was a short, middle-aged man who had dark hair, streaked with silver, and matching silver-gray eyes, brimming with a gentle curiosity.

After making some awkward small talk about the plants the priest was gathering, Jonathan got right to the point. "You really mustn't encourage the Irish to come to you. It's taking advantage of their susceptibility."

"Susceptibility?" the priest repeated in a soft French accent, slipping some more leaves into his satchel.

"Yes, you know…they are easily drawn back into their old ways, even if it means breaking oaths. Their upbringing is dependent upon superstition."

"So you think I peddle in charms, like a witch doctor?" the priest queried.

"It doesn't matter what I think about you," Jonathan replied. "It matters that they are committing a breach of duty by trying to serve two masters. We have reasons to be cautious when it comes to Ireland. It is the perfect platform for invasion, which foreign Papist powers have made the most of in the past."

"Are you English not the ones who have forced the Irish to choose between masters?" the priest asked calmly. "As I recall, it was a pope who first gave you Ireland as a fief, and encouraged the faithful to pay fealty to your kings. But you have since, how shall I say it…changed the terms of ownership?"

Jonathan shrugged. "From our point of view, it was a matter of reformation."

The priest smirked. "*La petite mort.*"

Jonathan wrinkled his forehead, the double meaning seeming to take him aback. "I admit I didn't expect that from a priest."

The priest chuckled. "Well, we all come from somewhere. Unfortunately, the little death to which I refer not only brought your King Henry his long-sought release, but also bastardized the faith of his realms."

"You are very blunt, monsieur," Jonathan said, circulating his shoulders in a show of discomfort.

"Are you offended?"

"I-I don't know. But I must return this conversation to the subject at hand. You are on this train because General Burgoyne was gracious enough to consider the consciences of his French volunteers…"

"But not of his Irish volunteers?"

"It is not advantageous to the national interest…"

"A pity."

"Please, will you just promise me to send them away if they come to you? They'll listen to you. Otherwise, I'll have to report any I catch from here on out. I don't relish it. They'll be punished, don't you see?"

"I am afraid in the same way you would not take orders from me on being a soldier, I cannot take orders from you on being a priest."

"But you are subject to our rules on this campaign…"

"God's rules first, Lieutenant," the priest stated. "I will turn no man away from me who wishes to confess his sins or receive the Eucharist. It would be a sin on my part to do so. It would be, as you said, a breach of duty."

"Monsieur…"

"But enough of this unpleasantness," the priest said, pointing up at a pine tree. "Would you be so kind as to shoot down that pinecone for me? We both seem to be vertically challenged…"

"What?"

"You have a pistol, do you not?"

"Well, yes, but…"

"Then you can shoot the branch and knock the pinecone free."

"I mean…sort of a trick shot, that…"

"I have complete confidence in you. I hear you are the clerk that shoots bears."

"A bear, but…well…" Jonathan drew out his pistol, took aim, and squeezed the trigger.

The pinecone ended up blasted to smithereens.

"You killed it," the priest said flatly.

"Told you it was a hard shot…"

"You murdered it…"

"I didn't mean to, but you know, if I had, this would be considered a ruddy good shot actually…"

"But my pinecone is dead now."

Jonathan groaned.

Soon the debate devolved into discussing other things Englishmen had killed, such as Joan of Arc and the Marquis de Montcalm. The usually tranquil Jonathan finally found his feathers ruffled, doubled down on the Maid of Orleans' witchcraft verdict, and accused Montcalm of war crimes. Ned, intervening, had to practically pull him away, but not without himself getting dragged into the Joan of Arc debate. Old Francis Southworth had always been a bit sensitive about the subject, as a descendent of Crecy and Agincourt veterans, and would give any Frenchman he came upon a piece of his mind.

It was incoherent to him that God would arbitrarily favor the French over the English when all of them were Catholics. While he did not deny Joan might have been personally pious, he was convinced that her visions of the saints, sending her off to slay her co-religionists over one of many dynastic disputes, were either the product of madness or possession. Besides, King Henry VI of England, within whose reign she was condemned, was himself saintly. But in the course of utilizing Francis' old arguments, Ned grew increasingly sick with himself. At this juncture, Joan of Arc, King Henry, and his father all had more in common than he had with any of them: They returned to ashes and dust firm in the faith he had abandoned.

An hour or so after the argument with the French priest had subsided, Jonathan regretted his temper, and decided to go back and make a peace offering in the form of a strawberry jam sandwich.

"I realize we have our differences, but there's no point in making this trek any more difficult than it has to be," Jonathan stated, extending the sandwich. "I…made a fuss, I suppose. This is my way of saying sorry for that."

"And sorry for the pinecone?" the priest surmised.

"Yes, well, I suppose…though I told you it was going to be a risky shot…"

The priest squinted at the sandwich. "It looks half-eaten."

"Look, I'm not a barbarian," Jonathan sighed. "I cut it with a knife."

"You people are good at cutting things with knives."

"Won't you just take it, please? I don't know how else to make up…" He sighed. "I suppose I lost my temper because my father was killed in the late war. I imagine we all lost someone back then, and maybe we forget how much it still hurts until something or other reminds us, and then we go off half-cocked."

The priest nodded. "I am not a stranger to your feelings. I was a young seminarian during the bombardment of Quebec under your General Wolfe. I had family and friends who perished in the city or on the field."

"I'm sorry," Jonathan said softly. "I mean…for your loss."

The priest smiled lightly. "I am not so unreasonable as to expect you to sorrow over your own victory, so long as you do expect me to celebrate it."

"Though I have never gone through it, I can imagine it must be a painful thing to be separated from one's king," Jonathan said. "But if it is any consolation, having another king is at least better than having such a hierarchy flattened, and the link to higher things broken, as the rebels are trying to do with their attempt to create a republic."

"Rather pagan of them," the priest admitted. "Though I believe your line of kings began this severing of links when they declared their own headship over spiritual matters. It has given rise to consequences you now find difficult to control."

"Well, all we can do is our best," Jonathan replied, extending the sandwich again.

And at last, the priest accepted it. Then he pulled a shiny circular box from his cassock pocket and extended it to the Britisher in turn. "Snuff, Lieutenant?"

Over time, Jonathan developed a more cordial relationship with the priest, whose knowledge of horticulture, love of chess, and determination to get passing acquaintances as addicted to inhaling pulverized tobacco as he was made him seem more like "a charming continental gentleman" than an oppressive Romish cleric. They were soon regularly exchanging sandwiches for snuff, playing board games, and discussing tree species, which Jonathan, reared on the edge of the New Forest, could hold his own about. They tended to avoid speaking about the "Irish problem," but did broach the torrid topic of European interactions with the Iroquois.

"We have gained many martyrs through them," the priest said. "Father Isaac Jogues went to work among the Hurons more than a century ago. He and his companions were captured by their enemies, the Iroquois, and led from village to village, where they were beaten, tortured, and forced to look on as their Huron converts were butchered. By the time Father Jogues escaped, several of his fingers had been cut, chewed, or burnt off. Ordinarily, a priest would not be allowed to offer mass due to such deformities, but the Holy Father in Rome gave him permission, saying it would be shameful to banish a priest who had shed his blood for Christ from the Altar of the Lamb. His zeal led him back to the wilderness, where he was once again captured by the Iroquois, then tomahawked and beheaded. René Goupil was tortured along with Jogues and was tomahawked for making the sign of the cross on the brow of several children. After these martyrdoms, the murderers ate the hearts and drank the blood of their victims."

Jonathan had listened quietly, then asked, "What would you say if an Iroquois child asked you to tell her about Christmas?"

The priest's eyebrow shot up. "Did an Iroquois child ask you?"

"Well, she asked her uncle. He said it was the day the white man's god became a man."

"You are thinking of trying to evangelize them, aren't you?"

"Nothing so ambitious," Jonathan said. "I just want to tell the story in a manner they are most likely to receive. Will you help me?"

The priest regarded him with admiration. "I think you are a braver man than I. Since my childhood, I have feared the savages and kept to my own people."

"I can hardly blame you for that," Jonathan replied. "But perhaps...I am in a position you could never be in. So tell me what you would say, and I'll see if I can find a way to say it."

The priest nodded. "*Oui.* Let us do a good deed together."

Later that week, Jonathan found himself in General Burgoyne's tent, being lectured by him in the presence of General Fraser for that very "good deed."

"Now then, Rawcliffe, it's not our job to play the role of missionaries with our tribal allies," the general said. "Their tribal healer was livid when he learned what you did."

"I only answered the child's question about what Christmas was and why it was so important for you to return to England for it," Jonathan replied. "I did my best to tell it in a way she would best understand it. I changed the shepherds to hunters, and the stable to a drafty lodge. I kept the star, and the three chiefs that come to the infant homage, but they give him animal pelts instead of gold, frankincense, and myrrh..."

"That sort of thing is well and good for French black robes trying to make martyrs of themselves. These people are most volatile when it comes to the fear of their children being converted. They tend to be more peaceful with us, since we are not Papist."

"You mean since we do not preach to them," Jonathan mumbled.

"Don't tell me you've let the French priest influence you."

"You did allow him to come along with us, sir."

"Only because these French volunteers refused to march without him!"

"General, in keeping with your own speech advocating Christian ethics on campaign, I happen to think a greater effort on our part to introduce these people to our faith is advisable, lest the employment we have provided them unleashes their baser instincts..."

"My dear Rawcliffe, as has always been my policy, I have spoken daggers, but used none," Burgoyne stated. "The natives are well under control..."

"They are men of spirit and passion, with their own intentions," Jonathan countered, "and I fear their heathen ways are yet too strong to restrain, for they know no better."

"I would not be reticent to bloody a few daggers, or have them bloodied for us," Fraser said lowly. "If it saved British lives, savagery unleashed might serve a purpose."

Jonathan winced. "But what of British honor?"

"My honor is bound up to restoring the King's peace without the needless waste of my men's lives," Fraser replied. "If that involves extending some leniency to our allies' peculiar customs, so be it. The rebels are most assuredly taking lessons from them in stealth and marksmanship. We, on the other hand, are dragging behind and being taken advantage of at every turn."

"'Tis not so dire, sir," Burgoyne countered. "In addition to the Hessian Jaegers on our flanks, your cousin, Captain Alexander Fraser, has been most innovative with the British Rangers. I know you've been personally involved in trying to arm Fraser's Company of Select Marksmen with those new rifles put together by your fellow Scotsman, Patrick Ferguson…"

"Drives a damn hard bargain, that one," Fraser sighed. "But even so, I've met canny Pattie's price at my own expense. They must be equipped with firearms that are esteemed for accuracy."

"The question is, to what extent should this type of warfare be expanded?" Burgoyne asked. "I know there has been increased inordinate targeting by rebels, but there's only so far we dare go without incurring censure, from God and men."

"There are certain merits to tribal ways of warfare," Fraser murmured. "If we refuse to accept this, we do so at our peril."

"But we should be showing these tribes a better way, not sinking to their level," Jonathan insisted. "They may be savage now, but they can become civilized. Yes, if education and the Gospel is made available to them, they may become good Christian subjects of His Majesty…"

"Better to leave them as they are, if it suits them," Fraser decided. "Some peoples are savage by nature. If that condemns them to hellfire, it's between them and their Maker."

Jonathan squinted. "*You* say this, General *Fraser*?"

The points of emphasis in Jonathan's question gave away his sentiments all too well. Fraser dead-eyed him in a manner that instantly summoned a sense of dread.

Jonathan mumbled a quick apology and excused himself from the tent.

When he was outside the tent, he went over to Ned, standing near the entrance, and counseled lowly, "Try not to make an enemy of our Highland general, Ned, as I fear I just did. There is something not quite right with him. I worry it will rub off on General Burgoyne through his counsel."

"Fraser of Balnain may have a dark side," Ned conceded, "but he has thus far shown me nothing but kindness."

"Yes, well, that's because you were…and he might have been…" Jonathan stammered out his thoughts in broken sentences.

"Papist?" Ned finished for him.

Jonathan exhaled, and laid a hand on Ned's shoulder. "Forgive me. I should not have said that. I have no proof General Fraser was anything but a Protestant his whole life. And you are no more a Roman Catholic than I am. Your past should not be held against you by fools like me."

"But you think Balnain's upbringing compromises him, don't you?" Ned queried. "You don't trust Highlanders."

"No, I suppose I don't, but…" Jonathan sighed. "I suppose I want to believe they can be civilized too. I just…worry the old ways die hard."

~

The time came for Tall Willow to give birth. It was a long labor that lasted all night and into the morning. All the while, she lie groaning on a bed of pine boughs while tribesmen danced around her, wearing terrifying masks and chanting loudly.

"What are they doing to her?" Jonathan asked when he visited the Indian camp.

"It is a healing ceremony," Red Elk explained, his eyes filled with concern for his sister. "The masks stand for the faces of our grandfathers, whose spirits have gone on to the sky world. They were carved into living trees, to make good medicine, then cut out and colored, to scare away the demons of illness. They are acting out dreams that the tribesmen have had about their ancestors."

Jonathan squinted at the scene, focusing on her belly. "I think…something's wrong with the baby. The position, think…" He glanced down at his hands for a moment, then turned and headed towards General Burgoyne's tent. He found General Fraser there as well.

"Sir, as you know, my stepfather was a doctor, and I have medical knowledge from serving as his assistant," Jonathan said. "Up in Canada, I helped two camp followers deliver their babies, a boy and a girl."

"So you did," Burgoyne acknowledged. "And?"

"And…intend to try and help our translator Red Elk's sister the same way," Jonathan informed Burgoyne. "She's been in labor more than a day, and I believe the baby is in the wrong position…"

"You can't help those who don't want it, Lieutenant," Fraser interposed. "They have their own ways of doing things, ways that have sustained them as a people for centuries. If you interfere, and the mother or child dies, or worse, you lose them both, the tribe will blame you for bringing the spirit of death amongst them, and then punish us all."

"General Fraser is right," Burgoyne stated. "We must not meddle in the affairs of the savages any more than is strictly beneficial to our cause."

Jonathan stared long and hard at the generals. "I can't settle upon that, sirs. I keep thinking…what if my Elizabeth were in such a position? What if someone could have stopped to help her, but passed her by on the other side, on a point of politics?"

"A point of national interest," Burgoyne clarified.

"If we set aside our humanity for such interests, then where will the nation go but to hell?" Jonathan blurted.

"Careful, Lieutenant," Burgoyne cautioned him. "You might be misinterpreted…"

"I speak frankly, sir, because you know me well," Jonathan countered, "and I know from experience your reputation for humanity is not ill-founded."

"But it must be tempered by practicality. There are serious risks involved…"

"What if it were your lady Charlotte?" Jonathan demanded, then turned to Fraser. "Or your lady Margaretha? Would all the risks in the world matter?"

"You are very free in making such crude comparisons to my late wife," Burgoyne snapped.

"I do not believe the comparison is crude, sir," Jonathan murmured. "We are all human beings, and thus have a duty to each other."

"Christian duty, hmm?" Burgoyne mumbled.

"Aye," Jonathan replied. "Where we all fall on the wobbly line of savagery and civilization matters little compared with that."

Burgoyne gazed at him for several moments, a glimmer of grudging admiration in his eyes. "Do you honestly think your ministrations could save that wretched girl?"

"I don't know," he admitted. "But I do know that if she's left in that state, there's no chance for her or the baby."

"General," Fraser addressed Burgoyne, "you could forbid him, lest he infuriate the natives…"

"If I did that, he would try anyway, and then I'd end up with infuriated natives, and one of my best clerks under arrest," Burgoyne sighed. "He's got a very hard head, I'm afraid."

Fraser raised an eyebrow. "So do I."

"There," Burgoyne exhaled. "You should understand each other perfectly."

Fraser gave Jonathan a wary look. "Even the best of intentions can go awry, Lieutenant."

"I am aware, sir," Jonathan assured. "All I can do is my best."

"And how good is your best?"

"No less than I would do for your own wife, if she were struggling to bring your child into the world."

Momentarily, the Highlander's stern expression softened. "God guide you," he murmured, "or they'll be hell to pay. No good deed, I fear, goes unpunished."

And so Jonathan headed off towards the Iroquois encampment. But before he got there, Gavin, Ned, and Eli intercepted him.

"We're coming with you," Gavin stated.

"Whatever are you talking about, Jones?" Jonathan inquired.

"Southworth overheard you with the generals. Did you really think I would let you face those savages alone?" Gavin folding his arms over his chest. "You have another thing coming, you saucy little clerk, if I have to sing or slaughter our way to safety."

"You'll only make things more precarious loitering about," Jonathan insisted. "They'll feel…threatened."

"Their braves will be loitering about, that's for sure," Gavin countered. "We're just offering counterbalance."

Jonathan exhaled. "You didn't have to drag Southworth and Thompson into this."

"We weren't dragged," Ned assured.

"We volunteered," Thompson finished.

"You two, agreeing on something at last?" Jonathan exclaimed. "Perhaps I am ushering in the end times after all!" He laid a hand on each of their shoulders. "But really, you must yield to common sense…"

"Common sense can go to hell or Connaught," Eli declared. "We'll go with you."

"Oh, my stars, you've gone full on Cromwell now," Jonathan exhaled.

Eli nodded, patting his pistol, tucked inside his tunic. "I've said my prayers, and kept my powder dry."

"Remember, Thompson, as much as you don't like pagans, they're just people," Jonathan said. "I don't want you to react too strongly to whatever we might see…"

"I told you before, our good Queen Mary did not want the savage tribes on British land to die in their sins, but rather hoped they might choose the promises of life found in the Holy Book. Perhaps the prologue to that is this act of charity. If they reject it, coals will be piled upon their heads, but we will be justified."

When the little party arrived at the Indian camp, Jonathan took Red Elk aside and spoke to him for a spell. The translator then went to the medicine man and spoke to him. The medicine man and those involved in the ritual dance argued hotly with Red Elk, but he argued back with a calm resolve.

Then Running River entered the fray, first engaging in the dispute in his native tongue, then addressing Jonathan in English.

"I do not trust you to touch my mother!" the boy declared. "I do not trust you upon our land! The ones who come from the French chief, and the ones who come from the English chief, and the ones that have cast off chiefs altogether, they are no different! They come, and they take, and take, and take!"

"Hear me, Running River," said his uncle. "If we intend to hold our own among the white men, we must learn from them, and turn their knowledge to our use. That is why I taught you their language and to shoot with their rifles. Why should we reject their medicine, if it is strong?"

"Medicine comes from the gods!" the boy insisted. "Whatever power the whites have is from their own god, the one born in a lodge meant for animals! We have always rejected that god, for he is foreign to us!"

"He is foreign to us too, Running River," Jonathan said, "but we accept Him and His gifts, all the same. This is true of other things as well. There was once a great empire called Rome that conquered those living on my island. In time, they declined, but we learned a great deal from them regarding medicine, science, and philosophy. The native Britons still kept many of their own customs, but they also ended up taking what was useful from the Romans, such as how they worked steel. Think of us like we thought of Rome. Who knows? Perhaps you will laugh as our empire crumbles, and you survive us. But that doesn't mean you can't benefit from what we once were, does it?"

The boy looked at him suspiciously, but Red Elk seemed amazed. The translator turned to the medicine man and told him what Jonathan had said. The medicine man replied in his own language, his expression matching Red Elk's.

"He says he has never heard of a white even considering that their empire may one day fade, or that ours would survive it. Your lot is too proud to ever suggest such a thing. He asks, why are you different? Why show such humility?"

"I will always be a proud son of England," Jonathan stated. "I am here in this land to uphold the honor of my sovereign, whom I love. But I would never serve my king or country well if not for the teachings of my foreign God, for all my obligations fall under Him. Empires will rise and fall, but not His Word. He commanded us to do good works to all tribes. That's why I want to help this suffering women, if I can." He gave Red Elk a meaningful look. "Also, because you are my friend, and she is your kin."

Red Elk appeared moved. The medicine man listened to the translation, then replied in his own tongue. Red Elk nodded and said, "He does not trust the others from across the great water. But he believes you, and so do I. He is fearful, not of you, but of the gods. Two different deities competing can bring evil upon us, and a curse may fall upon my sister."

"I will invoke the Father of Days," Jonathan replied, "the One who created all that is. You will not have any clashes with deities or spirits you believe in. To show you I am in earnest, I welcome your assistance. As you know, I was adopted by a man of medicine who practiced in my own village, and worked alongside him. I would be honored to do so again."

As Red Elk translated, the medicine man gave Jonathan a long look, then slowly nodded.

"What do you plan?" Red Elk asked. "How are you to work together?"

"Let me look at her first, so I can see what's wrong," Jonathan said.

At last, they allowed him to approach her. As he knelt down in front of her, the woman stared at him, wide-eyed and cringing as she clutched a medallion around her neck. It depicted the three sister goddesses, who were responsible for harvesting corn, beans, and squash, and thus nourishing the tribe. He tried to touch her but she pushed his hand away.

"Don't be afraid," he said softly. "I'm here to help."

Red-Elk knelt down by his sister and whispered a translation in her ear. She nodded slowly, then beckoned for the Englishman to come forward.

He examined her belly and her cavity, frowning and shaking his head.

"It's as I feared," Jonathan said. "The baby is in the wrong position. We have to turn it so it's head down. I can try to do so, but it will be painful for Tall Willow. Do you have anything to ease the pain and make her drowsy?"

The translation was conveyed to the medicine man, and he sent for his bag of herbs. Soon, he had crushed the leaves in a bowl, poured a mixture of water and alcohol into it, and then heated the blend over a fire. Tall Willow drank it down, and her eyelids soon began to droop.

As Jonathan went to work on her, pressing down on her belly to turn the baby, she still groaned through her delirium, causing Running River to lunge at him.

"You are hurting my mother! You are defiling her with your touch!"

"Boy, for the love of God, I'm trying to save her life!" Jonathan panted. "Red Elk, tell him!"

His uncle pulled him aside and translated, but the boy's eyes remained full of wrath.

Several other braves gathered around, clearly sympathizing with Running River, and started shouting and spitting at Jonathan.

Ned, Gavin, and Eli, who had been watching at a distance so as not to make matters worse, emerged now, hands reaching for the pistols, prepared for the worst. The Indians were well aware of the weapons hidden in the soldiers' tunics, and there was a cutting tension in the air.

"Please," Jonathan begged, perspiration forming on his brow. "Give me a chance. I just need…to concentrate…"

He swallowed hard, but continued working, despite his hands starting to tremble.

"Oh, Father of Days," he prayed, "steady my hands…"

At last, he knelt up and spread her legs wide. Her eyes flickered open, filled with tears.

"Now," Jonathan said, turning to Red Elk. "Tell her to push now."

The labor came on quickly, and he squeezed her hand as she cried out in pain.

"Sorry…I'm sorry," he apologized, helping her to lean up. "Just…push…"

After what felt like an eternity, a tiny body covered in blood and fluid slipped voicelessly into Jonathan's arms. The natives' eyes flared, and he saw their hands go to their tomahawks, seeming to think he had killed the child by way of some negative energy.

Jonathan cut the umbilical cord then smacked the child on the rump. A squeal rent the air.

Ned felt a wave of relief sweep over him to hear the baby cry.

"It's a boy," Jonathan said as he cleaned the blood off the newborn and handed it over to the medicine man, who proceeded to swaddle and chant over him.

After Jonathan had cleaned the blood from Tall Willow, he turned to Red Elk. "She's very weak, but I think she'll pull through. You'll just need to keep an eye on her, lest she develop a fever. You have herbs to prevent and reduce such things, yes?"

Red Elk nodded. He knelt down again and took his sister's hand, speaking words of comfort. Then she gestured for the baby to be put in her arms. Jonathan smiled as he watched her gaze down at her newborn and heard her start to sing a lullaby in her language.

"You know, that sounds like something Elizabeth sang, at such a moment as this," Jonathan murmured. "Maybe mothers all have the same tongue."

The Iroquois woman turned to him briefly and gave the redcoat a weary smile.

Running River, standing in the shadows, had been joined by his sister Little Crow, clinging to his leg, and watching their mother and new baby brother with wide eyes. Jonathan beckoned for them to come forward. They did so hesitantly, hovering over mother and child. Tall Willow spoke to her children, weakly yet tenderly, as she showed them the infant. Then she gestured to Jonathan, and the tone of her voice conveyed thankfulness.

Running River's eyes remained suspicious, but he gave an obligatory nod.

Little Crow, meanwhile, was far less reserved and gave Jonathan an impulsive hug, causing the clerk to giggle nervously and pat her on the head with one hand while keeping a firm hold on his spectacles with the other.

As the four British soldiers headed back to their own camp, thankful to still be in one piece, Ned turned to Jonathan and asked, "Will you teach me some of what you know about medicine? It might be useful in a scrape."

"Truth be told, I could teach you all I know in a day or two," Jonathan replied. "I can take a fair gander at setting bones, stopping bleeding, breaking a fever, and birthing a baby. But I'm no expert. I just…I didn't want her to die."

"And you didn't let her die," Ned said, admiringly. "You risked disaster for what you believed in, and made it a point of unity between two peoples. I…I would give anything to have that kind of courage. Maybe that's why I want to learn from you…learn to save people…"

Jonathan smiled. "I'll teach you. But I didn't save anyone. The Father of Days did that."

~

The next time the train prepared to make camp, it ended up running into a slight snag.

"What's the fuss?" General Fraser inquired, riding over to General Burgoyne's wagon.

"There's an obstinate settler tangling with several of our soldiers," Burgoyne explained. "He seems unwilling to let us camp here, though he has little enough choice under the present circumstances."

"Is he a rebel?" Fraser guessed, putting hand to his forehead to shield his eyes from the orange rays of the setting sun.

"He claims not to be," Burgoyne replied, "at least not in this war. Just doesn't want to get involved either way. We'd prefer to avoid a scene if we can, given the revolutionary zeal for propaganda. By-the-by, he's one of your fellow Highlanders, Balnain."

"Then let me try putting my Highland charms on him," Fraser replied.

Burgoyne gestured grandly. "The floor is yours, friend. But keep in mind, our Loyalist guide said the man's name was MacDonald. A history of feuding between you, no?"

"Dammit," Fraser grunted. "Forget that I ever offered."

"Now, now, you must see this business through, even with your ancestral foes," Burgoyne insisted. "At least you're not a Campbell!"

Fraser rolled his eyes, and urged his horse forward to where the wiry Highlander stood, his arms pinioned behind his back by two guards. The general began to converse with the man in Gaelic, and Ned found the manner in which he spoke it pleasing. Indeed, Fraser could manage to make most languages elegant. Ned had watched him chatting away in German with the comely Baroness Frederika von Riedesel, wife of the Hessian commander Baron Friedrich von Riedesel, and Burgoyne had teased that he might bring down her husband's wrath for working his tongue around her. Fraser assured his friend that he was in no way jeopardizing the alliance. He had already won over the baron by commiserating with him about Washington's horrendously unchristian attack upon Hessian troops on Christmas morning, which resulted in the mortal wounding and agonizing death of poor Colonel Rall near his post at Trenton.

The baroness, too, seemed to appreciate Fraser's condolences regarding her fallen countrymen of high and low degree. She could understand and speak rudimentary English, but Fraser preferred to put her at ease with her native language, just as he liked to do in the company of his German wife. Fraser also proved adept at making idle conversation with Burgoyne's French-speaking mistress, and it was evident he had a greater mastery of Gallic pronunciation than Burgoyne. It was undeniable he enjoyed female companionship and conversation, and the ladies seemed to take to him in turn. Now the question was whether such winning ways could work on his fellow man, as stubborn as the mountains of their mutual homeland.

At last, the deliberation concluded, and Fraser came riding back over to Burgoyne.

"Good news," the Scotsman reported. "You and I, along with our aides, have been invited to share supper with this fine family."

Burgoyne's eyebrow rose. "Do tell…how did you manage to so quickly pacify that Highland hound who moments ago was baring his teeth?"

"I told him that there was no point in ruining the memory of an old rising in favor of a revered age-old royal dynasty by supporting a new rising in favor of a rather dull self-appointed committee. It's just not a good look. Besides, I reminded him that George, our gracious sovereign, has a higher quantity of Stuart blood in his veins than another George, masquerading as a general."

"I'm not sure if I should approve of that line of argument, but…" Burgoyne began.

"If it works, it works," Fraser pointed out.

"Yes, if it works, it works," Burgoyne sighed.

"So now that we've settled that, shall I…er…get myself properly accoutered for the occasion?" Fraser queried cheekily.

"You are intent upon showing off your legs again, I can tell," Burgoyne exhaled.

"Well, if you've got what it takes," he beamed. "Besides, a little flourish couldn't hurt to smooth over relations."

"No, indeed," Burgoyne mused, glancing over at a comely young woman standing on their newfound host's porch.

Sure enough, within a few hours, Fraser was dressed in his kilt, sitting at the same table with MacDonald, chatting some more in Gaelic, while a hound lie under the table, periodically begging for scraps. Burgoyne was also provided with a table, and both the generals had their respective aides join them. The young woman, who proved to be MacDonald's daughter, placed a bowl of fresh strawberries on the table in front of Fraser, and he laughed brightly, returning Gaelic courtesies to her before offering a strawberry each to his aides, Alan and Donald, as a sign they were part of his family.

Then Fraser turned to Burgoyne's table, beaming. "General, will you let me borrow your young friend from Lancashire?"

Ned looked up, realizing he was the one in question.

"As long as you return him to me, hale and hearty," Burgoyne chortled.

"Haler and heartier, in fact," Fraser insisted, and extended the bowl of strawberries.

Ned walked over, a bit awkwardly, and stood in front of Fraser. "At your service, sir," he mumbled.

"'Tis I who am serving you," the general quipped, extending the bowl further. "Take and eat!"

Ned did so, and sensed he had been drawn into some strange adoption ritual. Yes, the sparkle in Fraser's eyes told him so.

"Strawberries are the symbol of the Fraser Clan," the general stated, setting the bowl back on the table. "Legend has it, in ancient days, we served up a bowl to a visiting king, and his pleasure at the fruit was such that he named us after the plant."

MacDonald chortled, then remarked in a heavier Highland accent than Fraser's own, "The symbol of the virgin and the harlot both!"

"The symbol that holds opposites together," Fraser responded. "Duality can be a useful quality in this world when it comes to survival."

"Your kinsmen know a thing or two about that, to be sure," MacDonald observed. "But it has a holier meaning as well…"

"It is the sign of the Blessed Virgin," Edmund filled in, as if the words lept unbidden from his mouth, "for she is both mother and maid."

MacDonald gave Ned a quizzical look, then asked Fraser a question in Gaelic, to which Fraser replied in kind.

The general turned back to Ned. "He asked if you were Roman Catholic, and if the British Army had changed its policy towards them." He lowered his voice, and added secretively, "You see, MacDonald is a Papist himself."

"Ye needn't whisper it," MacDonald replied. "I am not ashamed to have it said aloud. I fought to have a Catholic king restored and the persecutions revoked, so our priests could reside in the villages openly, instead of hiding amongst the heather. Yes, I was there from the beginning, when Ranald MacDonald, younger brother of the clan chief, swore to fight for Bonnie Prince Charlie, though no other man in the Highlands would yet draw his sword. I was there when the Stuart standard was raised in Glenfinnan, on the shores of Loch Shiel, where one of our priests offered benediction. I was there when the fiery cross was sent out to call the clans. I was there in triumph at Prestonpans, and I was there in defeat at Culloden. I served beside General Murray and Gentle Lochiel and MacDonald of Keppoch. I knew the despair of the prison ship, where my comrades were starved and our priests disgraced, and the misery of the long voyage over the sea. I bore the brand of indenture for seven years, and regained my liberty. Now, I accept my exile as it has come to me, in this land no more savage than the one I left, for the sake of keeping the faith, and with no coloring of my cheeks, as yours are colored, lad."

Edmund felt his face burn, and could not resist it, as their Highlander host's gray eyes, so much like his mother's, probed the sore spot in his soul. Then he realized, under the folds of his dull plaid shawl, the man was wearing a small crucifix carved out of wood.

Ned slowly shook his head. "I…am not one of you."

"I have already assured our host that you are like my kinsmen," Fraser said. "We catch a scent on the wind, like the stag on the moor, and respond accordingly, advancing or retreating as prudence dictates. I take no shame in that, and neither should you."

"You know how to survive," MacDonald admitted, his eyes still boring into Ned, who turned his own eyes to the floorboards.

"We know how to endure, when the night passes away and a new sun rises," Fraser corrected.

"And make many a concession," MacDonald remarked.

"Perhaps," Fraser acknowledged. "Though it seems even the Young Pretender chose to imitate my relative, called the Fox, in the end. Word has it that Charles Edward has since visited England under an alias and abandoned his popery for the Anglican Church, having been advised that it would give him the long-awaited chance to reclaim the three crowns. All very secretive transactions, mind you, for he would not wish to be turned into a roving vagabond in Europe, rejected by all Catholic powers, but you know…Paris or London has proven worth a mass, or the abolition of the mass, more than a few times in the past. It seems to have gained the Pretender little enough in the long run, but still…"

"There is no proof of his apostasy," MacDonald growled.

Fraser shrugged. "Perhaps it is my natural cynicism that makes me more willing to believe, in this case." His eyes softened a little, regarding MacDonald's own obvious pain at the prospect of his prince betraying their faith. "But all is not lost. For all the concessions we've made, there have been concessions made to us as well." He gestured to his kilt. "The ability to balance such losses and gains I'd call a damn gift."

"Or a curse," MacDonald countered. "Don't you ever see the shadow-side of your clan's so-called gift?'

"Sometimes we overplay our own hand, and must suffer the consequences," Fraser admitted. "Other times, we see what no one else wants to see, and they refuse to listen to us until it's too late. And yes, there is a shadow over us, reminding us of the things we abandoned to save ourselves, and readying us for the hour that comes upon each of us when we can no longer save ourselves…" Fraser cast a glance over to Ned. "That's one of the Fraser mottos, you know, surrounding the head of a stag on our coat-of-arms: 'I am ready.' The second accompanies the heraldry of strawberries: 'All my hope is in God.'"

Ned smiled slightly, fondly.

"What are you thinking, lad?" Fraser queried.

"When I met Major Pitcairn of the Marines in London, he told me the manse where he was born had a sign over the door, 'My Hope is in the Lord.'"

Fraser nodded once, in respect. "May that hope have served him well. I suppose the Creator has no preference between Highlands and Lowlands. Perhaps that is a lack of taste on His part, but…" He jutted out his chin a bit. "Do you see any connection between the two Fraser mottos, Ned?"

"Yes," Edmund admitted. "One must be ready to die."

Fraser smiled grimly. "You cut to the heart of it."

MacDonald leaned forward. "And are you ready to die, lad?"

Ned blinked. "I don't know," he admitted. "But I would not scorn losing my life for my king or my country."

"The highest goods for you, eh?" MacDonald prodded.

"Many men could do worse," Fraser replied, eating another strawberry.

"What are you two doing with poor Ned?" Burgoyne called over. "Trying to induct him into another Highland quorum you're plotting?"

"Of course!" Fraser chirped, raising his mug of spirits. "What else would we be doing?"

"Will you let me sit in, for security's sake?" Burgoyne teased.

Fraser pulled back his chair to make room for his superior. "Any man willing to drink what we're drinking is welcome."

"Oh-ho! Is that how it is?" Burgoyne laughed, pulling his own chair over to the table. Then he glanced over at the strawberries, and snatched one up.

"Och, I'm supposed to offer it to you before you take it," Fraser sighed. "You ruined the whole bloody thing."

Burgoyne shrugged, munching on the berry. "I can't wrap my head around your uncanny ceremonies. Besides, in addition to being flavorful, these are supposed to enhance a man's virility. No wonder you kissed your wife more heartily than might be deemed suitable for public consumption when we returned from that hunting trip."

Fraser rolled his eyes. "I love my wife. Take me to court over that, if you will. But either way, I don't believe you need much enhancement in terms of ardor for the fairer sex, Johnny."

"There's always room for improvement, even in near-perfection," he decided. "You Highlanders are supposed to be terrors in bed, if you even bother getting into bed. Some even say you bite. Not sure if that's a good or a bad thing, but…"

MacDonald muttered something in Gaelic, and Fraser laughed. Burgoyne raised an eyebrow.

"We, er, don't know any ladies who have complained over such terrors," Fraser chuckled. "Our enemies, aye…we've been known to fatally bite them…"

"Tear their throats out with our teeth," MacDonald chortled.

"But are lady-killers of a much kinder sort, I assure you," Fraser finished.

"Well, your Stuart prince had quite the reputation for such conquests, didn't he? He may have failed to take the crown, but he took many a maidenhead, rutting like a stag upon the moor…"

"He had more to recommend his fair person than Cumberland to be sure," MacDonald snorted. "Even in Whiggish Edinburgh, though most of the men were against him, most of the women were for him!"

"Yes, it's no secret he seduced many female rebels into enabling his bloody escapade," Burgoyne recalled. "There's one in particular I recall. What was her name? Colonel Anne? Betrayed her government supporting husband to lead her maiden clan out to battle for the Stuarts!"

"Yes, a Farquharson by birth, and a MacIntosh by marriage," Fraser confirmed. "Her husband was brought to her a prisoner-of-war. She greeted him, 'Your servant, Captain'. And he replied, 'Your servant, Colonel.' The name stuck."

"And then there was Miss Flora MacDonald," Burgoyne chuckled, "who ferried the Pretender over the sea to Skye so he could make his escape. She charmed all of London with her romantic tale. No one would dare cut off her pretty head, no, sir!"

"She emigrated to these colonies," Fraser stated, casting MacDonald a glance, "and declared herself for King George and broadswords in this contest. Better a royal from a different branch of the same tree than none at all."

"Depends on the fruit the branch bears," MacDonald mumbled.

"Speaking of fruit…enough with the berries," Fraser huffed, pulling the bowl away from Burgoyne. "It's time for the brew."

"Aye, if you can't hold hard liquor, General, you can't expect to conquer new lands for your Hanoverian laird," the Highlander stated, petting the great dog at his feet.

"We're here simply to reclaim that which His Majesty already owns," Burgoyne stated, petting the dog, rubbing against his leg under the table.

MacDonald chortled and muttered something in Gaelic. Burgoyne turned to Fraser for translation.

"He is trying to teach you an old Highland belief," Fraser stated. "No man, even a king, can truly own the land, not in the deepest sense. It is rather the land that owns us."

"Do you believe that?" Burgoyne pressed.

Fraser shrugged. "We do not choose where we are born nor where we die."

"So what is the relationship between the king and his lands then?"

"Marriage," Fraser stated. "The land is a lady, you see."

"Aye, and she must be treated as she wants to be," MacDonald insisted, "or she'll prove muckle unruly under the sheets!"

Both Fraser and MacDonald laughed out loud, and Burgoyne snorted.

"On you go, prattling about your superstitions," Burgoyne sighed.

"Surely you're used to it by now, trying to bring the wilderness savages to your way of thinking," MacDonald replied.

"Well, it seems you've managed to live in their midst unmolested somehow," Burgoyne observed. "Care to let us in on your secret?"

"Keep in mind, General, we too are savage people," MacDonald answered.

"Lucky us," Fraser snorted.

"The natives even recognize similarities in us," MacDonald insisted. "We are a warrior people who hold to our own chiefs, our own tongue, and our own customs. They have their beads and we have our plaid. And our young men dance to show their prowess. Perhaps most importantly, we both know what it is to be called uncivilized. Those who consider themselves the bastions of civilization either use us for their own ends, or pursue our end. But we do not die easily."

"I for one am not daunted by tribal tendencies," Burgoyne stated. "As for your people, well, my dear Balnain has sufficiently proven to me that you can be the most cosmopolitan of gentlemen if given the opportunity. As for these forest dwellers, while some may excel in intelligence, most are like children, simple and pliable, so long as a firm hand is applied. We shall have no trouble from them that we can't handle."

"The general gave them a Sunday school lesson," Fraser remarked sarcastically.

Burgoyne suddenly grew serious. "They'll not harm the innocent," he stated earnestly. "Not under my command."

MacDonald raised an eyebrow. "A rare sentiment, for one in red."

Burgoyne grew flushed, and looked likely to make a fierce retort. But Fraser interrupted.

"The general's gentlemanly sentiments are given weight by his untarnished record. His word is enough for me on the matter. Indeed, I drink to it." Fraser took a sip from his mug then handed it over to Burgoyne. "Now down the hatch with the rest of it!"

Burgoyne gave his friend a smile of gratitude as he accepted the challenge and gulped down the mug's contents, struggling not to spill. "Damn, that smarts!" he gasped upon finishing, rubbing his throat.

"There's more where that came from," Fraser assured cheekily.

MacDonald's daughter Caitriona was filling up the drinks again, her long tresses of dirty blonde hair flowing down to her waist.

Burgoyne leaned over towards Fraser and whispered, "Think you might be able to get that handsome young thing to sing us a song?"

Fraser rolled his eyes again. "What makes you think she can sing?"

"I thought all Highlanders could sing! You certainly can after too much of your native brewed beverage!"

Fraser sighed. "You know, General, I somehow don't believe your main interest is in her singing voice."

"Balnain, you don't trust me." Burgoyne made a pouting face.

"I just don't want you undoing everything I've done to keep the King's peace in this humble abode," Fraser retorted.

"Oh, come, Balnain, I'm genteel enough to know how to look without touching," Burgoyne insisted. "Unless, of course, things develop…"

"That's what I was afraid of," Fraser exhaled. "You'll try and coax her over to your knee."

"No, I won't."

"Then once she's perched there, pretty as a picture, your hands start wandering…"

"No, no, I'll restrain myself."

"On this brew? I think not!"

"You underestimate me, I tell you! I shall drink in her sweet nectar only with my eyes!"

Fraser sighed then mumbled some words in Gaelic over to her father. The old Highlander responded in kind, and Fraser laughed heartily. He turned back to Burgoyne. "There's a condition, General."

"Do tell."

"She must sing a Jacobite song."

Burgoyne raised an eyebrow. "Well, if it's in your mountain tongue, I can deny knowing the meaning of the words, can't I?"

"You can indeed," Fraser agreed, grinning.

And so Caitriona came out again. She tossed her long hair over her right shoulder, as if it were some gesture of good luck before beginning to sing. Her voice was raw, but not in an unpleasant way, and it had a way of cutting quickly to the soul. The audience was hushed. MacDonald's eyes grew misty listening to his daughter, and even his frumpy, hard-working wife who had been cleaning the platters paused to listen.

Fraser leaned over to Burgoyne again, who was clearly involved in looking over the charms of the young woman from head to foot, and whispered in his ear a translation. "Who will play the silver whistle? My king's son to sea has gone, on a ship with three masts of silver, and ropes of light French silk…"

"Stop it," Burgoyne grumbled, pushing him away.

But Fraser was enjoying himself too much. "A youth with blue eyes, enticing! Welcome to you, your fame and honor! Fiddles and choice tunes attend you!"

"God save us all," Burgoyne huffed.

"Who will sound the silver whistle? Yea, will I not myself be playing?" Fraser's eyes twinkled as he beamed at his friend.

Burgoyne gave him a scolding, cross-eyed look, and Fraser slapped him on the back.

Miraculously, after she had finished singing, Burgoyne managed to keep his hands to himself as he complimented her "ravishing voice" and flashed his lustrous eyes at her. Fraser seemed positively proud of him for exhibiting such restraint. But later on, as they were departing for camp, the Highland general had a cause to lecture his cousin Alan for having escorted their host's daughter out to the porch alone and getting more than a bit amorous with her. She didn't seem to be fighting it too hard, but Fraser broke them up all the same, fearing all his diplomatic efforts might be jettisoned. Alan cited the strawberries as the cause of his sudden ardor.

Chapter 22: PRIVILEGE OF THE SWORD

Possessing the abilities of both a clerk and a quarter master, Jonathan was sometimes sent along with foraging parties, though he found the duty distasteful. He did what had to be done without minimal complaint, grudgingly admitting to its necessity, but Ned could tell how it taxed his conscience. He once broke down and admitted that he considered it little better than theft, even when the general gave him leave to offer some compensation for the goods confiscated. It was British policy to give the colonials, even loyal ones, debased money to filter into the colonial economy to destabilize it. It would help disrupt the war machine and cause the revolutionaries difficulties when trying to purchase armaments from abroad. Jonathan still despised the deception, especially when dealing with the King's friends who they were supposed to be rescuing and had already suffered property loss at the hands of the rebels. But regardless of his sentiments, he had little choice but to barter with the coinage he was given.

One day, Jonathan took Ned with him on a foraging mission to several nearby farms. He also found the job undesirable, although Jonathan told him they could at least provide a good service to the locals by restraining any excesses the soldiery might be inclined to commit and assuring that at least some food remained to prevent civilian starvation. Nevertheless, it was a bitter experience encountering women and children, helpless to hold off the incursion, screaming insults at the soldiers as the men took possession of horses, food stuffs, and anything else that might be of use to the army. The women's husbands were off to join the rebels, most likely, and they interpreted this confiscation of property by the King's troops as yet another proof of his inherent tyranny.

"You bloody-backs trample upon the rights of the people, and leave America upon her knees, without sustenance or virtue!" one woman cried.

"Ma'am, unhappily, Pax Britannia has been disrupted, and the necessity of force initiated," Jonathan stated gravely. "As such, the right to commandeer is ours. However, your rebels, too, claim that prerogative, to keep their fighting men supplied whenever it proves necessary. It is no unique tyranny on our part, regrettable though it may be for us all."

His words did nothing to quell her rage, and she spat in his face when he tried to offer the meager coinage allotted to him for the task.

Another woman at a neighboring farm was caught trying to set fire to the barn and had to be forcibly restrained. Better to lose the stores to the flames, she said, then to have them feed the enemy, gunning for her husband. Jonathan could have arrested her; he told her as much. Her rebel husband had placed his family in immediate danger, and her efforts to aid and abet him only made her position more precarious. Indeed, another officer might have burned the house and barn himself. Ned could easily imagine Lieutenant Caldwell deciding upon such a course. But Jonathan seemed unable to bring himself to carry out the threats, especially when she broke down in angry tears and cursed him, pulling her little ones closer to her skirts.

Moving on, with increasingly heavy hearts, Ned and Jonathan found that a few of the farms had already been abandoned, and the stores partially destroyed before their inhabitants fled. But due to the rapid evacuation, the inhabitants had not finished the task of destruction and there was still enough remaining to collect for army use. At the final farm, they encountered a homesteading family that belonged to the Society of Friends, and were thus committed to pacifist neutrality according to their conscience. Ned took note of their plain attire, but more memorably, their honest faces. While the soldiers were set to work commandeering supplies, the man and his wife confessed to having already been visited by foraging rebel soldiers earlier in the week, from whom they had not begrudged food, clothing, or medical care for the wounded in their own parlor.

"Do you realize you might be construed as lending succor to the enemies of the King?" Jonathan queried.

"Friend, we did nothing but what any Christian should do on behalf of the needy, regardless of what flag they fly," the farmer stated. "Nor would we withhold such, succor, as thou hast called it, from thee."

"All that we ask," began the woman, gathering her teenage daughter and younger son close to her, "is that thou shouldst leave us enough to survive these troubled times." She gestured to the door. "In any case, thy friend and thyself are welcome to sup with us."

This generosity clearly moved Jonathan, and Ned felt further burdened with guilt.

"I assure you, ma'am, the cruel necessities that this conflict entails bring me nothing but distress, and I desire to be as moderate with the populace as I can be," Jonathan confessed.

"Then why art thou taking part in the war?" the Quaker boy blurted. "It is a sin…"

"Hush, Jesse," his sister scolded him. She looked at Jonathan pleadingly. "Please…do not harm him…"

"That is not my intention, miss," Jonathan assured. Then he turned to the boy. "I do not consider it a sin to restrain felons and restore order. It is an act of justice and, in the long run, of mercy. All the same, my most fervent prayer is that this unhappy affair is swiftly concluded and peace prevails throughout His Majesty's empire." He then turned to the boy's father. "Surely, sir, we can drink to the latter sentiment."

The Quaker gentleman smiled slightly. "We do not drink, at least not in the way thou intend it. But we can break bread to it."

"I did make switchel, Papa," his daughter added.

"Ah, yes," he confirmed, nodding at Jonathan. "Naomi stirred up with a fresh batch this morning. You are welcome to that."

"We would be honored to partake," Jonathan accepted for both himself and Ned.

An hour later, as they all sat down for the evening meal in the small but neatly furnished home, Jonathan seemed in his element in a domestic setting, eating home-cooked food and asking the children questions, especially the two youngest girls, ages seven and four. An amused smile spread over his face at their guileless answers, mixed with a strain of melancholy. The four year old even ended up scrambling into his lap at one point, and he seemed very pleased, looking upon her as Ned imagined he looked upon his own little Emma back in Hampshire.

They learned from the master of the house that the family name was Martin. Like most Quakers, he seemed to be an educated and industrious man, from a line of educated and industrious people who had abandoned Nottinghamshire for the New World some three generations before, seeking relief from the Test Act, which they had refused to take.

"But, friend," Jonathan queried, adopting their manner of speech out of respect, "the Test Act is, if you will, a preventative measure to preclude foreign intervention and preserve peace within the realm. I know dissenting Protestants in this army who have found ways to interpret in a manner acceptable to their beliefs. And Lieutenant Southworth, here, was raised Papist, but took the oaths out of patriotism. He wanted nothing more than to serve alongside his countrymen."

Jonathan laid a hand on Ned's arm in a gesture of brotherhood, and Ned blushed.

"Firstly, we do not believe in hierarchies amongst the people of God, be they king or commoner, man or woman, white or black or red," Martin stated. "Secondly, we do not believe religion can be maintained in men through compulsion, and that God intends for all persons to enjoy liberty of conscience. Thirdly, we do not take any oaths, regardless of their content. Our yes means yes, and our no means no, as Christ commanded."

"Is that not a rather literal reading of the passage?" Ned queried. "There are other interpretations that regard oath-taking permissible, so long that it is taken up with utmost gravity and sincerity…"

"Christ is a present reality to us," their host replied. "We are, indeed, literal-minded when it comes to following Him and what is written of Him in Scripture."

"And so Christ's words regarding living and dying by the sword," Jonathan surmised.

"Lay me by thy pleading; law lies a-bleeding," Martin recited. "Burn all thy studies down, and throw away thy reading. Small power the word has, and can afford us not half so many privileges as the sword has."

"Poetry from the Civil War," Jonathan remarked.

"Aye," Martin confirmed. "It was such strife that brought into being The Society of Friends. Our founder, George Fox, grew sickened by the carnage, with two armies professing a purer form of Christianity terrorizing their Christian brethren and abandoning all the mandates of Christ. And yet such strife is for naught, for there is only one, even Christ Jesus, that can speak to our condition and save us from ourselves."

"But there have always been Christian warriors, and the Bible uses martial language extensively," Jonathan said.

"Although, it must be said, the early Church was hesitant to canonize soldiers, lest a career of violence be unduly glorified," Edmund conceded. "Still, I agree with Lieutenant Rawcliffe that there are certain cases when war becomes a necessity for the greater good."

"I find that the excuses based upon extremity fail to stare reality full in the face," their host replied. "We are very canny when it comes to convincing ourselves that violence is justified, falling back upon nebulous greater goods. I can count many wars that have unfolded in my time, my father's time, and my grandfather's time, each with their own reasons, with both sides insisting God fought for them. Perhaps, in truth, God was pleading with them all to cease the slaughter and turn the other cheek."

"But there are times when honor itself demands it," Jonathan insisted, "

"Yet this inconstancy is such as you too shall adore," Ned quoted, "I could not love thee, dear, so much, loved I not honor more."

"Lovelace," said the Quaker quietly, glancing over at Ned. "Thou art a true Cavalier."

"And you are well-read, friend," Edmund replied with a smile.

"I used to work in a print shop in Philadelphia, before moving my family north, hoping to avoid the war," he stated. "It was founded by one of our own, William Penn, who wished it to be the city of brotherly love where all Christians, both Protestant and Papist alike, might live together in harmony. But now that has changed, and it has become a capital of strife."

"Then you are opposed to the actions of the rebel congress?" Ned surmised.

"I am opposed to the actions of any body that leads to men killing their fellow men, and particularly one that does so in the hopes of creating an earthly Utopia, based upon the ideas of the pagan Greeks and Romans. Still, I pray for them that they may be guided to the light yet kindled within them."

"And for King George?" Jonathan queried.

"For all men," Martin confirmed, "especially our brothers in Christ, whom I believe the King to be."

"But you do not believe it is laudable to fight for his honor?" Jonathan pressed.

"From both reading and living, I can only say that what we call honor should never contradict a man's conscience," Martin responded. "That is the inner light, and the pureness of divine presence, which we all experience. George Fox learned this in the sanctuary of hollow trees and lonesome places of Mother England. One day, Fox climbed to the top of Pendle Hill, said to be haunted by witches and demons, and beheld a vision of people in white raiment, coming to the Lord in throngs."

Ned smiled. "I've been up on Pendle before."

"Aye, thy accent is from Lancashire," Martin observed. "Some of us consider it similar to a place of pilgrimage."

"Holy ground," Ned concluded, "where heaven and earth meet."

Martin nodded. "Where they meet, and show us that all of creation is imbued with the presence of the creator, not least ourselves. Seeing the vision of a white-robed throng, Fox came to the conclusion that the people, not the steeple, is the church, and that the same Spirit which inspired the Scriptures is their true interpreter. For making such views known, he was tossed down church steps, beaten about the head with sticks, and bludgeoned with a brass-bound Bible. So he went out to preach at fairs and marketplaces, to the farmers in their fields and the prisoners in their cells. Soon, he too was jailed, along with his followers, under the Lord Protector and the Stuart kings alike. Some were even hanged in these colonies. But truth can live in the jails and outlives death. What is most imperative is that we be valiant for truth upon the earth and tread upon deceit."

"Tell the story of his meeting with the Lord Protector, Papa," young Jesse requested.

"I shall let thy mother tell it," Martin decided, gesturing to his wife with a smile. Then he looked back to their guests, and said with a wholesome pride, "She is a deacon, you know."

His wife smiled in return, nodding in assent. "When offered freedom from prison if he would accept a commission in Cromwell's army, Fox declined, insisting Christ had called him to enter into the covenant of peace. Those who embraced this same call left Cromwell's army to join what they called the Lamb's war. They would tremble at the word of the Lord, and for this reason, in addition to accusations of cowardice, were derided as 'quakers.' But the society grew, all the same, from servants, such as Mary Fisher, to nobles, such as William Penn, to the politician and military commander Freeborn John Lilburne. Cromwell was puzzled and displeased by how many had become Friends. But he was also fascinated by the preaching of Fox, and rumors of his visions and healings. Cromwell, too, it was said, had visions. So they met, the two men who were so close to each other and yet so far away, and the lord protector laid bare his soul with its many burdens. And so Fox preached a sermon to Cromwell, and advised him ardently, 'lay thy crown at Jesus' feet!' And the lord protector wept."

"Then you believe even a man of blood such as Cromwell could be touched by the inner light of which you speak?" Jonathan queried.

"Of course," she replied. "Any man." She gestured to the whole table. "All of mankind."

"And this is why you use familiar terms of friendship with everyone, and do not bow or curtsey?" Ned concluded.

"And why we abhor slavery of any kind," she added. "We are all equal, in our creation and redemption. Our comportment gives testimony of this."

"Do you consider the rebel hyperbole which uses the language of enslavement to depict the King's laws as having any merit?" Jonathan inquired, testing them.

"Friend, there are many modes of government which we find lacking, throughout the world, when compared to the ideals set forth by Christ," Martin replied. "But we distrust hyperbole as much as you do in this case, particularly when espoused by men who claim to be heralds of the gospel, but in truth have been converted to a secular cult. They may still preach Christ, but their goal is to usher in an apocalypse without Him, to create a new heaven and a new earth through their own Armageddon."

"You speak wisely," Jonathan said. "What are your thoughts on Nathaniel Greene, the rebel general who was raised as a Quaker?"

"They say he rebelled against our strict manner of living," Martin replied. "And it is true, we are simple people, not given to the frivolity of music and dance. Even our services are mostly held in silence. But his father curtailed the boy's reading, which I for one believe was an error on his part, and the main cause of the boy's rebellion."

"Literally and figuratively?" Jonathan snorted.

"I do not know what turned his hand to shedding thy blood, but it breaks my heart that he sins against thee," the man said, softly, sincerely. "Though he berates us as cowards now, what can we do but pray for him?"

Ned found that he could not help but admire these people. Even if he disagreed with particulars, their integrity struck his soul. He suddenly found himself wishing he had maintained similar fortitude in his convictions, even if he had been branded a coward by every other soul. But too late now, too late…

"So there is hope, even for us soldiers, in your eyes?" Edmund mumbled.

"There is always hope," said Martin firmly. He gave Jonathan and Ned a penetrating gaze. "Thou art yet innocent of much blood, I think. The killing times have not yet clouded thee. But a time will come soon when perhaps thou shalt understand us a bit better, odd as we may seem to thee now." He focused on Ned in particular. "Perhaps thou might yet have cause to break thy sword, and bury the pieces, before its privilege breaks thee."

"I fear we must wield our weapons until, by the blessing of God, tranquility reigns, and we can retire them with dignity," Jonathan replied, "but until then, we would appreciate your prayers."

"Thou shalt have them," their hostess assured.

"Thank you," Jonathan returned, smiling. "By the by…might General Burgoyne and his staff, of which we are a part, camp on your property over the weekend? I feel it would be safer here than in some other locations. Perhaps in the open field, behind the house? I promise not to demand any further services from you nor contributions from your stores."

"We do not object," Martin replied, "though I imagine thou need not have asked in order to make it so."

Jonathan shrugged. "I prefer to seek permission when possible."

Before leaving the house, Jonathan dug into his coat and produced several additional coins. "It will not make up the difference, ma'am," he said sadly, placing the coins into the hands of his hostess. "But it may help tide you over."

"Will thou not be given trouble by thy general for this if he were to learn of it?" she queried. "This be proper British coin."

He shrugged. "You have reminded me that I must abide by my conscience first and foremost."

~

Lounging on the peaceful spread of the Quaker's property, General Burgoyne and the British high command allowed themselves some respite from their toils. It was a tranquil scene, almost as if they were all spending a Sunday afternoon in the countryside back home. And Naomi Martin showed up with a pitcher of her switchel from the house to offer them. She was a bundle of nerves in front of General Burgoyne and his mistress, spilling some of the drink as she poured it for them. Said mistress scolded her for being clumsy, then seemed even more affronted, in a guilty sort of way, when the girl innocently assumed she was Burgoyne's wife. But the general joked in a good-natured manner over the girl's repetitious apologies, kissed her hand, and pronounced her "a sweet little field mouse," whatever that meant. That kiss caused her to turn pink and scamper away.

Several of the guards attached to the general's supply wagons saw her pass by, and startled to ogle her. One whistled, catching her attention, and she blushed crimson as one of the soldiers made a lewd gesture to his crotch and the others laughed, bandying about dirty words pertaining to her.

Thankfully, Jonathan intervened.

"Stop harassing the young lady," he ordered sternly. "You disgrace the King's good name with such behavior!"

"We were only funning, sir," one of the soldiers insisted, "not touching…"

"One thing leads to another with your sort," Jonathan retorted hotly. "Going forward, you will turn your eyes down and hold your tongue in the presence of any member of this family, until the time of our departure, or you will answer to me!"

Ned felt relieved that Jonathan decided to accompany Naomi back to the house for her own safety, lest any of the soldiers decide to straggle after her. Why were so many men so disgustingly rapacious? Where was the spirit element, meant to keep the animal element in check? He supposed that, for the moment, it was Jonathan. These Quakers could do far worse in terms of a guardian angel.

Major Acland seemed to be enjoying the sweet molasses-based beverage while sitting with his now-pregnant wife, who clung to his arm and gazed at him adoringly as he tossed a stick for his faithful dog to fetch back to him. The running joke was that the red-coated canine was the true love of his life and the most devoted soldier under his command. Indeed, some felt that he did not give Lady Acland the proper attention and took his delicate bride for granted. It was certainly true he tended to use her as an object of boasting among his friends, including about his success impregnating her on the road. Yet he sometimes seemed to have difficulty knowing how to deal with her own devotion towards him. But in this moment of restfulness, Ned saw Acland briefly turn to her, his eyes finding hers, and they softened, all the arrogance assuaged, and he tenderly kissed her neck. She nuzzled into his shoulder as he wrapped his arm around her, and Ned felt certain there was so much more beneath his usual bravado.

General Philips was also out and about with his dog Rebel, whom he was still training to heed him instead of his former revolutionary master, General Montgomery. Thinking upon that man, shot in a doomed assault to capture Quebec for his sham of a congress, Ned found it particularly distasteful that the rebels had tried to take the city which had cost so many British and colonial lives to capture, not least Wolfe of immortal memory. What was worse was that Montgomery had hailed from a prominent Ulster-Scots military family and had once served as an officer in the regular British army before absolving himself of allegiance to his king. Indeed, Lieutenant Caldwell had used Montgomery's ancestry to instigate Eli multiple times.

But regardless of the dead man's traitorous legacy, Ned still felt sympathy for his dog, who had curled by his master's grave and refused to be moved for days. Thankfully, Philips had taken pity on the creature, treated him with gentleness, and got him eating again. Now the two were inseparable, even if Rebel still needed training to learn whose voice he should obey. Some joked the dog was bad luck and Philips was risking life and limb adopting the cursed creature. The Welshman ignored them entirely, and Ned was pleased that he did so.

General Fraser, meanwhile, was having lunch with the Hessian Baron von Riedesel and his young family. Baroness von Riedesel was chatting vivaciously as ever, and Fraser was flattering her in German as usual, as well as periodically teaching her new phrases in English, equally complimentary to her person. Ned noticed how her pretty face was blushing. Contrary to Burgoyne's warnings of potential jealousy from her husband, the Baron seemed amused by the Scotsman's charm, and the two men exchanged winks, with the Baron laughing, deep from his belly. The Riedesels' two little girls had started off playing tag around the makeshift table, but after their mother scolded them for nearly knocking over a jar of jam, Fraser spontaneously picked the youngest one up and balanced her on his knee. For a man without children of his own, he seemed to have a natural way with them, and she quickly calmed in his firm hold, resting her head against his chest. He smiled down at her fondly and stroked her yellow hair.

Soon, the little girl was enraptured watching a duck splash about in a nearby pond, and tried to squirm down from Fraser's lap to befriend it. Her mother appeared markedly unenthused, most likely afraid her tiny child would either fall in the water or be devoured by said duck. Fraser, in order to avoid undue fatalities, volunteered to supervise the situation, and he and the two children ended up trotting over and tossing chunks of bread into the pond, with the youngest girl learning how to say "duck, duck, I want duck", repetitively, in a comical mix between a German and Scottish accent. Fraser could not help but burst out laughing.

And while all this unfolded, Ned observed Burgoyne sitting up in one of the wagons, where he had been napping with his mistress, watching Fraser and the little girls with a look of longing that was painful to behold.

When Fraser gave the child back to her mother and excused himself from the little family gathering to smoke his pipe, Burgoyne sauntered over to him.

"How have you managed to make such headway with that baroness?" Burgoyne queried. "She nearly bites my head off every time I'm around her!"

"She thinks you're a bad influence on her babes," Fraser replied, taking a deep draught on his pipe, then offering it to Burgoyne.

"Oh, come now, I'm not so very bad," Burgoyne scoffed, accepting the pipe and taking a draught himself. "It's not as if you don't get rather frisky yourself when enough liquor flows."

"That's because you're a bad influence on me!" Fraser snorted, taking the pipe back.

Ned couldn't disagree there. Everyone knew Fraser had finally ingested too much alcohol at Burgoyne's tent parties when he started to sing bawdy ballads like "The Trooper and the Maid" and "Eppie Morrie." By then, Burgoyne had usually passed out in the lap of one of his lady friends. No one knew how far Fraser went in that department himself when the lights in the tent finally went out. He was mad about his "dearest Margaretha", going so far as to call her the best of wives, and Ned sincerely hoped he was more physically faithful to her than Burgoyne had been to his "incomparable Charlotte." But even a devoted husband could grow lonely and loose in a far away land when his inhibitions were lowered. All Ned knew for sure was that Fraser would grumble the morning after about being corrupted by Burgoyne's parties, and Burgoyne, with an innocent bedside manner, would tell him what to do to ease the hangover.

"Maybe it's because you're good with children," Burgoyne mumbled, glancing back over at the baron's family.

"Easy to fall in love with them," Fraser replied with a fond smile. "They're like little German dolls."

"That come to life and break jam jars," Burgoyne chuckled.

"All part of their charm!" Fraser insisted. "I'd happily have a couple of them myself. They are particularly amusing when they come in pairs…"

Burgoyne continued to stare wistfully over at the family. "Regardless of what the baroness thinks, I'm not…well, I'm not altogether unfamiliar with children…not least of all girl children…sitting them on my lap and keeping them entertained, or even lulling them to sleep, you know…that sort of thing…"

Fraser lowered his gaze. "I know."

"Of course you do," Burgoyne sighed. "You must know everything about me, don't you?"

Fraser seemed unsure how to answer that, just stalled by tapping out the ashes from his pipe against a tree trunk. "John, I have a question for you," he said at last.

"Fire away," Burgoyne replied with a wave of his hand.

"Why did you pack half your house for the road?" Fraser gestured broadly to the twenty wagons of Burgoyne's personal baggage. "You're almost as bad as a woman!"

"I resent that," Burgoyne declared. "When we went hunting in the Highlands, you put me in a bind. 'Pack light,' you said. 'It'll be fun', you said. No. I'm an indoor cat by nature, and if it's at all within reason, I don't see why I shouldn't bring along a few comforts from home."

"I think you just want to turn this into a bloody party train," Fraser decided.

"Why complain, Balnain? I always invite you to brighten up my little social events with your troublesome plaid!"

"I show up in breeches more often than not," Fraser scoffed, slapping his thigh.

"Well, either way, it's better than whatever your sort would be likely to do in your natural environment," Burgoyne snorted. "You'd probably have me drinking out of broken shells in a cave somewhere!"

"Perish the thought," Fraser clucked. "We don't like foreigners there. It's just for us and the spiders to enjoy. And I know you don't like spiders…"

"If you're referring to my walking into that bloody spider web spread out from a tree limb when we were hunting…"

Fraser grinned.

"It just startled me, is all," Burgoyne insisted. "Also felt rather disgusting."

"Then you slipped on that wee bit of moss…"

"Which was wet," Burgoyne clarified, "and also disgusting."

Fraser chortled. "You were a good sport about it though, must be said. Slept out in the open for most of the trip, and only bailed out when your bronchitis acted up."

Burgoyne raised his chin. "I may have a history of vulnerability in my lungs, Balnain, but I also have a history of bedding down on the battlefield if duty bids me, you know…"

"I know…"

"Did so when I fought the Spanish dons in Portugal, bronchitis be damned…"

"So you did." Fraser beamed, then bowed slightly "Any man would be proud to serve under such an esteemed veteran as yourself. Just don't march us into any spiderwebs!"

Burgoyne shook his finger. "Keep in mind, Balnain, I proved my worth on that hunting trip too. Shot down one of your great red stags, I did!"

Fraser shrugged. "You wounded him. I had to finish him with a blade, lest he suffer."

"And you cannot abide the suffering of a fellow Highlander?" Burgoyne surmised.

"Let's just say that we understand the nature of majesty laid low," Fraser murmured, "and wish to make fast work of a bitter end."

"Yet even your mercies are dreadful," Burgoyne sighed. "You can lull children to sleep in your arms, and yet when you draw blood, even upon a dying stag, you…"

"I what?" Frazier challenged, just a little bit on edge.

"You…" Burgoyne paused, shrugged. "You get your own blood up over it. I see it in you, with the blood splattered on your hands and clothes. You show frightfully little, and altogether too much."

Fraser closed his eyes. "Sometimes this world needs dreadful mercies." He glanced back over to Burgoyne. "I suppose it's good that you were there, to help me clean the blood from my blade." His eyes darted briefly. "And my hands."

Burgoyne nodded. "Any time."

Fraser grew wistful. "Do you remember the colors we saw in the sky when you were assigned up at Fort William?"

"Indeed," Burgoyne replied. "The lights of the far north. We see such things periodically in Lancashire, but there was something more beautiful and terrible about it in the Scottish Highlands."

"It was orange tinted pink, and blue tinted green, and sometimes, when the colors overlapped, it ran red like blood…" His voice trailed off.

"I know," Burgoyne said softly.

"Is that why you put your arm through mine, to steady me?"

"I thought you were going to get sick."

"Oh, John," he chuckled. "I don't get sick from such things. I have learned how to subdue the memories when they become bothersome."

"I thought…you needed a friend," Burgoyne said softly.

Fraser gazed at him for a long moment, gratitude coming to his eyes. "There are few things that I treasure more."

~

The friendship shared by the two generals would be put to the test in the following days.

Lieutenant Caldwell began to stir up trouble by putting pressure on Burgoyne for advancement in rank and duties, which the general, to his credit, did not believe the arrogant and impetuous young man was ready for. Caldwell became increasingly embittered, and his bullying tendencies worsened towards the rest of the staff and beyond.

General Fraser's staff had long shared a sometimes friendly, sometimes contentious rivalry with Burgoyne's staff. There was always banter aplenty between them when they were thrown together due to their commanders' tent parties. The two young Highlanders, Alan and Donald, along with Irish Artie, were the most boisterous, though Donald was the most artful of the three in terms of roasting. They tended to target Jonathan frequently, having been convinced he held their general in contempt. Jonathan did his best to handle it with grace, even as Gavin frequently rose to his defense. There was nothing quite like having a crusty Welshman for a friend when fire had to be fought with fire, preferably also of Celtic extraction. Eli would sometimes throw himself into the fracas as well, or indeed be lured into it by choice words. But he did not excel at sarcasm, and usually came off like a humorless schoolmaster, lecturing unruly students, which only increased the merciless teasing.

But Lieutenant Caldwell, when he became the brunt of a joke, would respond with unfiltered rancor, attacking General Fraser's reputation and Highland pride in general. Alan was so provoked, he lept upon Caldwell and broke his nose with the pummel of his sword. A duel might have broken out if not for the intervention of both Jonathan and Donald, and later the two generals. It was Alan who received punishment for such behavior, having various privileges withheld from him, though everyone knew Caldwell had pressed him to the brink.

"Lieutenant, you went too far," Jonathan told Caldwell after the fact. "Whatever you think of General Fraser's origins, he has authority over us, given to him by His Majesty…"

"He is a mountain barbarian wearing the costume of a gentleman," Caldwell declared. "None can guarantee his allegiance. Loyalty is as foreign to him as etiquette. Treachery flowed with mother's milk."

"No," Jonathan countered. "He is a professional soldier who is committed to fulfilling his duties, under whatever flag he may be serving. I cannot judge his level of fidelity to the British state compared to his craving for personal gain, for I cannot read his heart, and he is unlikely to reveal it to me, but this much I know: He is loyal to General Burgoyne. I can see it in his eyes, and I would stake my life on it. He would go into the fire for him."

"I hope he goes into the fire," Caldwell growled, "just like his fellow rebels in the barn at Drumossie Moor!"

This violent imagery seemed to give Jonathan the impetus to take the matter before General Burgoyne.

"Sir, the Scriptures say that the father disciplines the son he loves," Jonathan murmured.

"And?" Burgoyne snapped defensively. "What has this to do with the issue at hand?"

Jonathan bit his lip, seeming to struggle to find a way out. "Sir, we know…you treat us all as family, including Lieutenant Caldwell. But he is disrupting that unity among us, and continuing to antagonize General Fraser's staff by abusing his name."

"I was not aware you had become one of General Fraser's defenders," Burgoyne replied. "I don't believe he has yet forgiven you for your remarks upon the humanity of savage peoples, even his own…"

"I will defend any man I believe wrongfully maligned, and feel a particular duty in this regard towards commanding officers," Jonathan replied. "Undermining them undermines the very business we are upon. If we are to combat discord in these colonies, we must not have it break out like a pestilence amongst ourselves."

"I assure you, Lieutenant, I have the situation in hand, and am more than capable of forcibly restraining those who fail to take a warning," Burgoyne stated.

The warning was just around the corner. Ned overheard Lieutenant Caldwell in the general's tent late one night, seeming to have abandoned decorum in favor of venom.

"It appears, sir, that the only ones receiving attention and favor on this campaign are erstwhile Papists and rebel Scots," Caldwell sneered.

"Do not dare to question my decisions regarding preferment, Lieutenant," Burgoyne snapped, "nor stir up rancor against any member of this staff, nor spread malicious gossip against a general in His Majesty's service! The memory of your mother won't cover your impudence and envy!"

Caldwell flushed. "General, sir…"

"By casting shade upon General Fraser's loyalty, you are not only treading the borders of mutinous ground, but casting that same shade upon the late King's choice of clemency and the current King's choice of reward," Burgoyne continued sternly.

"It was not my intent, sir," Caldwell protested. "I only meant to point out…"

"I know exactly what you were pointing out, and I will point out certain facts in kind," Burgoyne retorted. "It has been more than twenty years since General Fraser's return from his exile on the continent. He was a mere lad when his clan was dispossessed. Of his own free will, he came back to Britain to seek pardon and make peace with the government, like so many of his fellow clansmen. His petition was granted, and the King's mercy obtained. As an officer in one of our Highland regiments, he proved his fidelity to our constitution beyond reproach. He has not looked back, from that time to this, nor should any of us, especially in the midst of such a campaign as we are upon."

"He's still a Scot," Caldwell mumbled, barely audibly.

"What was that?" Burgoyne demanded.

"Nothing, sir."

Burgoyne's eyes flashed. "Keep in mind, Lieutenant Caldwell, that we have become one people. Perhaps we are still making sense of that, and sometimes going about it poorly. But it remains a reality, nevertheless. If he is a Scot, he is also a Briton. They fill our ranks, and I count quite a few of them among my friends, Lowlander and Highlander alike." He leaned forward. "By the by, I have an old-fashioned sense of friendship. If you find yourself involved in any intrigues against General Fraser, you will have to answer to him, but first, you will have to deal with me. I recommend not making enemies of either of us. Now you are dismissed."

Chapter 23: BOOTY AND BEAUTY

July brought good fortune for Burgoyne's expedition with the recapture of Fort Ticonderoga from the rebels. The legendary Ethan Allen and his Green Mountain Boys, allied with the brash social-climber Benedict Arnold, had captured it from the royal garrison in the name of "The Great Jehovah and the Continental Congress" a mere month after the skirmishes at Lexington and Concord. Cannons from the fort had then been used to besiege the British in Boston and ultimately force them to abandon the city. Ticonderoga occupied an advantageous position, and retaking the stronghold for King George had initially seemed an unlikely achievement. But General Fraser with his advance corps had spotted a weak point in the enemy lines, and General Phillips, the dauntless artilleryman, decided to accomplish the feat by dragging his cannons up the slope.

"Where a goat can go, a man can go, and where a man can go, he can drag a gun," the proud Welshman declared, and ordered his men to set to work hacking a path up the almost perpendicular ascent.

The rebels were caught off guard by the determination of their adversary, and when they saw that Phillips' cannons had been dragged into position on the aptly named Mount Defiance, they abandoned the fort to Burgoyne lest they be blown to pieces. Fraser, for his part, was determined to give chase to the fleeing revolutionaries with his advance guard. His Scottish blood was up, and his men craved action. So off they rode. After the hard pursuit that dragged on for days, a skirmish erupted which proved bloodier than anticipated, with Fraser in the thick of the fighting. There were hundreds of casualties on both sides, and Fraser's beleaguered force had to be rescued by Hessian troops. Ned sensed the mood in General Burgoyne's camp change from elation to dread as news trickled. Indeed, Ned himself felt a mix of apprehension over the bloodshed and desire to have been there himself, proving he was as much a man as his illustrious ancestors and as fit to hold a sword as a pen.

The next time Edmund saw Fraser was when he finally returned to camp with his diminished advance guard. There was a glazed look in his eyes, the same Ned felt certain they had held when the general went hunting in the Highlands. Scarlet splattered his steed's neck, which Fraser was stroking to calm the anxious beast. Ned could not tell whether the blood originated from man or mount or both, but the sight of it chilled him.

Burgoyne came out of his tent, his eyes wide, his face white.

"My God, sir," he exhaled. "I heard rumors you'd been struck down, and I knew not whether to believe them."

Fraser shrugged as he was helped as an aide assisted him to dismount. "Believe no such thing of me, General, unless you see it for yourself." He gestured to the tent. "Let us consult."

They both went inside, and Ned kept at a distance, not hearing clearly what was said between them in hushed tones, but judging from Burgoyne's face that the news was as bad as they had all feared.

Ned watched as both generals leaned on the table over the map, with Fraser gesticulating broadly, presumably to show the route he had taken. Then Burgoyne blurted, "Bloody hell, Balnain, you're bleeding all over the map!"

"Some of that is bull's blood, slaughtered and eaten along the road," Fraser explained. "And some of it is Yankee blood, also shed with my sword…"

"And some of it is *your* blood," Burgoyne finished for him. "Go to the hospital!"

"'Tis a scratch, and nothing more," the Scotsman grunted. "I've given and received far worse. Believe me, there have been many more grievously injured…"

"Simon, are you going to make me order you?" Burgoyne's voice was taut as he said Fraser's Christian name. "I'm not going to stand here and watch you bleed. Get a fresh tourniquet on that arm…"

"The rebels fought well, too well, even hard-pressed," Fraser cut him off. "That's how they managed to escape to fight another day. That's why we were forced to abandon most of our wounded." He gave his fellow general a grim look. "This may be a longer and costlier game to play than we first thought."

"Whether or not that is the case, we will give better than we get, and persevere to the end," Burgoyne declared. "In the meantime, we must think in the short term as well as the long. Now go and be bandaged. For my sake. You do not know what state of mind I was in today at the prospect of losing you."

In spite of the disastrous pursuit, the recapture of Fort Ticonderoga still served as a boost to imperial morale, both in practical and symbolic terms. Not only was the stronghold strategically placed, and secured their supply line, but it was regarded by many to be a sort of shrine, sacred to the memory of Lord George Augustus Howe and so many other brave Britons who had perished while campaigning to wrest control of the stronghold from the French in the last war. Ned noticed the way Jonathan seemed to tread carefully near the fort, as if it were holy ground, still rich with the blood of the slain, including his late father, buried in some unknown common grave. Back then, men from the mother country and the colonials had been joined in both purpose and grief. Not so now.

Nevertheless, Britons had struck home, once again, and it seemed that Gentleman Johnny's great gamble was at least partly paying off. Furthermore, Burgoyne's select subordinates had demonstrated their dynamism beyond doubt. Fraser had long been close with Phillips, since their time fighting the French together on the continent, and the two generals were seen celebrating the recapture of Ticonderoga together after Fraser return.

"Even a hard ride through the stinking heat and a hard fight with the stinking rebels can't dampen my joy at your achievement," Fraser beamed, wiping his forehead with a handkerchief, then heartily shaking his friend's hand. "We're going places, you know that?"

Philips laughed. "As if we haven't been places already, you damned old Highlander?"

"Welshmen and Scotsmen have certain commonalities of origin," Fraser chortled. "It's in our blood to be ever-journeying! And look at you now! Putting even goats to shame with your climbing! There's no telling how high you'll go from here!"

"As Britannia rises in the world, so do her sons who prove themselves resilient in rocky terrain," Phillips declared.

"You're the proudest man of the proudest nation on earth, and I toast your name, sir!" Fraser raised his tankard to him, and Phillips bowed.

Baroness von Riedesel, having developed a fondness for both Fraser and Phillips, invited them to a celebratory luncheon along with her husband the baron and her children. There was much good-natured competition over which general would be named godfather of the couple's next child. At last, they proclaimed the only solution was to take it up on the dueling, and seemed to revel in the shocked expression of the baroness as they loudly debated whether to use swords or pistols.

After the respectable celebration with the baroness had concluded, Burgoyne, who had not been invited due to antipathy of the straight-laced Germanic hostess, responded to the slight by doing what he did best and throwing an extravagant counter-party in his tent to outdo her in the eyes of his generals. The wine, women, and song mania lasted into the early morning, and Ned was amused to hear a very intoxicated Burgoyne lead them in an old Royalist ditty, originally penned in support of King Charles I.

"Three merry boys came out of the west
To make saltpeter strong
They turned it into gunpowder
To charge the King's cannon!
And so let his health go round, go 'round,
And so let his health go round, 'round,
And so let his health go 'round!
God bless His Majesty,
And send him victory,
Over his enemies, over his enemies,
For anon!"

After the song had finally finished, when the "three merry boys" ran out of breath and could not go 'round anymore, Phillips felt the need to confess that the one weak link in his lineage of loyalty to the crown came in the form of Sir Richard Philipps, who had held Picton Castle for Cromwell during the civil war. Burgoyne, ever a Cavalier to the core, groaned. Fraser then felt the need to admit that his clan had stayed true to themselves and been dead split during that contest, causing both Burgoyne and Phillips to groan in unison. Ned, listening to the banter outside the tent, laughed into his hands.

The more Ned got to know General Philips, as the artilleryman kept company with Burgoyne and Fraser at work or in play, the more he found him to be a fascinating fellow, well-suited to the risk-taking that was part and parcel with their current military adventure. Matching his unlimited verve and audacity was an explosive disposition, quick to violent rages, but also quick to compose himself, with a disposition that drew some people towards him and repelled others from him. Love him or hate him, he drove everyone zealously to their duty through his own industriousness, and none dared shirk on his watch. He might have a temper that flared like dragon fire, but he was undeniably warm and resilient. Besides, when he liked a man, or sought to impress a lady, he could be the most pleasant, unselfish, and courteous soul in the world. He would loiter in Burgoyne's tent sometimes and chat with Ned about music, his favorite hobby horse besides his big guns.

"A well-rounded gentleman should make it his business to know the mathematics of music," Philips states. "It possesses a sort of magic, really, unmatched by any other art form. Painting, sculpture, architecture…all wonders to behold. But when a man lies dying, it's music he remembers. I've seen it, with men out of their head with fever. They'll still remember a song. Aye, we see it all the time, with men staggering through the smoke of battle, driven on by martial airs. It is music which gives us the will to live, and eases us into the final sleep."

"I agree, sir," Ned assured, "though I lack the talent to perform or direct. I simply listen, and let the fever work its effects upon me. My sister, though, is proficient at the harpsichord. She's tried to teach me to play duets with her, but I always prove a poor partner."

Phillips grinned mischievously. "I would like to meet this sister of yours and perhaps take your place beside her so she can teach me a song or two!"

"Nothing doing," Burgoyne declared. "She's my dear sweet recusant songbird, and I will defend her innocence with my life!" He gave Ned a quizzical look. "Don't trust this ravishing Celt, my boy! He struggles to control his passions!"

Phillips guffawed. "You're one to talk, Burgoyne! Besides, as Fraser said, I may have Arthur's blood in my body! How could I be anything but chivalrous? Our honor was forged by steel and stone before the coming of Normans and Saxons both!" He pointed at Burgoyne and Ned respectively, then added in a more solemn tone, "We were a people who dwelt in the twilight of many ages, between the sunset of one day and the dawn of another. We have seen many empires crumble and kingdoms fall, yet still fight, and streak the sky red with the heat of our blood." His eyes gleamed like blades as he recited from ancient poetry, "Men went to Catraeth with the dawn. Their fears left them, a hundred thousand and three hundred clashed together. They stained their spears, splashed with blood. He was at the forefront, foremost in battle, before the retinue of Mynyddog Mwynfawr."

"So did your ancestors distinguish themselves in battle by wearing leeks, blessed by Saint David of Wales, when he made the valley become a hill?" Ned queried brightly.

"Mayhap," Phillips replied. "You know your lore, lad!"

"As you can see, our young friend is an expert on all matters pertaining to the ancient saints and sages of the Isles," Burgoyne said.

"I used to read translations of the old chronicles, including Gildas and Geoffrey of Monmouth, that my father kept in his library," Ned recalled.

"And they recorded this one's ancestors, riding into every fray with fire-belching dragons on their shields?" Burgoyne teased, gesturing to Phillips.

"Of course, every fray," Phillips boasted. "It's not in our nature to sit on our laurels or our leeks!"

"No, because they were the first of the Britons," Burgoyne conceded. "You passed on your courage to the rest of us, even when we gave you grief."

"The Blessed Lady, ever virgin, was upon Arthur's shield," Ned murmured, recalling the illuminated script that kept him mesmerized as a child when reading these ancient tales.

Phillips smirked. "Careful. I might file a report and dock your pay!"

"That's what the text said, sir," Ned returned. "I was merely recounting it."

"Besides, Phillips," Burgoyne interjected, "surely your chivalry is not so base as to run dry in the company of virgins?"

The old veterans laughed while Ned blushed. But in truth he was grateful the topic had ended in a joke instead of a more serious accusation. To be fair, the Welshman didn't seem like the tattling type.

~

As the march proceeded, Gentleman Johnny continued to maintain the lifestyle to which he was accustomed and periodically throw parties for his top-tier officers, who did not seem inclined to complain. The downside was that it had a negative effect upon all their sleeping patterns. That being the case, it was Ned's duty to rouse Burgoyne from his alcohol-induced slumber in the aftermath of every jamboree. One morning, upon entering the tent, Ned found the general tangled up in his blankets, in a state of undress, with a girl, also unclothed, at his side.

While Burgoyne spent most nights next to his French-Canadian mistress, he also "explored the charms" of various camp followers, including Maggie, a down-to-earth Cornish laundry woman who Burgoyne specifically selected to wash his and the other staff members' clothes. She was often seen in or around the general's tent, her flaming red hair and sturdy hips causing most of the aides to ogle, though most liked her best for her sharp sense of humor. But this girl, lying beside Burgoyne in his post-party stupor, was different from the others. Ned had never seen her before. Was she a local of the region?

She stirred, her sleep ebbing out apace, and opened her eyes. They were wondrously icy blue, and Ned found himself mesmerized. She sat up, and he saw more of her, milk-white skin over a curvaceous form, offset by long tresses of willow-brown hair, streaked with strands of summer gold. Ned stared and he stared and he stared, for God only knew how long. Then Burgoyne awoke and laughed.

"Well, my young friend, we have no secrets from each other now!"

Ned snapped out of it and jerked his gaze away, shame catching in his throat.

"I'm s-s-sorry, sir. I didn't realize you were…"

"Indisposed?" the general chortled. "Well, there's no time like the present to get me in a better disposition. Go on, lad, do your duty! Fetch me a change of underwear!"

By the time Ned returned with the underwear from the baggage carts, he was both relieved and haunted by the fact that the girl was gone.

Later that evening, as Edmund tried to forget what he had seen by going about his camp duties alongside Jonathan, including selecting what foodstuffs and champagne bottles should be brought up front for the general's new few meals, Burgoyne summoned Ned back to his tent.

When Ned arrived, he found the blue-eyed girl sitting on the side of the general's cot. Ned felt relieved that at least she and Burgoyne, standing nearby, were both dressed, but Ned's eyes still lingered upon her longer than intended.

"This buxom young thing—what's your name, love?" Burgoyne queried.

"Abigail, sir," she answered meekly.

"Yes, Abigail…well, I've decided to make her a present to you."

"What…what do you mean…?"

"I mean she's all yours, Ned, in the flesh."

Ned felt himself flushing. "Sir…"

"Now you can't tell me she does nothing for you," Burgoyne chuckled. "You give her the same look every time you set eyes on her. Dare I say, she rouses your manhood in more ways than one!"

"I-I didn't mean to…" he stammered.

"Of course you didn't!" the general laughed. "It's really rather adorable how hard you try not to gawk. But I'm wise to these things." He gave a naughty glance down to Ned's breeches and winked. "There's no point in tormenting yourself any longer. I'm surrendering her to the better man."

"But sir!"

"Now, now, what are friends for? Besides, she's been bandied about a bit, but is far cleaner than the sort who've been on circuit for a decade!" He cast the girl a quick glance. "How long have you been at it again?"

She shrugged. "A year…a little more…"

"There! You see? Freshly plucked! There's risk to everything in this world, but what's the fun of it without rolling the dice once in a while? Take it from me! Still fit as a fiddle!"

Ned made momentary eye contact with her, but was unable to read her emotions one way or the other. "Sir, I-I can't…"

"I think you can," he insisted. "In fact, I have unshakable faith in you. If you're man enough to serve your country, then you're man enough to bed a woman."

Ned stood there like a statue, unsure how to escape or proceed. Then he turned to the girl again. He rather wanted her to protest against it, and at the same time, he did not want her to do that at all. It was true; he could not look at her without desire being kindled.

But it was wrong. Wrong. He knew it was wrong…

Yet he had done other things he believed were wrong.

Perhaps he had already sold his soul anyway.

Perhaps such scruples simply did not belong here, in the wilderness of another world.

"Now, dear Ned," Burgoyne chortled. "You look as if I'd asked you to take her out and shoot her. I'm not quite that monstrous. Besides, she and I have made arrangements. She came asking a favor, and I promised to try and do it for her if she showed you a good time from here on out." He turned back to her on the bed. "Isn't that right, love?"

She nodded.

"Well, don't just sit there, girl," he sighed. "Go to him!"

"She doesn't have to," Ned murmured. "If-if she doesn't want to, I don't want to…"

"It's transactional, Ned," Burgoyne clarified. "I assure you, she's put the stakes high!"

"The general's right," the girl stated, standing up and walking over to Ned. "It's all been arranged. I'm yours until New York. I'll keep my end of the bargain faithfully. I am here, at your pleasure."

He thought to make another objection, if he could think of one, but she had taken his hand, and it was warm. And he felt that warmth spread through every part of his being. So Burgoyne shooed them both outside, observing that it was growing late, and the night was theirs.

When she undressed and lay beside him, outside under the stars, he felt as if he were facing a hail of bullets for the first time. Perhaps he should have waited until after his baptism of fire, when his nerves were stronger. But he was lonely. And she was beautiful. A gift, indeed, a gift for the taking. How could he refuse that any longer? So he stripped himself to embrace her, and tried his best to erase the memory of Burgoyne bedding her the night before.

Her body was inviting, firm and supple, pale as a lily opening in spring. But her eyes were cold, like blue gems, or the great gush of the sea, between here and home. He wanted her, more than anything, yet also struggled to take her.

"Sorry," he mumbled, over and over again, as he tried to make love to her. "Sorry…I've never done this…" He was conscious of his own nakedness and felt ashamed. It was a sin, but at least he wished he was better at it. He might have asked Burgoyne or Fraser or Phillips about it, but they would have laughed good-naturedly at his innocence. He might have asked Jonathan, but his chaste married friend no doubt would have tried to talk him out of it and made Ned lose his courage.

He wondered what she was thinking of him as he touched and kissed her all over. She was probably comparing him to much more capable consorts. So he said "sorry" yet again, and struggled to stop shaking. When he met her eyes once more, they were a little less hard. Worse, they were pitying. He knew he should hate that, but there was a melancholy to it that spoke of some deeper ache in her own soul.

"They usually don't…kiss this much," she informed him.

"Oh?" He shrugged. "Sorry."

"They just…get on with it."

"Sorry, sorry…I've never done it…"

"You don't have to apologize," she assured. "You can do it however you like it."

He swallowed. "How-how do you like it?"

For the first time she smiled a little. "You're sweet."

"I'm making a fool of myself, you mean," he sighed, his face burning again.

"No, I don't mean that." She touched his face. "Don't be angry."

"I'm not…not at you," he said.

She gestured beside her. "We can just…be together, if you want. We can hold each other and kiss…until you're ready."

He knew he should probably have taken it poorly, being unmanned somehow, but he found himself saying, "Yes…I'd like that…"

It was a strange night. He felt as if it had occurred outside of time, because he could not properly reconstruct the sequence of events or how long they lasted, the cuddling, and kissing, and clumsily mating. He had a guilty feeling he might have gone too rough, maybe even bruised her, lost in the act, and he apologized yet again after he had been satisfied. She said it was alright, that anything he did was alright. That just made him feel worse. So he cuddled her more afterwards, and they lay in each other's arms, listening to the sounds of the wild creatures till they both were asleep.

He was very tired the next morning when he was roused to his duties, but it somehow felt worth it. Her eyes were so pretty in the morning, so very blue, and he thought they might have lost a little bit of their chill, towards him at least. But as the day wore on, he again felt pangs of guilt, and was unsure how to absolve himself. So he went to find her again.

"Hello, Abigail," Ned greeted her bashfully when he found her sitting on a wagon.

She smiled ever so slightly. "People have only ever called me Abigail when they're cross with me. Otherwise, it's Abby."

"Abby," Ned repeated, savoring the name. "May I sit with you?"

She shrugged, and scooted to the side, making room on the wagon seat for him. He climbed up and sat down beside her. He felt his old embarrassment coming back and lost his voice for several long, excruciating moments. Then he asked awkwardly, "May I, ummm…h-hold your hand?"

She laughed shortly. "We went a bit further than that, don't you think? You can do with me whatever you wish."

Ned turned his eyes down. "But…may I?"

There was a pause. Then she slowly offered him her hand. He loved the feel of it slipping into his, and he found it gave him courage.

"Would you mind…if I asked you questions about yourself?"

She tilted her head. "What kind?"

"I don't know, I just thought…I could ask about you, and you could ask about me, and maybe…we might become friends…"

She took her hand away from his, and he saw that her eyes had grown icy again. "Lieutenant, I am yours in any way a bold young officer of the King could want," she stated tartly. "I will do whatever is in my bodily power to make this journey enjoyable for you. However…" She glared at him. "I will never be friends with a redcoat who has come into my country to subdue her."

"Oh…" Ned exhaled. "So you're a rebel then?"

"A Patriot," she countered. "Yes."

"You're the first one I've talked to properly," he said. "I admit I'm surprised. A girl like yourself…"

"Girls cannot love their country?"

"Of course they can. But…"

"You mean you doubt it because I've made a whore of myself?" she blurted.

Ned hesitated in his response. "General Burgoyne said you came seeking a favor from him."

She nodded. "For my father. He was a printer in New York City. He loved liberty and wrote about it, article after article. When General Howe came, you people arrested him and smashed up his press. Then you took over our home, and…" She stopped, clenched her fists. "Well, he's in a prison hulk now. And I'll do anything, anything at all, to set him free."

Ned very gingerly reached over and touched her hand again. "I loved my own father dearly. I fully understand how much you must love yours."

Her eyes softened again momentarily, then they lit up with something new and fierce and even beautiful. "He taught me to love America, and to hate tyranny. Every one of his articles I read, and he let me edit them with my pen, and suggest words, and rearrange sentences, and we would work long into the night trying to make each line sound just right, and I was the happiest then…" She squinted at him. "You aren't listening to me."

"Sorry," he mumbled, having only vaguely registered her self-incriminating reminiscences. "You just…you looked quite pretty when you were talking just then."

"Oh, that's such a man's excuse," she sighed, shaking her head.

"But your eyes were so bright, and cheeks got all rosy, because you were happy," he said. "I…hadn't seen you like that before."

She gave him a side glance. "Just like a man."

"I know," Ned confessed. "It's a curse from birth, I'm afraid."

She surprised him by giggling into her hands. "So…what questions did you want to ask me?"

"I-I don't know," he admitted. "I suppose…I would ask if your hair always had gold streaked in it, or if that was from the sun…and what you used to daydream about as a child, when we all dream secret things we never tell anyone about…and what makes you smile, so that I can make you smile, and…"

"Stop," she murmured, turning her face away.

"I would ask about your favorite color…"

She turned her face back to him, and he saw a flash of anger across her features, and she shoved her mouth against his suddenly, almost violently, and started to force her hand down his breeches. This caused him to recoil from her and wipe his mouth with a trembling hand.

"Don't you understand?" she rasped. "That's what men want from me. That's what men get from me. You shouldn't want anything more."

Ned swallowed hard. "I-I don't know how to do it that way."

"Well, you'll learn."

"I don't think so."

She wrapped her arms around herself and shook her head. "Please." After ignoring him for nearly a minute, she turned back to him and said, "Stop looking at me like that."

"Like what?"

"It's not…you're not…" She sighed, exasperated.

"I would like very much if we could talk," he said softly. "I've been…lonely. It's all…strange, this new world I'm in. And what I did last night…"

"What would we talk about? My favorite color?"

"Maybe. I don't know. Anything. Everything. Except politics, I suppose."

She giggled again, in spite of herself. Then she said quietly, "It's blue."

"Mine too," Ned answered, gently taking her hand yet again.

~

The next day, Ned once again went to find Abby.

"Might you be inclined to go walking with me?" he inquired, holding up his satchel. "I plan on collecting some natural specimens."

She gave him a mystified look. "You are a strange one."

"You mean wanting to keep your company?"

"Well…this way, yes," she confirmed.

"I'm a northerner, and from the country, at that," Ned replied. "We're friendly."

She chuckled. "And I am a city girl, so nature hunts are not my specialty."

"I can show you how it's done," he insisted, extending a hand to her.

Again, she giggled, and reluctantly accepted.

As they wandered deep into the surrounding woods, collecting bark, lichen, acorns, pinecones, and even a snail shell, Ned realized he still hadn't gotten used to the vastness of the country, and the sense that, if they just trod their own path without a care in the world, they could get lost in it for days without running into another person. He almost wished he could do just that, and be all alone with her, dispelling with all memory of the military encampment and the uncomfortable circumstances that had thrown them together.

Although unaccustomed to such excursions, she seemed to rather enjoy the romp, and Ned noticed she was just as wide-eyed about the length and breadth of wilderness beyond the road as he was. She also was rather good at using her long fingernails to help pry free loose bits of bark and lichen, for which Ned pronounced her an asset to his foraging. She also seemed dedicated to organizing the collection when they returned to camp as well, according to shape, size, or color, and pressing the perishable leaves and flowers she found. This feminine eye reminded him of Tessie. He missed her so much. Did she ever miss him?

Of course, there were also downsides to bringing a woman out into the wild, mainly to do with her skirts. Abby complained repeatedly about him walking too fast, so he needed to consciously slacken his pace lest he lose her in a thicket. She also nearly took a tumble whilst trying to scramble up a slope, and when he reached out to help her regain her footing, they both ended up going down.

"Y'alright?"

She made a frustrated noise and fussed over the mud on her dress. He chuckled as he pulled out his handkerchief and cleaned the smudges off her face. "You really are a city girl, aren't you?"

"You're the one who made me fall!" she snorted.

"Me? I was being gallant!" he insisted, fixing a piece of hair that had come loose from her ponytail behind her ear.

"Well, maybe don't be," she grumbled, swatting his hand away.

"Awww…" Undeterred, he offered her his arm, which she reluctantly accepted, and after a few false starts, slipping in the mud, they managed to get back up again.

Then, as they headed back for the road, she got her skirt caught on a thorn bush. Ned, again struggling to measure his strides, heard her squeak from behind him and returned to rescue her.

"Don't touch anything," he instructed. "I'll set you free."

"A servant of Pharaoh, playing at being Moses?" she blurted.

He gave her a scolding look, and she turned her eyes down.

"The servants of our most Christian king are called upon to represent him chivalrously," he stated. But as soon as the words were out of his mouth, he could not help but feel stung by the hypocrisy of the situation. She had been given to him for his pleasure by the general himself, and he had not resisted the temptation. No, he had failed as a knight even as he played at being one now, freeing her skirt from the thorns with his bare hands. He hissed slightly through his teeth on instinct.

"You silly boy," she scolded him, taking his right hand, with two of his fingers and his palm dripping blood. "You've gone and hurt yourself!"

"Eh, it's not so bad," he insisted.

She clicked her tongue, then bent to pick up a strip of her torn skirt that had fluttered to the ground. Soon she was using it to bind his fingers and palm.

"So is your intention to emulate Sir Walter Raleigh, throwing his cloak over puddles for Queen Elizabeth to walk over?"

"Depends how much it rains here," Ned chortled.

"You must be used to getting deluged where you come from," she decided.

"N-no, not really…I mean, only sometimes. Like earlier this year…we did have some flooding…rather bad, if I'm honest. A farm child got washed away trying to save one of the landlord's sheep…"

"You're doing a poor job convincing me that it's not as bad as I thought," she snorted.

"Fair enough," he chuckled. "But the grass is very green from all the watering. And when the clouds do pass, the sky is ever so blue, like your eyes…" He placed a finger under her chin.

"You know, just looking into them, I feel less homesick. The mother is not far from the child in you."

She shrugged. "I have never set foot there in all my life. This continent is my only home."

"But your lineage…"

"Part English, yes, through my mother," she admitted. "But also Dutch through my father. My family name is Vanderkamp. General Fraser seized upon that with fervor."

"Did he?" Ned snorted.

"Yes, at General Burgoyne's tent party, after drinking down a bottle of whiskey. He pulled me onto his knee and regaled me with tales of time in Holland and the saucy Amsterdam lasses who flocked to him." She rolled her eyes.

"He likes to tell stories when his head starts to swim, I've noticed," Ned remarked, not particularly wanting to know what else the old Highlander may have done with her to amuse himself.

"And like me, you've been obliged to endure it so as not to give offense and end up getting your head sliced off by a broadsword?"

"Oh, I could listen to him for hours and not tire of it," Ned replied. "He's seen so much of the world…"

"As a mercenary," she retorted, wrinkling her nose.

"His family were rebels, and he found himself exiled," Ned countered. "I thought you of all people would be more understanding towards him."

She shrugged. "They wanted to replace one dynasty with another. Such wars have raged since the dawn of time. What we want to do is different."

"Yes, your father wants to replace a king with a committee," Ned surmised, not hiding his distaste.

"And so begin the world again, on more egalitarian grounds," she insisted. "Monarchs are fickle and always have been. Elizabeth had numerous courtiers banished or beheaded when they fell out of favor with her, for all their past chivalry."

"Well, in truth, I never liked her much, having been raised a Roman Catholic, although one of my patron saints was favored by her as a student and continued to pray for her even when he was about to be executed on her orders," Ned admitted. "But…well, it doesn't matter anymore. I'm an Englishman now beyond question, and the old ways are left behind."

"You mean you took the Test Act to don the King's livery."

He nodded again. "It…was worth it."

"Was it?" Abby asked, seeming to sense his guilt. "You know, in New York City, we have quite a wide variety of people. Anglicans, Calvinists, Quakers, Papists, and even Jews. Father taught me that our strength in this new world must be built upon respecting the liberty of conscience, something rarely attained in Europe, where everyone gives themselves over to persecuting the other." She slowly placed her hand on his arm. "Perhaps you and I are not so very different after all. We are…forced to be things which we are not by those in power over us."

"I came here to serve alongside my friends," Ned states. "It is my duty towards them…"

"Your friends, Lieutenant, or your oppressors?"

Ned was taken aback. "You sound like my mother now!"

"Well, maybe she was right all along."

He shook his head. "No. I could not keep living her way, cut off from the world and turning a blind eye to its joys and sorrows. I could not go on as a man without a country."

"Just make sure the country to which you offer yourself is worthy of your allegiance," Abby remarked.

"Is that how allegiance to the motherland works?" Ned queried. "That we judge her merits before giving her our hearts? Nae, surely we cannot do that, any more than we can do it with a woman we love, but must cast our entire selves into it without reserve. Otherwise, it is not pure…"

"So pure you would sacrifice your conscience for her?" Abby challenged.

Ned found he could not form a retort.

She seemed to intuit his pain and unexpectedly kissed his injured hand. Then she giggled. "You're blushing, Lieutenant."

Ned smiled bashfully. "I suppose I liked it. Do it again."

And she did.

~

Their walks over the course of the next week became more frequent. Whenever Ned could take a respite from work, and the train paused in its progress, he was spending time with Abby. Despite her original determination to shun his friendship, she was becoming increasingly open to conversing with him on an intimate level, particularly about their fathers, who they discovered had more similarities than differences.

"I miss my childhood days," Ned remarked. "I remember how, after being put to bed, I would get up again and sneak down into the library. Father was always there, studying by candlelight late into the night. He would pull me up on his knee and read me stories from old tomes. I loved the ones with pictures most of all, the sovereigns with their crowns and saints with their halos. Such splendid stuff." He felt a wave of sadness. "How I miss everything he was to me!"

"My father was much the same with me when I was growing up," she reflected. "I spent so many hours with him in his study, and we would discuss the news coming in from the diverse colonies. He would ask my opinions, and I believe he truly appreciated them. He taught me everything he would have taught a son, for he believed I took after him. He nurtured not only me, but also my mind." She squinted at Ned. "Are you one of those men who don't believe girls should be schooled the way boys are schooled?"

"I haven't given it much thought, to be honest," Ned admitted, "but given how much my mother and sister taught me, I would be a hypocrite to oppose the cultivation of the female intellect. I think your father was right to see himself in you."

"Good," she replied. "If you were not a redcoat, we might almost have been friends."

Ned laughed, a little bit nervously, then tried to flirt. "Can we not at least be friends when I take my coat off?"

She rolled her eyes. "Was that you being naughty?"

"I suppose," he chuckled. "But…I don't know, I suppose I hope you could see past the coat."

"Men aren't looking for friendship when they take their clothes off, unless they are old and lonely and confuse ardor with affection."

"I think ardor and affection might easily go hand-in-hand for me, just like the body and the soul," Ned stated. He glanced over at the brook running nearby. "Come on. Let's find its source."

They discovered a pool beneath a small waterfall that gurgled down a slope. It seemed the perfect spot to bathe, which Ned openly remarked upon. He surprised her by producing a chunk of fragrance-filled French soap he had snatched from one of the general's wagons. She gave a little squeal of delight, swearing she had given up on ever seeing proper soap again since leaving the city.

Then she raised an eyebrow. "So this was your plan all along, hmm? To get me in the water?"

He swallowed. "Well…I thought…we might…"

"I was given to you," she reminded him. "It's not unnatural that you should expect it."

"I-I don't expect it. I…I want to know if you might…" He paused. "Might be willing…"

The truth was that he wanted rather badly to try making love to her again, to see if he had improved in his ability, and to feel the tension in his body ease.

She obliged him. Of course she did. It was contractual. He didn't like it, but there it was, and he could have her, and he was thrilled and disturbed and obsessed all in the same instant. Soon they were taking off each other's clothes, with him reddening far more than her, and slipping into the pool. The temperature of the water and the scent of the soap were both refreshing, and Abby's mood seemed to soar as she washed away the grime from the road. Ned, too, felt a bit more like his old self now that his skin, at least, had been scrubbed clean. But his old self would never be bathing alongside a young lady. Had this new self begun the moment he had set pen to parchment, killing the boy and becoming the man through the taking of the Test Act? Perhaps. All the commandments seemed equally shattered somehow, just as when Adam sank his teeth into the fruit, and it felt both terrifying and liberating.

Yes.

Drown the boy.

Give breath to the man.

He repeated that to himself as he wrapped her in his arms, their legs intertwining and their mouths joined.

Ned felt more comfortable with their intimacy in the water. But in the daylight, he observed more clearly how she became almost inanimate during intercourse, a thing being acted upon with as little agency as a log, her eyes glassy and far away. He thought to say something, but he did not wish to force her to engage, nor, more selfishly, did he wish to remain unsatisfied.

"Are you alright?" he panted when he had finished.

"Of course," she said flatly, focus returning to his eyes. "You needn't always ask. I'm used to it, really I am."

"But you don't like it?" he surmised.

"I don't like it, nor dislike it," she replied. "I just…take whatever comes."

He swallowed hard. "Maybe I could find a way to do it so you would like it more."

She laughed shortly as she sat up. "You're a silly boy."

"But I can try, at least, if you tell me what you think you need from me…" His eyes trailed down to the water which he noticed was tinged slightly red. "Abby, did I make you bleed?"

"It's nothing," she assured.

"But you're not supposed to," he blurted. "Not…now. I-I know that much."

She touched his face. "I'm fine. A few drops of blood look so much worse in water."

"But…"

She pressed a finger to his lips. Then she happened to glance down and fixated for the first time upon the scar that wove its way like a ribbon around his side. "Good Lord, what happened to you?" she gasped, running her finger along the scar. "Was it from us…err, I mean, is it from battle?"

"Oh, no, not from your rebels," he chuckled. "Nothing so exciting, I'm afraid. I was in a local horse race when I was sixteen, and a friend–well, he's sometimes a friend anyway–lent me a mount from his family's stable...we didn't have any proper horses, you see. Weren't allowed to have them, nor indeed could we afford them. So it was kind of him to let me in. He wasn't a very good loser though. Had too much pride and too hot a temper to be beaten by his own horse. So he came up behind when I'd crossed the finish line, called me a damn saucy Papist, and pushed me out of the saddle. My leg got caught in the stirrup and I was dragged."

"That's awful," she murmured.

"Yes, it wasn't pretty. I must've struck a stick or something on the ground, because my side got a good deep gash in it. They had to stitch me up like a ragdoll. Poor Jack…he hadn't meant for that to happen. He was the one who rode ahead and grabbed the reins to stop me from being dragged farther. Then he made quite a fuss seeing the wretched state I was in. I think all the blood on my waistcoat scared him. He thought he had right well murdered me…"

"Doesn't sound like a very good friend," she remarked. "He was more worried about himself than you."

"Oh, I think he was worried for himself and for me in equal measure. He was really rather sweet to me when I was recovering...well, sweet for him, anyway. I would be resting out in a little shack by our garden...needs to be renovated rather badly, but it's nice to hear the birds and smell green things growing. He would show up at the windowsill whistling 'Lillibulero' and drop off muffins from the family kitchen, because I didn't have much of an appetite for heartier fare. Then he would sit up there and tease me mercilessly like he always did, and tell me all the news in the village...that made me smile."

"Did he ever say he was sorry?" she asked.

"He was bad at apologizing for things...too much arrogance. But one day, all of a sudden, he asked if I had forgiven him. I made a joke. I thought he was just needling me. But he looked quite sad afterwards, so I told him that I had. He came over and hugged me...shocked me out of my mind, and made my side smart, but I didn't stop him. Felt good in its own way...I was still quite weak, so he just held me like that for a while, with my head on his chest." Ned smirked. "Then he pinched my cheek like he used to do in backyard fights when we were children. We would wrestle around until he had me straddled, then he'd mock me for my baby face." He shook his head and laughed. "He was always careful that my mother didn't see him when he came visiting, or she would have told the gardener to chase him off with a shovel. She considered him the worst influence. She even said the accident was God's way of warning me not to keep company with Protestant ruffians."

"Did you continue to keep company with them?"

"Yes, of course I did, if they let me. They were...my friends. Besides, Jack broke the rules and taught me how to fence on the slide. And I was bloody terrible at it. That's why he taught me, I imagine...his skill seemed to increase, just by comparison! And I suppose he reckoned this Papist wasn't too great a risk to the public good with a blade in his hand, for I could only cause injury by lucky accident!"

She laughed lightly. "And what's your troublesome friend up to these days? Getting himself embroiled in affairs of honor left, right, and center?"

"Well, actually, he's on this very train," Ned said. "Just on the far other end of it with his regiment. We've exchanged several messages since our arrival upon this continent, in which he continues to tease me mercilessly, but he's not the sort given to writing copiously. We've both been kept so busy, with me as a staff officer and him as a regimental officer, that we've not had the chance as of yet for a proper reunion."

"I'll be sure to stay out of sight whenever the reunion happens," she mumbled.

"Oh, but I would make sure he treated you like a lady," Ned insisted. "By all that's holy, that's what I'd do."

"A lady," she repeated, seeming to find the application of the honorific to be quite ironic, then blushed.

"Yes, I'd expect that from any friend of mine, or I'd blot them from my book." He smiled fondly. "You would quite like another friend of mine, Paul. I met him just before we all set sail, at a breakfast for recruits, but we got on as if we'd known each other forever. He's written me much longer messages than dear Jack, describing absolutely everything he sees in this new world. But he is busy with his own regiment, and I have yet to meet him on this side of the water. I think you'd like him, actually. The lad has a very kindly disposition."

She shrugged. "You're the only redcoat I'll bear up with on this march."

"For...the transaction."

"Of course."

She stared down at the grass for several moments, then unexpectedly, she leaned over and kissed along Ned's scar, as if that might heal it.

"Ha," he exclaimed. "It tickles."

They started to help each other dress, Ned pointing out that Abby always seemed to forget his second button, and Abby retorting he seemed to always miss her third. Spontaneously, he leaned over and kissed her on the neck, which seemed to catch her off guard, and she swatted at him. He tilted his head, puzzled.

"So you may peck at me, but I may not peck at you, is that it?"

She shrugged. "You can do whatever you want."

"Now, really, I'll never figure out what you like at this rate," he protested.

"I'm...particular. Like a cat, I suppose."

He chuckled. "I suppose I need to get used to the behavior of cats. I'm more of a dog person. Comes with the territory when you own sheep."

She smiled. "Sheep?"

He nodded. "Five of them."

"Do they ever let you hand-feed them?"

"Yes. We raised them from lambs for their wool. They trust us completely." He smiled in return. "I would have taught you how to do it without getting bitten."

She giggled. "I would have liked that."

As they walked back to camp, hand-in-hand, they spied a doe drinking from the stream. Behind her was a fawn.

"Oh," she breathed. "I wish I could feed them…with handfuls of oats or something…I'm sure their mouths are very soft…"

She sounded so full of innocence, his heart began to hurt. He nuzzled his face into her hair affectionately, and she leaned into his shoulder. Then he pressed his lips against her forehead, and she did not pull away.

~

As time passed, Abby became as important to Ned as food and drink and sleep. She was that one lovely thing available to him when there was little other loveliness to be had. He was willing to trick himself into believing he had won her favor, for he could make her smile and sometimes laugh, although she continued to look upon all other redcoats in the camp with the same stony stare. And sometimes, when he woke up beside her, he found that she had been watching him asleep with that very same terrifying look. But when their waking eyes met, she would seem to remember who he was and her gaze would soften. Then they would start to talk more about New York and Old Lancashire, distracting each other from their current situation, and nothing else seemed to matter.

Aside from their conversations, Ned liked doing nice things for her, like giving her flowers and beads he acquired from the Indians that matched the color of her eyes. She seemed surprised each time, and that just made him more eager to present her with tokens of his affection. He continued to take her on walks and sometimes spontaneous picnics. And she continued to let him release his passions upon her, flesh upon flesh, often fumbling, a strange awkward exhilaration always accompanying it. Maybe she would get to like it, he thought to himself. Maybe she would find her heart fluttering along with his someday soon.

Yes, the more time Ned spent with Abby, the more he wanted to find out how to please her when they made love. She told him not to let it bother him, for she was past the point of pleasing or displeasing. But this only bothered him more. So he broke down and asked Burgoyne for advice on how to satisfy women. The mischievous gleam in Gentleman Johnny's eyes made Ned regret his inquiry. The general clearly relished being sought after as some sort of expert on generating warmth beneath the sheets, and offered a litany of suggestions that made Edmund's cheeks catch fire. The more he blushed, the more Burgoyne seemed entertained as he acquainted his young charge with all manner of colorful phrases to describe colorful acts he had up to this point restrained himself from using in the youth's presence.

"Trust me, Ned, you'll have them eating out of your hand," the general insisted every time Ned questioned if one or another unorthodox method of love-making was really what women wanted. "It's been proven!"

Things only got worse when Fraser happened to stop by the tent, and Burgoyne immediately drew him into the conversation, despite all of Ned's best efforts to prevent it by excusing himself. Burgoyne would simply not allow him to be excused. Fraser had a smirk on his face as Burgoyne rattled on, then he leaned over and whispered something into his fellow general's ear, causing Gentleman Johnny to laugh heartily.

"Lord have mercy, Balnain, that's too much!"

"It works," Fraser insisted. "Take it from a respectable married man…"

"A Highland rogue, you mean! I'm not repeating it aloud, saints preserve me!" Burgoyne gestured to Ned. "Look at the poor lamb, embarrassed half to death already!"

Ned was indeed wishing he might sink even further down into his chair.

"Don't mind us, lad," Fraser consoled him. "We…uh…we get like this sometimes…"

"We need an intervention," Burgoyne exhaled.

"I suppose we should be each other's intervention, but…"

"It's not working, Balnain. We need someone from the outside…"

"General Phillips?" Fraser suggested, and Burgoyne guffawed.

By the time they finally allowed Ned to leave, Burgoyne and Fraser were giggling together like naughty schoolboys. He was decidedly unsure if he should dare to try any of their suggestions on Abby. The last thing he wanted was to repulse her.

A few hours later, General Phillips marched resolutely up to him, his dog barking at his side.

"Listen, boy," he said gruffly. "Don't follow the advice of those two perverted friends of mine. I love them, but they are being idiots."

Ned squinted. Phillips had garnered a reputation of his own for bragging about his conquests and producing illegitimate children.

"Alright, alright, maybe I'm no better in various ways, and I judge Fraser to be better than both Burgoyne and myself, thanks to his husbandly attachment. But I have enough intelligence to counsel beginners like beginners!"

"Thank you, sir," Ned mumbled, just relieved someone was making sense.

"My pleasure. Just wanted to prevent you from landing yourself or anyone else in a hospital tent. Besides, fantasy and reality are distinct, and I seriously doubt my illustrious commanding counterparts have tried even half of what they suggested, the show-offs!"

And so the Welshman offered his own earthy advice. At the very least, it did sound rather more doable than the previous options. Ned decided it would be best to simply keep it all in mind, and play it very much by ear.

But before he could even experiment with any of it, Abby refused him intimacy. She had a reason, though. It was her time of the month.

"Men always forget about such things," Abby mumbled, "or act as if we are making an undue fuss…"

"Oh, but I have a sister," he reminded her. "So I've been made more aware of such realities."

"Lucky you," she sighed miserably, curling up the blanket.

He smoothed out some wrinkles in the blanket tenderly. "I wish I could take you home right now to meet Tessie. I think she'd welcome you with open arms, and make you comfortable, and you could both talk about…girl things…"

She sorted. "You really are ridiculous."

He tilted his head. "Why?"

"Because…I'm not the sort of girl you'd take home to your family," she said. "Not now, anyway."

"I would do it, Abby," he said softly, stroking her hair.

She gave him a long look, one strained with sadness. "Ridiculous," she whispered, and he thought she might cry.

"May I stay with you tonight?" he asked. "Not for…well, you know. Just to…be near you."

"If you wish," she rasped.

So he lay down beside her, under the blanket, and held her in his arms, her face buried in his chest, and his face buried in her hair. And he thought he would be content even to die like that.

Jonathan, meanwhile, had become increasingly concerned about Ned's amorous adventure, and though he held his tongue for a while, he finally chose to confront him about it directly.

"This isn't like you, Ned," Jonathan remarked.

"What do you mean?" Ned retorted. "You haven't known me for that long."

"It's not necessary for me to," Jonathan decided. "You're not General Burgoyne, however much you think of him. Fornication doesn't suit you."

"You sound like Thompson now," Ned ground out, frustration cloaking his guilt.

"He's not always wrong," Jonathan reminded him. "You know in your own heart it's belittling both to her and to you, using her as you are."

Ned clenched his fists at his side. "I'm not using her."

"Oh, no?"

"No. I…care for her."

"Is this caring for her? Really? Her honor has already been compromised, and you do nothing but continue to compromise it. And what if you put a child in her belly? Have you given no thought to that?"

That possibility cut him to the quick, and he lashed out, "It's none of your affair!"

Jonathan was undeterred. "You should either put an end to this dalliance, or make an honest woman of her. You know that, under God. But you won't do the former because you've grown attached, in body and heart. And you won't do the latter because you're afraid of her."

"Afraid of her?" Ned repeated incredulously.

"Yes. I honestly don't know how you sleep next to her. I know I couldn't share a bed with Elizabeth if I thought she might stick a knife between my ribs any odd night…"

"I don't think that!"

"The girl is a rebel, with hatred in her heart for us all…"

"Not for me," Ned shot back.

"Sometimes yes, sometimes no," Jonathan countered. "We see her watching you sometimes, when she's at a distance, and there's something wrong with it. She loves you and hates you all at once. The fact is…I don't think she's alright in the head. Maggie has the same suspicion, and she spends more time with her than either of us, in the women's wagons. She says Abigail has outbursts, sometimes violent ones…"

"Maggie's just jealous of her because Abby used to be a lady," Ned blurted.

Jonathan squinted. "That's not being fair to either of them, and it's not like you to speak so."

Ned gave him a hard look. "Well, it's not like me to be on this march! It's not like me to be…" His voice trailed off, as a fresh wave of guilt over his apostasy swept over him. "What I mean to say is…I'm very different than I used to be, for better or worse, Jonathan."

Jonathan reached over and touched his shoulder. "I told you it would take time to adapt. You just mustn't hurt yourself too badly in the interim."

But Ned refused to heed Jonathan's words.

A week later, the train stopped for a brief respite, with the general's camp pitched nearby a large abandoned barn. Middle class British camp followers and Loyalist girls from families who had followed the train took part in an evening of entertainment with the young officers, where music and punch flowed. Ned insisted that Abby come along with him, and reluctantly, she obliged.

"Do you dance?" he asked her as they crossed the threshold, observing that the dancing was already well underway.

She turned up her nose at him. "You think all American girls are uncivilized, do you?"

"I didn't say that…"

"No, but you thought it," she decided. "I'll have you know that I was tutored by one of the finest teachers in New York City regarding etiquette and dancing since the age of nine. I excelled at both."

"Good for you, miss," Ned chuckled.

"And you?" She folded her hands over her chest. "Do you dance, sir?"

"We can find out." He offered her his arm.

She took it, a light coming into her eyes he had never seen there before. And suddenly he knew, without reserve, he was falling in love. She was destined to be his mate, it seemed, before either of them were born.

Yes, they both could dance, for he too had learned as a child, mainly in a large barn at communal country dances, so far from her city drawing room. She was more elegant at it than he was, and was soon scolding him for stepping on her feet. But she was smiling at him the whole time, and did not seem inclined to stop. They were lost in their own little world, and cared not a fig if they stuck out.

"The Tory women are staring at us," she observed as they danced.

"Let 'em stare," he responded. "I am content with my *belle rebelle*."

She snorted. "You're ridiculous."

"I know," he conceded. "Do you mind very much?"

She rolled her eyes and smoothed out several lumps in his coat. "The color displeases me, but I shan't be caught dancing with an untidy man."

"I appreciate your high standards," he quipped.

They did better at the reels than the minuets, for Ned enjoyed getting lost in the motion and the sound of his partner's laughter as he whirled her around.

But soon even Ned grew dizzy, to Abby's amusement, and after they both downed some punch, they agreed to escape the stuffy barn for the cool night air. They went meandering through the nearby woods, hand-in-hand, chatting lightly about Tory girls throwing themselves at this or that soldier, probably trying to lure them into a scandalously quaint bed-bundling ritual, where the man would sleep beside a woman, but only after being sewn into their sheets.

When they reached the edge of a small brook, they both tossed pebbles in for good luck. For a girl, he had to admit, she had a very good throw. Then sat himself down on a large smooth rock. "Come on, then," he coaxed her. "Sit with me."

"But there's no room," she responded playfully.

He tapped his upper leg. "Yes, there is. Give it a try." Ned smiled at her bashfully as she sat on his knee. He wrapped his arms around her back and sang in a wobbly voice, "Give me a kiss, pretty lady…"

They both laughed a little, and then he felt her lips brush his right cheek, then his left. The tenderness of it made him blush, and he nuzzled his face into her shoulder, kissing her slender neck. He felt her body settle in his arms, and felt her heart beating in time with his as his mouth met hers. As the moments melted together, and Ned put into practice some of the suggestions General Phillips had given him, she seemed to become more passionate, responding to his touch and moaning with pleasure. He too felt more heated at the prospect of having finally learned to please her. With his one hand already down her bodice, he started to reach up her skirts with the one. Then all hell broke loose.

He was not sure what he did wrong, but he knew he had done it, all the same. For a moment, her entire body went stiff. Somehow, he knew instinctively what was coming, but there was no time to protect himself as pain shot through his cheek from her fingernails and through his lip from her teeth. He felt as if his heart might stop from the shock, as he struggled to push her off of him, and they both tumbled into the grass, wrestling on the ground. He finally pinned her down, though she screamed and punched him in the chest over and over again. He managed to seize both wrists and stretched out her arms against the churned up dirt. She continued to spit and kick and writhe until at last, with a moan of defeat, she stopped fighting, her strength all gone.

Overpowered, she looked past Ned's face, up at the sky, as if trying to empty her mind of everything, trying to steel herself for what was to come. She started singing under her breath a macabre rhyme, "Stick, stock, stone dead…dye her petticoats rosy red…tie her up in a old mare's hide…lay her down and break her pride...beat her blue, beat her black…tie her up in an flour sack…drown her where the waves do roll…let the devil take her soul..."

She shifted slightly, in a last effort to free herself, then opened her legs wide in despair.

Ned felt sure he might vomit as he released her wrists and leaned up from her. She remained outstretched, unmoving, her eyes like glass, her breast heaving. Moved to compassion, he touched her tangled hair.

To his horror, she jerked upright, her eyes filled with savagery, then crouched, like a wild animal, and growled at him. It was as if she had been hideously transformed into something beastly, her back curved, her fingers like claws, dug into the ground, her teeth gleaming.

"Abby," he choked out her name, terror swelling his throat.

Slowly, his voice seemed to seep into her consciousness, and she began to resemble a human again, though her back remained arched, and her whole frame was trembling.

"D-d-don't hurt me," she stuttered, visibly scared almost to death.

"Abby," he repeated again, his heart breaking, reaching out to her once more.

"Stop," she pleaded. "Stop! Stay away! Stay away!" She curled up into a ball, hands over her head. "Don't touch me!"

Ned could bear the piteous scene no longer, and hurriedly struggled to his feet, then rushed back to camp, his stomach tied into a thousand knots. Perhaps Jonathan had been right all along.

Well past midnight, she came to him when he was bedded down for the night, her eyes bloodshot and face streaked with tears. But at least she seemed to have returned fully to her human form again.

"Ned," she whispered. "Don't hate me too much, please."

He sat up a little. "I-I don't. I just…I don't know what I did wrong, nor what I turned you into…" He touched the scratch marks on his cheek, and the incision on his lip.

"I'm sorry," she apologized. "I'm so sorry. I wasn't thinking when I did that. I swear I wasn't. I was just…afraid…"

"Why, Abby?"

She avoided the question, and begged, "Please, Ned. Forgive me. Please take me back."

"I forgive you," he assured. "But…I don't believe it would be wise to carry on as we have."

"But I won't do it again. I'll force myself to do better. I swear I will, Ned. I'll be a good girl…"

Something about the last line made him shudder. "Did someone you lay with before tell you to be a good girl, or else they would hurt you?"

"Oh, they all want me to be a good girl," she giggled, eerily, "even though they are bad boys. And when I'm not good enough, well…they teach me a lesson. That's…just how it goes…"

"How many have you lain with?" he blurted. He knew it was rude, but he felt some burning need to understand the origin of her agonies.

"I don't know," she admitted. "Three or four the first time, God knows how many since. It's a blur."

"What?" he gasped.

She gave him a quizzical look. "You're too nice, Ned. Altogether too nice for that coat of yours."

"I'm proud to wear it," Edmund retorted. "I'm proud to serve my king."

"All I see is a bloody butcher's apron, I'm afraid," she croaked. "I like it better when we're naked, then I don't have to think about it anymore. You have a way of making me forget about it sometimes, even when you are wearing it, but…" Her voice trailed off. "I-I'm rather broken inside, you see, and I do not know if I can ever be fixed. Still…" She swallowed hard. "Back before the wars, I used to dream of a charming young man who would come and court me with flowers and pretty words…like you've been doing. Hard to believe now, isn't it?"

"No," Ned answered gently. "Not hard at all. There is nothing you deserve more."

She wiped the tears away with her sleeve. "Well, such dreams were stolen, along with my virtue."

Edmund leaned up a little. "What happened, Abby? I mean, the first time?"

She shrugged. "The redcoats occupying New York…well, they're out for booty. I was booty to them. They took my father away, then robbed the house. I was part of the house to them. And…they took me, all at once."

Ned felt his stomach flip yet again. "Did you ever report them for punishment to their superior officer?"

She snorted. "Their officer was with them. He congratulated me on bearing up with it. Said we Yankee women were made of sturdy stuff. The truth was I froze. It hurt too much. But he just took my room for his own and broke me in further, every night afterwards for weeks. I only stayed sane by going numb. After that…I was passed around…then started passing myself around…until there was very little of me left…"

Edmund found himself at a loss for words for a long, long time. At last, he asked quietly, "General Burgoyne…he didn't hurt you, did he?"

"He wasn't mean about it, if that's what you're asking," she answered bitterly. "He's the sort who doesn't like to break his toys, credit where credit is due."

He winced. "I-I don't think you're a toy, Abby."

"Don't you?" she laughed, and there was no mirth in it.

"No." He bit his lip. "Please believe me."

She turned her eyes down. "I want to, very much. But perhaps along with my virtue, I have lost my faith."

"It was not your virtue that was lost," he replied. "It was their honor and humanity."

"But don't you see, Ned? It's so very common for soldiers to view women as creatures incapable of feeling, mere spoils of war to be used and cast aside. More girls are suffering what I went through every day this wretched war lasts...the shame and the pain and the prayers they would just be killed instead…" She inhaled. "When it's happening to you…you can't quite believe it. Yes, maybe this sort of unspeakable thing happens to other girls, ones you don't really know, but surely it would never happen to you. You keep expecting someone to stop it, someone to come in and rescue you, like in stories you grow up with. But…it doesn't happen…"

"I won't let anyone hurt you again, Abby. I swear it." Edmund sighed and added, "That includes myself."

Her eyes took on a strange sheen. "I remember one night, when that officer forced himself on me in my own bed. I had submitted to him for almost a month out of fear…and numbness. But that night…I broke down and begged him again and again to stop. I thought maybe, just maybe, he would remember I could feel too. But all he did was call me nothing but a Yankee whore and punish me by going harder. Then he said a rhyme in my ear, every time I asked him to stop, and made me repeat it to show I was going to be…a g-g-good girl…" She shuddered. "It-it hurt so much, Ned…in my body, in my heart…whatever was left of either." She stared at him for a long moment. "That's what I thought of, all of a sudden, not even wanting to...when you were touching me…"

Edmund pressed a hand to his face for a long moment, his cheeks burning. At last he murmured, "Then I won't touch you again."

"But Ned," she rasped. "I must...must get help for my father, Ned. The treatment of the men on those prison hulks is monstrous. The soldiers torment their prisoners, like demons guarding the gates of hell. They mocked my father when he was too weak to sit up, because he was no more than skin and bones. They're not even human, not doing what they do."

Ned swallowed. "There must be a great influx of prisoners they don't know what to do with. But General Howe and his brother the admiral always sympathized with these colonies. Surely they would not approve…"

"Don't defend them, Ned, please!" she blurted. "The ones doing it know exactly what they are about, and Howe washes his hands like Pilate!"

Ned winced. "I'm sorry. I didn't mean to doubt you. I just…I don't like to think about people being that far gone, is all."

"Well, they are. They're letting Americans, their brethren in blood, die by the thousands, from starvation and disease, then burying them quickly in the mud flats!" She tilted her head. "If it was your father wasting away in there, what would you do?"

"Go a bit mad, most likely," Ned admitted.

She laughed shortly, strangely. "Yes, my dear, I've gone a bit mad!" Then she buried her face in wrists, as if trying to block out memories from her mind. "Please, Ned, please...I don't want to have to hate you...you're a fool farm boy with a silly, honest face, and I can't hate you!" At that, she started to weep into her hands.

Ned wasn't sure how to respond without making things worse, but found himself saying softly, "Thank you." He paused for a moment, then added, "But you don't have to lie with me anymore to aid your father. There's another way."

"But General Burgoyne..."

"I will tell General Burgoyne only what he wishes to hear on the matter. He will still help your father based upon his pledge. And as far as any other soldiers know...you are still under my protection. If they try to touch you, they will have to answer to me."

She blinked. "You would do that for me?"

He nodded.

"But why, Ned?"

"Because," he said, "you're a lady."

A tear trickled down her cheek. "And you're a gentleman."

"There are gentlemen in this army, Abby, not only brutes," he assured her.

"When I first got here, the guards wouldn't let me get near Burgoyne till I had pleasured them," she informed him bitterly. "They roughed me up something terrible. I-I was in a state by the time I reached the general's tent..." She shook her head. "A good man is hard to find, Ned."

Edmund felt a deep pity for her and shame over the behavior of his fellow soldiers. Not sure what else to do to comfort her, he opened his arms, and she looked at him in a dubious manner. He waited, not wanting to frighten her, but hoping she might come to him.

After a long while she did, gingerly easing into his embrace, her head resting on his shoulder. She shivered, and he tucked the blanket around her. They cuddled like that for the remainder of the night, and he felt her trust in him growing as the hours passed by. It was such a precious thing to gain.

"Ned," she murmured after a while. "Will-will you still...bring me flowers and...keep me company? I-I'm all alone, Ned..."

"It will be an honor," he replied.

She sniffled. "I get...so very scared sometimes...like the world is a monster out to devour me, wherever I turn...sometimes I can't tell what's real and what's not..."

"Don't be afraid. I'm here," he assured, gently stroking her hair, "I'm real. And I would rather cut off my right hand than hurt you."

"I believe you, dear Ned," she whispered, and held him close.

Chapter 24: THE WOOING

In the following days, General Burgoyne's staff made camp on the property of the Reverend Isaac Sexton, a Loyalist vicar who had been driven from his parish by his mostly rebel congregation. Fearful they might drive him from his home next, Sexton welcomed the arrival of the King's troops with open arms. Burgoyne found himself not only wined and dined by the vicar, but also approached with petitions from the local Tories for all manner of redress, as if he were the King himself. Most had lost something or other to the rebels, be it some piece of property or manner or bread-winning, and while it was clear Burgoyne sympathized with their plight, he was in no position to restore them to their former estates, not yet. He would have to win the long game first. In order to do so, he needed the Loyalists to support him before he could compensate them.

Reverend Sexton was a widower, with four children to his name, first a boy aged twenty-one, followed by two girls aged eighteen and sixteen respectively, and then another boy, aged ten. Andrew Sexton, the eldest son, was a strapping lad who pleased Burgoyne immensely by his willingness to take up arms for the royal cause, promising to follow the British wagons when they rolled out. Fidelity Sexton, the eldest daughter, got on the wrong side of the general, however, when she quite bluntly protested Burgoyne's intention of sharing the guest room with a woman who was most assuredly not his wife.

"My father may no longer have a parish, sir," said Fidelity, "but he is still a man of the cloth and a preacher of the Gospel. It is unseemly that adultery should take place under his roof."

Burgoyne flushed from a mixture of anger and shame, then blurted to his host, "Reverend, you should teach your daughter to curb her tongue. Does she not realize we are here to punish those who exiled you from your pulpit?"

"Forgive my daughter's impetuousness," her father sighed. "Like many women, she leans towards enthusiasm…"

"Surely, General, I have spoken no falsehood against you," Fidelity countered. "She is another man's wife…"

"And I am an officer of the King," Burgoyne snapped. "I represent his will, and as such could commandeer any room I wished for whomever I wished."

She gave him a long, unyielding look. "I believe, sir, that the King would be on my side. Yes, even if you and you alone secured him an empire, destined to last for a thousand years, he would still abide by the truth. If you represent him here, then represent him in truth."

Burgoyne stared at her in return, then chuckled. "I suppose His Majesty's penchant for chastity and distaste of that which falls short is well-known, even on the far end of the empire."

"Yes, sir. I hear he is positively stubborn about the subject…as am I."

"Hell, someone should make you a lady preacher, protocol be damned!" He turned to her father. "Yes, you get the parish back, and let her run it!" He laughed heartily as the vicar blushed. "Now, my good sir…set aside a room for myself and another for my…traveling companion. Not too far apart, though! You see, I'm willing to compromise between honor and comfort if you pious folk are!"

Eli, meanwhile, stood at the door, watching the whole exchange with rapt fascination, which had now turned to a thrilled admiration at the slip of a girl taking on the general.

She was plain-faced and pink-cheeked, with intelligent brown eyes that were often circled by spectacles, balanced on her small nose for reading. And after the first day, she was regularly seen by the general's staff, usually reading, in the house or in the orchard. She seemed to truly savor her devotional books of poetry and prose. Her clothes were always tidy but unostentatious compared to the dresses worn by her younger sister Penelope. Her hair was always tied up tightly, usually under her bonnet, except on some truly lovely days when she took it off, sitting on a bench outside and letting the breeze blow through a few of her loose locks.

And Ned had noticed Eli continued to watch her whenever she appeared, a look of bliss on his face, then flushing, he would march off.

Jonathan seemed to pick up on the younger man's affliction, and took it upon himself to have a little talk with him. Ned watched from the other side of the wagon so he would not be spotted by either party.

"You think Miss Sexton is comely, don't you, Thompson?" Jonathan queried.

Eli turned red again. "You're making fun of me."

"No, no, I'm not," Jonathan assured kindly.

Eli swallowed awkwardly. "I wasn't thinking anything dirty."

"I didn't say you were," Jonathan countered. "It's a natural enough thing for a young man to admire a young lady."

"Yes, but…" Eli paused. "It's hopeless."

"Why do you say that?"

"Because...I'm me."

"Nonsense," Jonathan replied. "You haven't even tried yet."

"I'd just make a fool of myself. She's of finer quality than I have a right to hope for. And I'm not...charming. You know that."

"I'm not exactly Lovelace myself, but I'm a married man," Jonathan replied.

Eli tilted his head. "And how did you go about wooing your wife?"

Jonathan cleared his throat. "I, uhh...I'm not entirely sure that I did."

"Well, you must have caught her attention somehow…"

"Yes, but that was entirely by accident. You see, our regiment was at a local social, and I was sitting in the corner, contemplating how I didn't want to be there, when up she marched, telling me I had an ink blotch on my coat. Then she started dabbing at it with a napkin, making it much worse. It was all rather embarrassing, but before I could stop her, she was telling me my specs were in such a state, and soon she had snatched them up and was cleaning them too, and I just sat there blind as a bat till she gave them back. I could see better, I had to admit."

"So you married her because she was good at cleaning spectacles?"

"Well, no, or at least not right off. We got into a little fight when she made me dance with her, and tried to get my opinion on the bread pudding she had torn me away from eating. I did not report as well as I should have, and she demanded to know if I could do any better. I gave her some very sound suggestions on how it could have been improved upon, and she said I should have been a cook instead of a clerk, and off she stormed red-faced, for I realized now it was her pudding. Next morning before our regiment went off to Dover, she had come looking for me to inaugurate an exchange of recipes which we would conduct by mail."

"But it didn't remain just recipes?" Eli surmised.

"No, it didn't. It gets quite lonely out in Dover. And the castle we bunked down in sometimes was said to be haunted by Saxon ghosts. So I told her about the ghosts, and we started this little game where we would make up stories about who the ghosts were and how they got there. It got quite melodramatic at times and comical at others. It was a pleasant distraction from the paperwork I was supposed to complete."

Eli raised an eyebrow. "So...how did you propose?"

"Well, when my we got back from Dover around Christmas, and I thought to pay her a visit, her village being a stone's throw from mine...she said that she wasn't sure I intended to ask, but given how nervous I was acting, it might be so, and if it were, I should really get it over with, because she had her heart set on being married in spring where she could get the kinds of flowers that would be out of season if we lagged about until summer. There was so much to be done, so it would be prudent to plan ahead. She asked if I saw the prudence in getting an early start, and I said...yes. She took that as a yes for everything, and the rest is history. Oh, and as a footnote to history...she had me make the bread pudding, but she was much better at roasting the duck I shot in the New Forest."

Eli blinked. "I'm not sure any of that is repeatable."

"Well, no," Jonathan concurred. "But the point is, if it could work out for an army clerk complaining about a young lady's bread pudding, it could work out for a horse soldier complimenting a young lady on her taste in Bunyan."

Eli smiled slightly, then looked disconsolate again. "But...my face…" He gestured to the marks from his childhood illness.

Jonathan brushed a finger down his cheek in a more affectionate way than Ned had seen anyone behave around Eli. "You have an honest face, dear. That's what counts."

Before the smitten Ulsterman had a proper chance to make his play for the pious damsel, however, he had to win over her youngest brother, Joshua Sexton. He was ten years old, and exceedingly curious, though a clubbed foot hampered his movements, and usually used a crutch to pull himself forward. It made his father and older siblings protective over him, but also patronizing of him, and he seemed desperate for some sort of excitement to break the monotony. The arrival of the army gave him this opportunity for adventure, and he was often seen spying on the soldiers drilling or doing chores on his father's property.

One afternoon, Ned observed Joshua trying to sneak up on Eli as the horse soldier brushed one of the steeds, beautiful and black with a white star on his forehead. As he worked, he sweet talked the stallion in Ulster Scots. For Joshua, sneaking around with a crutch was a difficulty in itself, but Eli seemed too involved with the horse to notice him.

"You talk mighty funny," the boy declared, after watching for some time, "like you have a clogged nose…"

Eli turned abruptly to the boy and shrugged. "Each man has his own accent. It's what he says, not how he says it, that matters."

"And your face has spots all over it," the boy blurted.

Eli reddened, his pock marks only becoming more visible. "Well, you walk funny, like your one leg is shorter than the other," he shot back. "How do you like that? You don't, do you?"

The boy blushed in response and shook his head.

Eli sighed and patted the horse's nose. "The good news is that Orion here doesn't care much if our nose is clogged or our face has spots, or even if our legs are uneven." He gestured to a nearby stool. "Now, do you want to make yourself useful? I'll show you how to brush his tail."

They developed an odd bound over the next few days. Eli was gruff with the lad, but Joshua seemed to appreciate being put to work alongside him. It was not in Eli's nature to patronize anyone, nor be overly reverential towards anyone, and as such he was thoroughly himself with Joshua, regardless of the boy's age or disability. And Joshua seemed to revel in it.

When he had demonstrated himself a dependable assistant in terms of brushing manes and tails and cleaning horse shoes, Joshua got up the courage to ask Eli if he could join him in the saddle when he was exercising the stallion. Eli hesitated at first, worried he might get on the wrong side of the boy's father, their host. But ultimately he relented to the notion of Joshua riding, since Eli himself was riding at that age.

"Hold on to Orion's mane," Eli instructed, settling the boy into the saddle in front of him and placing the boy's hands where they needed to be. "We're going to go fast."

"Oh, I've always wanted to go fast!" Joshua exclaimed.

And so they did, first at a canter, then at a gallop. They went along the route Eli had been using daily, around the barn and out into the orchard, then circling back after jumping over a stone wall or two. When they returned, it was evident from his glowing face that the boy had loved every minute of it. He also seemed determined to somehow return the favor

"Want to see something queer?" Joshua asked, as Eli got out of the saddle.

"What sort of queer thing?" Eli queried cautiously, lifting the boy down as well.

"Our barn cat had kittens this morning," the boy explained. "But this was different from any other litter. Come on. I'll show you."

Eli sighed and followed him over to the nearest barn. There, now far from the door, in a pile of hay all by itself, sat a tiny kitten, mostly white with brown patches. Eli took one look at the puny feline, then said, very matter-of-factly, "It's got two heads." He squinted. "Or…faces, anyway."

The strange creature was mewing from its two mouths, and had an eerie third eye set in its forehead. Whenever it tried to move from the spot, it would fall over.

"Penelope says it's from the devil," Joshua reported. "Its mother wouldn't let it suckle. I guess she thinks it's from the devil too. Father was going to have the farm hand kill it."

"But it's not been killed," Eli observed. "Did you bring it out here?"

Joshua shrugged. "I...I guess I didn't see why being born with two heads should get you killed. It's not like it's done anyone harm."

"No more than being born with a clubbed foot," Eli responded bluntly.

The boy turned red, pulling himself forward on the crutch a little. "My...mother turned over on me, when she died," he mumbled. "She was like that all night, and it twisted my foot. So I wasn't born this way, it just...happened."

Eli gestured to the scars on his face. "I wasn't born this way either. Whatever killed my parents gave it to me. Though some folk fancy I must have come out ugly."

Joshua stared at the kitten. "I fancy we all must be hard to kill."

"Aye," Eli sighed. "That much is clear. But that wee thing will need some milk if it's to keep pace with us."

"So you don't think the devil is in it? Like the swine in the Bible?"

"Why? Because he has two heads? The swine didn't grow extra heads." Eli shook his head emphatically. "Besides, it's not animals half so often as people who fall under the devil's sway. Animals worship God by their living and dying. It is mankind in rebellion in our living, and even more so, in our dying. But maybe the beasts might yet teach us a thing or two about fulfilling our duties to the Lord, without resistance, unworthy though we are."

Joshua smirked. "You should meet Beelzebub, one of our goats. He's full of resistance."

"Really, you shouldn't name him that," Eli replied.

"But he's black, with horns, and bucks anything nearby it, on account of him being so crotchety."

"That's his nature," Eli said with a shrug. "Besides...people say much the same about me, in the latter regard."

Joshua laughed. Then he asked, "So you don't think Negroes have the mark of Cain on them, like Old Barnaby?"

"It's not the blackness on the outside that matters, but the blackness inside, which is in all our hearts," he said. "We give the Lord a paltry offering and murder our brother, all the time. But God can cover any of us over, until our hearts are made white as snow, if he wills it to be so."

"You think God would save a Negro when he could save a white man?" Joshua asked. "I mean, Papa says Negros have fewer smarts than white folks, so being a slave doesn't bother them the same as it would a white man."

"God," said Eli, "can save any man over any other man, if He wills it. He can set a man free from whatever binds him in the darkness, and cast another man who thought himself of higher degree into the dungeon. Having smarts is neither here nor there. It is the Lord alone who gives wisdom to whoever He desires, and confounds whoever He desires. Blessed be His name."

"Do you think women are as smart as men?" Joshua queried. "Penelope is as stupid as a box of rocks, but Fidelity is the really smart one around here, nose always in a book and going on and on like a schoolmarm."

Eli shrugged. "God can cleanse the heart of a woman from her folly just as well he can do so for a man, if He wills it. A pious woman reminds men of God's wisdom always."

Joshua squinted. "I've seen the way you look at my sis. You know, the smart one. You've got it for her, bad."

Eli blushed. "I'll not lie. Her countenance is…most becoming to me." He cleared his throat, and glanced back over at the kitten. "But we have more pressing matters to address. Where can we get fresh milk?"

Joshua directed Eli into the goat pen where he set about pulling up a stool and a bucket and milking a doe. Beelzebub, kept shut up in a nearby stall, seemed jealous of anyone going near his lady friend, and butted his head against the enclosure repeatedly. Eli just sighed and marched over to the stall, staring down at the infuriated creature defiantly.

"You are not Beelzebub," Eli stated firmly. "You are Oliver." And with that, he shoved a handful of clover in the buck's face and, marvel of marvels, he ate it. Then he stroked the goat's horns and gave Joshua a little lecture about the wondrous way blood vessels kept the horns warm and regulated Oliver's temperature.

Afterwards, the two of them went back to the barn, found a bottle to put the milk in, and set about trying to get the two-faced kitten to take turns drinking from each of its little mouths. Then they found a basket, stuffed it with horse blankets, and folded them in such a way that the tiny creature would be able to bury inside for warmth and safety without having too much on its wobbly limbs. The kitten might not have a long life, but Eli and Joshua seemed determined it should be as comfortable as possible, and Joshua kept stroking its fur with his finger until it fell asleep for the night.

The next day, while on lunch break, Eli taught Joshua several different games that he grew up playing with marbles, usually by himself, since he had very few playmates nearby his grandfather's farm. It was rather sweet to see both of them, lonely in their own ways, warming to each other like brothers, and it was funny listening to Eli recite several nursery rhymes in his Ulster dialect and trying to teach them to his younger companion, who would try to mimic Eli's turn of speech and end up giggling.

A couple of days later, Ned spied Joshua coming to find Eli again.

"One of the baby goats is caught in the bog," he panted, hobbling up on his crutch. "He'll drown in no time if he's not gotten out."

Eli put down his polishing rag he was using on a saddle. "You were supposed to keep the goats from straying while they grazed, weren't you?"

Joshua nodded guiltily. "I-I wasn't fast enough to stop him when he slipped under the fence. Please don't tell my folks. I want to prove I can do things by myself, without any mishaps, like you were teaching me."

Eli sighed. "Take me to your goat."

Edmund and Jonathan watched him head off on the mission into the unknown, and when he had not returned in fifteen minutes, Jonathan insisted they should track him down.

When they arrived at the bog, they found a very muddy Eli standing nearly waist deep in the murky waters, struggling to hold the squirming young goat in his arms, and it began to baa in complaint. "Hauld, ye crabbit wee thing," he muttered in Ulster-Scots. "I be thran, forebye!"

"Need some help?" Jonathan queried.

"He does," Joshua insisted, sitting on the bank. "He wouldn't let me go get any for him, though."

"I grew up around bogs," Eli insisted.

"That's lovely, but doesn't prove a jot," Jonathan exhaled.

Eli blinked.

"You're stuck aren't you?"

"Not very," Eli insisted, as the goat thrashed some more in his arms.

"Right, alright, we're getting you a rope," Jonathan decided. "Ned, go fetch a rope from one of the wagons."

"There's no need, I know how to deal with bogs, I grew up in Antrim…I don't need any secret Papist to get me out of a bog…they were the ones who drove us into bogs…"

He was still going on like that by the time Ned returned, rope in hand, and dutifully deposited it with Jonathan.

"You're a gem," Jonathan thanked him, then turned back to the bog-bound Ulsterman. "Eli, listen," he sighed, taking the rope from Ned and looping it at the end. "This cradle Protestant is going to throw you a rope, alright? You're going to put this around your waist, and we're going to pull you out."

Eli stared at the rope as it was thrown to him, and reluctantly plucked it up before it sank in the bog. Then he struggled to slip it over himself and the goat without losing his grip. The goat very nearly got away, but seemed to lose its own nerve upon ending up part way in the bog, and realizing it was doomed to sink without its beleaguered rescuer's arms for security.

Finally when the rope was settled snugly around them, Eli gave a tug to indicate his own rescuers could get underway.

After a lot of huffing and puffing on the part of Jonathan as well as Ned, who Jonathan kept giving pleading looks to assist with the salvation of his antagonist, they managed to drag Eli and the goat to the bank.

"Ughhh, I think I've thrown out my back," Jonathan lamented.

"I burnt my hands," Ned observed, glaring as the red rope marks destined to become blisters.

"Well…I lost my boot," Eli reported, "but I saved the goat." He held said goat aloft as if he was Moses, just returned from Mount Sinai with the Ten Commandments.

Jonathan chortled. "You're a real Billy boy now, aren't you?"

Eli looked as he might be offended, then seemed to think better upon it, and actually smiled.

"Good," Jonathan exhaled, patting the goat on the head. "You're adjusting to my sense of humor!"

"Joshua," came a female voice from behind them. "Whatever is going on?"

Joshua blanched. So did Eli. It was Fidelity.

"Sis, don't tell Papa on me," Joshua pleaded. "I was watching, honest I was, but…"

"I saved your goat," Eli blurted, mechanically setting the goat down in front of her, then pointing at it. "That goat."

The goat went "baaaah" very loudly, seemingly glad to be on dry ground again, and shook the mud off its coat, splattering some on Fidelity's skirts.

"Sorry," Eli offered, "for him, I mean." He started to turn bright red. "I-I think I had best go find another boot," he stated. "You-you look very pretty, in that dress, even with mud on it…I'm off now, goodbye…" He nearly tripped on a root as he gimped off in the direction of the wagons.

Jonathan and Ned both gave each other a look and rolled their eyes.

Fidelity, however, ever-so-slightly smiled.

After seeing Eli and Fidelity together, Jonathan seemed to make it his mission to play cupid, and had a very particular idea of how to bring them together.

"Lieutenant Thompson just needs to loosen up a bit," Jonathan declared to his unwilling confederates, Edmund and Gavin, over lunch of some rather nice summer vegetable soup Jonathan had managed to cook up. "All he needs is for us to nudge him in the right direction!"

"Why do we care?" Gavin grumbled.

"Because, it's decent of us," Jonathan said. "Also perhaps the young lady will help alleviate some of his frustration at the world and the fullness thereof."

"So do you have a plan in mind, or are you picking our brains for one?" Edmund queried, beginning to get comfortable enough to tease.

"Well, I was thinking, since it's getting rather hot anyway, we could suggest that he…take off a few outer layers while exercising the horses," Jonathan suggested. "And maybe get her to see him like that on horseback, by accident, of course."

"Is he even appealing to look at that way?" Gavin queried.

"I don't know," Jonathan replied with a shrug.

"Is this something you've tried yourself then?" his friend pressed.

"Not a method I've personally utilized," Jonathan admitted, "but I have the misfortune of resembling a potato."

"And Thompson looks like a string bean," Gavin noted.

"We're leaning into the vegetable analogies rather hard now, aren't we?" Edmund remarked, glancing down at his soup.

"Look, we may not have an Adonis in our back pocket, but we must be resourceful," Jonathan insisted. "He does ride quite well. Can't take that away from him. Perhaps, now bear with me…we can get her to cast a glance in his direction while mounted…"

"With the collar of his waistcoat unbuttoned?" Gavin surmised.

"Precisely!"

Jonathan pulled out a scrolled parchment from his knapsack and held it open for his comrades.

"What *is* that?" Gavin queried, squinting.

"The plan," Jonathan explained, using a clothespin to attach it to a nearby board originally used to mark the route to the latrines. "I admit I'm not a natural artist but…"

"Is that stick figure on a cow supposed to be Thompson?"

"Yes, well…on a horse…"

Just then, General Burgoyne came strolling by with his fancily dressed French mistress on his arm. Then he caught sight of Jonathan's parchment and pointed at it with his walking cane. "Is that…a storyboard, Lieutenant?"

"Umm…you might call it that, sir," Jonathan allowed with a guilty grin.

"I am an author, Rawcliffe! I can sniff out a story-in-the-making miles away! Such things are why mankind has the will to stay alive!" He waved his cane around some more. "A romance, am I right?"

"Y-yes…"

"Tragedy or comedy?"

"I…don't know yet, sir."

"Oh, make it a comedy, if you can manage it. There's enough tragedy in this world." The general squinted at the drawing. "He loves her, but she doesn't know if she loves him. You must find a way for the girl to realize, in spite of herself, that he has latent charm…perhaps even a deeper thing, namely virtue…" He turned to Jonathan. "You know the plot of my last production, *Maid of the Oaks*, acclaimed by critics and audiences at its grand opening at Covent Garden, do you not?"

Jonathan froze.

Ned mouthed some words to him.

"Cinderella…but…if she was a witch…" Jonathan tried to take the cue.

"What?!" Burgoyne blurted unhappily.

Ned rolled his eyes and tried again.

"I mean…" Jonathan squinted. "If she was rich."

Burgoyne stared at him. "You just gave away the twist."

"Oh…sorry, sir…"

"Also, it's not the same as that French folk tale you referenced…fine, there may be a few extremely passing similarities, but…"

"Pardon my lack of literary discernment, General," Jonathan apologized. "I'm afraid that I'm positively boorish."

The lady hanging on the general's arm made a few annoyed remarks in French, and he sighed.

"I don't despise Cinderella, *mon ami*. It is a quaint fairy story which should absolutely receive a musical treatment someday. But my production was the essence of originality!"

Ned shunted aside the memory of a few threatened legal suits Burgoyne had nearly been sucked into based on accusations of shameless plagiarism. Burgoyne, of course, had rambled a bit about being willing to take the matter up on the field of honor, while also insisting everyone imitated everyone when it came to storytelling motifs. That's what made them resonate with the public. Ned had to agree, at least to a point, and was glad the charges were dropped before pistols were drawn.

"Question, though, Rawcliffe…why is your protagonist riding a giant rabbit?" Burgoyne inquired.

Jonathan grimaced. "It's a horse, sir."

"Oh…I thought you were perhaps going for medieval calligraphy…"

"Afraid not."

Burgoyne gazed at him piteously and snatched up a nearby pen. Then he started sketching on the parchment. When he was done, the horse looked impressively superior, and Gavin and Ned spontaneously clapped, to Jonathan's chagrin. The general bowed slightly.

The lady at his side rolled her eyes, then a mischievous grin came to her face. She took the pen from his hand, went over to the parchment, and drew a unicorn's horn onto the horse. Burgoyne burst out laughing, and she joined him. Then he took the pen from her and added wings to the horse. She clapped in approval, praising him in French, and he playfully pecked her on the cheek.

Jonathan looked dismally at his "plan", rather like he had given up on living.

"There, now, dear Rawcliffe," Burgoyne chortled. "We've just made your production a bit more magical!"

Jonathan, in spite of himself, cracked a smile. "Emma and Jeffrey took great pleasure in the book you purchased for them last Christmas."

"The collection of fairy stories?" Burgoyne recalled brightly.

"Yes," Jonathan confirmed. "I read it to them twice now, and told their mother to do the same, since it's their favorite."

"Your offspring have marvelous good taste," he decided. "I really must meet them after all this is over."

"And read to them," Jonathan suggested. "I am sure they would be thrilled. You have an excellent voice for it."

"Well, I am a professional," Burgoyne replied, puffing out his chest. "And I am not a total stranger to charity readings."

"My house will always be open to your charity, sir," Jonathan assured.

"Good. Make sure you have a bottle of champagne on hand for the occasion."

"Elizabeth is more likely to serve you tea…"

"I like to mix it with my tea," he stated with a shrug. "A substitute for cream."

Just then, Eli returned to camp. He saluted Burgoyne stiffly, then tilted his head, studying the strange picture.

"Go ahead, Thompson," Burgoyne randomly coaxed, dipping the pen in the nearby inkwell and shoving it into Eli's hand. "Add something to the picture."

Eli looked puzzled, but did as he was instructed, adding something to the Unicorn Pegasus.

"What's that supposed to be?" Burgoyne asked.

"A feed bag, sir," Eli explained. "It looked hungry to me."

"How very…pragmatic," Burgoyne sighed.

"Thank you," Eli replied.

"At any rate…I am off," Burgoyne declared. "Let me know if you ever want to adapt your literary foray for the stage, Rawcliffe. And if you want music put to it, I say, the more the merrier."

"That would certainly be…an adventurous endeavor, sir," Jonathan acknowledged.

"Of course it would be," the general said as he departed. "All my endeavors are adventurous!"

With no further interruptions by their colorful commander-in-chief, Jonathan continued to plot over the next couple of days how to set his match-making conspiracy in motion. But before it could be unleashed, fate intervened.

"I…I asked her to go…on a picnic," Eli divulged.

"How did this come about?" Jonathan queried.

"She was out reading up in a tree…it's her favorite tree, it turns out…and a soldier started making trouble for her, on account he could see her petticoats…" Eli blushed. "Must have punched him. All a bit of a haze. Then I got her down and told her she should be careful wandering about alone, as she does…and she said it was her father's land, so she could do as she pleased. Not that she was wrong, but…I said I'd be happy to be her guard, when she wanted to go walking. So…we were walking, and…talked a bit about what she was reading, and then…I upped and did it. I brought up the notion of…a picnic…"

"Oh, good for you," Jonathan chirped.

"Not good," Eli blurted. "I never should have done it. I'll ruin it. I know I will…"

"Now, dear…"

"We're all going to die!"

"What? Why would we all die because of your picnic?"

"I mean…mortality, in general…"

"Oh. So this is just a philosophical reflection…"

"We're all going to die, and then no one will remember what happens on this picnic."

"Right…alright. If that makes you feel better…"

"I've never gone on a picnic before," he lamented. "I don't even know why I suggested it! I don't even know how people are expected to behave on picnics!"

"Look, she said yes, correct?"

Eli swallowed. "Tentatively."

"All women are tentative! Just humor her. And impress her with food."

"How?"

"Well…I do have access to twenty baggage carts…"

"But those are the general's…"

"By the time we get to Albany, he won't miss a ham here or there…"

"But…"

"Trust in the power of culinary persuasion! I'm good at what I do!"

Jonathan kept his word, and threw himself into a flurry of preparations, cooking up a storm from the supplies on hand. When the mission was complete, he stuffed all the victuals into a basket and presented it to Jonathan with as much solemnity as if it contained the crown jewels.

"This is your primary path to the damsel's affections, so…guard it with your life," he instructed gravely.

"You're making me nervous," Eli complained.

"Oh, hush, you're already nervous, dear. So am I, for that matter."

"But…"

"Just trust the process. That's my advice."

"What does that even mean?"

"I don't know. Just feed her. I put extensive labor into the peach glaze for that ham."

When noon rolled around, and the highly anticipated picnic finally commenced in the orchard, Gavin and Ned found Jonathan a short distance off lying behind some mulberry bushes, flat on his belly, with a spyglass held to his eye.

"What in heaven's name are you doing?" Gavin exhaled.

"Spying," Jonathan stated simply.

"You could get hanged for that sort of thing," Gavin reminded him.

"Or at least end up in the stocks as a Peeping Tom," Ned added.

"It would be worth it to see how this picnic pans out," Jonathan decided, adjusting his spyglass. "Now, get down, you two, or we'll all be caught!"

Reluctantly, Ned and Gavin obliged, lying flat on their bellies next to Jonathan behind the bushes. A few moments later, he smiled. "He's reading to her! How positively romantic!"

"It's probably 'Sinners in the Hands of an Angry God,' to be fair," Gavin sighed.

"No, better than that! I believe…it's Bunyan! It's really rather sweet!"

Ned couldn't help but smile a little as he listened to the distant sound of Eli's nasally Ulster accent recounting the Pilgrim's Progress.

"Then said he, 'I am going to my Father's; and though with great difficulty I am got hither, yet now I do not repent me of all the trouble I have been at to arrive where I am. My sword I give to him that shall succeed me in my pilgrimage, and my courage and skill to him that can get it. My marks and scars I carry with me, to be a witness for me that I have fought His battles who now will be my rewarder.' So he passed over, and all the trumpets sounded for him on the other side…"

Eli looked up from the book and smiled bashfully at Fidelity.

"You read very well, Lieutenant Thompson," she complimented him. "It's soothing."

"R-r-really? I mean…thankee," he stammered. "I've always been fond of Bunyan."

"Me too."

"You know, there's a story about the great Puritan divine John Owen, who served as Oliver Cromwell's chaplain, being asked by King Charles II why he, a learned scholar, went to hear the uneducated tinkerer John Bunyan preach. Owen said, 'I would willingly exchange my learning for the tinkerer's power of touching men's hearts.'"

"I read Owen as regularly as I do Bunyan," Fidelity said.

"Do you?" Eli queried brightly.

"Aye," she confirmed. "He taught most clearly that it is holiness alone which is honorable. The more we abound in the fruits of the Spirit, the less we are concerned with the works of the flesh. Our minds, by love, are then changed into the image of what we contemplate, and we endeavor that our lives be conformed thereunto."

"Indeed," said Eli breathlessly, in a sort of rapture, "because the Christian's goal must not be merely external conformity or mindless action, but a passionate love for God informed by the mind and embraced by the will."

She placed a hand to her breast. "Yes, brother. A heart that is inclined to converse with Christ is a thriving heart, and nothing else but a sight of His glory will truly satisfy God's people. We are made like unto God, that we may live unto God. A dungeon with Christ is a throne, but a throne without Christ is hell."

"And a righteous woman is more precious than rubies," he blurted out, and both their cheeks turned ruby red.

The trio of Peeping Toms in the bushes glanced at each other.

"What's happening?" Gavin asked.

"They're flirting," Jonathan decided.

"And it's getting warmer," Ned added.

Fidelity was fiddling with her hands in her lap now. "I…umm…I have long considered the marriage of Christian and Christiana to be of great encouragement," she stammered. "The young men of means who my father has encouraged me to wed do not dwell upon the things of God as much as I should wish. I thought, at least, there might be hope that such a spouse would follow me on my own pilgrimage to the Celestial City, even at a later date, if I offered a good example."

"But your father is a preacher," Eli remarked. "Surely he would not wish for you to marry a godless man."

"Not godless," she said, "but paying heed to the Lord as if He were some earthly potentate to placate, for the sake of polite society."

"So your father is like that too then?"

She blinked, seemingly taken aback.

"I'm sorry for my forthrightness," he mumbled.

"I am usually the one scolded for forthrightness," she admitted.

"Then we make a pair," he said, flashing an awkward grin. "I mean…in a manner of speaking, that is."

She nibbled on a piece of ham. "It's not proper for a daughter to speak ill of father."

"No, of course not…"

"But I dare say, I wish his religious convictions were as strong as his political ones. Indeed, if he would defend the King of Heaven with the same fire of fortitude as he defends the king on earth, he might be another Augustine."

"Perhaps that is for you to do," Eli suggested. "Be a lady Augustine. Or like Queen Mary the Second…you know, she was a great Christian queen…and wife…"

She giggled, and her cheeks flushed again, not quite red, but pink.

He swallowed. "I think…you know, you should wait and marry someone who knows just how fine you are…someone who appreciates the treasure of a pious wife…"

"Oh, I don't suppose I am as good as I ought to be," she dismissed.

"None of us are," Eli replied. "But still…" He blinked. "My grandfather…he always said that the most important thing in marriage is to be joined in a single purpose under God."

She smiled, then picked up another book from her little pile and flipped it open. It was Thomas Gataker's *Marriage Duties*.

"A Christian married man is bound to believe and to persuade himself, not that his wife is the wisest, or the fairest, or the best conditioned woman in the world," she read, "but that she is the fittest wife for him, that God hath allotted him, and therefore rest himself contented in her and satisfied with her, and live with as much alacrity and cheerfulness with her as may be. And as parents love and delight in their children, not because they are fair or wise and witty, but because they are their children and therefore howsoever seeing better parts in others, they could be content to change quality for quality, yet they will not exchange child for child: so a man is to love and delight in his wife even for this cause because she is his wife, and howsoever it may be he could wish some of her parts bettered, yet to rejoice in her as they are."

Upon finishing the excerpt, she smiled at Eli again. And he smiled back. Then they finished eating Jonathan's ham.

All things considered, the picnic seemed to have been a success, so much so that, when a farewell dance was held in the barn for the staff officers of Generals Burgoyne, Fraser, and Phillips, whilst the generals themselves were wined and dined in the house, Eli appeared with Fidelity at his side. Not to dance, however. The two were in accord about the temptations occasioned by such frivolity, so decided to sit it out, on a hale bale, rather close together. Jonathan appeared more than a bit pleased by the development as they periodically chatted and cast embarrassed smiles at each other.

Ned wished Abby had agreed to attend with him, but he supposed he understood why she declined. The last dance had not ended well, and she wished nothing but to forget about it. So, for the sake of being social, Ned had to struggle through with the local Tory girls, though he longed for her face the whole night and felt like more of a clodhopper than usual in her absence.

Fraser's aides Alan, Donald, and Arthur had formed a band of impromptu musicians along with Richard, one of their friends from a Welsh regiment who had been assigned to lead Loyalist insurgents against the rebel government. Alan played the piles; Donald alternated between whistle and drum; and Alan and Richard both played fiddle. The entertainment was well-received by most of the audience. As the night wore on, and much alcohol had been consumed,

Alan vanished with one of the female attendees and Arthur, his Dublin blood roused, got out on the floor and started dancing to Richard's fiddling. Everyone watched as he showed off, intrigued by the unusual display. Donald sat on a hay bale, a broad smile on his face as he clapped in time to the jig.

"Is that a known Irish dance?" Edmund queried.

"Partly so and partly not, I would reckon," Jonathan mumbled, munching on the last of the roast corn Red Elk had brought. "He's probably had one too many to know which is which."

"He is bad at it," Red Elk declared. "Any brave could do better."

"I shan't argue the point, my good man, but we're not Irish," Jonathan countered. "Thompson, do you recognize anything he's doing…or trying to do?"

"I've never seen the likes of it," Eli sniffed. "But of course, I've not gone native."

"Watch your mouth," shot back Red Elk.

"I didn't mean you," Eli clarified with a shrug. "Then again…"

Jonathan stepped between the two of them. "Look, let's just enjoy Talbot making a spectacle of himself. He's a Fraser staffer, after all, so we need feel no embarrassment…"

"Is that a fact?" came a voice from behind them, and Jonathan nearly dropped his half-eaten handful of roast corn.

"G-g-general, sir," he stammered.

Fraser, with a glass of wine still in hand, gave the assembly a stern look, and gave Arthur in particular a perplexed stare.

"Lieutenant, I don't pretend to know what you were doing, but don't do it again." He turned again broadly to the young officers and stated, "I would have preferred sending an orderly to make my will known, but unfortunately, they all seem to have vanished, absent without a leave…" He promptly spotted the young men he was referring to, pointing to them in sequence. Then his eagle eyes darted up to the hayloft. "Shake a leg, Alan!"

Alan tumbled out of the hay, revealing one of the family maids beside him who was hurriedly pulling her dress back up her shoulders.

"It seems to have slipped your collective minds, but you were all supposed to be out of here a good quarter of an hour ago. Yet lo…you are still here, and needing to pack for the road in the morning. General Burgoyne wants you all out too…but he's as intoxicated as I am, and he becomes lenient, whereas I become impatient. So move!"

The assembly, disheartened, began to disband, and Fraser gave them their marching orders.

Fidelity, possessed by a sudden determination, strode up to General Fraser, and declared, "Why, sir, do you deem it acceptable to present yourself publicly without breeches?"

His eyebrow shot up. "Why, miss, do you accost me with a question you have not posed to the others so arrayed?" He gestured to Donald and Alan.

"Because you are a British general, and have a higher responsibility to set an example of due propriety," she declared.

Fraser drew himself to his full height, and took several slow steps in her direction. It could not help but appear menacing, and she swallowed a lump in her throat, but did not retreat. She was indeed as stubborn as any royal or noble. Soon, the general was directly above her, towering over and glowering down at her.

"But, my dear young lady, I am deemed to be a most improper general," he stated in an icy tone. "My upbringing, you know, is unique. Some even say…savage."

Eli and Jonathan both came closer to Fidelity, flanking her on either side, concerned, it seemed, for the girl's welfare. Had Ned also been concerned about the Scotsman's dark streak putting Fidelity in danger, he would have joined them. But he found he was not concerned in the least. Fraser would never harm a lady. Only scare her a little, like poor Nevison used to do. Oh, how he missed that highwayman…oh, how his memory still burdened him with guilt…

Fraser snorted at the sight of her defenders, then took her hand in his and kissed it. "Lieutenant Thompson, since you are so eager to be Miss Sexton's guardian angel, and are not already spoken for in holy matrimony like Lieutenant Rawcliffe, why not escort her back to her father's house?"

"Aye, sir," Eli agreed promptly, offering Fidelity his arm and departing.

When they were gone, Fraser turned back to the soldiers.

"We have a basic arrangement with these people: don't burn their barn down! I want every light in this place doused! Besides the chance for accidental arson, it's a waste of bloody expensive candle wax!"

He turned to Donald, who was collecting the band's instruments. "Aye, Stewart, gather all that together and…maybe burn the pile instead of the barn…"

"Sir!" Donald feigned shock. "I thought you liked music."

"Who said anything about music?" Fraser snorted.

"But the Bards were in rare form tonight," Donald insisted. "I thought my whistle sounded as blythe as a bird…"

"Is that what you're calling yourselves now? The Bards?"

"The full name, sir, is The Bards Across the Water," Donald declared cheekily.

Fraser gave him a scolding look, belied by a wry smirk. "Think you're so clever, don't you?"

"Well, we are across the water, so…"

"It's not funny," the general insisted, with a glimmer in his eyes. "It's playing with fire!"

"Well, I'll just pack up these bits and pieces so they can't become kindling," Donald decided, stuffing Arthur's fiddle and Alan's bagpipes into a box.

Fraser sighed. "Why can't you all be more like Lieutenant Blanding? There's a good lad…worked steadily until I bid him retire, then went straight to bed early without complaints so that he can have his full faculties tomorrow." Fraser drank down the last of his wine, just a little hypocritically, then added, "Look, someone needs to be spared a headache come morning, and he's the one with intelligence and diligence among you…"

"Teacher's pet," Alan mumbled under his breath, but the general either did not hear or preferred not to respond.

"You, Southworth, make sure the doors are closed," Fraser instructed, then turning to another soldier, apparently on a quest for booty, he barked, "And you, whoever you are, release that chicken this instant! This household is loyal, and that makes the chicken loyal too! Besides, you clearly have no capacity for holding a chicken without inflicting injury upon your greedy self!"

~

The next day, General Burgoyne and his staff officers had gathered in the entryway of the house to bid a fond farewell to their hosts. The general, of course, had launched into a flourishing speech about the untarnished generosity and stalwart endurance of loyal Americans, worthy of a closing monologue on stage.

Just as he was concluding, the sound of a squeaking wheelbarrow made everyone turn towards the porch. Eli stood there, at the helm of said wheelbarrow, which contained some unidentified object under a horse blanket.

"I-I apologize for this intrusion," Eli stammered.

Reverend Sexton raised an eyebrow. "That…is our wheelbarrow."

"Thompson, get away from the man's wheelbarrow," Burgoyne ground out.

"I'm sorry…I only meant to borrow it. To deliver…this." He pulled the blanket away to reveal a cage, containing a rather annoyed looking flying squirrel that was trying to gnaw its way out of the orange ribbon tied in a bow around its middle.

"That, I believe, is our gopher trap," Reverend Sexton observed.

"And that's my hair ribbon!" shrieked Penelope. She turned to her little brother and demanded sharply, "Joshua, did you have anything to do with this?"

Joshua looked down guiltily.

"It was my fault," Eli mumbled. "He just…helped it be my fault."

"Thompson," Burgoyne hissed. "Return the gopher trap and…whatever's left of that ribbon, at once."

"Oh, I am, sir…to her!" He pointed at Fidelity, making her turn even pinker than usual, and Jonathan could not help but put a hand to his face in despair.

Eli stepped forward a few paces, directly in front of Fidelity, and cleared his throat. "I-I am not much for words…to say what I've got on my mind. But Lieutenant Rawcliffe here—" He pointed at Jonathan, who had his face buried in both hands now. "He said a gift might be the best way to show…how much I admire you, and how I thought you'd take good care of Jenny here, instead of me rattling her on the road."

The squirrel was climbing up to the roof of the cage then falling to the bottom repeatedly, landing with a squeak and bounce on the nest of rags Eli and his miniature accomplice had assembled for her. Fidelity stared at the cage, with one eyebrow raised, but said nothing.

Burgoyne just rolled his eyes. "Are you quite finished, Thompson?"

"Yes, sir," he said softly, sadly. "That's everything I had."

"Then you may return to your labors, before inflicting any further embarrassment upon the young lady," the general declared.

Eli bit his lip, then reached over and briefly patted Joshua on the head before saluting and leaving the house.

Back outside Jonathan and Edmund watched him preparing the horses to get back on the road, and Ned could not help but feel pity for him. He had lost Jenny and failed to gain Fidelity. And now he was doomed to receive a hyperbolic lecture from the man in charge. Jonathan went over to him to try and soften the blow.

"That went rather wrong, didn't it?" Eli mumbled.

"It was from the heart," Jonathan decided. "That's the important thing."

"But you were just as embarrassed as the others," Eli noted.

"Well, right now, I…I'm proud of you."

"But I failed."

"It doesn't matter. That took courage."

Eli smiled slightly. "At least Jenny has a good home now…"

"Lieutenant Thompson."

They jumped a little and turned to find General Burgoyne looming dramatically behind them, a few steps ahead of his other aides.

"I have one thing more to say upon this subject, and then we will do our utmost to forget it ever occurred and have no repetitions," he stated, leaning closer as if to keep others from hearing the rest. "In all the days of man since Adam knew Eve, I have never once heard of a woman being seduced by the acrobatics of a squirrel! I know you're Irish, but…"

"Ulster Scots, sir."

"Yes, Irish…but what could you possibly have been thinking…?"

"That Jenny's a very good squirrel," Eli said meekly.

Burgoyne groaned. "I should have had more beer with my breakfast…"

"Excuse me," said a female voice.

Eli's eyes lit up to see Fidelity standing there. He raised his hand in a highly awkward wave.

"I…asked my father for permission to…receive letters from you on how best to care for Jenny," she said, fluttering her eyelashes behind her spectacles. "And, if you would find it no bother, I might…write to you as well, so as to appraise you of her health. Would-would that be agreeable?"

Eli stared for a few seconds then blurted, far too eagerly, "Yes!"

"Good," she said, reaching out her hand daintily. He took it, very awkwardly, and shook it. He turned red, realizing his misstep, and just kept holding it, frozen. She turned red too, and likewise froze.

Burgoyne, his eyes now sparkling with amusement over his own defeat, and apparently allowing himself to indulge in his penchant for romantic comedies, leaned towards them. "Perhaps, Lieutenant, you could keep Miss Fidelity abreast of the goings on during the course of our glorious expedition to restore the King's justice," he suggested grandly. "Maintain a fruitful correspondence for posterity and all that."

"Yes!" blurted Eli once again.

A faint smile touched Fidelity's lips.

"Right…well, I must get back to crushing rebellions now," Burgoyne declared. "Adieu." He glanced at Fidelity, touched his feathered hat, and left the premises.

After she had scampered back into her father's house, Eli hurriedly finished preparing the horses, and he and the staff quartet prepared to hunker down for the road.

"So when you get around to marrying the girl," Jonathan counseled as he got in the wagon with Eli, Ned, and Gavin, "I'd advise you to forgo carrying her over the threshold. I tried it. Threw out my back, like when I pulled you out of that bog."

"How is that even possible?" Gavin queried. "Your wife is no bigger than a garden fairy from children's nursery rhymes!"

"Look, it's all about angle. I was at the wrong angle. It can happen to anyone…made our wedding night more awkward than it might have been…"

Gavin rolled his eyes.

"Well, I wouldn't carry anybody over the threshold, on account that it's pagan," Eli decided. "Also, I wouldn't want to throw out my back…"

"Then my wedding ring got stuck on my finger," Jonathan continued reminiscing. "Had to get it off with soap. Took two or three hours soaking my hand in a wash basin. 'Tis the price that comes with having fat fingers."

"Well, aren't you Don Juan," Gavin sighed.

"I'll have you know once I got to it, we really got to it," Jonathan insisted. "All's well that ends well!"

Chapter 25: LIBERTY'S CHILDREN

In the coming weeks, Ned kept his word to Abby, doing nothing further than holding hands and exchanging chaste kisses with her, even as he continued to assure the inquisitive General Burgoyne that his needs were being met. His mentor would coax him to divulge naughty bits of information about the girl so they could compare their experiences with her. Burgoyne seemed to think it was all just a bit of a lark, but Ned resisted his efforts at playfulness and simply stated repeatedly that Abby was beautiful to him, yes, so beautiful sometimes it hurt. And the general was taken aback by his earnestness. When Burgoyne noted the scratch marks on his face, Ned insisted it was Eli's cat that liked to lounge about in the supply wagons. He also proved quick to defend Abby if any other soldiers circled around her like crows after fresh meat. He would not allow anyone to manhandle her again, not after what she had been through.

Then one day, Ned's made-up excuse had a real-life parallel when Abby ended up sucked into a row with Eli over the very same cat. She had come upon the feline lapping up milk from a bowl that Eli had set up among some crates. She reached towards it, her fingers poking its back, which startled the creature badly enough to make it go on the attack.

"Look what you've done, you godless woman!" Eli berated her, scooping up the cat into his arms. "You scared Lucy!"

"I did not!" Abby yelped, clutching her bleeding arm. "I just wanted to pet her, and then she scratched me!"

"You did too! You snuck up on her!" Eli insisted, as Lucy made a funny squeaking noise instead of her usual meow. "See? You scared her so much, she can't even talk!"

"She's a stupid cat, far too stupid to talk!" Abby hissed, her eyes glistening. "Mean and stupid, just like her master!"

Eli blushed. "You don't know anything about how cats go about talking. And you don't seem to know what scares them. So you're the stupid one."

"Am not! You're nothing but a half-wit Irishman foaled in a stable somewhere! My father taught more useful things than how to talk to horses and cats!"

"Yes, the sort of things he could teach will get him hung up to dry, and you'll be left selling yourself from man to man like a ragged old shirt," he growled.

"Shut your dirty mouth!" she shrieked.

"Well, it's true!"

"Stop!!!"

Tears spilled over from her eyes now, and she sobbed almost involuntarily, turning her back on the soldier and his cat.

Eli watched her for several moments, then slowly set Lucy down. He took a handkerchief, wet it with his flask, and took a few steps closer to her.

"You should wash your arm, you know."

She said nothing, just cried into her apron.

"Could get infected. Then they'd have to cut it off. Then they'd blame Lucy, and it's not even her fault..." He shrugged. "Besides, if you think a scratch hurts, just think of what a saw would feel like..."

"Leave me alone..."

But Eli didn't listen, and took hold of her arm. "You'll thank me for this...ouch..."

She had turned and thrust her knee up into his groin, then spit at him.

"Your cat is afraid of me, you say?" she snarled, tearing herself away from him. "That ugly face of yours would be enough to scare anyone! Your little Tory girl must be blind to look at you and not get sick! Your own mother probably does!"

Eli blushed an even deeper red than before. "Take that back," he demanded.

She shook her head defiantly.

"You take it back!!!"

Enraged, he shoved her hard against the ground, then pounced on top of her and shook her by the shoulders.

"Take it back!"

"Let me go!" she screamed, trying to squirm away. "Let me go, let me go!"

"Not until you take it back!"

The defiance in her eyes had melted into terror as she struggled against his grip. He shook her some more, and she started to cry again.

"Don't," she choked. "Don't do it, don't do it, don't..."

Eli paused momentarily, seeming to realize all at once the way his legs had inadvertently pushed open hers in the tussle, and then retracting from her like he had touched something hot.

At this point, both Ned and Jonathan got involved, pulling Abby and Eli apart. Ned, seeing that Abby was in tears, threw a wild punch at Eli, and both were soon wrestling on the ground.

"Southworth! Thompson! Enough, in the King's name!" Jonathan barked. "You should be ashamed of yourselves as officers!"

The reprimand brought both young men to their senses. Ned felt guilty for upsetting long-suffering Jonathan, and based on his expression, Eli did as well.

"I didn't hit her," Eli blurted. "I-I just...pushed her. She...she mocked me for my face..."

"I hate you!" Abby rasped, wrapping her arms around herself. "Oh, how I hate you!"

The intensity in her voice caused Ned to shudder as he took her by the arm and pulled her to the side. Jonathan briefly leaned over to Ned and whispered, "I'll do what I can with him; do what you can with her."

So Ned tried his best to pacify Abby.

"Can you not apologize to him for your harsh words?" he queried.

"Why should I?" Abby demanded. "He started it!"

"I'm not saying he didn't, but...his parents perished when he was a child, and he has always been very conscious of the scars upon his face. They remind him of all he's lost..."

"So?" she snapped.

"You know something about loss, Abby. So do I. So does he. We all suffer in different ways, but that we all know what it is to suffer should fill us with compassion."

"He's your enemy!" Abby protested. "You told me that he hates you for being raised Papist, and that he's done nothing but undermine your position since you came onto Burgoyne's staff! Why should you feel compassion for the likes of him?"

"Because," he murmured, "it's the Christian thing to do, Abby…"

"And you fancy yourself to be such a pure Christian boy?" she challenged him, the bitterness in her tone stinging Ned.

"N-no," Ned stuttered, blushing. "I'm a sinner. All the more reason I…I must not hate my enemies."

Abby let out a frustrated sigh and hung her head. After about half a minute of silence, she mumbled, "I'm sorry I tried to shame you about…well…"

"My breaches of chastity?" Ned mumbled.

"I am in no position to judge you."

Ned shrugged. "It's not a false judgment."

She touched his arm. "Ned, listen to me. No one has ever done what you're doing for me. I said it once, and I'll say it again: you are a gentleman."

"Then…will you apologize to Lieutenant Thompson, for my sake?"

She blinked. "You're afraid he'll cause trouble for you, aren't you?"

"Tempers have been roused," Ned said. "But besides that…" He kicked at the dirt. "He's been a better man than I am in matters of chastity. He's the last sort of man to ever take advantage of you that way. He doesn't deserve your hate. If you say that you cannot hate me, do not hate him."

Her eyes softened a bit, and she touched his cheek. "For you," she said at last.

And so Abby apologized to Eli.

And Eli blushed, the scars on his cheeks appearing almost scarlet as he nodded in acceptance.

"Thank you for what you did, getting her to apologize," Jonathan said to Ned later. "I know Thompson seems odd to us, but he does feel things, I'm sure of it, just deals with it in his own way. He rather reminds me of my wife's youngest brother Matthew. She's always fretted over him because, well, he's different. Folk say he lacks wit and wherewithal. I think they underestimate him. He's just a bit…airy, you know? He loves poetry and the like, thinks he sees things others can't in nature, like the Fair Folk. He is pious in his own way, though, and asks all sorts of questions about God. Some think his enthusiasm is a product of his unstable mind, but I think perhaps they judge something they cannot hope to understand, for their hearts are not in the right place."

"And you believe his heart is?" Ned surmised.

"Oh, yes. He goes up for communion every Sunday, which I suppose makes sense, for he is pure, far purer than those that disparage him. But he gets overwrought easily, then he can end up having fits, and shout and cry and rock back and forth, like a child. Apparently I have some sort of soothing effect on him, or that's what Bitty thinks. She says I have extra patience, though I fancy I have only a normal amount. We used to go walking in the woods, and he would ask me to explain passages in devotional books. I did my best. He loves the writings of William Law. Some call Law a mystic, others a heretic, but he speaks of the love of God in such a way that puts Matthew in rapture."

"What is heretical about it?" Ned asked.

"Well, Law has been called a universalist. It put him at odds with the Wesley brothers who used to respect him. But Matthew respects him all the more for it. He once said to me that God would save all of his creatures, angels as well as men, plants and trees and rocks, all raised up to sing the divine praises. I know not what to make of such whimsy, but I cannot fault him for the innocence of it." Jonathan exhaled. "I hope he's doing well. He didn't want me to leave, and he had a rather bad fit when I did. I'm sorry for that. Thompson, I have a feeling, would be just the type to start ranting about the Fair Folk being pagan, and belief in universal salvation to be blasphemy, and set poor Matthew into a fit but, I don't know, I think they're more alike than different sometimes. I could imagine them fighting and then making over the cat. As you probably guessed, he loves animals too." Jonathan smiled a little. "Matthew could never work like Eli does, but all the same, they are both different. It's not so terrible, being different, though. God makes us like that so we must care for each other."

"Yes," Ned said softly. "I suppose we must."

~

One afternoon, Ned overheard Burgoyne and Fraser joking with each other as they sat outside the tent, drinking brandy and playing checkers.

"I swear, that Irish horse boy insists he's a Scot," Burgoyne chuckled.

"No, you can't saddle me with their queer kind," Fraser snorted, puffing on his pipe. "The Ulster folk are mostly from a reactionary Lowland strain that morphed into something altogether inscrutable upon crude Irish soil."

"Their descendants make up a fair portion of the rebels I hear," Burgoyne noted. "I suppose, out of generosity, we cannot expect our adversaries to put up with them all by themselves. See, I have done my Christian duty by surrogating at least one of their breed upon my staff!"

"Aye, but your surrogate isn't even the sort of Ulsterman who can drink a man under the table," Fraser complained. "He downs a beer for breakfast, and that's the end of it."

"You think I'd let a drunk handle my precious horses? Never, Balnain! I'd prefer to humor his Cromwellian tendencies, even if I am a consummate cavalier!"

"Such sanctimonious types give me a headache," Fraser groaned.

"No, it's that dreadful northern brew you guzzle down on an empty stomach that causes your ailments," Burgoyne decided. "Perhaps a bit more religion would cure you!"

"You're one to talk…"

"Besides, there's hope for Lieutenant Thompson to find some sweet release and perhaps loosen his collar just a bit. His Loyalist lady friend, I've heard tell, is still writing to him."

"That wee school marm is far from the sweet release sort," Fraser snorted.

"Oh, you just don't like her for condemning your kilt as uncouth and being markedly unimpressed with your legs," Burgoyne decided.

"It's not my fault if she was raised with no taste for the manly form!"

"So then you had to go and scare her, according to Lieutenant Rawcliffe."

"What did your be-speckled clerk say I did to terrify her so?"

"You stood up to your full height and gave her that hard look of yours," Burgoyne declared. "It appears mortally perilous to those unaccustomed to the ways of the mountain clans…"

"After which I kissed her hand and behaved like a perfect gentleman," Fraser replied.

"And that scared her more, no doubt."

"No doubt," Fraser chuckled.

"And probably inflamed the jealousy of our dear Irish horse soldier. Who knows though? Perhaps he'll win this contest, and she'll be making more of him soon…"

"Oh, that's just what we need…ten more little Puritans, reared to have too many sermons in their heads and little enough drink in their bellies," Fraser exhaled.

"You must have a few children yourself before it's too late, Balnain," Burgoyne decided.

"Must I?"

"Yes, make some more Frasers to fight in His Majesty's service. Name all ten of them Simon! Keep tradition alive!"

"God, no," Fraser snorted. "Too much confusion on that front already. No, I'll have a daughter to start things off, just like those wee Von Riedesel bairns. She'll be like her mother and sing pretty German songs and bless my old age."

"That's the sweetest thing," Burgoyne said. "And you berate me for being a romantic!"

Fraser shrugged, moving one of his checkers. "I suppose I can manage to be the most romantic as well as the most cynical man alive. Comes with the territory I was raised upon."

"Well, either way, you must tell your wife what you want," Burgoyne replied.

"I have," Fraser said quietly, tapping the ashes out of his pipe. "It's just…I've not been home very much, in case you've noticed. I've spoken with Margaretha far more often with my pen than with my mouth. But…I'm a soldier, and a struggler. I don't know how to do anything else, to be anything else, even if the climbing costs me."

"We both have ambition," Burgoyne replied. "It can be a virtue."

"Perhaps." He paused momentarily, then added solemnly, "Or else, it consumes us until there is nothing left."

"You have plenty left, and don't you forget it," Burgoyne replied. "A fair lady who adores you, and laurels soon to adorn your offspring. Yes, the future will be in full blossom for you, and you will know peace as well as war."

"Why this sudden interest in my chances for domestic bliss, General?" Fraser queried, folding his arms over the checkerboard. "Are you intending to include me in one of your plays?"

Burgoyne smirked, considering the move. "I don't know. Incorrigible Scot! Why do you ask me these things? I suppose I simply like to think of you being happy, Balnain."

"You like to think of everyone being happy," Fraser said. "It's why you favor comedies over tragedies. You may have a stomach fit for battle, but your heart…och, soft as a pillow."

"Yes, well…" Burgoyne shrugged. "The army is my only family now, you know? It does me good to plan things for my friends."

Fraser smiled, a bit sadly. "You're just determined to plot out the best outcome for each and every one of us, whether fate agrees or not."

"Is not an author, and a general, doubly in touch with the secrets of fate?" Burgoyne queried brightly. "Can he not at least bend its rules a bit?"

"So now you are a mix between a match-maker, deciding who's to mate with whom by the village well, and a good fairy, mediating the destiny of man?"

"Look, if I can't have happiness, at least…others should be able to. Thinking about it like that makes me feel better, somehow."

Fraser's eyes were sympathetic. "Surely you can take some small comfort in the memories that have been made, never to be unmade, with your wife and child…"

"No," Burgoyne blurted. "They are of no comfort."

Fraser took the pipe out of mouth for a moment. "You know…where I come from, there's a saying…"

"Oh, God, don't start trying to teach me your Erse tongue!"

"Perish the thought!" Fraser retorted. "You'd butcher the pronunciation, and probably spit in my face while trying."

"Like you haven't done that to me before?" Burgoyne raised an eyebrow.

"I will translate, upon your insistence," Fraser conceded, then grew solemn. "We say…the very worst thing that can happen to any soul is to be forgotten. Even when we're gone from this world, we still desire something…someone…tethering us to it. So our worst curse reads, 'May your name be forgotten forever.'" He leaned forward a little. "I just…I don't want that to happen to Lady Charlotte. She was far too…alive for that. I have such fond memories of her as a hostess…her love of gossip and banter…her warmth, her wit, her kindness to Margaretha, her devotion to you…" He gestured broadly. "You know all this better than I do. She would never want to have that tether to this world, and to you, severed, and her name never spoken again."

Burgoyne moved his own piece across the board absently. "We all must deal with such matters in our own way."

"I've known you long enough to observe how you bottle things up," Fraser said. "I've also known you long enough to see very little good come of it. It pains me to see you pained, and it only gets worse…like this."

"What you do not see…well, that, my dear Balnain, is the good outcome," Burgoyne replied. "There are some things no one wants to see, nor show."

Fraser gazed at him silently for a spell. "I believe I could bear up with it, if you wished to show me."

"Do you?" Burgoyne scoffed.

"Aye," Fraser assured. "It is certainly better than just…more women and more drink…" He lowered his gaze. "What else are friends for?"

"Perhaps not to impose themselves in areas where they have not been invited," Burgoyne snapped. Then he shook his head dejectedly. "Sorry…I didn't mean to…look, let's not quarrel. I hate it when we quarrel. You're wrong about me, anyway. I do not seek to drown my sorrow in pleasure alone. At least the war came along to save me. A God-send, I think."

Fraser's eyes widened. "Is it, John?"

"For me, absolutely."

"But it took you away from her…"

"Yes, well…" Burgoyne shifted uncomfortably in his chair. "Couldn't be avoided, could it? And nothing to be done for her, either. Watching her waste away wouldn't stop it. I'd have done anything, if anything could have been of use…yes, cut off my hand or any other part of me, to save her. But to watch, or run away from watching, and for her to know I had done so in her final moments…no, God sent me this war. If it had not lasted this long, where on earth would I be? Well, whoring, yes, more whoring, but afterwards? I don't know. But here we are…I could almost kiss that traitor Washington, before we hang him, that is…" He laughed oddly. "Come, Balnain, don't look at me like that. All I crave is glory now. I feel true zeal for king and country in my blood, and would happily spill it along with any man here as my brother. That's a lofty enough sentiment, is it not? I choose glory over pleasure as my motivation, and nothing shall withstand me. I have thrown away the scabbard!"

Fraser winced.

"What is it?"

"Charles Edward Stuart…he said that, you know, about throwing away the scabbard."

"You're on the winning side now, Balnain," Burgoyne assured. "Neither of us need fear not being remembered! And…Charlotte…" His voice wobbled slightly now. "She will be remembered through the honors I gain. History will remember her along with me."

"History never mattered to her," Fraser murmured. "You do."

Burgoyne shrugged. "Here we are, about to become the most esteemed soldiers of our generation, and we're arguing about what ghosts think of us!"

"These are matters of the heart, John. We can treat them as incidental, but they will have their way with us, one way or another." Fraser's eyes grew glazed. "My mother once told me that, since life is full of woes, we each have three unseen hearts, so that if the first two are broken, the third will still beat true."

Burgoyne asked, "What if all three unseen hearts are broken, Balnain?"

"Then that means death." Fraser answered, "The third unseen heart beats alongside the heart in our chest."

Burgoyne was quiet for a moment, then teased, "I think we've both broken more than three hearts in our time, being so devilish when amongst the fairer sex!"

Fraser chuckled, then looked at Burgoyne wistfully and extended his pipe to him. Burgoyne smiled in gratitude at the gesture, and puffed on it contentedly. "Our peace pipe," he teased.

"Aye," Fraser agreed. Then he tilted his head. "You will remember me, won't you, John?"

Burgoyne's eyes flashed with momentary shock, then he laughed again. "Bloody impossible to forget, I'm afraid, though you're not going anywhere. And what about me? Eh? Would you call to mind my scandalous legacy once clods are put upon my head?"

"I would remember you, always," said Fraser softly, sincerely.

"Well…now that we've settled that," Burgoyne decided, gesturing to the board, "I can claim my victory over you!"

Fraser squinted. "You cheated!"

"Yes, but it was fun!"

~

That evening, Ned found Abby stirring her share of the laundry in a large pot, humming a very familiar tune.

"Since when did you become so ready and willing to cheer on our British grenadiers?" Ned chuckled.

She looked up and rested a hand on her side. "It's called 'Free Americay', with words by the martyr of liberty, Doctor Joseph Warren."

"Clearly an original man," Ned remarked, tongue-in-cheek.

"Now don't be glib," she huffed.

"Alright, I'm curious," he said. "Sing it for me, won't you?"

"What? So you can arrest me?"

"Oh, we can say it was not a matter of endorsement on your part, but rather mere demonstration," he decided cheekily.

She let out a sigh, and began to sing.

"That seat of Science, Athens,
And earth's proud mistress, Rome,
Where now are all their glories?
We scarce can find a tomb!
Then guard your rights, Americans,
Nor stoop to lawless sway!
Oppose, oppose, oppose, oppose,
For North America!

Proud Albion bowed to Caesar,
And numerous lords before;
To Picts, to Danes, to Normans,

And many masters more.
But we can boast, Americans,
We've never fallen a prey!
Huzzah, huzzah, huzzah, huzzah,
For free America!

Torn from a world of tyrants,
Beneath this western sky,
We formed a new dominion,
A land of liberty!
The world will own we're freemen here
And such will ever be!
Huzzah, huzzah, huzzah, huzzah,
For free America!

Lift up your hearts, my heroes,
And swear with proud disdain,
The wretch that would ensnare you
Shall spread his net in vain!
Should Europe empty all her force,
We'd meet them in array,
And shout huzzah, huzzah, huzzah, huzzah,
For brave America!

Some future day shall crown us
The masters of the main,
Our fleets shall speak in thunder
To England, France, and Spain,
And the nations over the ocean spread
Shall tremble and obey
The sons, the sons, the sons, the sons
Of brave America!

"Ambitious intentions," Ned remarked. "Though I think we sons of Albion have done a rather fair job bringing together our Romans, Pictish, Danish, and Norman strains to make us a force to be reckoned with. They came to conquer us but, well, we just kneaded the ingredients into the dough. I thought surely our colonists, in all their diversity, might appreciate that."

She rolled her eyes. "You missed the whole point of the song."

"No, I didn't," he insisted. "I very distinctly heard something about fighting France and Spain! That's why we have the British Grenadiers, celebrated by that fine tune!"

"Oh, you're hopeless," she exhaled. "For your information, I avoid your grenadiers like the plague. They're terrifying in height alone. Those fur hats don't help matters."

"I can't disagree with much there," Ned admitted. "I'm far too miniscule in size to go boldly without the fear they might think to eat me up for supper. I much prefer keeping company with freedom-loving Americans chanting curses against us over a cauldron."

She smiled slightly, shaking her head at him. "I have enough trouble not getting eaten alive by the camp women around here. They hate me."

"Oh, I'm sorry to hear that."

"It's alright. I hate them too," Abby huffed. "They are barbaric and vulgar, wives and strumpets alike. They shove me about and mock me whenever they get the chance, because I'm of better birth, and they know it. I do my best to avoid them whenever possible."

"Maggie's not so bad," Ned offered. "A bit crude, to be sure, but cheerful and kind, for as long as I've known her. She'd give her supper up to a stray dog if he came begging. Perhaps she could take you under her wing…"

"She's a whore," Abby blurted.

Ned gave her a look. "I…find it hard to judge her on that account."

"You mean I should count myself no better?" Abby demanded, her face growing red. "Nothing I've done was for myself, not even to keep body and soul together! It's been for my father, and him alone!"

"What I meant was that *I* count myself as being no better when it comes to…" He blinked. "Sin."

Abby cast her eyes to the ground. "I hope you aren't still thinking of what I said about you when we quarreled over Lieutenant Thompson."

"I am only thinking of what I am, and what I have failed to be," Ned said softly. "I have few delusions on the subject. But all the same, when I'm with you, I feel…" He extended a hand to her. "Come on. Time for a walk."

"I'm not your dog," she reprimanded him, hand on her hip.

"Regular walks work wonders for the two-legged as well as the four-legged," he insisted.

"But I'm not finished…"

"Oh, let the stuff soak. It's a beautiful evening."

She shook her head in exasperation, then relented and took his hand.

They strolled through the woods that way, and Ned felt his palm grow warm through her touch.

"I'm still not used to so much wilderness," Ned remarked. "A man could walk for days and not run into another person. I'm not sure whether to be thrilled or disturbed."

"You're the farm boy," she teased. "I'm the city girl, and hardly used to so much grass, much less all these trees!"

"Do they scare you?" he queried.

"Absolutely!"

He smiled. "Good. I'm not alone…"

"Oh, look, another doe," she said, pointing at a deer in the thicket that looked up from eating and then bounded away.

Ned laughed. "Still want to feed one?"

"Of course I do."

"You would fall in love with our sheep."

"Are they friendly?"

"Frighteningly so," Ned confirmed. "There are only five of them now, and they seem quite convinced they are dogs thanks to our real dog who keeps them company. And they'll eat anything. One of them tried to eat General Burgoyne's cloak when he came visiting!"

She giggled. "And what did he say to that?"

"Oh, he just complained about Papist creatures out to eat him."

"It's funny to think about him…back there, not here," she remarked, then tilted her head. "So he's the one who convinced you to come to America to put us down?"

"To restore the King's law," Ned replied candidly, "yes. Though as you know, with me it's more restoring order to the general's filing system and baggage carts."

"You think a lot of him?" she pressed.

"It is not every man who can count their commanding officer as a friend," he said. "I try my best to show him loyalty on both counts. I believe most of his men do not find devotion to him too great a chore, however, for he has been, in every respect, the soldier's friend."

"But not the American's friend," she replied tartly.

"He means only to do his duty, but he bears you no ill will otherwise," Ned insisted.

"Same with you?" she queried.

"Oh, I'm afraid I've grown far more invested in your well-being than that," he chuckled, "duty notwithstanding."

She was quiet for a little while, then asked, "So you had no sweethearts in England?"

"Not serious ones," he replied.

"Did you ever kiss a girl back home?"

"Well, yes…on a dare. I was fourteen. Some boys from the village said that I should either tell them if we had any relics in the house, or else that I should sneak up to the innkeeper's daughter and steal a kiss. So I did the last thing. She slapped me for my trouble!"

Abby giggled. "Served you right!"

"I suppose it did," he conceded, grinning. "And what about you? Have you had any sweethearts?"

She shrugged. "Maybe. Maybe not."

"I refuse to believe you didn't, unless all the lads in New York are blind."

She blushed. "Flattery…"

"On my honor," he said, touching his gorget.

She squinted at the chivalric item and shuddered.

"What is it?"

"The lion and the unicorn," she mumbled. "They are dreadful beasts, poised to maul or gore, red in claw and horn."

"But power restrained is the basis of virtue," he argued. "The lion represents courage and the unicorn purity, two virtues we are sworn to show as officers and gentlemen in the service of the sovereign."

She shrugged. "I saw little enough restraint in the subjugation of my city. I saw little enough restraint when…that awful little crescent moon with the two beasts kept hitting into my teeth when the officer in command of my home was poised on top of me. He didn't even bother getting out of uniform some nights…didn't even bother putting the little beasts to bed…"

Ned winced. "Abby, I…"

"You know, I always used to think I would miss my house if I ever had to leave it. I loved it dearly, with all its happy childhood memories, until it became my prison. I felt nothing but gladness when the terrible fire sweeping the city burnt it down. God only knows whether it was caused by looting lobster backs, giving themselves over to a frenzy of destruction, or patriot citizens, burning their own dwellings to deprive the enemy of shelter. It was stunning to watch it spread. I was still a prisoner, dragged off to my wicked captor's new quarters, and when I laughed at the way they were driven out by the flames, he slapped me. But…it was worth it. It felt good to laugh at him."

"Abby, dear Abby…"

"But returning to your original question," she cut him off. "I was courted after a fashion, not long before the city fell. I don't suppose I ever found out for certain if he loved me."

"What was his name?" Ned asked, suddenly curious about the young man whose memory made her cheeks redden like a chaste schoolgirl.

"Joseph," she said softly. "Like Doctor Warren…"

"Or like the Spouse of the Virgin," Ned said almost without thinking.

She giggled. "Still a Papist at heart."

"Well," he said, blushing, "he surely loved you, your young man. We boys are just silly about saying what we feel."

"He held my hand a few times," she recalled. "I liked it. It used to feel soft, but got rougher as he trained. He joined one of Washington's regiments, you see, and was gone for a number of months. I don't think he ever picked a gun before then. He was a student, a clever one too. Everyone listened to him when he spoke."

"About politics, you mean?" Ned guessed, trying to limit the edge in his tone.

"He's the one who took me outside when the Declaration of Independence was being read," she said. "Father had predicted it would come to this for so long, yet it was still hard to believe it was really happening. It was thrilling, and frightening, and I couldn't get my heart to stop pounding like a drum. It only beat harder as everyone rushed off to the statue of King George on horseback and threw ropes over it to pull it down. They said they were going to melt it down into musket balls for our American soldiers…"

Ned winced, wondering if she was indeed content with the notion of one of those balls striking him, or if she had made an exception for him she was unwilling to articulate.

"I met the King once," he blurted.

Abby gave him a quizzical look. "Did you?"

"Yes. He was quite kind to me, Abby. He gave me a button off his own coat."

"So does the King own your soul, in exchange for the button?" she queried.

"Every subject's duty is the king's, but every subject's soul is his own," Ned quoted from Shakespeare.

"What does that mean?"

"I…don't know," he admitted. "I suppose I'm still trying to understand the particulars of it and put it into practice according to my station in life."

"The children's primer has changed here, you know," she said. "It used to read: 'King Charles the Good, a man of no blood.' Now it reads: 'Queens and kings are gaudy things.'"

He sighed. "I-I don't believe in the change, Abby."

"Charles I was not so very different from George III, you know," Abby said. "As Patrick Henry said, the current king might profit from the former's example. It is well known that his influence among the members of parliament is substantial to implement his designs."

"A king must exert some force of will, or he is merely one in name instead of truth."

"Kings are by nature strong men who force their wills upon weaker men, then tell a better story about their ancestors," Abby decided. "No king rules by divine right, but rather by his own will. That is why, for every good king, there are a hundred tyrants."

"I would argue that God calls us each to be something beyond ourselves, often by way of inheritance, and that includes kings at the top of the earthly chain of being," Ned replied. "That's why sovereigns have been called God's stewards, like Adam in the garden, from whom we inherit bliss and woe. Of course, we are all stewards, at the end of the day, just by existing. Whatever we are, whatever we receive, we are called by God to do good with it. The most worthy kings and queens were those who tried the hardest to be just and merciful and righteous regardless of the outcome. It is the striving under the burden of responsibility that made them admirable."

"So you choose which kings you serve, or are you compelled to serve the one enthroned?"

"Each man, king or subject, is bound to a fate which they must fulfill. His Majesty does his part, as do I."

"And so you are compelled to live as a servant?"

"I do not scorn being a servant, even as a noble," Ned replied. "Neither does the King, and he is more kingly for it."

"But loyalty is not the same as fealty."

Ned squinted. "What is fealty if not an oath of loyalty? Come, Abby, even the revolutionaries in arms must submit to authority, or else submit to chaos."

"They fight for an idea, not for a man."

"And what about George Washington?"

"It is not the same," she said. "Washington is, well, different. You would have to meet him to fully understand that."

"I hear he is a mightily ambitious man."

"But his ambitions are directed beyond himself, towards an end that transcends his own role in the liberation of man. He does not seek after his own aggrandizement, for America is his greatness. It is fostered by a vision, in which people of all origins and espousing all creeds have been created to determine their own destiny and be given equal protection under the law. We would be governed as a virtuous republic, under principles of enlightened reason for the common good."

"How do the negro slaves Washington owns fit into this scheme?"

"He knows the institution is a blot upon us," Abby admitted. "My father spoke out against it in his paper, and earned rebuke from some. But please understand, the general has resolved that the institution should not outlive him, as have various others among our representatives. We may not yet be perfect in realizing our ideals, but surely the seed is worth fighting to nourish."

He smiled slightly. "You defend your people well."

"Do I? Oh…" She seemed to grow excited, almost like a child being praised. "Well, it's easy for me. I met General Washington myself. I was wearing my best dress when he rode through the streets of New York. He is a most accomplished horseman, on his great white charger. He was clad in his uniform from the last war, complete with the scarlet sash willed to him by the dying General Braddock."

"Why would he wear a British sash when he has repudiated the crown?" Ned asked.

"Because," she said, "the authority has passed to him now, and he wears it well. It is a sign that we are inheritors of what once was, and what is now passing away except for us. I remember studying that sash when the general and I danced together and noticing where it was dyed darker with old Braddock's blood."

"You danced with Washington?" Ned queried.

She nodded. "Seven young ladies from Patriot families in the city received the honor. I was among them. He is a tall, stately man with a graceful stride who proved adept on the dance floor. Afterwards, I entertained the guests along with another girl. I sang patriotic songs like 'Free Americay' and she accompanied me on the harpsichord. I don't think she was happy about it. She wanted to sing herself, but everyone knew she couldn't!"

"Well, I'm sure you spared the house cruel and unusual punishment, like I inflict whenever I try to sing," Ned teased.

Abby giggled. "I would have forced you to do a duet with me."

"Oh, no, no…"

"Yes!"

"That really is cruel and unusual, my lady."

She laughed again. "Well, they seemed to like my singing."

"Then they had good taste."

"The general's entourage flattered me when we sat down for supper and even raised a toast to me, as well as my accompanist, though she still pouted. But I'll always remember the main toast that Washington made more vividly. He said that the cause we were engaged in was so just and righteous, that we must try to rise superior to every obstacle in its support." She grew glassy-eyed. "General Hugh Mercer was with General Washington upon the occasion. He was a Scotsman who had supported Charles Edward Stuart. He acted as a surgeon for the prince, then eventually found his way to the colonies after the clans were massacred at Culloden."

"Ah, an exile," Ned noted, "like General Fraser used to be…"

"But they chose such different paths," she said.

"Yes, clearly," Ned sighed. "Though I heard tell they both served under the Union flag during the last war against the French and Indians…"

"Mercer served alongside Washington, it's true, for the defense of the colonies. It's how they became friends. But that friendship was lent greater meaning when they both embraced the cause of independence. It made them not only friends, but brothers, and that brotherhood extended to all lovers of this land. At table, they talked about our fellow patriot, the late General Richard Montgomery. Mercer said the poor soul was never so happy in all his life as when he married his Janet, but felt certain such happiness could not last, and told her they should enjoy each other for as long as they could and leave the rest to God. Montgomery had not wished for the military appointment from Congress, but said he would put aside the quiet scheme of life he had prescribed for himself in order to obey the will of an oppressed people, compelled to choose between liberty and slavery. It was not long before he perished crying out to his men that Quebec would be theirs if they would just push on."

Ned bit his lip, withholding his sentiments regarding such a flagrant attempt of a British defector to undo Wolfe's legendary victory. "I…am sorry for his wife."

She nodded sadly. "At the time, I thought…well, if I married in the midst of a conflict such as this, would I end up like her? And if I did, would I have the strength to make the sacrifice for my country without complaint? I must have said it aloud, for Joseph, who was my escort at the dinner, gave me a strange look. Then General Mercer patted my hand and insisted that, while Montgomery's death was lamentable, and the city could not be taken, his widow could draw comfort from his lofty motives. 'We are not engaged in a war of ambition,' he said. 'We serve not for ourselves, but for our country. For my part, I have but one object in view, and that is the success of the cause. God can witness how cheerfully I would lay down my life to secure it!' And then we all toasted his courage."

"The way you talk about your revolution sounds like it's some sort of religious movement," he remarked.

"Like a reformation," Abby decided. "My father believed that we were endowed by the Creator with the ability to reform ourselves and move past superstitions that clouded our faculties. He had a pew at a Dutch Calvinist church, but he did not agree with everything the minister said. It was fitting, he said, to cultivate our minds through freedom of thought."

"Ah, a freethinker then," Ned surmised.

"This new world is suited for them," she said. "We are a people of free townsmen and yeomen, bound together by a common experience, though espousing different creeds. The type of freedom that might flourish here is all but impossible in Europe. There's more land for the taking, you see, especially after the last war, though crown officials bend over backwards to keep us from claiming what is ours by right of conquest in the west…"

"It was set aside for the Indians, Abby," Ned said. "They are the King's subjects too."

"Equal to us?" she queried. "Savage tribesmen who murdered and enslaved our people over the children of Englishmen?"

"They might argue that the white man has done his own fair share of murder too," Ned replied. "Whatever they are, they are no different from us in wanting a home where their families can live without fear. If your compatriots are so dedicated to universal brotherhood, why do they struggle to accept this, unless it is for worldly gain?"

She shrugged. "The King only gave the land to the Indians for the sake of politics, not humanity."

"For both, Abby," he insisted. "He takes his role as sovereign over every color and creed that inhabits his empire seriously."

"I say it was done to keep us from expanding, lest we realize our own continental power," she declared. "Unlike those in Britain, we are not encircled by the sea or subject to your Enclosure Act. The old systems of class, based upon land ownership, are not as rigidly upheld here. Similarly, old religious hierarchies and prejudices cannot be sustained."

"I have come to see America as England overflowing," Ned replied. "She is a spirit which cannot be contained within her island bounds. That is why, in your eyes, I see the English sky. We did settle you here, after all, and nurtured you as you grew."

"We nurtured ourselves, too, through our own sweat and toil," she said. "And now…perhaps we are grown up and ready to settle matters for ourselves. We may have needed you in our infancy, but no more."

"Are we ever absolved from devotion to our parents, even if we have spats with them?"

"We do not remain in their home forever. We become mature enough to govern our own households without outside interference."

"I seem to recall hearing this argument before," Ned murmured, thinking back to Jonathan's defense of the religious schism. Was such a line of reasoning coming back to bite them?

"It suits you. Did you not leave your parents' house to follow your own path?"

Ned stiffened. "The scriptures say…those who obey their parents will be blessed with a long life…I wonder what that means for me…"

"Don't," Abby blurted.

Ned smiled softly. "Thankee."

She shrugged. "So many people come to this land, trying to make sense of their past and figure out who or what they are. General Mercer was one of those men, who discovered his allegiance to liberty after absolving himself from submission to royals, Stuarts or Hanoverians, who seemed to care only for themselves while their subjects paid the ultimate price."

"Well, I suppose we shall see how well being without a lord to serve shall serve him…"

"Mercer is already dead," she blurted. "He was unhorsed in a skirmish that broke out when he was on the way to the Battle of Princeton. Redcoats surrounded him and demanded he surrender as a rebel. He cried, 'I am no rebel!' Perhaps he was sick of the disparagement found in the term, having served in two separate rebellions. He wanted to meet death as a citizen soldier, on his own terms. And so he continued to fight with his sword, until the enraged enemy pierced him through with their bayonets seven times. It took the poor man nearly ten days to die. But even dead, he has a country, and we will always keep him alive in our remembrance. His character was marked with all the traits of one of the heroes of antiquity, and the manner of his death was equally honorable to himself and to our cause."

"Washington must grieve him, if their friendship was as strong as you say," Ned surmised, imagining what it would be like for Burgoyne to lose Fraser.

"No doubt," Abby concurred. "I believe that General Washington deems friendship as dear to him as his life. The only thing that can sever them from him is death or betrayal on their part."

"I heard that he cut ties with quite a few British military friends from his days in the service of Georgius Rex," Ned remarked.

"They betrayed him," Abby said, "by betraying America."

"How so?"

Abby shrugged. "At dinner, Washington and Mercer made conversation about their old army days. Washington brought up his time as an aide to General Braddock, and his memories of that horrible massacre at Monongahela. The loss of life still clearly haunted him, especially because he tried to counsel Braddock, but the British general insisted upon fighting as if he were still in Europe and said he would not listen to any colonial, particularly a beardless boy. It was then, Washington said, he realized that British arrogance might be a mortal weakness. He had hoped that some younger officers in the regular army might be different, but it was not to be. When the colonies were beleaguered and their rights in jeopardy, they took up arms against us."

"It was their duty, Abby," Ned offered. "They took oaths…"

"A lesser duty, I think," she said. "There are higher oaths, Ned, ones that bind the very hearts of men to each other, no matter what a monarch commands. Yes, I think we all must make certain oaths to ourselves not to lose ourselves. Do you understand?"

Ned swallowed hard, and not able to form an easy rebuttal, nodded.

"I knew you would." She smiled slightly and continued, "Then General Washington talked about his previous visits to New York, and how he had stayed with the royal governor Thomas Gage in happier days, before he became an instrument of our subjugation, just like the Howe Brothers. The general said he had indeed counted them among his friends, but no more, for they had yielded their integrity to despotism, and as such were no longer true men."

"I know Gage," Ned said.

She gave him yet another odd look.

"He's probably my cousin."

"Probably?"

"Recusant families interbreed like mad," he chuckled. "His family used to be Catholic, like mine, but his father…well…" He hesitated for a moment. "His father was…like me. He…took the Act…" He shook his head. "His son is a good man, though. He was kind to me."

"Oh?"

"Uh-huh. He and I have much in common. We're even-keel sorts, whose feathers rarely get ruffled, and our weakness is the charm of American ladies…"

"Oh, stop."

"Well, it's true…" The joke died on his tongue as he thought back upon the rumors that Margaret Gage had chosen the revolution over her husband.

"I think you even get men who have sacrificed their conscience to be kind to you, because they look at you and want to be you," she mumbled. "There's no guile in you, and you hardly say a bad word about anybody."

Ned shrugged awkwardly. "Umm…do you know where your young man Joseph is now?"

"Dead, like Montgomery and Mercer," she blurted. "Killed by Highlanders in the service of the crown, like your General Fraser, while defending Fort Washington."

"I'm sorry."

"I don't suppose you should be…"

"But I am."

She touched his hand in gratitude. "What would you have done if I said he was alive?"

"I-I don't know," Ned mumbled. "I thought…well, if you knew where he was, maybe there might be a way a message could be sent through the lines, to let him know you were alright…"

"Why would he have cared, being what I am now?"

"I mean…I would, if I were him."

"But you always knew me dirty, never clean," she said. "So…it wasn't a shock, like it would have been for him. Maybe it was some small mercy he died thinking I was still unsullied…"

"Shocked, or not, I'd have gone looking for you anyway." He gave her a long look. "You mustn't blame yourself, Abby."

She shook her head. "You haven't heard half of the awful things dirtying me, Ned."

"Do you want to tell me?"

"Oh, Ned…"

"I won't run away from it," he assured. "I…won't run away from you."

Abby took a deep breath. "There was one British officer, a major, who used to come for pleasure at the tavern where I had been left to fend for myself," she said. "One night, another customer was…well, he seemed to take pleasure in causing pain, and the major…he saved my life. Then he asked…if I wanted to form a connection with him…if I wanted to…live with him. I said I would do anything to get out of that evil place. So…our connection was formed. He was a silly old man, balding under his wig. But his carnal passions had not subsided. No, sir. It was his distraction, he said, from danger and boredom alike." She glanced over at Ned wistfully. "You remind me of him, sometimes. I mean, not in the body…you're so much more bonny, but…he never swore around me. All the others did up to that point, but he wouldn't. And he had tea and toast with me, and read to me, sometimes, when I was crying and couldn't sleep. And sometimes he just wanted me next to him, on the chaise by the fire, so he could hold me and touch my hair…" She giggled. "He treated me rather like a cat, something soft to keep him company and warm his bed. But…he never hurt me. And he's the only one, besides you, who I could fall asleep beside. I suppose that's something, even for a dirty old man."

Ned swallowed hard, embarrassment heating his cheeks. "Why didn't you stay with him if he treated you well? At least it would have been safer than coming out here…"

"Because he couldn't save my father," she said simply. "The best he could do was let me visit him a few times and bring him baskets of food and blankets. I never told Daddy how I got permission. It would have broken his heart. And he was already so reduced, I could hardly bear to look at him. I…I tried to kill myself after one visit, then the major wouldn't let me go back."

Ned's eyes widened, and he gripped her hand. She turned her wrist over to show him, and he saw the scar.

"He did…try to be nice, I think. That was when he…read to me, most of the night, when he wasn't scolding me. It was so silly. He read *Love in Excess*! He was the last sort I ever thought would own novels like that. You know, I think he was actually worried about me, the fool man. Or maybe he just got used to the way I finished him off when he was in heat. I-I don't know, but I think…he wanted to save me, all over again. And when he was like that, I could wheedle other favors out of him, if I really tried…"

"What kind?" Ned asked.

Her eyes grew hazy. "I had heard they'd taken a new prisoner, a spy. He was a young officer from Washington's army sent out to gain intelligence in common clothes, pretending to be looking for work. He didn't have much of a chance, really. He'd never gone on a spying mission before. Some said he was betrayed by a Tory cousin who recognized him. General Howe wouldn't even allow the prisoner to be tried. Once he had confessed to the deed, the orders were to hang him, no further ado. The rules of war, it was said. No room for justice or mercy, only death. But I wanted to see the poor soul before the end. I don't know why. I suppose I fancied I could help somehow, little me, with my ideals in spite of everything. I had a feeling the old major would indulge me if I played him right. And he did. So I ended up going into the greenhouse of Howe's headquarters where they had the prisoner locked up. A greenhouse…isn't that sick? It should be a place only for thoughts of life, among green and growing things. At first the prisoner thought I was…well, that I'd been sent to get information from him in exchange for a final few hours of pleasure. He was just a bit beyond twenty, and he was afraid, though trying to be brave about it, I could tell. I imagine another sort of boy might have tried to have some fun with me, just to distract himself, maybe feel a little more alive for a while through the rush of his blood. But not this one. He told me he wanted none of it, and prayed to God to guard him against temptation. I started to cry. I knew what I was, sleeping with the enemy, but…I hated to have him think of me like that, especially because…I-I never meant to tempt him…and I tried to explain that I just wanted to see him, because I…I…" She placed a hand over her heart, her eyes glistening. "I was a patriot too, and the daughter of a patriot, and I had not given it up, not yet."

A tear shone like a jewel on her cheek, and Ned tenderly brushed it away with his finger. She reddened. "You wouldn't understand."

"I think I do," Ned said softly. "Whatever I am, I know what it is…to love."

She swallowed hard. "The prisoner changed after that. He had heard of my father's name and read his articles. I got so excited, and told him that I'd helped Father write some of them, that we'd have long discussions and I'd make all sorts of suggestions before the pieces went to print. I would always be so proud to see my ideas he included. The prisoner said he believed in the education of women, that his fellows too often underestimated us, and that such a story as mine was proof of it. He said that some of the sentiments expressed in those articles Father and I wrote had kept his zeal burning bright through long months of disappointment and inactivity. He said he had even read excerpts to some of his friends as they perished from wounds or illness, and he would hold their hands afterwards to pray for them and the cause."

"I…understand why you were pleased to hear that your writing had been of comfort to the suffering," Ned tried to sympathize.

"I don't know if I was pleased or not," she admitted. "I rather thought I might cry, then and there, and as he spoke upon it, I thought he might join me. Perhaps it seemed to him the cause was dying, as his friends had died, and as he would soon die, and as my virtue had died. It seemed as if we had come so far, and had sacrificed so much, yet it was all coming to nothing. Yes, the dream of America was dying. I said as much, and he replied that true liberty was found only in God, and no matter how many tyrants triumphed or how many shackles were placed upon those who dared to resist here below, the Far Country promised to us would be our new birth of freedom and our eternal allegiance. Every good thing about America would be refined and immortalized. The dream would be like a jewel in paradise, he said, because of the purity of its conception in the hearts of men and women who yearned for liberty over life. God would honor that, he said, and the blood of patriots, no matter the outcome of the war, would color the gem like a ruby."

"It is a fine thing to find oneself able to have hope beyond this world," Ned murmured.

Abby. "I suppose it is. The things he said were so very beautiful, and so very sad, I finally gave in and cried on his shoulder, and he didn't push me off. Nor did he cry, though his breathing fluttered. He said…it wasn't over yet, even here below. Then he told me things…how his father was a church deacon, and how his mother died when he was young, and how they always taught him to read the Bible when he was afraid, and he wished he had one then and there. Then he said…he hoped his mother would be the first one he'd see on the other side, or maybe somehow, she'd come to him before, when he was…between one world and another, earth and sky…and soften the sting by her touch, because…he remembered, when he was very small, how she would tenderly touch his hair and his cheek…"

Abby brushed the back of her hand across her eyes. "At dawn, they came for him. It seemed so short a time we had together, but also so long. I felt him shivering as he got up. Oh, Ned, I'd have offered my own life in his stead if I thought they'd take it, just to stop his shivering! His voice was wobbly when he asked for a chaplain, which they denied him. Then he asked for a

Bible, but they refused him even that. They said he was an unrepentant traitor to the King, governor of the Church, and so had cut himself off from its ministry. His voice grew wonderfully steady, and he responded that a far worse treason was against God Himself, which they were committing by refusing him spiritual consolation. The soldiers were unmoved, and shoved him hard against a wall for his insolence. He asked to write to his family. One officer said no; but another said yes. They fought over it as he penned the letters, which then got confiscated or torn up. It was horrible. The look on his face was horrible. But then he started to recite what his parents had taught him, the scriptures he had committed to memory."

"What verses did he recite?" Ned inquired.

Abby's eyes took on a haze, as if she were seeing a glimpse of things beyond the veil. "'Why art thou cast down, O my soul? And why art thou disquieted within me? Hope thou in God: for I shall yet praise Him, who is the health of my countenance, and my God!' I was so moved, I pushed my way through to him and dared to hold his hand, then his sleeve, for as long as I could, to console him…or maybe console myself. How does one console someone about to be deprived of their very breath? I was so sick over it, I could hardly breathe either!"

She shuddered. "He was led out to an apple tree. When I saw it, I thought he might panic, but he remained serene, even though he was very, very white. I was the one who started panicking, when they were pulling me away from him. He turned to look at me one more time, and I thought, all at once, he was rather pretty, with his fair face and blue eyes, and a sort of schoolmaster's intelligence shining through his countenance, because that's what he was before the war…a teacher of children. And…he smiled at me, with so much kindness, as if to thank me for the company, and whispered, 'We are yet children of liberty, you and I.'"

Now she wrung her hands together. "A soldier read aloud his sentence, and some nearby Tories started to mock him. One man spit at him and swore, 'May God damn your black soul along with your black cause!' But the prisoner didn't flinch. He made a little speech to the redcoats surrounding him and the crowd gawking at him, and he told them all that one should be prepared to meet their death in whatever form it came, and he hoped they might be as content as he was when their time arrived. Then they made him climb the ladder. He started to quote Cato up there, and I heard him say, 'I only regret that I have but one life to lose for my country…' Then…they pushed him off before he could say anymore. Oh, Ned…I heard him choking, and I screamed. Then…I was senseless to everything, in a swoon. And when I woke up, young Nathan Hale hung there, unmoving, like a slab of meat at the butcher's shop, or a twisted apple upon the tree. Yes, he had become that terrible sign upon the Bible they would not give him. And filled with the knowledge of good and evil, I threw up in the grass."

Ned didn't know what to say. He was too distressed by the thought of her distress. And he hated hangings too, for all their supposed necessity.

"That night, I paid my debt to the major in his bed," she continued dismally. "But I hated him more with every second he touched me. I wanted to punish him for poor Nathan's body, sentenced to hang out there for days as a deterrent. I wanted to end his wretched life with my thoughts, because he was one of them, a killer of my people. He noticed I was crying my angry tears, and scolded me, feeling guilty, I think. He said…it was custom of nations to deal thusly with spies and traitors. I screamed at him that I did not care, for a boy had been killed, and all mankind was killed with him, yes, in one life, all our lives were lost. He muttered that I sounded like his mother, who taught him war was a sin. Then, suddenly, he demanded to know if I'd given the dead boy my body. He was jealous, the stupid man, as if we were husband and wife. And I told him, no, not every man was filth like him!"

She bit her lip. "I wanted him to hit me or something, I suppose. He didn't though, just rolled off me. Then after a while, he said that he knew what it was like to faint the way I had fainted, to feel so broken-hearted the whole world goes black as ink, like a little death. I said I didn't believe him. Then…he told me a story from when he was a boy. His father was a weights and measures man along the Sussex coast. His mother was a Quaker, whose parents hadn't approved of her marriage to someone outside of the Society of Friends. The family was a middling sort, sometimes sinking lower when his father gambled down at the wharves. I suppose it's why the major kept to himself so much and took so long to rise in the ranks. He didn't much fit in with those better connected. Growing up by the sea, his closest companion was his younger sister. She was an angel, he said. She was beautiful, he said. She was…like me, like his mother, and felt too much."

"Perhaps it is a blessing to feel too much," Ned mumbled, "even if it is painful."

Abby shrugged. "He said they would go collecting washed up seaweed and shellfish for soup when money got scarce. They would also climb the cliffs and look for gulls' eggs. Then one day…she slipped and fell, all the way down. He said that he should have run for help. He should have, but her head was bleeding so much, and he saw the light in her eyes flicker, and he thought she might slip away from him. So he just stayed and…kissed her dear little face…and she kissed him back. Then…she was gone, and he swooned on top of her. I think…he never forgave himself, even though it wasn't his fault, and she died loving him…"

She was quiet for a long while. "Ned, I…I don't know what came over me. But when he finished rambling to me, I held him. It shocked me. It shocked him too. He fumbled to hold me back. And he apologized. That is the saddest part. One of the cleanest things the old man did that night made him apologize. But he seemed too afraid to let go, as if he might dissolve into that black ink forever without me. So I let him cling to me like that till morning…and I even fell asleep with his heartbeat in my ear…" She looked at Ned for a long while, then choked, "Why must we all be so broken?"

Ned swallowed hard. "Perhaps so that we might be moved to pity."

"There's little enough of that in this war, even to those most deserving of it." She turned a pebble over with her shoe. "Take the case of Doctor Warren. His virtues endeared him to the honest among the great and the good among the humble. His father was a devout man, and he saw to it that his son was raised to memorize the scriptures, for which the youth had no equal. Such was the tender sensibility of his soul, that he need only to see the distress of others in order to feel it and contribute his healing skills without any hope of material reward. He took pleasure in silencing the wants of his penniless brethren through his charity. The pillar of his life was the love of mankind, far above his own health, interest, and ease. He resisted all temptations towards preferment among the elite and gave himself over fully to the inflexible purpose of his soul, animating us with his pen and sword alike when our liberties were threatened. And yet at Bunker Hill, where he sealed his principles with his blood after a stern resistance, his corpse was subjected to barbarous usage and scarce privileged with earth enough to hide it from the birds of prey. Yet monuments are risen to him in every faithful American breast. His glorious wounds marked illustrious relics, proclaiming salvation to his country."

"Sounds like you deemed him to be a saint," Ned remarked.

"He bade us act worthy of ourselves and our ancestors, who cast themselves upon the bosom of the ocean to be free of tyranny," she said. "He said we were the generation upon which the fortunes of America depended. We were the ones to decide the important question on which rests the happiness of millions yet unborn."

"In England, he is remembered as a radical incendiary stoking violence against His Majesty's troops," Ned stated, then added softly, "They say he caused good men to die before their time. I was friends with one of those men, slain charging Bunker Hill…" He flexed his fingers just thinking of Major Pitcairn's strong handshake no one would ever feel again.

"I told you, Warren was a humanitarian, according to every meaning of the word. Don't you see? That is the essence of our cause. It is not only for ourselves that we fight, but for the whole world! Though he was a great patriot, like Philip Sidney or John Hampden among the English, receiving their mortal wounds, he transcended their legacy by espousing a perfected vision of liberty here in a new world. Though he idolized James Wolfe in his youth, whose life's blood was shed upon the altar of victory, he rose above the legacy of that passing conquest…"

"How so?" Ned demanded, protective of the memory of his hero.

"The heights of Charlestown shall be more memorable for Warren's fall than the Plains of Abraham are for that of the hero of Britain," Abby insisted, "for while Wolfe died contending for a single country, Warren fell in the cause of mankind, and thus even his defeat was turned to triumph. He died even for the posterity of the men he killed."

Ned grimaced. "I assure you, my friend's family did not benefit from such a gesture at the expense of his blood." Then he added softly, "I would not benefit from it. When human beings are cut down for the sake of humanity, I think everything has gone to rot and ruin."

Her eyes told him that his words had penetrated her defenses, even if for a mere moment. "Warren's family suffered too. He was a father of four, you know."

"No, I didn't," he admitted.

"Their mother was already in the grave. So it left them orphaned."

"I'm sorry."

"Again?"

Ned nodded. "As sorry as I am for my dead friend's children."

"The children of Warren, at least, know their father died for something more than to keep the past upon the throne or to receive a nod from a crowned head or put an extra shilling in his pocket," she stated.

"Do you really think you can sum me up in such a way?" Ned retorted, a tinge of anger clawing its way into his tone now.

"No," she said softly. "I think you are…better than this." She cleared her throat. "I got a look at your sword one early morning while you were sleeping. There are words on the blade, Latin ones. My father taught me bits and pieces of it, so I know it's the maxim, 'Do not unsheathe me without reason. Do not wield me without valor.'"

"Correct," Ned replied. "General Burgoyne gifted me with it…"

"But you are not Burgoyne," she insisted. "You…are different." She touched his arm. "Each man must decide what he stands for, Ned, and what justifies drawing the sword. When the blade is sheathed again, he must find satisfaction in himself, or live a lie forever."

Again, Ned felt unable to respond, only nodding and wishing he could keep his face from flushing and knees from knocking as she burrowed into his soul.

"So…have you lain with anyone else since, well…we stopped?"

"No…it's just not my sort of thing, really."

"You're a healthy enough young man," she replied. "Of course it's your sort of thing…"

"I mean…I can't just keep doing it over and again, with people I hardly know, and not feel sick inside," he explained. "General Burgoyne would call me very old-fashioned. And most men in uniform would have a cause to laugh me to scorn. But there you have it. At least I get to work with people rather old-fashioned themselves. Jonathan and Gavin are fine family men, and Eli…well, he's even more straight-laced than I am. But sometimes I think I am simply too sheltered to be a soldier."

Abby smiled wryly. "And sometimes I think I am too sheltered to be a whore."

Her bluntness made Ned wince. "Well," he said softly, "we've got each other at least. We can…shelter each other." He squeezed her hand. "Would you accompany me to Sunday service this week?"

She snorted, seeming to think it was a joke.

"No, I mean it. I feel uncomfortable every time I go, but…you put me at ease."

"I used to be a good girl, in church with Father every Sunday," she said. "It was a lovely big pew, and we would joke about being a king and a princess." Her eyes sparkled for a moment, then grew dull. "I don't fit anymore. It's not just because of…what I've become. It's because…I don't believe in God these days. Or at least, I don't believe He very much cares what happens to any of us. As a child I did, but not now. Maybe He's still out there, somewhere, beyond our wildest hopes of understanding. But He no doubt takes as little interest in us as we take in beetles in a heap of mud and dung. Maybe that's what we all are in the end."

Edmund paused and looked into her eyes for a long moment. Then he said, "You make me believe in God more every time I look at you."

She blushed and turned her gaze down.

He put a finger under her chin and lifted her head up again. And in that instant, he felt swept up in an intense passion, and desire for her that rushed through his whole being. And he thought, just maybe, her eyes betrayed some small hint of desire as well. He wanted to wrap her in his arms and kiss her all over. But he restrained himself. Instead, he touched his fingertips to his lips, then briefly touched her own.

"Ned," she whispered.

"Please believe me," he said. "It's God's truth, and no mere flattery."

Her eyes shimmered. "I know that, Ned."

"Never forget it," Edmund pleaded, "no matter what happens."

Chapter 26: THE MARKSMAN

As the summer wore on, the rebels increased their efforts to impede Burgoyne's march. Trees were cut, crops were scorched, and riflemen picked off British soldiers left and right before melting into the woods again. Indeed, the inordinate targeting of officers, marked out by their ornamental gorgets, gold braids, and brighter red uniforms, was particularly disturbing and tended to cause confusion among the ranks. Some of the attackers were part of local militias incorporated into the rebel army, while others seemed to have been acting alone. Burgoyne did not take kindly to them either way. While he was in awe of their skill, he viewed such tactics as being outside honorable modes of combat, especially when it came to the inordinate targeting of officers. Thus far, the attacks had all occurred further down the lines from the general's camp. But the shots were still near enough to be heard, making the staff officers grow in uneasiness.

Swift reprisals were taken by the British and their allies. Smoke hung thick in the air from burning buildings deemed to have been a source of aid to the rebels within nearby settlements. Ned saw in Jonathan's eyes the same guilt that he felt, knowing civilians turned out of their homes would suffer privation in the coming months, perhaps desperately so if they could not find new lodging by the time the seasons turned. Some had not even helped the rebels directly; their houses were simply under suspicion, or at a perfect leverage point for marksmen to make use of, and Burgoyne was unwilling to gamble with the lives of his soldiers for no greater gain.

There were other prices to the conscience accumulating as well. Once, after riding out for forage, Lieutenant Caldwell was heard bragging to his friends in the camp about entering a nearby cabin and slashing a boy in the face with his sword when he refused to clean his boots and went on a rant against King George. Then he had pressed the boy's comely sister to "please him" in order to spare her brother further harm. While the soldiers nearby laughed, Jonathan was sickened by it, and was not afraid to say so.

"Lieutenant, you are encouraging your men to license as no officer or gentleman should," Jonathan scolded him. "Foraging to supply the army may be a bitter necessity, but there is no call to force our will upon the unoffending inhabitants further than that."

"I won't take lessons on gentlemanly conduct from the son of a village quack," Caldwell shot back. "I didn't force myself on her. It was…transactional. Besides, I kept my word. The boy still lives, though he really shouldn't, given his treasonous attitude. I didn't even haul him back here to press into service around the camp."

"You gave the poor girl a choice between her family or her virtue! Do you honestly think our King would approve of such a debased course of action, however much his name was maligned?"

"Virtue held too long in a woman turns sour," Caldwell decided. "She must be put to good use, sooner than later, lest she spoil. Country doctors should teach their offspring as much."

Jonathan grimaced. "You are incorrect about my origin. My father was a regimental captain, slain in the attempt to capture Ticonderoga in the last war. He died with his face to the foe, charging the French stakes. I probably walked over his bones, buried there, somewhere, in a common grave." He shuddered slightly. "My stepfather…yes, he was a country doctor, and Lord bless him, he drilled into my head something about the sacredness of human life and dignity. He taught me that whatever warrior blood I inherited should be tempered with humanity, because in the end, our common nature trumps all divisions. The general, when he heeds his better angels, believes that too." He bit his lip. "You…robbed the dignity of these people, brother and sister alike, not out of any courtesy towards the King's person, but for your own pride and pleasure…"

"Don't preach to us, Rawcliffe!" one of Caldwell's friends complained, rolling his eyes. "You're getting just as bad as your Ulster pet. Besides, we've had more than enough sermons floating around of late! These rebellious bumpkins need to be kept in line lest their preachers make mincemeat of us all!"

At first, Ned didn't know what that meant. But not long after, he learned that a series of sermons had been preached in local churches, then spread around the countryside in pamphlet form, to rouse the inhabitants against the soldiery. One such pamphlet came into their hands by way of some prisoners-of-war who Jonathan made a point of seeing properly fed, despite the protestations of the officer who had captured them and believed they would be more likely to divulge military information on an empty stomach. Freddie the messenger boy had been sent to deliver the bowls of stew. When Ned next saw him, he had one of the pamphlets in his hand and was reading it by the light of a low-burning campfire.

"As poison to a snake, or warts to a toad, are the monstrosities of this royal brute upon the people, inherent to his nature, manifest in his action, proven by his obstinacy, spurning of all modes of redress. He grasps us at the throat to choke us, and forces our faces to the ground, his foot upon our necks. His ministers are villains; his soldiers, heathens. Burgoyne, the lap dog of the despot, sits in the lap of luxury, devoid of godliness. A drunkard and a whore-monger, he proclaims our overthrow in his pomposity, not seeing the pit prepared for him since the beginning. Let them come to us, with all might. They will reap their own destruction, for God is on our side. Let no man fear arming himself for the day of battle in the cause of righteousness. Let no man fear the shedding of the blood of a tyrant's slaves more than submitting to slavery themselves."

When Jonathan got hold of the pamphlet and scanned it over, his face burned, and he cast the paper, as a crumpled ball, into the open hearth. Then, after asking Freddie which prisoner had given him the pamphlet, he went to confront the guilty party.

"You abused my kindness," Jonathan blurted. "You tried to twist the mind of that boy away from his duty…"

"He has a right to read what's been written and decide for himself the truth of it, as much as you, as much as me," the man replied. "He should know what he's doing here, what cause he's serving, and how we see it…"

"The contents were nothing short of slander and sedition," Jonathan replied. "It had no right being printed in the first place, much less passed around!"

"That is your opinion," the man stated. "Others would say it simply cuts through the ermine-trimmed robes to test the substance of the mortal shrouded within. The reason I believe in freedom of the press is so that the people will never be subject to such opinions as yours, at the expense of all others."

"You speak of freedom, yet use it as a shield to hide behind when challenged over spreading lies to your countrymen, based upon the pettiest propaganda," Jonathan retorted. "Freedoms, unfettered, drag men down, not raise them up."

"And who chooses what fetters are to be applied? Your general, hmm? He seems free enough in terms of his own conduct, with his Papist paramour and flowing champagne…"

"He would have the flesh torn from your back by the scourgers if he read what I just read," Jonathan shot back.

"Perhaps he should get a thicker skin before shredding that of others," the man retorted.

"It wouldn't be so much to avenge himself as to avenge the master he serves," Jonathan replied. "Britons have no cause to scorn that service, for we are freemen, not slaves."

"In case you've noticed, your colonial kindred feel otherwise regarding their own situation," the prisoner retorted. "The laws passed by men like your general have reduced us to little better than a conquered race…"

"You bandy naught but hyperbole," Jonathan responded. "Colonials under allegiance to other nations have long considered you some of the freest and most prosperous in the world. Still, you remain dissatisfied …"

"With anything less than equality with those who happen to be born across the sea," the man finished. "Yes, proudly dissatisfied to be considered less worthy of a voice in parliament than your wine-drenched, copulating general…"

"Touching upon the general, well…he is a sinner," Jonathan acknowledged, "as are we all. You know something else I am? His family. He has never ceased to treat me and my colleagues as such, with a decency that is rare, and we give him our fidelity in return. But beyond his staff, ask the men of the line. They will tell you the worth of their leader. They will defend his honor with their blood…and indeed, with yours, if you insist upon pressing the point at your peril."

The man shook his head. "Beware to whom you give your loyalty. You may receive poor recompense for the wearing of your livery."

"I have no reason to complain of ill usage thus far," Jonathan stated, "either in terms of king or general."

"And what of your immortal soul?" the prisoner demanded. "What if you discover yourself dying in a ditch one day, only to realize too late that God does not smile upon your colors?"

"As I said, you are in no position to throw stones," Jonathan replied, "at me or any other man. No, you are in no position to condemn my colors, for under God, they are yours too, though you assault them! You besmirch them simply because you resent being a colonial and are jealous of those who are not!"

"I will combat the devil as he appears to me, as well as the snares laid by his servants to keep a man from rising up on his own two feet, whatever his origin," the man replied. "I left my congregation for nothing less."

"You?" Jonathan squinted. "A preacher?"

The man nodded. "I took off my robe and bands, and lo and behold, a uniform from my militia days was underneath." He smiled thinly. "There are many of us, particularly despised by your kind. We set an example for our people and tore up our hymnals to use the pages for wadding muskets."

Jonathan winced. "That's sacrilege."

"To everything there is a season, and a time to every purpose under heaven," the preacher replied. "The time to preach and pray has passed away…"

"Not while there is yet a time to be born and to die," Jonathan countered. "Not until the old world passes away, and we see God face to face. To abandon your ministry any sooner reveals you as a false minister."

"There is a time to fight, and that time has come now, for the old world is indeed groaning to be made new. The Lord commands, and we obey." His smile broadened. "You know of Isaac Watts?"

"The Congregationalist hymnist from Southampton," Jonathan answered. "He wrote of Christ, from crib to cross…"

"Well, 'give 'em Watts, boys' and 'put Watts into 'em' was the cry of the battle, when the hymnal pages were stuffed down the barrels," the prisoner chortled darkly. "A bit funny, using the hymns of an Englishman to send other Englishmen to their maker."

Jonathan stared for several moments. "You're sick."

"It is a sick world."

"Then preach and pray, as Watts would have you do," Jonathan retorted, "and remember, you are killing your own people!"

"I served in the last war, when I still believed being British was a badge of honor," the man said. "That was long ago, before I fully realized that the Mother Country deemed me to be a lesser creature. I have since kissed my wife and children goodbye, and have not looked back, lest my resolve weaken to fight you to the end so my little ones might lead a life at liberty. But I have vowed to myself and to heaven that they will yet see the mighty cast down from their thrones, and the day will be glorious. Who knows? Perhaps, even as we resist you, we are doing a service to your children as well…"

"You mean kill me," Jonathan rasped, "and leave my children fatherless?"

"You and I are inconsequential in the end, regardless of our personal sentiments," he replied. "We are passing away, right or wrong, on one side of history or the other. Our children are the future, and their children after them, a generation yet unborn who will benefit from the sacrifices we make today…"

"Including sacrificing the lives of those already born on the altar of your cause?"

"If the worst in England will not listen to the best in England, and continue to unleash their dogs of war upon us, we will continue to put those dogs down with a clear conscience!"

Jonathan exhaled. "You should be grateful for General Burgoyne's restraint. According to the laws of nations, rebels taken in arms against their rightful sovereign may be put to the sword en masse, if the commander suppressing the rising gives the word. Our commanding officer has chosen against such measures, except in extremities, because mercy appeals to him, whenever possible to show it."

"Yes, I've heard of the tender mercies found in your prison hulks," the preacher remarked bitterly.

"And our Loyalist friends have told us how your cells are akin to apartments in paradise," Jonathan snarked.

The man chuckled again. "Well…perhaps that is something for both of us to concede, at the end of the day."

"Perhaps it is."

"There. We agree, at last." The preacher tilted his head. "Are you going to deliver me up to your general as an extreme case in need of more immediate punishment?"

"I would, but in my anger, I burned the evidence that would have convicted you," Jonathan stated. "I happen to be scrupulous about such things. You may thank providence for that. It is more than you deserve."

The prisoner gave Jonathan a knowing look. "The Lord indeed works in mysterious ways."

In the subsequent weeks, with the help of Loyalist guides, the British and Hessians burned a number of rebel sympathizing churches and arrested or even executed more such preachers, often spontaneously, without clear orders. Again, Jonathan acted as the conscience of the camp, and this time took up the issue with the general.

"Sir, I fear good conduct is in jeopardy," Jonathan stated. "When men are given leave to destroy houses of worship, and impale men in clerical guard, they will take it as a sign that nothing is forbidden to them. And the Hessians are proving a poor example to our own troops, given a freer hand when it comes to immediate execution without any sentence being passed from an officer in command."

"I will remind the Hessian commanders of the need for due process while they remain under my authority," Burgoyne responded. "Most of them are rather passionate Lutherans, if you could tell from their hymn-singing on the march. But when their blood is up…well, they have a tendency to go straight for the kill, no questions."

"We all do," Jonathan replied, "without restraints imposed."

"Do you think I enjoy burning churches, Rawcliffe?" Burgoyne sighed. "On the contrary, when I served the King upon the continent, I even tried my best to spare Papist religious houses from the ravages of war. But the radical preachers in this country, having forsworn their obligations, both spiritual and temporal, owed to His Majesty, are inciting their congregations to violence against us. They are turning their flocks of sheep into packs of wolves. The church buildings are being used as recruiting stations for rebels and vantage points for riflemen. The nests must be destroyed and the birds shot down or put to flight. It is a matter of self-preservation and an implementation of justice. Black robes cannot protect their wearers from the consequences of their own treasonous actions."

Ned wondered sometimes what Abbey made of all this. Yes, she was still as staunch in her cause as ever, and he saw the mix of pain and anger in her eyes when the glow of fires glazed the sky orange. But did she deem his life so worthless she would rather he be shot by a farmer firing out a window or from behind a fence? He fancied that she really had come to care for him by the way she looked at him, the way her hand grew warm in his, the way she was always doing little things for him, like cooking bits of snared meat or mending tears in his clothes. She laughed when he tried to be funny and kept insisting he was ridiculous. He always took it as a compliment from her.

One Sunday, in the early hours of the morning, Edmund dropped by to see Abby briefly and gave her a daisy chain he had woven while off-duty. She giggled, slipping it over her head.

"I had no idea you had so much time on your hands, Lieutenant," she teased, fingering the flowers.

"Well, I don't," he sighed. "That's why some of the daisies are more wilted than others. But it's a talent I learned young. My sister taught me when we were both small."

"Did you give them to little country girls you fancied?" she queried.

"No," he chuckled. "We would make necklaces for the sheep, and they would always end up eating our gifts."

She rolled her eyes. "I'm flattered that you count me in the ranks of your sheep."

"I told you, you'd love them!"

They both laughed together.

"Are you sure you won't come with me to the service today?" Ned asked.

Abby looked down. "I don't feel ready, that's all."

"Alright," Edmund relented. "I'll be thinking of you the whole time, though." He leaned up on the wagon where she was sitting and pecked her on the cheek before returning to the general's camp.

Ned still felt desperately awkward at Sunday services. He even struggled to pray these days, though he never stopped trying. If God was not angry with him for being Anglican, surely he was displeased with him over his fornication, but prayer had been so instinctive for Ned in his early years, he plodded on regardless of divine wrath. To be fair to himself, Ned would gently remind God that he had gone without for weeks now, but he still felt guilty, knowing in his heart he would not have stopped if she had not revealed her past. There was no hope of receiving a priest's absolution either. So he just kept saying "sorry" and shuffling along.

One of the more interesting aspects of the services for Ned involved watching General Burgoyne's reactions. Sometimes, he seemed almost as nervous as Ned, fumbling with the prayer book and fidgeting in his seat as the Reverend Brudenell launched into a fairly academic sermon about soldierly duties. Other times, he seemed more attentive than anyone else there to the ceremonial proceedings, rapt, as if an epic drama were unfolding before him on stage, and demonstrative in his responses, desperate to be involved, somehow, but tragically hindered, even at the height of his sincerity, then embarrassed and he tried to decide whether or not to present himself for communion, and usually deciding against it.

Ned, too, usually chose against it, even as his heart went out to his commander, at war with himself. He knew what such internal battles felt like, when the body and spirit felt ill at ease together. This Sunday, Jonathan had to hold his hand down again to keep him from crossing himself once or twice. Oh well. At least he didn't make the mistake of genuflecting again. But Eli went on a rant anyway, as they all knew he would. He had decided Edmund was a spy for Portugal now. Gavin still favored Naples, though by now his insinuations were clearly tongue-in-cheek. Eli just lectured him for not taking the security threat seriously enough.

Now there was luncheon. At the crack of dawn, Jonathan had got out into the woods alone, probably ill-advisedly, to shoot for small game. Yes, rebel snipers were a risk, but he was convinced they had all been cleared out of the vicinity by the time the general himself made camp. Unfortunately, this would also mean most of the game would have been scared away too. But Jonathan returned in triumph with what looked like a gigantic hedgehog with longer spikes slung over his brace.

"It's going to taste like suckling pig!" he declared, and swiftly recruited one of the off-duty guards to assist him in removing the spikes.

Now that luncheon had rolled around, Jonathan was busy roasting the creature on a makeshift spit, slowly pouring a quarter bottle of wine over it that he had managed to snatch from the aftermath of one of the general's parties. He was positively enthused and seemed determined to make something of a production about it, describing what he was doing to the entire camp.

Gavin rolled his eyes. "You've made your point. We bow to the culinary expert in our midst!" He bowed from the waist dramatically.

"You'll thank me when you taste it!" Jonathan declared, holding aloft his basting brush. "The bounty of the wilderness is best tamed with Burgundy!"

"Unless you can get me rabbit stew with leeks, my palate will remain unsatisfied," Gavin declared.

"Oh, you're so bloody Welsh," Jonathan huffed. "General Phillips should recruit you as one of his bannermen when he declares himself the one and only Prince of Wales at some future date…"

"I also except you to make me Pwdin Eva," Gavin added.

"Sorry, I can't produce apple crisp in the middle of summer," Jonathan replied. "I'm not Merlin the Magician. But if you show proper appreciation for my porcupine, come autumn…we'll see."

Just then, Eli came over, and his eyes widened in horror. "It looks like a cat!"

Jonathan groaned. "No, no, it doesn't!"

"Actually, if you squint…" Gavin concurred squinting. "Maybe if you try looking at it without your smudgy specs."

"My specs are not smudgy, and porcupines don't look like cats! Their tails are completely different, for starters…"

"Begging your pardon, sir," said the guard, still nursing a spike wound on his hand. "But I've seen a skinned cat, and it ain't too far afield…"

"Where-where did you see a skinned cat?" Jonathan asked, cringing.

He shrugged. "Grew up rough in London, sir. Sometimes, a body has to make due, or do without altogether."

Jonathan sighed, shaking his head. "Well, I believe you will find this more digestible than that, at any rate."

The guard's eyebrow went up. "I...didn't expect to be getting any, sir."

"Call it compensation for being wounded in the line of duty," Jonathan said, gesturing to his hand. "Now enough of all this. I'm not letting any of you people dampen my spirits in this, my hour of victory. A cat is a cat, and a porcupine is a porcupine, and never the twain shall meet!"

And with that settled, it was now time for the mail call. Gavin always made a bit of a drama over such things, calling out names in his sing-song Welsh lilt as he read them on the packages. The letters scented with perfume resulted in the recipients being teased mercilessly.

"Southworth," he called. "A miracle has been seen by our eyes, and marvelous it is!"

He tossed Edmund a parcel, and he suddenly felt more alive than he had in months, seeing his beloved sister's elegant handwriting. He tore open the package, his heart beating faster as he saw a green woolen scarf and a letter. He tore open the seal and drank in the words, feasting on the squiggles of ink on parchment.

She cared. She still cared. She wanted to know how he was faring, said she had not stopped praying for him, said he would always be her little brother. That was all that mattered. Tears came to his eyes. Then he saw she had told him to reach inside the envelope, so he did so, and found a small Agnes Dei wax seal, melted down from a Paschal candle, blessed by the pope, with the Paschal Lamb imprinted upon it. On the back was attached a tiny swatch of red cloth. He knew it had to be a relic containing the blood of one of the martyrs, perhaps Campion himself. Yes, she had sent him something forbidden to a soldier in His Majesty's service, something which had caused men and women to be arrested for wearing back home. She would never give up, would she?

He felt a hand on his shoulder, and turned to see Jonathan had momentarily abandoned his roast. "Alright?"

Ned nodded, quickly wiping his eyes with his sleeve and stuffing the seal inside his coat. "Yes...all is well."

"Good, good." His friend patted his arm. "You'll be quite fetching in that scarf, come Christmas in New York…"

"Rawcliffe," Gavin called, extending a box to Jonathan, who tested the weight of it in his arms.

"I have a very bad feeling this is Betsy's fruitcake," Jonathan surmised, starting to open. "And...yes, it bloody well is."

"Send it to the artillery," Gavin suggested. "The rebels won't know what hit them."

"I suppose we could break it up with a bayonet and eat it alongside the meat," Jonathan suggested.

"No, cheese needs to go with it," Edmund chimed in, happy to finally have something to add to banter. "Crumbly cheese from the north."

Jonathan clicked his tongue as he started to open his letter. "Barbarians, you northerners…"

"Careful, you'll get roast cat grease on it," Gavin cautioned, pointing to the paper. "And speaking of cheese, when are you going to pull some Welsh rarebit out of your hat?"

"Oh, button your gob," huffed Jonathan, swatting at him as he sat down to read. His eyes darted back and forth over the lines, and a smile came to his lips as he finished, folding it and placing it inside his coat.

"Why are you grinning like Mari Lwyd?" Gavin queried.

"Mari Lwyd?" Edmund queried.

"Yes, the Christmas horse head," Jonathan chuckled. "They parade it around in parts of Wales during Yuletide."

"A mare cast out of the stable to make room for the Virgin on Christmas night, wandering the realm between life and death," Gavin explained, in a low, ominous voice. "She comes, her bones come, seeking us all…" He cast a teasing look over at Eli. "Shall we borrow one of your horse's heads to celebrate Yuletide in New York City?"

Eli flushed absolutely red, and Gavin laughed, then started singing a ditty in Welsh that Ned imagined was some sort of beckoning of Mari Lwyd. Eli stepped closer to his favorite cart horse, a dappled gray mare dubbed Winifred, and patted her nose. She nuzzled his cheek in response. "We don't hold with pagan superstitions like that in Ulster."

"But Ireland is full of it, under every rock, so I'm told," Gavin needled him.

"Not where I come from!" Eli shot back. "We've done away with such vile things wherever they've cropped up!"

"There now, dear," Jonathan said kindly, turning to Eli. "Don't let his twisted humor get to you." He turned back to Gavin. "Now am I allowed to tell my news?"

"The floor is yours," Gavin acknowledged with a flourishing hand gesture.

Jonathan smiled again. "It seems I have the magic touch after all."

"You've made apple's grow out of season?"

"No. Better." He beamed even brighter.

Now Gavin smirked. "I see. You're having another one, aren't you? Trying to keep pace with me. Must have had a very good night before marching off for the docks, eh?"

"Night and morning," Jonathan added cheekily.

Gavin laughed. "Lusty little clerk!"

"Your wife is expecting?" Ned realized.

Jonathan nodded. "She's sure it will be a boy, as he's making her very sick in the stomach. That's what happened with Geoffrey, but not with Emma…"

"Shall we have a toast?" Gavin queried, standing up. "I for one think we should have a toast."

"You just want the last of the wine," Jonathan surmised.

"No use wasting it on all that poor burnt creature."

"It is not burnt!"

Gavin snatched up the bottle, then went over to a rock next to where Ned was standing and climbed on top. He held it aloft.

"To my inestimable colleague, who has kept my vile tongue from swearing too much lest I get myself horsewhipped by our gentleman general…"

The little company laughed.

Then the Welshman's eyes shone with an unusual sincerity. "To my friend, to the best of us, and his family. Iechyd da…"

A sudden, loud, terrible sound punctured and reverberated through the air.

The wine bottle smashed on the rock, and Gavin's hands were pressed against his face, reddish-purple liquid spilling through his fingers as he reeled and fell.

Edmund was frozen to the spot in horror. He felt a warm trickle down his own face, and touched it. When he took his hand away, it was stained with the man's blood.

He couldn't move, couldn't think, as the shock gave way to panic with screams to take cover ringing through the camp. He saw most of his comrades lying flat on their bellies, but the guard who just a few hours ago had helped Jonathan take the spikes out of his porcupine remained erect and reached for his gun.

It was too late. Another shot rang out. The guard was thrown to the ground from a bullet impacting his chest. He moved no more.

Suddenly, Ned found himself on the ground too, but not from a shot. He turned and saw that Jonathan had tackled him.

"Stay down," his friend rasped. "Just stay down, all of you stay down…"

But Jonathan did not heed his own counsel, and sprinted up, seizing his hunting gun that had been leaning against a nearby tree. His hunter's senses had clearly given him a good idea where the sniper was concealed, and his eyes now fixed on a certain tree as he hurriedly loaded his weapon.

"Jonathan, don't…" Ned begged. "Get down…"

As Jonathan shouldered his weapon, yet another shot rang out from the tree, but it missed him. There was a screaming sound from poor Winifred the cart horse, and she collapsed on her side, tipping the cart to which she was tethered in the process.

It was the last shot this marksman would ever get off.

With a calmness that amazed Ned, Jonathan closed one eye, steadied his aim, and fired. There was a rustle in the tree branches as the sniper crashed from his perch and landed on the tangled roots below. Jonathan took several steps forward, and then stopped short staring. Edmund followed him and saw at the same instant that their assailant was a mere boy, thirteen or fourteen at most, shaking like a leaf as he stared at the wound in his stomach, spurting dark blood, and struggling to staunch his bloodied, broken nose with his grotesquely twisted arm from the fall. Jonathan turned away for a moment, as if his own act was too much to take in.

Then he stared at his dead friend, his face unrecognizable. He let the rifle fall from his hands, and swore, for the first time Ned had ever heard, in a voice verging on tears.

Soldiers from around the camp had been drawn over by the shots and quickly surrounded the fallen young marksman. Ned briefly saw his eyes go wide with terror. Then they descended on him in a frenzy, kicking and punching and spitting at him. One smashed the butt of his musket into the boy's side. Bones snapped, and he screamed. Another blow from the musket fell, this time in his face. Ned saw the boy's body writhe convulsively, and wondered if it had been a killing blow. But no, in spite of the blood everywhere from his nose and mouth, and the teeth he spit out, the boy was not dead. It had been calculated. The soldiers wanted it to make it slow, yes, wanted to beat him to death, and for their victim to be aware of it happening. Helplessly, the boy curled up in a ball, covering his head with his hand as more kicks caused him to moan.

"Stop!" Jonathan shouted, pushing his way through the soldiers. "I order you, stop!"

When he had managed to finally get them under control, they stared at him as if he had two heads as he crouched down by the boy. The young rebel was still curled up, his face buried in his arms, and when Jonathan laid a hand on his shoulder, he made a low growl like a wounded wolf, about to be finished off. Then he lifted his head, curiosity, it seemed, overcoming everything else. He stared at Jonathan, and it was evident he expected to be killed any moment, his frame shaking, and his dark brown eyes wide, as if the clerk were some monster from myth.

Suddenly, the boy reached into his common brown coat…and drew out something shiny. Jonathan yelped, a red gash appearing across his hand, and a fresh flash of anger upon his face. He was soon wrestling the blade away from the boy, flipping him over on his belly, and holding the weapon to his throat. The rebel froze and shut his eyes tight, then groaned in pain. Jonathan shook his head, bit his lip, and threw the knife away.

Just then, a shot rang out behind them, drowning out a desperate whinny. Ned turned and saw Eli, standing over the motionless form of Winifred, a smoking pistol in his hand, pointed at the dead horse's bloodied head. There were tears streaking the Ulsterman's face. Then his eyes narrowed, focusing on several muskets nearby, with bayonets shimmering on the ground besides them. He charged over to the muskets, snatched one up, attached the bayonet, and marched towards the tree. There was deadly earnest in his eyes as he stared down at the boy, pointing the bayonet at his back.

"Thompson, no! No!" Jonathan cried, knocking the bayonet aside.

"In the Lord's name, and by His might, the wicked shall not go unpunished!" Eli cried. "He should be pinned upon the tree!"

"And vengeance be mine, saith the Lord!" Jonathan shouted, his voice cracking. "He was pinned upon the tree!"

Eli winced. "But-but there must be justice…"

"Yes, justice," Jonathan conceded, "and that is for the general to decide, not us!"

Then he turned back to the boy, curled up between the roots of the tree, and seized hold of him. The boy squeaked and squirmed as Jonathan pulled him up into his arms, but he was too weak to resist for long, and let his head limply fall against his captor's chest.

"As an officer of the King, I hereby take this rebel prisoner!" Jonathan declared. "He is under my charge, do you hear? My charge!"

With that, he pushed past the soldiers and carried the boy off to one of the supply wagons. Ned trailed after him, watching as Jonathan moved to tend to the boy's injuries, an instinct learned at the side of his physician stepfather. When he finished his basic ministrations, Jonathan stared at the boy, then at his own bloodstained hands, then at the boy once again.

"Why?" Jonathan rasped, seizing the young rebel by the shoulders and shaking him slightly. "I must know why…"

The boy sucked in a breath, his face twisted by agony, and Jonathan released him.

"I…didn't mean to…" Jonathan's voice faded and he shook his head. "But I must know why! Why?!"

"You invaded us first!" the boy choked. "I only fought back! What else did you expect?"

"You shot down my friend in cold blood!" Jonathan blurted. "He had no chance!"

"He fought for a tyrant," the boy spat. "You bloody-backs came here to force your king's dirty laws down our throats, then set your Hessians and savages on us if we wouldn't yield! You all deserve whatever you get!"

"Has no one taught you fear of the Lord, boy?" Jonathan snapped. "His Majesty holds authority over you, and all others within his realms, by the grace of God…"

"Kings are not made so by God," the boy panted. "They are not born that way! They are no better than any other babe in the cradle! They only become kings by the words of men, and hold power through the submission of men! The King does not speak for God!"

"Render unto Caesar that which is Caesar's," Jonathan replied, "and all the more so to your worthy Christian sovereign, defender of the faith and governor of the Church!"

"No man is head of the Church, be he king or pope!" the boy declared.

"Ah, a dissenter, the fanatical kind this country seems to breed by its nature," Jonathan hissed. "I like to think myself tolerant of my Protestant brethren of differing persuasion, to which this army is no stranger, but your kind proves that rejecting the King's spiritual authority leads, often enough, to rejecting his temporal authority…"

"We have our own authority God has given us as His people!" the boy countered. "Yes, and we are our own authorities too! We chose them for our own, lesser magistrates who have the right to protect us from tyranny!"

"All authority in this land is either transmitted by way of the King, or it is a sham, used by cunning charlatans to seize power for themselves!" Jonathan rebutted. "The King is the one whose task it is to safeguard liberty and law, not men trafficking in the sentiments of the mob!"

"We're not a mob," the boy returned, "but an army! You'll realize that soon enough…too late for you, too late…"

Jonathan winced. "It's clear you've been educated by radicals from childhood. Who taught you to reject royal authority?"

"My grandfather," he replied in a wobbly voice. "He taught me…to recognize no sovereign but God, and no king but Christ…"

"Then the millstone is around his neck, for taking Our Lord's name in vain to corrupt children, and using pious language to encourage anarchy," Jonathan ground out.

"He was a man of God, a preacher," the boy shot back.

"A man of the devil, preaching blasphemy!" Jonathan shouted. "That's what your black robed regiment is made up of!" He clenched his fists, struggling to control his emotions. "You…you killed my friend…and another poor man…he helped me make lunch…"

"And your Hessians killed my grandfather, and pinned him to a tree with a bayonet!" the boy screamed, biting his lip. "Then you burnt down his church!"

Jonathan let out a shaky sigh, then silently watched the boy as he started to squirm again, in pain. He took the boy's chin in his hand and forced him to meet his gaze. "You fool…you little fool…" He rasped. "Don't you know what they'll do to you?"

The boy swallowed hard, then fighting against his own fear, he blurted, "I would have shot you instead, if the other one hadn't gotten up on the rock! I-I said to myself, 'I'll shoot the fat one, with four eyes!'"

Jonathan just shook his head. "You…shot my friend," he whispered, near tears. "And…I shot you. Do you think silly names could hurt me now?"

The boy, for the first time, looked ashamed.

Ned heard voices behind them, and turned to see General Burgoyne, standing over Gavin's corpse, a strange expression on his face. Then Burgoyne fixed his gaze upon the wagon, his eyes gleaming with fury. He marched over, with a couple of his battle aides on either side of him in a show of power.

"Did you come for me, boy?" Burgoyne rasped.

The boy forced himself to sit up a little, then hissed, "Yes."

"Who sent you to assassinate me? Tell me truly, or your death will be a hard one!" The general clenched the hilt of his sword.

The rebel bit his lip, but would not answer.

"Were you sent, boy, or did you come of your own accord?" Jonathan joined the interrogation. "Are your people trying to murder our general?"

"To harass you," the boy blurted, dead-eying Burgoyne. "Those are the orders. I'm the one who chose…who tried…to get as close to you as I could. I wanted to take you down, however I found. But when I didn't think I could get any closer, without being caught…I took down whoever I could…"

"That aide of mine you shot, he was no fighting soldier," Burgoyne ground out. He gestured to Jonathan and Ned. "These people here, they're not fighting soldiers! They're part of my family! They sort my luggage, take dictation, mix my brandy. Why slaughter them?"

"Because," the boy spat, "they're yours! And they're here!"

Burgoyne just stared for a long while, blood rushing to his face. "You should have thought better of it, boy. You should have come after me, and not stopped till you reached me. Alas, for you, I am still here, and I will make you suffer! As God is my witness, I will not let you go easily into hell!"

~

Ned watched as the boy was pulled along roughly, the rope around his neck like a halter around a dog. His hands were bound behind his back. Some of the soldiers made mocking barking noises. Short of their destination, he fell down, and was dragged along the ground. More laughter and barking. Finally reaching the tree, he was forced upright, and the rope flung over a high tree limb. His clothes were smeared reddish-brown with a mixture of blood and dirt and he was trembling as the noose was fitted around his neck.

General Burgoyne was sitting on a chair that had been brought out for him to observe the spectacle. One of the aides began to read out the condemnation from a parchment.

The boy was no proper soldier, it had been decided. His common coat did not designate him as such. Yes, most of the rebel volunteers came out like that, in their workaday clothes. The makeshift American army could little afford such uniformity. It didn't matter. This boy was a despicable assassin, and would pay the ultimate price.

The boy managed to make his faltering voice heard over the reading. "When will the preacher come to pray over me?"

"He will not," Burgoyne declared icily. "Treason against the crown makes one's life, and soul, forfeit. You have lost the privilege of spiritual consolation from ministers of the Church, over whom His Majesty is Supreme governor…"

"No man should think to stand between another man and God!" the boy shot back. "Not you, nor the one who sent you!"

"You fancy yourself to be a man, boy?"

"More so than you!"

"You are nothing but a cowardly murderer!" Burgoyne growled. "Yes, you have murdered men, and murdered yourself, by abandoning your rightful allegiance!"

"I am no traitor to the King!" the boy screamed, obviously in great pain. "It is the King who is a traitor to us!"

"Silence!" Burgoyne commanded.

But the boy would not be silent.

"This king is nothing but a royal brute! It is each American's duty to take up arms! It is each man's right to be free! Go ahead! Kill me! I'm not afraid!"

"Good!" Burgoyne blurted. "For you have lost even the hope of having your legs pulled down upon, when you're up there, dangling from the rope! Nature will be left to take its course!"

The boy turned even more ashen at these words. But his eyes remained defiant as he cried, "Free America!"

Ned could not help but feel a grudging admiration for the boldness found in one so young, no matter how twisted by insidious propaganda, no matter how dishonorable his attack. Whatever else the revolutionaries were, the rank and file seemed profoundly obstinate in their cause, yes, even with a bullet in the belly or a rope around the neck. It was a compliment to the powers of persuasion manifested in so many seditious speeches and sermons, spewed up and down the length and breadth of the colonies. It was also a compliment to their strength of will. They were, after all, Britannia's children, misguided, but a part of her, flesh and bone, heart and stomach. And seeing such an inheritance wasted grieved Ned. He wished he could leave.

Then, once again, the boy's knees buckled and he slumped down, causing the noose to start crushing his throat. Ned grimaced as the rebel struggled to regain his footing, with the rope cutting off most of his air, leaving him gasping and wheezing. He cast a piteous glance at the ones watching him suffer, pleading with his eyes for help, even as one of Burgoyne's aides continued to read out his sentence, unmoved.

Then Jonathan stepped forward from among the general's staff officers. Before anyone could tell him otherwise he was at the boy's side, pulling him upright with his bandaged hand. The young rebel gagged, trying to get a breath. He was soon choking so hard vomit and blood came up, and he nearly fell down again, but Jonathan kept a tight grip on him. The boy looked up at him, watery desperation in his hazel eyes, afraid of being allowed to fall again, afraid of being left to choke again, and then seeming to know that is exactly what was destined to be when they hanged him, and fighting in vain against the ropes binding his arms. His broken arm had no strength in it, and he was in too much pain to continue the struggle for more than a few seconds before shuddering and starting to lose consciousness.

Jonathan continued to keep him upright, taking out a handkerchief from his coat and cleaning off the blood streaming from the boy's broken nose. The young rebel wriggled slightly, shutting his eyes tight, tears standing out on his eyelashes, then his cheeks, bracing himself, it seemed, for the rope to yank him up and dangle him from the tree limb, his life draining out slowly while his enemies watched him suffocate, his wound tearing open. Some of the redcoats laughed as it became clear the boy had wet himself in his panic, and his face turned red as he bit his lip, drawing more blood. But Jonathan did not laugh. He just wiped the boy's mouth with his handkerchief. Then he turned towards General Burgoyne.

"Sir," he said, "may I ask a favor of you, as you said I might?"

Burgoyne gestures with a gloved hand. "Ask, Lieutenant."

Jonathan swallowed hard. "Let me have the boy."

"No," Burgoyne denied him. "He has merited death, and will suffer it."

"But sir, he cannot survive this wound," Jonathan countered, holding up a hand, red with rebel blood. "All I ask is that he be allowed to die with some measure of dignity, not like a dog…"

"He deserves no such consideration," Burgoyne replied. "He attacked the King's troops, yes, my own family, just like a wild beast. He has not ceased to profane His Majesty's name. Tell me why he should be shown any leniency?"

"The boy has been deluded by his grandfather, a preacher in these parts, who was in turn deluded by wicked men who seek to be petty kings in their own right," Jonathan insisted. "They are the ones who have maligned His Majesty with the epithet of tyrant in their preachings and writings and used their influence to mislead the gullible."

"There are some all-too-eager to be misled," Burgoyne retorted coldly. "And others all-too-easily tricked into sentimentality on their behalf."

"Sir, with all due respect, I am the one who brought the rebel down," Jonathan reminded him. "Look, even now there is blood on my hands!"

"He brought himself down," Burgoyne stated, "by his own villainy. His blood, and the blood of those he slew, is on his head, and his head will remain in the noose…"

"But General, what kind of an example are we setting to the Natives who fight alongside us if we show ourselves incapable of mercy to the wounded?" Jonathan tried another angle. "You expressly forbid the killing of injured men, or even dying ones, because of your consciousness of Christianity, and because you serve a Christian Prince, who understands the merit of mercy. You said that you would view it as the height of wickedness to harm a man in such a state of weakness, even if he had been in arms against the King…"

"Assassins and incendiaries deserve whatever barbarism they receive," Burgoyne snapped.

"Are we to become barbarians then?" Jonathan shot back. "Are we to reflect our King to the people as barbarous in his edicts?"

"Careful, Lieutenant…"

"Surely, sir, now is the time to show that His Majesty's justice is tempered by a paternal affection for his subjects, even grievously erring ones. Surely this is a means of proving the rebel leaders to be liars when they accused the sovereign of brutality and despotism."

"I'm afraid there is no time to petition His Majesty for clemency," Burgoyne replied.

"But you, sir, are the King's voice and hand in this campaign," Jonathan shot back. "The power to pardon is yours…"

"Which I do not feel inclined to use!" Burgoyne growled. "He sought my life and assaulted my staff!"

"Sir, please, this one favor I ask to repay my good aim, please…"

"I thought you and Lieutenant Jones were like brothers!" Burgoyne blurted.

Jonathan winced. "Yes," was all he said.

"And you still want custody of this murderous little wretch?"

"Yes."

Burgoyne looked around him. "Is there any officer here who agrees with Lieutenant Rawcliffe that the hanging should not take place?"

Some laughed. Some shook their heads. A few said "Swing him high." Some remained still as stone, staring at the boy with death in their eyes.

But Jonathan was not through.

"Ned," he cried. "Ned, please!"

Edmund winced. He did not want to be called upon. He did not want to lift a finger. He was too sick in his spirit to pity the little monster who had torn up his world, spraying blood everywhere.

But Jonathan was looking at him, beseeching him, with his kind, honest eyes shimmering in pain behind his spectacles.

Edmund moved closer to Burgoyne, leaned down, and whispered, "Sir…a word…in private?"

"Surely what you have to say may be said for all to hear, Lieutenant," Burgoyne retorted.

"Sir…but a moment of your time…please?"

Burgoyne remained seated, strumming his fingers on the table in front of him. Then at last he relented. "A moment," he said, "in my tent."

Once inside, Ned blurted, "Sir, Lieutenant Rawcliffe is only asking for the smallest of mercies…"

"He is asking me to pardon the unpardonable," Burgoyne replied. "He has too soft a heart for this business, and so do you, I fear…"

"The boy is already condemned by his wound," Ned countered. "He is young and afraid to be hung up like a slab of meat and strangled for the pleasure of an audience…"

"Many younger than he have suffered the same penalty for lesser crimes!" Burgoyne declared.

"Yes, but you never liked it," Ned shot back. "You are not cruel."

"Are you so sure?" Burgoyne chortled bitterly. "Perhaps you have not seen enough of me at war…"

"Remember, sir, that you are a Christian," Edmund said, struggling not to let his voice shake.

Burgoyne turned on him, his eyes flashing. "Now, don't go pulling that one on me, Lieutenant. Not at a time like this."

"Especially at a time like this," Ned retorted.

"This is not a game," Burgoyne retorted.

"I never thought it was, sir."

"We're not in England anymore!"

"She did not specify a location to me," Ned rasped.

Burgoyne shut his eyes. "Stop it, Ned. You press me to the brink…"

"Her prayer book," Ned blurted. "You brought it with you. I saw you with it the other night, when you thought no one could see."

"Become a regular Peeping Tom, haven't you?" Burgoyne said bitterly. "Couldn't you limit yourself to spying on my sensual excesses?"

"I saw you run your fingers across an open page, then kiss it, before you put it away."

Burgoyne stared at him for several long seconds. Then he responded, in a voice unlike his own, "She...annotated it…"

"What part of it?"

"It was…the Beatitudes."

Again, a long silence elapsed between them. Then Burgoyne seemed to notice something and came closer to his aide. He touched Ned's cheek and his fingers came away bloody. "You were that close, weren't you? It could have been you…"

"Sir…" Ned's voice wobbled.

"It could have been you!"

"Please, sir…take pity on Lieutenant Rawcliffe. If you hang the boy, you'll destroy him. He already suffers from losing his best friend and being the one to have to shoot down a mere youth."

"By the living God, youth or not, he deserves to hang!"

"I know," Ned rasped. "But I love Jonathan more than I hate the rebel. Please, sir…let Jonathan see the boy die with some dignity."

Burgoyne exhaled. "Alright. We'll let nature take its course this time. Whether it is a mercy or not is yet to be proven. Perhaps the little assassin will wish for the rope to put him out of his misery before the end."

"I do not think he will," Ned said softly.

"He will not be grateful, either way," Burgoyne scoffed.

"But I am," Ned replied.

Chapter 27: UNDER ORDERS

That evening at twilight, Edmund found himself leaning up against a tree a little ways off from the camp, struggling to stop himself from shaking. A drizzle of rain was coming down, and drew his cloak tight around his shoulders, and adjusted his hat. But his hands were exceedingly clumsy at their small tasks.

He could not manage to get his mind off the horror he had witnessed. A man, a colleague, a comrade…almost a friend…gone. It was hard to fathom. And it felt utterly without gain. His poor family…

And Jonathan. He was still in the wagon, soaking that wretched young rebel's burning face as the boy thrashed from the fever and groaned from the pain. Whenever he came to consciousness, he would make a fool fight of it, decrying the invaders and insulting the King. Jonathan would leave him for a while, to discipline him, but always ended up returning when he heard the boy starting to vomit, as he had been doing every little while. And Jonathan would sit him up, and clean him up, and try to get him to swallow some brandy and laudanum to ease the pain and get him to sleep. Edmund marveled over it. Truth be told, had it been his best friend killed, he doubted he would be half so generous. Indeed, if Jonathan had been killed, he would not have been nearly as generous…

"Ned!"

He heard Abby's voice calling his name through the pattering rain, and saw her searching for him frantically around the campground.

"Here!" he called, and winced at the frog in his throat.

"Ned!" she cried again, catching sight of him and then sprinting towards him.

"Oh, Ned! I thought you might be dead! I thought…oh, I thought…"

"No," Edmund replied numbly. "Not me…Lieutenant Jones…he was hit, standing to the side of me…and then a guard, and poor Thompson's horse...then Jonathan got his gun, and shot the rebel down…and I was afraid he'd be killed trying…" His voice cracked.

"But not you! Thank God, not you!" She flung her arms around him, weeping in relief and kissing him all over his face. He wrapped his arms around her waist and squeezed her tight, afraid if she left him, he might dissolve into the abyss and never see her again.

"Ned," she said softly, "you're shaking…"

"Mmm-hmm," he agreed, and was soon sitting down on the grass lest he fall down, and she was cradling him in her arms.

"Don't be afraid, my dear," she tried to calm him. "I'm here…I won't let anyone hurt you…"

He very nearly laughed at this. How in the world could she protect him from a bullet in the face or in the back? But he was grateful for her words all the same, and the sound of her heartbeat.

She took his face in her hands and started kissing him again, this time on the mouth. It grew passionate, and Ned felt heat course through his body.

"Abby," he gasped, but she kept kissing and touching him. "Abby, please…I am only a man…"

"And I love you!" she blurted.

He swallowed hard. "No, no…it's all just…this madness all around us…"

An expression of pain came to her face. "I can still love, Ned," she murmured. "I may be broken, but…but I love you, I know that now, I do…oh, Ned, let me love you!"

He felt tears come to his eyes, and as she continued to kiss him, he did not resist any further as she pulled him deeper into the woods.

She undressed him very tenderly, and touched him more than she ever had before, as if she wanted his body to feel more fully alive since his life was almost ended. Soon she was on top of him, flesh against flesh, and she encouraged him to roll in the wet grass with her, to get on top himself.

He did so. And he lost himself to her, lost himself in this sweet distraction, and for a few fleeting minutes, forgot the blood that had stained his face as they were washed clean by the rain.

"Are…are you alright?" he panted when he had been satisfied.

She nodded.

"Are you sure?" He leaned up a little and grimaced. "Abby, you're bleeding…why didn't you stop me?"

"Because I love you," she insisted, taking his face in her hands again.

"I-I went too hard," he lectured himself. "I forgot myself…"

"Ned, you're the gentlest man I know," she rasped on the border of crying again. "Sometimes I bleed a little, that's all. Ignore it."

"I can't," he choked. "I love you…I can't stand to think of anybody hurting you, I can't stand it…I wish I could find them and kill them for whatever they did to you…"

"Ned," she whispered, and buried her face in his shoulder. "Don't worry about that now. Stay alive, please, just stay alive…"

And Ned promised himself that he would, at least for as long as he could, just to lie in her arms again.

~

Later, Ned went to look for Jonathan, who himself had gone to find Eli. The awkward young Ulsterman had run off from the wagons after the hanging was called off, and was now sitting on a log by the remains of a campfire, shivering in the chill air as he cradled his cat for comfort. Jonathan was standing over him, speaking kindly to him, which Ned thought was even more soothing to the ear than the sound of the cat purring.

"Thompson, you shouldn't be all alone at night like this," Jonathan insisted. "It is an invitation to be made a target."

"Lieutenant Jones was a target among us all, in broad daylight," Eli mumbled, continuing to stroke the cat. "It doesn't matter, does it?"

Jonathan sighed and sat down next to him on the log, and petted the cat's head as a sign of solidarity. "You're very angry at me, aren't you?"

Eli shrugged.

"I couldn't just stand by and let you stick a bayonet through the boy's throat."

"Why not?" Eli demanded. "The others were just as likely to do it!"

"I-I couldn't let any of you do it," Jonathan stammered.

"He's a murderous traitor, and full-well deserved it!" Eli retorted. "God only knows why you're coddling him now!"

"Because…I shot him," Jonathan said softly. "I've never done that before…not up close like that, at least, where I got to see who I hit. In Massachusetts, and later in Canada, there were several rebel raids on the supplies I helped fend off, and in Boston, an attempted assault upon the general's person which I am proud to say failed. But it was all quite chaotic. Myself and the others fired a few rounds to scare off the attackers. I think I may have wounded a man or two, maybe killed someone…but I don't know. Their comrades always bore them away before we knew for sure. In each instant, either they made a hasty retreat, or we did. And there was considerable smoke, wrecking bloody havoc on my specs. So you see, this was all quite new to me, what I did today, shooting down that boy…dreadfully new…"

"But he shot your best friend!" Eli blurted. "And a guard, and-and my horse!" Now tears came to his eyes. "You should have at least let the general hang him!"

"He's dying," Jonathan murmured. "There'd be no point in it. And…he's a boy. My youngest half-brother isn't much older, and…has those same eyes, round and scared when he's done something he shouldn't. I was always getting him out of mischief…so…"

"So there is a point in it for you," Eli said bitterly. "You don't want this one to die like an animal! Well, I say animals are much more deserving of consideration! They always have been! They're innocent, while we're evil! We alone draw the wrath of God among all His creatures! And-and that cursed rebel made me lie! I never lie!"

"What do you mean?" Jonathan asked calmly, seeming to sense Eli was bordering on a breakdown. "When did you lie?"

Eli swallowed hard as the cat leapt out of his arms. "I-I talk…talk to the horses. In my way, in my tongue, you know? Ulster talk. They understand me. I can calm them…I can make them think everything will be alright…" A tear ran down his face. "And I shot Winifred. After talking her down like that. She was gentle and trusting and…I-I shot her…"

"You ended her pain," Jonathan said softly.

"I ended her life," Eli retorted. "Don't you think she wanted to stay alive, like we want to stay alive? Don't you think she was afraid? She was always such a sensitive creature…" He rubbed a sleeve across his face. "I know, I know, you think I'm touched in the head. I know that's what you think. I don't care. No one cares what happens to me out here anyway."

"That's not true," Jonathan said gently.

"Yes, it is. I'm just a fool Irish farmer with a ruined face to you. No one would care if a rebel bullet took it all the way off."

"Eli, lad," Jonathan sighed, exasperated. "Must you think the worst of everyone, even yourself?"

"Am I the only one who sees our depravity for what it is?" Eli snapped.

"But there is goodness too," Jonathan insisted. "Can you not open your eyes to it?"

Eli shuddered a little. "I-I wonder sometimes if my parents liked me. I don't remember."

"No memory of them at all?" Jonathan queried.

He shook his head. "Little, very little."

"What is the little you can call to mind?" Jonathan coaxed gently.

"Mother had a special bonnet for church," Eli mumbled. "And Father smoked a pipe. I remember the color of one, and the scent of the other. That's all. I used to remember their voices a little, or think that I did, because Mother sang sometimes, but that's gone now. Their faces went away much earlier than that." He leaned forward and hugged his legs. "I-I remember…being sick. And knowing they were dead, and I was all by myself." She smiled slightly. "The cat…the cat was there. She kept me company. She kept me warm. I-I was afraid…it felt like my face was on fire." He touched his cheek self-consciously. "Next thing I remember was Grandfather, come to fetch me. He wasn't afraid of anything, said God had chosen the date of his departure, and no pestilence would hurry it along if it wasn't already ordained."

"And he nursed you?" Jonathan surmised.

Eli nodded. "He put wet rags on my face and prayed over me. He said that the Great Jehovah should take me or leave me, according to His decree. But if He left me, then Grandfather said he would see to it I was raised a good Protestant, to fear God alone, and…to prophesy."

"Prophesy?" Jonathan repeated. "What did he mean by that?"

"I don't know," Eli admitted. "But his voice, saying that, I do remember. He said that I would be…the salt of the earth. And so I lived. And he taught me about God, and about horses."

Jonathan chuckled slightly, then said sincerely, "It seems you spoke often to both."

"And barn cats," Eli added, and the innocence in his voice was palpable. "I worked in the stables every day but the Sabbath, and they were always there. If I was well-behaved, and I tried very hard to be, Grandfather would read to me, about the Siege of Londonderry, and our Protestant martyrs. And I thought…it must be terrible to really have your face burn off like that."

A disconcerted look came to Jonathan's face, and he asked, "Were you sent off to school?"

"Yes, as often as Grandfather could spare me. But sometimes I got sick, and had to come home from the schoolhouse early, or skip going altogether. The teacher said I was just pretending because the boys made fun of my face. But my grandfather, he knew me. He told the teacher none of his kin were shirkers. He knew I never lied, especially if put to the oath. He knew I'd never say I was sick if I wasn't. Besides…he got to know when I was sick after a while just by looking at me, and he'd tell me to go lie down before my face swelled up again. And he would read to me then." A wistful look came to him. "He did like to fish in the summer, usually alone. It cleared his mind, he said. But when I was very good, when I applied myself to the stable and the schoolhouse very hard, he let me come with him. And I was…happy."

"He loved you," Jonathan stated gently.

"I-I don't know. He never said it. I had a hard time reading his face most times. He was missing an eye, you know. A Papist outlaw, a Gael from the old nobility, came to collect the black rent on his family's homestead when he was fifteen. His mother was afraid of the threats, and said they should pay for protection, but his father said it would never end if they gave in, and it was hard enough to keep the farm going with the tithes Presbyterians had to pay to the established church. Most of the Protestant lords proved worse than useless in protecting us, though they were the ones to insist upon settlements of the Lord's people in Ulster, for their own benefit. Some even formed alliances with the outlaws, taking a cut from the raids. It was horrible. And in retaliation for his father's refusal to pay, my grandfather was taken by the brigands and had his eye put out. They burned the barn too."

"How dreadful," Jonathan sighed.

Eli shuddered. "Eventually, men and boys of the settlement, Grandfather amongst them, managed to fight off the animals, after finally getting a pious lord of some gumption to aid and arm them. But not before many good folk died. Grandfather never forgot any of this. He told me the story so often…yes, I think it was the last story he ever told me too, to make sure I was always careful where I kept the key to the strongbox, lest the Papist raiders should ever come back. When he died, he had lost his speech for days. I took care of him…but he never talked again. I wished so much that he had. But I'd like to think…I didn't disappoint him too badly. I tried…believe me I tried."

"Of course you did," Jonathan consoled him. "And he appreciated it. I know about such things. My stepfather was not one for wearing his feelings on his sleeve either. He was a fine old gentleman, and showed his love through deeds. Your grandfather was the same."

"But he's gone now." Eli turned his eyes down. "And I've nowhere to go. My mother's family in England say that I have no manners, and my accent is rough. They want nothing to do with me. That's why Fidelity's family will likely not let me have her, you know." He looked back up at Jonathan. "Even if I'm not shot, I don't…have anywhere to go."

"You can come and visit us, when we've all gone home again, and bring your lady," Jonathan said. "I'll introduce you to my new son…or daughter." He smiled. "Thompson, have you ever been a godfather?"

Eli shook his head.

"Well, there's a first time for everything."

There was a little clicking noise in Eli's throat. "You don't mean that."

"Why not?"

"You don't have a good recommendation for me," Eli replied.

"Yes, I do," Jonathan insisted. "You're a God-fearing young man who never forgets your prayers."

"But I'm nobody."

"I'm nobody too. We make a pair."

Eli brushed at his face again with his sleeve. "I-I could read to him. About the martyrs. The burnings and the drownings."

"Right…alright," said Jonathan, clearly not wanting to defuse the happiness Eli took from this idea even though it struck him as being slightly macabre.

"Lieutenant," Eli said softly. "If I should ever marry...if I should ever have a son…" His voice faded out and he blushed.

"Yes, go on, dear," Jonathan encouraged him to continue.

"Would you mind very much if I had him christened with your Christian name?"

Jonathan smiled a little, pulled Eli close, causing him to tighten, then relax. No words were necessary.

When Jonathan finally got Eli back to bed down in the tents in the main camp, and headed off towards his own tent, Edmund intercepted him.

Jonathan looked at him with concern. "Are you alright, Ned? You should be bedded down for the night by now."

"I was going to say the same thing about you," Ned chuckled nervously. "Are you alright?"

Jonathan shrugged. "I don't suppose any of us are alright at the moment, nor are we likely to get much sleep." He gave Ned a sympathetic look. "First time you've seen a bloody death like that, isn't it? And so close to you, too."

Ned nodded.

"I suppose this is what our Quaker host meant when he said that, in time, we would better understand them…" Jonathan placed a hand on Ned's shoulder. "I thank God the bullet missed you."

"But it hit Jones," Ned blurted. "You were on closer terms with him than with me. Surely you'd rather I took the bullet instead…" Ned's voice cracked.

Spontaneously, Jonathan gave Edmund a hug. "I would never make a choice like that. All I know is that I am glad you were protected from harm." He leaned Ned up again. "I fear we'll have a rougher time going forward. Stay close to camp, alright?"

Again, Ned nodded. Then he rasped, "Jonathan, don't you hate the boy in the wagon?"

Jonathan blinked. "I don't suppose it matters, does it? We each must do what we must do."

"What do you mean?"

Before Jonathan could respond, he seemed to spy something over Ned's shoulder. Ned turned to see Red Elk standing there.

"Excuse me," Jonathan said, and went over to the Iroquois.

"I came to praise your aim," Red Elk stated. "You have proven that you are truly a warrior, not merely a man of medicine."

Jonathan winced. "A bitter necessity."

"What is bitter about it?" Red Elk asked. "The spirits of those slain beside you will rest easier now, having been avenged."

"I cannot speak on behalf of the dead," Jonathan replied, "but it does not make me rest easier to see the boy writhing and vomiting blood from the bullet I put into his body."

Red Elk was quiet for a while, then stated, "Your brother soldier was right just now. You should hate that boy. You should have let your chief hang him, or stake him to the ground and leave him to die that way. That would put fear in the hearts of your enemies."

"Firstly, in a way, he too is part of my people," Jonathan replied. "And secondly, though more importantly, I must…" He closed his eyes. "I must do what I must do."

"But why?" Red Elk pressed. "Why are you tending to the one who shot down your brothers?"

"You wouldn't understand…"

"No," Red Elk said sarcastically. "We are savages. We would not understand."

"Of course, you can't bloody well understand me," Jonathan blurted. "And I can't bloody well understand you! God help me, I'm thick in the head, a common country bumpkin from the forest's edge, the simple sort accustomed to the ways of Hampshire village folk. Yes, our lot understands each other well enough. Beyond that, the world seems to me a God-forsaken mystery! No, far be it from me to understand any sort of American, tribesman or colonial. The whole pack of you terrifies me! I have no better luck with the Germans and their brutish manners or the French with their ritual hocus pocus or the Scots and Irish, always about to bash each other's brains in, or the Welsh…" His voice cracked. "No one on this side of eternity should attempt to understand the Welsh! It's part of an ancient revenge, keeping the Saxons forever in the dark! They are inscrutable and infuriating and…oh, my God…" He pressed a hand to his mouth and bent over as if stricken by a sudden pain. After recovering himself he stood up straight again, and continued in a rasping voice, "You see what an utter fool I was…thinking I could somehow come to understand what makes that rebel boy tick…no, no, fool's errand that…I don't even think I'd want to understand him, the little fiend…"

"Then I ask you again: why did you not let your chief hang him?" Red Elk demanded.

Jonathan swallowed hard. "Because I am under orders from a higher chief."

"Across the water?"

"No, greater yet," Jonathan replied. "They are both His servants. And His command is not that I should understand, no…but that even when I have no understanding left to me, I should…" He sucked in a breath. "I should give the hungry man bread and the thirsty man drink and the sick man aid and the lonely man company and the doubting man encouragement, and when I have nothing left to give, if the occasion calls for it, well, then I should give away my life as well, so that another might live. Those are His orders I live under, and please God, in His mercy, I shall die under. We love because He first loved us."

Red Elk stared at him for a moment. "Your foreign god has such a hold over you?"

Jonathan nodded.

"Some would call you weak because you follow such teachings."

"Do you?" Jonathan asked.

Red Elk shrugged. Then he said lowly, "Most of your kind do not believe those things you said. Or if they do, they have not shown it, have not lived it."

"I cannot judge them," Jonathan replied.

"But I can," Red Elk snorted. "And you…you are different." He gave him another long look. "I trust your weakness more than I trust their strength."

Jonathan swallowed hard. "Thank you."

Chapter 28: I SHALL NOT WANT

The next morning, the young rebel remained mostly in a feverish coma, tossing about under the blankets Jonathan had wrapped him in. The exhausted clerk kept checking on him periodically and wiping the sweat from his brow. But when he had to leave for a longer span to attend to his work, one of the guards crept into the wagon and began to torment him with a pen knife. He had cut the boy's face several times and was threatening to cut off his fingers when Ned happened to overhear the man growling and the boy yelping, and went to fetch Jonathan. By the time they both got to the scene, and dragged the guard off the lad, one of his fingers was bleeding profusely and his eyes wide with terror.

"Think yourself so brave, private?" Jonathan blurted.

"He-he shot Private Billings, sir," the guard panted. "We-we got on alright…could have been me out there just as well, sir…could have been you, even, sir…he shot your mate too…so I thought…I'd give the bloody Yankee his dues…in blood…"

"No, soldier," Jonathan rasped. "He is a prisoner of the King, under my watch, and you had no authority to harm a hair on his head! Now return to your duties. I'll decide how to deal with your misconduct later."

Jonathan quickly bound up the boy's finger and cleaned the blood off his face with a wet cloth. Then he decided to move the rebel out from the wagon to his tent so that he could keep a closer eye on him. The boy did not utter a word the whole time, just stared at Jonathan with a strange expression on his face.

By afternoon, the boy was vomiting again. He would fall into convulsions and could not stop himself until he brought up blood. This round was particularly horrendous, causing blood to seep through the bandages on his wounded abdomen and gush from his broken nose. Ned heard the awful noises and wandered over to Jonathan's tent, watching from the open flap as his friend tried to help the boy in whatever little ways he could. Ned heard a couple of the guards nearby chortle darkly and say it was music to their ears to listen to the rebel wretch in such a state.

But Jonathan was Jonathan. There was something in that man that could not help but be decent, even if everyone else was drowning in their dreams of revenge, for what the young rebel did or might have done, and whenever his eyes would gleam with resentment, they would soon after shimmer with pity for a boy, assassin or not, that he had shot out of a tree like a perched bird. Yes, he defied and shamed the whole camp with that frustrating decency.

"Alright," Jonathan said, holding the boy up as he gasped for air and shook violently, keeping him from falling into his own vomit. "It's alright…get it up."

The boy spit up more saliva and blood, as there was nothing left inside him. When he was done, tears were running down his cheeks, as if the exertion and pain of it all had finally broken his defiant will. Still he struggled against the sobs, biting hard on his lip, pressing a hand to his bleeding stomach, the dark purple liquid spilling through his fingers and down his chin. At last he fainted against Jonathan's shoulder, and Ned saw his friend spontaneously hold him.

"There…there…" Jonathan murmured, moving his hand up and down on the boy's back. "There's a brave lad…whatever else you are, you take it like a man…"

Ned heard the rebel gasping harder and saw his white hand clutch at Jonathan's sleeve.

Jonathan glanced over at the boy's hand, then squeezed it tightly with his own bandaged one. The boy could restrain himself no longer and sobbed convulsively into Jonathan's shoulder.

"Shhh…I know, I know…" Jonathan whispered. "Easy now, easy does it…"

When the boy had tired himself out with tears, he just lay against Jonathan, resigned, quiet, shivering. Waiting to die. And Jonathan rubbed his back some more.

Then the boy stammered weakly, "Why…why didn't you shoot me…h-h-higher?"

Jonathan winced. "It wasn't my intent to make it slow. But everything was happening so fast. I-I wouldn't have done this on purpose, even to an animal. I…" He shuddered. "You believe that, don't you?"

Ned didn't hear the boy say anything in response, but thought he might have seen a slight movement of his head, nodding.

There was a clicking sound in Jonathan's throat as he used a rag to clean the boy's face. "We can't…go back. Can't change a blessed thing. God will judge us, and his judgments shall be just. But we can try, all the same, to have mercy on each other, as He told us to do. Try to…forgive. Can't we?"

Again, after a few moments, Ned saw the boy's head move.

"Right then," Jonathan exhaled. "We won't talk about it anymore."

He laid the boy back down on the blanket, plugged up the bleeding wound as best he could, and helped him drink a bit of brandy mixed with laudanum, though the boy could only get down a few swallows before turning his face away, too sick to get more down. It did have its effects, though, and he did not have any strong seizures after that. He just rested silently, watching the enemy who was trying to ease his suffering.

When the boy finally spoke, he asked a question.

"Did he have a family?"

"Who?"

"Your friend."

Jonathan hesitated for a moment, then answered, "Yes, he…yes. He was a busy man." Ned thought he saw Jonathan almost smile. "I think five was the last count when I visited Wales. There was a sixth, but she died when she was very small. It was terribly sad…" He was quiet again, then finished, "Please God, they're together again now."

"I'm one of five," the boy said softly.

"Oh?" Jonathan was shivering a little now, his teeth chattering slightly, as if trying desperately to keep his emotions in check. "Brothers? Sisters?"

"Sisters."

"All of them?"

"Yes."

"Your mother's only son then." Jonathan dabbed the sweat from the boy's forehead with the rag and brushed back a few locks of his damp hair with his hand. "Does she know where you are?"

"I-I don't know. Not...that I'm here, now."

"Just that you ran off to the rebels to make a hero of yourself."

The boy inhaled sharply. "Don't...burn them out. They didn't do anything to you."

Jonathan didn't respond. Ned doubted he knew how. He just muttered, "Worried sick, no doubt, poor woman."

Then the boy looked distressed at this. "I-I'm glad she'll never see my face all cut up."

"It's not so bad," Jonathan countered gently. "Seems to have been a dull knife."

"Really?"

"Yes, really."

The boy swallowed hard, then asked timidly, "Do you have a family?"

"Yes. Not as many as Lieutenant Jones, but two already, and a third on the way. I haven't had as much time with them and their mother as I would like, but perhaps when this is over, there'll be more to come. Besides, I want to be there to teach my son to hunt when he's a little older..." He chuckled wryly. "You know...I got in trouble with the law at your age too."

"How?"

"Poaching in the New Forest. I was caught with a grouse and hauled in by the gamekeeper. My stepfather had to pay me off. He said I was never to do a troublesome thing like that again...unless I could get away with it as well as he could."

At this, the boy actually smiled. Then the smile faded.

"The other man...did he have a family?"

"I don't know. He was a guard here. But surely we all either have a family or want a family, no matter our rank. It's part of being human. It's the beauty of life. And...he was a man." He touched one of the cuts along the boy's face. "I think the guard who hurt you was his friend. He wanted to avenge him...and I suppose he was afraid. It could have been him instead."

The boy sucked in a breath. "Were you afraid?"

"Mmm-hmm," Jonathan responded.

"Maybe...you'll make it back alright," the boy offered.

"Oh?"

"Yes...maybe you'll be alright."

Jonathan laughed shortly, as if he might cry. "Fool boy," he said, almost to himself. "You're not as hard as you put on."

The boy shrugged, then mumbled, "Tell me something, won't you?"

"What do you wish to know?" Jonathan responded.

"I-I was just wondering if...if you had an opinion on angels..."

Jonathan snorted. "I admit that was not the question I expected from you..."

"It's just that my mother used to tell me the angel of death was beautiful to the righteous, but terrifying to sinners. I…umm…I was just wondering how he might appear to people…well, like us…"

"People who have killed?" Jonathan surmised.

"I…I don't know, I suppose that's what I mean…"

Jonathan exhaled. "We are all sinners, in one way or another. As such, we all have blood on our hands. But no death is ugly if the soul casts itself upon the grace of God."

"I…I hope you're right," the boy replied, then after a few moments of silence, said, "Would you tell me something else?"

"Ask it."

"Will you...will I be strung up when I'm dead? To make an example?"

Jonathan sighed. "I'll see you buried, if I have anything to say about it."

"Will anyone...say a prayer?"

"I will say a prayer."

And for the first time the boy said, very quietly, "Thank you."

Jonathan touched his cheek. "Will you tell me your name?"

"I can't," the boy protested. "You'll hurt my family…"

"Your Christian name," Jonathan clarified. "That's all I want. God knows who you are, but I want to…well…" He shook his head. "I want to pray, using your name, that's all."

The boy said nothing for a while. Then mumbled, "David."

"David," the clerk repeated, smiling slightly, sadly. "The boy with the sling, taking on Goliath. That's what you thought you were doing, hmm? Oh, don't answer that. It doesn't matter now. For you are David, and I am Jonathan, and God brought us together, and only God knows why. And I will stay with you until God takes you."

The young rebel did not live more than an hour after that. Sensing his end coming on, he had asked for a drink, and after having a flask of water held up to his lips, he started reciting the 23rd psalm:

"The Lord is my shepherd; therefore can I lack nothing.
He shall feed me in a green pasture, and lead me forth beside the waters of comfort.
He shall convert my soul, and bring me forth in the paths of righteousness for his Name's sake.
Yea, though I walk through the valley of the shadow of death, I will fear no evil; for thou art with me; thy rod and thy staff comfort me.
Thou shalt prepare a table before me in the presence of them that trouble me; thou hast anointed my head with oil, and my cup shall be full…"

He continued on until he was too weak to speak. Jonathan was still there with him, as promised, and taking the boy's hand, he finished the psalm for him, as David closed his eyes for the last time, drifting off peacefully, as if to sleep:

*"Surely thy loving-kindness and mercy shall follow me all the days of my life;
and I will dwell in the house of the Lord for ever."*

~

    Jonathan saw to the boy's burial himself, just as the sun's light was fading in the sky. He selected a spot not far from where poor Gavin Jones and the guard had been buried under a spreading maple tree. He reasoned that the dead of any conflict would not scorn proximity to each other beneath the earth for they would all be judged equally under God, and had no further quarrel with one another. He recruited Ned to help him with the digging, hoping to have the task completed before anyone could stop them. There was a real possibility the general might still deem it fitting to leave the boy's body hung up to rot as a warning. It was not a very deep grave by the end of it, but it was dignified enough, and Ned and Jonathan managed to find several sizable stones to discourage animals from digging it up again

    Abby happened to come around just as they had placed the body into the hole. Ned at first tried to dissuade her from looking, but she would not be held back.

    "He's just a boy," she blurted, her eyes glistening. She looked at Jonathan accusingly. "You shot a boy."

    "A boy who was shooting at us," Jonathan ground out, "who killed two of us, and a horse, and would have killed more if he wasn't taken down…"

    "He wouldn't have been doing any such thing if you hadn't marched into his country to suppress his people!" she shot back. "If you hadn't taken the side of a king who—"

    "Stop," Jonathan commanded her. "You border on treason!"

    "What if there are other kinds of treason, worse than against one man sitting pretty on a throne somewhere?" she continued. "What about treason against your fellow man? What about treason against your conscience?"

    "Ned," Jonathan snapped. "Rein her in now, or I may have to report her."

    "Abby, please," Ned exhaled. "You don't know what you're saying."

    She looked back and forth between them. "You both really believe the King is the highest good, don't you? That anything he says is from the mouth of God?"

    "He is our head, in matters spiritual and temporal," Jonathan replied firmly. "All loyal subjects affirm the same, as should you, and accept his God-given authority."

    "And what about Ned?" Abby challenged. "He used to prefer the pope to the king!"

    "He doesn't anymore," Jonathan replied calmly. "He's sworn otherwise."

    "And what if you're wrong? What if you found out he was a secret Papist? Would you turn him in?"

    "Abby," Ned hissed, taking her arm, but she pulled away.

    "Well, would you?" she challenged Jonathan again.

    Jonathan sighed. "Yes, I would. But I trust his word. He will not break his oath."

Edmund felt a sudden weight upon his chest. Jonathan did not know about the relic from Teresa, the one Ned had sewn inside his coat. It was a small enough infraction, surely. No one needed to know. It was simply for sentimental reasons, a manifestation of homesickness. But still…it was there, over his heart, where no one else could see it.

Jonathan put a handkerchief over the boy's face, then picked up his copy of the Book of Common Prayer that had been lying beside the grave and quietly started to read from it as Ned shoveled earth back into the hole. When the shoveling was complete, and the rocks dragged into place, Jonathan was still reading.

"For none of us liveth to himself, and no man dieth to himself. For if we live, we live unto the Lord, and if we die, we die unto the Lord. Whether we live, therefore, or die, we are the Lord's. Blessed are the dead who die in the Lord; even so saith the Spirit, for they rest from their labors…"

"Lieutenant Rawcliffe," came a booming voice from behind them. It was General Burgoyne, with Lieutenant Caldwell at his side. Of course, he would be the one to tattle. "That's quite enough. Close the book. You know perfectly well it's against regulations…"

"He felt contrition for having taken lives, sir, I could tell," Jonathan stated. "I thought we might err on the side of mercy before the throne of God…"

"You have gall even to be burying the corpse," Caldwell spat.

"He's right," Burgoyne admitted, though with a certain hesitance to agree. "You received no permission from me."

Jonathan closed the book and lowered his gaze. "I will humbly accept any discipline you deem fitting, sir."

Burgoyne stared at him for a long while, then muttered, "There's no time. We leave this place at the first dawn. I need you to prepare."

Burgoyne turned to leave, and Jonathan cast Ned a look, indicating he thought it would be wise if they followed. The funeral, if it could be called a funeral, seemed to be over.

But Abby was still standing there by the stones, pulling up the hood of her worn cloak as rain started pattering down. And then she began to sing, in a voice as heavy as the night and as fierce as the dawn.

"Why should vain mortals tremble at the sight of
Death and destruction in the field of battle
Where blood and carnage, where blood and carnage,
Clothe the ground in crimson, sounding with death-groans?

Death will invade us by the means appointed,
And we must all bow to the king of terrors;
Nor am I anxious, nor am I anxious
If I am prepared, what shape he comes in.

*Then to the wisdom of my Lord and Master
I will commit all that I have or wish for,
Sweetly as babes sleep, sweetly babes sleep
Will I give my life up when called to yield it.*

*Now, Mars, I dare thee, clad in smoky pillars,
Bursting from bomb-shells, roaring from the cannon,
Rattling in grape-shot, rattling in grape-shot,
Like a storm of hailstones, torturing ether.*

*Still shall the banner of the King of Heaven
Neither advance where I'm afraid to follow;
While that precedes me, while that precedes me,
With an open bosom, War, I defy thee!"*

Abby turned towards Burgoyne, who had himself turned back to listen to her song, enthralled, it seemed, by the drama of the moment. He was too much a theater man, attuned to the language of song and stage, to react any other way.

"War," she repeated the hymn's final line, "I defy thee!"

Then she picked up her shirts and headed off into the clearing.

When Ned went to find her, the tears were falling from her eyes like the rain from the heavens, and his heart bled for her.

"Abby, I understand how you feel," he murmured.

"Do you?" she demanded, brushing the tears from her cheeks.

"Yes, because I understand what civil war does to people," Ned replied. "It tears us all up into little pieces inside, knowing that win or lose, we are destroying, or being destroyed, by our own. Look at Jonathan. Can you not see his pain? Even if he had caused suffering to a foreign boy, French or Spanish or from some other enemy nation, he would still have suffered, because he's a decent man. But this is ever so much worse. And for me…it's worse in yet another way…"

"What do you mean?" she demanded.

"My family found themselves a part of more than a few rebellions down through the years, usually failed ones. You're right to mark me out for my Catholic rearing. It makes me see things in a different light than others. I know what it is to earn the wrath of those ruling the roost. I know what it is to have a legacy of strife, with neighbors killing neighbors because of what king they own or how they worship God. It breaks my heart that it's happening again. And yet…here we are…"

"And what sage counsel do you have for me then?" she queried bitterly. "To kiss, and make it all better?"

"Nothing so trite," he murmured, tears stinging his eyes. "All I can do is mourn with you, for this is an unnatural and accursed war that must end soon or ruin us all. We are the same people, Abby, and we are bound to the same fate…"

"The old world and the new world are separated by more than an ocean now," she retorted. "The chasm is in ourselves and the wounds we have delivered and borne for different dreams! Perhaps we do not wish to be the same people or be bound to your fate! Perhaps we have higher aspirations! Perhaps my blood has changed from British to American!"

"But we should not be making each other bleed, for any dream under heaven," he insisted. "Blood binds, whether we like it to or not, and knows nothing of distance, over land or sea. We belong to each other. We should…love each other…"

"Have you not heard? Those who love each other draw each other's blood," she mumbled.

He swallowed hard. "We must learn how best to care for another…how best to serve each other's needs…"

"And you think Britain has done that with her colonies?" she challenged, turning her back to him. "I say that the King and parliament, like most men around a comely woman, think only of our submission for their own benefit."

"Perhaps we are all to blame, one way or another," Ned suggested, choosing to ignore her treason yet again, even as he prayed his own treasonous relic would never be uncovered. "If we loved each other as we ought, we would put everything else second, and no sacrifice would be too great to make. We would rather bleed than draw blood."

She chuckled ruefully. "You sound like some sort of Romish priest, Ned."

He felt a twist in his stomach. "I-I fear I would have made a poor one…"

"Alright, so you're not perfectly chaste," she conceded. "But still…you're good and kind and you talk about everything as if God were in it…like you know some great secret the rest of us keep forgetting…"

"Well, I know God is in you, especially after hearing you sing just now," he said softly. "You cannot tell me that you do not believe in Him after that. No…your voice was too true…"

"He is still a mystery to me, even as I sing of Him," she murmured. "You seem to walk in the light, Ned, while I walk in the shadows."

Edmund took several steps forward, with her back still turned to him, and wrapped his arms around her from behind. "Surely it is the other way around…I sleep in the dark, and can only wonder whether or not I shall live through the next day…"

"Don't," she blurted. "You'll make it happen if you say it out loud."

"But then whenever you have come to me, it's as if stars have gilded the blackness, and I am simply thankful to be alive, for as long as the moment may last." His body instantly grew warm beside her own, craving to be as close to her as she would allow. "I suppose not knowing what will befall me makes me feel…an almost violent need to love and be loved, whenever possible…" He linked his hands around her middle. "Abby, do you still feel the way you did yesterday? Are we, at least, one people?"

He squeezed her tighter, and she sucked in a breath, placing her hands over his. He relished the feeling. She had explored him so lovingly with those hands the day before. He wanted to do the same with her.

"Let me come to you tonight," he whispered in her ear. "Won't you?"

He kissed and nuzzled her neck, and she let out a sigh. Was it yes? It certainly wasn't no.

And in the night, he did come to her.

"May I have you?" he rasped, never having felt such intense desire before. "Abby…I want you…please…"

He did not know how else to say it, even as he felt his face burning from shame and his throat tightening with longing for her, all of her, this night and forever.

She did not punish him by holding him at bay, but welcomed him into her embrace. They rolled in and out of each other, like the tides that rolled between their homes. Yes, they were England and America, part of each other, flesh and bone, breath and blood, and they were the ocean's turmoil too. If they could resolve the tension, or even let go to it, somehow, he thought, there was hope on the other side of the bloodshed.

She moaned as he became one with her, the moon reflecting in her eyes.

And somewhere, far off, a wolf howled.

In the end, he asked if she was bleeding this time, asked if he had done better, gone softer. He had tried, truly he had, in spite of his lust. He wanted to prove his love for her.

She answered everything the way he wanted her to answer it, and kissed his cheek.

He wondered if she was lying.

As Edmund returned to his tent, he passed by Jonathan, sitting with the guard who had tried to cut off the rebel boy's finger. The guard's face, he noticed by the lantern light, was taut and blanched. It was certainly unusual for an officer to sit beside an enlisted man in such a manner, as if they were equals.

"He killed your friend," Jonathan was saying to him. "He could have killed you. So you wished to punish him for it."

"Isn't that natural, sir?" the guard mumbled.

"Yes," Jonathan answered, "for one who fears death."

"Don't we all fear death, sir?" the guard pressed.

"It is altogether natural," Jonathan conceded, "for men born once of women." He paused, then added, "You're young. But you've seen your fair share of death haven't you?"

The guard hesitated, then murmured, "Yes, sir."

"And you are afraid of the dark," Jonathan said.

"No, sir," the guard denied, shrinking back, closer to the lantern. "I am a thing of the dark. Like a rat in the alley, I live off scraps and corpses, all rotting things. Wilcox, my mess mate…he understood that. He grew up the same as me…orphans."

"Yet you are not far from the light," Jonathan responded.

"What do you mean, sir?" He blinked. "Oh…the lantern, sir? Is that what you mean?"

"I mean that you fight against the final darkness of death," Jonathan said. "That is why you attacked the boy. He might have killed you, and bound you to that same darkness, and you did not want it. You wanted to bring death upon death."

"I-I suppose I did," he admitted. "Not even rats want to die, do they?" He laughed shortly, then grew serious. "No disrespect, sir, it's just that…most of the time, when death's come to someone close, it was by way of a thing that couldn't be killed, like…like the pox, or no food…you can't make those things pay, can you, sir?"

"Yet death comes for us all, no matter how we fight it, or try to make it pay," Jonathan noted. "No matter birth or rank, no matter if our purses or our bellies are full or empty. She comes, and we cannot defeat her darkness."

The guard shrugged. "Then…there ain't much point in anything, I suppose."

"I said *we* cannot, being born of nature," Jonathan clarified. "But there is another nature, another birth."

"What do you mean, sir?"

"Charity," Jonathan said.

"I never took no charity, sir," the guard defended himself.

"No, not that kind," Jonathan countered. "It is a flaming coal that burns our lips and our hearts. It brings us pain, but casts out fear. It is stronger than death."

"I-I don't know much about religion, sir, if that's what you're on about," the guard confessed.

"What is your Christian name?"

"Mine? Oh, Samuel."

"Samuel," Jonathan repeated. "You have been named after a boy who the Lord called out to in the dead of night."

"Really?" he chuckled.

"Yes," Jonathan said. "The Lord called his name in the dark, 'Samuel, Samuel, Samuel.' And he would not stop until the boy answered."

"That wouldn't happen to me," the guard mumbled.

"Oh no?" Jonathan challenged.

The guard blinked. "What happened then? When he answered, I mean?"

"The coal," Jonathan replied. "A foretaste of greater things."

"What greater things? You mean that he couldn't die?" The young guard bit his lip. "I know it doesn't matter, not for me…I'm likely to be flogged…then sometime or other, die…and that will be that. I'm not your kind, not pious. I don't like folks pretending to be what they ain't…but I'll think about it now, though I might mock it in the morning, for I don't know how to handle holy things…" His voice wobbled, and he pressed his hands briefly to his face. "Do you think…do you think my friend is…gone, just gone for good? And that'll be me too?"

Jonathan touched the guard's arm. "Charity," he repeated again. "When all else fades away, charity shall endure." He pointed to the lantern, burning through the night. "Charity," he repeated again. "For our neighbors and our enemies alike. It is an altogether unnatural thing. And the darkness cannot put her out."

The guard's eyes were shimmering now. "Your friend's dead too. Do you think he's still…?"

"Charity," Jonathan rasped sorrowfully. "I know, by her light, that death has been trampled down by death already. God loved the world so much…" Then he cleared his throat. "I don't suppose you can read, lad?"

The guard shook his head. "I'm good at remembering things, though."

"Well, I can read," Jonathan said. "And you can remember. We make a pair." He handed the soldier some dried meat wrapped in a handkerchief. "I had little appetite tonight."

"But-but I don't take…"

"It'll just go to waste otherwise. Take it, out of respect for me."

So the guard nodded once, took the dried meat, and began to nibble on it.

Jonathan, meanwhile, pulled out a book and began to read.

"Though I speak with the tongues of men and of angels, and have not charity…"

Chapter 29: BUMPS IN THE ROAD

The British march continued south, and the harassment by the rebels grew worse. Toppled trees lay everywhere, obstructing movement, and efforts to remove them invited marksmen to take aim from the underbrush with deadly effects. Worse yet, the revolutionary army, under General Philip Schuyler, was systematically destroying both crops and stores in Burgoyne's path to prevent foraging. In retaliation, the British burned more buildings, including Schuyler's own house. But this did little to control the damage being inflicted on the King's troops. Everyone knew that the supply lines back to Fort Ticonderoga were being stretched dangerously thin, and the more the unexpected delays and lightning raids wreaked havoc with the schedule, with means to replenish the army dwindling, the more desperate the situation became. Some soldiers started roving off on their own to forage from houses along the route, terrorizing the inhabitants, regardless of whether they were Loyalist or Patriot. Punishments were duly administered if they were caught, lest order collapse. But it was a hard thing to put a halt to altogether. The men were growing hungry, and the hunger made them unruly, no matter how many times Burgoyne shrugged off the troubles afflicting his campaign as mere "bumps in the road."

The men had other appetites too which they often sought to satisfy on such independent ventures. One night, as Ned sat taking dictation, a farmer brought his daughter to Burgoyne's camp, claiming she was ravished by a grenadier a week or so before, and he had been chasing after the train in quest of justice for his name. *For his name.* Ned didn't like his choice of words, didn't like how the poor girl cowered before him, didn't like how her hesitation to identify the man responsible caused her father to slap her. The poor thing was bruised and broken in spirit, and Ned felt his heart bleed when she said, "He has a missing finger…I made him a glove…with only four fingers…"

He had come to the house hungry, she said, his hand still twitching slightly from a terrible wound that had cost him that finger. She had felt sorry for him, and fed him, and made him the glove. She was lonely and they talked. He came back the next day, and again she fed him, and again they talked. It was only on the third day, when the train was about to move on, that he decided to rob the house and her virtue, leaving her crumpled on the floor, bruised and bleeding, her clothes torn from her back. Her father, of course, blamed her for feeding the soldier to begin, and said she got exactly what she deserved, though he intended to avenge his own honor.

The guilty party was finally identified, and first tried to deny the charge, but when the girl was pressed for further identification beyond the missing finger, she mentioned a mole on his left shoulder. It was found where she said it would be. The grenadier changed tactics.

"She was asking for it, sir," he insisted. "She let me in every night of her own free will…"

"After you went looking for pillage," Burgoyne stated gravely.

"Forage, sir…"

"Without orders, private!" Burgoyne snapped. "Without orders!"

The grenadier swallowed hard. "She-she fed me of her own accord after that first night, sir. Honest."

"And to repay her, you stole her maidenhead," Burgoyne surmised.

He shrugged. "She wasn't fighting it when I put my tongue in her mouth."

"Vulgarity aside, why was there a struggle, private?" Burgoyne demanded. "If she received your advances willingly, why was she found bruised and bleeding, with her clothes torn off, sobbing on the floor?"

The grenadier lowered his eyes. "She…lost her nerve, sir." He cast her a condescending look. "I thought she was woman enough to take it. But no, she tried to hold back on me, the prudish little wench."

"It hurt," she rasped. "I-I didn't think you were going to…"

"What else did you think I would do?" he scoffed. "Think I just came back to hear you prattle at me? You asked for it, and I gave it to you. No crime in that." He turned again to Burgoyne. "Besides, sir…she ain't nobody special. What honor did she have to lose?"

Burgoyne stared at him, disgust spreading over his features. "Soldier, you dishonor your livery. And so it shall be taken from you. You will be removed from the grenadiers, whose noble name you have tarnished, and transitioned back to the battalion company of your former regiment for trial. If they have any sense of dignity for their regimental honor, they will make you suffer a penalty of equal weight to your misdeeds."

"But sir…" He gestured to some guards.

"Do not dare, private, if you have any hope of saving your life," Burgoyne snapped. Then he gestured to guards nearby. "Get him out of my sight."

When the soldier was taken away, the farmer stepped forward and slapped his daughter with such force that the sound caused both Ned and Burgoyne to jolt.

"You damned hussy," her father spat. "Smear my name, will you? You've been filth since the day you were born, since you killed your mother!" He raised his hand again.

The poor girl, blood dripping from her nose, doubled over in pain and fear, sobbing.

Ned had enough and stood up from his desk in the corner, planting himself between the weeping girl and her irate father.

"You'll not lay a hand on her again," Ned ground out. "Not in front of me."

"She's from my body, soldier, not yours," the man declared. "She's mine to discipline as I see fit!"

"You're little better than the man just taken away for being an animal," Ned rasped. "Bullies and brutes, both of you!"

The man lunged forward, and Ned pushed him back, drawing his pistol.

"Ned," Burgoyne tried to calm him. "Easy does it, lad…"

"General, keep your bloody fool of an aide off of me," the man growled.

Burgoyne raised an eyebrow. "Me, sir? I am not accustomed to taking orders from farmers, nor allowing a young gentleman to be insulted by them. Also, I…am getting old. My back hurts. I am weary of this whole business. And if you expect me to exert myself further by rising from this chair to restrain Lieutenant Southworth from dislodging your remaining teeth, you are insane." He leaned forward, arms folded over his desk. "So I can only advise you not to strike your daughter again, and thus avoid arousing the dear boy's chivalric streak, as out of place as it may be in this savage wilderness of yours."

The man snorted and stepped back, gesturing dismissively at his daughter. "She's dead to me. Leave her here to fend for herself or take her along with you. It doesn't matter to me either way." With that, he marched out of the tent.

The general sighed, then cast his gaze upon the girl, one which Ned could not help notice contained a flash of attraction. "Ned, better let Maggie get her some clean clothes and something to eat. We'll sort things out from there."

Ned obeyed, and Maggie, good-hearted and down to earth, was kind to the poor girl who struggled to stop shaking, and kept asking if she was bound to be left behind in the forest.

"Naw, sweeting," Maggie assured, dishing her out some stew. "The general's not the type to let a pretty face or skinny waist pass him by." She winked.

The girl swallowed hard. "Maybe…I shouldn't eat then. I might get fat."

"You don't eat on your own, and I'll have to force you myself," Maggie declared. "Skin and bones, child! Too much of a good thing, you know!"

Reluctantly she started to eat, and Maggie pulled out a crude bone comb to get the knots out of her hair.

Late that night, the girl made her way back to Burgoyne in his tent. There was only ever one reason for that. And Edmund knew the general was drunk. His carnality was in a perfect position to conquer his morality, and it made Ned feel sick.

"I-I want you to…take me on the train, s-s-sir," she stammered. "And if you do, I can…I can give you…"

"The cuckoo's nest," he slurred.

"Sir?" she asked innocently.

"What you're offering me…is a hand in the cuckoo's nest. Maybe you did entice that grenadier after all!" He laughed at his own dirty joke, and slapped his knee. "Come along, little bird, settle on your perch!"

She very nervously skittered over to him and sat on his knee.

"There's a good girl," he encouraged her, his eyes gleaming lustily. He wasted no time in starting to undo her dress. "Let's see what goods you have to barter with…"

He ran his hands along her open front, then followed the motion with his mouth, and she gasped, her cheeks flushed. Then he followed it up by reaching one hand up her skirt. Again she gasped, and squirmed a little.

"I think I'll be wanting a quick fix," he decided, his voice thick with desire, as he started to undo his breeches. "Hold firm, little one, and open up wide…"

"Wait, please," she yelped. "Please, please, I…" Her teeth chattered. "Please wait…wait, and I'll kiss you…I'll kiss you for a long time, and make you like it…he taught me how before…" She sucked in a breath. "Please, please, please…wait…"

He just stared at her for a moment, then chuckled a little. "Such a virgin…"

She took his face in her hands, in a way that seemed to shock him, and started to kiss him. Something about it made him turn red, even though he had ventured so much farther with his hands under her skirt. As if to prove something, he leaned her down suddenly and kissed her passionately until she squeaked. "There, you see?" he sighed. "A virgin…"

"I-I'm not, though," she reminded him. "Not…anymore…I'm just…afraid, please…please…"

He took his hand out from under her skirt. "You're…shaking…" he murmured.

"I thought…he just wanted to kiss me, really, I did," she whimpered. "I thought he liked me. I liked to think…someone had gotten to like me. But then…then…" She broke down in a sob. "He h-held me down…he held me down, so hard, and he hurt me…I told him to stop…I did, I told him…but he…h-hurt me…and I couldn't make him stop hurting me…"

Burgoyne just stared at her hazily for a moment, then whispered "Shhhhhh" and leaned her into his shoulder, his hand bracing her back. She cried even harder and spontaneously threw her arms around his neck. He seemed to stiffen, not expecting it. Then he touched her hair.

"Believe me, child…I won't hurt you. I couldn't…your hair, it's like…another little girl I knew…the most beautiful thing I ever did see…the most beautiful thing God ever made…" His voice wobbled. "And she had a little girl, with the same hair…no, no, I could never hurt you without…hurting myself…" He took her hand and kissed her palm, then her wrist. "Now, go on, little bird, fly away."

"I'm lonely," she rasped, her arm still wrapped around his neck, her face nuzzled into his shoulder.

"Is that why you let the soldier back into your father's house, you wanted him to teach you how to kiss?" he asked softly.

She nodded. "You…you wouldn't know what it's like…you always have people around you, giving you attention…"

Burgoyne snorted. "You know nothing, child." He kissed her forehead, and leaned back into the cot with her. "So…if the cuckoo's nest is not for me tonight, it's time for me to sleep. Must be up at a reasonable hour tomorrow. You may go or stay, as you please."

She didn't say anything, but stayed with her head on his chest as he pulled up the blanket.

"You sad little thing," Burgoyne sighed. "Should I kill him for you?"

"Who?" she queried.

"The brute who said he was going to kiss you, then put marks all over all your poor body. Yes, I saw. Black and blue on lily white."

She blushed. "He-he said I shouldn't have squirmed so much. It-it just hurt me worse."

"Want me to kill him then? I have the power, you know."

She shrugged. "Killing him won't fix me. Besides, Father added a few marks too."

"And that's why you want me to take you along with us?" Burgoyne surmised. "You're relieved he's left you behind, but you've nowhere else to go?"

She nodded. "I'd be no trouble."

He laughed. "I'm sure you won't be."

She clutched his sleeve. "Tell me…what do you like to do, when you're not fighting?"

Burgoyne smirked. "I imagine you have a fairly good idea."

"That can't be the only thing," she insisted.

"Oh, no?" he chuckled. Then he grew wistful. "I like to…tell stories."

"Happy or sad?" she asked.

"Happy," he said. "Life has enough sadness already."

"Well, I like to listen to stories," she replied, "so you really must tell them to me."

"Yes," he murmured, "so I must."

And so she stayed on the train. And he would call for her, sometimes. And he would sit up with her half the night, telling her about his plays still being written, and weaving romances about the Lionheart and his noble crusade or Arthur and his peerless Round Table. And she would watch him adoringly with her pretty violet eyes, and they would embrace, and share chaste kisses, sometimes even ardent ones, but that was as far as it went. She was his little pet, and sometimes she fell asleep with him like a pet, and rose with him in the morning. And he said her hair was golden, even as the sun.

Then, for several nights, the girl excused herself from coming to him, saying she was ill. On the third, he sent over a physician to check her, and he determined she was with child. Again, Burgoyne had her come to him, and her eyes were swimming when she sat down on the edge of the general's cot.

"There now, child," he sighed, sitting beside her. "You mustn't weep."

"Why not?" she choked.

"Because…you've been ill enough, and besides, you…you're going to be a mother…there's something wondrous in that, no matter how it happened…"

"My mother died when she had me," she sniffled. "I-I think that's why Pa hates me…"

Burgoyne gently pulled her up on his knee. "Yes, some mothers have died, but so many don't. It's a percentage sort of thing…some people get run down by carriages, or get struck by lightning, or get bitten by adders, or never recover from a passing chill. And we soldiers live with such odds most of all. Can't go through life in constant fear of it, can we?"

She smiled sadly. "I don't think you know how to be afraid of anything."

"That's…not true, love." He smiled slightly in return. "But listen…my mother had me, and afterwards, she was right as rain. A great lady, my mother, always the center of attention at operas and galas, always courted by admirers…she didn't let a little thing like birthing keep her long confined. A great beauty, indeed, and I loved to look at her face as a child, though she didn't stay put long. It was…like a phantom in the mirror, full fair and fleeting…"

She looked at him, a bit piteously, and kissed his cheek. "You must have been a delightful child."

He blushed and chortled. "An active one, to be sure, always playing with my toy knights on horseback dragging their little catapults into position on the heights of my pillow, well past my bedtime…"

She beamed. "And was your mother proud to see she was raising a soldier, even then?"

"Oh, she was rather too busy to ponder such things overly much," he replied. "My lady wife was rather more contemplative about what our daughter's future might hold…" He absently rubbed the girl's knee cap, and briefly nuzzled his face into her hair, as if for comfort. "She too gave birth without a hitch, and she was fit as a fiddle afterwards. Remained that way for years. We went everywhere together, you know…even on campaign…I could only go so long without her, and then…there was such an ache in me…"

"You loved her," she murmured, "just like the characters in your stories love each other."

"Oh…I wish I managed to love her like that, the way she deserved to be loved. But…I'm an easily distracted man, who doesn't know half the time what's good for him. Still, whenever I returned to my senses, she was always there. She was just that faithful to me…the most faithful friend to me…"

"You're the only friend I have in the world," the girl blurted.

Burgoyne stared at her for a moment, seemingly struck dumb, then burst out laughing.

The girl flushed and bit her lip so hard she drew blood.

"Oh…poor little bird…" He brushed the trickle of blood away with his thumb. "I was not laughing at you…no, I was laughing at myself…the shame is on me…" He held her close to his chest, and she wept again. "Please…please, don't take on so…it breaks my heart, so help me…"

"Are-are you going to…to give me to him?" she sobbed.

"Him, who?"

"The one who…put a child in me?"

"Is that what you want?"

She shook her head vigorously. "He'd hurt me. And maybe the baby."

"Then no."

"Are you…going to send me back to my father?"

"Would that be any better for you?"

Again, she shook her head. "I-I think he'd kill me."

"Then we must find someone else worthy to look after you," he said kindly.

"I-I could stay with you, maybe," she squeaked. "I know I'm not like your French lady in lace, or even the washer woman with red hair, and I know I…I'm probably not even to your liking anymore, with a child in my belly, but…if you wanted…"

He laughed a little again, then quickly stopped himself, and took her chin in his hand and kissed her on the lips. When he had finished, he said softly, "You'll make some man the sweetest little wife. I've even taught you how to kiss for real now. We just have to find him for you."

She shook her head. "No one…would want me like this, surely…"

"Have more faith, love," he assured. "I'm an incorrigible optimist when it comes to piecing together happy endings. It's a selfish delight of mine, seeing others happy, if I can make it so."

She tilted her head. "Do you think your campaign will have a happy ending?"

He snorted. "Well, we've never talked about that, have we?"

"We don't have to talk about it now," she assured. "I just…I can tell you're tired…very tired." She ran a finger under each of his eyes, as if to indicate dark circles there.

"Part of the job, my dear," he sighed, "as much as battle scars." He raised an eyebrow. "And have you any ardent political persuasions, my little bird? Not spying on me for the rebels, are you?"

She smiled and shook her head.

"Well, one can never tell in this country," Burgoyne sighed. "The most unexpected sorts become political to a suicidal extent. I interviewed a handful of farmers turned rebels back in Boston just to pass the time. They were positively rabid in their opinions, though honest souls beneath the surface, I can't deny…just easily manipulated by more learned men…"

She regarded him softly. "Maybe men who spend their lives in the soil are learned in ways other men will never know. Maybe…the really important thing is that they are all men. God makes men…and women, too."

Burgoyne chuckled. "Very egalitarian of you. Are you quite sure you're not a little revolutionary?"

She shrugged. "I don't think so. My father doesn't have a side, and I don't suppose I have one either. Except…whatever side loves you, I suppose, if that's a side. You're the first man in forever who hasn't hurt me."

The color in Burgoyne's face drained, and he cupped her chin in his hand. "If anyone tries to hurt you again, well…I'll hurt them instead. That's a promise." He started kissing her again, on the cheek, on the lips, and down along her neck, his hand tangled up in her hair. Then he paused, and asked, almost like a little boy showing off a secret treasure, "Would…umm…would you like to see what my lady wife looked like?"

She blinked, a bit perplexed, then nodded.

He turned towards the table at the side of the bed, and opened a box sitting there. Then he took out a miniature, the portrait of a youthful Lady Charlotte surrounded by tiny sparkling gems.

"Here…here she is," he said, his face flushed. "I always used to take this with me, whenever we were apart, and I'd write home and tell her how I kissed it every night."

"She's beautiful," the girl on his knee murmured. "Like a princess. Like a fairytale."

"Mmm-hmm," he agreed. "My daughter…she looked very much the same. Even as a baby, she did somehow. That's why we called her Little Charlotte." He cleared his throat and turned the miniature over his palm. "There's a piece of my lady's hair in the back, see? It-it matches yours…" He held it up to demonstrate the comparison. Then, after pressing it to his lips, he put the miniature back in the box and took out a delicate gold chain. "I-I bought this in Italy, long ago." He smiled bashfully and slipped it around her neck, almost as if he were dressing up a doll.

Her eyes widened as she fingered it. "What's Italy like?"

"Positively balmy," he said. "I started to miss the sweet relief of good English rain." He ran his fingers along the chain, imitating her. "It…would have gone to my daughter, had she outlived her mother. I…took it along to remember them…"

"But…I'm nothing so special to you…" she murmured, tears welling up again.

"You…have their hair, gold, like the chain, and…" He lifted her chin, gazing into her eyes. "Something inside…is the same too. It has made me less…lonely…"

She embraced him again, weeping into his chest, and he kissed her hair.

The next day, Burgoyne called Jonathan to his tent for a consultation.

"Look, Rawcliffe, you know I'm not like you, a clean man," Burgoyne sighed. "I've had plenty of pretty young things give themselves to me for favors, either to get a chance to perform on stage, or to gain a promotion for a relative in the service, or to obtain a pardon to a condemned party, or sometimes just because…well, I had money, at least for a short span. Let's just say…I readily pressed most advantages of that kind when they came my way. But this girl…well, she…she's been poorly used. She doesn't deserve…me, alright? I'll just cause her grief, and I don't want to do that. She doesn't have the thick skin to take it. Do you understand?"

"Yes, sir," Jonathan replied. "You've come to care for her."

Burgoyne sighed. "She's…a good girl. I want her to be happy. Surely you can make sense of that. You're…a good man. I've always known that about you…always liked that about you. You must know someone, out of this whole army, that could manage to make a kindly husband for her? Surely there must be some man amongst us without a hankering for beating women or making small animals squeal?"

Jonathan looked thoughtful for a moment. "I…may have a candidate."

"Do you?"

"Yes. Private Samuel Woodroffe."

Burgoyne squinted. "Correct me if I'm wrong, but isn't that the same man who tried to cut off your little rebel's finger in the wagon? You know how I can be about remembering names…"

"Ever astute, sir," Jonathan replied. "They are, indeed, one and the same."

"Right, so…I feel like we must have had some sort of a miscommunication," Burgoyne sighed. "I want to put her with someone kind, and you want to put her with someone who cuts off other people's fingers for the fun of it…"

"He did it to avenge his friend," Jonathan clarified. "That shows a fair measure of devotion to those he loves, protectiveness even. And I dare say…you, sir, I am no stranger to the sentiment."

Burgoyne exhaled. "And you are, Lieutenant?"

"No, sir," he replied. "That, perhaps, is why I think I have come to understand what makes Woodroffe tick. But aside from fidelity in friendship, it is my opinion he suffers most from fear."

"Fear?" Burgoyne repeated.

"Yes, fear of death," Jonathan repeated, "rendering life meaningless. But love casts out fear. And I think he would prove a better man and braver soldier for it."

"You're willing to risk the child's wellbeing, and my wrath, on that?" Burgoyne challenged.

Jonathan exhaled. "May I at least introduce them under supervision? I will take full responsibility."

"Yes, you will, Lieutenant," Burgoyne replied, a warning in his tone even as he conceded to the plan.

Now the difficulty was getting Samuel to agree to the experiment, which he initially adamantly rejected.

"Sir, you can't order me to do it," Samuel blurted. "You can't make me pick up where another man left off and own his offspring!"

"I can't order you, it's true," Jonathan admitted. "But you said you wanted to be a new creation."

"No, sir," the guard protested. "I said…I thought everyone wanted it, one time or other…we could never sort out how…"

"When you took the King's shilling, you kissed the Holy Bible," Jonathan said. "That was an opportunity for you to become a new creation, a man of honor, in the service of your king. It's up to you to make use of it."

"But what does that have to do with play-acting fatherhood over a child from another fellow's seed?"

"Do you really think fathering just comes down to planting one's seed, Private?" Jonathan queried. "It is not so. Besides, becoming a new creation is an act of being adopted."

Samuel was silent, scuffing the first with his boot.

"Will you at least meet with her, for my sake?" Jonathan asked softly. "You are not obliged to go further than that."

Samuel hesitated, then nodded.

Ned only heard bits and pieces of what transpired after that from Jonathan.

During the first meeting, the girl found her soldier sitting on a log, nervously whittling with his knife. She sat down a ways off from him and pestered him with questions about what he was making. When he confessed he didn't know, she suggested carving a bird. Then she asked if he would teach her to carve too. Samuel seemed annoyed but reluctantly complied. The eager pupil accidentally cut herself, making Samuel further annoyed, but she kept apologizing to him on the verge of tears, and something inside him seemed to soften as he used a strip from his blanket roll to bandage her finger.

"What's your name then?" he asked as he went about the task.

"Charity," she replied with a hesitant smile. "My mother's name."

Samuel looked stunned, and indeed, Jonathan had a similar reaction himself. Some things could not be planned by man.

He agreed to a second meeting, and this time produced for her a small carved amulet in the shape of a bird, with a metal loop affixed to the top so she could slip it onto the chain she wore around her neck. She seemed so very moved by it, fingering the bird between her fingers as if she was afraid it might fly away, then pecking him on the cheek.

"I made up a story, once, about a girl who could turn into a bird. It was a very sad story, I heard told by some children from another farm, but then I made it happy. Her father shoots her down with a hunting gun and bakes her in a pie when she eats magic berries to grow wings and fly away from home. But her soul gets to keep the wings, and she flies off to a better country where she marries a prince from among the fair folk." She giggled to herself. "I-I know you think that's very silly of me, but…I was very lonely, so lonely I couldn't sleep some nights. And I was afraid of Father drinking in the kitchen. So…I'd tell myself stories to distract myself."

He glanced down. "I used to do that too. When I thought I might die, a few times when I was little, I did it to take my mind off of what I thought was coming. It was winter, and I had almost given up fighting the hunger in my belly…I curled up in a corner and thought to let myself freeze…it would be painless, I thought, going numb…" He shook his head. "I made up silly adventures about pirates and that sort of thing, and somehow I didn't want to go numb anymore. I-I fought to get up…and stole some pie…" He chuckled. "So I…I know how it can be…"

She leaned over and kissed his other cheek, causing him to blush. "Maybe we could tell each other stories," she said gently. "We must be good at it by now, with such practice."

"Aye, with such practice," he murmured, gingerly running a finger along a lock of her hair.

During their third meeting, they walked down to a nearby stream together, and he let her hold his hand. She had finally taken the bandage off, and he studied the scab along her finger in a concerned manner. Then he opened up and talked about the Thames River, how he nearly drowned as a boy after getting into a scuffle with some other boys looking for jobs down by the wharves. She asked what the ocean was like.

"Wet," he said. "And always moving. Like a river, but bigger and angrier. I think water is alive, in its own way."

"I do too," she said, and ran her hand along the current of the stream.

On the fourth meeting, they took another walk, and several soldiers Samuel was acquainted with spotted them. They made several choice remarks about her rumored pregnancy, accompanied with snickering. Samuel turned beet red and fell to blows with one of them, but Charity pleaded with him to stop before he got into trouble.

"Please, don't…you don't have to see me ever again…you needn't have anything to do with the baby…just please, don't get yourself flogged… I couldn't stand it…"

Then she ran away into the woods.

When Samuel next found her, she was hunched over a log, throwing up. The poor thing was still in the throes of early motherhood. Appearing unsure what to do at first, he went over to her, and helped hold her hair out of the way.

When she was finished, turning red from embarrassment, he awkwardly patted her back, and she offered him a tentative smile. "You're very nice."

"Not really," he sighed. "I'm a nasty sort. Lived rough for so long, there's no other way it could have turned out. Alley cats don't know how to be nice. They just scratch up other cats and eat rubbish."

"But you're nice to me." She blinked. "Unless it's because…they offered you something to pretend…"

"No," he blurted. "I've more pride than that. If I didn't wish to see you again, I wouldn't have bothered coming after you."

She blinked. "Thank you. I-I'm glad. I like being with you."

"Do you?"

"Yes. These past few days, when I've been sick in the morning, I make myself feel better by thinking of the next time I'll see you."

Now his face flushed.

"Did I say something wrong?"

"Charity," he addressed her earnestly. "Do you believe in the New Creation?"

"You mean about all things being set right in the end?"

"Or even now, in a man, if he's born a second time?" Samuel shook his head. "I-I ain't sure I believe in it myself. But…I want to, very much. I'm not…a clean man, but maybe…I can become one, just maybe…"

"I think you can be whatever you want to be, Samuel," she assured him, fingering her amulet. "You're kind and strong, I can tell. And you made me a bird."

He sighed. "Didn't the man who took advantage of you treat you nice at first?"

"Y-yes," she admitted. "But…you're not him. Or at least, I don't think you are. You have different eyes."

"No, I'm not him," Samuel admitted. "I'm many other things, but not him."

She put a hand under his chin. "I-I think you are being born again already. I can see it, clear as day."

And so, then and there, Samuel proposed marriage to Charity. And she accepted.

Burgoyne made sure the bride had a dress, and Maggie fixed her hair. Jonathan, meanwhile, remained glued to Samuel, who polished his uniform buttons to excess out of nerves. He made sure the temptation to desert never overcame his charge. After the simple ceremony performed by Samuel's regimental chaplain, the new groom went to Jonathan for counsel before their wedding night, planned to be shared in a nearby abandoned barn for the sake of privacy.

"I-I've only ever bedded whores," Samuel blurted. "How should I do it with her?"

"Be patient," Jonathan told him. "Be kind. Remember? That's what love is. And you're taking a vow to love her for all her life."

"I think that damned grenadier scared her half to death," he mumbled.

"I imagine so. Wouldn't we be scared too if we were handled so? Hurt and shamed and afraid of it happening again, no doubt." Jonathan gave him a long look. "But I don't think you'll let it happen again. I think you'll be good to her, and she'll come to trust you, even with her body. Just…give her time."

"Is it even safe to do it when…I mean, when she's so…?"

"With child?" Jonathan filled in. "I did it during my wife's past two pregnancies, if that's any consolation. Mother and babies both came through fine. Your bride should as well, so long as you are gentle and think about what you're doing."

Samuel gazed down. "May I…tell you about it afterwards, Lieutenant?"

"If it would help," Jonathan replied.

And so he did, the morning after their wedding night.

"We kissed a lot," he reported. "But she was shaking so much, I couldn't bring myself to try anything else."

"Time," Jonathan assured. "Let her get used to you."

"She said...I could," he mumbled, "if I wanted. She opened her legs to me. But..." He winced. "She closed her eyes so tight, like I had a knife to stab her with, and I just..." He shook his head. "I couldn't."

"You chose well," Jonathan responded.

"Not much of a wedding night, though, was it? I mean, does it even count as one?"

"You put your wife before yourself, so...yes it does."

The next time the couple had the opportunity to try again, between his duties and her sickness, Samuel once again reported to Jonathan.

"Very close," he rasped. "Very close to it, we were. But I touched her in a certain way, maybe the way he touched her somehow, and she curled up in a ball, shuddering, and then..." He sucked in a breath. "She kept saying sorry...over and over again, and...that she didn't want me to hate her, to leave her alone...and I didn't know what to do so she wouldn't be afraid of me, so I just...petted her hair..." He swallowed hard. "The thing is, I don't hate her...not at all. I hate the ones who did this to her. I hate them, and I want to kill them, all of them." He clenched his fist in rage.

"That won't fix what's been broken," Jonathan stated. "Besides, the man who forced her to his will I hear has already received the punishment of two hundred lashes for both the assault and looting. It is unknown whether or not he will survive it."

"If there is any justice in this world, he will not," Samuel retorted.

"I think we might all have some cause to rejoice that perfect justice is not meted out here below in every respect," Jonathan murmured. "We may yet be surprised by grace, tearing open the veil."

Samuel let out a shivering sigh. "And what of us, sir? I cannot mend what's torn her."

"Patience," Jonathan advised once again. "Kindness. That's the only medicine for this."

At long last, the following week, there was a simple, yet meaningful report.

"She trusts me," he said. "We are man and wife in every way."

And Jonathan smiled brightly, laying a hand on Samuel's shoulder. "God be praised!"

Ned had caught a glimpse of the newly married couple not long afterwards, and was pleased to see Charity smiling as she stitched a tear in her husband's sleeve, while he proudly showed her how well he had memorized Jonathan's latest lesson. Yes, it was devoutly to be hoped they had gotten their happy ending after all. Only time would tell.

~

Later in the month, there was another rebel attack not far from the general's camp. This time it was a raid on the horses behind the baggage train. Some mounts were driven off; some were killed. It was the same with the men. And when Jonathan heard what had happened, he immediately rushed to the scene, rushed to find Lieutenant Thompson, dead or alive.

"He needs me, one way or another," Jonathan murmured. "To bind him up or pray over him…I know not which. I must find out."

Ned felt compelled to go along with him.

The scene they came upon was an ugly one, with corpses of man and beast strewn about an overturned wagon. But at least Jonathan managed to locate Eli fairly quickly, lying beside a slain stallion, blood soaking his leg scarlet and spurting from his shoulder down into the dirt.

"Thank God," Jonathan breathed, as he saw him twitching. "He's alive…"

Jonathan started to go to him, but Ned grabbed his arm and blurted, "Wait, there might still be riflemen about…"

But Jonathan would not wait. He hurried over to Eli, and took the boy's face in his hands. "It's me, dear…all will be well…"

Eli winced. "I-I shot at them…"

"Of course you did, Lieutenant," Jonathan said, gingerly sitting him up and starting to pull open his uniform to get at the shoulder wound. "You're a good soldier."

"But my hand…it was wet," Eli mumbled, holding it up, the blood from his shoulder dripping down from his fingers. "My pistol…it slipped…and-and they kept shooting…till I fell down…" He looked around him at the dead horse and the dead soldiers. "I-I shouldn't have let it slip. I should have kept shooting, somehow. Maybe…maybe they wouldn't be dead…"

"It was out of your hands," Jonathan assured.

"But-but it slipped…I should have held onto it…I should have…" His eyes were glistening, and he touched the dead horse's mane. "I should have…done something…"

"Eli, look at me," Jonathan said firmly. Eli did so, rather blearily, and Jonathan repeated, emphasizing each word, "Out of your hands."

Eli swallowed hard, then glanced down at his leg. "Do you think it's ruined?"

"We'll get it sorted," Jonathan promised. He glanced around, then cupped his hand to his mouth and called, "Is anyone else alive?"

"If they were alive, I think they left," Eli said simply. "By running or dying."

A haunted look passed over Jonathan's face as he stared at the motionless bodies, and the way a breeze suddenly toyed with a neckerchief one of the soldiers had been wearing, likely to shield his mouth from the dust of the road. It was a dingy white…now spotted red. Ned squinted, realizing it was the young Irish soldier Jonathan had caught sneaking over to the priest. Afterwards, Jonathan had made good his intention to give him lessons to speak better English, usually at night, after the others had gone to bed. Jonathan, sleep deprived on the following mornings, would grumble about the Gaels being naturally slow learners, and question aloud whether any of the seeds he was planting would take root, or simply lie dormant among rocks.

Now, Jonathan knelt beside the stricken boy and pulled free his neckerchief, muttering "sorry" as he did so. Ned was standing over Jonathan's shoulder now, and saw, at the same time as his friend, that the boy was not, in fact, dead. His eyes opened slowly, and they were glassy with pain. He tried to speak, but choked on blood. Words spilled out at last, but they were an incoherent jumble in Gaelic.

Jonathan leaned down. "English, boy," he said, sadly now.

"Don't…let me…" The boy choked on more blood. "…drown…"

Jonathan pulled him up and leaned his head against his chest as the Irish soldier spit up blood in a violent flow. Ned noticed the boy had his hand inside his tunic, as if he was clutching something. Jonathan seemed to notice too, and pulled the coat open slightly. He sighed, and shook his head, but did not try to take whatever he had away from him.

"Ned," Jonathan addressed his friend hoarsely. "Come. Help him stay sitting up while I tend to Thompson."

Ned knelt down and took Jonathan's place, taking the boy's body in his arms and leaning his head against his shoulder. He felt the front of the boy's tunic, wet and warm. He turned his hand over, and saw it was stained, carrying his mind back to his youth, when he would go berry-picking with Tessie, and would come home with hands colored a reddish-purple from the juice of the berries and blood drawn by thorns.

"Should-should I try to staunch the wound with something?" Ned asked.

"It's too late for that," Jonathan said quietly. "Just…keep him upright, hear?"

The clerk gave the dying boy a last, long look as he started murmuring in his native tongue again, slipping into delirium, his breathing sputtering. Then Jonathan touched his face and said solemnly, "May God, who knows all tongues, take you to Himself."

Ned felt a lump in his throat as Jonathan went back over to Eli, and he was left alone with the dying boy, his chest pumping up and down as he recited in Gaelic what Ned knew in his heart must be prayers. Then the language changed.

Latin. He was praying in Latin.

Edmund swallowed hard as the boy looked at him, through him, and there was a knowing in those eyes, emerald as the isle of his birth, that terrified him even as they spoke to him.

You were one of us.

Then the Irish boy took Ned's hand in his own tremulous one and slipped it under his soaking tunic.

Beads.

A string of five beads.

And a cross.

Ned felt his eyes grow blurry with tears as the boy pressed the cross into his palm.

And then…he was dead, though his open eyes remained a lively green.

When Ned had wiped his tears hurriedly away and returned to Jonathan, he saw his friend had used the neckerchief as a tourniquet for Eli's leg and was cutting off a piece of a horse blanket with a knife, presumably to use for Eli's shoulder.

Jonathan looked up at Ned. "Is the boy…?"

Ned nodded.

Jonathan exhaled. "He was like Tall Willow, clutching her heathen talisman for comfort when I delivered her child. I thought I'd managed to cure him of it, but…"

"The natives never change," Eli ground out, giving Edmund a suspicious look as Jonathan slipped the material over the shoulder wound to staunch it.

"I suppose I just gave myself too much credit," Jonathan said. "But he died as he lived, in superstition…"

"Don't hate him," Ned blurted.

"I don't," Jonathan said softly. "He was afraid. I may not be a Gael, disposed as they are to ignorance, but I know what it is to be afraid. Fear is no respecter of persons and makes silly little children out of us all. We must hope God proves an indulgent Father towards our foolishness."

You don't understand, Ned wanted to shout. *You don't understand what he was doing, what all our ancestors were doing, what is in our very blood to do! But I do! I do! Oh, Lord, have mercy, I do!*

But Edmund did not say anything of the kind, even as his palm burned with the imprint of the cross. He just helped Jonathan get Eli to his feet, taking one arm while his friend took the other.

"Come on, dear," Jonathan coaxed his wounded comrade. "Lean on us. It's back to camp for us, eh?"

Once they made it to the hospital tent, Jonathan spent hours with Eli, staying with him as the physician extracted the bullet from his leg, and the other from his shoulder. Poor Eli handled the pain as well as could be expected, given that he had refused any strong liquor so he could keep his wits about him and pray. He just bit hard on a stick and clung to Eli's arm.

The leg proved easier to bear up with then the shoulder, and pain from the latter nearly caused him to vomit. He instinctively pulled away several times, and Jonathan had to hold him still. He calmed rather quickly when Jonathan did so, as if he did not wish to cause trouble for the one person who had thought to rescue him.

"No one came back for me," Eli murmured later on, as Jonathan stayed stalwartly beside him, keeping up the pressure of the tourniquets. "No one but you."

Jonathan shrugged. "They were in a panic. Don't take it to heart."

He blinked. "Do I have to stay at the hospital all night?"

"You shouldn't be moved, dear," Jonathan said. "You need looking after."

"But I can't sleep here," Eli mumbled, glancing over at another wounded soldier who had been less fortunate than himself and was just now having his face covered over with a sheet. "Death is here."

Jonathan exhaled. "What if I stay here with you?"

"All night?"

Jonathan nodded.

"Then…I might sleep after all."

So Jonathan brought his bedding into the hospital tent and lay down at Eli's side.

And Eli slept.

~

More unsettling events stalked the British advance in the coming weeks.

Ned remembered the night when a fire broke out among the officers' tents, with Major Acland's taking the worst of it. No one was sure at first if it had started by accident or through some infernal onslaught by the rebels. Everyone's nerves were on edge, dreading marksmen coaching somewhere in the shadows, who might use the ensuing chaos and the eerie glow to their advantage.

Major Acland stumbled out of his tent, choking and sputtering, his smallclothes blackened and his face and hands singed from the blaze. Then he turned back around, his mind seeming to clear from his smoke-induced stupor, and dove back into the tent once more. When he came out again, he had Lady Acland cradled in his arms this time. He fell to his knees, choking some more, then seized his wife by the shoulders.

"Harriet!" he screamed, shaking her limp form in desperation. "Oh, God…please, no, please…Harriet! Harriet, my love, my only love, wake up!"

She stirred slightly, and he buried his face in her breast, his hand over her pregnant belly. "I'm sorry…I'm so sorry…" he sobbed. "Oh, my angel, I need you so!"

Still struggling to get a full breath, and sustaining a ragged cough, she reached up and stroked her husband's hair.

"I didn't mean to leave without you," he wept. "I wasn't myself, waking to the smoke and fire…oh my dear, forgive me…" He pressed his ear to her belly. "Is…is he alright? My dear, will our baby be alright?"

"John," she rasped. It was all she seemed able to manage, stroking the burns on his cheek with her delicate hand. He kissed that hand, once, twice, ten times. Then he saw the burn marks along her arm, and fresh tears came to him. "Oh, I love you so…if you were dead, I'd have thrown myself into the flames…"

As soldiers struggled to douse the fire, Acland's red-coated dog came limping over to them, a guilty look in its watery eyes. Acland took one look at him, turned a livid shade of red, and drew out his pistol, which he had kept strapped to him even in sleep in case of a rebel raid.

"John, no!" Harriet cried, placing her hand over the mouth of the gun.

"This bitch's runt knocked down the lantern," Acland spat. "It deserves to be destroyed…"

"No, John…you love him!"

"Not nearly as much as I love you!"

"I left the lantern burning to journal before falling asleep! I am to blame as well! Please, don't hurt the poor creature!"

Slowly, Acland lowered the pistol. The poor dog whimpered, clearly hurt by his master's reaction, and nudged its nose into Acland's shoulder. Acland seemed determined to ignore it.

Harriet petted the dog sympathetically. "Husband, please, don't break his spirits. I am alive. The baby is alive. He is as frightened as we are. Look, his paw is singed."

Acland took the paw in his hand on instinct, then met the dog's sad eyes and scratched behind his ear. "You really are my angel, Harriet, whispering only good things in my ear," he murmured. "You keep the demon perched on my other shoulder at bay."

After both of them were escorted to the hospital, and it was established the burns were not severe, Acland wandered off by himself, trying to drown his guilt and fear with liquor. He always seemed so undaunted, in parliament or among his troops, but now he had become like a broken little boy, trying to find some means of comfort. Burgoyne took it upon himself to talk to him.

"Acland, for heaven's sake, put down the bottle, and embrace your wife. She's had a terrible fright, and needs you to be with her, yes, to be strong for her, not to drench your senses and feel sorry for yourself."

"I should never have brought her to this godforsaken place," Acland murmured. "I should be strung up by my thumbs for such selfishness."

Burgoyne hesitated, then said quietly, "If I could only…go back, and be in your place, with a wife who adores me waiting to embrace me, for all my faults, I would smash every bottle, tear up every map, abandon the whole world…" He bit his lip. "She's glowing with your offspring inside her, yours and hers, a testament to all you share. Oh, Acland, don't waste such precious moments on regrets. *Carpe diem*, my good man."

And so Major Acland returned to the arms of his lady wife.

~

Later that week, Ned was given the opportunity to consider whether he too might be ready to start a family. Abby had been sleeping at Ned's side most nights, and he had broken down and showed her Tessie's relic inside his coat. He asked if she thought he should burn it. She shook her head and helped him put in an extra line of stitches, just to be on the safe side. Ned felt incredibly grateful to have her not only as a paramour but as a confidante. Yes, it was a sin, but a gentle sin surely, compared to all the horrors that surrounded them, and one which perhaps might be set to rights sooner than later. He was pleased that Abby seemed to be adjusting to camp life, and had even established cordial relations with several of the other camp followers who she did chores alongside. She even volunteered to babysit their children, and she seemed to take genuine joy in doing it.

It was a pleasant summer's day, and Burgoyne came outside to find Ned and Abbey together, with a baby making demonstrative noises in a laundry basket. "What's all this?" the general queried. "What are you two doing today?"

"Abby and I sorted out how to spend more time together," Edmund stated. "I'll do this paperwork outside, and she can look after the baby by me."

"That's…sensible enough," Burgoyne chuckled. "And whose moppet is this?" He pointed to the baby who had tipped the laundry basket over and was crawling across the ground.

Abby scooped her up in her lap, and the baby swung her little arms around in protest. "Oh, just one of the soldier's wives. She's doing washing down by the stream today, so I said I'd keep an eye on Baby Sally."

"Ah."

Ned opened his arms and Abby handed him the baby. "We've been taking turns," he explained. "This one is very active and doesn't much like being held by anyone who's not her mother, but we're training her."

"An accomplishment, I'm sure."

Ned stood up, babe in arms. "Would you like to hold her?"

Burgoyne blinked. "I…no."

"Even for a minute?"

"I don't see the need…"

"It could be fun."

"Why am I, commander of the King's hosts, being recruited to double as a nanny for an absentee laundry woman?"

"Because it requires authority," Ned stated. "You'll find that out around Sally…"

"He doesn't know how to hold her," Abbey said under her breath.

"Of course I know how, girl! I was a father myself, once…"

"Was?" Abby repeated.

Burgoyne stared at her for a moment, then blurted in a flat, emotionless tone, "Typhoid."

Her eyes grew briefly piteous, after which she turned her gaze to the ground.

"Here," Ned insisted softly, handing him the baby. "You have more experience than I."

Burgoyne scrambled to get a good grip and remained somewhat frozen as the baby gazed up at him with her big blue eyes, then started to squirm. "I…don't think she is happy with this arrangement…"

"Be more confident, and she'll settle," Abby instructed.

"I am the picture of confidence, young lady!" he retorted.

"Then act like it! Show her who's the general around here!"

"Alright, what in the name of Mars is she doing?" Burgoyne inquired, as the baby started to try to claw her way up his shoulder.

"Told you she didn't like to be held," Ned noted.

"Then why did you people hand her off to me?" Burgoyne huffed, struggling to pull her back down into his arms, as she squealed in protest. Then she got distracted by something shiny which she grabbed in her little fist and stuffed in her mouth. "She's eating my button…"

"She's teething," Abby reminded him. "Just make sure she doesn't swallow it…"

"It shouldn't detach…oh, damn…"

"Get it out of her mouth!"

"Look, just…take her back…"

"Don't let her swallow it!"

Burgoyne rolled his eyes, then grimaced as he pried open her mouth to retrieve the slimy button.

"Don't break her neck either!"

"I know how to support an infant's head, thank you very much!" Burgoyne assured, doing exactly that. "Ouch! She bit me!"

"How could she bite you without teeth?"

"Well, a few are breaking through…besides, malevolent intent…"

The baby started wailing, wanting her button back.

"Shoosh," Burgoyne instructed the child in monotone. The child did not obey. He turned back to Abby, exasperated. "Give me that basket before…ugh…"

Sally promptly spit up on his uniform.

"I'll hold you both responsible if I perish from disease! My ghost will haunt you…"

"Very Hamlet of you, sir," Ned remarked, struggling not to laugh.

Abby sighed and went over to the general, who tried to hand the baby off to her, but she simply repositioned his arms. "There," she said. "Now pat her on the back."

"I say, can't you just…?"

"Go on."

Reluctantly, Burgoyne did as instructed, and wonder of wonders, the baby calmed. On his own impetus, he started humming a tune which Ned was fairly certain he first heard on the opening night of Gentleman Johnny's play. The baby seemed to fall into rhythm and made tranquil gurgling noises.

"This one is destined for the theater," Burgoyne predicted. "Musical theater, at that!"

Sally seemed instinctively pleased, and gazed up at him with a toothless smile.

"Now we've formed a meaningful association!" Burgoyne declared to her. "Yes, we have!"

Sally laughed.

Abby smiled in spite of herself, and petted the red fuzz on the baby's head. Then she sang softly, "Hushabye, don't you cry, go to sleep, ye little baby…when you wake, you shall have all the pretty little horses…the blacks and the grays, the dappled and the bays, a coach and six white horses…"

Burgoyne looked wistfully at her. "You…have a lovely voice."

"She does," Ned confirmed. "I have her sing me to sleep sometimes…"

"I'm not entirely sure that's a compliment," she sighed, making cross-eyes at Ned. "But…I remember my mother singing to me when I was young. Almost the only thing I remember about her."

"Well…she gave you a lasting gift, it seems," Burgoyne remarked. He cleared his throat. "Perhaps you two should think about…making some babies of your own to sing to. You know…get a house and garden and…have a brood. And I could…volunteer as the most irresponsible godfather alive…"

Ned felt his heart melt. He cast a quick glance at Abby who was blushing.

"A sort of grandfather, really," Ned mumbled, smiling bashfully at Burgoyne.

"Yes, well, I…I suppose I have tried to…pick up where your father left off. Badly, lad, badly, but…I could imagine spoiling your children, I suppose." He looked over to Abby again. "He really is a fine boy, you know. You should…hang onto him."

She swallowed hard. "I-I'd like that."

Ned felt warm inside and took her hand in his own.

The baby started squirming again. "Hell's teeth," Burgoyne exhaled.

"Now, sir, you mustn't get in the habit of swearing in front of young ladies," Ned chided him, gesturing to both Abby and Sally.

Burgoyne grumbled under breath at the rebuff, then glanced to the left, over Ned's shoulder. "Major Acland, perfect timing! Come hither!"

Acland did as he ordered, a perplexed look on his face. The expression only intensified as Burgoyne promptly thrust the baby into his arms. "You're going to be a father, so you'll need practice."

"Sir, I…I can well afford nurses for the children I bring into the world…"

"That's beside the point," Burgoyne replied. "You must hold them yourself too, as often as you can. If you don't, you'll regret it." Burgoyne adjusted Acland's arms. "Now whatever you do, don't break her neck! I've become invested in this one's future on stage! Also, guard your buttons with your life!"

With that, the general made his exit, disappearing back into his tent and calling for Lieutenant Rawcliffe to help him clean his uniform. Poor Major Acland, meanwhile, was left to be schooled by Abby about infant maintenance while Sally acted out all over again, seemingly quite enjoying her little rebellions against the top brass.

Later that evening, Ned watched Abby wistfully as she combed out her hair and readied herself to bed down beside him. "Abby," he said, "would you, umm…"

"Would I what?"

"Would you be very upset if you came to be full with child by me? I mean…do you think you would love what we made?"

She turned her eyes down. "Would you?"

"Oh, yes. So much." He stroked her cheek. "And I'd want to give them a house and a garden to grow up in." He took a deep breath. "Abby, what would you say if I asked you to…?"

"I wish I had pretty nighttime things to wear for you," she remarked, seemingly determined to change the subject from babies, houses, and gardens. "You seem like the sort of man who would like that."

Ned chuckled. "Do I?"

"Yes, like the silly old man I last lived with in New York. He liked to dress me up, like a doll. He bought all sorts of things for me to wear for him, silky things he liked to stroke."

Ned reddened a bit, wishing she would not tell him so much about her past paramours, but unwilling to shame her by saying so. Then he put a finger under Abbey's chin. "When we reach Albany, and my pay comes through, I'll buy you whatever pretty nighttime things you want."

She smiled sadly, then shook her head. "You'll tire of me by then. That's why I wish I had such things now…to keep it fresh…"

"If you think I tire so easily of love, you do not yet know me," he replied, and then started to kiss her tenderly.

"Oh, Ned," she whispered. "I wish you were the first one…I wish we met years ago, before the war…I wish I could have given you my innocence. Instead, I'm just…used goods…"

"No," Ned blurted, taking her face in his hands. "Never, ever say that. You are…my lady…"

A tear slid down her cheek, and Ned kissed it away. Then he rolled her into his arms, nuzzling her face with his own, and kissing closed her eyes. "I want to make you feel things, Abby," he rasped. "Tell me what you want from me…"

"From you?" she murmured. "Oh, all of you, Ned…"

He held her closer yet, running his hands along her form as he kissed her exposed shoulder. Then he felt her take his hand and place it on her lower belly.

"Make it feel better, Ned," she pleaded. "Touch me here…" She moved his hand in a circular motion over her womb.

Something about it startled him, something he could not put his finger on, but he did as he was asked. She relaxed further, smiling softly as he massaged her.

"Abby," he said at last. "Have you been bleeding again when you shouldn't be?"

She batted her eyelashes as if to distract him from the question.

"Abby, you need a doctor…"

"You're my doctor," she teased him.

"Abby, I'm afraid," he blurted. "I might…hurt you. At least let Jonathan check you. His stepfather was a physician, you know…"

She reached a finger up and pressed it to his lips.

"Abby, please…"

"I thought you were going to make me feel things," she pouted. "Good things…"

"Ab—"

She leaned up and kissed him quiet.

Chapter 30: HANGING TREE

Another Sunday rolled around, and Edmund was asleep. He dreamt of sunlight glinting upon armor, the silver reflection obscuring his sight. There was Latin chanting, coming deep from warrior throats, and there was an earthy taste upon his tongue. His heart was pumping old blood, noble blood to match his noble name and the names of those with eyes upon him, gazing through the visors of their helmets, reading into his soul. It burned him, oh, how it burned him, to hear them whisper in accord:

The second death is worse than the first.

Ned sat up suddenly, and finding that he was naked, he felt ashamed.

Yet he also felt struck by the strange, fresh glory of the world around him. The sky was light gray, the grass glistening with dew, and Abby's chestnut hair curling down her swan-white neck as she lay snuggled beside him. He thought she was as beautiful as the coming dawn, and could not restrain himself from leaning down and pressing his lips to her locks over and again. She opened her eyes, bright blue, sparkling like the dew drops.

"What on earth are you doing, Lieutenant?"

"Kissing your hair."

"Why?"

"Because," he said. "It's soft. And it's yours." He brushed his hand down her pearly cheek and neck, smiling bashfully.

"Now you're gawking."

"I can't help it when I wake up to find you next to me. It's new every time. It's as if you've been taken from my rib!"

"So you think this is paradise?"

"With you by my side, it might as well be."

He kissed her forehead. "What shall we do today? My free day is all yours. Well...every day of mine is yours, really, even if we can't always be together."

She blushed. "What would you like for us to do?"

"Whatever you want."

She chuckled and kissed him on the mouth. "Ouch, you need to shave," she teased him, brushing a thumb along his stubbly cheek.

"Will you help me?" he said playfully, kissing along her neck.

"What am I, your servant?" she sighed, lightly pushing him away.

He pulled her back. "Oh, you do have a rebellious streak, don't you?"

She rolled her eyes. "You're mighty foolhardy to offer the enemy a chance to put a razor to your throat, I'll say that much."

He laughed. "I suppose I'm feeling daring!"

"Show me just how daring you feel," she coaxed him mischievously.

He did not disappoint, and they lost themselves in each other, time becoming irrelevant, and dreams dissolving with the darkness. In the end, they were panting from a feverish pleasure.

She playfully pulled the sheet up over their heads and cuddled with him.

"You know, when I was younger, and my body was just blooming, I used to get hot at night and have all sorts of naughty thoughts." She giggled. "I used to bury my head under the covers, as if to hide myself from myself, and think of what it might be like to lie naked next to a man, and for him to be naked too! I thought I might laugh out loud to see a fellow with nothing on at all! And just imagining it, I would blush under the covers and grow even hotter!"

Ned laughed along with her. "And how was it really?" he said, before he had a chance to think of the implications. "Sorry…sorry, Abby, I didn't mean to…"

"I know you didn't," she said softly. "I suppose…I didn't think much about it at all in the beginning. I was dead to the world, if you will. Things were happening to me, but I could not reflect upon them. The first time I really thought about it was with the old major who took me in. I suppose it was because I got to know him better than the others. So…it embarrassed me more, lying with him, naked as the day he was born. I think, sometimes, when he would touch me all over, it embarrassed him too. He could not seem to decide if I was his lover or his daughter. But I got to know his body well, for better or for worse, I'll say that much. He liked the distraction, and would not give it up. It was just routine for me, and other possibilities were fair worse. And he…he tried to be gentle about it, because he had seen me treated so poorly. He could be so funny, when he was tender towards me, and used his mother's old Quaker language, calling me 'thee' and 'thou' like in prayers and poems. Maybe…that's why I felt worse than I thought I would when he was wounded on a mission into New Jersey. I didn't expect to, truly, but…I suppose I felt his pain. Isn't it awful? His body had become an extension of mine, and I didn't want him to suffer…"

"I don't think it's awful, Abby," Ned said softly. "I think…you got to care…"

She snorted, then said in a low voice, "I didn't really care. If I did, perhaps the only really merciful thing I could have done for him was put a pillow over his face or a blade into his throat when he was weak enough not to fight it. I thought about it, sometimes, when he slept beside me and seemed almost happy. I thought…there, you could repay him for both his kindness and his crimes, for the darkness would be a reward and punishment alike. If only the other wretches before him had fallen asleep beside me long enough for me to find a knife! Oh, how I dreamed of slitting the first one's white throat and watching the dark blood choke him! But I suppose…when I imagined doing the same with the old major, I just…I couldn't bear for his last moments to be filled with fear of me. To imagine making any officer afraid thrilled me sometimes, but to watch him dying because of me, knowing it was me, would have broken his heart before it stopped beating. He…relied on me, you see. Now he will die, slowly and alone. So I really should have found a way to do it… perhaps I was a coward not to do it. It would have been fitting, for the only thing more intimate than lying naked with a man is to cut the cord of his life and watch him cease to be. But…" Her voice trailed off. "I couldn't."

Ned felt his stomach flip, deeply disturbed by her ramblings and the strange glaze over her eyes. But he found himself asking all the same, "So you never felt anything when he made love to you?"

"He tried to please me, sometimes, but no, I never felt anything, or at least not the sort of thing a woman hopes to feel in her body at such a time. It was just…" She exhaled. "After he was hurt, he struggled to even do it. I suppose I felt relieved when he could manage again, for it meant he wouldn't die. Besides, I felt sorry for him when he tried and failed, and would turn red with shame. I thought to mock him, but again, I couldn't. I held him and made him feel better, and his breathing wobbled and he kept touching my hair. He was like clay in my hands then, so utterly vulnerable. I, on the other hand, was…powerful."

"Powerful because he could not make you feel things in your body?"

She was quiet for a few moments. "Perhaps."

"And yet…" Ned paused. "You've grown to like it when I make love to you. By all that's holy, I can feel it."

"Or unholy," she countered. "You've learned to sin well."

He winced, leaning up on his elbow. He thought back on Jonathan's renewed advice, once he realized Ned and Abby's relationship had rekindled, and found himself determined to set things to rights.

"We could…become honest, Abby."

"How?"

"There are ways."

She gave him a long look. "You don't know what you're saying."

"Yes, I do…"

"No, you don't," she blurted. "Trust me, you don't." She turned away from him.

He touched her shoulder. "Is it because of the red coat?"

She didn't answer.

"Damn it, Abby," he mumbled. "I'm still me underneath it. You'd be taking me for who I am, not the uniform I was assigned…"

"Can the two truly be separated?"

"You once said you don't think about it when I'm not wearing it…"

"Oh, Ned," she sighed. "It's more than the dyed wool, and you know it. It's…what you stand for, what you represent…"

"And what's that?"

"We've had this conversation already…"

"But you said you love me," he argued, "and you let me make love to you, even when I said there was no need…"

"That's not the same as…submitting to you forever, with no way out. A ring upon the finger can be like shackles upon one's wrists."

Ned felt pained. "You make it sound so cold, Abby…so brutal. You know it wouldn't be that way with me, surely."

"But don't you see? If I submit to you, then I am also submitting to that which you submit to. And that would make me, in all truth, an enemy of my country." She turned to look at him. "Have you thought about anything I said that day when we went walking? About our cause?"

"Abby, I'm not an enemy of your country," he insisted. "It's impossible to love the mother, yet hate her offspring that she took such pains to bring into the world…"

"Then why were the rights of Englishmen withheld from us, if our spirit is bound to the original clay?" Abby challenged. "Why did the King and his ministry choose to debase us as less deserving of English liberties than those born across the sea? The taxes passed without our consent, the dissolving of our assemblies, and the trading and production regulations that stifled our economy were not worthy of the freedoms our fathers fought for in this great expanse."

"The taxes were levied across the empire to pay off the debts incurred in the last war," Ned countered. "Surely you can see the justice in that…"

"We Americans prefer to be asked, not told," Abby replied. "Can you not see the principle behind that?"

"And you apply that same principle as a justification for smuggling goods to and from foreign nations? All great powers monopolize trade with their colonies and regulate the manufacturing of certain goods therein…"

"But we thought we were different," she said. "Yes, we thought England was different, more given to liberality. How wrong we were, and how wrong she is. We do not see ourselves as a subject race or a conquered people, as this ministry has chosen to treat us. That is why we chafed under the breaking of even English Law, the searches without warrants and trials without a jury of the accused men's peers. Smuggling may be a crime in your eyes, but surely it does not justify equally unlawful actions in response."

Ned hung his head. "I suppose not."

"Tell me, is it not true that the greatest and most important right of a British subject is that he shall be governed by no laws but those to which he, either in person or by his representatives, hath given his consent?"

"Many insist there is a constitutional imperative when it comes to maintaining parliamentary supremacy, Abby…"

"But surely the great basis of British freedom is interwoven with the Constitution, and whenever this is lost, the Constitution must be destroyed. Do you really think that should have applied less to us, your kindred?"

Edmund sighed. "You may have a point."

Her eyes brightened. "You think so?"

"Yes. Perhaps, at least in the long run, the question of dependence or independence should be answered by…interdependence. I don't know what form it would take exactly, but if it might be achieved without doing violence to the constitution, it might prove a stable bedrock upon which the empire can rest secure for generations to come. Many of my countrymen disagree, but…"

"But you are more enlightened," she decided. "I always knew you were, deep inside yourself."

"Unfortunately, in most civil wars, decent men on both sides make valid points, but are too stubborn to admit it, much less do anything about it," Ned said cautiously.

"Stubbornness can be lethal, it seems." She sucked a breath through her teeth. "What a court hath old England of folly and sin…"

"England may be sinful, in many ways," Ned admitted, "but she is still the Mother of Liberty. And…I love her with all my heart…"

"Well, then why be shocked when we carry the trait?" Abby challenged.

"I'm not," Ned admitted.

"That's because you know history, Ned. Remember when I spoke to you of John Hampden, called 'The Patriot', in light of Joseph Warren? On the eve of the Civil War, when he took a stand against King Charles' Ship Tax, he proclaimed that if an English king had the right to demand, an English subject had the right to refuse, and that the Lord would level to dust those bent upon depriving the people of their liberty. He was a gallant man, an honest man, and an able man who would surely be appalled by what is being done in America. And remember John Lileburn, who they called 'Freeborn John' because he protested the tyranny of the Star Chamber? He, too, would have seen our cause as justified."

Ned smirked. "Until Lileburn became a Quaker, and disavowed all warring."

"That's neither here nor there…"

"Oh, I don't hold it against him if it brought him peace. An easy conscience is to be coveted above all else. But on the subject of that late civil war, you might get on with Eli better than you think. My people were Royalists under Charles, but he is a latter-day Cromwellian if ever there was one."

"Washington will be better than Cromwell," Abby said. "He is more enlightened and is tethered to the ideals of republicanism."

"He was not always so," Ned reminded her. "He used to be a King's man, like me…"

"Men can change for the better, when they embrace the right cause," she said. "They can be redeemed from whatever has come before. Now, he would rather die as the last British freeman, bearing the new title of American, than live as the first of British slaves. But I do not think he will die, not for a long time. He has some protection keeping bullets from touching him."

"Like General Burgoyne," Ned remarked.

"That is yet to be seen."

"In both cases," Ned reminded her.

She grew melancholic. "I wish my father had that sort of protection around him."

Ned took her chin in his hand. "Listen to me. I promise to do everything in my power to see that your father's sentence might at least be commuted to house arrest where he may receive decent treatment."

There was a little squeaking sound in her throat, and she leaned forward and kissed him on the cheek. He found himself blushing more than he had during their passionate love-making.

"Help me get dressed?" he coaxed her. "Then we can go walking."

She did so, pulling on his waistcoat and then his uniform, trying hard not to look at it, even as she felt her way down the buttons.

"There," she sighed. "I've made you a lobster again."

"No," he chuckled, as he slipped her shift over her head. "I'm always a man with you."

Again, she kissed him, this time on the lips, and ran her fingers through his flaxen hair. As she tied back the strands with a black velvet ribbon, she sang sweetly to him.

"Here I sit on buttermilk hill
Who could blame me, cry my fill?
And every tear would turn a mill
Johnny has gone for a soldier

With fife and drum, he marched away
He would not heed what I did say
He'll not come back for many a day
Johnny has gone for a soldier

I wish, I wish, I wish in vain,
I wish I had my heart again,
For if I did, I'd not complain.
Johnny has gone for a soldier.

Me, oh my, I loved him so,
It broke my heart to see him go;
Only time will heal my woe.
Johnny has gone for a soldier.

I sold my rod, I sold my reel
I sold my only spinning wheel
To buy my love a sword of steel
Johnny has gone for a soldier.

I'll dye my dress, I'll dye it red,
And through the streets I'll beg my bread;
Until my parents wish me dead.
Johnny has gone for a soldier.

The one I love from me has fled.
Johnny has gone for a soldier..."

"Did you ever sing that to your first love, when he went off to fight?" Ned asked.

She shook her head. "No. I wasn't so forward then."

"Would you be angry with me if I said that I was glad I'm the only one you sang it for?"

She smiled, rather sadly. "No," she said. "I'm not angry."

When they were both dressed, they linked hands and wandered into the surrounding woods until they came to a height overlooking sprawling wilderness below. They watch the sun rise, with her head on his shoulder.

Then he opened the book he had brought along his nature specimen satchel, the one Burgoyne had given him about Richard the Lionheart. He read from it aloud, about stories of the Crusader King rescuing Christian slaves, wrestling a lion and eating its heart, refusing water at a parlay when his knights were refuse refreshment, ennobling a dying steward's son on the battlefield and a talented cook in the kitchen, romancing a jailor's daughter while he lay imprisoned, making alliances with outlaws to reclaim his kingdom, and Burgoyne's favorite story about Blondel the minstrel discovering the King's prison cell by playing a tune they had composed together beneath the window. It concluded with the story of Richard forgiving the boy who mortally wounded him. She seemed to enjoy it.

"So Burgoyne imagines himself to be the Lionheart?" she surmised.

"Perhaps, just a little bit," he chuckled. "He can really be quite chivalric, when approached the right way."

She squinted. "What do you mean by 'the right way'?"

"I mean…when he's asked in a manner that makes him feel like a knight from a storybook."

"So flattery," she surmised.

"Not quite," he said. "Yes, he's susceptible to that sort of thing to be sure, but…what I'm saying goes deeper than that. It's about reminding him that he has goodness inside of him, that he can be noble, in the purest sense of the word, like Saint George, vanquishing a dragon to redeem a damsel. I think perhaps that's what makes him most like the Lionheart. Both very badly want to be worthy of higher things, and as such, both can be very generous to those who see the best in them."

"Well, he had one thing in mind when he saw me," she snorted.

Ned tilted his head. "Did you ever just…ask him for help?"

"What?"

"I mean, ask him out of the goodness of his heart, not in exchange for anything?"

"I would never grovel to him so!" she blurted. "I would rather sell my body than my soul!"

Ned was quiet for a long moment, then said, "I think he would have helped, without any sale being made, had you just asked."

"I don't want to talk about it anymore," she decided, standing up. "Let's walk."

So they did.

As they strolled near General Burgoyne's tent, they both jolted at the sound of a woman's hysterical screaming, and the Iroquois language being shouted.

"Go back to the women's quarters," he instructed Abby hoarsely. "Something's amiss..."

With that, he rushed over to the tent. Upon entering, he saw four Iroquois braves standing in front of both Burgoyne and Fraser.

A man with streaks of red running down his body was holding a woman by the hair as she shrieked and tried to pull away. Another one, also streaked with red, deeper in color, had long, bloody, blonde hair, tied with a blue ribbon, hanging from his belt. Ned grew cold at the sight.

"Payment," the first man grunted, "or she die! Pelts, guns, fire water. Give, or she die!"

"You come here, with a woman's bloody scalp on your belt, and General Fraser's cousin held hostage, and expect me to pay you?" snarled Burgoyne. "You've broken your oaths to us!"

The Indian held his scalping knife close to the woman's throat.

"John," Fraser blurted, laying a hand on Burgoyne's arm, his look desperate. "Not now…"

"Simon! Please! Give them what they want!" screamed the woman. "They already killed Jane! Please, please, make them let me go!"

His face turning white, Burgoyne turned to Ned, and instructed with stiff lips to gather some supplies for these raiders from the baggage train.

Having received their demands, they turned the woman loose, and Fraser immediately took her in his arms to comfort her. Ned felt sick, realizing who the scalp on the brave's belt surely belonged to. A week or so before, a young woman named Jane McCrea had asked if she could journey out to meet the British train and tryst with her fiancée, a Loyalist officer under Burgoyne's command. Fraser had suggested that she stay with his cousin since the train would be passing by the vicinity. It would be safer than having her make the full journey out, he reasoned. Clearly it had not been.

"They were raiding houses," she sobbed convulsively into Fraser's shoulder. "Burning! Kidnapping! Killing! They scalped her! They argued about who should be the one to bring her in, then they pulled us apart, and look! They scalped her! God only knows what they did to her before that!"

"Shhh, *mo chridhe*," Fraser tried to calm her. "Easy, easy…you're safe now..."

"What made them do it, Simon?" she asked. "That poor girl never did them any harm! She was a gentle soul! They're monsters! How could you have armed them?!" She looked up at her cousin, then frantically over to Burgoyne. "You have to stop them!"

Burgoyne's eyes were shimmering wildly, caught up in the swirl of chaos. "Yes!" he cried. "We must act now!

Frasier seemed at a loss for words, his face showing absolute shock, as well as guilt. It was his well-intentioned suggestion that had led to the dead girl's undoing.

Just then, a guard came running into the tent. "Generals! A fight is breaking out between our Tories and savages outside! What should we do?"

Ned felt his blood grow warm and his head spin as they all rushed outside the tent. Having experienced sudden violence before, his body and spirit were readying him for renewed danger. At the center of the camp, he saw a group of Loyalist soldiers pointing muskets at the Iroquois raiders. Jonathan was already on the scene with hands raised, trying to calm the angry soldiers, while Red Elk seemed to be trying to reason with the Iroquois in their language.

"That's my fiancée's hair!" the leader of the soldiers screamed, pointing at the gory memento. "I recognize it, and the ribbon she wore in it!"

Red Elk stepped forward. "You misunderstand. They didn't mean to kill anyone. They just wanted to take prisoners for ransom. A stray bullet killed this Jane woman, and they didn't want to waste the power of her hair. She did not suffer from the scalping. She was already dead."

Jonathan's mouth dropped open, aghast, but no words came out.

"You butchers," the Loyalist ground out.

"Why would they lie?" asked Red Elk, "How could they collect ransom on a dead woman? It must have been an accident."

Burgoyne strode forward, regular soldiers flanking him on each side. "I will be the judge of that. These braves will be handed over to me for trial."

"You will not try them, General," sneered Red Elk. "Not under your laws."

"They harmed my people, so they will face my laws," Burgoyne retorted.

"If you dare it, the Iroquois will sever ties with you, and you will lose us in your petty war!" Red Elk declared.

Fraser took hold of Burgoyne's arm and pulled him to the side. "He's right," the Scotsman admitted. "If we press the matter, first they'll attack us and loot the train, then they'll leave us to go it blind in the wilderness. Afterwards, God knows what they'll do as they flee to who knows what, and we will have no way to stop them."

"That was your kinswoman they threatened!" Burgoyne exclaimed. "Family has always meant so much to you, Balnain! How would you feel if she were the one who had been scalped, and maybe ravaged beforehand? No, we must send these savages a message, or we'll control them altogether..."

"We will have more blood on our hands if we pursue this!" Fraser countered. "If they go rogue, they will have nothing tethering them to our laws at all! They go out for booty alone, and cut down whoever they come upon, Rebel or Tory!"

"Simon..."

"You know I speak the truth! We can't bring back Jane McCrea, but we can at least try to prevent this madness from escalating!"

Burgoyne swallowed. "And what of our honor?"

Fraser exhaled. "We knew the risks of allying with the tribes. I defended the practice. So did you. Perhaps this is our punishment."

Burgoyne gave Frasier a long, pained look. Then he stepped forward and reluctantly waved his hand, beckoning the natives off.

That night, Ned went looking for Jonathan and found him talking with the unfortunate woman's fiancée. The Loyalist had headed off into the woods alone with a loaded pistol.

"Please, put away the gun," Jonathan pleaded.

The Loyalist hand shook. "They defiled her...cut her up into pieces...I'm going to kill them...then myself..."

"That won't bring her back," Jonathan insisted. "It will unleash a further outpouring of innocent blood."

"But they'll be beyond earthly pleasure, and I'll be beyond earthly pain," he murmured. "You know…it's not just Jane that's dead. It's our children that never will be. I always wanted our children…to have her hair…her beautiful hair..." He gave Jonathan a hard look and rasped, "What would you do if it was your wife?"

Jonathan grimaced. "I would want to do the same thing as you do."

"Then you have no right to stop me!"

"But in such a case, I would also not be in my right mind," Jonathan argued, "just as you are not in your right mind." He took a step closer. "Are you a savage like they are?"

"Maybe we all are," the Loyalist mumbled.

"Yes, but we are also soldiers, and have been taught discipline and restraint for the greater good. Besides…" Jonathan reached out his hand towards the man. "She wouldn't want you to throw your life away. You know that. She was willing to brave every danger to see you. Such a love does not end in death, so long as it is not cheapened by an act unworthy of it."

"But Burgoyne will not punish them," the man murmured.

Jonathan managed to slip the gun away from him, and the Loyalist let his hand fall at his side in defeat.

"General Burgoyne is a just man, who has always taken care to protect women and children from outrages," Jonathan said. "If he is staying his hand now, it is only out of that desire to protect other women and children. I know that is little consolation, but I trust him completely."

The Loyalist said nothing for a long while. Then he started to weep.

With nothing left to say, Jonathan embraced him. And Ned saw in the moonlight that tears were on his friend's cheeks.

~

News of Jane's scalping spread like wildfire. Horatio Gates, the English-born turncoat who had once served with the regular army but now was a general among the Continentals, wrote a manifesto blaming Burgoyne for allowing or even encouraging atrocities. If the Indians could get away with murdering a Loyalist officer's fiancée, what hope did Patriot civilians have? Loyalist support dwindled, and the Patriots became more impassioned to stop the British advance at all costs. As the train continued to move south, the rebels felled more trees, burnt more bridges, and targeted more soldiers with their squirrel guns. Loyalists were also targeted more viciously by their neighbors, and anyone who helped Burgoyne risked being lynched. Indeed, Burgoyne was disgusted to find two of his Loyalist couriers disfigured and hanging from trees where the rebels knew the train would pass. British reprisals were swift, and smoke from burning settlements hung thick and hot in the summer air, making the soldiers' throats grow parched and lips crack.

Eventually, the British train came to a mostly abandoned settlement. After scouring it for rebel infiltration, Burgoyne settled upon a large, well-situated house to use as a safe location to confer with his generals. Both General Fraser and Ned were with him when he entered the house for the first time. They found a Negro woman, a baby that looked decided mulatto, and a white girl around ten or eleven years of age.

"Sirs, we don't want no trouble," the woman insisted. "The massa's away from the house, and his lady's long gone to the grave, so it's just the three of us."

"If you don't want trouble, then you'll have no objections to us using this building for our temporary headquarters," Burgoyne decided.

"You have no right to just move into my father's house like you own it!" the girl cried.

"But we do, lassie," Fraser said. "These colonies belong to the King, and we are the King's men. We are here to take back what is his own by birthright."

"The King has more than enough! He lives in palaces! He doesn't own this house! He doesn't own the people in it! We own it, and this land, we, the people!"

"Careful, child…"

"This country is done with him! We want to be free from him! We won't stop fighting till he lets us go, no matter how many Hessians and Highlanders he sends over!"

"Mind your tongue, young lady!" Burgoyne reprimanded her. "Given your father is more than likely a raving rebel, and has planted such notions in your addled little head, we could have burnt this place to the ground by now. Might still, if you don't behave."

Fraser sat down in a chair and regarded her thoughtfully as she bit her lip, anger marring her youthful features. "Come here, girl."

She blinked, but did not move.

"Afraid of Highlanders?"

"I'm not afraid of anything."

"Prove it."

She swallowed hard, and marched up to him, staring him down. They remained like that, in some sort of silent contest to see who could out-stare who, until Fraser finally broke down and laughed.

"Well, it seems your father raised you to have a manly spirit, even if he has a poor cause."

She shrugged.

Fraser gestured to the portrait on the wall. "Your mother? You look rather like her."

"No, I don't," she mumbled. "She was pretty."

"You have the same nose. It's…petite."

She blushed.

He took something out of his coat, a miniature of a lady with shoulder-length curls. "My wife, a German, wed to a Scot. Your worst nightmare, no?" He chuckled again, then in a gesture she clearly didn't expect, let her hold it for a moment. "It's dear to me."

She gazed down at it. "Father has one of these."

"I recall that the Prince carried two," Fraser reflected.

"Who?"

"The Young Pretender," he clarified. "Charles Edward Stuart. He carried a miniature of his mother, and another of his mistress, both named Clementina. I suppose they gave both the boy and the man in him some sort of grounding amidst the stormy seas he embarked upon…that he embarked us all upon…"

She looked perplexed.

He leaned forward a little as if confiding in her. "My clan turned rebel, don't you know? Paid the price for it too. And yet…our story didn't end there. It need not be for your kind either." He leaned back in his chair. "Do not hate me so, child, for I do not hate you. So long as I am under this roof, no harm will come to you. "

The baby in the corner crib made a squealing noise, catching Fraser's attention. He smiled in an amused manner, then squinted. "Is that…a duck?" He pointed at the toy the child was holding.

"Y-yes, sir," the Negro woman stuttered. "I made it, sir, out of an old pillow…"

"I would like to have it," Fraser stated.

Burgoyne's eyebrow shot up. "Balnain, why in blazes do you want to commandeer a pillow duck?"

"I have my reasons."

"Need I remind you that robbing babies of their chew toys is not the primary function of this expedition?" He gestured dramatically to the baby, who was chewing on the duck's wing.

"I don't want to rob it," Fraser retorted. "I'll pay for it…"

"Dear God," Burgoyne exhaled. "This is getting extreme for any Scotsman!"

"Look, it could save a life…"

"Oh, wait a minute," Burgoyne sighed. "I remember now. Your little Hessian sweetheart…"

"She's going through a phase that could lead to her untimely demise if she chases ducks into ponds. She's two-and-a-half. Her wee self would be underwater and out of sight just like that." He snapped his fingers. "So…if she has a duck of her own, it might satisfy her needs until the phase passes."

"Ummm…I'll concede you've given this a lot of thought," Burgoyne responded, "and it might indicate you need some time off to unwind…"

"But it's logical," he insisted, then turned to the woman and queried, "Isn't it logical?"

"I reckon it is, sir," she replied meekly.

"Excellent." He dug into his pocket and produced a coin. "Buy a new pillow. Make a new duck."

"I feel like such words should have a deeper symbolic meaning," Burgoyne mused. "I'll give it a think…"

"Don't quote this in a play…"

"I should quote this in a play…"

"John!"

The baby started crying over all the racket. His mother now arched an eyebrow herself. "General, I put one point upon this business of the duck," she said, a sparkle of confidence springing to her eyes. "You'll have to be the one to retrieve it."

Fraser raised an eyebrow. "Strange stipulation." But he didn't balk further and headed over to the crib. He glanced back over his shoulder. "Umm…does it bite?"

"The duck? No, sir."

"I meant…"

Burgoyne groaned. "Must I do everything around here?" He went over and dangled his watch chain in front of the baby, who followed the swaying motion with wide eyes. "That's it, baby. Now be greedy. Reach out and take it."

"Always the tempter," Fraser sighed. "Oh…he's going for it…"

"Of course he is! I know human nature! Now grab that duck!"

Fraser did so. "Alright, so how will you get the watch chain back?"

"We don't," Burgoyne sighed. "I have replacements."

Now the mother rushed over to make sure her child didn't swallow the chain, and the generals chuckled to see her struggle to get it away from him.

~

The next day, Fraser was sitting in the parlor smoking his pipe, when the girl came bursting through the door, being chased by a soldier. She ducked behind the chaise, clutching a sizable wooden box in her arms.

"What's happening here?" Fraser inquired.

"They took it out of the barn," she said. "They were gonna steal it."

"We found it under a loose board!" the soldier said. "Could be contraband!"

"But it's mine. They can't have it."

"Well, you heard her, private," Fraser sighed, puffing on his pipe. "Sounds as if you can't have it."

"But sir…"

"I'll deal with the matter, soldier."

"Yes, sir," the soldier conceded, saluting and exiting the room.

Fraser glanced over at the girl. "What's your name anyway, lass?"

"Amelia," she said.

"Oh. That's a nice name."

"I've never liked it," she said. "It sounds like…oatmeal or something."

Fraser burst out laughing, and she frowned scoldingly.

"Sorry," he apologized, then gestured to what she was holding. "What's in the box?"

She held the box closer to her chest. "You want to steal it too?"

"Don't be silly…"

"Well, you stole the duck…"

"I paid for it, actually!"

"I'm not selling this…"

"I don't want to buy it!"

"Then why do you want to look inside?"

Fraser groaned. "Stubborn creature, you be! Did your father ever tell you that?"

"Yes," she said. "He's stubborn too."

"I can imagine!"

She blinked. Then hesitantly, she opened the box. "It's beads."

"Oh." He leaned forward to look at them. "You've got them sorted by color, I see."

"And by what they're made of. The glass ones are more expensive than the wooden ones." She pulled out a compartment in the box to show off the glass selection.

"You must have been collecting these for a while."

She nodded, kneeling down and starting to take out all the compartments and lay them out on the floor.

"So you string these?" he guessed.

"Sometimes," she replied, "or I use a tool to hook them onto the links of chains."

"Well, that's clever of you."

She nodded.

"So where did you get all these?"

"The wooden ones from Indian traders," she explained. "The glass ones my father got me from New York City." She gazed at them with satisfaction, like a bird that had carried off a colorful trinket to its nest. "I would like some more green ones."

"Green? But it's bad luck for a pretty girl to wear green," said Fraser.

"Who says?"

"It's a known thing where I come from," he insisted. "Makes the fairies jealous, and they can cause all manner of mischief."

"That's silly," she scoffed. "And anyway, I'm not pretty."

"You're too hard on yourself," he chuckled.

"Well, the point is, green is my favorite color," she said. "That's why I want more green beads."

"Fair." He rested his chin on his fist. "If I make it down to New York City in the next few months, would you like me to fetch you some glass beads for Christmas?"

She looked genuinely taken aback. Then she blurted, "But I don't want you to go to New York City."

"I didn't imagine so," Fraser sighed, "but if I do end up there, it's a silver lining for you."

She blinked. "My father can get them for me after he wins the war."

Fraser chuckled and shook his head.

She pulled out a necklace from the bottom compartment of the box. "See? This one is with a chain. And there's a medallion on it." She held it out towards him.

"It's a turtle," he observed.

She nodded again. "The Indians think they bring good luck, that the whole world is like a turtle shell, covered with mud."

"You should wear a mouse medallion," he decided.

She bristled. "Why?"

"Because you're like a wee mouse, always scurrying about."

"And what would you be?" she challenged him. "A wolf?"

"No, lass," he said. "All the wolves are dead across the sea. Only the foxes remain, who are their children. Many of them have died too, but…" His eyes grew hazy. "We remain."

She pulled out the bottom compartment farther and pulled out a loose medallion. Then she handed it to him.

"There," she said. "A fox."

The general smiled. "It's like looking in a mirror."

Later that evening, Burgoyne and Fraser were eating supper together when Amelia came into the dining room.

"You're not supposed to be here, young lady," Burgoyne sighed. "Go to your room."

She raised her chin defiantly, even though her voice came out like a squeak. "It's my home! Why should I be locked up in my room as if I did something wrong?"

"Oh, let her stay," Fraser said. "What harm can she do?"

"Balnain…"

Fraser drew out a chair next to his. "Your house, your table."

A bit skittishly, she went over and took a seat, still holding her head high.

Fraser cut a slab of meat, set it on an extra plate, and passed it to her. He scooped something out of a pan that had been placed on the table and put it on the plate as well. "I'm not entirely sure what this is…"

"Corn casserole," the girl said. "Belinda is very good at making it."

"Good. Glad you could identify it." He scooped out some green beans.

"I don't want any," she mumbled.

"Besides the point, lassie," Fraser sighed, putting the greens on her plate. "They're good for you." He took the pitcher of milk and poured her a cup. "This too."

"But I don't…"

"Look, you've gone too long without parents in the house, so it looks like I'll have to lay the law down," Fraser said. "Now do as you're told, young lady."

She pouted, and played with her food on the end of her fork.

"Bloody hell, these Americans," Burgoyne snorted. "Won't eat their greens, won't pay their taxes…"

"You're not supposed to swear at the table," she lectured him.

"Then they turn around and scold you for breathing," he exhaled, "especially the female kind, doubly obstinate, and in need of a good spanking…"

"Let a Highlander handle it, John," Fraser chuckled. "We're just as obstinate."

"None more so than you, dear Balnain."

"I'm afraid I must take that as a compliment, however you intended it!"

The girl finally shoved a forkful of green beans into her mouth. "Why are you called Balnain? I thought you were a Fraser."

"Yes, a Fraser of Balnain. It's my home. Would you like me to tell you about it?"

"Not really."

"Don't be so rude, girl," Burgoyne lectured. "Bad enough you talk while chewing."

She shrugged.

"Balnain is not so terribly different from this place," Fraser said wistfully. "I grew up near forests and lakes and the shadow of the mountains, looming gray-blue, like the silhouettes of giants, just over the horizon."

"So why not stay there?" she asked.

"Things happened, lass. I told you, I come from a clan that earned a rebel brand."

"But now you work with…with him?" She pointed at Burgoyne.

"Rude!" Burgoyne exhaled.

"Aye, I work with him," Fraser answered, eyes sparkling. "He's not so irredeemable when you get to know him, even if he is rather too English for his own good, and always been a government man…."

"You're not helping, Balnain," Burgoyne lectured.

"We're from the same island, you see," Fraser continued. "It's a matter of necessity that we either learn to work together, filling in where the other party lacks, or we are no good to anybody, least of all ourselves."

"We're entwined together," Burgoyne sighed.

"The thistle and the rose," Fraser chuckled.

"Roses still have thorns, for all their beauty…"

"And perfume!"

"Is that why you made me hunt in the Highlands?" Burgoyne queried. "To fill in where I lack and make me smell more natural?"

"And to put some color on your cheeks, grown pale and pasty from too much time spent in theaters," Fraser said. He turned back to the girl. "Unlike me, Johnny here is a city man from birth. Zigzags from London in the south to Preston in the north. I had to learn to adapt to city life over the course of my travels. But I suppose the wild streak never left me."

"You mean like eating raw meat?" Burgoyne queried with a smirk. He turned to the girl. "You're lucky you met him indoors. Outdoors, he's an absolute ghoul. Up in the Highlands, he shot a stag, killed it with his sword, then cut a chunk right out of it. He started to eat it, right then and there. He tried to give me some too, but it was dripping with blood, and I politely declined."

The girl grimaced and dropped her fork.

Fraser rolled his eyes. "Johnny…"

"Well, it's true! Then you did the same thing with a bull you skewered during your madcap chase after Ticonderoga!"

"When you've gone through times when meat was scarce, and fires a risk, you learn that you have to do what you have to do to nourish yourself," Fraser said.

"But you have surprisingly good table manners, it must be said, so long as you're sitting at a table," Burgoyne admitted.

"Well, I'm afraid we don't always have the niceties of tea and crumpets at our disposal, do we?" Fraser challenged.

"I could really use some tea right now," Burgoyne sighed, then glanced accusingly at the girl. "But some practical jokers in face paint had to dump an ungodly amount of it in saltwater."

"I don't like tea," Amelia decided.

"Drink your milk then," Fraser coaxed. "Now on the count of three…"

"Alright, already," she huffed and drank it down.

"There," Fraser said, satisfied. "That wasn't so hard, was it?"

She shrugged, wiping her mouth with her sleeve. "Do you force everyone to drink milk?"

"Whenever milk is available, aye," he replied, pushing a napkin closer to her for future use. "It isn't always. There was a time we had a shortage back home."

"Why?"

"Because livestock that gave milk were being driven off or shot," he said gravely, and Burgoyne dropped his gaze guiltily.

"On account of the rebellion?" she surmised.

"Yes, lass, on account of the rebellion." He cut her a piece of raspberry cobbler the maid has provided for dessert, then cut a piece for himself. "Now, would you like me to tell you a story?"

"About what?" she asked, going at the dessert with verve.

"About…the prince among the heather, on the run in the Highlands…"

"Oh, no, Balnain," Burgoyne groaned, pushing back his own plate of cobbler, as if losing his appetite.

Nevertheless, the Englishman let the Scotsman have his way, and Fraser managed to capture Amelia's rapt attention with his string of yarns about the Charles Edward Stuart and the folk who hid him from his pursuers. Fraser would never give away names, of course, but he spoke broadly of farmers, fishermen, and fair ladies, all willing to risk their lives for the sake of their chosen royal. And it seemed certain that, little by little, he was at least winning her away from the Congress. Burgoyne could not help but smile at unfailing Fraser stealth.

~

The next morning, the British high command prepared to get back on the road. Fraser glanced up at Amelia, watching them from the stairs. She was still in her nightgown, her arms wrapped around her legs.

"Good morning, wee mouse," he chuckled. "Going to come down to say goodbye?"

She shook her head.

"What, you're afraid of me again?"

She bunched up her fists at her side now. Then she came down the stairs and stood in front of him, staring up at him defiantly.

He laughed at her pluck, then regarded her more softly. "You've been crying."

"Have not," she blurted, lowering her eyes.

"Little girls shouldn't lie."

"I'm not little. Haven't been for years."

"Alright. Young ladies shouldn't lie." He tilted his head. "What's wrong?"

She said nothing, just bit her lip.

"I think I know what it is," he said. "You miss your father."

She winced. "I don't care what you think he's guilty of, or what he's done against your king, I just…I…" Tears filled her eyes, and she hurriedly brushed them away with her hand. "I don't want…I don't want him to get hurt…I'd do anything…"

"I know," he said quietly.

"Anything…"

"I know."

She broke down and sobbed.

Fraser sighed and pulled out a handkerchief. He held it up to her face, and she winced.

"There now, lass. Blow your nose."

She reluctantly did so, and he dabbed the tears off her cheeks.

He smiled a little. "I should lecture you, but I find it hard to do. I suppose it's because…I'd rather fancy having a daughter who hoped I wouldn't get hurt, regardless of my indiscretions. In that, your father is blessed beyond what he deserves. Let's hope he lives to be a former rebel, like me."

She kept her eyes down, refusing to meet his gaze. Another tear rolled down her cheek.

"There now, dear," he said kindly. "Won't you look at me, hmm?" He placed a finger under her chin and gently lifted her gaze to him. "You alright?"

"Yes."

"You're shaking."

"I'm cold," she said. "You-you made me come down before I got properly dressed."

"Alright, my fault, I was just…well, we're leaving, so…" He shook his head, then glanced over at a coverlet draped over a nearby chaise. He snatched it up and put it around her shoulders like a shawl. "Better?"

She didn't answer, but did pull the coverlet closer around her.

"I'll see what I can do about getting you those glass beads in New York City," he promised, "if I don't get a taste of hot lead first…"

Her face turned white as a ghost, and her eyes grew wide.

"Sorry," he said. "I have a black sense of humor…"

She appeared even more shocked when he took her hand and briefly brought it to his lips.

"Well, we're off, lass. Give me a smile, hmm?"

"No," she choked, but it wasn't even angry, wasn't even defiant, just sounded like she would cry harder than ever, then turned and ran back upstairs.

And Ned noticed Fraser's eyes were gleaming too.

As the two generals walked outside, it seemed that Burgoyne sensed Fraser's mood.

"I swear, Balnain, if your indulgent attitude of brats keeps up like this, you'll be sure to spoil any children you have with Margaretha," Burgoyne predicted.

"And you have no experience with spoiling children?" Fraser queried.

"Well..." Burgoyne blushed.

"You just need to win over the baroness. I think you'd fall in love with her children even more than I have, given the chance."

"I shan't grovel to her," he said with a shrug.

"No, but you could put out a little..."

"Alright, fine. When we go shopping in Albany and New York City, you must remind me to pick something up for her Hessian ladyship and brood of hapless moppets..."

"How did I get press ganged into your future shopping ventures?"

"I need someone to restrain me if I spend beyond my means."

"You know you will, and you won't listen to anyone who tries to stop you..."

"Oh, then I suppose I just want company. It's bloody boring shopping alone."

Fraser smiled. "You miss buying up half of Europe with Lady Charlotte, you mean."

"Well, France, Italy, and Portugal, at any rate," he giggled awkwardly. "London doesn't have bad shops either. It was...fun."

Fraser's expression grew sad. "Fine, I'll go along with you, just to scold you like a parent when you act like a child in a sweet shop."

Burgoyne beamed. "Besides, you'll need to buy Christmas presents for your wife anyway, and I've got a list to appease..."

"Right, so you'll be jumping onto *my* shopping trips," Fraser sighed.

"Why not? I'll let you jump on my victory train!"

Fraser snorted. "You're taking years off my life, Johnny..."

"Years well wasted! It'll be, well, fun!"

"Good God! What would you do without me?"

"Be a lesser man!" Burgoyne started to pull on his riding gloves, flexing his fingers. "You know, I really should have had a few extra pairs of these made...elegant yet functional..."

Fraser chuckled, then suddenly grew serious. He glanced over to the building, alarm glinting in his eyes. Then he turned back to Burgoyne.

"John." His voice was taut, his face white. And before Burgoyne could respond, Fraser had lunged forward and shoved him backward.

A mere second later, a shot rang out. A soldier nearby cried out, clutching his arm. The attacker darted back into the building, and soldiers charged in after him. Burgoyne and Fraser both had their respective pistols drawn as their aides rushed to their sides.

The pursuit proved brief, and the assailant was taken alive with a bullet in his shoulder and dragged before the generals. After searching the attic where he had been seized, papers were found under the floorboards, intended for the rebel high command.

Burgoyne glanced over the letters, then glared at the prisoner coldly, who stared up at him defiantly. "Not only did you attempt to assassinate me and my fellow general, but you are clearly a courier, albeit a terrible one, having put your own mission in jeopardy. Do you have any idea how my couriers have been handled by your own commanders?"

The man did not respond, just kept his dark brown eyes upon Burgoyne, resentment and resolve blending together.

Burgoyne stuffed the letters in his coat. "No answer for me? Then you must know, but are afraid to say."

"I do not fear unjust punishment, for I have a clear conscience in the defense of my land," the man stated in a voice as clear as a bell.

"Pray tell, how am I being unjust? You tried to murder me in cold blood, with my back turned," Burgoyne spat. "You nearly murdered my friend!"

"I am not cowed by your hierarchies," the man replied.

"You contradict your own philosophy," Burgoyne declared. "If you cared nothing for hierarchy, you would not have targeted us in particular, nor prided yourself for having attempted to bring us down. Besides…" He gestured towards the house, where the Negro woman was staring anxiously out the window. "It appears you are part of a hierarchy yourself!"

The prisoner lowered his gaze slightly. "Belinda…she's more like family."

"Oh, I imagine she is very intimate to you," Burgoyne surmised. "I know well how such things go."

The man flushed at the inference, but he did not deny it. "Will I be tried?"

"Do you deny your crime?"

"No, nor do I see it as a crime."

"Then no is my response in kind."

Soon, the man was standing on a ladder that was leaning up against a sturdy tree, with his hands bound behind his back and a noose pulled tight around his neck.

"Permission to speak," the man said hoarsely.

"I see no reason to grant it to you," Burgoyne replied.

"Come, sir, if you have settled upon making a dead man of me, allow me command over the few moments remaining to my allotted time in this world…"

"To speak treason?"

"To offer a defense, since no one else will defend me, just as these colonies were not allowed to defend herself when declared seditious by parliament."

"You have been condemned by your own seditious actions," Burgoyne retorted.

"Actions in response to other actions must be judged according to the law," the prisoner retorted.

"And you are a man of the law?"

"Yes, I was, until the law itself was laid low," he declared. "The die was cast long ago, and not by me."

"How so, hmm?" Burgoyne queried, seemingly relenting to his curiosity over what type of defense he would muster. "How do you defer responsibility for your attack upon the throne?"

"The throne has stained itself with everlasting infamy by its determination to defend the usurpation of our rights by parliament," the condemned man declared. "Britain has become infatuated with her so-called prerogatives, to the distress of her offspring, America! Together they might have grown, like the oak and the ivy. Britain, united with these colonies, by commerce and affection, by interest and blood, might have mocked the threats of France and Spain! She could have been the seat of a universal empire! But one part of the empire sought to enslave the other! By seeking to bind America in a state of vassalage, Britain must lose her ascendency! We, meanwhile, must make this the season when we seize again those rights which, as men, we are by nature entitled to, and which, by contract, we never have and never could have surrendered, and which no king, nor all the lords and commons put together, can revoke!"

"It is fitting that the child should submit to the parent, not as a slave to a master, but out of filial devotion," Burgoyne replied. "Britain required only what was just to expect!"

"The blood that once joined the parents honored and the child beloved has now been spilt thanks to your expectations," the man replied. "All milder entreaties to redress our grievances being rejected, the sword has become our dreadful alternative to bondage!"

"Bondage, you say? In what way has a master such as yourself ever been enslaved?" Burgoyne challenged, his eyes glinting, seeming to be invigorated by the debate he felt confident of winning.

"When the parent demands that a child never grow, the child becomes a slave," the man replied.

"Spoken like every petulant child," Burgoyne scoffed.

"We can only humbly hope that the Supreme Being whose justice is unyielding will engage on our side, and deliver those of us who go forth in defense of our injured and oppressed country from the hands of those that persecute us. We will repel the unprovoked assaults of the enemy, and you will suffer the cost of presuming to fight against freemen!"

"We are an army championing the rights of law-abiding citizens," Burgoyne stated. "It is your revolutionaries who subject the people to arbitrary dealings and rapacious intrusions!"

"And what are you doing, marching through this territory, devouring the fruits of our labor like locusts? Do you truly marvel that people risk everything to inhibit your progress?"

"We tried to make peace with you, on numerous occasions, with offers of pardons if you would but lay down your arms, but you would not have it," Burgoyne replied.

"Can we with indifference behold so much valor already laid prostrate by the hand of British tyranny, while the King sits in his palace, surrounded by the ensigns of despotism?" the man demanded. "Can we ever grasp that hand in affection again? Shall we still court a dependence on the nation from which we sprang which has forfeited not only every kindred claim, but even their title to humanity?"

"You, an assassin, speak of humanity?" Burgoyne queried.

"The spirits of our valiant countrymen who fought, bled, and died for freedom demand that we hold our lives cheaply until it is attained! Go tell the king that we and the Britons can be friends no more! Tell him, to you all tyrants are the same! Yes, we ought, and will—we will assert the blood of our murdered heroes against thy hostile oppressions! With you, rude Britons, we will wage life-scorning war till you admit your fault, and like hell fall off!"

"You will be the one to fall off," said Burgoyne flatly, and signaled for the ladder to be removed.

The condemned man stiffened, preparing for the worst. "Before you cut short my life, General Burgoyne, I must know…will you preserve my family?"

"Your family?" Burgoyne repeated.

"Yes," the man replied, "Belinda and both my children."

"So you own the mulatto as being of your blood," Burgoyne said. "First time?"

The man nodded.

"Better late than never, I suppose."

"What are you going to do with them?" the rebel demanded.

"Provide them with greater protection than you did," Burgoyne answered, "not because of any request made by you, but because of who I am."

The man looked slightly relieved. "Something else," he added. "I want to see a chaplain."

"There's no time," Burgoyne blurted. "Talk to your Maker when you see him face to face. If He's just, he'll know exactly where to send you!"

"I am a religious man…"

"Clearly you didn't read the passage of Scripture that reads 'render therefore unto Caesar the thing which are Caesar's', nor the passage that reads 'fear God, honor the king,'" Burgoyne shot back. "As such, you have forfeited the right to receive succor from the Church of England, whose rightful governor is His Majesty, King George III. You have disavowed our head, and are no member of our body."

"You really believe that a king is what stands between a man and his God?" the man challenged. "My ancestors came to this land as Separatists…"

"Then you'll die as ignorant and unruly as they were."

"I dread to think what will happen to your kind after you've murdered all the men of conviction in your midst!"

"Conviction?" Fraser spat. "Is that what made you use your own daughter to cover for your crimes? How low can a man go without ceasing to be a man? The lass could have been hurt!"

"Don't you dare speak of my daughter, you Highland dog!" the man retorted fiercely. "I know you had your eyes on her, and wanted to get your hands on her! I know all about your kind and their backward ways! Doesn't matter how young, you still go after them!"

"What?" Fraser blurted.

"Even the cursed crown views you mountain barbarians as a menace, especially the shiftless Frasers! That's why they sent you here, to terrorize us! It proves how far England has fallen! You thought I was aiming for Jack Brag, but it was you I intended to dispose of, first and foremost, to prevent your perversions!"

"Silence, filth!" Burgoyne shouted. "General Fraser thought first of saving my life, without any concern of his own. But you? You slunk about like a coward, waiting for your chance to shoot us in the back! You accuse him of unspeakable things, yet he protected your daughter, and even your female slave, from any harm that might have befallen them. Now you insult his honor, when your daughter's innocence was shielded by him and he treated her with nothing but kindness! You deserve everything you are about to suffer! You deserve the shame! Now we will watch as you soil yourself as you die!" Then he guided his horse backward several paces and announced, "General Fraser will take command here. He will give the order for the execution."

Fraser gave his friend a brief, grateful glance at this show of solidarity. But he did not give any command. Instead, he rode up to the man who had sought his life and insulted his name, staring at him with a stony intensity. Then, with his own strength, he seized the ladder, wrenched it to the right, and caused it to topple over. The rope tightened around the victim's throat, and he choked.

The hanging proved to be gruesome, but it was Ned's duty to watch justice take its course. He fought the instinct to turn his eyes down as the man kicked and writhed and gurgled, the life being squeezed out of him for his crimes. But Ned found that all the crimes in the book could not make him wish this on anyone, not as ten minutes ticked by and the man still struggled, his face a hideous purple shade. Alan Fraser, the general's kinsman and aide, with warped humor, started whistling a tune about a hanged Scottish brigand, but General Fraser, to his credit, ordered him to stop. Yet there was a terrible gleam in the Highland commander's eyes as he watched the man suffer, seemingly intent upon the rebel's last sight being a Fraser glowering down at him. Indeed, he appeared determined to take in every moment of this execution until the enemy was no longer a man, but mere hanging meat. And Burgoyne was staring too, but at Fraser rather than at the strangulating man.

Just then, Amelia ran out into the yard, screaming at the sight of her father's agony. Her voice caused Fraser to wrench himself around, and the look of dark hatred was replaced by one of dawning horror as she reached the side of his horse, clawing at his leg and begging him to make it stop. His horse whinnied and sidestepped as she was seized by one of the soldiers and pulled away, but she fought hard against his grip, continuing to shriek and plead.

The man dangling from the rope finally went limp, his suffering finally extinguished.

Amelia screamed yet again, louder and longer than ever, until her voice cracked. Then she crumpled to the ground and wept.

Fraser kept staring down at her, his face having gone blank. He seemed to have forgotten about his previous fixation on the execution and was now utterly absorbed in the aftermath. Ned saw him chew on his lower lip.

"You killed him!" she sobbed. "I hope you die! I hope it hurts!" She struggled to her feet, a clump of loose earth in her hand, torn from the ground with her fingernails. She flung it at Fraser, and the soldier who had previously restrained her swore at her, then, in an act of impulsive violence, struck her in the forehead with his gun, knocking her into the dirt. She whimpered in pain.

"Put up your weapon, soldier!" Fraser bellowed. "We do not make war on children!"

"But sir, she might have known about—"

"She's a child!"

Amelia knelt up, hands pressed to her forehead. When she took them away, she saw they were stained red. She looked up at Fraser, her eyes flickering with fury. "Blood for blood!" she cried. "Blood for blood!"

Then she fell backward in a swoon.

The blood drained from Fraser's face as he watched. Then he rode closer and extended his handkerchief to the soldier who struck her. "Staunch her wound," he ordered hoarsely. Then he looked over at the house, and then at Burgoyne, who simply nodded. "Fire the house," Fraser commanded, and five soldiers hurried off to start the task.

A few minutes later, they shoved the slave woman outside, with her baby held close to her breast, and tossed touches through the windows and into the doorway. She gasped and put a hand to her mouth when she saw her master's corpse, turning eerily on the rope, and used her other hand to cover her child's face, as if to shield him from the sight he was surely too young to understand or remember. Then she saw the man's daughter on the ground and rushed over.

"Miss Amelia, honey…what'd they do to you?" she fretted, wiping the girl's face with her apron before being pushed away by a soldier. Burgoyne nodded his approval

"Keep them apart," the general ordered. "They may have had a hand in the attack."

Just then, Abby, who had been part of the crowd watching the hanging, pushed past the guard to the girl's side as she slowly regained consciousness. She hovered over the child protectively, drying her tears with her skirt. Then she shot a furious glance up at Burgoyne and Fraser. "Think yourselves so brave, invading men's homes and murdering them if they fight back? Think yourselves heroes, molesting children?"

"Be quiet, girl," Burgoyne snapped. Fraser merely grimaced.

She raised a fist. "Silence is for the dead! I am not dead yet! You can't kill us all!"

Ned sprang forward and clamped a hand over her mouth.

"Please, sirs, permission to escort her elsewhere," he panted. "She is overwrought…"

Burgoyne exhaled. "Very well, Lieutenant, but we will not endure this type of outburst from her again. Is that clear?"

"Yes, sir," Ned replied. "Thank you, sir."

Fraser stared for a few moments at the blazing building, then gestured broadly to Amelia, the slave woman, and her baby. "Take them with us." He cast Burgoyne a glance. "We cannot leave them amidst the ashes to be murdered by anyone who comes upon them."

Anyone? Ned thought as he pulled Abby away. *Loyalist neighbors? Straggling soldiers? Roving Indians?*

Fraser was, no doubt, weighed down by all possibilities. Especially the Indians.

Burgoyne nodded. "Very well, General. Your generosity of spirit does you credit."

Again, Fraser stared at the house as the roof came down with a crash. "Hardly, General," he murmured. "Hardly…"

Chapter 31: TORN ASUNDER

Later that evening, General Burgoyne stepped into the surgeon's tent, and the young soldier who had been struck by the assassin's bullet flinched, instinctively sitting up straight.

"There, now, lie back, soldier," Burgoyne instructed. "The surgeon tells me you've lost a good deal of blood."

The soldier hesitantly let himself slump down again.

Burgoyne stepped closer. "Ah, I remember your face," he said in his easy-going manner. "You've guarded my tent some nights ago."

"Yes, sir," the young man mumbled. "You-you have a very fine memory, sir."

"I am a playwright as well as a general, you know," he reminded him. "It is habitual for me to mind all those on stage, major or minor." He smiled a little. "And you're a Preston lad. I can hear it on your tongue."

Now the soldier smiled a bit too and nodded.

"Now we come to this business about the arm," Burgoyne said, gesturing to the blood-soaked bandages. "The surgeon tells me there is little choice but to take it off."

The soldier swallowed hard. "I do not wish for that, sir."

"Well, I hardly thought you would, but it is your life at stake, private. You would do well to submit to whatever the surgeon says should be done," Burgoyne stated.

"Is this an order, sir?" the soldier asked meekly.

"No," Burgoyne admitted, "but it is my counsel, and I do not believe a man with any courage or wisdom would reject it. I myself would not reject it in your state."

"But if it were you, then you wouldn't need…" His voice faded, and he bit his lip.

"Wouldn't need what?"

"Nothing, sir."

"That's not good enough," Burgoyne retorted. "Now talk to me."

The boy winced, then continued quietly, "Begging your pardon, sir…but you wouldn't have to fear needing a begging bowl or landing in the poorhouse." He was trembling a little now. "I'm sorry, sir, but that's how it is."

"Ah. Well…perhaps you underestimate my near-brushes with the latter, but…" The corner of his mouth twitched. "What was your work before you took the king's shilling?"

"I was a weaver's apprentice, sir," he said. "That's-that's all I'm good for, that and fighting the Yankees, and I can't do either without my arm, my right arm, sir…" His voice cracked. "I-I don't mind dying so much as dying less…less than a man. Does…does the general understand?"

Burgoyne sighed. "Yes, the general understands. But…you needn't fear the begging bowl. It will not come to that."

"But sir, I–"

"Do you think your general is a liar?"

"No, sir!"

"Then it will not come to that," Burgoyne repeated softly. "I will not permit it to come to that. Now save your life. It is no unmanly thing to be marked by your service to the king and country."

The boy was shaking as he finally submitted to the saw. The surgeon gave him a stiff drink, then had him bite on a bullet wrapped in cloth. Then he was pushed flat on his back and his arm pulled out in preparation. His breathing grew faster and faster until his chest was heaving in panic. But Burgoyne was soon above him, looking down to meet his fearful eyes, and making calm nonsense talk about Preston.

Then the sawing started.

The boy screamed in muffled agony. There was a horrible grating sound of saw against bone, and blood sprayed everywhere.

But Burgoyne stayed. He didn't flinch at the horror of it all, just kept talking, his eyes never leaving the boy's as they watered from the pain.

He stayed there till the weaver lad had fallen unconscious and the arm was off. He stayed as the stump was cauterized. And he stayed to make sure he had the soldier's name from the surgeon. Ned heard him repeating it to himself as he left the tent, like some minor character in a play he was determined not to forget.

When the general saw Edmund standing nearby, he went over to him.

"I know how hangings sicken you, Ned," he said sympathetically, "but you handled it well, as a soldier should when called to witness the execution of the King's justice. You showed yourself manly, and for that, I am proud of you."

"I did not feel like very much of a man, watching another man strangulate in front of his child, and standing by as if it had no effect upon me," Edmund mumbled dismally.

Burgoyne exhaled. "Do not think yourself a monster for it. Treason is the monster in this scenario, one which we have no choice but to slay, for the common good. You should feel no qualms about that, for the guilty party brought it down on his own head."

"But…" Ned's breath caught in his throat. "He…couldn't breathe…"

Burgoyne regarded him softly. "I didn't say you must take pleasure in it."

~

That night, Burgoyne visited Fraser in his quarters, both of them having taken up residence in the next abandoned house they came upon.

"You're up late," Burgoyne remarked.

"So are you," Fraser returned.

"It's been a rather rotten day."

"You handled it well, though"

"So did you."

"Did I?"

"Well, you gave me a shove in the right direction when I needed it," Burgoyne reminded him. "It was altogether decent of you."

"It's my job to be a service to you, is it not?"

"Hopefully not an obligation that runs too strongly against the grain."

"Not strongly at all," he replied kindly.

"Whatever you do, Balnain, you throw your whole self into it."

"And that concerns you?" Fraser queried. "I see the furrows in your brow."

"Sometimes, yes. But I don't suppose I would change you if I could."

"Thank you for standing by me, anyway," Fraser muttered.

Burgoyne raised an eyebrow. "My dear Balnain, there are favors I do for you based upon my personal consideration for you. But this was not one of them. Correct me if I am wrong, but you are no less a representative of the King's authority and majesty in this restless land than I am. Affronts against you are to be interpreted the same as affronts against me."

"Yes, but…"

"No buts."

Fraser bit his lip. "There's a little girl who thinks me a murderer."

"Couldn't be helped. He was guilty."

"She can't help who her father happened to be." He blinked. "I…went to check on how she fared earlier. I made sure to stay out of sight of her, of course. It might have thrown her into another fit."

"How is she?"

"Sleeping, when I was there, poor creature. They say she has a concussion. But she's bandaged up, that's something." He closed his eyes for a moment. "I…never wanted her to be struck like that, just for throwing some mud."

"I know."

"After all, I didn't just execute her father. I wanted him to suffer, for his words against me. You know this. My pride can be a deadly thing."

Burgoyne sat down next to him on the bed. "I wanted him dead too."

"Are you saying that you never shared his sentiments about Highlanders?"

"Some of them, once. But then…I met you. We had fun."

"We did," Fraser chuckled, "for all your Whiggishness."

"Still do," Burgoyne said, "even at war. Not only do we have a healthy respect for each other's skills, but we…cheer each other up."

Fraser sighed. "Do you ever find that you have grown afraid of yourself?"

"We all do, some time or other. But after such nightly terrors, the morning comes, and we rise to greet the day. It is our soldierly duty." Burgoyne tapped on the book in Fraser's hands. "So…what are you frittering away your hours with this evening?"

"Frittering away? You're the one who gave me this!" Fraser waved the book under Burgoyne's nose.

"Tch, tch, I'm teasing you," he clucked. "You know I advocate all my officers should steal away some time to read daily. You are setting a sterling example for them!"

"Thank you."

"So what did I bequeath to you then?"

"The poetry of Ossian. I forget upon what special occasion you deposited this with me, but…"

"I don't require a special occasion to gift books to my friends, Balnain," Burgoyne retorted. "Nor indeed, to my enemies. No one should ever have to offer an explanation behind the giving of books beyond the pleasure of it. They are a perpetual solace to the mind."

Fraser chuckled. "Spoken like a true scholar."

Burgoyne nodded eagerly. "I read that volume and thought of you, the kinsman of chieftains."

"Unlucky chieftains, it must be said," Fraser sighed.

"Unlucky in fate, but noble in blood," Burgoyne reminded him. "Now…read something to me, why don't you?"

Fraser smiled wistfully, then began to read, "Raise my white sails, raise them to the winds of the west. Let us rush through the foam of the northern wave. Let us be renowned in the battles of other lands." He glanced over at his friends. "Though claimed to be of ancient origin, some say these poems are fraudulent."

"No art is fraudulent if it produces some higher sentiments in our breasts," Burgoyne insisted. "No work is false if it speaks some deeper truth."

"And that deeper truth is…?"

"Our destiny, Balnain."

"As knights of the round table?"

"Yes, we're here to keep Camelot from falling this time! We're mocking the catastrophe of Camlann!" Burgoyne beamed. "And a great racket was made by the arms of those who came," he recited, "and often against the arms struck the branches of oaks and hornbeams. Resounded the woods of the shields and hauberks! Resounded the iron of the shields and clashed against the hauberks!"

Fraser chuckled. "Well, you know what they say…if nothing else, you Englishmen are brave. Brick-headed, but brave."

"The unifying factor binding us two together is our Norman blood and our Norman names," Burgoyne stated. "Yes, yes, it's been a bit diluted by the Saxons on my side and the Gaels on yours, but all the same, the conquering streak is alive and well in us both! We are the descendents of Norman knights, and they will boast about our deeds in the afterlife!" He lifted a bottle on Fraser's bedside. "Thank the Lord! 'Tis wine!"

"I use it as a sedative," Fraser stated.

"Please tell me you have glasses so we can drink like civilized people!"

"You ask too much from a barbarian like me. But I aim to please…" Fraser opened a drawer and pulled out two glasses.

Then Burgoyne poured the wine. They raised their glasses, and clicked them together, first the top of Burgoyne's glass to the bottom of Fraser's, then the top of Fraser's to the bottom of Burgoyne's. "To our union," Burgoyne toasted. "From Orkney to Dover,"

Fraser smiled. "To my general. A long life."

And so they drank the first round together, and went on to have a second, and a third. By then, Burgoyne's eyes had grown glassy, and his thoughts reflective.

"I think Charlotte liked to think of me as a knight," he mumbled. "I mean…in the beginning, at least, when she was young and…besotted with me…"

"Well, you were a cavalryman," Fraser reminded him. "A cavalier…"

"Yes, I always sat a horse damn well." He smiled wistfully. "When I was courting her, I…I would play up to her expectations, collecting favors from her, a lock of hair, a comb, an earring, a kerchief…that sort of thing. Her father and brother said I was trying to seduce her. And I was. But…well, I suppose I was getting quite besotted myself, and thus treasured everything I took from her."

"None who knew her would find that hard to understand," Fraser remarked.

Burgoyne glanced at the floor. "I think even later on, when all my failings became apparent to her, she sometimes still saw me as her knight. Maybe not at the very end, but…"

"Why would she not, at the very end?"

"I was not there," Burgoyne blurted. "God help me, I…I was not there…"

Fraser tilted his head. "Now then…you know how we are? When we haven't seen each other for a span, no matter how long, we have the tendency to just pick up wherever we last left off."

"Yes, a talent of ours!"

"Well…Lady Charlotte always struck me as the same type. She could not easily forget her own feelings…no matter the length or breadth of separation. And there was never a moment spent in her company when I did not see her eyes shine when they were upon you."

"She…confided in you, didn't she? Women always trust you."

"Sometimes she did, when she was concerned about you," Fraser admitted. "I suppose she knew…I'd try my best to be of good service to you. I was honored by her confidence in me, given that, well…she was ever an Englishwoman!" He chuckled. "It took her time to trust outsiders. But when she trusted, she did so fully. She was…a pure woman in love and friendship. That is why I know…you were always her gentle knight, no matter the dents were in your armor."

Burgoyne swallowed hard, then smiled softly. "By the by, I received a letter from a pretty German lady recently."

Fraser raised an eyebrow. "Should I be concerned that she might succumb to your seductive spellcraft?"

"Oh, I've tried my magic on her, Balnain," Burgoyne teased, placing a hand to his heart dramatically. "But I'm afraid it's no use. My promise to whisk her away to a castle in Portugal was rejected out of hand."

Fraser laughed. "No doubt because she found out about the state of your finances!"

"The lady knows what she wants, and it's a Scotsman in her bed." He tapped Fraser on the shoulder. "Clearly Highland manners have merit when the door's shut and the candle's blown out!"

"Mayhap," Fraser said with a grin.

"More than mayhap! She's merely toying with my poor heart so that I'll protect you for her! And being of such a knightly disposition, I have sworn to do just that. So you see…you must promise me that you'll remember to duck next time a squirrel hunter tries his aim. I can take care of myself."

Fraser exhaled. "You are my superior. My duty forbids me from…"

"None of that," Burgoyne cut him off. "Just duck!"

Fraser regarded him for a moment. "Getting shot….hurts, John. Believe me. I've been there a few times myself, you know. So…" He shrugged. "I didn't want to see you like that."

"You must learn to leave a man alone to his fate, Balnain," Burgoyne insisted. "I thought you Frasers had a reputation to maintain!"

"We have contradictory impulses," he mumbled, "pulling us to and fro." He gazed at Burgoyne wistfully. "It seems fate itself has pulled me in your direction. No sense fighting it now."

"Is that what you were thinking when you said my name back there, before the shot was fired?" Burgoyne asked.

"I was thinking…" He paused. "Thinking…one of us would perhaps be gone, in an instant, and I was…sad. With either of us no more, that would be the end of…us."

Burgoyne winced, then put on a brave face. "Well, that would be a tragedy. We have too many jokes between us no one else would understand!"

"Exactly. We'd be locked up if we tried them on anyone else."

Burgoyne snorted, then grew serious. "Listen…you must not let yourself fall into the hands of the Yankees."

"Well, yes, a basic principle…"

"No, I mean…they worry me. What they might do to you. You in particular, Simon. They may not…or at least, some of them may not…"

"See me as a proper British officer?" Fraser finished. "No, instead they may see me as a mercenary, brought out of savagery in the mountains purely for the love of gold and gore, set to trample down their English liberties because I am…an animal, frothing at the mouth, that must be disposed of…"

Burgoyne shuddered. "Simon…if anything happened to you like that, I would…" He bit his lip. "I don't know…freeze up, or go for blood. You know me…I can get set off, sometimes. It wouldn't be a good look. So you see…you mustn't fall into the hands of those who…don't know you like I do…who don't respect you like I do. You mustn't…get yourself hurt…"

The Scotsman clicked his tongue, then said in a tone glazed with sarcasm, "But John, remember the words of the Fox, *dulce et decorum est pro patria mori*…"

"Don't," Burgoyne blurted, and the sincerity was palpable. "Please."

Fraser was quiet, then whispered simply, "Thanks, Johnny."

And Burgoyne squeezed his arm.

~

The British train got back on the road, with Amelia, Belinda, and baby Malcolm in the women's wagons. Their exact status remained complex. The infant, of course, was innocent of conspiracy, but the hanged man's daughter or his slave might have known what he was about. As such, they might be called political prisoners. Amelia was deliberately kept separate from the slave and her baby, for fear of some type of collusion, but Abby continued to nurse the injured girl and see to her needs.

Burgoyne, meanwhile, had Belinda brought before him for questioning.

"So," he began, "were you a part of the plot?"

She blinked. "Plot, sir?"

"Don't be coy. You hid the failed assassin, that much we know."

"Sir, I am a slave, and nothing more," she said. "I must do what my master bids me…"

"Nothing more, you say?" Burgoyne repeated. "Think me blind? Your offspring is from your master. You were his pillow girl."

She winced. "I did what my master bid me, sir. I don't want no trouble, is all. Folk like me can find themselves in a whole peck of trouble, if they fight too hard. I know the kind that fought it, and it did them no good, just got them a bloody back. I am made of weaker stuff, maybe. God made me, so I hope He understands. Will you judge me for it?"

Burgoyne sighed. "Did your master beat you?"

"I gave him no cause," she said, then added softly, "He was more lonely than cruel. His lady died, you see. He wanted…a warm bed. I'd been brought in to tend his little girl. So…one thing led to another…"

"And so he put a child in you."

She nodded.

"You may be a slave, but firstly, you are a woman," Burgoyne remarked. "And I've long held that women are far shrewder than we men like to think. It's the same with Negroes in general. You can use that against those over you. It is our own assumptions that doom us"

"I ain't trying to use nothing against nobody, sir," she replied. "I just don't want me or my baby getting hurt."

"Again, you are a woman, like any other," Burgoyne said. "You want what is best for your child, and maybe even to believe that his conception was not merely a product of coercion, but that his father had an atom's worth of good."

She bit her lip. "I knew he had that already. Sometimes I think he felt…sorry. So he'd get me pretty things, at least on occasion, like hair combs, or a new bonnet, or once, a necklace…"

"So he was not solely your master, then. He may have owned you, but he still bothered to flatter your femininity."

She swallowed hard and shook her head. "I dunno…I'm all mixed up. I suppose I thought…"

Burgoyne leaned forward. "Go on."

"I-I don't know why you'd be interested in what I thought, sir…"

"Call a fascination with human nature," he replied. "I am a writer, you know. Pray continue."

She glanced down. "I'd given him a boy child, something even his wife couldn't give him, something he wanted. Once or twice, when we were alone, he looked down at him fussing in the crib and called him, 'our boy', and I could tell he loved Malcolm after all, at least after a fashion. That's why he let me pick that name for the baby…it was his own middle one. I thought maybe, with time, he'd think less of me as a slave, and more of me as the mother of his boy. And maybe Miss Amelia would get more and more used to the notion of Malcolm as her baby brother, and we could all find a way to…"

"Be a family?"

"In so many words, sir." She glanced down. "I-I never wanted him to die like that."

"His death was his own doing, I'm afraid," Burgoyne said curtly. "Despite your efforts to keep him from the law."

"You gonna punish me, General?"

"I don't know yet."

"It's true I wasn't gonna tell on him, hiding upstairs," she admitted. "But I didn't know he'd be fool enough to take a shot at you. That's God's honest truth."

"I am inclined to believe that much," Burgoyne said. "He put you all in danger through his fanaticism, including his own flesh and blood."

She glanced down to the ground. "Miss Amelia must be hurting something awful, to lose her mama and now her daddy like this. Will you let me go see her, sir?"

"No," he replied. "You may still be capable of collusion. But I'll have you know she's being cared for, so you needn't imagine we're tormenting a child for her father's crimes." He tilted His head. "If you want to do something beneficial for yourself and your own child, you should enlist yourself in His Majesty's service and point out other rebel households in the vicinity to me. I am sure you can identify quite a few of your master's seditious friends…"

"So you can hang 'em, or burn their houses down upon their families' heads?" Belinda surmised.

"So we can prevent them from harassing our men and impeding our march," Burgoyne clarified. "For payment, you might appeal to us for your emancipation. You certainly won't receive it from a deadman, even if he ever would have been so inclined for the sake of the child. You're crown property now."

Belinda winced. "I may be a slave, sir, but as you can tell, I ain't no tattler, neither on runaways or rebels," she declared. "I'll not help you hang or burn."

"Even in exchange for freedom?"

She squinted. "And how free would I be, gaining it like that?"

"What about freedom for your child? Or would you rather he be sold away from you? He is mine to do with as I please, you understand, just like you."

Her eyes widened. "Don't…don't take my baby…please. Even my mama's massa didn't take me from her when I was such a little 'un…he took me when I'd grown up some, seven or eight years on…oh, please, please, General…he's such a bitty thing…"

Burgoyne stared at her for several moments, then said quietly, "I do not steal babies from the arms of their mothers. I rather wish I could more convincingly threaten it, to make you more helpful…but it's not in my nature." He shrugged. "Until further notice, you will be put to work, washing, sewing, and completing other tasks for the officers around the camp. If you change your mind about my offer, you may come to me. Now you are dismissed."

After she curtsied and left the tent, she passed by General Fraser, who was coming in. He raised an eyebrow at Burgoyne.

"You don't like this slavery business, do you?" the Scotsman surmised.

"Not much," Burgoyne admitted. "I find the hypocrisy amongst these so-called revolutionaries to be particularly rank when they engage in the practice. Remember Richard Montgomery, the Ulster defector? He went about claiming the colonies were bound by royal chains, yet kept Negroes in shackles. Same with Washington and Jefferson and so many others groaning under the weight of their many privileges."

"It has of course been argued the Negro is not fully a man," Fraser noted. "Their minds are feebler, more like the ape, it is said…"

"Similar arguments are made regarding countless sorts of people we do not understand at first glance," Burgoyne remarked. "I have learned from experience to question such conclusions, at least."

Fraser winced, then nodded.

"Perhaps some forms of men are lesser in the chain of being, incurably savage and created to be governed by their betters," Burgoyne postulated, "or perhaps they find themselves on the lower end of that chain simply because we labor to keep them ignorant, for thinking beings will resist lash, chain, and master, and demand that his sweat should merit a wage."

"Many insist the economy of the empire cannot be sustained without the slave trade," Fraser stated. "They say the flow of money enables common men to climb…"

"Ah, the argument based upon necessary evil. Such a premise may be rested upon temporarily, but never indefinitely. The more we become dependent upon evil, the more it corrodes society. What, in the end, will be left of us?"

"And in terms of voting?" Fraser queried. "Would you do the deed, if you thought you could end the trade?"

"Oh, I imagine I'd do the deed even if I didn't think I could end it," Burgoyne replied. "It's that annoying little voice inside me, that wakes me up from the comfort of a brothel bed, and says that perhaps it's inhumane to stuff poor devils into a ship's hold so tightly they can barely breath, where nearly half are doomed to choke to death on their own vomit and tossed over the ship's side. I know, I'm not the reformer anyone wants. I'm not the sort to wear social betterment on my sleeve, nor partial to sitting down to tea with a lot of wrinkle-faced Quakers and raving Methodists, even if they bothered to invite me! But I am that which I am, for good or ill, and so help me, if I could strike a blow against something I deemed incompatible with fairness and humanity, I'd do it, even if I were the only one who bothered."

"Even at the risk of being branded a champion for lost causes?" Fraser queried.

"A risk we all must take, one time or another, especially those of us who like to stand out in a crowd…"

"Even at the risk of being targeted by the mob?"

Burgoyne shrugged. "I'm used to handling mobs."

Fraser chortled. "More power to you!" He raised a glass in a toast and drank down the contents.

Burgoyne did the same, then grew wistful. "Humanity fascinates me," he murmured. "Always has done. It is the question of mind and matter unified, albeit often struggling. We each possess worlds within us, wondrous and dreadful. None of us are beasts, no matter how primitive, for the One, who made us, fashioned us with purpose, to reflect that Mind, however distantly, however poorly, by making our mark upon reality. We do not submit to sound and fury, signifying nothing, but dare to tell stories, yes, to live stories, and bring order out of chaos by chronicling the patterns. In that, all of us, however base, are like God, and I think He delights in that. It is thrilling to contemplate, isn't it?"

Fraser smiled sadly. "General Wolfe once said all human beings were in essence the same, and so deserving of compassion. You demonstrate that."

"And you." Burgoyne smiled a little. "I saw that little Hessian doll of yours, running about with your pillow duck."

Fraser nodded. "The one resounding success from a disastrous stopover. The dear little thing even kissed my cheek when her mother told her to thank me."

"There you go, winning over the ladies!" Burgoyne chuckled.

"Indeed!" Fraser laughed, then grew quiet. "I-I'm worried about Baroness von Riedesel and Lady Acland. Both are delicate creatures, growing full with child, in the midst of these conditions. I worry they'll miscarry. You know, one of the guard's wives in my camp miscarried a week ago, and woke up all covered in blood in the wagon. The terrain was too rough. The husband came back from seeing her blood on his hands and shock in his eyes. It was terrible. And now she's got a fever. Why do these damn husbands bring their wives out here? If I ever brought Margaretha out here, I'd tell you to put a bullet through my head."

"Because you'd finally get to work making her pregnant on the road?" Burgoyne chirped. "You're taking forever, and I want to be a godfather…"

Fraser sighed. "We'll get there."

"We will," Burgoyne agreed.

"I mean, we always do…"

"We've survived tavern crawls and hunting trips and are working on surviving a rather silly war just to get us into a church, with an infant, who will be receiving a name and bawling over the cold water!" said Burgoyne.

"I need to have twins," Fraser decided, "to pacify Phillips too. He is not without godfatherly aspirations."

"Either that or we'll have to follow the example of King Solomon and…"

"Don't you dare!"

Burgoyne took his sword lying nearby and unsheathed it, ridiculously and dramatically. "Damn," he swore. "My finger…"

"Serves you right," the Scotsman snorted, going over to help him staunch the cut with a handkerchief. "What would you do without me?"

"Kill myself, quite obviously!"

~

That evening, Ned went to check up on Abby. She was tending to Amelia, trying to get the poor girl to eat, though the girl was resisting. She seemed to have all but given up on living.

"You must eat, dear thing," Abby coaxed her, running her hand through the girl's hair, a bowl of porridge in lap. "For your father's sake."

"Father's dead," she choked. "What he would have wanted doesn't matter anymore."

"That's not true," Abby insisted. "You have to live for him…yes, we must live to win, for those we love, living and dead…"

"We're not winning," Amelia said dejectedly. "We're going to lose, just like the Scotsman's clan lost when they rebelled against the last king. I'd rather we die now than become what he's become…"

"No, it's not over yet," Abby assured. "Maybe nothing changes in the old world, but this is the new one. We've been raised breathing different air. We can prove ourselves stronger than the Scotsman if we do not bend the knee. He may be alive on the outside, but is dead on the inside. Your father may have died, but there was no man more alive." She set the bowl down beside the girl. "I expect that to be empty when I come back."

When Abby climbed down from the wagon, Ned took her by the arm and escorted her out of earshot of the girl.

"You shouldn't tell her those things," Ned said. "It'll cause her to do something indiscreet."

"You mean like I did?" she snapped.

"Yes, like you did," Ned replied.

She gave him a harsh look, then mumbled, "She needs to eat, doesn't she?"

"Of course, but…"

"Then I'll tell her what I feel she needs to be told to that end."

"Perhaps I can talk to her," Ned suggested.

"You?" Abby blurted. "Whatever could you hope to say to her that would help?"

"I-I don't know," Ned admitted. "I just thought…well, back home, I was considered to have a way with local children…"

"She saw you stand there and watch as her father perished! I'm the one with a father who…" Her voice drifted out. "I know what it's like, Ned. My father is made to suffer by the same powers that made her father suffer."

"You know I don't take pleasure in anyone's suffering," Ned replied, "especially that of a man who, at least in death, proved brave. But it was my duty as a soldier of the king to put my own feelings secondary. It was my duty to bear witness to the King's justice, and your interruption of it only put you in harm's way..."

"The King's justice?" she sneered. "Fraser's vengeance, you mean. That's what it turned into by the end of it!"

"I cannot blame the general for his wrath," Ned responded. "Both his life and that of General Burgoyne had been imperiled, targeted inordinately after having behaved as gentlemen to the inhabitants of the house and sparing it from the torch. Besides, I understand what it is to deal with prejudice, the constant calling into question of one's honor, the inability to fully trust…"

"He's a monster!" she blurted. "Did you not see the way he stares at that poor man as he was being strangled? Everyone knows that Highlanders, when they bow to their former oppressors, become tyrants twice over, for their savagery is infused with power!"

"He's a man, like any other," Ned retorted, "charged with implementing royal law, according to the oaths he has sworn upon the reception of his pardon. He knows all too well what it's like to be on the other side of that law, so he must go above and beyond to clear his name."

"And you think that's so very manly of him? To serve the ones who destroyed his people and betray the oaths he made to his precious prince?"

"Manlier than to support another rising, and assure more torrents of blood are spilled," Ned argued. "We're one people now, Britons all. Besides, the Stuart prince abandoned the clans to their fate first..."

"Like your king abandoned his colonies to slavery, then declared war against them for resisting bondage?" she snapped.

"Abby, don't…"

She took a step closer to him. "That was what the man you hanged was trying to make clear to you with his last breath! If we are outlaws, you have made us so!"

"He tried to murder men with their backs turned to him, and cost a boy his arm! He brought death upon his own head, and fire to his own roof!"

"If you can understand why Fraser has sacrificed his humanity to redeem his name, can you not understand why Amelia's father sacrificed his life to redeem his country?"

"This is not redemption, Abby," Ned retorted. "It's Cain and Abel, all over again, crying out to heaven. And heaven weeps!"

"If there is a heaven, then any weeping is for the righteous below! My father once printed in his gazette that, where justice is the standard, heaven is the warrior's shield, but conscious guilt unnerves the arm that lifts the sword against the innocent!"

"And who is innocent in the midst of all this, Abby?" Ned queried wearily.

"Can you not tell the difference between a man who changes kings for his own advancement, and a man who embraces a higher call to break the wheel of subjugation? Or has everything become relative to you since you left your faith for a commission?!"

"That's not fair, Abby!" Ned ground out, her words striking a nerve. "What I did, I did for my country! Treason does not charm my ears, and if you are wise, you would not let it charm yours! It is a siren's song that wrecks boats upon the rocks!"

"Or that guides us to a brighter shore than other worlds can offer!" Her eyes simmered, in a way Edmund found both beautiful and disturbing. "A new day is dawning, Ned. Our land can be an empire of liberty, the seat of virtue, the asylum of the oppressed, a name and a praise in the whole earth, even when the last shock of time buries all other empires in one common undistinguished ruin!"

Ned felt his throat grow dry. "I am British," he rasped, "and so are you. It's in our blood, it's on our tongue, it binds us to the past…"

"The past is dead," she retorted. "Only those who love the future can endure!"

"No, Abby," he said, "the past is very much alive, and it makes demands of us…"

"I thought you said you could see yourself making a life here, like your cousins who settled in Maryland," she said.

"Yes, I suppose I did, but…"

"Come with me, Ned!" She seized his arm. "You are not at peace with yourself where you are, for your loyalties are split already! You are better than these people around you. They are easily convinced of royal supremacy, but you are not! In your heart of hearts, you resist, in manners great and small! That's why you had me sew that relic in your coat! It is your own little defiance!"

"Abby, stop…"

"I have always sensed it, always seen it in your eyes! You have the strength of will to rebel! You have the spirit to break away from the rest, before you are destroyed along with them! Don't you see? It is only by a timely amputation of a rotten limb that the mortification of the whole body is prevented! England is lost! Let us be free of her! Let us be rid of her!"

"No!" Edmund refused hotly, clutching his gorget. "If you thought you were leading me astray from my allegiance, you were sorely mistaken! I took oaths, Abby, before God and men, to serve my gracious sovereign, King George, the third of that name, by my life or my death. I am not one to put my hand upon the holy book in vain!"

"Though you would break every other commandment?" she shot back. "Though you can't make me an honest woman because your soul is already sold for the price of the King's shilling? How cheap is that!"

"England must be my first lady!" he replied. "I am descended from English knights, and my blood still runs true! I will not betray her, though every temptress in the world bid me to do so!"

Abby's face flushed with anger and embarrassment alike, then she turned and retreated towards the wagon.

The next day, after mail call, Ned went back over to the women's camp, hoping to make things right with Abby. She may have provoked him with her attempts to lure him into treason, but he knew the execution had deeply unsettled her, and perhaps her outburst would have been better handled with greater diplomacy. He needed to learn how to handle her with more patience, especially if his intention was to put a ring on her finger in Albany, if she was willing.

When he reached her wagon, she was nowhere to be found, but a letter was lying open among her belongings. The words "your father" caught his attention, and though he knew he should leave it where it lay, he found himself picking it up. Water drops had made the ink run in places, but he was able to make out most of the message.

Dearest Abigail,

It is with sorrow I pen this letter, though you may not believe me. Please, dear, think better of me, no matter how base I am. I would rather lose every faculty remaining to me than see you hurt. And yet I must hurt you with the tidings that your father is no more. I did not forget my promise to you, and made sure that your baskets continued to reach him. I made sure the guards did not steal anything. That is how I learned he succumbed. They had buried him with his comrades in the mud flats three days before. I spoke to another prisoner, who told me the old man's thoughts were always of you. I know not if that will bring you comfort or more pain, but I feel you should know that, as the best of the daughters. I gave the prisoner who told me some of the food. I thought you would want it that way.

Abby, my dear one, do not grieve unto sickness. Do not blame yourself for what was beyond thy power to cure. It will not revive him, nor punish us. Believe me, I for one am already being punished. I miss thee daily. Oh, my girl, I am dirty. God knows how dirty I am, as thou must. But I have never felt such affection swell my heart as it swells for thee, and the memory of thy sweet face is ever in my mind. I struggle to sleep without thee by my side. Food and drink bring me little pleasure without thee to share it with. Thy letters, whenever they come, are my only consolation. And I kiss them. Does that disgust thee? I am a fool, such a fool, Abby.

But I miss thee, yet, and the softness of thy lips and hair. And thy words, whether kind or cruel, were better than this silence. I have even grown fonder of the scar on my cheek. Thou couldst not kill me in thy anger. I flatter myself that it counts for something, and keep on living. And the most foolish part of me, that tiny voice belonging to a silly little boy, waits for thee to come home. I know thou cannot think of me as home, but I think of these as home, and so I wait. Then I pray to my mother's God, her inner light Who is nearly a stranger to me, to keep thee in His arms, even if I never see thee again.

But Abigail, please hear me out. If there is no further cause for you to stay in the north, get yourself away from the fighting. It is a dangerous game Jack Brag is playing. If you return here, I promise I will place no obligations upon you. Say the word, and I will send you anywhere that is safe at my own cost. You know I would never imprison you. I let you go the first time, did I not? But if you thought, perhaps, you might see me as I believe you once saw me, when you cried over my wounds, and you held me, though I was all but unmanned, then for the love of the God I do not know, come to me, and we will find ourselves a house, and share everything as one. I will never let you want while I live, and when I am dead, you may take whatever I have in this world. I may not be a rich man, but I would consider myself suddenly to be so if thou came to me. I don't deserve it. But I would delight in thy sweet company, my dear, dear girl.

I remain
Yours

Harold Leslie, Colonel

Ned felt a mix of emotions swirl in his chest. He had not managed to make peace with any of them when he went to look for her, and found her standing at the the top of a little rise, gazing out into the tangle of trees.

"Abby," he rasped.

She did not turn.

"I…found the letter in your wagon. I know I shouldn't have read it, but I saw it mentioned your father, and…" He took a deep breath. "Oh, Abby, I'm so sorry."

"Why should you be?" she croaked. "He was nothing but dog's meat to your kind."

He winced. "Whatever he was, and whatever he did, I wanted him to live, for your sake, just as the man who wrote that letter did. We…worry about you…"

"It was for nothing," she murmured. "Everything I've done, all the humiliation, all the hurt, all the sacrifice, all the times I told myself I wasn't a bad girl, not really, because of why I was doing it…all for nothing…"

Ned shook his head. "Love isn't 'nothing.'" He swallowed. "I think…Major Leslie is sincere in his condolences and profession of love for you…"

"I wish that disgusting old fool would choke on his own drooling!" she lashed out. "It's people like him and you who tortured my father and tarnished my soul!"

"Abby, please…"

"My father never did your kind any harm! He never even owned a gun!"

"His pen was his gun, Abby," Ned retorted. "With that, he incited countless others to take up arms and shoot down His Majesty's soldiers…yes, soldiers like me…"

"If you come here to suppress Americans in hopes of rising through your ranks, then that is exactly what they deserve," she hissed, "perhaps you, most of all, for betraying everything you ever believed in to wear a red coat!"

Ned felt a dagger plunged into his heart at her words, but retorted through gritted teeth, "We are servants of the crown, and are honored to go where our master sends us…"

"Then your master has made slaves of you as much as us!" she spat. "He who hunts the woods for prey, the naked and untutored Indian, is less a savage than the king of Britain!"

"Do not presume to insult our King to my face!" Ned shouted, loud enough to make her flinch. "I am his true man, from this day to my last day, and I will defend his name against any man or woman who besmirches it! Your father spread treason like a disease, and you are proving to be no better!"

Crack.

She slapped so hard, and so unexpectedly, he fell backward against the wagon.

"Yes, I am my father's daughter," she cried, "and you will yet see me make the most of it!"

On instinct, Ned bunched his fists as he stood up straight again. The flicker of fear in her eyes startled him almost worse than being slapped by her. Suppressing his anger, as he had long trained himself to do, he turned and stormed away.

The following day, Jonathan came to talk to Edmund. Ned widened his eyes at the sight of the horrible blistering along Jonathan's left cheek. "Dear Lord, what happened to your poor face?"

"It was…an accident…of sorts," Jonathan said haltingly. "Well, a bit more deliberate than an accident, but…"

"Just tell me what happened!"

"You won't like it," Jonathan sighed. "But…I went to talk to Abby about…well, leaving the train when we reached the next settlement."

"What?"

"I saw her slap you, Ned. Heard her speak treason, too."

"You were eavesdropping on us?"

"You vanished when there was work to be done, Ned," Jonathan gave him a measured scolding. "I came to fetch you back to your duty. But believe when I say I was proud of you for the way you resisted her when she tried to sway you from your allegiance."

"Her father's dead, from our filthy prisons," Ned countered. "Her heart's broken, from the life we stole from her. Can we blame her for feeling as she does?"

"Perhaps not, or at least not altogether, but that doesn't mean her behavior could be left to continue here. It's not good for her, or us…" He shook his head. "Suffice to say…she didn't like what I had to say much. She…is attached to you. So…she called me some rather choice names, then seized the coffee pot, and flung the contents in my direction. It was, well…scalding, as you can see."

Ned examined his friend's disfigured cheek more closely. "Will you be alright?" he asked worriedly.

"I think so," Jonathan replied. "Her aim was imperfect, so it could have been much worse. My second pair of eyes protected my first one as well." He tapped on his coffee-stained spectacles, and Ned noticed his hand was red and puffy as well.

"I'll go talk to her," Ned mumbled, turning to leave.

"Wait," Jonathan stopped him. "She…she's already been brought before the general."

"You…reported her?" Ned rasped.

"No. Eli did. He saw what happened, then came over calling down the wrath of heaven on the girl, who spat at him. He sat me down, handed me a towel to nurse my face, then went straight to Burgoyne before I had the chance to calm him."

Ned felt the blood drain from his face. "Why did you have to get involved?" he snapped. "You've made everything worse!"

Jonathan winced. "I know. Forgive me."

Ned felt guilt twist in his chest. "It was my fault too," he admitted. "I am a weak man, Jonathan."

"We all are," Jonathan assured. "And she…she's hurting. I didn't want to make her hurt worse. But I didn't want her to hurt you worse either, so…" He shook his head. "I erred in judgment. And Lieutenant Thompson can be unyielding in his. Though I suppose in this case it is because he cares for me, meaning it is my fault all over again."

Ned exhaled. "I'll intercede with the general on her behalf."

"I'll join you, if you'll have me," Jonathan offered. "Perhaps two voices will have more clout than one."

Ned glanced down and mumbled, "Thankee."

And so they went to see the general.

"Why is it always you two trying to beg someone off?" Burgoyne sighed when they made their appeal in his tent.

"Sir, as the wronged party, I do not wish to press the case," Jonathan insisted.

"That's irrelevant, Lieutenant," Burgoyne replied. "She must be punished for attacking an officer of the King."

"But not a very important one," Jonathan offered.

"You know it doesn't matter," Burgoyne replied. "Your livery represents the King's honor. She has compromised that honor, and satisfaction must be had. Whether or not we like it, the Irish boy is correct in his judgment this time."

"Sir, I believe it to have been an act of impulse, not premeditation," Ned insisted.

"And she didn't lay a hand on me," Jonathan pressed a technicality.

"Surely you know that in this army, if a man were to even fail to salute an officer, it might cost him twenty to fifty lashes. If he were to raise his hand against an officer, even out of impulse, without ever laying a finger upon his person, it might cost him fifty to a hundred lashes," Burgoyne stated. "If he actually injured an officer's person, well…the last might fall anywhere from two hundred to five hundred times."

"That's a death sentence," Ned blurted.

"It could be, though some are sturdy enough to endure it."

"But it's inhuman…"

"We can debate the particulars day and night, and the humanity or lack thereof implicit in such punishments, especially in response to lesser infractions. But keep in mind, our army is lenient in its disciplinary measures compared to others, such as the Prussians. Britons are not so likely to yield to the whipping post like brute beasts as other peoples. And yet…an army runs upon order, and blood is shed to keep it." Burgoyne gave Ned a long look. "My own feelings about floggings should be plain to you by now. I approach them with reluctance, and even distaste. But I am still in command, and as such…"

"But she's a mere girl," Ned protested.

Burgoyne let out a sigh. "Yes. I am aware. But this is not her first offense, Ned. I have eyes about the camp, and you know I speak the truth."

"She was overwrought on the day of the hanging, and has been in a fragile state of mind ever since," Edmund insisted. "Her father's suffering and death torments her, as it would any devoted daughter, regardless of the man's wrongs."

"And you think she considers her father to have been guilty of any wrongs?" Burgoyne queried dubiously. "Come now, Ned. We all know she's a brazen little rebel, no matter how tidy she is between the legs."

Jonathan and Edmund both blushed.

"She's still a woman," Ned murmured. "And she's been poorly used…very poorly used by our own men, stationed in New York. You know of what I speak."

Burgoyne drummed with his fingers on the table. "I do not relish brutality against the weaker sex, no matter the meanness of their condition nor the indiscretion of their behavior. Given this, and other factors you have submitted, I am willing to be as merciful as I can be. Ten lashes. That's down halfway from twenty, Ned. We can only hope the sting will tame her rebellious passions before something worse befalls her. That's my final word on the subject."

Edmund winced at the prospect of what was to come, but still said, "Thank you, sir."

"And you, Rawcliffe," Burgoyne said, pointing at Jonathan, "do have some salve fetched from the baggage for your poor hand and face. Lucky you had your specs on. Couldn't afford to have one of my best clerks blinded!"

~

Edmund watched as Abby was brought out, her hands bound behind her back. The whole camp seemed to have been brought out to watch the example that was to be made.

Abby looked around in a panic as her sentence was read by one of the soldier's. Then her eyes latched onto Ned, and he felt immediately sick.

"Ned, please, please!" she screamed, and he felt every fiber of his being tighten as she struggled against the guards.

They threw her down on the ground roughly, and Ned involuntarily started forward but Jonathan held him back.

"We did all we could," his friend reminded him sadly. "There's no stopping it now."

"Ned! Ned! I'm sorry, I'm sorry, please!" She was sobbing now as they held her down and pulled open her dress so her back was exposed. She strained hard against the cord binding her wrists, and one of the guards grabbed hold of her hair. Then one of them raised the lash.

Edmund jerked as the first strike fell, and she let out a piercing cry, like a small animal being seized by the talons of a bird of prey. The sound repeated each time the lash tore her skin. For the first five strikes, she continued to intermittently call his name, piteously.

"Ned, please…oh, please, Ned….Ned…"

Then she seemed to give up trying, and simply wept convulsively as the strikes continued to fall, and purple blood trickled down her white back.

"Stop, please, stop…please…"

Ned felt his heart break as she pleaded with the guards, knowing all too well what memories were assaulting her. He turned to Jonathan, and saw he had his fists clenched, and his face turned away. Ned steeled himself for the last few strikes, for she was *his*, and he could not turn away.

Eight. Nine. Ten.

Thank God, at last, the end.

He tried to comfort himself, tried to tell himself that this was a comparatively light punishment, but he felt it was such a hollow victory, as she lay face-first in the dirt, beaten and bloodied, shaking like a leaf as the cord binding her wrists was finally cut.

Then one of the guards took it upon himself to add to her humiliation by slapping her on the rump. She curled up into a ball as they started to spew mockery and vulgarity at her.

Ned was about to charge forward and punch the first man he came upon.

But Eli was there before him, with horse blanket in hand.

"Get off with ye, lechers," he spat, covering her back. "That's not part of the punishment!"

When the guards dispersed, Eli reached a hand out to her, but she retracted and hissed, "Go away…leave me be…"

Eli, in a voice softer than was usual to him, replied, "There now. I mean you no harm. Justice is done, and to be learned from. There's no further debt to be paid."

"Leave her to me," said Maggie, coming over with a look of unexpected sympathy on her face. "She's not ready to deal with the likes of you men."

Chapter 32: WITHOUT MERCY

For the next few days, Maggie tended to Abby in one of the women's wagons, soaking the stripes on her back with damp rags and keeping her wrapped in blankets so she wouldn't catch a chill in her vulnerable state. She also brushed out Abby's hair for her, and Abby, for the first time ever, set aside her self-righteousness and thanked Maggie for her kindness. At last, she seemed to have realized that, no matter their differences in origin, they had been brought to the same place. As such, they were sisters.

Ned went over to the wagon several times, hoping against hope that Abby would allow him to explain himself, but Maggie would insist she was in no state of mind to see him. Most of the time, she simply lay on her side, staring into nothing, as if her heart had been shattered beyond repair. Besides, he knew deep inside any explanations would ring hollow. He had stood by and watched her be whipped, stood by and listened to her scream. That was all she would ever remember, and perhaps all he would ever remember either.

Then at last, towards the end of the week, Abby sent a message to Ned, asking to be let off the train with young Amelia, claiming she had some cousins living on a homestead nearby. She even suggested it would be a good place for forage. He had an immediate gut reaction against the prospect of going off the beaten path, and found it strange she had never mentioned any such cousins before. But when he expressed his concerns in writing, Abby replied with another message, claiming that he is holding her there against her will, despite her own misery, and that she regretted deluding herself into believing he was a gentleman. Disturbed by her reaction, he found himself asking permission from Burgoyne to drop her off, which the general reluctantly granted, so long as soldiers were taken along, both for security and forage. Jonathan, concerned about his friend, volunteered to go along for the ride.

As the wagons were being prepared for foraging, Red Elk came to see Jonathan.

"I know we have had some disagreements lately," the Iroquois admitted.

"Your people scalped the corpse of a helpless woman they may or may not have murdered en route to seeking ransom for her hair and caused the entire region to take up arms against us!" Jonathan exhaled.

"Again…disagreements…"

"Where is this going?"

"Look, you shouldn't go off the trail, that's all. It will come to no good."

"Evil spirits at work again?"

"Maybe." The Indian glanced across the clearing towards the women's camp, where Abby was sitting on the edge of the wagon, staring at Jonathan with glassy eyes and a strange, slight smile.

"He's right, you know," said the French priest, suddenly appearing on Jonathan's other side. "It is most unwise."

"I feel like you two shouldn't be sharing the same space together…"

"Maybe you will listen to one or the other of us," Red Elk decided.

"*Oui,* that is fair," the priest agreed. "Listen, my heretic friend…"

"Heretic friend?!"

"Well, we have sort of become friends…you gave me a jam sandwich that one time, and I got you addicted to snuff…"

"A very sound basis for friendship, yes…"

"I think we are closer friends, if we are still friends," Red Elk argued. "Remember…the bear…"

"Yes, we're still friends," Jonathan sighed. "You just…concern me sometimes." He gestured to the priest. "Like there are moments I get the feeling you want to jump him and cut out his heart so you can eat it…"

"Did your people not cut out the hearts of priests?" Red Elk queried. "They make powerful medicine, especially if they die well…"

The priest gave Jonathan a quizzical look.

"Alright, that wasn't why we…I mean…it wasn't like that…"

"No?" the priest queried, folding his arms.

"No…uhhh…we never…you know, ate hearts…"

"You put kidneys in pies," Red Elk argued.

"Not human ones!"

"I cannot help that you are wasteful…"

"Dear Lord, I'm friends with a cannibal!" Jonathan shook his head.

"One who is trying to save your life," Red Elk replied.

"All the same, I have to go," Jonathan insisted. "I might be able to…intervene somehow, if things go sideways…"

"But you have a family," the priest reminded him. "Your first responsibility is to them over your friends."

"But I am a soldier too. I have a responsibility to my comrades."

"If you're worried about your friend and that mad squaw with large hips, there are other ways to save him from her…" Red Elk's hand slipped to his knife hilt.

"No! No more scalping!" Jonathan pleaded.

"Oh, I would not scalp her," Red Elk assured. "Just stab her. That one's hair is probably carrying evil spirits, and besides, it's rather ugly…"

"It's unchivalrous to call a lady's hair ugly," Jonathan lectured him.

"Fine, I am just too mild by nature to want to deal with her kind of crazy…"

"All the same, stabbing people is not the right way to break up things like this!" Jonathan insisted.

"Must agree with the heretic on this one," the priest remarked.

"Thank you!" Jonathan sighed.

"Better her than you," Red Elk decided.

"Listen, despite everything, I…appreciate you," Jonathan informed Red Elk, laying a hand on his arm. He laid his other hand on the priest's arm. "And you, believe it or not. I mean, you both terrify me, and have a history of burning people like me at the stake, but…"

"I am the one who should be terrified!" the priest retorted. "Either of you could cut out my heart!"

"For heaven's sake, no one's going to…oh dear…" Jonathan squinted as Eli came limping over.

"*Mon Dieu*," the priest sighed, crossing himself. "I'm leaving."

"Probably for the best," Jonathan agreed.

Red Elk didn't even verbalize his planned departure, just made a few exasperated gesticulations and stormed off.

"*Adieu, mes amis*," Jonathan called after them both, expending most of his French lexicon.

By then, Eli was in front of him, panting from the pain in his slowly mending leg. "Please. Listen to me. You mustn't go off the trail…"

"Not you too, Thompson," Jonathan exhaled.

"Please, please. Hear me out. That woman…there's evil in her. I can feel it."

"There's evil in us all," Jonathan replied, "as well as goodness. Besides, Ned is involved…"

"That secret Papist isn't worth the risk…"

"Whatever you may think of him, he's my friend," Jonathan replied softly. "He may need me at such a time as this."

"But-but I need you more than he does," Eli protested. "I-I'm…odd. I know that I am. Everybody does. It's just the way God and His fever made me."

"We all are a little odd, my dear," Jonathan assured kindly.

"Aye, but…well, me more than most." He glanced down. "I…don't make friends…"

Jonathan put a hand on his shoulder. "You're a blessing to me, Eli."

He squinted. "Surely not…"

"Surely so," Jonathan replied firmly. "And I expect you to return the favor and make me godfather over one of your babes, after you've saved up enough to buy Miss Fidelity a ring."

Eli laughed, in his awkward way. "I-I umm…I did think about that…the ring, I mean…"

"Of course you did," Jonathan beamed.

"Haven't managed to gather up the courage or money yet, though…"

"Well, I can make you a loan of one of those two things when we reach Albany!"

"That…would be right decent of you, to be sure." He smiled sheepishly. "I suppose, for the courage, I'll just…pray, and then…drink more beer for breakfast…"

Jonathan laughed heartily at this. "That's the spirit! In devotion and drinking, you Scotch-Irish come second to none!"

"Well…" Eli shrugged. "If we put our minds to it, that is…"

Jonathan laughed again and pulled Eli into a brief embrace. "Now, then, dear, I must be off. Say a little prayer for me."

"I'll say a long one," Eli mumbled.

"All the better! Till then!"

With that, Jonathan headed off to help ready the wagons.

General Fraser, meanwhile, appeared at the women's quarters, intent upon speaking to Amelia one last time.

"Go away," the girl choked, turning her back to him. "Leave me alone."

"Child…"

"I don't ever want to see you again! I hate you! I hope you die!"

"I know you do," he said softly. "I just…I had to see how you were faring. Does your head still hurt?"

She was quiet for a long time, then blurted, "No."

"Good." He blinked awkwardly. "I hope you believe, at least, I never intended for you to be injured. I made a promise, remember? I said you would be safe as long as I was there, but then…" He exhaled. "I suppose the courtesy didn't go both ways. You knew he was going to try to kill me, didn't you?"

"Not till the end," she mumbled. "I-I didn't want him to…not back then, anyway…"

"Oh, well…I'm glad of that, I suppose. Makes sense why you didn't want to look me in the face…" He gave her a long, penetrative look. "Did you lie to him about me? Did you tell him I behaved in an untoward manner in your company?"

"What do you mean by untoward?" she rasped.

"I mean...never mind. Judging from the look on your face, I don't think you told him any such thing. I fancy you just said some things in a rush, and he construed the rest, because he wanted to construe it, because I was a savage to him…"

"You are a savage!" she shouted. "I didn't think so inside, but outside, you proved it!"

Fraser lowered his gaze. "Maybe so. Maybe we all are, a little bit."

She bit her lip. "You…killed him."

"Yes, I did," he said quietly, "and you'll probably always hate me for it. He was your father, after all. I put an end to his life. I think he deserved what he got. But that doesn't make you love him any less, nor should it. So I respect your hatred. In my country, loyalty to family is prized above all else. And I know a thing or two about hate. I've carried it inside for decades. It's done all sorts of things to me…" He gave her a long look. "Don't let it eat you from the inside out, lass."

She winced. "Why do you care?"

"Because," he said, "you have your whole life ahead of you, on the other side of this cursed war. And your father would want you to live it. Please. Don't hate me unto death."

~

When they reached the settlement, the people proved to be polite, and true to Abby's word, there was a middle-aged couple who acknowledged her as their cousin. Amelia was also treated warmly and assured a place among the settlers. Everything seemed to be going smoothly, almost too smoothly. Jonathan had a suspicious gleam in his eye as he instructed the soldiers to search the vicinity and make a tally of supplies the army intended to take for forage. The settlers did not even protest. Jonathan leaned towards the nearest soldier to him and whispered some short instruction in his ear. Then the soldier ran off towards the woods.

Ned intended to go over to Jonathan and ask if anything was amiss. But then he felt eyes upon him, and turned to see Abby behind him, staring at him.

He swallowed hard.

"Well…do you like it here? I mean…"

She continued to stare at him, her eyes like gems, her body like stone.

"S-s-sorry, I know it sounds…foolish. I just…"

Something flickered within those gems, something he could not read.

"I'm sorry, Abby," he blurted. "I'm so sorry...for everything."

She blinked.

"I know, I know, you hate me. Maybe you should. There's so very much between us, yes, an ocean roaring between us, and I don't know for the life of me how to swim it without sinking. And yet…"

He dared to take a step towards her, dared to approach her across the divide, dared to walk on water. Soon he was in front of her, so close to her he could hear her breathing.

"Please believe me, Abby. No matter what happens, no matter how wicked the waves, my heart will be yours till my dying day…"

He felt tears filling his eyes and causing her form to lose distinction before him. He turned to go to his men, but she seized his arm. The trickle of saltwater ran down his cheeks, and he saw that her eyes were glassy now. She moved her lips, as if to speak, seemed to think better of it, and started to kiss him passionately. He felt warmth rush through his body, but tried to break free. Then she pulled him towards the barn. Again, he tried to disentangle from her, insisting his place was with the others, but she thrust her hand down his breeches, causing his cheeks to burn. Before long, they are under the rafters, rolling in the hay.

He lost himself entirely to her, perhaps more than during any other encounter between them. She was the one on top of him, in control of him, drawing some sort of energy from him, like a creature from myth. It terrified him, yet he did not want it to end. She was devouring all his resistance, swallowing his very identity. He felt the anger in her body as she pinned him down, and scratched and bit and drew blood. He allowed it, but it hurt.

"Abby," he whispered at last.

She froze.

"Ned?" she choked, seeming to remember who it was, taking her face in her hand.

Then she weakened, relented, allowed him on top.

"Be mean to me, Ned," she mumbled. "I was mean to you…"

But he was kind to her instead, cuddling and kissing her like he had on their first night, their bodies entwining naturally, as if they alone could complete each other.

When it was over, he realized he had scraped his hand against something sharp, perhaps a rusty nail or a shard of glass, and he saw blood dripping down onto her breast. Abby, eyes wide, seemed to regard it as some horrible omen. She kissed his hand, and there was blood on her lips.

"Abby, I don't want it to end this way," he panted, "not rutting in a barn like beasts! I-I want us to have a bed and a house and a garden and babies together…"

"Ned…"

"I want you to be my wife! I may not deserve it, but…"

She covered his mouth with her hand, tears filling her eyes, but he took her hand in his own and kissed it.

"This war is a passing thing compared to what we are to each other," he insisted. "Must we let this conflict kill the children we might have borne?"

"That…could never have been anyway," she said dejectedly.

"Why not?"

She was silent for a long time. Then at last she blurted, "They fixed me."

Ned felt himself grow instantly cold. "What do you mean?"

She bit her lip. "The first officer…he lost me in a card game to one of his friends. He was growing tired of me anyway, so it was no great loss to him. The second officer, well…he discovered, after a while, that I was with child. He didn't know if it was his or his friend's. All he knew was…he didn't want to deal with it. So…he got someone to…" She shivered. "I almost died. He was even shocked when he saw me afterwards, and all the blood. I think he meant to leave me there at first, but then I screamed for him to help me, and…he tried, in his way, to help. He got an old midwife to come and patch me up, then in the days that followed, spoon-fed me soup. It was…strange. He would make foolish conversation, and take his mind off…what he'd done to me…yes, to his own child…" She sucked a breath through her teeth. "I couldn't get my mind off it, though. I was going rather mad. In the end, he dropped me off at that horrible inn, where I played the harlot, till the old man got me out…" She closed her eyes. "So you see, I don't think it could have been…you and me, making a family…"

Ned felt his stomach flip.

"Even so," he rasped, "we would still have each other. And who knows? War leaves many children in need of parents. Perhaps we could–"

"Stop…"

He started to kiss her once more, her skin hot against his lips.

"Stop," she pleaded, turning her face this way and that to avoid his kisses. "You must stop…stop loving me…"

"I can't…"

"Please, Ned…"

"But Abby…"

Just then, the sound of shots punctured the air. Many guns were being fired at once. Ned's heart caught in his throat. Something had gone wrong, very wrong. He could hear Jonathan outside, shouting orders to get down, get down. Then he saw Abby's eyes, blue as ice, boring through him like the condemnation of his own conscience. Yes, she was the punishment for all his sins. She was having her way with him.

"What have you done?!" he blurted.

"What I had to do," she choked, "for freedom." Another tear rolled down her cheek. "We each must choose what we stand for…"

"Damn you," he swore, shaken to the core. "Damn you to hell!"

He struggled to get up, but she grabbed hold of his arm.

"Ned, for God's sake, don't…it's too late for them…"

Ned felt panic squeezing the air out of his lungs. Jonathan was out there. He had to save him.

"Let go, you rebel bitch!" he spat, furiously shoving her back and getting to his feet.

Ned staggered out of the barn, pulling up his breeches and buttoning his coat as he ran towards the sound of the shooting. He imagined he might have looked comical had anyone been watching. Yes, the whole thing might have been a comedy, if not for the fact that an evil fate was upon them, and the kiss of betrayal still bittersweet on his lips.

He had no plan, simply following the dictates of his own panic, his legs carrying him faster than his mind could calculate the odds of his own survival if he threw himself into the middle of an ambush. He simply knew he had to be there. He had been the one to bring them to this place. He could not live with himself if he alone was left unscathed.

When Ned reached his destination, he saw scarlet corpses littering the green, bullets still tearing into them, though they were now still as stones. He heard the bullets whizzing by his ears, coming closer to death than at any point in his life, but did not duck. He just stood foolishly erect, gazing at the gully nearby, where a few survivors were crouched down, returning a withering fire. He felt a momentary relief wash over him, seeing Jonathan was among them, a musket cocked at his shoulder. Then Jonathan saw him, and shouted at him to get down.

Ned did not know why he kept standing there. Perhaps some small part of him wanted to die. He stared down at the dead all around him, and simply could not move from the spot.

The next thing he could remember was Jonathan, out of the gully, yanking him forward, out of the line of fire, and tackling him to the ground, just as he had after Jones had his face shot off.

There was a thudding sound, and Ned felt Jonathan's weight shift forward, his friend's face smashing against the ground. Then Jonathan swore, only the second time Ned had ever heard him do it.

"My-my specs, Ned…they broke…" He drew in a shaking breath, and groped with a clumsy hand along the ground. "It's a blur, dear…help me…is there glass in my eyes?"

"N-no," Ned rasped. "J-j-just...blood…"

What happened after that was also a blur to Ned. He knew there was lots of blood, everywhere, more than could be accounted for by the broken spectacles cutting into poor Jonathan's face. The sound of the thud kept playing over again in his mind. He knew before Jonathan seemed to know, knew without any proof of whose blood it was or where it was coming from, knew the bullet meant for him had been blocked. He knew, but was too terrified to admit it, so he embraced a sort of willful ignorance, fixating on gathering the fragments of glass scattered in the wet grass.

"Oh…oh, sweet Jesus…" Jonathan gasped, a sudden awareness sinking in. "I've been hit…" He shifted on the ground slightly, unable to pull himself up at all. "I-I can't…feel it…oh, sweet Jesus…it's all over…"

Ned felt himself shaking convulsively, staring at his friend's blood staining his hands, unsure what to do, how to help him. He knelt up with his back erect, intent upon gesturing for help from one of the other soldiers still shooting from the gully.

Then there was a whizzing sound, and a burning sensation across his forehead, and time was suddenly suspended.

When Edmund regained some semblance of consciousness, blood was running into his eyes, turning the world around him red. But he soon realized that the crimson hue staining his surroundings was partly due to the color of uniforms milling around him. More British troops had arrived at the settlement to reinforce their beleaguered comrades. Jonathan must have sent for aid, suspecting the worst might be about to unfold. Now some of the settlers were running in and out of the buildings, seeking shelter while the rebel soldiers offered a withering fire from various windows. The largest house in the settlement seemed to be the main bastion for resistance. It also was where most of the settlers chose to barricade themselves for protection.

Overcome with a blinding passion, his head throbbing fiercely, Ned seized a musket and cartridges from one of the dead soldiers lying nearby. Then he joined the other soldiers pouring shot into the main building. Over and over again, he fired and reloaded, as Jonathan had taught him to do months before, until he lost all sense of sequence. He felt too much fury coursing through his veins to resist the cruel seduction of events, pulling him under like a leaf caught in a whirlpool. She had done this to him; that was all he knew for certain. She had destroyed him, from the inside out. Yes, she had destroyed them all. She would pay. They all would pay. Through smoke and fire, yes, through smoke and fire…

God have mercy on them, he thought. *God have mercy on me…*

He squeezed the trigger yet again, and heard a woman's scream. Whether the sound came from his mind, or from reality, he could not tell. Everything seemed to be playing out in a hall of mirrors, a chamber of echoes. Was he awake or asleep? He didn't know; he didn't care. His ancient Saxon blood, fiercer than civilized Englishmen wished to admit, had taken over.

By the time his mind cleared at all, there were dead bodies of settlers and soldiers alike sprawled on the ground and in the thresholds of the buildings. His fellow redcoats had sunken into a total frenzy, and anyone found moving on the ground or in the houses was being shot or bayoneted. Then the houses were set on fire, and more screaming filled the air. Dead to all feelings, Ned did nothing to stop the horrors unfolding. He just stood there, staring, the wound in his forehead dripping down his face. Then he looked back to the spot where Jonathan had lain, but he was nowhere to be found. Only a pool of dark gore amid the bent blades of grass remained.

When Ned finally made his way towards the main house, with the lurid haze heavy over his vision and the scent of death causing his nostrils to flare, he found himself tripping over corpses, men and women alike. Then he saw her lying motionless inside, her willow brown hair splayed across the bloody floorboards, calico dress riddled with holes and splattered scarlet. Her blue eyes were open, empty, and there appeared to be a third red eye drilled into her forehead. She was clasping the limp hand of Amelia, the hanged rebel's daughter, whose clothes were also torn to shreds and dyed crimson. She lay still at Abby's side, her eyelids drooping drowsily but her mouth still gaping, blood trickling down her lips, as if she had tried to cry out before the end came, but before she could manage, she was gone.

Ned felt unable to move, watching as the fire ravaging the building caught their clothes and hair. The smell of burning, melting flesh caused him to lurch forward and vomit on the floor. He fell to his knees, then collapsed onto his side, shuddering.

He wanted to catch fire.

He wanted to die, in agony.

He wanted to return to ashes and dust.

Yet some instinct beyond his own despair forced him up again. Some urgent voice within him insisted that he keep soul and body together for yet a while longer.

Yes, his ancestors were speaking again, knightly eyes piercing through helmet visors: *The second death is worse than the first.*

And so he stood, turning his back upon the slain, and wandered aimlessly towards the forest, where men and devils lie in wait.

Chapter 33: DEATH, BE NOT PROUD

When Edmund finally came to his senses and staggered back to the British camp, the sun had sunk low in the evening sky. He found Jonathan, white as a sheet, stretched out on his back in the tent they shared. His wig was off, revealing his cropped copper-brown hair. His spectacles, of course, were gone too. Maggie was next to him, trying to comfort him with some wet rags, nursing the cut along his face. He was telling her she was a good girl, and she was telling him to shut up, though her voice wobbled.

"Ned?" he murmured when his friend stepped closer. "Oh, thank God...you're alright..."

"Yes," Edmund rasped, but couldn't bring himself to say more.

"My specs broke when I fell, remember?" he chuckled. "I'm down to just two eyes like the rest of you..."

At this, Maggie suddenly leaned over and kissed his cheek. Then she stood up and rushed out of the tent.

"She's a good girl," Jonathan repeated wistfully, and shivered a little. "The surgeon said...it's my spine. I knew that already, to be fair. Can't feel much of anything. Can only move my hands a little before they grow tingly, then numb. Can't move my legs at all. It's an odd way to be, but it doesn't hurt. Suppose I'm a lucky dog."

Edmund tried to respond, tried to say something, but couldn't.

"How's...Abby?"

"Dead," Edmund blurted. "All of them are dead and burnt up."

"Oh, Ned..."

"I'm not sorry! I don't feel anything! The animals deserved it! I hate her! I hate..."

"Ned..."

Edmund felt tears burning his eyes at the way his friend said his name, as if trying to call him back to himself.

"She...she did care for you, I'm sure of it," Jonathan insisted. "She got you alone in the barn to save you..."

"But she killed you!" he blurted. "*I* killed you and the others..."

"Don't hate her on my account, Ned. Please. She was just a girl, and life dealt her a poor hand. So she got to hating. It's an easy enough thing to do, isn't it?"

Edmund exhaled. "What makes you like this?"

"Knowing my limitations. I'm no hero, so I try not to judge." Jonathan smiled a little, sadly. "Ned...I've got a few things. I'd like you to keep them for me. One is...well, it's some odds and ends I've scribbled down..."

"You kept a journal? "

"Well, badly...when I still had my specs. I just don't want to torture Betsy with the chicken scratch, because she'd get sentimental and would try to read it, and then she'd need spectacles herself. So it's yours to do with as you see fit." He twitched. "There are some other things for you, and some for Lieutenant Thompson. Do try to be patient with each other…I fear it's going to be a hard road ahead…" He twitched again. "And…if you ever meet my Elizabeth…do tell her…to marry someone….like my stepfather, who likes children…who loves our children…" His voice faltered. "Tell General Burgoyne…I am grateful for his courtesies to me, for I always found him to be a true gentleman…and tell him that, if he is satisfied with my services to him and to our country, I would be obliged if he would assure my family's needs are met…as I feel certain he will…" He closed his eyes for a few moments, then opened them again. "I'm sorry…I'm tired…"

"It's alright," Ned assured, kneeling down next to him. "You don't have to talk…"

"I was just thinking…I won't lie in the churchyard…back home…no, I never thought about that before…no one will know where I am out here…hell, I don't think I know where we are out here…oh…poor Bitty…"

"Shhh," Ned quieted him, placing his hand on Jonathan's forehead, realizing his friend could feel frightfully little from the neck down.

Jonathan regained his usual composure quickly. "Oh well…God knows where we are…" Then he drifted out of consciousness.

Ned lay beside Jonathan in the tent during the long night, listening to his friend's fitful breathing. There was no hope of sleeping. He did not even know how to pray anymore.

Then, in the wee hours of the dark morning, he heard his friend's voice.

"N-N-Ned?"

It was shaking.

"Here," Ned said quickly, sitting up and grasping Jonathan's tremulous hand, unsure whether he could feel it or not. "Right here."

"I-I think…" He inhaled sharply. "I think my lungs…are failing me…"

Edmund felt numb, as if he were the one paralyzed.

"Listen, Ned…listen, it's alright…" Jonathan's body spasmed. "I wanted to…say something, that's all. You and I, on occasion, discussed religion, though not often…it was a tender subject to breach, and I wear very few things upon the sleeve, but…but I want you to…to know…" He gasped hard. "I'm afraid…but I'm not afraid. I believe…that my redeemer lives…and death has lost her pride…that's all, Ned…"

Edmund swallowed a lump in his throat. "I did this to you…"

"No, no, it's alright. Don't go on about it. Everything's forgiven…" He lost his voice then and started gasping again, then writhing.

Ned reacted by holding him as he struggled, feeling so sick he feared he might vomit again.

When Jonathan managed a few shallow breaths, he whispered, "Thanks…thanks, Ned…but it's alright, I'll be alright…I'll see you, Ned…"

He never talked again after that, just fought to breathe till he couldn't anymore and went limp in Ned's arms.

Edmund stayed, frozen like that, with Jonathan in his arms, for a very long time, yes, so long his arms began to ache. When he finally set his friend down, he tenderly kissed his wounded cheek, closed his sightless eyes, and covered his face with a blanket. Then he left the tent, wandering off to a clearing next to the camp. Maggie was there too, her red hair luminous in the gray morning. Her eyes were red too.

"Dead, ain't he?" she guessed. "Some ten minutes past?"

"How did you know?" Ned croaked.

She shrugged. "Cornish folk know things."

Ned tilted his head. "What was between you two?"

"Nothing. He was no customer of mine. But he always said hello and good morning and how's your day. Bloody stupid talk, like he saw nothing wrong…" She shook her head. "And he looked me in the eyes. Men always looks lower, as is fitting…I've wares to sell…but no, no, he had to look me straight in the eyes…and I should have hated him for it, but no, no…just on account of him saying my name nice, like it meant something, I go to pieces…" She pressed a hand to her mouth and turned away. "There's more," she whispered. "I don't care what you do to me. Someone should know."

"Tell me," Ned pressed.

"Well, you know…he knew doctoring, more or less. So I went to him because…I was bleeding after I…stuck something between my legs to get rid of…" She blinked. "I couldn't go to a surgeon, not without him suspecting what I'd done. Your lieutenant suspected right off. He had a look on his face like it was Judgment Day, but…I told him it didn't matter, it couldn't be, not in my line, not in this place…and who would own it? No one, to be sure, not from my body. And I'd be out of work…"

"What did he do then?" Ned rasped.

She gazed at the ground. "He helped me. It was a risk. He could have been accused of doing the deed. But of course he wasn't the one. He would never. But he wouldn't report me either. He was a gentleman, he was. He patched me up, and he wouldn't let me work for weeks…said I'd get myself killed. So he made sure to slip me food…from the general's kit, if you can believe it! Imagine me, eating general's food!" She laughed shortly. Then she grew melancholic. "He said…his wife was full up too. And I said, well, yes, full up with something that would be valuable. Mine wasn't, on account I'm not. He said…that it wasn't so…and I think it pained him…to see me pained…" She shrugged. "Yes, he…he was a gentleman…"

~

The Reverend Brudenell conducted the funeral for Jonathan the following morning, his comportment solemn and restrained as he thumbed through the Prayer Book and read the liturgy over the open grave. But General Burgoyne seemed to be struggling to maintain similar composure. Just as when Gavin was taken down by the sniper, he seemed strained and agitated, his mind obviously struggling against a wave of some deeper sentiment he was unwilling to give ground. He kept shuffling loose dirt with his boot, but would not allow himself to gaze down into the gaping chasm about to swallow another member of his family.

Ned saw most of the general's camp had turned out for the funeral, from fellow staff officers to guards and camp followers. Maggie was there, dabbing her eyes with her apron, and the guard Samuel who Jonathan had counseled, standing beside his wife Charity, biting his lower lip. And of course, Eli was there, standing like a statue, staring down where Burgoyne dared not look, down, down into the grave, as if waiting for the day of resurrection. Ned also noticed several of the natives, including Red Elk, watching from amidst the trees. Not far from them stood the French priest in his black robe, blessing the grave with the sign of faith from afar. Jonathan had been well-loved by so many, indeed, more so than he would have probably imagined. Ned did not struggle to understand it at all, and his heart broke with guilt.

When the chaplain finished the designated prayers, Samuel stepped forward and blurted out in his thick Cockney accent, "General, sir, I-I would like to read something…"

Burgoyne blinked. "You can read?"

"No, sir…sorry, I didn't mean it like that," he countered. "I mean…say things from my mind, that he taught me to say." He gestured to the grave. "He-he taught me well. Matter of fact…he saved my soul. That's why I want to…well…"

Burgoyne hesitated for a moment, then nodded in assent.

The guard cleared his throat, then began, his accent growing thicker yet from nerves, "Though I speak with the tongues of men and of angels, and have not charity…I am become as sounding brass, or a tinkling cymbal. And though I have the gift of prophecy…and understand all mysteries, and all knowledge…and though I have all faith, so that I could remove mountains, and have not charity…I am nothing. And though I bestow all my goods to feed the poor, and though I give my body to be burned, and have not charity…it profiteth me nothing. Charity suffereth long, and is kind. Charity envieth not. Charity…" He paused, clearly struggling for the next word.

"Charity vaunteth not itself," Burgoyne said softly.

"Yes…charity vaunteth not itself, and is not puffed up…doth not behave itself unseemly, seeketh not her own, is not easily provoked, thinketh no evil…" He swallowed. "Rejoiceth not in iniquity, but rejoiceth in the truth…beareth all things, believeth all things, hopeth all things, endureth all things. Charity never faileth…"

His wife came to his side, and he put an arm around her for comfort.

Ned saw a lump rise in Burgoyne's throat now. "Very good, Private." Then he finally glanced down at the grave. He was quiet for several moments before he began to recite, in a deep and dark voice, from the recesses of memory, the words of John Donne:

"Death, be not proud, though some have called thee
Mighty and dreadful, for thou art not so;
For those whom thou think'st thou dost overthrow
Die not, poor Death, nor yet canst thou kill me.
From rest and sleep, which but thy pictures be,
Much pleasure; then from thee much more must flow,

And soonest our best men with thee do go,
Rest of their bones, and soul's delivery.
Thou art slave to fate, chance, kings, and desperate men,
And dost with poison, war, and sickness dwell,
And poppy or charms can make us sleep as well
And better than thy stroke; why swell'st thou then?
One short sleep past, we wake eternally
And death shall be no more; Death, thou shalt die."

Burgoyne glanced back over at the guard, who said quietly, "Very good, General."

Burgoyne smiled slightly, sadly. "I owed the man a thing or two myself."

As the funeral seemed about to draw to a close, Eli, who had been staring silently in some sort of shock the entire time, turned towards Edward, and shouted, "You killed him! Aye, as if it were by your own hand! You brought the punishment for your sin down upon an innocent man! You put the flesh before the spirit, and how many lives has that cost?" His lower lip trembled, his eyes watering. "He was a better man than you…a better man than both of us!"

Ned grimaced, the truth of those words harrowing up his soul.

"Lieutenant Thompson," Burgoyne snapped. "You will control yourself!"

"Remember, you are at a funeral!" the chaplain scolded him. "Show respect for the dead!"

"A funeral, yes! Our funeral! We are far more dead than the man we bury! We are destroying ourselves for naught!"

"I said that you were to control yourself, Thompson," Burgoyne repeated.

"Is this secret Papist not to receive punishment for his crimes, sir?" Eli demanded, gesturing angrily at Ned. "After all he's done? Is he to be pardoned for traitorous fornication and the murder of his comrades?"

"Your hyperbole will gain you nothing," Burgoyne snapped. "I alone will decide the case, and you are in no position to question it. Now return to shoveling manure where you belong!"

Eli was shaking, like some earthquake was erupting within him, and he fell down upon his knees before the grave. Then he started to laugh, like a madman, digging his fingers into the earth. Suddenly, he stopped laughing and pointed at the assembly.

"We have strayed," he rasped in a voice not quite his own, "yes, strayed from the way of the Lord! We were given the Covenant to seal in blood, but we have forsworn it, and been deluded by our carnal lust, our worldly pride! We no longer serve God, but ourselves! And so we will be chastised! If we will not be Israel, then we will be Babylon! And Babylon shall fall, unless we repent!"

"Get up, you Irish fool!" Burgoyne snapped at him. "I will not be preached to by a half-witted stable hand!"

Eli's eyes flickered eerily. Then he spat in the dirt, dug up for the grave, and smeared it upon his pock-scarred face. "The rod of iron will crush us," he murmured, bowing his head. "Blessed be the name of the Lord."

"You're mad," Burgoyne spat. "You disgrace your rank, mucking about like swine!"

"I am making restitution…"

"Mind yourself, Lieutenant!" Brudenell cried. "This sort of display is not what God wants!"

"I am submitting to His holiness!" Eli declared. "We cannot escape our sins, no, not one of us, not of high or low degree! The Lord of Hosts levels us all, just as he drew us up from the dirt! We should all be on our knees, in the dirt, repenting…"

"You would do well to watch your words, Lieutenant, lest you be misunderstood as throwing your lot in with the radicals!" Burgoyne chastised him. "Your mind may be lost to a hopeless enthusiasm, but remember, you're as much a part of this train as the rest of us! If we are to be punished, so are you!"

Eli's face drained white. "Yes," he choked. "For my sins. To God alone be the glory."

Burgoyne shook his head, then gestured for several guards to take Eli away. Eli did not struggle against them, but simply stared at Edmund, his eyes chilling him like ice.

When Ned finally dared to turn away, he was surprised to see General Fraser upon his gray mount, watching the proceedings. His face, too, was pale. One of his aides, the one who had won the dancing contest, was with him, and helped him dismount.

Burgoyne caught sight of him, then glanced over at Ned. "You will come to my tent, Lieutenant Southworth," he said. "General Fraser will deliberate with me upon the matter."

"Yes, sir," Ned responded meekly, and did as he was told.

When the generals had seated themselves accordingly in the tent, Burgoyne gestured for Edmund to speak. "Report, Lieutenant. Leave nothing out."

"Before I begin, sir," Ned rasped, "I must tell you what Lieutenant Rawcliffe told me to tell you…that he always found you to be a gentleman towards him and hoped you would consider the needs of his family…"

"He needn't have asked," Burgoyne replied, his voice wobbling slightly. "He must have known it would be done." Again, Burgoyne gestured, impatiently this time. "Now…report, Southworth."

Ned winced. "The enemy was waiting at the settlement for us, sir. It was a slaughter." He bit his lip. "I…should have been at my station when the first volley came. I should have been out there, with the others, searching the premises. I…was not."

"Where were you, Lieutenant?" Burgoyne demanded.

Ned swallowed. "In the barn, with…her. I thought…it was her way of saying goodbye…"

"And she was the one to set the trap?" Fraser surmised.

"Yes, sir," Ned croaked, the words hurting his throat. "I…led everyone into it, because I was blind to her…"

"And you think that's an excuse?" Fraser countered harshly.

"No, sir!" Ned blurted. "I think I deserve punishment!"

"What kind, Lieutenant?" Burgoyne asked lowly. "How would you have me punish you?"

Ned trembled. "Break me," he rasped, "in all the ways I can be broken."

Burgoyne closed his eyes momentarily. Then he murmured, "Finish your report, Lieutenant."

Ned started to shake. "I-I ran outside, when I realized what was happening. Then…Lieutenant Rawcliffe knocked me down to save me…" His voice broke. "He was hit in the back…then a stray ball grazed my forehead, either from the rebels or our own men. I saw only red. The next thing I knew…I was shooting…yes, at anything, everything that was moving, in and out of the buildings…then I was shooting into the barn and the main house, along with the survivors from our party and reinforcements that were sent…we all were doing it…" He pressed a hand to his forehead. "I…wasn't even thinking…just…shooting. And it went on and on and on…and then…they were dead, they were all dead...then the buildings were set ablaze…"

"The girl," Fraser blurted, "I mean…the hanged man's daughter…Amelia…was she amongst the slain?"

"Yes," Ned rasped. "There were no survivors."

Fraser's face turned ashen and eyes hazy.

The thought of Abby's corpse clutching Amelia's limp hand amidst the flames assaulted Ned, and he felt like vomiting. "I am guilty…of terrible things…"

"You're not fully culpable if you didn't know what you were doing," Burgoyne replied softly.

"Yes, I am!" Ned exclaimed, clenching his fists. "I…I killed…"

"Ned," Burgoyne rasped, leaning over the table. "Defend yourself."

Edmund shook his head.

"Please, Ned…"

"I deserve anything," Edmund replied. "Everything."

"No, there are mitigating factors," Burgoyne countered. "I gave you permission to take her out there, and your being shot down alongside the others during the first volley would not have prevented what unfolded after. You did not transgress any particular orders."

"But I should have been outside…"

"Yes, you should have," Burgoyne agreed. "What you did was far from laudable."

"It's much worse than that!" Ned declared in anguish. "Those settlers…they didn't all deserve to die! Not all of them were guilty, like she was! But we…I…"

Burgoyne exhaled. "You were provoked to extremities. You know I do not condone attacks upon the innocent, even under provocation. Inquiries will be made and penalties delivered accordingly. But knowing your own abilities as I do, I highly doubt your aim was so very accurate as to do great damage. Your state of mind would have made it even less so."

"But I shot," he cried, "I shot!" Unshed tears burned his eyes. "And Abby, she…she's dead!" He buried his face in his hands.

"Lieutenant, you will look at me."

Ned obeyed, taking his trembling hands from his face.

Burgoyne gave him a long, penetrating look, then waved his hand towards the opening of the tent. "Step outside, Lieutenant, while General Fraser and I discuss the matter."

Edmund did so, his heart pounding in his chest as the generals spoke.

"It is wrong of me to say it, but I am grateful her blood is on someone else's hands," Ned heard Burgoyne confess. "If she had been taken alive, I would have had to hang her. And that would have haunted me. Of course she deserved it for her treachery, but…she was a slight thing. I remember, in bed…she was very slight. I was almost afraid of breaking something…" He sighed. "She'd have either gone very quickly, with a broken neck, or taken very long to go, not heavy enough to end the struggle. I would have had to watch her, dangling…but worse than that, Ned would have had to watch her like that. It would have killed him."

"He may have killed his lover, by his own testimony," Fraser said darkly.

"One bullet among many," Burgoyne blurted. "An accident!"

"Or a crime of passion," Fraser croaked. "Though perhaps crime is the wrong word. She'd be dead either way, and if the settlers enabled that ambush, they brought it on themselves…"

"Not women and children," Burgoyne countered.

"She was a woman, was she not?"

"That's no proof the others were involved," Burgoyne insisted. "Certainly not the children."

"If these rebels had any care for the welfare of their families, they would never use a civilian settlement as a shield to attack us," Fraser countered. "They asked for it."

"Balnain, you could not even watch that little rebel girl crying without being gutted," Burgoyne sighed. "Now you blame yourself for her death. I can read you easily enough, no matter how you try to put up a false front…"

"I hanged her damn father in front of her, didn't I?" Fraser ground out. "I killed her innocence. What remained of her was twisted by hatred, and now…" His voice wobbled. "She wasn't a bad girl. She loved her father, that was all. She wanted him to come home in one piece, and to have the chance to fill up her box of beads, to get some more pretty glass ones from a fancy store in the city…" He pressed a fist to his mouth. "She could have been…ours, John…"

"You're the hardest and the softest man I know," Burgoyne murmured.

"Well, perhaps young Lieutenant Southworth lives with the same dichotomy. Perhaps we will make a bloody-minded soldier out of him yet…"

"He doesn't even clearly remember what he did, beyond reacting in panic and confusion," Burgoyne insisted. "I believe that. He still has the pure eyes you saw in the beginning. He's not guilty, not of murder. Besides…" Burgoyne paused. "I could have stopped him from going to the settlement. But I didn't. I granted him permission."

"What's done is done," Fraser dismissed.

"But it's not," Burgoyne rasped. "Not for…him. Not with poor Rawcliffe in the ground, on top of everything else." He was quiet for a moment, then said, "That Irish fool, he's right about this much…Rawcliffe was a better man than most of us. That's why he was so good for Ned. But now…"

"John," said Fraser in a low voice. "Give the boy to me."

"But this is my burden to bear," Burgoyne retorted. "He's my responsibility."

"It will do neither of you any good for him to stay here," Fraser countered. "I can take him into my family until this scandal blows over. He will have a chance to start over."

"Banish him from my side, you mean?" Burgoyne asked wearily.

"It's a lighter sentence than the alternatives," Fraser reminded him.

"Not for him," Burgoyne murmured.

"He must be toughened if he is going to survive," Fraser insisted. "He must be hardened if you expect him to stand up against the winds blowing. You cannot expect to make a man out of him and also keep him an innocent. Besides, no matter his eyes, those days of innocence are already gone beyond recall."

Burgoyne snorted. "You once warned him that I might corrupt him. Well…I may have started it, yes. But it seems you may be the one to finish it."

"Aye," Fraser replied with a tinge of melancholy in his tone. "So it seems."

Burgoyne was quiet for a long moment. Then he said softly, "Will you be the father to him I can no longer be?"

"I will push him and protect him in equal measure, as if he were one of my own country, my own clan," Fraser replied. "That is the most I can give any lad under my authority."

"Will you promise me not to send him onto the field when the confrontation comes?" Burgoyne asked.

"I cannot promise to hold him back," Fraser replied. "But I will not rush to put him out."

"Balnain," Burgoyne rasped. "I…told him to come here. And I told him to take that rebel harlot to himself."

"We either learn from our mistakes, or perish with them," Fraser declared. "There are no two ways about it. I for one intend to give Young Southworth every opportunity to live and learn."

There was another long silence. Then at last Burgoyne said, "So be it, Balnain. Southworth is yours."

And Ned remained standing like a statue outside the tent, feeling as if his heart had been turned to ice, even colder than Eli's eyes.

~

That night, Edmund listlessly packed his possessions to relocate to Fraser's camp, then sorted through Jonathan's personal effects, including his books. His Bible and Book of Common Prayer were filled with scrawls of ink, with the corners of many pages bent back. Tellingly, the page bent furthest back and annotated the most in the Bible read, *"Though I speak with the tongues of men and of angels, and have not charity…"*

Jonathan had willed the Bible to Eli, and the Prayer Book to Edmund, along with his diary. Ned found himself reading through the latter all in one night, realizing it was mainly a prayer journal. It seemed a day had not gone by since the march began when Jonathan had not scribbled something down. They were usually short entries, but each one broke Ned's heart a bit more.

Lord God, let Thy light be made known by this weak sinner, he had written. *Make use of Thy simple instrument.*

Another day, he had scratched down, *Comfort my dear Elizabeth and our little ones. I would give all the world if I could wake up at her side again!*

Again, a bit of scripture, and a morning offering: *This is the day the Lord has made. I give Thee everything, poor as my everything may be.*

There was a more formal passage for the King's birthday: *God in Thy great mercy, grant health and long life to our gracious sovereign, that he may govern his subjects and the Church within his realm with the wisdom of Solomon. May we scatter his enemies and dispel all treason.*

Then there was talk about the war: *Sweetest Jesus, may this unhappy and unnatural contest swiftly end. I am counting out the provisions we have commandeered, and shudder to think of the children who may starve. May the rightful government be restored quickly and mercy shown to the erring.*

And more talk: *My God, I can smell the smoke rising so thickly. The peasants of this vicinity may freeze come the winter. I cannot sleep for the thought of their pains, especially the women and the young. They are not guilty of the faults being committed by their husbands and fathers.*

Some pages later, there was a happier passage: *I give thanks for the dream about my little Emma and her baby teeth. I hope they come out easily, and she keeps them for me to see.*

Ned could not help but smile slightly when Eli was mentioned: *Give me patience with Lieutenant Thompson. The Irish boy sometimes rubs me raw. Make me kinder than I am inclined when he rants and rails, and then my feelings may follow suit. He is a good lad at heart, though given over to enthusiasm. He needs a friend. I suppose that it must be me. So make me better suited to the task.*

Then there was something about the other Irish boy: *Lord, make me a better teacher. I feel like I am getting nowhere with this stubborn Gael. Rocks for brains, clinging to superstitions. Still, I think it is my duty to try.*

Then Edmund saw himself mentioned: *Make me a good example to dear Lieutenant Southworth. He is a decent lad, and away from the faulty attachments of his upbringing, he will become all the better.*

He brought up the Indians: *Savior of Mankind, may the peoples of this country who still dwell in darkness be brought to light through Thee. Thou came no less for them than for me, despite their savagery. Please, bless my hands, that I may labor to do them good, for I have little enough faith in myself. Make my poor efforts worth the risk.*

Then Ned came to the day of Gavin's death. There was one line only: *Jesus, Jesus, take away my hate.*

Ned saw drops of water marking the following page: *My friend is gone, my dear, dear friend, gone. And I want the boy to die. I want all the rebels to die. I fear I cannot pray.*

But not long after, he wrote: *I talked with dear Lieutenant Thompson for much of the night. He shall be godfather to my child.*

And then he was praying again: *Please, Lord, don't let the boy suffer anymore from my shot. It hurts me to see him shaking like this. Take him to Thyself.*

And the next day: *Lord God, pity the boy, whose Christian name was David, now departed from this world. In Thy mercy, absolve him of his grievous sins of murder and treason. He was so young. Surely he did not know what he was doing. It is the rebel leaders who have millstones around their necks for leading astray these poor impressionable people. God, pity them, and us!*

He added an addendum in the evening: *There is a guard whose Christian name is Samuel. His soul is restless about the last things. I endeavored to introduce him to the only source of felicity to be had in this world and beyond it. God knows I have little felicity to share at this time, but at least I might share this man's sorrow, and hope for better days to come. I have chosen not to report him for attacking the prisoner, for I believe he will not repeat his misconduct if shown mercy. I have read to him from the scriptures and shall teach him verses to repeat to himself, as I do throughout the day. I feel more peaceful now, even in pain.*

There was a pensive statement from some time later: *There are too many children who come into being unwanted, and then go out of being again, and never know a moment's love. How is it that mine should be loved, and others not? Surely every creature born of God deserves love, no matter the pedigree.*

The last entry stuck out with particular poignancy. *Dearest, Ever-Adorable Christ, guard my friend from any who might bring him harm, and forgive us for anyone we have harmed. Kiss my dear babes for me, born and to be born.*

Amidst his belongings was also a letter Jonathan had been writing to his wife:

My pretty, pretty Bitty, there is little to tell you about the goings on here, but that cannot stop me from writing to you! Praise God, after the loss of our dear Lieutenant Jones, no marksman has dared approach the general's camp. We are taking every precaution under heaven, so you mustn't worry yourself. We are halfway to nowhere, as far as I'm concerned, but a nobody like me shouldn't mind that overly much. I'll say no more about it, lest I bore you to tears, but I remain as fit as a fiddle, clerking with zeal for the king's honor and shilling.

Tell me all the news. Is the baby kicking yet? I am grieved you feel so ill. Do try to take some chicken soup, though you lack the appetite. He is going to be a soldier, I fear, and is causing you to fret already! How are poor little Emma's teeth? Has the swelling gone down? Try to keep Jeffrey from teasing her. It's not her fault she has squirrel cheeks! Tell him to be good, and I will buy him a little sword. Don't worry, Betsy! It shan't be sharp enough to skin the cat! I might as well ask after the cat too. Has he brought you any more mice and birds for presents? He's simply trying to court your favor, and I can hardly blame him for that gentle sin!

How is the garden? I hope the rains haven't drowned it out nor the rabbits eaten it up! What were the strawberries and raspberries like this year? Have you and Annie baked any pies with them? Has the poor girl broken any more dishes? Even if it is so, I think it was the right choice to employ her. She's very good with the children, and they seem to have taken her to be another aunt. Without any other family, she could do much worse than being our little sister.

Sometimes I wish I had thought to set up shop in my own house with you and the children and be a dull little village clerk. But you love your man in uniform, and don't try to deny it. Still I would give much to have that sort of life, and this Sunday be beside you in the pew, listening to the rain at the window and Reverend Maphet hypothesizing something theologically obscure for an hour or more, like he did at our wedding. I don't suppose either of us know to this day what he was going on about. I'm afraid we don't deserve him, dear man! Perhaps he can find some way to get me to turn in my livery on a point of conscience!

Has Mrs. Harbold had her baby yet? Do see she has everything she needs, as I know the family has fallen hard. See if there is anyone that can be done to find the husband some position that can be accomplished from home. You are mightily persuasive. See also if you can convince the man that drinking will not restore the legs lost to him outside Boston. It only grieves his poor wife. Give him my feelings as a fellow soldier, and tell him I will do whatever I can for him upon my return. Keep his lady in good company, as you are able. And of course you are more than able, as the best companion a man or woman ever had.

I may add more to this, for the rascals in arms against us have made it their life's work to disrupt our mail, so I leave it open upon my desk and keep jotting away every spare moment. I should not laugh, but I do, when I consider that one of the rebels might intercept this and think, "what silly people we are fighting"! I must try harder to be more terrifying on His Majesty's behalf. But I shouldn't mind for anyone, friend or foe, to know my feelings for you.

Give my love to my mother, and tell her to expect a letter from me as soon as I can manage it. Tell my brothers and sisters not to give her any grief, lest I come home and box back their ears. Tell your family I am still not worthy of you, but they know that already. Tell Matthew I miss him as much as he misses me, and that I daily speak to Heaven about him. Give all my fondest thoughts to our friends. Perhaps we shall spend Christmas together, but if I find myself stuck twiddling my thumbs somewhere in New York, at least for Easter.

Keep in mind, my darling, that such worldly separations between us must be borne up with resolution. Our Lord tests those whom He loves in manifold ways. He refines us with His fire. He conforms us to Himself, and empty ourselves, just as the Son did in obedience to the Father. As Watts said, we must kiss the Son in the manger, where no royal, shining things are to be found. We must survey the wondrous Cross, and pour contempt on all our pride. We must silence the spirit of complaint before this love beyond degree and submit ourselves to be tested.

We must prove ourselves to be Emmanuel's friends by raising up our hearts up to Him. Only then will our love for each other be blessed. You, as well as I, must be valiant souls, and live and die as soldiers, striving, watching, and praying until our sweet hope of glory is realized and we meet those who have gone before us. Then we will never more be parted, and all our tears will be wiped away. Believe me, Bitty. We shall yet have our victory, shall yet gain the day.

I have kissed this letter and shall keep doing so before bed until it can be sent off to you, so you shall have all the kisses I can give you for as long as I can give them! Here you are, my sweetest Elizabeth, another kiss!

Edmund found his hands trembling, but he still could not cry. It was as if all his emotions had run dry, and he wondered if it would always be so for him. He felt sick unto his soul, and lay down to try and catch even the briefest sleep, but his eyes refused to close. Blood was on his hands, and he feared the ghosts would never permit him rest, no matter how sincerely Jonathan had assured him of forgiveness. The man had simply been too good for the war and, perhaps, for the world

When Ned left the tent in the wee hours of the morning, the books he had inherited tucked in a blanket under his arm, he found Eli, also tucked up in a blanket, lying beside Jonathan's grave, like a loyal dog, unwilling to leave behind his master, even shrouded in death. The gleam of the first morning campfires cast a flickering light over his scarred face. His eyes were open, and they too, were gleaming. His lips were moving; whether with morning prayers, or with words for his dead friend, Ned could not tell. But Edmund sensed in his soul that this unpredictable prophet from the Antrim glens had indeed been burned by the fever, and a deeper fire yet, one infused with both wrath and love. Yes, it was alive in him, through all his strangeness and suffering, and the words he had spoken at the funeral rang with a terrifying truth.

Yes, no matter where the weary road led them all, Edmund found himself desiring with all his heart that he too might be burned like the bush that was not consumed and brought back to life again. Yes, if Babylon was falling, he wanted to be among those who clapped their hands and blew the flames. And he touched the place over his heart, where the Lamb of God concealed the blood of the martyrs, stitched into his scarlet tunic. And his fingers burned.

ABOUT THE AUTHOR

Avellina Balestri is a Catholic author and editor from the historic borderlands of Maryland and Pennsylvania. Her stories, poems, and essays have been featured in over thirty print and online publications. Prior to *Gone for a Soldier*, she published two books: *Saplings of Sherwood*, the first book in a Robin Hood retelling series, and *Pendragon's Shield*, a collection of poetry. She is the Editor-in-Chief of Fellowship & Fairydust, a magazine inspiring faith & creativity and exploring the arts through a spiritual lens. Under its auspices, she hosted two literary conferences, one in Oxford University and the other in Cambridge University. She also represented the state of Maryland at The Sons of the American Revolution National Orations Contest in Greenville, South Carolina. Avellina believes that the Trinitarian divine dance and Incarnational indwelling mystery are reflected in all things good, true, and beautiful, and that the image of God is wondrously woven into every human heart. These themes are at the forefront of the stories she chooses to tell.

For more information about the author and her various projects, please visit the following websites:

www.fellowshipandfairydust.com

www.avellinabalestri.com

Printed in Great Britain
by Amazon